THE MYSTERY

OF

MARLBOROUGH HOUSE;

A TALE OF TRIAL AND TEMPTATION.

LONDON :

PUBLISHED BY E. HARRISON, MERTON HOUSE, 135, SALISBURY COURT,
FLEET STREET.

CONTENTS.

THE SECOND EPOCH.

CONTENTS.

THE MYSTERY
OF
MARLBOROUGH HOUSE.

A TALE OF TRIAL AND TEMPTATION.

CHAPTER I.

FAIR LIZ THE BALLAD SINGER, AND THE NOC-
TURNAL VISIT TO THE HOUSE OF DEATH.

IT was a dismal night in the December of 1780, and the great city of London was wrapped in silence.

The snow was deep upon the ground, and the pale moonlight fell on a scene of singular stillness and beauty, the snowy shroud wrapping the streets in a guise of supernatural appearance, and lending to the houses a quaint and grim aspect; speaking of death, decay, and the mysterious hereafter.

It was a night for feasting and merriment for the rich, snugly ensconced in their well-furnished chambers, but it was a time of sorrow and despair for the poor; grovelling in their hovels and wrapping their threadbare rags about their emaciated bodies in the vain hope of conveying some of the warmth they could not procure by artificial means.

The clocks of Westminster tolled forth the hour of midnight, and, save an occasional shout from some disorderly tavern-revellers, or the monotonous cry of the old watchmen going their rounds, all was still.

This tale opens in a small street forming one of those many veins connected with the main artery of traffic leading to the old Abbey of Westminster.

The only sound that breaks the silence comes from a little tavern, whose appearance would indicate that its customers were of a class which may be briefly and pointedly termed, disreputable.

The inn was visited by high and low, rich and poor, but all who made it their haunt must come under the same category. They were all dissolute, unprincipled, and lawless. At the moment we introduce the reader to the exterior of this den of vice and misery, a loud rapping of glasses, clapping of hands, and shouts of approval disturbed the quiet of its immediate neighbourhood.

"Come, wench," a voice within was heard to exclaim; "come, wench, one more song and then you may go; but by Jove you do not stir until another sweet ballad is warbled from that pretty throat."

This speech was hailed with reiterated shouts of "That's our sentiments, that's the way to put it: bravo! bravo!" And then, when the tumult had in a measure subsided, a woman's voice uttered—

"Not to-night, gentlemen, not to-night; I must go home, indeed, indeed I must; some other time—to-morrow, perhaps, but now I must get home."

"That be cursed for a tale," was uttered in the loud and harsh voice of a man, "that's but poor repayment for our money and kindness. No, no; another song."

"I cannot sing."

"You must."

"Then I will not sing."

"By George, you shall."

"By Heaven I will not."

There was a sound as if some struggle was progressing.

"Close the door, block up the passage; the devil has taken half the skin off my face. Stop her."

The door of the house flew open, and out started a young and very beautiful girl, and a youth of about eighteen years, whose sumptuous dress bespoke high rank and position, but whose coarse, sensual face told of the very lowest order of humanity.

"Come, fair Liz," said the gallant, catching the girl around the waist, "this is all nonsense. Stay with us but for an hour and I'll give you another guinea."

"Indeed, sir, I dare not; pray unhand me," the girl replied.

"Unhand you be hanged! What a devil of a show of modesty for a tavern ballad singer."

"A tavern ballad singer may have such a thing as modesty, although a gentleman may not always be overburdened with courtesy."

"Come, that's smart; I don't mind a sharp answer when it comes from a pair of pretty lips, so I'll not be offended."

"You may be offended if you choose, and the more you show it the better I shall be pleased; now unhand me, or I'll call the watch."

"Call the devil. What do I care for the watch!"

"Will you unhand me?" cried the girl.

"If I do I'll be eternally cursed."

"Then I will shriek until assistance arrives."

"I should not advise you to shriek too loud, as you will spoil that pretty voice of yours, and that would be a pity."

"Monster, unhand me: help! help!"

"Shut up your bawling, or I'll gag you."

"Help! help!" was the girl's only response.

"Curses on you! the whole neighbourhood will be alarmed in another minute: hold your infernal row."

"Help! help!" still shrieked the girl.

"Why do not those fellows come out and hold the wench?" yelled the man.

Lights were seen at the end of the street, and there was every sign of the watch approaching.

"Ah," cried the girl, "they hear me at last; the watch is approaching."

"The watch be cursed; the sooner they come the better, for they must lend me a hand since those drunken wretches will not come out to do so."

"They will release me and arrest you," said the girl, still trying to free herself.

"We shall see," returned the man, with a sneer. "They must be much altered if they will not lend me a hand in a case of emergency."

"If that is the case," cried the girl, in an agony of terror, "there is nothing for it but this——"

Uttering these words she bent her head, and, catching the hand of the man who held her firmly between her teeth, she administered such a bite as made him yell with pain, and instantly release his hold.

As soon as free, the poor terrified girl sprang away from her captor, and with the velocity of lightning sped from the spot.

"Ten thousand devils," cried the man, "the little brute has nearly bitten my hand off!"

At this moment a watchman came up to the persecutor of the poor ballad singer.

"What was that noise?" asked the guardian of the peace.

"Oh, hang you; why not have come sooner and seen for yourself?" replied the man.

"No imperence, feller," said the watchman, "no imperence; or I'll shop you for contempt!"

"Bah! Hound!"

"Hound! Hound to the watch! Oh, this ere's too bad; but we must see who this awful rioter and imperent brawler is."

With this the watchman lifted his lantern to the face of the man with whom he conversed, and took a long and fixed stare at him, but no sooner had he done so than he fell back a pace, and, pulling off his hat, stood bowing respectfully and silently.

"Now," said the other, "now; have you anything more to say?"

"Oh, if I had only known it had been your Highness—"

"Hist! The devil take your tongue. Do you think I want the vile set who hang about this place to know who is among them? Call me Wentworth—Mr. Wentworth."

"Well, your—that is, Mr. Wentworth—in the first place I'm very sorry. In fact, Mr. Wentworth, I never expected it was your High—that is, I didn't think it were yourself, or I'd have been here all the quicker. But can't I do anything now to assist your—that is, you?"

"Yes, yes; you can."

"Who attacked you, Mr. Wentworth? Only tell me who it was, and in an hour we'll have him safe under lock and key."

"Oh, no one attacked me, you old fool. It was simply an affair with a woman whom I did not choose to part with."

"Do I know her?"

"How should I know who you number among your acquaintances? but this was the wench they call Fair Liz, the ballad singer."

"Ah!—everybody knows Fair Liz."

"Well, where is she to be found? I've not done with her yet."

"I know her house full well, and will take you to it, if that's all your—that is, you want."

"That is all. Now let me get those fellows out of the tavern; after that I shall want your assistance."

The mysterious personage went to the door of the tavern, and knocked hurriedly. He was admitted immediately, but we must now leave him and follow the girl who had occasioned the foregoing conversation.

No sooner had she freed herself from the man who had so suddenly assumed the name of Wentworth, than she rushed away at a terrible rate through the deserted streets and lone alleys of Westminster. Crossing the Abbey churchyard she rushed into one of the many turnings which branched from the main road, and entered a squalid court designated the Abbey Buildings. This was the home of squalid misery and unblushing vice, sheltering, as it did, a whole host of the worst of pickpockets and cracksmen, and a gang of the lowest class of unfortunates. Here stopped the ballad singer, and entering through the door of one of the very worst of these rotting old houses—they are all swept away now—she hurriedly closed it, and sprang, three steps at a time, up the creaking stairs.

She ascended to the very top of the house, and lifting the latch of the door of one of the attics, stepped in.

The only thing that could be said in favour of the apartment she had entered was that it was clean; beyond this its aspect was most repulsive. The small diamond-shaped panes of glass were nearly all broken out of the frame-work, and replaced by old rags and paper. The walls were bare and grim, and the ceiling blackened and defaced by the smoke of a candle, with which a former occupant had displayed his artistic abilities by tracing the outlines of gibbets, pistols, and handcuffs in great variety.

The only furniture of the place was a broken deal table, and two old chairs. On the former stood a candle flaring away in a black bottle.

In a corner of the attic was a heap of straw and rags, and on this lay the form of a pale, emaciated woman, apparently of about forty years. She breathed very hard, and the brilliancy of her eye and the hectic flush upon her cheek told too plainly the ravages of consumption.

"Who is that?" cried the woman, as the singing girl entered.

"It is I—Liz," replied the girl. "I should have been home full an hour before, but a company of gentlemen detained me at the Black Swan. Oh, I longed to fly back to you, mother, and bring what I have earned, but they persecuted me so, I could not escape. Oh, God help me! You know not what I suffer!"

"You suffer!" cried the invalid, "you suffer! Psha! What can you know of suffering, who spend your days and nights in warm, well-lighted rooms; who can have every comfort for the asking —who feel not pain, and know not the misery of lying here alone from morn till night? You suffer! Ha! ha! suffer, indeed!"

"Oh, mother; you talk wildly—you know not what you say. But I will not distress you now: see, I have brought you two guineas, obtained from the men at the Black Swan. I could have thrown it in their faces, and the only thing that made me take it was the thought of your sufferings."

"Give me the money."

"What will you do with it, mother?"

"Give it me. Hide it here Did they know we had so much they would kill us in the night, and take it away. Oh, I know them—I know them."

"But let me buy something for you, mother. You must be faint from want of food, for you have tasted nothing since I left this morning. I will get some wine."

"No, no; I can wait until to-morrow. I can wait. You must not change gold in this neighbourhood. It is dangerous, I tell you, dangerous, so you shall not do it. Come to bed, and hand me the gold."

The girl did as she was ordered, and the invalid clutched the coins in her wasted hands and buried them deep in the straw.

The poor singer watched this act with tears coursing down her cheeks.

"Poor mother," she murmured, "perhaps she will not need sustenance to-morrow. Her breathing is terrible, and she sinks lower and lower every hour."

"Are you coming to bed?" demanded the sick woman.

"Yes, mother; yes," answered the girl.

"Quick, then; and do not put out the light. I hate the darkness. I see such terrible things in the gloom."

"Poor mother," murmured the girl, as she stripped off her torn and tattered outer garments, and prepared for bed, "poor mother, hers is indeed a hard fate."

A footstep on the stairs here startled the girl, and made her pause to listen.

On it came, nearer and nearer, and by the stumbling and uncertain steps the girl divined that a stranger was approaching.

"Who is that?" cried the mother.

"I do not know," said the girl, her cheek blanching with terror, "I do not know."

"Bar the door!" cried the invalid, "do not let them enter!"

"Alas!" said the girl, "there is nothing but the latch."

"Keep them out!" almost shrieked the invalid, but the singing girl was too terrified to move hand or foot. Casting her garment about her shoulders she stood glaring at the door.

In another moment the step was on the landing, and a hand was on the latch of the door.

"May I come in?" said a voice from without, "may I come in?"

Not waiting. however, for any reply, the owner of the voice raised the latch, and stepped into the apartment, revealing the figure of a tall, sallow-faced, blear-eyed man.

"It's all right, my dear," he said, looking at the poor girl in a manner which clearly indicated that he had been indulging very freely in drink, "it's all right, my dear, so you needn't be alarmed. I only want a word with Madge Maydock, that's all. I s'pose you don't remember me, but Madge does, I'll bet a guinea!"

The sick woman raised herself with some difficulty, and, gazing at the intruder, shouted wildly—

"Back! back! Come not here! Oh, God! that I should see him again after all these long years! Back, back, I say, and let not my last look be fixed upon thee!"

"Come, I say," said the man, "that's cruel, thundering cruel, to say such things to your husband. But I won't complain."

"Her husband!" said the girl. "Are you, then, my father?"

"Hav'nt that pleasure, my love. You see, it's a long story, and if Madge don't mind, I'll take a chair and run it over."

"No, no," screamed the sick woman; no! Not a word, I beg—I entreat. Oh, God! that you should have come back after all these years! Get hence!

"I can't, and that's the plain truth," said the man. This is just how it is: I'm wanted, and have been looked after for some time. Turned out of all my nests, one after the other, I at last got to the crib called the Smutty Quaker, at the bottom of the court, there. Well, the last half-penny was gone, and I didn't know what to do for any more, when luck turned up your neighbour of the next attic, and says he, 'Old Madge Maydock's worse to-day. I've heered her breathin' away like anythink all day, and I'll be hanged if I don't think she's a croaking,' says he, and oh, thinks I if I hav'nt fallen across the missus I'll be kicked; and so I determined to hunt you up, just to say how do ye do, and to borrow all the money you can conveniently part with."

"I have no money. I am ill—perhaps dying; so get thee hence, and never come again to this house. Get hence, I tell thee; I cannot bear thy presence!"

"That's all very well, but I'm going to tell the young woman about her father. Why, you really ought to have told her that her father was—"

"Silence, silence; and you shall have gold—yes, gold! I have two guineas here, and they shall be yours, only open not your mouth!"

"Oh, it's all snug; only it's right the young woman should know—"

"Nothing! Here is the money. Take it and go!"

"I will. And I promise not to come back again—until I want some more money. Well, I'm going to go, you see, my dear; but the missus won't be trifled with. I'm off. I may come back and spin that yarn about your father one day. But at present I suppose I must keep the secret, and let it remain THE MYSTERY OF MARLBOROUGH HOUSE. Good night!"

With this the drunken man reeled from the attic, and the girl closed the door after him.

"Come here," shouted Madge, "come here, girl! Heed me, for I am dying. Avoid Yellow Maydock — heed not his boasted secret. The knowledge of it has been ruin to me, but to thee it will be death!"

With this the invalid sank back upon her couch of rags, and became insensible.

She never spoke again!

The exertion she had undergone had proved too much for her remaining strength, and the interview with the man who claimed to be her husband was her last earthly effort.

A thin stream of blood issued from her mouth, and trickled down her white face and saturated her pillow. Her eyes became glazed, and after a few convulsive movements of the feet and hands the spirit took its flight, and all was over.

The singing girl bent over the corpse, and tried to catch the breath. She placed her hand over the heart, and then tried to move the body.

It was full a minute before she could realise the fact, but at last it came upon her, and she screamed, "God of Heaven help me! for she is dead!"

Uttering these words she fell insensible over the body of her mother.

CHAPTER II.

HUNTED DOWN.

AN hour after Liz had arrived home a group of men might have been seen in the old court wherein stood the house in which she resided.

There were four in all—first, the stripling we introduced to the reader in the last chapter; second and third, his companions, two dissolute wretches whose faces bore traces of the havoc committed on the health by a life of debauchery and criminal indulgence; the fourth was the watchman, than whom, it will be conceded, a greater scoundrel could not exist. This little group of worthies stood in the shadow of the wall, and conversed in a low tone.

"That 'ere's the house; you had best mind what you're arter; its a queer place to get into at two o'clock in the morning, I can tell ye. Just be as leary as a fox, or ye'll get such a herd down upon ye as 'll considerably disarrange yer weak stomichs, and no mistake about it." Thus spoke the watchman.

"Never fear," said Wentworth, "this is not the first errand of the kind on which we have been engaged, and if we don't accomplish it successfully you are at liberty to speak. Now Portman, Lawrence, are you ready?"

"We are," replied one, while the other nodded.

"Then follow me," continued Wentworth. "The front attic, you say, Dawes?"

"Yes; the front 'un."

"All right; remain you here, and if necessary, give the alarm. See that the carriage still stands at the corner, and mind, above all, to give the signal for its approach directly we heave in sight."

"I understand," said the watchman, as his companions disappeared into the low lodging house. "Well," he continued, "this here's a fine bisness for a peace guardian to be arter, but the young 'un pays like, like—well, like only a prince can pay, and that's saying a great deal."

The three men crawled stealthily into the passage, and, with a cat-like step, ascended the creaking stairs.

Nothing arrested their progress, and they at length reached the attics; here they paused for an instant to reconnoitre.

Hearing nothing, Wentworth motioned his companions to enter the front apartment.

"There is not a sound," he whispered; "surely the whole lot are asleep or dead drunk. Now, make short work, and do not bungle."

"We never do," replied Portman, while Lawrence raised the latch.

A gust of fetid air greeted the three visitors as they opened the door.

"Pooh," cried Wentworth, "what a den! For Heaven's sake be quick." They entered.

The sight which greeted them was one they might well remember. There, on the heap of rags lay the corpse of the mother; across it, insensible, was prostrated the form of the daughter.

"By George," said Wentworth, "I never bargained for this; look to the girl, Lawrence, is she dead?"

"Nay, she only faints; but the old woman is stiff enough. What the devil can have been done here? Ah! blood from the mouth. I see: a blood vessel has been broken; the hands are clenched, and the teeth still set; the old hag has been terrified to death, and to judge from appearances, the young one isn't many doors removed from the undertakers."

"O, curse the undertakers, pick her up: now the cloak; its heavy folds will stifle a cry should she give utterance to one, which, by the way, does not seem likely. Bear her swiftly but gently over the stairs, and then away. By George! the work has been done much easier than I anticipated."

The two men raised the form of poor Liz, and, enveloping it in a large cloak, proceeded with it down the stairs.

Securely they reached the door, and gained the snow-covered court; and securely they crossed it, and gave the signal to the watchman to call the carriage.

The expectant peace guardian was ready, and uttering a long, thrilling whistle, the signal was conveyed, and a large, heavy, and sombre coach drew up.

Into this the inanimate form of Liz was placed, and after her sprang the three men who had borne her from the attic.

Wentworth looked through the window, and "tipped" the watchman handsomely, and then gave the signal for starting.

"St. James's or Kew?"

"Neither—are you mad? Go to Marlborough House, and put some life into the horses."

A slash of the whip, a little snorting, a slight swaying of the body of the coach, and the start was made.

"All's right!" said the watchman; "the girl's nabbed, the Prince is pleased, and I'm well paid —and never a soul the wiser."

"If yer excepts me," murmured one in a low tone, who stood concealed in an angle of the court, and who stepped into the open space as the vehicle drove off, and the watchman disappeared; "if yer excepts me! Hillo, Pipey, my covey," continued this individual, holding an animated conversation with himself: "this ere's a rum start, aint it, Pipey? You should think so, Pipey? Vy, in course you does. Old Brandy-nose saw the gal nabbed, and the Prince is pleased. Vell, if yer puts this and that together, Pipey, yer nat'rally draw a kinclusion to the effect that a prince of some breed or other has bin and bolted vith Singing Liz; and if yer asks yerself, Pipey, vy yer fixes upon Singing Liz as the likely 'ooman, yer replies that she's the only von in the court that a prince is likely to bolt vith. And so, as the Old Bailey lawyer says, by a perfectly nat'ral line of argument, it must be she. Yes, and you vould have stepped out and demanded toll, Pipey, only it vere not conwenient for yer to face the vatch jest now, and so yer jest kept dark and marked it all. Yes, Pipey, and von day the evidence you shall give the bench, or anybody as 'ull tip up for it, upon this matter, shall be the truth, the whole truth, and nothing but the truth—according to the rate they pay!"

This soliloquiser proved to be a very short and very slim young gentleman, who was dressed in clothes made for a man of three times his size. He was well known in the neighbourhood of the theatres, and had several times appeared, with more or less *eclat*, in the docks of the King's courts of law. The youth was a promising specimen of the light-fingered fraternity; and, being rather eccentric in his manner, was a great favourite with the *elite* of low Westminster. This was the individual who marked the abduction of Liz. He will play a prominent part hereafter, and so the reader had better remember this slight sketch of his peculiarities.

CHAPTER III.

MARLBOROUGH HOUSE.

THE town house of the present promising Prince and virtuous and well beloved Princess of Wales was not always the pure abode of domestic bliss we now behold it. With the present, however, we have nothing to do ; our duty is to chronicle the doings of a former generation ; would we could say, of a better one !

Silently the heavy carriage containing Liz and her captors rolled over the snow-covered streets. Silently it passed along under the grim shadow of St. James's, and, unheeded save by a few dissipated revellers, it entered the gates of the Pall Mall mansion.

"Who waits ?" cried Wentworth, springing from the carriage at the door of the house.

"Lord Mountcressy and the Earl of Larvelle, your Highness."

"Are the rest retired to bed ?"

"No, your Highness," said the porter to whom these questions were addressed, "there is cards and music in the green chamber : several gentlemen dropped in after the theatres, and Madame Toulafatte and other ladies drove here from the opera house, and said they would await your Highness's return."

"Oh, the devil take them. They must not see this girl, or there will be a noise. Here, Portman—Lawrence, run to the green chamber and allow no one to leave it until I have established the girl somewhere ; and you, sir, find some people to assist me."

Portman and Lawrence bowed and retired, whilst the porter ran off in another direction to find the required assistance.

With ease the son of George III., for such Wentworth really was, lifted the singer from the carriage, and bore her along the spacious corridors into a bye passage which, by an unfrequented staircase, led to a suite of rooms above. Here he was met and followed by a group of pages, or women masquerading in the guise of pages, who relieved him of his burden.

"Here, pretty ones," said the Prince, "here is a new mate for you, take care of her."

The women—poor wretches, they had all found their way into the house by similar means to those used to decoy Liz—swarmed about the still insensible singer, and removing the cloth which enveloped her fair form, commented on her looks.

In truth she could well bear the scrutiny.

A flood of golden hair poured over a neck as white and graceful as ever sat on human shoulders : her symmetry was perfect, and the dazzling fairness of her complexion spoke of better birth than that to which her humble, if not disreputable, calling would point. She was apparently not more than eighteen years of age, but there was a womanliness in her look which led many to suppose her slightly more advanced in years. The development of her form was faultless, and the expression of her features firm and dignified. Her mouth seemed formed for smiles, but it was just such a mouth that could, by the merest motion of the muscles of the lip, express the most supreme contempt and scorn. Her eyes were of a light blue, and of great depth and brilliancy. Well did she deserve the name of Fair Liz, for a fairer ne'er was seen.

Supported in the arms of the girl pages, Liz slowly recovered her senses. At first her great eyes wandered about wildly, but as consciousness returned their expression became more fixed.

"Where am I ?" cried the poor girl, staring at the magnificence which surrounded her. "Surely I am enchanted."

"Say rather enchanting, mistress," said one of the women.

"Who are you ?" asked Liz ; "by your voices I should take you to be women, but by your habits you should be men."

"It does not matter what our habits make us. We dress as it suits our tastes. You may not prefer trunks and hose, but we do ; they are so much more comfortable to move about in."

Poor depraved creature ; a few short months ago she would have shrank from such a guise as from a plague.

"Whoever you are," continued Liz, "explain to me where I am, and on what errand I came here. I dare not stay, for my mother—oh ! my poor mother ; do I remember rightly ? Was it a vision ? The man in the attic, the strange conversation, and the horrible death. Right ! it was no dream. The terrible reality comes strong upon me, and I can remember all. Oh, let me go ! My mother dead—dead from want and misery, lays without a soul to close her eyes, or watch over her. Oh ! let me go, I pray thee."

"Nonsense ; you will be better off here than watching over the body of a starved mother elsewhere. Shake off melancholy, and hey for the life of pleasure your fine face marks out for you."

"Well advised," said the Prince, stepping forward, and encountering the gaze of Liz for the first time, "well advised ; and you had better follow it, fair Liz, without any affectation of modesty or grief. It's an old game, and it has no effect."

"Who art thou, and what have you to do with this place ?"

"Not much," replied her captor, "not much ; but I make free with it when in town, that is all."

"Will you explain how I came here ?"

"Readily," replied the Prince, "to that I cannot have the slightest objection. You see, sweet, in spite of your coldness, I could not make up my mind to leave you without another glimpse of your transcendent face ; and so I followed you to some vile den they called your home. I found you insensible on the corpse of a horrible old woman ; and pitying your miserable condition, and being, moreover, madly in love with you, I thought the best thing to do was to bring you away with me. Acting on the impulse of the moment, I did so, and here you are."

"And what is your name ?"

"They call me George."

"And what is your calling?"

"Ah, ah ! upon my soul, that is charming ! My calling ? why, I have none as yet : but in time I shall have a great many, that is, if I survive my father."

"A light breaks in upon me : I see now who thou art. Yes, this place, these liveries, all confirm it."

"Well, dear, having opened your eyes to the facts, I trust you will not complain of the change I have taken the pains to make in your position.

I have positively expended one whole night in tracking you—I, who could bring half the noble blood of England at my feet by the beck of a finger!"

"That is possible: but the half you mean must hold their honour light. But mistake me not : fine houses, fine dresses, and fine words will not affect me. I am proof against all the temptations you can throw in my path, and I demand an instant release. I cannot breathe the air of this place : I would return to a purer atmosphere."

"Oh, hang it! you can't be talking of that cursed dead-house from which I snatched you. A purer atmosphere! By George! I shall never get the stench out of my nostrils."

"At least it was free of the taint of sin. I cannot say as much for this."

"Well, you have a miserable taste; but it is useless to argue with me. I can't stand it: moreover, I am used to be obeyed, so no more."

"Yes," cried Liz, "more and more—much more, unless you consent to my immediate departure. I tell you I will not remain here; so let me pass."

"Never."

"Then I will expose you."

"Do. To whom?"

"To all mankind."

"That is to say, to all the mankind and womankind you are ever likely to see until you become more tractable. Well, do so. I have no doubt they will be very charmed with the revelation."

"Oh, villain! can I not move thee? Will not prayers and entreaties suffice to ransom me?"

"They will not."

"Then my curses—"

"Oh nonsense! ladies do not curse: and, if they do, it makes no great difference, for they always rub them out with a blessing immediately after uttered."

"Stoney-hearted monster!"

"My dear, you are getting extremely personal; and so, for a while, I must say adieu. I shall see you again soon; and, in the meanwhile, do try and collect yourself a little. Do, there's a dear."

With this the youth turned on his heel, and, with a final word of direction to the women, walked away.

"Come," cried one of the *soi disant* pages, "come, Liz—since that appears to be your name, come to your chamber; for we really want to go to ours, and, until we have disposed of you, that is an impossibility."

"Oh, if you are women, let me leave this place," cried Liz, in an agony of grief; "let me quit this house, and I will bless you."

"That would do us but little service," said the one who had previously spoken; "I am afraid that we could set no more store on your blessings than the Prince does on your curses, for we have grown quite indifferent to such things. Oh, a few months within these and similar walls will teach you, as it has done us, to look to more tangible things than blessings or curses."

"God of Heaven!" almost shrieked Liz, "I cannot stay here. Oh! be merciful, and let me depart. You cannot be dead to all sense of womanly feelings. Will not your hearts plead for a young and innocent girl?"

"We were innocent ourselves once, and that not very long ago; but no one pleaded for us, and we are—well, you can conceive what we are. A life such as we have led has deadened most of the womanly feelings nature gave us; and, ere long, you will become as indifferent as we are. You may hold out for a while—most of us did—but it was useless, TRIAL and TEMPTATION everywhere: we could not withstand it, and from being indignant we became indifferent; and, then, all that had once disgusted us served to please—then to delight, and now to intoxicate. No mortal woman could withstand the fascinations of this place. Wait till the perfumes steal into your brain; wait till the light and glitter of jewels affect your sight; wait till the delicious music drowns the sorrows of your heart, and wait till the voices of a thousand brilliant flatterers flow into your ears, and the sparkling wine excites the brain, and then will come your time. Better than you have fallen ere now; better will fall every day to the end of time. But, psha! what detestable moralising this is; come, rouse thee, fair Liz, and think no more of the future. Care is a dull knave, let us drive him away."

Liz saw that appeal to the women into whose charge she was given was perfectly useless, and so she ceased her importunities, and followed her new friends without another word.

She was trapped now.

Yes, fairly in the toils of the cunning hunter.

CHAPTER IV.

A LAWYER ON A SCENT.

THE Smutty Quaker was the sign of the little, dirty public-house at the corner of Abbey Buildings: it was quite on a par with the rest of the salubrious neighbourhood, and its frequenters were persons of no particular claims to respectability or high social standing. In fact, they were no less than a gang of Westminster thieves of the worst class. On the night of the opening of this story this notorious house of entertainment was, as usual, crowded with its regular customers. The rooms were full to overflowing, and brutal mirth was running riot.

One of the most conspicuous of the customers was the gentleman to whom we have already been introduced in a preceding chapter. This was Yellow Maydock, the supposed husband of the woman who died so terrible a death on the heap of rags in the old attic.

Yellow Maydock was a tall, coarse man, with long sandy hair and beard. He looked every inch a ruffian, and his behaviour corresponded with his appearance.

On returning from the chamber of death with the two guineas, he commenced drinking inordinately, and in a short time had disposed of one of the gold pieces.

"Steady," he cried at length; "steady, Maydock, you'll want some of this swag to-morrow, and you won't get any more out of the old woman, so be careful.''

If he could have only acted up to the good advice he offered himself he would have done very well; but the love of drink overpowered every other feeling, and in less than three hours after his visit to the attic in Abbey Buildings he was reduced to his last shilling.

This made him surly, and he retired to a quiet corner and fell into a profound slumber.

Meanwhile the diversions of the thieves were being continued with unabated fury around him. Dancing was the chief amusement, but singing was also popular; and several flash ditties were carolled forth in a variety of tones, ranging from the gruff bass of the house burglar to the shrill, cracked notes of the gin-soddened street ballad-singer. Most of these ditties were accompanied by a chorus, in which the whole vocal strength of the company lent its powerful but inharmonious aid.

One of the songs will serve as a specimen of all the rest; and so we select a sample, given by a youthful thief, whose vocation was plied at the theatres.

In a miserably cracked voice, the young gentleman sang as follows:—

THE LIFE OF A PRIG.

I.

Oh, a merry life is the life of a gent
  As lives on the gents as he meets,
And *borrows* the svag vich never vos *lent*
  By the friends he finds in the streets.
Off he goes to the play, but don't care a jot
  'Bout acting nor actors—not he;
He comes there, you flad, to make a great pot,
  And the best of all actors is he.
    Chorus:—Then here's to the prig:
      His health in a swig
      Of the best hops, malt, and bar-le.

II.

Oh, he comes 'fore the beak, if the case is weak,
  Vy, he treats it as light as you please;
If t'other, my lads, vy he comes the meek,
  'Cos he don't like soup made o' peas.
He objects to the jug, and hates mills to tread,
  He don't like his hair to see
Chopped off, my boy, right close to his 'ed,
  'Cos he would a nobby svell be.
    Chorus:—Then here's to the prig,
      His health in a swig
      Of hot, sweet, and strong bran-de.

The young vocalist was about to commence another verse of this charming effusion when a loud knock at the outer door startled the whole of the company out of their propriety.

"Hist!" cried the landlord; "lights down, and the vonted 'uns below. That's awfully like a Charley's bang."

Bang, bang, bang! again fell the blows upon the door.

In a few seconds the "wanted" gentlemen disappeared, the lights were lowered, and the landlord approached the door.''

"Who is there?"

"A friend."

"What friend?"

"An old one."

"We're werry *old ones*, all of us in here. How old do you happen to be?"

"Come, cease your jaw, Job Winchurch, and let me in."

"You vill just let me in as to who you is, and then I may return the compliment."

"Curse the fellow! Do you think I'm going to shout out my name in the streets for every fool to know that I am here?"

"I'm afraid you'll have to, my sweet child, before I opens the door."

"Don't you know my voice?"

"I think I does, my 'andsome baby; I think I does. 'Av'nt I heerd it at the Old Bailey afore now? I think I has an uncommon quick ear for detecting the wocal notes of my friends the Charleys."

"Oh, d—n the Charleys! Since you will let the world know who is here, it's Grimer."

"Grimer!" said Job, lowering the chains and drawing the bolts with all alacrity. "Grimer! Vell, to think I didn't remember yer voice agin. Light up, my beautiful infants. Yer's yer precious friend and parient, Mr. Grimer, come for to see yer. Lights up there, and make him welcome!"

"Hurrah for Grimer!" shouted the mob. "Hurrah for the friend of the poor purfessional!"

The object of this ovation was a little, podgy fellow, in a very seedy suit of black, much the worse for wear, and still more for snuff, with which the garments were literally tanned.

Mr. Grimer was about the lowest of a very low set of Old Bailey lawyers, and his practice was derived from the defence of such petty criminals as those to whom he was now paying so late, or, rather, early and mysterious a visit. He was a man of undoubted ability as a lawyer, but from his low and debased tastes and habits, and a miserly love of pelf, he had degraded himself so low that the respectable members of his profession would have as soon taken by the hand one of the thieves he defended as himself.

Such was the man who came to the Smutty Quaker on the chill December night and morning of the opening of this tale of mystery and misery.

"Vill you valk in vith the children?" asked the obliging Job of his guest.

"No, Job; no. I'd rather not. Just take me into your private bar, will you? I want to ask you something."

"Valk in and velcome," said the magnanimous innkeeper. "Can I offer you anythink in the shape of refreshments, sir?"

"I don't mind taking the least drop of brandy—warm, Job; but don't make it too strong, or it will get up in my head. Ha! ha!"

This was a standing joke of Mr. Grimer's, and all his clients were supposed to laugh at it. The point of the thing was to be found in the fact that Grimes could drink a bucketful without being made drunk.

Grimer had his brandy warm and sipping it he said:—

"Job, I know it's not in your line to sell any friends of yours when they are inquired after."

"No one can ever lay sich a dirty action as

that at my door ven I'm a dead un," interpolated Job.

"Just so, but you see, Job, in an emergency you wouldn't mind saying to me, Job—to me, that you knew where to put your hand on a certain party if I wanted him."

"Vell," said Job, "if he vere vanted for any think not connected with his purfession and alvays understood that there vasn't not never a beak or a Charley in the case, I might be indooced to say I does know vere he could be found."

"Just so, Job, just so," said the lawyer; "that's precisely the case, Job. Now, I particularly want an acquaintance of yours at the present moment. Do you mind telling me where he is?"

"And no gammon?" demanded Job.

"Honour!" said the lawyer.

"Vell, then, I don't mind telling—always per-wided that I knows."

"Just so, Job, just so."

Of course, if I don't know you vouldn't expect me tell?"

"Just so, Job, just so."

Just so, then, Mr. Grimer."

"Well, Job, I want to see your friend Yellow Maydock very particularly."

"Yes; but I say, you know the yellow boy *is* a vanted, and no mistake."

"Yes," said Grimer, "so I believe, but I have no hand in the matter. This is a private affair, which we could settle in a few minutes."

"Vell, then, I trusts in your honour, and I tells you he is here."

"Just so, Job, I knew that; I have been on his track for the last week, but could never get at him until now. Just tell him that I am here."

"Now, Mr. Grimer, there *is* no gammon?" asked Job, very impressively.

"Honour!" said Grimer.

"Then I'll hunt him up," said Job, leaving the private bar.

"Good," said Grimer; "now to see if there is any hope."

Job went to Yellow Maydock's corner, and endeavoured to awake him, but this was a work of time that required patience. After a severe application of cold water, however, Maydock opened his eyes.

"Now then," cried Job, "now then, you're a vanted."

"Am I?" asked Job, "then I shan't come."

"Oh, wake up; here's a genleman arter you on pertickler private business; says he must see you, and no mistake."

"There will be a mistake if he does," said Maydock, determinedly.

"Nonsense; its Mr. Grimer, and he really vants you on business of his own."

"Oh! that is it. Then Mr. Grimer may as well go again, for he'll get nothing out of me. No, no, Grimer; I'm not so green as to part with my secrets, so that you can coin a fortune out of them."

"Vy, vot does the fellow mean?"

"Oh nothing—nothing that you can understand."

"Vell, you needn't be uncivil, yer warmint, more specially to Grimer; he knows as you're vanted, and if you can do him a good turn you'd better, as p'raps he may take it into his 'ed to tell certain parties as shall be nameless vere you're to be found. Now, are ye going to see the gemman?"

"Oh, I s'pose I must," sulkily grunted the anything but pleased Maydock; "I s'pose I must: where is he?"

"Come on," was Job's reply.

They entered the private bar and found Mr. Grimer comfortably seated, with his feet on the fender of the grate and his glass in his hand.

On the entrance of the worthy host and his guest the lawyer looked up, and exclaimed:

"Well, Yellow Boy, I've found you at last."

"Yes," replied Maydock, "and much good may the discovery do you."

"Oh, that's a kind wish," was the lawyer's quiet reply, "a very kind wish: yes, much good may it do me. I think it will do me a little good, Maydock."

"I doubt it," said that worthy, taking a chair.

"I do not," remarked Grimer, coolly; "but we shall see. Job, give the Yellow Boy some brandy."

"No he don't," said Maydock, with a grin, "no he don't. I shall want all my wits in dealing with you, and so no brandy."

"As you please."

"Well, that s as I please."

"Good: now Job, get out; our conversation is strictly private; remember, no admision, under any pretence."

"I'm fly," said Job, winking and quitting the room. "I'll just lock the door on the other side,

so ven you vants to cut the confab just knock and I ll shoot the bolt and show you daylight."

With this Job disappeared.

"Now then," said the lawyer, turning to Maydock, "now then, my friend."

"Now then," remarked Maydock.

"I suppose you know what brought me here?"

"No"

"That's a lie!"

"You're a gentleman."

"Bah! no fooling; I've no inclination nor time for it; it is now four, and at seven I must be at Newgate, so I have no spare moments to expend in child's play."

"You came to please yourself and you can go when you please: you can talk as much or as little as you like, or you needn't talk at all but take your hook at once, I aint particular."

"Oh, hang the fellow!" cried Grimer,

"I must come to the point at once; now what about that will?"

"Which will?"

"*The* will: I know of but one."

"I know of a whole heap; you must name the particular one."

"Well, if you will be so cursed obstinate, the Duke's will."

"What of it?"

"That is what I am asking you: what of it?"

"That's my business."

"By God, fellow, you shall soon find that it's mine; where is that will?"

"Where you, nor nobody like you, is ever likely to get at it; aint that enough?"

"No, it is not. I must and will have it."

"How will you get it?"

"You will give it me."

"Will I?"

"You must."

"Must!"

"Yes, must!"

"Where's the necessity?"

"Just here—listen: I see your memory wants touching up a little. I'll run over the necessities, one after another, and if you fail to appreciate them the result will be upon your own head."

"It won't give me a headache."

"We shall see."

"We may."

"Now, seventeen years ago you and your wife were servants at Marlborough House, and wore the livery of the Earl of Portville, who then had a suite of rooms in the house. On a November night in the year I have mentioned, a lady was brought in a mysterious manner to the house. She was conveyed to a chamber, and there, in the course of the night, gave birth to a child."

"You seem well up in the story."

"You will say so before I have done. Although you were professedly in the interest of the earl, who at the time was little more than a boy, you were in reality no better than a spy upon him—the paid spy of his father, the old duke. Now the lady who was conveyed to Marlborough House on the November night of which I speak was the wife of the earl; poor and lowly she may have been, but still she was his wife. You know it, for you were a witness to the ceremony."

"Bah! a false priest, a mock ceremony. It was all a sham, to settle a few qualms of conscience."

"You thought so; but I can prove that that marriage was legally solemnised. The false priest was a real priest after all, and the ceremony, therefore, perfectly valid. But to return to the tale. The wife of the earl was delivered of a child in Marlborough House, and soon after its birth the old duke arrived, and you had an interview with him; what passed you best know, but what followed I can tell you: you went to your wife, and, by dint of persuasion, temptation, and force, you induced her to make away with the infant; whether she did so or not you best know. In the next place you failed to send for medical aid, and the poor young countess was permitted to die from the absence of professional assistance. She died and was buried—I know where—and soon after her decease the old duke followed her, leaving the earl sole possessor of the estates and titles; but there was a death-bed scene, to which you and your wife were witnesses. You may remember that in an agony of remorse at the crimes of which he had been guilty the old duke made a will, leaving the bulk of his estates to the family of the woman whom he had been instrumental in murdering. The will was signed by you and your wife, and it was deposited with *me*. You may remember doing so."

"I can't say that I do."

"You won't say that you do, but that is immaterial. You deposited the will with me, and persuaded me that it might be as well to keep it dark, in order that we might be enabled to make something out of it — either through the woman's family, or by flashing it in the eyes of the young duke whenever we should be in want of money or interest. I consented, and locked the will away. The duke went abroad, and the will rested for a while. Then we made search for some clue to the woman's friends, but all our efforts only tended to prove that she was alone in the world, and that there was nothing to be got from that quarter. Some three years passed, and you came to me and demanded the will. You had evidently heard something which made it necessary for you to regain possession of the document. I know not what that something was, but I shrewdly suspect that *the child was not disposed of by your wife;* in fact, that it lived, that you knew where to put your hand upon it, and that you thought to make a good thing out of it, and keep it all to yourself. Ah, you start! I think I have touched you at last. Well, I declined to part with the will, and then *you stole it.*"

"Did I?"

"You did. It's not worth denying. I say you stole it; but as I saw no immediate sign of its being of service to me I kept quiet, determined to wait my time. Years I have waited, and now I tell you the time is come! I have you in my toils; a word from me would hang you at any moment. I have a long score of robbery, forgery, burglary, and other crimes of more or less magnitude against you, and the day of reckoning has come. All shall be wiped off if you produce that will."

"Shall it though? Well, that's kind; but, excuse me, I don't see it."

With this Maydock applied his fingers to his nose, winked, and whistled derisively.

"Well," said the yellow one, "you are a generous old swell, to be sure. And so you would wipe off all my little crimes if I would give you the will? Of course you would; but I ain't so green. No, no. Look here. I know where the will is; you don't. I know where the parties are as would like to get hold of that will, you don't; and I know all the circumstances connected with the affair, and you only guess at 'em. What could you do without me? S'pose you hanged me. What are you the better for that? Why, all your hopes is bottled up at once. With my death your prospects die, and so you'll keep me alive. I know you will, cos if that hadn't been your game you would have scragged me long ago. Now we understand one another, and you had better tell Job to shoot back the bolt."

"Devil!" muttered the lawyer.

"Well, the same to you," said Maydock, "and I don't care how many of 'em; you see, you're done, and so good morning."

"Don't tempt me too far, Maydock; I tell you I may yet hand you over to the hangman, in spite of all."

"Do; I'm ready."

"You may soon be called upon."

"Good; and now open the door."

The lawyer knocked, and the bolt was shot back. Turning on his companion as he left the bar, Grimer exclaimed,

"Mark me, it is now a race between us. I am on the scent, and its hard if I don't run the fox to earth."

"Go it," said Maydock; "I shall be handy at all times."

With this the men separated.

After Grimer had gone Maydock exclaimed, hurriedly,

"So, so; it's fortunate I dropped upon the pair of women to-night. Grimer's threats musn't be despised; he's a devil when he's roused. What's to be done? The first thing is to remove the women."

This had already been done for him. One was removed for ever by the hand of Heaven; the other was carried off by the libertine

"Yes," continued Maydock, "they must be got far away from the clutches of old Grimer."

CHAPTER IV.

THE GAME IS UP.—GRIMER GETS THE START.

GRIMER strode out of the house and into the streets.

At the corner of the court called the Abbey Buildings, wherein the unhappy wife of Maydock resided with Fair Liz, the ballad singer, stood the youth who had witnessed the abduction of the latter.

He had evidently no taste for bed, and, in spite of the intense coldness of the morning, prowled about with evident enjoyment. No sooner did he catch sight of the figure of Grimer than out he pounced upon him.

"He may have a vatch, and he's sure to have a vipe," uttered the youthful thief.

But he had mistaken his man, for no sooner was he within reach of the lawyer's stick than he felt it across his shoulders.

"Hillo, young Newgate," cried Grimer; "you had better keep your distance or I'll crack your skull open for you in no time."

"Vot did you go for to hit a poor kid like that for?" demanded the young hopeful.

"Because I didn't choose to have the poor kid dipping his hands into my pockets. Now, jail bird, what brings you about at this hour."

"Vy, it's Mr. Grimer," said the youth; "it's Mr. Grimer, I declare. Vell now, who would a thought to find you here?"

"Not you, evidently, or you would not have come within reach of my stick."

"Vell, this here is a blessed surprise and no gammon."

"Never mind the surprise; what has brought you out at this time, I say. Can't you answer?"

"Vell, I've been vorried in my mind ever since I got away from the vest end last night. I tell you vot, Mr. Grimer, there's been the devil's own games 'a going on here to-night; if there ain't—kick me."

"What do you mean, dog?—speak out."

"Vell, I vill, if you'll jist listen. Now, in the fust place, a young 'oman as lives next door to me, in the sky parlours of yonder house, has been a boned, valked off, cut vith, by a lot of svells. I see the start myself."

"The deuce you did; who were the parties?"

The gal they call Fair Liz, the Vestminster ballad singer, and the svells I don't name, but you may guess who they is ven I tells you that they ordered the coachman to drive to Marlborough House,"

"The deuce!"

"Yes."

"Well, proceed."

"I thought, arter I seed the cut, that I'd jist step upstairs, and see how the old 'oman, her mother, liked it, so up I goes, and tries the door—it vere a-jar, and in I valks. 'Meg,' says I, 'Meg, how about Liz?' but there vos no answer. She's asleep, thinks I, and knows nothing of the affair. The light vos out, and so I goes in and strikes one. Down I goes on my knees at the bed-side, and sings out again 'Meg, Meg! there, the svells have a bolted vith Liz; vake up, I tells ye!' but it vos no go, there warn't no answer, so I puts the light down close to her face, and vot does I see but a blessed corpse. Meg Maydock vos dead.

Grimer clutched the lad's arm.

"Here, you're a sqveezing my arm off," cried the youngster "let go, vill ye?"

"What name?—what name?"

"Meg Maydock," I said; "Meg Maydock; ain't that plain enough?"

"Yes, yes; but you interest me. Go on."

"Go on! I ain't a going on any further, that's all I knows; Meg vos dead, and so I stepped it out here."

"Yes, yes," cried Grimer, "it must be so; he here, the same name—and the girl, ay, the girl! At last I am right; at last I have a fair starting point; at last the game is in sight, and I can work in daylight."

"Vot the deuce are you a chattering about?" asked Pipey.

"Here, boy; you have done me a good turn to-night, and I will not forget it. Here's a guinea for you, and if you want to earn more you have only to obey me and keep a quiet tongue. Mention what you have seen to-night to no one; above all, breathe not a word to the man Yellow Maydock, who is now in the public-house yonder. Do you understand?"

"I'm downy."

"There's money to be made out of this—lots of money, and you shall have your share; but only act on my orders, or you will spoil all."

"That's right enough, but I don't care about vorking in the dark. Just give us a hint of vot's a going on, so that I mayn't put my foot into it through floundering about in the gloom."

"Briefly, then," said the lawyer, "I believe that this girl—this Liz—is not what she seems. These Maydocks know it, and have done their best to keep her out of the way because of certain circumstances into which I cannot enter just now. However, I may tell you that there is a will in the case, and that will I must have."

"Vere is it."

"I know not, but I think it is in the possession of Yellow Maydock; at all events he knows where it is to be found."

"I'll soon let you know vether he's a got it about him. In five minutes my hand vould cross from the top of his 'ed to the sole of his boots, and if he had about him a scrap of paper no bigger than a lady's note I'd get it from him."

"I believe you are quite capable, but do nothing hastily; Maydock is a dangerous man, and may thwart us if we are not careful: nevertheless, you may stick close to him, and keep your eyes open. What you may hear communicate to me; and mind, no blundering—I trust in you."

"You know you can do so with safety. Im as downy as a monkey."

"All right, lad; and now, good morning; you know where to find me when I am wanted."

"At the old shop?"

"Yes; or, if not there—"

"At the Old Bailey; I know, but I hopes you'll always be at home ven I calls, cos I has some qualms of conscience about mixing in such low society as is found in them 'ere courts of justice; besides, ven they gets hold o' me they falls so desperately in love vith my society that the devil himself can't persuade 'em to let me go again."

"Ah! ah! you're a funny boy, and deserve encouragement. Good morning."

"Good morning, Mr. Grimer; good luck to ye."

With this the pair separated.

"Vell," said Pipey, "I've got a job at last, a reg'lar engagement; I'm in a plot to do somebody out of something, but it's all the same to this 'ere cove, so long as they tips up the browns."

At this moment Maydock staggered out of the public-house and ran against the downy one.

"Hillo," said the former, "what's your game?"

"Vot's yours, 'andsome?"

"Hillo, it's you, is it? Don't you remember my face? We met a few hours ago in the public there. You told me that Meg Maydock was ill."

"Did I?" inquired the youngster. "Oh, is that all?"

"That's all; good morning."

"Good morning."

Maydock entered the house where he had left his wife, and stumbled up the stairs. The lad followed him.

The brutal husband felt for the door of the attic, and staggered in.

It was still dark, so dark that he could discern nothing.

"Here, Meg," he cried, "show us a light. Hillo, young 'oman, get up and show us a light. Thunder and lightning! are you both dead?"

It appeared so; there came no answer.

"Hoy! Meg! I say, curse you, won't you answer me? Show us a light."

Still no answer.

"Come, you'd better wake up," continued the bully, "as you'll feel my fingers at your throat in another minute."

Still a dead, unbroken silence.

"This is too much for me to stand," yelled the fellow. "I'll soon bring you to your senses."

Uttering these words, he groped about until he felt the heap of rags which served for a bed.

"Oh, here you are, are you? Now I'll see if I can't put some motion into you!"

He stretched forth his hand and felt for the recumbent form he imagined to be there. He felt it, and then, raising his heavy fist, he dashed it down twice or thrice heavily.

"There, curse you! won't that make you speak?"

The fist fell with dull, heavy thuds on the body, but there was not a sign of motion.

Maydock was startled.

He stretched forth his hand again, and now it touched a cold, clammy face, which he knew must belong to a dead body.

With a shriek he jumped to his feet, and in the first agony of terror cried,

"Help! help!"

Pipey, who had followed him into the room, now advanced, and called out

"Vot's up, man alive?—you're a raising the house vith yer noise!"

"Who are you?"

"The cove you saw in the court just now," replied the lad.

"That's well. For God's sake show us a light."

"In a moment," said the promising juvenile. "Here yer are."

He struck a flint and steel, and in a moment had ignited a large piece of paper.

They advanced to the bed and looked down upon the ghastly features of the corpse.

"She's a gone case at last," said the youth. "Poor Meg!"

"Poor Meg!" muttered the other; "yes, poor Meg, indeed! But the girl—where's the girl?"

"Vot gall?"

"Why, her girl—the girl who was with her to-night?"

"Is she a gone?" asked Pipey, innocently enough.

"Yes, gone!" replied the other.

"Vell, that's a go," remarked the youth. "But p'raps she's off for the vorkhouse doctor, or some other equally talented gemman. I s'pose she vont be long."

"The deuce she wont!" said Maydock; "why, look here—see this, here's all her clothes."

"So there is! Vy she must be a valking in her sleep."

"Fool!" cried Maydock, "cease your nonsense."

At this moment the eye of the ruffian fell upon the ground, and there he beheld a glove and a lace ruffle.

He snatched them up, and examined them minutely,

"Ha!" he cried, "I see it all!"

"Vy, vot does you see?"

"Look here—a glove and lace ruffle, which could only be worn by a nobleman. The girl has bolted with some swell."

"A werry sensible proceeding on the young 'oman's part," observed Pipey.

"Curses on it," cried the other; "her disappearance ruins all."

"Does it though?" asked the youth.

"Yes, yes; but you don't understand it. You don't know the meaning of all this."

"Oh, don't I though?" thought the wide-awake young gentleman. "Oh, don't I, though; that's all you know about it."

"Well, there's no help for it, but it's thundering bad luck, just as I had made all so square; howsomever, I'm not done yet. Sudden lose sudden find, p'raps. It mayn't take me long to drop upon the gal if I keep my eyes open."

"P'raps not," remarked Pipey.

"Look here," continued Maydock, "you knew her, and seem to be a leary one, just keep your eyes open, and try and drop across the wench. If you find her it may be good for you. Can I trust you?"

"Can't you?"

"Well, then, there's money hanging to the wench, and I must get hold of her. Do you understand that?"

"I am there, or thereabout."

"Good. Do we understand each other."

"We does."

"Then all's right. I daren't leave the crib yonder for some time to come. I'm wanted, but you can run about and keep yer eyes open."

"I can."

"Then don't by any chance shut 'em."

"Right."

"Now let us get back to the crib, it's near daylight, and it's dangerous for me to be out."

He then blew out their light, and without another glance at the corpse passed from the apartment.

In a few moments they were again in the public-house. Maydock procured some brandy on trust, and the men providing themselves with long pipes commenced a carousal. They both drank freely, but Maydock, who had not yet recovered the effects of his recent fit of drunkenness, soon dropped off to sleep, leaving his young companion to amuse himself as he best could.

The house was by this time perfectly still. The landlord slept behind his bar. The "wanted" gentlemen were dead asleep on the benches, and the others had gone forth to business again. "Now," said the juvenile, "now's my time. Let's see if this will is to be had."

The hand of the young thief glided over the dress of the slumbering Maydock, examining every part of the costume with the greatest care, but so carefully was this done that the man felt nothing.

"Vy he's as poor as a church mouse, not a scrip nor a screw about him. Hillo, vot's this?"

He drew forth an antique key attached to a small chain.

"Vell, it don't look of much account," said the boy, "but ve may as vell take an impression" Holding the key in his hand he concealed it in the hollow of his palm, and then dived into his coat pocket and drew forth a crust of bread. Breaking off a small piece he put it into his mouth and chewed it slightly. He then put it between his fingers and worked it into a paste. When he had done this to his own satisfaction he placed the purloined key upon it, and took a perfect impression. This he placed on the dying embers of the fire, and then returned the key to the pocket of its owner. He was but just in time, for as he returned it the man turned in his sleep, and with a start dived his hand into his pocket and felt for the key. It was there safe, and so he slumbered again.

CHAPTER V.

A VISION IN THE HAUNTED CHAMBER.

LIZ was dragged away through innumerable passages, and at length reached the quarter of the house set apart for the pages.

"Now," said one of those who conducted her, "now, then, let us know one another. I'm Adele, that's Louise, there's Florence, and that's Lavinia. In public I'm Adolphe, Louise is Horace, Florence is Francis, and Lavinia is Edward."

As she spoke she pointed out her companions. Adele was a splendid girl, scarcely more than nineteen years of age, with hair dark as night, and large lustrous eyes ; her form was as perfect as possible, and was well set off by her neat dress. Louise and Florence were brunettes, of scarce more than twenty summers ; they, too, were of excellent symmetry. Lavinia, like Liz, was extremely fair, but her hair was of a perfect auburn hue, and her figure slighter than that of the others.

"Now," continued Adele, "what is your name?"

' Liz,'' replied the ballad singer.

"Liz! you mean Elizabeth, I suppose?"

"No ; I have never been called anything but Liz."

"Well then, Liz, how did the Prince find you?"

Liz briefly repeated her history.

"Ah!" said Louise, "that is the old, old tale."

"Yes," said Adele, "that is his usual style.

Not one of us came here of our own consent— few do. However, one day we will tell you our stories, but now to bed."

"Where shall we put her?" asked Florence.

"Where? why, there is but one room for her; you know that."

"Yes, but she can't sleep there."

"Why not?"

"Because the place is haunted."

"Psha!" said Adele, with a contemptuous smile ; "who believes in ghosts. Do you, Liz?"

"Not I," said Liz, "not I."

"Well, then, the haunted chamber be it."

They conducted the girl to the chamber, and pushed her in.

"There you are," said Louise, "there you are ; and if you see the White Lady be sure and tell me in the morning what she is like."

A lamp was left with the girl, and she was alone.

It was a grim old room, furnished in the style of a bygone age, and a heavy gloom hung around it.

The bed was massive, and was covered with heavy and faded curtains, which hung in massive folds from near the ceiling to the ground.

The other material was entirely of the same character, and the whole chamber wore a dis. heartening and singularly oppressive look. The walls were decked with large mirrors, which reflected back the images with which they came in contact until the room seemed full of figures, flitting about in a miserable gloom.

Liz was awed, and sprang into bed without a moment's delay. She did not, however, extinguish her lamp, for she had a great horror of the darkness in such a place.

Once on the pillow she reviewed the singular events of the night in the order in which they occurred ; in imagination she went back to the public-house, then came the meeting in the street, then the scene in the attic ; next, the unconsciousness, and then the awakening in the mysterious house among the still more mysterious women. These events confused and perplexed her, and, exhausted nature getting the better of her, she at length mingled them in a phantasmagoria of horrors, and then dropped into a profound slumber.

All was still as in a chamber of death, and she slept soundly. An hour must have passed when the poor girl was startled by experiencing a sharp, cold breathing over her face and bosom.

Half awake, she turned her face and drew close her clothing, but the cold blast still penetrated to her heart and made the teeth chatter in her head.

As this became unbearable the girl raised herself on her elbow and gazed about her.

Her eye fell upon the retreating form of a woman clad in white. It was a figure of the middle height, but of singular grace and beauty ; the face would have been positively grand and enrapturing but for its expressionless eye and want of colour. The movements of this apparition were quiet and mechanical It advanced and retreated, extended an arm and bowed its head, and then opened its lips as if to speak, but no sound escaped it.

At first the girl was horror-stricken, but

gradually this feeling deserted her, and terror gave place to admiration.

She felt stealing over her a mysterious sympathy for this vision which she could scarce comprehend; certain it is that her heart yearned towards it, and that she would have embraced it had such a course been practicable.

The spectre stood before the girl for more than a minute, and then it moved away; and as it altogether faded from her sight Liz heard it utter the word "daughter" thrice in a deep hollow voice.

Liz shrieked aloud and then fell back fainting.

In a minute her chamber was besieged with the women who had conducted her thereto: they crowded about her and strove to bring her to by every means in their power; at length they succeeded and Liz opened her eyes.

"What has happened?" cried the girls in a chorus.

"Hush," said Liz, "I have seen it."

"What?"

"The White Lady, as you term the spectre that haunts this chamber."

"Oh nonsense," cried Adele, "nonsense; you have been dreaming."

"Would to Heaven I had: I tell you it was no dream but a terrible reality. As surely as you are here so surely did I behold the spectre at my bedside: I not only saw it but felt its icy breath on my face and bosom and heard its deep supernatural voice."

"Strange," said Adele; "are you sure your imagination has not been playing you tricks?"

"I am sure that I have not been deceived."

"I can scarce credit your words, but you appear collected and truthful."

"Yes, yes," cried Liz; "I am collected—I am truthful. What should I gain by a lie?"

"What indeed?" asked Adele.

"She cannot remain here," cried Louise; "the poor thing will be frightened to death. She must come with one of us."

"No, no," said Liz; "I am not afraid—pray leave me. The vision will not alarm me again should it appear. Indeed, indeed I was not frightened at it, and know not why I shrieked. Return to bed and rest without fear of being again disturbed by me."

"Well," said Adele, "have your own way; but if I had seen a ghost you would not get me to remain in the spot where it appeared."

"Nor I—nor I," cried the women.

"I fear nothing," said Liz, again resting her head on the pillow as the others withdrew.

CHAPTER VI.

A NIGHT OF REVELRY.

It is now time we returned to the youth through whose instrumentality Liz was brought to Marlborough House. Having disposed of the girl as hereinbefore detailed, he turned to the apartment indicated by the servant as being the one wherein the guests had assembled. Entering a brilliantly lighted and gorgeously furnished chamber, the youthful Prince found himself in the presence of about a dozen men and women, who were in the midst of a deep and wild carousal.

The tables were covered with choicest fruits and confections, and wines of all descriptions; and by the confusion of the scene it was evident that the revellers had not cared much how they served the articles placed for their use. Gorgeous salvers and choicest glass lay strewed and broken over the floor, and the table was in itself a perfect chaos of empty and broken bottles and half-eaten fruit.

The participators in this scene were mostly women of great personal beauty, whose moral parts were scarcely on a par with their other charms; they disported themselves about the apartments with the most reckless *abandon*, and seemed as drunk with excitement as they were heated with wine.

The men were in the same condition and wild jests and obscene anecdote was the order of the day.

On entering, the youth was received with a shout of delight.

"Here is George," cried the women; "here is our darling George at last."

"Yes, at last," said the men. "Why, we thought you were never coming."

"I did not expect you, or I should have returned earlier."

"Not expect us?" cried the women; "not expect us? as if we could stop away from so charming a house and so charming a prince. No, no, the temptation is far too strong for poor, weak women."

"And now," demanded one of the men, "where have you been?"

"Oh, nowhere; that is, nowhere of any importance."

"He has been breaking the hearts of some poor women, whom we do not know; that is what he has been doing, and he can't deny it. Ah, me! he makes some fresh conquest every day, and entirely forgets his oldest and most devoted ones."

This speech of one of the women seemed to tickle the vanity of the boy to a great extent, and it was evident that he was susceptible to flattery, even of the grossest kind.

"Oh," said one of the men, "he is a confirmed heart-breaker; there is no withstanding him, is there, Marie *mia*?"

This question was addressed to a fine, dark-eyed girl who sat a little apart from the others, and appeared interested in anything but what was progressing about her.

"Who is our new acquaintance," demanded the Prince.

"Oh, I forgot that your Highness needs an introduction; this is our Marie, who has created such a sensation at the opera. Your long absence from town has as yet deprived you of the pleasure of hearing her voice; but you will avail yourself of an early opportunity."

"I shall be charmed."

"Of course you will; we are all charmed—every body is charmed—enraptured—enslaved! The little gipsy has a perfect *troupe* of admirers, have you not, Marie?"

"I believe you, yes, thank you—how you do?" returned the girl, in a sweet, Italian accent.

"There is a flow of beautiful English for you," cried one of the women, "positively Marie is becoming quite a linguist."

"I don't well see how it could be otherwise," said the man who introduced the Italian to the Prince, "since she keeps the society of such a set of parrots as you are."

"Now don't be rude, General, or I shall positively break my heart. You know I will."

"I know you never had a heart, and therefore that it is impossible to break it," returned the General.

"You are complimentary."

"No, only truthful. Now, sweet Marie, speak up, this is to be your new adorer; say, what do you think of our Prince?"

"It is a grand Prince," answered the arch gipsy.

"There, Prince," said the General, "you hear what they say of you, 'its a grand Prince;' why the devil don't they say I'm a grand General; nobody takes the slightest notice of me as soon as you arrive."

"Be satisfied, my dear General, be satisfied; see Rose sitting over there dejected because you will not speak to her."

"So she is, I declare," said the General, rising and walking away.

This was a *ruse;* the General sat next Marie, and as the Prince wished to gain possession of his chair, he gave him a gentle hint to evacuate it.

"How long have you been in England?" asked the Prince of Marie.

"Three weeks," said Marie.

"No longer! And what think you of London?"

"I like London ver moch, I thank you; oh yes please, not if I know it; how you do?"

This singular answer really puzzled the Prince, who looked quite at a loss how to proceed.

"See, Marie has astonished the Prince by her eloquence," cried the General; "really it's too bad of the little baggage to display her volubility in that way. Poor Prince."

"Oh my poor Prince," cried Marie, throwing her round white arms about his neck, and kissing him, "what they say? Me fright you! Oh, no; me love you too moch to fright you. No, no, I no fright my grand Prince; that would be too cruel. No, no, I would not, I think; I know; how **you** do, very well I tank you; never say die; keep up your peck-aire, *mon enfant.* Oh it is a grand Prince."

"Dear me," cried the General; "the little wretch is madly in love with him already. Here, I shan't allow this to go any further, or something serious may happen."

"Oh, nonsense, General," cried the Prince, in an ecstasy of delight. Don't talk nonsense; you are a foolish fellow, that you are."

And the very delightful Prince ruffled up his feathers like a peacock, bursting with pride and self-satisfaction.

These scenes were of almost every night's occurrence with the Prince. The person addressed **as** the General, an old libertine of the name of Rooker, was the chief administrator to the depraved tastes of the youth. He used to conceive

the most sensual enjoyments man could devise, and in all of these the youthful heir to the throne would join with heart and soul. The women who were present at the saturnalia, with which we are at present dealing, were of the most part from the theatres, and bore characters distinguishable for anything but virtue. They had each in turn been the prime favourite of the youth, and as he grew tired of them so he cast them off, and they were content to play secondary parts in the scenes of nightly dissipation to which they were invited.

It never touched their hearts to know that they were deposed. Their vanity may have received slight wounds, but nothing more serious occurred. All they cared for was money, and the splendid dissipation in which they took part.

No longer able to entrance the Prince themselves, they sought, by every means in their power, to find others to fill their positions rather than abandon the scenes in which they took so much delight. The last victim to their machinations and cruel designs was the young Italian girl, called Marie, from whose behaviour the reader may be inclined to draw conclusions little to her credit, but the fact was the poor creature was acting a part entirely repugnant to her feelings and inclination, but imposed upon her by a sordid father who would have sold her precious soul for gold could he have realised upon its barter.

A few hours before we find the poor girl in the precinct of the den of vice, the General had waited upon her father at Covent Garden, and proposed to take the girl to his patron.

"A splendid career is open to her," said the old villain; "money she can have in any quantities, and her name will be made on the instant."

"Good, good," said the father.

"Let her come with me to-night, she will not repent it. The youth cannot withstand beauty, and the charms of Marie will enrapture him."

"Good, good," remarked the father; "but I fear Marie will care not to go. She love one Phillipe Morlavine, the tenor, who is now speak to her in her room."

"Psha! you must settle him, and stifle her qualms. Think of the future!"

"Ah! ah! it would be a grand future."

"So it would," said the General, "so it would. Go and see what you can do, there's a good fellow, and I will wait."

A scene which we will not repeat, lest its intensity should wound the sensibility of the reader, followed this conversation. The daughter implored, the father stormed. At length, aided by threats and curses, the girl consented to barter her honour for money.

The General bore her away in his carriage, and, having seated her at the table before described, contrived to excite her by wine and the conversation and example of her companions, all of whom were professionally known to her, to give up regrets and sighs for pleasure and dissipation.

The warm temperament of the Italian is soon fired, and in a few short hours the girl really began to take pleasure in the scene in which she was playing so conspicuous a part.

It is astonishing how speedy is the downward course when the foot once slips. The depths

of degradation may reached in a moment ; but, on the other hand, how difficult is it to approach the opposite extreme !—it is an upward course, each step a work of time ; and as we advance the goal seems to recede. Yet how bright and glorious is the prospect we enjoy when once attained !

Downward we may glide upward we must climb. The following tale will illustrate this truism.

We introduce two young females of an age, but of very different temperament ; the one a poor ballad singer of obscure origin and mean education, but possessed of all the moral strength to withstand temptation and endure trail ; the other a fierce, passionate, high-blooded girl, whose excitable temperament would at any time tempt her into folly or crimes had she not been led into their precincts by example, and forced into their depths by the iron will of a parent.

Our heroines start together—the paths of good and evil lay before them. Let us observe which they will pursue, and mark the incidents which befal them on their journey through life.

To return to Marie, whose surname, we may mention, was Lavrouffe. In the embrace of the Prince she appeared perfectly content, and even volunteered to warble an Italian *aria* for his pleasure.

She possessed a lovely contralto voice, and as

it gushed forth and filled the large apartment, the listeners were wrapt in attention. The glorious volume swelled until the very glass vibrated, and the air seemed charged with delicious melody.

The whole audience, critics as they were, became enchanted, and listened with wrapt attention.

The words breathed of love and passion, and they flowed from the girl's coral lips with a fluency which proved that she felt all she uttered.

In the midst of this enrapturing melody a servant entered the room abruptly, and by a gesture commanded instant silence.

" Now, fellow, what do you require ?" demanded the General.

" If you please—" .

" But I do not please, "cried the Prince; " what means this intrusion ?"

" So please your Royal Highness, there is a man below who demands instant speech with Signora Marie Lavrouffe. He says his errand is of importance, and that delay may be worse than death."

" Oh," screamed Marie, " let him not come; it is he !—it is he !—he will kill me ! Oh, Santa Maria, let him not me find."

" What does she mean ?" demanded the Prince of the General.

" Hist ! I know what it means. A poor devil of a lover: a little jealous, that is all. Here, fellow, just pitch him outside the gates and give him in charge as a thief; anything—only get rid of him."

This was addressed to the servant, who was about to withdraw to execute the order of the General, when his passage was checked at the door by the entrance of the very individual he was ordered to eject in so summary a manner.

" How dare you enter here uninvited?" demanded the Prince, indignantly.

" Begone, fellow !" said the General, rising to his feet, " begone, or I will eject you through the window."

" No, no !" screamed Marie, " do not touch him, he will go; he means no harm. He will go, I say."

" He had best," said the Prince.

" He will go," said the intruder, " when he has heard what he came to hear, not before."

" How ?"

" Nay, look not big at me ; you may keep your frowns for those who heed them, I am proof against them. Now," he continued, turning to Marie, " now, Marie, I have to ask you, did you come here of your own free will ?"

The girl hung her head and answered not.

" You do not speak; I would be answered. Did they use force in bringing you here ?"

Another pause.

" Quick, I say : your answer."

At length the girl returned a faint and tremulous " No."

The young man started as if stung by an adder. He passed his hand across his brow, and then, looking Marie straight in the face, he proceeded :—

" Well, if you admit you came of your own free will, I have but one more question—"

" Oh," interrupted the Prince, " I shall not allow this questioning to proceed."

" You will have no choice !" cried the young man. " Dare to move, and I will plant a stiletto in your heart! Move not, I say ; I am desperate ! Now, Marie, one other question : Having come here, and having seen the place and those who inhabit it, I want to know if you desire to remain ?"

Still a pause.

" Speak !"

" Really," said the General, " this must not proceed. Remove him."

" They dare not ! Quick, Marie, will you answer ?"

" Spare me !" cried the girl.

" Your answer !"

" Oh, spare me, and depart !"

" I require your answer. Once more, do you desire to remain ?"

" She does," said the General. " She came here of her father's knowledge, and with his free consent. After that what right have you to question her ?"

" The right of loving her—the right every honest man has to snatch a victim from the libertine and seducer ! You are answered, but I am not. Marie, Marie, answer me ! Oh, God; if you do not speak my heart will burst ! Will you remain here to sink into degradation and shame, or fly with me to happiness ? One word and all will be over."

" Bid him go," murmured the Prince; " bid him go. What is his love to mine ? What can he give thee compared with the gifts I will lavish upon thee ? I will ennoble you, and place you among the great and wealthy. Wealth, station, title, shall be yours for ever. With him you can get but poverty and seclusion. Bid him begone."

" You still hesitate, Marie. Will you not answer ?"

The girl raised her head, and, fixing her gaze upon the young singer, murmured in Italian—

" Let us part : it will be better for me, better for you. My father dislikes you, and only a life of poverty presents itself to us. Leave me to my fate."

" Is that your answer ?"

" Yes."

" Then heaven have mercy upon you. I leave you to your fate—great God, what a fate !"

" Come, no impertinence," said the General, " no impertinence, fellow, You have your answer, and now depart."

" I am going," said the young Italian, in a broken voice; " I am going. Would to heaven I had never come. Had I not seen her here I might have been able to have thought her dead : now I can only remember her as living the life of a —"

" Silence !" cried the Prince; " silence, or it will be the worse for you."

" You threaten, do you ? Well, you can do so with impunity, but a time must come when it will be my turn."

Turning to the General, he continued—

" As to you, villain, beware; for you are ten times my enemy. My reckoning with you will be a long and terrible one."

With this he turned on his heel, and, without another glance at Marie, stalked from the apartment, through the house, and into the street, a peal of laughter following him from the revellers in the chamber.

"Laugh on !" he cried, as he stood gazing back on the house ; "laugh on ! but a time will come when your mirth will change to sorrow, when your smiles will turn to the grin of idiotcy, and your pleasure to pain. Laugh on ! your days of re-joicing are short."

There was a deep prophetic air in his bearing, and an earnestness in his words, which would have induced a listener, had there been one, to have regarded him as gifted with a supernatural power of foresight.

As he strode away the moon disappeared, and snow began to fall. Wrapping his mantle about him, he hurried rapidly through the streets.

CHAPTER VII.

A TIME OF TRIAL.

NIGHT passed, and the darkness gave place to the light of day.

The advent of the Italian had been a diversion in favour of Liz, for in the first transports of a new passion the Prince thought but little of the poor ballad singer, who trembled like a newly-caught bird in its cage. The grand house to which she had been brought was to her little better than a cage, and so for days she beat her wings against the bars, and sought by every means to effect an escape.

But her attempts were in vain ; neither persua-sion nor force could effect her liberation from her hateful prison. She had not seen the Prince, although six days had passed since her arrival. Not being called upon to quite her apartment, she took good care not to stray from it of her own accord, and so she avoided coming in contact with any one, except the girls in the guise of pages, and they were con-stantly with her, for, save on the occasion of some night revel or mummery, they were never required to be in attendance on their master.

During their hours of relaxation and quiet they, of course, resumed the habits of their sex, and none would deny but that they gained in appear-ance by the change.

It was to these girls that Liz was indebted for the explanation of her comparative repose.

"Fortunately," said Adele, on the second day after the arrival of Liz, "fortunately for you, but unfortunately for her, George has found a new flame—one of the General's *proteges*, I presume ; a fine, dashing Italian girl, whose success on the boards of the opera has been the town talk for many a day."

"Thank goodness !" said Liz, " oh, thank good-ness ! I may now be permitted to go."

"Oh, nonsense," said Louise ; "you talk like a silly child. Why, this new fancy will not last a month, and then—"

"And then ?"

"He will turn his attention to you, as a matter of course."

"The villain !"

"There, there, do not excite yourself ; I thought you had got over such weakness. Six days

here ! why, I became resigned in twenty-four hours."

"Resigned ! to what ? To infamy and degra-dation ! Resigned to such a fate ? I cannot under-stand you."

"Well, you appear dull of comprehension ; but wait your turn. It's all very well for you to talk morality now, for you have a kind of right, but wait—wait ; you will forget such trash after a while."

Liz answered not ; she regarded those poor creatures with too much horror to converse with them on such themes, and it was only when under great excitement that she allowed herself to be mastered by her feelings. But what she never ceased talking of was her desire for liberation from her perilous position. By every argument she could think of she tempted the girls to effect her release, but it was useless ; they were not to be persuaded.

"No, no," cried Louise ; " you are given into our charge, and we must keep a sharp eye upon you. A breach of trust is unpardonable."

" But not so unpardonable as the keeping an injured woman for degradation."

" Now, nonsense," said Adele ; "what stuff : a poor street singer to talk of degradation when a prince has fixed his attention on her. There, do not let me hear any more of it or I shall get so snappish as to make your life here anything but as comfortable as you have hitherto found it."

"Oh heaven !" cried Liz, " to whom shall I look for assistance ? where shall I turn for aid ?"

" This is dismal, girls," cried Louise ; " really this continued wailing is becoming unbearable ; let us leave our young Madame Modesty until she becomes more reasonable."

"Ah," said Adele, " such croaking is enough to make one sick."

With this the girls left the apartment of the singer, and sought their own rooms ; where in a few moments they commenced singing, laughing, and dancing in the most unrestrained manner.

Liz felt dejected, and sank down by her bed-side and wept aloud.

A footfall near her induced her to raise her head, and there, within a few paces of her, stood the man she so much dreaded.

"What ! weeping, my charmer ?" cried the Prince ; "weeping at my absence and neglect ? Never mind ; you see I am come to console you now."

"Oh, leave me—leave me," cried Liz.

"Leave you ! oh, be not so cruel ! There, smother your resentment, and give me one word of encouragement."

" Will you not go ? I tell you I cannot endure your presence. You have wronged me, you have done me a bitter injury, but all that is of the past, and I will forgive ——"

" I knew you would."

" But on one condition."

" Oh, name it."

" It is that you permit me to depart at once."

" The devil !"

" You refuse ?"

" Refuse ; of course I do. Why, you silly little fool, you do not think I could spare you so soon— do you ?"

"Why not? There are others here who enjoy the life you lead and feel pleasure in your countenance and kindnesses; these for me have no charms. I could never reconcile myself to living here, I feel nought but disgust at all I see and hear, and therefore I beg you to grant me permission to depart."

"Psha! Do not talk such rubbish to me. I thought you had become more reasonable, or I would not have wanted you so early. I had imagined that the example and teaching of your companions had had its effect; but I find that I have been deceived. However, do not misunderstand me. I tell you that you are mine; and that, until I speak the word, you will remain here. I am not to be trifled with; for I can hate as well as love. I cannot—will not be thwarted; and so I bid you shake off your folly, and change your tactics. This show of grief annoys me. You forget that I am a Prince."

"How can I remember that when you forget that you are a man?"

"It is because I remembered that I am a man, and no more, that I stand prating with thee."

"Then hence, for I hate the very sight of you. I feel nothing but intense loathing and disgust when you are near. I tell you that nothing but the bitterest hatred will be evinced by me towards thee, and so it is better that you let me go in peace."

"By heaven, you put me on my metal and touch my pride! Is it to be said that I, a Prince, was beaten, cowed, and turned off by a wretched street ballad singer? No! It shall not. I will first of all tame you, and then let you know what it is to incur my displeasure. Before I have done you shall grovel at my feet!"

"Never!"

"I swear it!"

"You can kill, but you cannot subdue me.'

"We shall see."

"We shall; but remember, should you one day enter here and find but an inanimate body to receive you, that my death would be on your head, and that you would have to answer for it."

"Answer for it! To whom?"

"To God! A judge who will forget your rank and power when you stand before him."

"The devil take you! I can't stand such talk as this," cried the enraged Prince, "but I warn you that I am not to be trifled with!"

"I reiterate that warning. Your day is to come!"

"If I do not curb that spirit of yours," said the Prince, "I will suffer hanging!'

"Begone, coward!" screamed the enraged girl. "I spurn and defy you!"

The Prince went his way.

"Beaten," he cried, "beaten by a wretched street singer. A good joke, should it become known. But I must curb this dragon. Why, did I not bring her to my feet I should be a laughing stock. Yes, she must be tamed and won; but meanwhile I must solace myself with Marie. Ah, sweet Marie! She, at least, loves me!"

It did not appear so, for when not plunged into the depth of exitement the Italian girl gave way to fits of gloom and melancholy and might have frequently been heard to heave a sigh, and breathe a regret for her Phillip.

But of this the Prince knew nothing; before him the poor wretch was all smiles and gaiety, all love and enthusiasm: she had need be, for she was solely in his power. He could cast her off with a breath, and could get her hooted from the boards should any manager be found courageous enough to engage her against his will; and so she had to conceal the bitterness which sometimes arose, and smother her emotions in a giddy round of dissipation and excitement.

CHAPTER VIII.

GRIMER VISITS A DUKE, AND THE RESULT OF THE INTERVIEW.

THE Duke of Grasmount resided in St. James's-square, and kept one of the finest establishments in London. He had but recently returned to the metropolis from the Continent, where he had resided some years in consequence of the delicate health of the Duchess. As the Earl of Portville, the Duke was said to have been a wild and dissolute man, but, on succeeding to the titles and estates of his father and marrying, he became very differently disposed. His life was spent in retirement, and a gloomy sullenness took the place of his former dashing and uncontrollable characteristics of temperament.

He was known as a harsh, severe, unapproachable man, and one who seldom mixed in society or took delight in the occupations and amusements of those in his own position.

He did not frequent the clubs, and it was seldom that the House of Lords was graced with his presence. When he came there he would give a silent vote and retire without a word, and, in general, he was avoided as much as possible. On the other hand, the Duchess was full of life, spirit, and gaiety. Since her appearance in London she had been hailed as the leader of fashion and the belle of the season. She was certainly worthy to fill her high position, for a more magnificent woman could not be seen. Just turned thirty, she was, as may be imagined, at the very prime of a beauty of a most uncommon caste.

The daughter of an earl and herself extremely rich, she had married the Duke, who was full ten years her senior, simply for position and *prestige*; affection had but little to do with the matter—it seldom has in unions in high places. The Duke was eligible to the Duchess because his title was acceptable, and the Duchess pleased the Duke because her father's name was spotless, her property so near his own that an amalgamation was a desirable consummation, and because her brow was quite lustrous enough to set off his coronet.

"As the Duchess of Grasmount, I shall hold a splendid position," thought the lady.

"She will improve my property and will not disgrace my name," thought the gentleman.

And so the union was effected. The Duke generally kept his own apartments, and remained there in comparative solitude, while the Duchess was seldom without a house full of people in her own quarter. The Duke did not object. His wife's tastes were not his, but nevertheless she was at liberty to pursue them uninterruptedly, for he well knew that they, in a certain degree, became her position, and further, that, although he was no participator in them, they reflected some lustre on his name.

Had it not been for the Duchess society would have forgotten the Duke; but as it was, the Duke's name was literally in every one's mouth.

His wife's entertainments were of a most brilliant description; her set was the most select in Europe, and men and women of every degree of rank, from royalty down to the humblest artist, strove with might and main to enter it. Her recognition was the passport to universal recognition for those who aspired to position; and her patronage of an artist, musician, or author, was sufficient to place him at the topmost height of popularity and renown.

People did not care much about the Court at that period, for, truth to tell, the Court was no such desirable place; but society was bound to have some rallying point, and so it made the Duchess the centre of fashion. It set her up as the goddess; and rank, talent, and beauty fell down and worshipped her.

Her rank was the adoration of poverty-stricken gentility, her beauty the lodestone that brought the young and rich, and her power the attraction for the talented. The Prince himself was the constant guest of the Duchess. He attended her balls, dinners, and parties with unremitting attention; and people even went so far as to say that he borrowed her money in rather large sums. Whether he did or not we do not know, but we may say that such a proceeding on his part was a more than probable occurrence, since he seldom had sufficient to keep up his expensive habits.

Such were the Duke and Duchess of Grasmount, two of the most prominent characters in this tale.

At the present moment we have only to do with the Duke, and must confine our attention to him.

On a wretched morning, about a week after the date of the commencement of this tale, a little man, of remarkably shabby appearance, wended his way from the City towards St. James's. This personage was dressed in a suit of shabby black, and carried with him a large blue bag, which hinted plainly that the law was his calling.

Muttering to himself as he plodded on in the heavy rain, he appeared to be deeply engaged in some matter of importance. His thoughts were evidently fixed upon some absorbing object, for he heeded not those who passed him in the street, nor did he notice anything that occurred during his journey; the thousand incidents of the street having no interest for him.

He passed through the Strand and into Pall Mall, and then pursued his journey into St. James's-square.

It was not eleven o'clock, and St. James's proper was not yet awake, for there was none of that activity and bustle which characterised the place at a later hour. Casting a hasty glance about the square, the lawyer selected one of the largest of the houses and approached it. "Yes," he said, "this is it; and now for it."

His hand was on the bell, when a youth of un-prepossessing appearance approached, and said hurriedly—

"Grimer, I'm avake. The hawk is abroad, but I'm near him, Grimer; he can't do Pipey."

"Good," muttered Grimer, for it was that respectable individual, "good."

"I'll hang about," said Pipey, and with this he started off—disappeared would have been the better word, for in a second he was out of sight.

Grimer rang, and, after some delay, the door was slightly opened by a very gorgeous hall porter.

"We don't want any, my man," said this individual, as he looked at Grimer; "go away."

"'Don't want any; go away!' why, what do you mean? I've nothing to sell."

"Oh, haven't you?" said the flunkey; "then I s'pose you've come a begging, which is worse. Get away, we don't encourage beggars."

"Curse your insolence! I want nothing of you. Look here: I wish to see the Duke at once, on matters of importance; just tell him he is wanted."

The flunkey opened his eyes and moved not a step.

"Are you going?" inquired Grimer.

"Have you an appointment?" asked the servant, slightly recovering his equanimity, which had been much disturbed by the supposition that such a being as Grimer could possibly have an appointment with the Duke.

"No," said Grimer. "I have no appointment, but my business is important, and you had better convey my message."

"Oh, nonsense, my man. You can't see the Duke unless you have an appointment; so go away."

"Go away!—not likely. Look you here, idiot. It will be as much as your place is worth to send me away. Convey my message, and here is a guinea for you; refuse, and I promise you that your place is not worth five minutes' purchase."

"But it's so early," urged the man.

"It is never too early for business of importance. Carry my message."

"I can only call the Duke's own man," said the flunkey; "he must judge for himself of the nature of your business."

"Ah, is that it? Well, I'll make the one guinea two, and then, perhaps, I may obtain an audience."

The flunkey smiled, and escorted Grimer inside the door. He then went for the Duke's footman, and on that individual appearing, the message and one guinea was handed to him.

"What name?" asked the footman.

"Oh, no name. A solicitor from the City on business of the greatest importance."

Probably the footman had never before seen a solicitor from the city, for he stared at Grimer as if he had been some unknown animal. His impressions of solicitors had been derived from another class of the order.

Nevertheless he withdrew.

In a few minutes he returned, and said—

"The Duke will see you, but I expect that I shall catch it for admitting you."

Grimer made no reply, but followed the servant.

After threading a number of passages they at length stopped before a door, at which the servant knocked.

"What name?" asked the servant.

"Grimer."

The servant entered and announced "Mr. Grimer," and that gentleman and the Duke stood face to face.

The servant remained.

Grimer stood bowing awkwardly, and. as he was not invited to sit, he felt remarkably uncomfortable.

He found the Duke a tall, dark, morose-looking man, over forty years of age, and looking even more than that.

"Now, sir," said the Duke, who appeared considerably surprised at the appearance of his visitor; "now, sir, your business."

Grimer glanced uneasily at the servant. The Duke took the hint, and ordered the man to retire.

"Now, perhaps you will be as brief as possible."

"Yes," said Grimer, regaining some of his old impudence and presence of mind; "as brief as possible, but I fear our interview will not be a short one."

"It must be," said the Duke.

"It will not be," continued the lawyer. "If you have other business I am sorry, but this of mine must take precedence."

"You are impertinent."

"I am sorry you think so, but you must excuse my abrupt professional habits. A lawyer in pursuit of his business is not in the habit of standing upon any ceremonies. And now, by your permission, I'll take a chair, and commence business. You had best be seated.

The Duke signified, by a wave of the hand, his disinclination to sit, and bade the lawyer commence.

"Well," said Grimer, "your Grace has been some time out of England."

"What has my absence to do with you, fellow?"

"Much; every action of your life has to do with me, and that you will find ere long. I said you had been long out of England."

"Yes."

"Of course. And now to business."

"You had best."

"Had I? Ah, my lord Duke, I shall bring down that haughty air presently."

"Insolent villain! you shall be immediately ejected."

"You had best not."

The Duke rang the bell violently.

"The servants shall throw you into the street."

"I hear them coming," said Grimer. "I have but one word to say, and remember you are playing with a determined man.—AGNES VILLIERS. Here are the servants: did you ring for them?"

"Yes—that is—no," said the Duke, in a frenzy of anger and amazement.

"The Duke did not ring for you, consequently you may retire," said Grimer.

The men looked at the Duke, and finding that he expressed no orders, withdrew.

"And now that they are gone," said Grimer, "we may resume."

The Duke spoke not.

"Returning to Agnes Villiers, whose name I casually uttered just now," continued Grimer, "your Grace does not forget her."

Still no reply.

"I believe the said Agnes was married to your Grace."

"It is false."

"A youthful indiscretion, perhaps, but still a fact."

"It is false!"

"I say a fact!"

"Fool! In my days of folly I perpetrated some mad mock ceremony of marriage with a woman of the name you mention, but nothing more."

"Yes, plenty more—much more than you dreamed of; listen: A dissolute wretch, of the name of Wisbech, was your constant companion. Through him you became acquainted with Agnes Villiers, a young and virtuous girl. You won her affections, and, I believe, grew to love her in return, but her humble position was an obstacle in the way of your union. Am I right?"

"Yes."

"Yes: you loved her, but would not marry her. You could not lose her, and had recourse to a trick to secure her. Wisbech was desired to personate a priest. and to perform a mock ceremony. He faltered, and desired to be excused from the performance of the task; but you were not to be denied, and he undertook it. Was it not so?"

"Yes."

"Then I am perfectly right when I assert that Agnes Villiers was your wife."

"How?"

"Your wife lawfully made—Wisbech was in holy orders at the time."

"Impossible!"

"It may seem so; but I possess proofs."

"You lie!"

"Nonsense, nonsense; do not excite yourself unnecessarily. I tell you I am right. Wisbech was in orders; but, being of a dissolute turn, he was deprived of his living, and commenced life afresh as a man of fashion—a position in society which he maintained by preying upon such fools as you were. I may not be complimentary, my lord Duke, but we can't always be so and speak the truth."

"This is some vile plot," murmured the Duke.

"I think not," continued the lawyer. "I have the whole of the papers connected with the affair; and, on investigation, you will find them correct. Here is a copy of Wisbech's ordination; here his university degrees; and here, most important of all, is a certificate of your marriage with Agnes Villiers. They are quite correct. Are they not?"

"I am astonished," murmured the Duke.

"Yes, doubtless," said the lawyer; "these revelations do come out in an unexpected manner, but we must bear up against them."

"Well, sir," said the Duke, after a pause, "I presume that this is the extent of your business with me. You have a secret which you wish to sell: name your price."

"Stop, stop!" cried the lawyer, "I have not yet done. We have only yet had one act of our drama; we must rehearse the whole, painful as it may be to your feelings. Now, the next act begins with the birth of a child at Marlborough House: you remember the circumstance. I think it was a little girl; was it not?"

"Yes."

"Well that child is legitimate."

"It appears so."

"It does; and I think it will take a great deal of evidence to disprove the fact. You had servants of the name of Maydock?"

"Yes."

"To them was entrusted the keeping of your wife: they killed her."

"Killed her!"

"Yes. You were no party to the deed, but your late father was. He bought over your servants to make away with the child, and to let the mother die of neglect."

"He could not have done so."

"He did: but on his death-bed he repented of his sins, and, by way of atonement, left the bulk of his property to the family of your wife."

"You confound me."

"No doubt. The will was witnessed by your servants, the Maydocks, and by one of them, the husband, secured. It was then placed in my hands, but was stolen by the depositor when he found that your child had not been killed by his wife, but was still alive, and ready to put in her claims to the estates you have for years wrongfully possessed. I have nothing to add but that I derived much of this information from the man who performed the ceremony of marriage when, a convicted and short-lived felon, he breathed forth his last words in the condemned hole of Newgate; and further, that I know where the will and your child are to be found."

The Duke turned ghastly pale, and shook from head to foot.

"My God!" he cried, "is it to come to this at last? Have I not suffered enough for years and years to atone for the one great error of my life? Is it come to this, that now, in the prime of life, with the golden vision realised, I should be called upon to undergo this terrible punishment? What will the world say—what will Catherine, my wife, say—when my crimes are blazoned forth to the public ear? Oh! it is too horrible to contemplate!"

"It is," said the lawyer, drily; "and, therefore, I should dismiss such a picture. Men in your position do not usually give way to grief in these cases; they act and endeavour to avert such impending calamities."

"What can I do?"

"What can you not do? Except Maydock no one but myself knows of this secret. I can be bribed to silence, and the other can be disposed of as soon as he has served our turn. This is how the matter stands: he has the will, and his object will be to drag it to light in order that he may become possessed of the property through the girl, should he succeed in finding her; whilst I will guarantee, for a consideration, not only to keep your secret, but to return the will, and, by a satisfactory arrangement, keep your child for ever in ignorance of her true name and position."

"What are your terms?"

"We will name them hereafter; at present I shall only require sufficient to prosecute my search for the will, and to employ the necessary agents for securing it."

"What sum?"

"A moderate one."

"Name it—name it; I am in your power."

"I am your slave, my lord Duke."

"Psha! do not madden me. Name your sum."

"Well, to commence with, I will draw £500."

The Duke spoke not a word, but opening a drawer he drew forth his cheque-book and filled up an order for the amount; he then handed it to the lawyer.

"That is right, my lord; and now I can commence operations in earnest"

"Go, and let me not see you oftener than is absolutely necessary: I cannot endure your presence."

"Perhaps not," said the lawyer, coolly, "perhaps not: it's just like the world; the bearer of ill news, though he be the best of mortals and acting under the best of motives, is liable to be considered in anything but a favourable light: but I am not offended, and as a proof, there's my hand."

The Duke shuddered as he contemplated the outstretched paw of the lawyer. He would fain have spurned it, but he was in the man's power and therefore he placed the tips of his fingers in the lawyer's palm. The long bony digits of Grimer closed over them, and in that calm clammy grasp the Duke felt that he was for ever in the power of his visitor.

"Now," said Grimer, "we understand each other, and so for the present adieu. In my hands your case is safe. Deal fairly, openly, and honestly by me and I will save you; act deceitfully, and I shall crush you without compunction. Good bye."

With this the lawyer gathered up his papers and thrusting them back into his faded blue bag prepared to go.

"Perhaps," he said, as he stood hat in hand, "you will ring for a servant to show me the way out, and at the same time give him orders to have me more civilly treated when next I come."

The Duke rang and a servant entered.

"Now, your Grace, the order," said the lawyer, pointing to the servant.

"You will, for the future, admit this gentleman whenever he may call, without any hesitation; we have business to transact, and he is ——"

"Yes, my lord," said Grimer, "proceed; he is—"

"A friend of mine," said the Duke, his face becoming suffused with crimson.

"You heard that, varlet," said Grimer to the servant, when he reached the outer door; "you heard that; I'm a friend of the Duke's, and now don't expect any more guineas from me, for you will never get any."

The servant gazed after the retreating figure in wonder and surprise. He had never before seen so remarkable a visitor at the town mansion of the Duke of Grasmount.

From under a portico in a turning into Pall Mall the lawyer was suddenly aroused by a voice.

"Stop," said the voice.

The lawyer stood still.

"Pretend to buckle yer shoes on the step, vill yer?"

Grimer obeyed.

"It's me, Pipey; I'm a watching the yellow von, who's a looking on all the vile, somevere's near. He has seen yer get into the Duke's crib, and he's on the scent. Take care o' that blue bag if you've a got anythink in it, for the chances are some von may take a vi'lent fancy for it presently. Are you fly?"

"As a hawk," muttered the lawyer.

"Right you are then. I say, just drop a odd gold piece on the door step, for I'm hard up, and dodging about in this here vet don't do for my constitutional veakness unless I serves the inside as the rain's a serving the out. D'ye twig?"

The lawyer cunningly did as he was desired, and pretending that he had secured his shoe to his satisfaction plodded on.

Pipey was right: as soon as Grimer resumed his walk, from a portico in the immediate neighbourhood Yellow Maydock darted out and followed at a distance.

There were several severe tugs at Mr. Grimer's blue bag on the return journey to the city, but it was held fast, and Grimer merely smiled at the vain efforts of his antagonist.

CHAPTER IX.

A GREAT BALL AT MARLBOROUGH HOUSE.

It was Christmas eve, and all who possibly could be gay and happy were enjoying themselves to the full bent of their dispositions. It was Christmas eve, and feasting and revelry progressed throughout Old England. High and low, rich and poor, gave themselves up to mirth and festivity, and the season was duly observed, as it ever was back in the good old days. There was a great ball at Marlborough House, and the number of *invites*, and the magnitude of the arrangements exceeded anything of the kind ever known in the chronicles of Christmas feasts. At this entertainment the Prince intended to introduce Liz as his last new conquest, and being determined that she should eclipse in magnificence and beauty all others; he purchased for her robes of singular magnificence and jewels of the greatest brilliancy, and these he caused to be conveyed to her through Adele, with strict orders that she should be ready to enter the ball-room at ten o'clock.

In the meantime the Prince had to dispose of Marie, who had set her heart upon being present at the entertainment.

"It will be a splendid sight," said the Italian, "and I will come and dance with my grand Prince, and he will be proud of his Marie."

"Oh, yes," said the Prince, "he would be proud of his Marie, but the fact is Marie cannot appear at this ball."

"Why not?" asked the Italian, her eyes flashing indignantly the while.

"For several reasons. It would be noticed—the King may be there. I should not like it. Psha! a thousand reasons, which I cannot enumerate. Suffice it that I do not want you to be present. Go to Kew, and I will join you as soon as possible after the ball; I will indeed. There, do not plague me, Marie; I dare not ask you to the ball."

"I see; you would be ashamed of me."

"No, no—nothing of the kind. There, if you promise me not to grieve about the matter, I will order the coronet of rubies you spoke of the other day. It will half ruin me, but you shall have them if you give way this once."

The eyes of the Italian glistened, and her countenance brightened.

"Well," she said, "if I may not come, I must be content to remain at Kew. But it is hard to stay away from the ball. I had set my heart upon going."

"Yes, yes; no doubt. But what's in the ball compared with the possession of the rubies. There, be a good girl, and I promise you all sorts of things. Now, go; there's a darling."

"Yes, I will go. Adieu, and remember you do not leave me longer than you can help. I am desolate when you are away."

The carriage was ordered, and in a few minutes the Italian was on the way to Kew.

* * * * *

At first Liz protested that she would not attend to the order of the Prince, and declined dressing for the ball.

"Take away these things again," she said to Adele; "I will not wear them, and nothing will tempt me to appear at this ball."

"I don't think there will be as much temptation as force used should you decline," replied Adele; "however, that is not my affair. My orders were to bring you the dress and jewellery, beyond that I have nothing to do. I leave you to reflect on the matter, merely remarking, by way of farewell, that I think you an obstinate little fool."

Adele withdrew.

Tossing the fine clothes on one side, Liz sank into a deep reverie.

Long and uninterrupted was that communion with her own thoughts, and one who could not see the working of her features would have thought her to be in a deep slumber. At length she sprang to her feet and clasped her hands, a deep glow illuminating her hitherto pale features.

"Yes," she cried, "I will go to this ball, for there I may find the means of deliverance from the fate hanging over me. I will be there, and perhaps Heaven may send me a deliverer."

* * * * *

The day passed rapidly over, and the hour of ten was fast approaching. Marie sat alone in a magnificent chamber in the Prince's establishment at Kew. She was reading, but her thoughts ever and anon wandered from her book to the grand ball.

"It is unbearable," she cried, "it is unbearable, and I would rather lose the rubies than remain here. Ah, he will appear at that ball with some one whom I am not to see—some new love, some

fresh attraction. By Heaven, I cannot bear the thought! it consumes me! my warm nature will never withstand such a trial."

The clock struck nine.

"I cannot read," she continued, "I am too much distressed; but what can I do to pass away the dull hours?"

Nothing suggested itself, and, almost despairing, Marie resumed her seat and again fixed her eyes upon her book.

She was startled by a loud ring at the bell.

"Who can it be at this hour? I should have thought all our visitors had been, ere now, in London."

The door opened, and a servant announced Lord Polington.

"Admit him," said Marie.

In a few moments a young man of prepossessing appearance, and dressed in a truly gorgeous evening costume, entered the apartment.

"Well, mi lord," said Marie, in her sweet broken English, "why you come at this hour?"

"I have just called to ask if I can escort you to town. My people told me that you had come down this morning, and I learned just now that you had not yet returned, so I imagined you would not object to my company to Marlborough House; but you are not dressed."

"No; I did not contemplate going. It is so far, and the Prince could not escort me."

"Ah, just my case. I wavered about going because my sister wished me to take her, and not wishing to burthen myself with her I contemplated remaining at Kew; but as the lady changed her mind I changed mine, and resolved on going."

"Then you have tickets ofr two?"

"Yes."

"Well, I think my mind change too; yes, I lose my ticket and think I would not trouble to see for one other, but as you say you have two I will go with you."

"I shall be delighted," said Polington.

"Then wait while I dress. I will not be long."

His lordship bowed, and Marie withdrew.

"Oh!" he said, as soon as the singer had left the apartment, "our little Italian has had a quarrel with the Prince, or she would not be here—unless he intends to introduce that mysterious beauty to-night, of whom his satellites spoke. At all events Marie will go with me, and that is sufficient to make me a town-talk for the next six months."

In a few minutes Marie returned, dressed in the most fascinating manner.

Truly she was a lady with whom a lord might have been proud to be seen; even at such a brilliant gathering as that at Marlborough House on that Christmas eve.

"Now I am ready," said Marie, and Polington led her to his carriage.

While they journey to London we will return to Marlborough House.

As the hour of ten approached Liz commenced her toilet.

She required but little artificial aid to make her thoroughly beautiful, and cold water was the only cosmetic to which she had resort.

Her dress fitted to a miracle, and the beautiful turquoise and diamond jewels set off her complexion exquisitely. To have seen her clasping these gems about her hair, neck, and arms one would have imagined that she had been used to them all her life: they did not embarrass her in the least, and her appearance, when the last touch was given to her simple toilet, was that of one of nature's own noble-women.

She could not confine her hair in the fashion in which the head was dressed at that time: so she permitted it to fall in a bright golden flood over her fair shoulders, simply keeping it from her face by looping it with her tiarra.

When thus arrayed she certainly presented a most remarkable appearance. She evidently felt this, for she surveyed herself with marked amazement, before she could reconcile herself to the metamorphosis.

The hour of ten struck, and Adele, Louise, and the others, all clad in rich costumes of their own sex, burst into the chamber.

"Now, then," cried Louise, "has Mistress Modesty changed her mind?"

Liz turned upon her visitors, and they fell back in amazement.

Such a transformation had never been contemplated, and it was some moments before they could recover their self-possession. They felt awed in that glorious presence, and the burst of ribald jests and unwomanly taunts with which they would have greeted our heroine fell dead upon their lips, and they simply asked if they could render any assistance.

"None whatever," said Liz, "I am quite ready."

"We shall be proud to show you the way."

"I must dissemble," said Liz to herself, "I must dissemble now or they will suspect my purpose and take means to frustrate my plans."

They threaded the brilliantly lighted passages, and descended to the grand floor, and thence to the private reception room of the Prince.

Here Liz was met by the author of her misery, but so well did she conceal her indignation and anger, that the Prince was quite delighted at the change in her disposition, and more especially with the magnificent appearance she presented.

He had not anticipated any such wonderful effect, and for an instant stood gazing in silence and admiration. At length he advanced, and bending over her hand, kissed it with the greatest show of courtesy, and then complimented her on her appearance.

"Oh," he whispered to himself, "there is nothing, after all, that will soften a woman half so much as fine clothes and sparkling gems. Here is one whom sighs and threats could not affect, tamed and won by the expenditure of a few hundred pounds."

He was mistaken.

"And now," he said aloud, "let me lead you to the ball room." Then, sinking his voice once more, he continued, "Tell me, fair Liz, am I so hideous now? Does my presence prove such a torture to you now as heretofore?"

"Time," replied Liz, skilfully evading a direct answer, "time works wonders in us all."

"It does, indeed," said the Prince.

They approached the grand entrance to the ball-room. A crowd of fashionables were pouring in; a gust of perfume filled the warm air, and a magnificent band saluted the ear with a burst of melody.

The approach of the Prince was the signal for a general falling back of the crowd, who made a passage for him to approach the room. Bowing carelessly on either side in answer to the mute salutations of the company, the Prince proceeded, with Liz hanging to his arm, into the ball-room.

For an instant the poor girl was overpowered. Anything so entirely magnificent she had never before looked upon, and her equanimity was shaken as she contemplated it. The Prince felt her tremble, and whispered "courage."

The sound of his voice recalled her power of control, and, with unapproachable dignity, she continued her walk to the end of the room.

It is needless to say that she was the observed of all observers; for that, under the peculiar circumstances of her introduction to the gay assemblage, will readily be comprehended.

"Who is she? Who knows? Who has met her before?" Is she English? and a thousand other similar questions were buzzed about from mouth to mouth, and Liz was the cynosure of all eyes.

During the progress of the ball Liz danced frequently with the Prince, and he was seldom an instant from her side."

"Really," one lady observed to another, "the Prince appears to be desperately smitten at last; I positively think this is a genuine case; but how singular that no one can tell who she is. How remarkably few have been introduced."

Such tattle as this filled the room, and, on the arrival of Marie and Lord Polington, they found that in that vast assemblage there was but one centre of interest, and that that was to be found in the little group in which the Prince and Liz were the principal figures.

The eyes of the Italian glared wildly at her rival, and muttering in her own tongue, "This, then, is the reason why I was to remain at Kew to-night," she advanced with her escort to the upper part of the room.

Marie attracted considerable attention from the fact of her known intimacy with the Prince, and as she walked up the room people said:—

"That is the Italian. Her reign was but a short one; she really looks as if she would kill her fair rival on the spot. A splendid girl, is she not? How proud Polington appears to be at having to escort her."

Marie heard some of these remarks, and they went to her heart. Her face burned and her fierce nature spoke through her eyes in unmistakable language. On seeing her the Prince was somewhat disconcerted, but recovering himself with admirable adroitness he carelessly called a gentleman who was standing near to approach.

"Lord Lovelace," said the Prince, "Pray know the Marchioness De Pratique," (this was the name he had given Liz;) "you will be delighted with each other's society; I must leave you for a while, I see some friends." Bowing deeply the Prince retired and joined Polington and Marie.

"Well, Marie," he said, "you have changed your mind, have you. How did you come?"

"Lord Polington called to know if I intended coming, and I took advantage of his kind offer of a ticket and a seat in his carriage."

"Indeed! Well I am glad you are come; had I known that I should have been so much at liberty I should have induced you to have remained in town, so that I might have had the pleasure of bringing you here. However, Polington has anticipated me. Lucky rascal."

The Italian was fairly deceived by this consummate effrontery, and accepting the proffered arm of the Prince, they walked away. In a few minutes the Prince, by dint of many professions, more promises, and a deal of coaxing, had restored Marie to something like good humour, and fully persuaded her that Liz was some distinguished German upon whom the King had desired him to bestow his best attention. Poor deluded Marie!

Lovelace proved a very acceptable companion to Liz; he was a very different being to the one who had left her so recently, and by his unaffected, gentlemanly behaviour he had in a few minutes ingratiated himself entirely in the girl's good graces. On the other hand Liz soon made a profound impression upon him, and after an acquaintanceship of but a few minutes they were conversing together as if they had known each other all their lives.

At length Liz became slightly overcome with the heat and the exertion of the dancing, and signified her wish to leave the room for a few moments.

"There is a conservatory at the end of the corridor; may I lead you there."

"Thanks," said Liz, "anywhere so that I may procure a little fresh air."

She accepted the proffered arm of Lord Lovelace, and they quitted the room together, attracting universal attention as they passed.

The conservatory was a charming place, filled with the best of statuary and the finest of exotic plants, it was illuminated by a perfect canopy of coloured lamps, which threw a brilliant but subdued light upon the scene. It might have been a fairy haunt, so beautiful was it in its detail.

Seating themselves on an elegant lounge, Lovelace and Liz commenced a conversation.

"How do you like England?" asked the young lord.

At first Liz was confused, but at last she answered—

"I should like it well, for it is the only country I know."

"Indeed, I thought you were a German—at least your title would lead one to suppose that you were a foreigner."

"My title!" said Liz. "Great Heaven! my title!"

"Why, what mean you?"

"Simply that my title is but a creation of an inventive brain. What titles have I—a poor, friendless, deserted, English girl?"

"You amaze me!" said Lovelace. "Pray explain."

"No, no: explanations were useless; I should not have said so much."

"There is a mysterious meaning in your speech which I cannot fathom. Are you unhappy?"

"Can you ask it?"

"Why not? I thought you a lady of title, enjoying every luxury, and basking in the smiles of a powerful Prince. I have listened to the gossip of the ball-room, and by what I could gain from that source I understood that you had made a complete conquest, in which you gloried; that you were the most envied woman in London; that for you the Prince had sacrificed all others, and that you were the belle of the coming season.

"Then you are not in the confidence of the Prince?"

"No, no; his ways are not mine; his mode of life is distasteful to me. And I believe he regards me with contempt, but that is a matter of total indifference to me."

"Yes," said Liz, "I can understand that feeling. It must be far more pleasing to be regarded with indifference by him than to be the recipient of his smiles."

"Then you do not love him?"

"Love him! how does the lamb regard the wolf that takes it to his lair with intent to destroy it? Surely not with feelings of affection."

"Surely not. But is this your case?"

"May I confide in you?"

"You may, indeed."

"You appear truthful; and, yet, how am I to know that this is not some trap devised only to sound me?"

"I can offer no proofs of my honesty; but if you will not trust me without hesitation do not speak at all. I would rather not hear your story— much interest as I take in it—if you accompany the narrative with a doubt of my trustworthiness."

"You do not speak the language of deceit," said the girl, "and I will relate the tale. If it should not interest you, when you find how poor and deserted a creature you listen to, I shall not be hurt, for I have learned to bear misery, and a little more added to the load will make but little difference."

Then, in a few simple words, she told her story.

"And now," she said, as she concluded, "and now that the mystery is divulged, confess that you take but little interest in it."

"I cannot confess that which I do not feel. No, poor, friendless ballad singer or powerful marchioness — it little matters to me which — my interest is centred in yourself, and not the name or social position you hold. Oh, I confess that I love you ! Sudden and unaccountable the passion may be, but I know it is true and enduring. I love you, but not as *he* loves. To me you should be an angel, whom I could worship. To me your purity should be a shrine, the violation of which should be sacrilege. Oh ! if you will permit me to love you—if you will give me the right to protect you, I will take you from this spot on the instant, and in the face of those powerful men. There are laws for all, and I will invoke their aid in your behalf. But say the word, and you quit this house to return no more."

"You speak wildly," cried Liz, "yours is the language of frenzy, not love. Oh, I dare not listen."

"You must listen. Oh lady, do not remain here to be sacrificed thus. Come with me; I promise you that a retreat shall be found for you where you will find ample protection. Let me persuade you."

"And you will promise that you mean me no harm ?"

"I will swear it by my honour—by my name, which is as spotless as driven snow."

"Enough," said Liz, "I believe you; but, oh ! reflect on what you risk by this."

"I have reflected ; I risk nothing."

"Then I will go with you."

"Come then : every moment is an age ; my carriage will not be here, but I can procure a vehicle. Come, no one will dare dispute our passage."

They quitted the conservatory, and as soon as they were gone a figure, in a rusty suit of black, started from behind the pedestal of a statue and darted through an open window into the garden, thence to the gates of the house.

It was Grimer.

Immediately outside the conservatory, and in the corridor, Lovelace and Liz were met by the Prince and several gentlemen.

"Oh, we have found you, have we ?" said the Prince. "Why, we were all afraid that our Lovelace had disappeared with the Marchioness."

"Not yet," said Lovelace ; "but that will be the case in less than two minutes."

The Prince was surprised ; he did not appear to understand whether the young lord was in earnest or merely indulging in a jest ; but he was soon assured of the real state of affairs.

"This lady," said Lovelace, "informs me that she is detained here against her inclination, and has placed herself under my protection to see her safely hence : I have accepted the office."

"Indeed," said the Prince ; "this is a strange proceeding."

"That, your Royal Highness, is just the impression I have formed," said Lovelace ; "and that would doubtless be the opinion of the public should this affair gain the notoriety it promises. We beg to take our leave."

The Prince was amazed ; he had not contemplated such a *contretemps*, and was powerless to remedy it.

The seeming complacency of Liz had led him blindly into a terrible trap, and now he floundered about therein in a manner which indicated his inability to extricate himself.

As Lovelace passed away with his lovely charge he could only look after him and mutter,—

"Very good, my Lord Lovelace, there must be a day of reckoning for this."

To which Lord Lovelace replied,—

"The sooner the better."

And in another moment he was gone, leaving the Prince and his companions in perfect amazement. Without the house and in Pall Mall, Lovelace ordered a servant to procure a hackney carriage, but before the porter could move a driver, closely enveloped in a large muffler, came up and tendered his services.

"Yes, you will do, if you have a good vehicle."

"An excellent one, sir," said the driver.

In another moment a boy led up a rumbling old hackney coach, and into this Liz was placed, Lovelace following closely.

"Where shall I drive ?" asked the coachman.

"To Brixton—across Blackfriars Bridge."

"I know the road."

"Quick, then, for there is not a moment to lose."

"I will do my best," said the coachman, who, we need scarcely say, was Grimer.

On hearing the determination of Lovelace to convey Liz from the house, he had rushed into the street and secured a vehicle, the owner of which was personally known to him.

A bribe silenced the man, and he resigned his mufflers to the lawyer, and his horse's head to master Pipey, who was in attendance.

In a few minutes the old coach was in full swing, rattling over the rough stones of Pall Mall.

CHAPTER X.

THE ADVENTURES OF MR. GRIMER IN HIS CHARACTER OF HACKNEY COACH DRIVER.

PIPEY watched the disappearance of the coach in great glee.

"Vell," said he, "that vos as neat a thing as ever I see'd : who'd a thought to see old Grimer a drivin' of a hackney coach. Oh, the sly old fox ! Vell, he did manage it a good 'un, and no mistake."

As Mr. Pipey gazed after the coach he saw something which somewhat disturbed his mirth.

"Hillo !" said he "vy, there's a feller a hanging on behind the coach. Now, vot can his game be ?

nothing good I'll bet ; however, I'll just foller up and see the end of it."

Mr. Pipey had his work to do; the coach moved somewhat rapidly, and it was as much as he could do to keep pace with it.

Through the Strand they rattled, and then into Fleet-street : a few minutes would bring them to the bridge.

Still the coach rattled on ; still the mysterious man clung on behind, and still Pipey kept up the chase.

The light gleamed from the lamps ; the horse steamed and snorted and clattered over the hard frozen road, and the foot of the bridge was reached. The man behind slipped off and ran nimbly beside the carriage.

Pipey observed this, and put on a little more steam.

"Hillo !" said he, " that feller means business ; I'll be up vith him."

But suddenly the inestimable youth changed his mind, and dropped back.

"Vy," said he, " blow me if it ain't the Yellow Boy. I ain't going to have anythink to do vith *him* this journey."

Acting on this resolve, Mr. Pipey withdrew into the shadow of the bridge.

The moon was shining out in great brilliancy, and it was almost as light as day.

Pipey kept his eyes open.

"The yellow 'un," he said, " means to capsize the Jarvey."

No sooner said than done. Maydock, for it was that worthy, suddenly sprang upon Grimer, and, catching him a severe blow with a short staff which he drew from his pocket, the unhappy lawyer was brought to earth.

This did not, however, disturb the occupants of the carriage, and it was not until the horse was brought to a stand-still that Lord Lovelace was aware that his journey was interrupted. Putting his head out at the window to ascertain the cause, he was caught round the neck by the powerful arm of Maydock, whilst a handkerchief, saturated with a potent drug, was held to his mouth and nose.

The young lord struggled violently in the grasp of his powerful opponent, but it was useless ; overcome by the effects of the drug he soon fell senseless, and was instantly dragged from the carriage.

Liz shrieked violently, and clung to the senseless form of the young lord as long as she was able.

As soon as Maydock had disposed of Lovelace, he turned his attention to Liz.

"You remember me ?" he asked.

"Yes, yes, I remember your terrible looks. Oh! what are you about to do with me? What has tempted you to this desperate act ?"

"You."

"I ?"

"Yes, you."

" What am I to you that you should be induced to do this through me ?"

" What are you to me? Everything : wealth and power ; ease and peace of mind. I have waited day and night for this opportunity. I have sought you high and low, and now that I have found you I have risked all to keep you. Such a desperate act was never before attempted. But this is no time for talk : keep silent, and I will not interfere with you ; shriek again, and I will serve you as I have the other. I mean you no harm, and so do not tempt me to treat you ill."

" I know not who or what you are, but I will not submit to this. You shall not convey me from this spot against my will. I will alarm the neighbourhood."

" You had best not."

" Leave me, then."

" Never."

" Then I will summon aid."

" If you dare speak I'll take an effectual step to stop your mouth."

" Will you leave me ?"

" No, fool—idiot, no : again, I say, do not tempt me."

" Help, help !" shrieked Liz.

" You will have it, then ?"

" Help, help !"

" Curses on you ! this shall stifle your shrieks."

He attempted to force the handkerchief over her mouth, but Liz struggled violently, and a desperate encounter followed, the girl shrieking during the whole time.

" Devil !" cried the man, " I'll strangle you in another moment."

His hands were about her throat, but she fixed her nails into them, and tore away the flesh, until, maddened with the pain, the ruffian was obliged to let go his hold.

Again and again this was repeated, each time a perfect stream of blood issuing from Maydock's lacerated hands, and covering the splendid robes of the girl. At length the ruffian, by dint of the exertion of the whole of his prodigious strength, succeeded in forcing the handkerchief over the mouth of the girl.

She struggled long and violently, but it was useless ; nothing could withstand the terrific grasp of the man, and, as he succeeded in keeping the mouth and nostrils entirely covered with the handkerchief, in a short time the girl dropped into a state of insensibility.

" Now," said Maydock, closing the door of the carriage, and drawing the prostrate form of Lord Lovelace on one side, " now for the Rookery."

In his excitement he had forgot Grimer, who, recovering from the stupor produced by the blow, suddenly sprang to his feet and seized the ruffian.

" Villain !" cried the old man ; " I will have your life or you shall have mine before we part."

" So be it, then," cried Maydock, getting a firm hold of the lawyer ; " a struggle for life be it. I would not have gone so far, but, since you force me to it, take the consequences."

They were both desperate ; both collected and calculating.

Maydock saw that he had to deal with a man of iron will, and the lawyer knew that he was in the grasp of a man with iron power, and so both determined to lose no chance. They at first struggled with the wariness of two experienced wrestlers, neither showing the other the faintest opportunity of closing or gaining an advantage. It was a fearful scene.

The moonlight poured down on two livid faces

glaring at each other with the fiercest malignity, and it revealed the sinews of each stretched to the utmost point, and well nigh bursting through the thin covering of skin that held them.

No human eye, save that of the boy Pipey, witnessed what was progressing, and no human being was near to end the mortal strife.

The lad, hardened and used to such scenes though he was, fairly trembled with awe at that terrible encounter, and held his breath in deep suspense to watch its issue.

He could not have stirred hand or foot to have saved his life. He was rivetted to the spot by a dark and awful fascination, which he could not shake off.

And the strife continued. At last the lawyer seemed to gain some slight advantage, and then the form of the ruffian would tower over him, and it would appear that all was ended.

Yet anon, with cat-like power, the old man would spring to his feet, and secure a faint advantage; but this was but momentary. On all occasions he had to succumb to the miraculous strength of the younger man.

At length they closed in a deadly lock. Their arms encircled each other's bodies, and it was a question of who could hold out longest.

Had either been able to grasp a weapon, and wield it for an instant, the struggle would have had a sudden termination; but in that terrible embrace it was merely a question of power of endurance, and in this Maydock certainly had the advantage.

Seeing that he could not shake the lawyer off, the ruffian, by dint of terrific exertions of strength, succeeded in forcing him against the side of the bridge. Getting Grimer's chest well against the projecting stonework, Maydock pressed with all his might against his back until the old man fairly shrieked with agony.

It was evident now that nothing could save him.

"Oh, horrible!" shouted the lawyer; "this is too horrible! Spare me—spare me!"

"No; you said it was to be a death struggle, and so be it."

And again the ruffian used all his strength in squeezing his antagonist against the stonework.

"Oh, God! I cannot endure this," shrieked the old man, his eyes fairly starting from his head in the agony he was undergoing.

"You said it was a death struggle," was all Maydock replied. "You chose your fate—abide by it."

Again and again he pressed, and at last the blood spouted from the old man's mouth, eyes, and ears, and with one or two more appeals for mercy he ceased to struggle. Sickened and fainting with the pain, he dropped down.

"Now," said his conqueror, "now to complete the work."

With this he raised the old man in his arms, and advanced with him to the edge of the bridge.

"Just find a long night's lodgings below, and thus meet the reward of all who meddle with Yellow Maydock."

The poor old wretch knew that he was about to be precipitated into the water, and, in the terror of the moment, clutched at Maydock's hair, over which his fingers closed with a grasp of iron.

"Let go! curse you—let go, I say!" shrieked Maydock," but the lawyer was insensible to all appeals; "let go, devil—curse you, let go! Oh! if I had a knife!"

He had not, and yet he was obliged to tear out his own hair by the handful, a proceeding which conveyed the most exquisite pain.

Again he raised the prostrate form, and this time he succeeded in dashing it over the bridge and into the water.

It fell with a dull splash, and was soon speeding down the river. This last act in the fearful drama he had witnessed called Pipey to his senses.

"The old 'un's vorsted," said he; "he's over the bridge, and, unless I goes after him, he'll drown, and that vont pay. No, no, Mr. Grimer, Pipey vont let you sink for vant of a hand to help you out, so here goes."

In another moment the boy was over the bridge and battling down the stream after the fast sinking body of the lawyer.

"Hillo," said Maydock, alarmed at this sudden and unexpected appearance; "hillo, here's an alarm. What's to be done? I can't leave the girl after such a fight to get her. The swell is still insensible—the coach right?—yes. I must trust to the horse."

With this he seized the reins, and, springing upon the box, dashed away over the bridge at a great pace.

Meanwhile Pipey struggled gallantly after the lawyer, and in the course of two minutes had grasped him.

The sudden immersion had partly recalled the old man's senses.

"Villain! villain! villain!" he cried, as Pipey seized him. "Villain! we have not yet finished; at least we will sink together."

"Hillo," muttered Pipey; "hillo, old 'un, vot's yer game; come, let go, vill yer? or else I'm hanged if we shan't sink together, and no mistake. Let go, and let me get yer by the hair, or in another minute it'll be all over."

Still fancying himself struggling with Maydock, the lawyer persisted in impeding the movements of the lad who was making such a gallant effort to save him.

He clung about the limbs of the boy and sought to drag him down, and it was only by the exercise of all his skill as a swimmer that poor Pipey could shake him off.

At length he succeeded, and the lawyer relapsing again into a state of insensibility gave the boy an opportunity of aiding him effectually. Half supporting the now inanimate body, the lad kept himself above water and struggled for some of the barges moored on the Middlesex shore.

To reach these was a work of time and difficulty under such circumstances; but at length it was effected, and the boy got into one of them and dragged the lawyer after him.

He deposited him at the bottom of the barge, and then proceeded to wring out the water from his own clothes.

"Vell," he said, as the cold air struck into his very marrow, "vell, if this here aint a pleasant vay to spent a Christmas morning I vish some 'un vould tell me wot is. No means of getting ashore, and never a drop of brandy or bit o' baccy about me. Kick me it ever I comes a vater journey again vithout fust perviding the creetur comforts."

He stooped over the body of the lawyer.

Hillo, Mr. Grimer!" he said, "Hillo! ain't you avake? Vot an old sound sleeper he must be to doze on such an infernal morning. I should say that he had nothink on his mind, and that his precious old carcase vos cold proof, or else he'd be glad to jump up and beat his feet. Hillo, Grimer! aint you a' going to vake up?"

No answer.

"Vell," continued the youth, "you are an old character, and no mistake. Vake up!"

"To the death," muttered Grimer, "to the death"

"Yes, to the death," repeated the boy, "and bless me if that aint vot ve are both a coming to, and no mistake. Vy, I'm nearly gone already. In another hour I shall be a precious corpus, and no von to take pity on me. This here comes o' bein' a precious orphin."

"It must be one of us," muttered the lawyer, "it must be one!"

"Vy, yer old cripple," said the lad, "don't I tell yer that it 'll be the death of both of us if ve stays here. Oh, don't I vish some luminous genius vould only now take it into his 'ed to set the Thames a fire. Vould'nt he deserve the thanks of all his feller citizens, and of Mr. Pipey in per-ticler. Oh, how jolly cold."

The morning air was biting fiercely, and as the moon went down there was every sign of another snow-storm. At length Grimer recovered slightly, and began to gaze about him.

"Where am I," he cried to Pipey.

"Vere are yer? Vell, as near as I can make it out ve are jist off London Bridge, vere ve have been for the best part of an hour."

"How came I here?"

"Picked up at sea, and brought on board by Captain Pipey," said the young gentleman, curtly.

"Ah, yes," said Grimer, "I remember all now; the death struggle and the plunge into the water."

"Yes, a nice cold bath yer vos a having vorn't yer? and a nice mess yer'd a made of going bathing if I hadn't jumped in arter yer, wouldn't yer?"

"How came you at Blackfriars?"

"Follered yer."

"For what purpose?"

"Cos I see a cove get up behind the carriage what hadn't no right there."

"Then you know all?"

"I do."

"And the carriage and the girl, what—what became of them—speak—quick!"

"Now, yer are a cool old dodger; vy, how should I know anythink about the carriage and gal If I had stopped to see vere vould you a been? Answer me that; vere vould you a been?"

"True, true."

"I should think it vos true."

"You are a good boy, Pipey, and I will not forget you, depend upon it."

"You didn't ought for to, if you sets any walley upon yer precious life, and that's a fact; for if I hadn't been a game 'un you'd a been enjoying the prospect of a Christmas dinner in another vorld long afore this."

"That is true. Help me to rise."

The boy hastened to his assistance.

"Oh, the horrible pain in my chest! The villain nearly did for me."

"I aint a doubt of it. Spiled yer digestion for a few weeks, hey?"

"But I will be even with him yet; yes I will take an ample revenge. My time is yet to come."

"Vy, vot a horrible old fire-eater you is," said Pipey. "Aint you had enough of fighting yet?"

"Not until I have finished him."

"Vell, I vishes yer succes; but, if I vere you, I should shirk another tussle with the yellow von."

"Yes, yes; the next time we meet I fight him with my own weapons, not with his."

"Vell done, old 'un," said Pipey, in an ecstacy of admiration; "that's the way to get at him. Only lay it on with the saw, and he'll have to knock under; everybody does."

"Yes, I will have a deep and terrible revenge; yes, deep and terrible."

"So I vould; meanwhile, I think ve had better get a boat and try to find our vay to dry land again, for I can't stand this here no how."

The river was beginning to show some slight signs of life, and after waiting for about another hour Pipey discovered a row-boat passing near him, and, hailing it, a bargain was soon struck for conveyance to the shore. The boatman could scarcely make up his mind as to the nature of his fare, but as he was paid well he did not bother his head about the matter.

We must now return to Lord Lovelace, whom we left insensible on Blackfriars Bridge.

It was long before he recovered his senses, and when he did he could not comprehend the events of the night. All that had passed seemed to him the terrible phantasmagoria of a dream, and it was long before he could bring himself to believe that the whole affair had not been the creation of a disordered fancy. But as the cold air cleared away the fumes of the potent drug, a vivid picture of the whole of the night's work came upon him, and he was staggered by the number of incidents which thronged upon him.

His first impression was that he had been followed and set upon by the minions of the Prince, and, acting under the impulse of the moment, he was about to set off at once to demand what had become of the girl he had taken under his protection when the traces of the struggle between Maydock and the lawyer attracted his attention.

These and other signs proved to him that he had been attacked by one individual only, and recalling the description of Maydock given by Liz in the short story of her life, related to him in the conservatory, he had no doubt that it was to this man he was indebted for the attack and all that had followed.

"She is lost to me as soon as found," he cried, "but I will never desert her. No, my time shall be devoted to her, and I will search for her until I have exhausted the hiding places of the world; and woe betide the man who has injured one hair of her fair head."

Dispirited and sick at heart, he quitted the bridge and returned westward through Fleet-street.

CHAPTER XI.

AN UNPLEASANT INTERVIEW.

THE conversation between Lord Lovelace and the Prince on the departure of the former from Marlborough House with Liz was listened to by no less interested a party than Marie, who, livid with rage, and boiling over with anger, stood near the entrance of the ball-room surveying the scene

In a moment she comprehended the relative. positions of the parties in the drama, and her heart leaped to her mouth, whilst the pang of jealousy fired her brain and drove her to a pitch of desperation.

"Fool that I have been," she said, in a low voice. "I have fallen a victim to a wretched trickster. I have sacrificed all for a being who makes the honour of my sex a common sport, and laughs our misery to scorn. Smooth-tongued villain, I have now unmasked thee!"

The Prince turned and saw that awfully-expressive face regarding him.

He gazed into those eyes, and he felt that he was comprehended.

"Marie!" he said.

"Yes, it is Marie," said the Italian. "You are doubtless much surprised to see me. It is Marie. Have you aught to say to her?"

"Much," replied the Prince; "but nothing now; some other time I will explain all."

"Some other time! Do you, then, require time for the framing of falsehoods? Do you wish to prevaricate and attempt to deceive me again? Oh, beware!"

"Marie!"

"Prince!"

"Pshaw! girl, you are excited—mad."

"No, only desperate. Remember what I have sacrificed for you, and now see the reward. Can you wonder that I speak?"

"Marie! Marie!"

"Nay, you must hear me."

"Yes, yes, I will hear you, but not at this hour, not in this place; remember, a thousand eyes are upon us; a thousand ears listen to every syllable."

"The more the better; there cannot be too many to hear the story of my great wrongs."

"Marie, for Heaven's sake forbear."

"Why should I?"

"For my sake."

"For your sake?"

"Yes, for mine."

"And what have you done that I should spare you?"

"I have loved you."

"Do not misapply the word. You love?"

"Yes, I have loved you deeply, devotedly; only let thefe people depart; only wait for a few short hours, and I will explain all."

"Good," said Marie; "I will wait. But be not long, or I may not endure the delay."

"I promise to explain all in a few short hours —will not that suffice?"

"It must."

"Then retire; you need not return to Kew, go to the blue chamber."

"The blue chamber be it then; there I will await you."

With these words words on her lips, the Italian flew along the corridors, and ascending to the upper floor, sought the blue chamber—the one usually occupied by her during the short time of her residence in Marlborough House.

The Prince returned to the ball room, and entered into conversation with his immediate friends.

Those who had witnessed the little scene just described pretended not to notice it, and the Prince was satisfied that the *faux pas* was unobserved.

With the old General, who played so conspicuous a part in the introduction of Marie to Marlborough House, he entered into a conversation on the subject of Lovelace's conduct.

"I ask your advice, General," said the Prince, "because I am inclined to abide by it. You know the world far better than I do, and can tell me what course to pursue in the matter."

"Yes, you do me justice. I can advise you, and will do so to the best of my ability."

"The insult cannot go unpunished."

"It cannot."

"Then we must fight."

"You ought."

"We must; there is nothing for it but a meeting; that is inevitable."

"Not inevitable," said the General. "Really not inevitable. I said you ought to fight, but add that you cannot do so."

"How?"

"You must not do so; the scandal would be too great."

"Am I, then, to allow the insult to be passed over unavenged?"

"No."

"Then what is to be done?"

"A meeting must be convened, but your rank precludes the possibility of your going out. You must depute some one to represent you."

"And appear a coward."

"Nonsense. No one will imagine that you are the party to chastise such an insult. To pass it over would be unpardonable; but you may look upon the matter as only worthy the consideration of a humble friend, even your devoted servant."

The General bowed.

"I understand you," said the Prince, "and am grateful, but believe me I would rather meet this fellow myself.".

"I have no doubt of that," said the General, "but you must not do so. Leave all to me."

"I will."

"Then you may depend that I will do you justice and now I must retire. I see that the last guests are disappearing, and as this business will call me from bed rather early in the morning I think that the sooner I reach my pillow the better. My dear Prince, I beg to take my leave."

"Good night, or rather good morning, General, and success attend you."

"Thanks, and farewell."

The General withdrew, and the Prince was almost alone.

A few servants flitted about, and the gaieties of the night were over.

"I shall have plenty of work to do before I pacify her. Curses on this ballad-singer, I wish I had never seen her."

A servant approached, and tendered his services to conduct the Prince to his chamber, but this assistance was dispensed with.

"Get you gone, fellow," said the Prince, "I require no aid."

The man withdrew, and the Prince lolled languidly towards the blue chamber. Arrived there, he found that Marie had divested herself of the greatest portion of her robes, and that she stood pale and livid as a marble statue, awaiting his arrival.

"Well, Marie," said the Prince, "is the fit over? Come, kiss me, fair one, and say that I am forgiven."

"Back," said the girl, "back, and mock not my anguish." There was something dignified and grand in her look, as with outstretched arm she waved the Prince from her.

"Now," continued the Italian, fiercely, "tell me in what relation you stand to the woman who left the house with Lord Lovelace: no prevarication, no falsehood, no hesitation or attempt at deceit. I ask for the plain truth; no more, no less."

This outburst was hurled by Marie in her own tongue at the Prince. It was accompanied by the fierce gesticulation and impressive pantomime peculiar to her country, and still more peculiar to the stage of which she was an acknowledged ornament.

It fairly staggered the one to whom it was addressed, and the stock of impertinence and coolness he had treasured up to carry him through this interview quite deserted him, and he made no direct answer.

"Psha!" he said, "do not let us quarrel: we have no occasion to do so. I swear I love you."

"That is not to the point. I asked you not in what relation you stood to me, but to the woman who quitted this house with Lord Lovelace. Is not the question a simple one?"

"No; it rather puzzles me."

"Why?"

"Because *I do not know in what relation* I stand to her."

"This is folly."

"I am of your opinion."

"No trifling, Prince. I am a determined woman."

"Well, dearest, I have no wish to trifle. In fact, I have no wish to continue the interview. You asked me a question, and I have answered you to the best of my ability. Are you not satisfied?"

"Far from it."

"Then what more am I to say? What can I tell you?"

"The truth."

"I have done so."

The Italian shook her head.

"You do not believe me?"

"No."

"Then I repeat it, and will prove it to you."

"Do so."

"Listen."

"Oh, I am all attention."

"Then you will hear nothing of importance, and the rehearsal of the apparent mystery will arouse no interest."

"I cannot comprehend how that can be."

"You will soon understand. This woman of whom you are so unreasonably jealous, I met on the very night you came here. I will confess that she pleased me, and that, had I not seen you, she would, perhaps, have become dear to me. She came here, and has resided here since the evening in question, but I solemnly declare that only once during that time have I seen her, and that, in our interview, no word of affection, no sign of love, passed between us. I did wish her to appear with me at this ball to-night, but the reasons for this I cannot detail. Is not this sufficient?"

"Sufficient deceit, yes. You must think me a poor blind fool to believe all this. You must think me an idiot of the worst degree to credit such a story. But no more of it. We must part."

"Part?"

"Yes, part. I am not yet fallen so low as to remain here as one of your many mistresses. I must have a whole heart or none. You have not a heart to give, so I will go."

"Whither."

"To my old home."

"You cannot."

"I shall do so."

"Nonsense. Your father would not sanction it if I protested against it."

"But you will not protest."

"You do not know me."

"Oh, yes; it is because I know you that I say you will not protest. You dare not do so. You *must* let me follow my own inclinations, or the world will know you too."

"You threaten?"

"Do I? I only meant to warn."

"But you will not go? Let this stupid nonsense have an end."

"It is about to end, but not as you desire. See, I have stripped off your fine clothes and jewels; there they lay. In this wardrobe hangs the dress in which I entered this house."

As she spoke she went to the wardrobe and drew forth a dress.

"It is here," she continued, placing it over her shoulders. "I will quit you as I found you—no richer, no poorer—save in honour; oh, Heaven! save in honour. And now, Prince, we separate. It is morning, and I can go home without escort."

"Marie! Marie! cease this folly, or you will drive me mad! I have been indiscreet—forgive me! I implore pardon, and promise that no such case shall ever arise again."

"It does not matter to me. You know not the nature of an Italian. You know not how she feels when injured, and therefore you cannot comprehend why I leave you thus; but you may learn hereafter."

"Marie, you shall not go!"

The Prince placed himself against the door of the chamber.

"Stand aside!" cried Marie.

"No!"

"You shall;"

"Marie, this is absurd. Govern your passion and listen to reason."

"I will listen to nothing you may have to say; so stand aside and allow me to pass."

"Are you in earnest?"

"Desperately so."

"Then I will not detain you; you may depart. I am sorry it must be so; but if you have decided I can say no more. But you will think better of this when you reflect, and will return again."

"Never!"

"Then leave behind something by which I may remember you—something that I may think of when I cannot see you."

"Oh, I shall leave behind a palpable memento of our intimacy; something which you will many long years have occasion to think upon."

"And pray what may that be?"

"My bitterest hate. Think of that, Prince. It may appear a trifle now, but the time shall come when you will know its full value. Farewell."

The Prince was so staggered at this unexpected termination of the interview, and so confounded at the terrible malignity with which the Italian conveyed her last sentences, that he uttered not another word, and permitted Marie to quit the chamber without even raising his eyes from the spot on the floor whereon he had fixed them.

"A nice night's work," he said at last; "a nice night's work to reflect upon. I have lost them both, and have made myself a town talk for many a day. Jilted, scorned by a beggar and an opera singer! Great Heaven! it will not bear thinking upon!"

It appeared so, for going to a cabinet he drew forth a small decanter containing Burgundy, and pouring out a large draught swallowed it, and then fell stupified on the bed.

CHAPTER XII.

MR. PIPEY GETS HOLD OF AN IDEA.

PIPEY never ceased for two whole days to keep up a hunt for Maydock. Grimer had told him that Maydock must be found, and so he set off to seek him.

"Mind," said Grimer, "not a hint of what has passed—not a syllable of the scene on Blackfriars Bridge. I rely on you, and if you are incautious in one particular we lose all."

"I tell you vot, Mr. Grimer, I'm not to be got at; and I thinks as how you'll say of all the downy coves as is, Pipey is the downiest. I'd take the eyelashes off a sleeping weazel, and he'd be never a bit the wiser for it, and I'd stand a month's cross examination by the combined forces of all the judges and lawyers as ever sat, and never lose my line. Them as catches me on the hop has to come to me and take lessons how to do it. Of that you may take your oath."

"Oh, yes, you are a clever fellow—a very clever fellow, Pipey, and I shall not forget you—I shall not forget you."

"Vont you, though? Vell, it's something to be remembered by a gemman like you, but if it's all the same you can forget me as soon as you like, only leave vord vith some vun to supply me vith all the ready I may vont. If you vonts to vin my heart, give us the ready."

"You surely can't want any money now?"

"Oh, can't I? Can't I, my beautiful old fogey? You've made me retire from business; you vont let me foller up the purfesshion to vich I vos sich a ornament; you don't let me do nothink for myself; and yet you asks if its possible I vant any money! I'm surprised at you, Mr. Grimer! I'm really surprised at your ingratitude!"

"Ingratitude! Why, it was only yesterday that I gave you two guineas!"

"Vell; and vot's two guineas to a gemman as has to run about into every flash crib in London a picking up information for you? Vot's two guineas to a svell as is a dodging another svell, and has to get on like a real tip top gemman of quality, and get filthy drunk at least three times a day, and go on vith a lot of other high-bred amusements of a similar sort? Vy, yer aint reasonable no how."

"Nonsense, nonsense, you have no occasion to get drunk: all you have to do is to track my man: follow him like a bloodhound; dog his steps day and night; hunt him down, and find for me the will and the girl; I want and I must have both: mark me, both. When you have secured them your fortune is made. Do you understand that?"

"I ought, for you din it into my precious ears often enough. Vell, I grants the striking nature of your argyments, but you forgets that as yet I aint a found the feller to dog and that the girl aint left a trace of her whereabouts. Once let me find the scent and I'll be on it: until then I must trouble you to let me go on in my own vay. I must visit them cribs vere the Yellow von is likely to be found, and I must spend money ven I goes to'em. If you dont like it, say so, and let me go to work again. If you still vants my services all you has to do is to stump up and say nothink."

"I suppose you are right," said the lawyer, "but it is hard to part with so much money, and stand a chance of never seeing back a penny piece. That, you know, Pipey, makes me a little tenacious!"

"Oh, fiddles!" was Mr. Pipey's reply, "I aint sich a green 'un as you think. Vy, d'ye suppose I dont know that you bleeds that old Duke to no end, hey?"

"Nonsense, nonsense, I get nothing from the Duke."

"Oh, dont yer; vot a pity. Vy, vot a nice charitable, good-natured old Christian martyr you must be. Oh, come, I say, just put your finger on the exact spot vere you beholds the bit of green in my eye, vill yer!"

With this Mr. Pipey screwed up his face, and inserted it directly under the nose of Mr. Grimer, who, in spite of himself, could not help bursting into a loud laugh.

"Ah, ah, Pipey," he said, "there is no doing you, I see. Well, well, you must have money, I suppose. How much do you want?"

"Five guineas."

"Then you will not have them."

"Very well; it's all one to me. I can return to the sweet pursuits of my younger and happier days. I can vonce more adorn my beautiful purfesshion. Let me go. Give me my discharge. Say you've done vith me. Tell me to take my hook, and I'm off. I'll forget the past. I'll not ask you for anythink for saving your precious old life. I'll veep to myself in private, and no von shall know how I've been wronged, and all 'cos I asked for the small sum of five guineas from the man who, by force of argyment, pervented me from earning fifty times that amount vithout any trouble at all. Oh, it's too awful; it vont bear thinking upon!"

And here Mr. Pipey pretended that he was deeply affected at the treatment he was undergoing.

"Now," said Grimer, "stop that nonsense, and just talk reason. For what do you require five guineas?"

"For vot? Vy, to go into the houses across the vater, to be sure. Aint I a stranger to them genlemen over there, and aint I forced to stand all round for 'em? I suppose all that can be done on nothink."

"I did not say so."

"No; but that's vot you mean."

"It is not."

"Vell, it's very like it, that's all."

"Never mind what it is like. You say you want five guineas."

"Never a von less."

" Say three."

" I vould not take four and a-half."

" Why not ?"

" Because I've made up my mind to five, and ven I've said a thing I stands to it."

" Well, here are the five guineas."

The lawyer told them out into the palm of Mr. Pipey, but he really did not appear to be particularly pleased at parting with them."

" And now," said Pipey, " I'm off."

" Where ? "

" To Mother Whistler's hop ?"

" Why there ?"

" I'll tell yer. I saw Wat Hammer this morning, and he said as how he should be glad if I could lend him a hand in a small job he had to do."

" What was it ?"

" Well, I think as how it concerns a smash."

" Where ? "

" I don't know."

" Well."

" Vell, I said I'd meet him at the hop and talk it over."

" Why, this is shameful," said Grimer ; " shameful. Have you not promised me never to mix up in anything of this kind until I have finished with you."

" I have."

" Then how dare you undertake this, and how dare you take my money for such a purpose. Am I being tricked ?"

" Vell, if ever I heard such an old sky rocket ? Only to think how he's going on."

" Explain yourself. What do you mean by this ? "

" Vot do I mean ? Vy, I means that this here Wat Hammer is a old pal of the Yellow Boy's, and that, if this game is anythink big, they vill both be in it, and, therefore, I stand a chance of dropping across the cove I'm a vantin'. Don't you see ? "

" I begin to have my eyes opened. Go on."

" Vell, you ought to know what a game it is to find the Yellow von ven he's scarce ; and, as I've been at it two days without coming across a sign of him, vy I jumped at this chance like vinking. Let me get hold of him, and he's sure to blab. He believes in me, and, as he aint aware of our engagement, vy, as a matter of course, ve vins by the move. Now what does yer see ?"

" I see that you are a clever fellow, and that I cannot do better than trust you."

" Vell, that's my opinion, and now that I've blabbed I'll cut. It's quite dark now, and the owls are awake. Here's off to their nests."

With this singular speech Mr. Pipey took himself off.

The above dialogue took place in the office of Mr. Grimer, which was situated in a miserable little court within a stonethrow of Newgate.

The court was dismal enough, but the office was ten times worse.

It was a dilapidated chamber on the ground floor.

The walls had once been painted, but time had worn all that off, and in many places the plastering had come away in large patches, showing the solid masonry of the structure. The ceiling wa° black with age and smoke, and in all four corners the spiders had spun enormous webs, on which the dust had accumulated until the webs bore resemblance to large patches of black cloth hanging to the ceiling. The grate had, in all probability, been unused for years, for it was rusty and broken, and the wind rushed down the great chimney in such gusts as proved that no fire could live under its power.

There were large cupboards and shelves, all laden with heavy masses of old yellow documents, the records of misery and misfortune for many a long year. A massive table was placed in the centre of the room, and this, too, was covered with papers ; but they were of more modern times, and bore an air of freshness which all the rest lacked.

The floor was completely covered with dust and filth. At one time it had evidently been carpeted, for in some places a few rags pointed out that such an article of comfort had once rested there.

In the wall was fixed a large iron safe, and to this, on being left alone, Grimer went, and drew therefrom a small bundle of papers, which he perused with apparent avidity.

" Yes," he murmured, " they are here, every one of them, certificates and all. They are mine, and I will hold them. Ah, the girl, the girl ! that is the sole point. I have dreamt for years of the joys of a home with a young and beautiful wife —a fair thing to clasp and kiss and call one's own. A sweet head, covered with silken tresses, through which the fingers may wander ; a cheek soft and lily white, a little hand which one's fingers may clasp, and whose slightest touch can send a thrill of pleasure through the heart. Of this I have dreamt for years ; and when I knew that the Duke's daughter lived, I thought that my dream would be realised ; and when I saw her—when I heard her voice in the conservatory at Marlborough House, I knew that the realisation was not an impossibility. One so exquisitely beautiful I never beheld. And then, the money—the money ! Ah, what money she would bring ! Yes, that—that is not the least important part of the thing. The money—the money, and these papers—these papers left me by the felon in the condemned hole, put her within my power. They give her to me, and I will have her. I will, I will."

These were the thoughts which Mr. Grimer gave vent to when left in his old chamber by Pipey.

These were thoughts which possessed him day and night, and to these he had become a slave.

Whilst he was yet gazing on his packet of papers, there was a knock at his chamber door, which startled him from his pleasant occupation.

" Who is there ?" he cried.

" Quick ; open the door. It is I. Do you not recognise my voice ?"

" Yes, yes," cried Grimer, starting up and going to the door ; " yes, yes, my lord duke ; I should know that voice among a thousand."

The door was opened, and the Duke of Grassmount, muffled in a large cloak, entered the apartment.

" Good gracious," said Grimer, " how it snows.

"Why, your Grace is almost buried in it. What could have brought you here on such a night ?"

"My thoughts, which torture me day and night—my thoughts, which have almost driven me to distraction !"

"What has transpired ?"

"Nothing new, that I am aware of; but as time rolls on, and this terrible uncertainty continues, I grow mad. I cannot rest. I cannot sleep. I have lost appetite and am fevered. It is to hear something from you—something definite—something that will end this suspense, that I come here."

"Indeed."

"Yes, indeed; and now what have you to say ?"

"Nothing ?"

"What! Has all my money been spent to so little purpose ? or are you tricking me ?"

"All the money I have had from you is not yet spent, and I am not playing you false. What should I gain by doing so ?"

"I do not know. Heed not my words; but speak, give me some hope."

"I cannot."

"Say not so."

"I repeat, I cannot. I know nothing, although the affair has never been from my mind one instant."

"But have you heard nothing—have you no clue to the girl—to the will ?"

"The girl I have seen, and in an attempt to secure her I was all but murdered. But that is nothing to you. I have a duty to perform, and must go through with it at all risks."

"Have you no idea where she is to be found ?"

"At present not the least remote. But one of my emissaries has but just left me on what he thinks to be an excellent scent. To-morrow I shall know of his success or failure. See here, my lord Duke; even as you entered my mind was full of you. I was perusing these papers when you knocked."

The eyes of the Duke were fixed upon the documents. At that moment he appeared capable of strangling the old man where he sat in order to possess himself of the coveted documents.

"There they are," said the old man, "every one of them, and now to return them to their place of safety. Ah, ah, my lord Duke; they are too valuable to leave about."

He rose as he spoke, and walked to the iron safe, in which he placed the papers, and turned the key upon them.

"There they are, my lord Duke; and now we can talk again."

But the Duke seemed little inclined to resume the conversation.

He placed his hands over his brow, and appeared lost in thought.

Thinking he was unobserved, the old lawyer quietly slipped the key of the safe into a small drawer in the table.

The Duke saw the movement, and held his breath in suspense.

"What ails you, my lord Duke ?" asked the lawyer.

"Nothing, nothing," replied the Duke; "at least nothing that you can comprehend. You say you may have something to communicate to-morrow."

"I said I may hear something. I did not say I should communicate what I heard. The fact is it does not do for us to reveal all we may hear. Everybody, fortunately, or unfortunately, as the case may be, does not make the law a profession; and therefore may be liable to drop a word or two which may defeat their own ends, not knowing its value; so that until his plans are matured it becomes a good lawyer to keep his peace. And so, my lord Duke, I am afraid you will have to wait for information."

"But this unbearable suspense !"

"Must still be borne if you cannot shake it off. I tell you all will be well in the end, though the end may be a long way off as yet."

"I am glad to hear you say so, but I am far from being convinced."

"That is a pity, for the sake of your own peace of mind."

"It is, but I cannot help it, and now good night: I must return."

"My business is ended," said the lawyer; "I will walk with you as far as St. Paul's, and there take my leave."

"Be it so," said the Duke; "my carriage waits at the foot of Ludgate-hill."

The lawyer secured his locks, arranged his loose papers, put on his rusty overcoat, then put out his flickering oil lamp, and departed from the office, securing his door after him.

"It is bitterly cold," said Grimer, as he stepped into the street, followed by his noble client.

"It is bitterly cold, and it grows very dark."

"It does. Let us walk fast, the air bites piercingly."

They hurried on without uttering another word, and soon arrived at St. Paul's, where they separated.

"Good night," said Grimer, "I shall expect to see your Grace again within a week."

"Shall I not come sooner ?"

"Not unless I write to you."

"Very well; good night."

"Good night, my lord Duke, and more pleasant dreams to you."

They parted, the Duke turning down Ludgate-hill, and the lawyer dashing under an archway leading into one of the courts which lead into the churchyard.

CHAPTER XIII.

A NOBLE BURGLAR AND A MYSTERIOUS WITNESS.

THE Duke walked quickly down the hill: at its foot he found his carriage awaiting him.

"Return home," he said to the coachman, "drive as fast as possible, or the horses will get chilled. I shall not return yet."

The coachman touched his hat, and drove off up Fleet-street, leaving the Duke on the hill.

It was miserably cold, and clouds had gathered over the moon, and completely obscured it.

Not a soul was to be seen, and the Duke commenced retracing his steps.

"Yes," he said, in a low voice, "I must possess myself of those papers. They are of vital importance, and appear to be this man's stock-in-trade. Once out of his possession, I am almost relieved from his power, for unless they could be produced against me his evidence would be scouted. I would have him imprisoned as an impostor, detected in an attempt to extort money by intimidation. Yes, I must have the papers."

Muttering these and similar sentences to himself, he hurried over the snow-covered road as fast as possible, and soon re-appeared at the door of the house in which the lawyer's office was situated.

The passage was left open in consequence of the number who had to pass in and out, the house having at least a dozen occupants.

Unobserved, the Duke entered, and approached the door of the lawyer's chamber. He tried to open it but the attempt was vain. The door was of solid oak, and the lock stoutly resisted his efforts. He then drew from his pocket a knife, and commenced chipping away at the wood work, but this he saw would be too great a work to accomplish before the probable arrival of some one belonging to the premises, and therefore he was about to give up the task in despair, when a footfall arrested him.

Some one was opening the outer door, and the Duke withdrew to a remote part of the dark passage in order to escape observation.

He saw the door pushed gently open, and a tall figure closely muffled in a long cloak enter by it.

This figure paused at the door of Grimer's office, and the Duke heard a low voice exclaim,

"Yes, here is the very door; years have passed, but the old place is unchanged. Now to effect an entrance."

The Duke heard the rattle of some steel implement and in another moment he saw the tall and mysterious figure stand in the lawyer's office. "What can he want?" thought the Duke. "It must be some burglar seeking to rob the old man's office."

The Duke saw a bright light in Grimer's office and heard a rustling of papers.

The light suddenly disappeared, and the figure stalked out again, and passed into the street.

For a few moments the Duke moved not hand or foot, but at last he drew himself up and listened.

"All is silent again," he said, "all is silent and the attempt must be made. It is a desperate game, but I must play it out now." Not a sound to be heard. It is well, I may yet effect my purpose."

Stealing along, he approached the door of the office and found to his delight that the mysterious visitor had left it open!

"Now," he said under his breath, "Now for the work."

He entered the office and groped about for the drawer in which he had seen the lawyer deposit the key of the iron safe. At length he found it. A severe wrench served to tear it open and in another moment he felt the key in his grasp.

Clutching it eagerly he approached the wall and felt for the safe until his hand encountered it. After awhile the key was in the lock and the iron door flew open. The Duke knew exactly where to place his hand upon the documents, and without any fumbling he found them and tore them out of the safe.

What was it that sent that horrible cold shiver through his frame, as he grasped the papers? what made him sicken and induce every limb in his body shake as if ague striken.

There was no sound, and he had not turned his head from the safe, but there was a something which made him conscious that he was detected in the act of committing a burglary. There was a something that unmanned him, and it was this—

The chamber was full of light!

He dared not turn his head, for he felt that his eye must encounter the gaze of an accuser.

"So," said a voice behind the Duke, "so, we meet again. Move your head and look upon me."

Mechanically the Duke obeyed.

On turning around he beheld a tall figure holding a lantern, from which poured a brilliant light, which revealed a face livid white and as immovable as if carved from the solid marble.

It was the face of a man, but it was as inanimate as stone.

"Do you not know me?" demanded this mysterious personage.

The Duke, terrified beyond measure, uttered an almost inaudible "Yes."

"You remember when we last met?"

"Yes."

"And what has brought you here to-night?"

"I dare not say. Great Heaven preserve me, does the grave up its dead?"

"Yes; but you have not answered my question. What has brought you here?"

"I must not tell."

"Then I will tell you. You came to hear news of your child and your father's lost will. Am I not right?"

"Yes,"

"You came, and was tempted by the sight of the documents you now hold in your hand to possess them."

"Yes."

"I knew all this, for I have watched you. I, too, came here to possess myself of those very papers; but I knew not where to find them. I followed you to your carriage, I saw you return, and marked your ineffectual attempt to effect an entrance here. I opened the door for you, and retired that you might procure the papers, and that through you I might possess myself of them. They are in your hands, give them to me."

The Duke moved not.

"You hesitate. I will take them."

With this the mysterious man advanced and plucked the documents from the Duke's grasp.

"They are mine. You have played your part well, and I thank you. I shall retire, and should advise you to follow the same course, or you may be detected here. Do you comprehend?"

The Duke, by a slight movement, signified that he understood what was intended to be conveyed.

"That is well," continued the man, "and now

I will go. Adieu, my lord Duke, adieu; we shall meet again.

With this, the mysterious individual withdrew. It was long before the Duke recovered sufficient consciousness to follow.

He staggered to the table and fainted. How long he remained in that state he knew not, but some considerable time must have elapsed.

At length, weak and ill, and with his brain reeling, he staggered forth, and into the street, almost unable to persuade himself that the whole affair had not been a dark and terrible dream.

CHAPTER XIV.

THE FURTHER ADVENTURES OF MR. PIPEY, IN SEARCH OF INFORMATION.

PIPEY sauntered away from the office of Mr. Grimer, and struck out in the direction of the Minories, in which respectable locality was to be held a hop, at which he expected to meet the man Hammer.

An hour's sharp walking brought him to the neighbourhood of the place to which he was bound.

He entered a low, filthy street, in which a number of persons was loitering about, evidently with no good intent. There was a palpable freemasonry among these people by which they at once recognised those of their own order, for Mr. Pipey walked through the place unmolested; a feat which would not have been accomplished by any other stranger to the locality. The people seemed to understand that he was one of themselves, and by a common consent allowed him to pass without let or hindrance.

At most of the window lights were burning, and it was evident the neighbourhood was holding high festival, for sounds of joviality burst ever and anon from almost every house Pipey passed.

"These kids enjoy themselves," said Pipey, as he plodded on through the snow. "They seems to keep up their peckers pretty vell, and come it stronger than ve vest-enders can."

He paused at the door of what appeared to be a private dwelling house, but what, in reality, was a place of public entertainment for all the vagabonds of the east of London.

This was the Mother Whistler's to which Pipey informed Grimer that he was bound.

After listening attentively for a few moments, Pipey knocked twice.

There was a slight stir within, and then someone said, "Patchwork."

And Mr. Pipey thereunto replied—

"Stitch it."

After which the voice within continued—

"All right, my covey; ve'll open the door in a kipple of seconds."

In almost less than that time Pipey stood on the other side of the door.

He was received by a great, brutal-looking fellow, dressed in a suit of vulgarly brilliant clothes, and decorated with more jewellery than would have been considered absolutely necessary for the adornment of three persons ordinarily fond of ornament.

This was Flash Toby: a very noted cracksman of the time.

"Vell," said that gentleman, eyeing Mr. Pipey attentively.

"Vell," reiterated that hopeful juvenile, returning the stare, and assuming his most impertinent air, "Vell, handsome; vot's in the vind?"

Mr. Toby did not seem to understand what was in the wind, and so he evaded the question by reiterating the word, "Vell!"

"Did'nt I hear you say that afore?" asked Pipey, looking very attentively at the flash one.

"You might."

"I thought so. Ain't you got any other remark to make?"

"No."

"Oh."

"You seem to have lots of cheek, you do, for a youngster," observed Toby, after a pause.

"Does I?" said Pipey; "vell, it's all a owing to the tooth-ache—it's svelled up."

"Ah! you're one of those sharp Vestminister boys, aint yer?"

"I have the honour of belonging to that amiable neighbourhood," said Pipey.

"Vell, you'd best get back to your own quarter again, or the chances are you'll get kicked out, in two minutes."

"Shall I?" said Pipey, "then it won't be by you."

"No cheek," said the other, working himself into a passion; "no cheek, or I'll wring your neck."

"Vill yer?" said Pipey, "I begs to doubt that werry much."

The flash one was about to give Mr. Pipey a practical illustration of his intention, when another individual put in an appearance on the scene, and interfered,

"Hillo!" said this person, a brutal six-foot ruffian, "hillo, what's up? No putting upon little Pipey, or I'll smash in your daylights, Mr. Toby."

"Oh, if he's a friend of yours it's all right. I didn't know he was a pal."

"A pal—he's the prince of pals, and so no touching him. There, shake hands with him, and no more squabbling."

"Proud to make your acquaintance," said Mr. Toby.

"Ditto, repeated," said Mr. Pipey, walking away with his friend, who, as the reader may suppose, was no other than the man Hammer, with whom he had the appointment.

They traversed a long passage, and then descended some stairs which led them into a large vaulted apartment, in which they found at least a hundred men and women, drinking, smoking, singing, and dancing in the most uproarious manner.

"Here we are," said Hammer; "here we are, Pipey. Ain't it jolly?"

Mr. Pipey exclaimed,

"Stunning!" and allowed his eye to wander over the place.

The scene was an extraordinary one.

Every individual present was more or less a

criminal, and evading the law. The place in which they held their revelry was what was known as a thieves' kitchen, and a more disreputable place could scarcely be conceived.

It was as filthy as possible, and the accumulation of tobacco smoke, for which there was no exit, made it intolerable.

Tables ran round the room, and benches were fixed close to the wall for the accommodation of those who chose to sit; a party in a decided minority, for the bulk of the company stood in the centre of the floor, engaged in dancing and singing.

At the top of the apartment was a rough made bar, at which liquors were retailed to the company. About half way down the apartment, seated at a table, were two or three musicians, who kept up an incessant flood of sound—we had almost committed ourselves by writing melody—to which the heels of the company kept time. Such was "Mother Whistler's Hop."

Very few of the company seemed to be known to Pipey; but he, nevertheless, displayed the greatest familiarity with all assembled, more particularly with the women, in whose good graces he was not long in establishing himself.

"You're all angels," said Pipey to about a dozen of them, who gathered round him for the purpose of obtaining liquor. "You're all angels, and I'm only sorry I can't be the fancy man of the whole lot; but the fact is I'm engaged to a lady of title, who has thrice attempted to commit suicide on my account, and so I'm obliged to be werry partic'ler."

This explanation was far from satisfactory to those assembled, who would not be beaten off with such an excuse.

"It won't do, my little man," said one; "it won't do. We've all taken a fancy to you, and you'll have to stand."

"Oh, I don't object to that," said Pipey; "only don't visper it to any marquis or duke in the Vest End, or it may be my ruin."

As it was not at all probable that these poor creatures would have a chance of doing this, they all promised secresy, and Mr. Pipey appeared much relieved. After this *badinage* the party drank at Mr. Pipey's expense, and that young gentleman now ingratiated himself into the good graces of all present. At length he was left alone with his friend Hammer, and then they turned their attention to the real business of the meeting.

"Now," said Hammer, "you know why I asked you to come down here to-night?"

"No, I don't," said Pipey, "cos you haven't as yet taken the trouble to tell me."

"But you know it's a crack as is meant."

"I think you said so vonce afore."

"Werry well; then you're jist the covey as ve vant to do the fancy business of the job.'

"Ve? Then you aint alone in the job?"

"In course not: there's another—a fust-class 'un, and an old pal of mine—Yellow Maydock."

"I knows him."

"In course yer does; everybody does. Vell, he's in the fake."

"Is he?"

"Yes."

"Then it's wery likely to be a good 'un; for the Yellow Boy isn't a duffer at the work."

"Not he. I should think not. Vell, vill you jine us?"

"You haven't yet told me vere or vot it is, and you don't suppose as I'm a going to run my head into a halter vith my eyes shut, does yer?"

"No."

"Vell, then, speak up."

"You're richeous?"

"As a bird."

"Then ve'll let you in. You know Kew?"

"I should rather fancy I've heard of it."

"Vell, at Kew the Duke of Grassmount has a villa."

"Hillo!" exclaimed Pipey.

"What's up?"

"Nothing. Go on."

"Vell, the Duke's a livin' in town, and there ain't never nobody but two or three sarvints at the willa, and the amount of plate that's there aint to be credited."

"Aint it?"

"No."

"Vell; go on."

"That ere plate, my friend the Yellow von knows vere to put his hand on; but it aint that vich takes him to the willa."

"Aint it, though?"

"No."

"Vell, vot is it?"

"I don't know, but I has my s'picions."

"Has you?"

"I has."

"Vell, out vith 'em, can't yer?"

"Are you a dummy?"

"I'm speechless."

"Vell, lately I've a heard the Yellow von a talkin' like old boots about a vill?"

"A vill?"

"Yes, a vill. The last vill and testiphant. Don't yer know?"

"I don't think I ever heerd of a testiphant. You don't mean a elephant?"

"No; testiphant, or testimum. Don't yer understand that?"

"Yer mean a testiment."

"Vell, ain't it all von?"

"Not quite."

"But it's pretty much the same, any how. Vell, he's been a talkin' in his dreams about this here vill, and do you know I think the dockyment is a hid avay somevere's at the Duke's willa."

"Ah!"

"Yes, that's just it. Vell, let him have the vill, say I, as long as he lets us have the svag. Vot say you?"

"Vell, I says as long as I has vot I vants, he's quite velcome to all that's left."

"That's the style, and now vot does yer say?"

"I'm game."

"Then it's understood?"

"Yes, as far as I'm concerned."

"Give us yer paw"—Mr. Pipey extended his hand—"And now ve're pals?"

"Yes," said Pipey, and then he added in an undertone, "yes, pals as long as it serves my turn, my covey, but no longer."

They joined the crowd of revellers, and were soon deep in the wild and dissipated pursuits of the throng.

Such a scene of reckless abandonment has seldom been seen. Each one attempted to outvie the other in debauchery, and very soon the place became a scene of corruption and vicious pleasure to which we, in the present day, are comparative strangers.

The march of intellect has led us from these scenes, and we now turn our attention to higher and better things. Education has taught us that enjoyment does not mean pandering to the worst animal passions of our natures, and the progress of the age has left far behind the brutalising habits of former generations. In every particular, from court to hovel, we have improved, until we can now boast of being the most moral people in the wide world.

Those who deem it wrong to bring to light and repaint those scenes of the past make a sad mistake, for it is only by comparisons such as they present that we can estimate the true blessings we enjoy.

It was about an hour after the conversation we have just recorded had taken place that an incident occurred which entirely disturbed the equanimity of the assembly.

The mirth was at its height; wine and brandy fired the brains of most of those assembled, and the fascinations and unconcealed charms of the women had done their work, when a sudden silence came over all: a low whistle without had stopped every mouth, and stayed every foot.

This was followed by the sudden appearance of a tall man, dressed in a suit of black velvet, elaborately trimmed with bugles of the same colour. He was over the average height, and had a most commanding air; but his greatest peculiarity was in his face, which was not a little singular. It was shorn of every hair, and was as white as sculptured marble, and as expressionless as that of a corpse; this was shaded by a quantity of long black hair, which, in accordance with the fashion of the period, reached his shoulders. He was altogether a most extraordinary being, and quite the sort of individual one would expect to meet in a charnel-house.

This being was accompanied by Flash Toby, who cried—

"Hist, all of ye! keep quiet, there's a whole force of Charleys outside, and if ye don't mind there'll be a row."

"Oh," said the mysterious new-comer, "don't mind them; they have followed me for the last two hours, and I am the only one they want, but I rather think they know better than to attempt to take me from this place: so resume your merriment, friends, and fear nothing."

Need we say that this voice was the same which so startled the Duke in Grimer's office? It was the same, and a more terrible one never sounded in human ears.

It was all very well to recommend the company to resume their mirth, but that was effectually checked; the appearance of this individual threw a complete chill over all there assembled. In vain they struggled against it, they could not shake it off.

"Vy, who is that rum 'un?" asked Pipey.

"Don't yer know him?" asked Hammer, in reply.

"Mo."

"Vy, that's the Black Captain, as they calls him here; I b'lieve his name's Rook, but they only dubs him the Black Captain in this quarter: he's on the road, and in about three months has done more vork than every other highwayman could in twelve. Vy, he's a perfect terror, and they do say that he's as bloodthirsty a villain as ever lived. He generally blows a man's brains out first, and then asks him for his purse afterwards. It's a sure plan, but a bad 'un. Give me a club, and let me catch 'em von on the nut, that they'll get over agin, say I."

"Yes," said Pipey; "but this Black Captain, vere's he from?"

"That's vot puzzles everybody. He come, no von knew how, and not von dared ask vy. He come, and with as much cheek and coolness as you see him a using now. He dubs himself Captain, and there aint von amongst us but vot has let him stick to his title."

"And you all vork under his orders?"

"Yes."

"Vy?"

"That's vot none on us knows."

"Does yer mean to say you're afeard of him?"

"Vell, it's somethink werry like it."

"Vell, it's a rum go," said Pipey; "but I'll be hanged if he aint just the sort o' cove as looks as if he could make people foller him vether they vanted to or not."

"Only you just come over and try it for a veek or two."

"Not if I knows it," said Pipey. "No Black Captain for me. Vy, vot a awful vite mug he has a got."

"Yes, its always like that," continued Hammer; "you never sees the beggar change countenance; he never laughs nor cries, frowns nor appears pleased. He's always vot you see him, and never nothink else."

"It's my opinion," said Pipey, "that he's a got a china head stuck on. I never did see sich a vite mugged 'un afore."

"Vell, never mind him, look here. Do you see who this is?"

Mr. Hammer pointed in the direction of the door through which Yellow Maydock entered.

"Vy, Yellow von," said Hammer, "vot brought you out to-night? I thought as how you vos afeered of the Charleys?"

"I was; but I grew sick of remaining at home, and determined to seek you here. Well, young one," he continued, turning to Pipey, "how have you been since last we met at Westminster?"

"Oh, as vell as can be expected."

"That's all right."

"And how have you been?" asked Pipey.

"Capital."

"That's a comfort."

"It is—to me. Why, what makes the people all so quiet to night?"

"It's the Black Captain."

"The Black Captain?" said Maydock. "Oh, I have heard of that being, but have never yet seen him. Where is he?"

Hammer pointed him out.

"Why the deuce don't he look around and let us see what he is like?" said Maydock. As if in anticipation of, or overhearing his wish, the Captain turned full upon the trio, and his eyes fell upon the face of Maydock.

There was still no expression in the face of the former, but the latter exhibited the utmost consternation; in fact, he was just as much terrified at the sight of this being as was the Duke when he encountered his gaze.

The Black Captain never took his eyes from the face of Maydock, and Maydock at length, unable to bear the rigid scrutiny any longer, shrank back, whispering in a hoarse, hollow voice, to his companions—

"Come away! Quick! quick! come away! Take no notice, but leave the place!"

"Vy, vot's the matter?" asked Pipey.

"Do not speak! Do not breathe! Do not look! but come away!" muttered Maydock, as he stepped backward to the door, with his eyes still fixed upon those of the Black Captain.

In this fashion they reached the passage, and here Maydock fairly turned and fled, never stopping until he had reached the street.

"Why, what the deuce frightened you?" asked Hammer.

"Frightened me! Aye, I was frightened! Good God! *that was no living man!*"

"What the Old Scratch are you a talking about?' asked Pipey.

"I say it was no living man! The owner of that form died years ago! Died, I tell you, died! I know it! Oh, what can this mean?"

"That's just the question I'm going to ask you. Vot does this mean—are you drunk?"

"No."

"Then vot are yer arter?"

"I cannot explain. Oh, curse the hour that I left my house to look upon that terrible phantom!"

"Vot *are* you a driving at?" asked Pipey, in blank astonishment.

"You will know all, one day; but I cannot tell you now, Come, let us hasten to my crib."

Without another word, they sped out of the street, and turned into a dark alley, wherein was the habitation spoken of by the terrified Maydock as "my crib."

———

CHAPTER XV.

PHILLIPE DETERMINES TO QUIT LONDON FOR EVER.

THE Italian, Phillipe Morlavine, had day by day, from the one on which Marie had quitted him for the Prince, grown more weary of London.

At length the place became unbearable to him, and he threw up his engagement and determined to spend a few months at a cottage he had purchased at Cobham, in Surrey.

The little place had been bought in the hope that, one day, Marie would share it with him; but that dream was gone, and there remained nothing now for him but to go there alone, and strive to forget the one who had proved so unworthy of him.

It was on a dark afternoon in the month of January that he set out on horseback for the village.

He had intended a much earlier start, but circumstances had detained him until an hour when it was dangerous to travel so far on the lonely roads; but he determined to go, and as there was no one to dissuade him, he set forth, mounted on an excellent horse.

He rode for many miles without the slightest interruption or discomfiture, but at last a terrible storm broke over his head, and his horse became startled at the continued peals of thunder and lightning.

He had but another mile or two to ride, and he kept on persevering; but at length had to turn into a secluded road, under an avenue of large trees, which moaned and sighed over his head.

The place was sufficiently desolate, but the thoughts of the Italian made it even more so, and it was with misgiving and doubt that he entered it.

He pressed forward until the end of this desolate place was almost reached, and then he was suddenly stopped.

As if she had sprung suddenly out of the earth to arrest him, there appeared before him a tall and truly hideous old gipsey woman, dressed after the style of the Italian Zingari rather than in the habits of an English tribe.

"Stop," said this being, "stop, Phillipe Morlavine, until I have questioned thee."

The words were spoken in the purest Italian.

"What would ye with me?" said Phillipe; "I know ye not."

"You do not," said the gipsey, "but I know you. I heard that you were coming to-day to take possession of your cottage in the village yonder, and I determined to remain here and confront you."

"For what purpose?"

"In order that I may have information on a subject as dear to me as life itself. Some weeks ago I heard it whispered that you would bring with you a young and beautiful wife in the person of Marie Lavrouffe, and then I heard that the engagement was broken off, and that you would come alone."

"What has this to do with thee?"

"Much; the girl is more to me than thou dreamest of, so I ask thee is what I have heard the truth?"

"It is."

"And why have you left her?"

"Ask, rather, why has she left me."

"Is it so?"

"It is."

"Then to what end has she left you?"

"To a bad one, I fear."

"Say not so! Oh! great Heaven, say not so!"

"It is so. She left me—forsook me—for the arms of one who, if he has not already abandoned her, will soon do so."

"His name?"

"The Prince of Wales."

"Oh! the curse still hangs over us—the terrible curse still clings to the name! Oh, God! first myself, then my child, and now my grandchild: all fallen—all degraded."

"Your grandchild!—what can you mean?"

"It is so, Phillipe, it is so. There has been a curse upon us for a century and more, and this is another and still worse proof of its terrible intensity."

"Will you explain?—your words are to me most mysterious."

"I will do so. Fifty years ago the Vendetta was the proudest of the families of Italy—fifty years ago we were rich, powerful, respected: but adversity came upon us through the instrumentality of the males of our house, and we soon lost caste, and became poor and abandoned. Severely tempted by a villain I fell, and became an outcast from society. I was deserted by my betrayer, and then fled to a secluded place with the child he had left me, in order that I might bring her up in ignorance of the world and its ways; and to this purpose I laid down such a course of study as I deemed best to effect my purpose. But in order that I might impart knowledge to the child I was tempted into study myself, and soon became a proficient, not only in the literature of the time, but was induced to go and increase my store of knowledge by a study of the occult sciences. I am afraid that in pursuit of these studies I lost sight of the grand idea that led to them; for the child formed acquaintances, and became so imbued with the spirit of the world and worldliness, that when I discovered the error of which I had been guilty, it was too late. She would not be tempted to study—she would not undergo confinement—and so she grew up to be a beautiful but uncontrollable girl. In an evil hour the tempter came, and she fled with him—fled, and became the thing I had been. After years of search I found her once more; she was still with her betrayer, still comparatively happy. But at length her eyes opened to the guiltiness of her life, and repentance came upon her. Well, I will not prolong my tale by telling you of the course of sufferings she underwent. I will not tell you how, step by step, she sunk into the grave, but I must tell you that she reached that home at last, and her sorrows were ended in the sleep of death. Before she died, however, she made her betrayer swear to bring up her infant in the paths of honour and virtue, and never to leave her until she was the wife of an honest man. Lavrouffe, her father, my child's betrayer, took that oath, and now I ask you how has he kept it? Has Marie fallen by his knowledge and through his neglect, or has she strayed by evading his watchfulness and care? For years I have followed her about from country to country, but without her knowledge. For years I have watched over her to see that Lavrouffe kept his oath, and I only slumbered when I heard that the child had loved, and was loved by you, and that she was to become your wife; and you tear my heart asunder by telling me that she is fallen, degraded—lost for ever. Oh Heaven! it is too terrible to reflect upon, but speak, man, speak; is it, I say, through the neglect of Lavrouffe that Marie has fallen?"

"Not only by his neglect," said Phillipe, "but through his direct connivance."

"You do not tell me so! I dream."

"It is true. He bartered away her honour as if it had been his goods and chattels to do with as he pleased."

"The villain! the accursed monster!"

"Yes, ten times accursed villain, I know him to be so."

"Oh! I could weep, weep, weep; but no, this is no time for grief, it is the hour to act."

"What will you do?"

"What will I not do?"

"You will commit no violence, no wrong?"

"I will fulfil the curse laid upon his head by my child in the event of his not fulfilling his oath—that is what I will do."

"Stay! stay!" cried Phillipe, "let him meet with his deserts from another—from me! Have I not a right?"

"Ah! You have! Then be it so. Here I give thee the curse to fulfil! 'Wrong for wrong,' said my dying child, 'pang for pang, wound for wound, life for life!'—will you fulfil the dying malediction?'"

"I will be the avenger of Marie's honour!"

"Swear it!"

"I swear!"

"Remember! Wrong for wrong—"

"Life for life!" cried Phillipe, "I will not forget!"

"We shall meet again and again," said the woman. "Seek for Estelle Vendetta, the Italian hag, in the camp of the gipsies yonder, and thou shalt find me. Adieu!"

"Farewell!" said Phillipe, dashing his spurs into the sides of his beast, and springing onward. Thus ended this singular and most unexpected interview.

CHAPTER XVI.

PIPEY'S DISCOVERY.

THE burglars, accompanied by Pipey, hastened into the house of Maydock, and closed the door after them.

"There," said Maydock, "I feel safe now. Ugh! I would'nt have the eyes of that cursed spectre on me again for the whole world."

"Vy, you're still on to that ere spectre, are yer?" asked Mr. Pipey. "Vot does yer mean by a spectre?"

"Never mind, that is my business; you will hear no more of him from me, and if you want to keep in my good graces, never recur to the subject again. I never wish to hear of it as long as I live."

"Oh, if it's so serious as all that," said Pipey, "vy, I'm mum."

They entered a room on the ground floor, and Maydock struck a light, and revealed a most dilapidated and unenticing apartment. Its characteristic was filth; of comfort, there was but little.

An oil lamp flickered on the table, and threw a light upon a variety of black bottles scattered about in lavish confusion. It was evident that Maydock had been indulging rather freely before he left home for the hop.

"Come," he said, "here is the stuff, and plenty; sit down and make yourselves at home."

"Vith all the pleasure in life," said Mr. Pipey; "there never vos an occasion, as I can remember, ven good lush vos offered me and I vos known to refuse it. I vos suckled upon gin, relieved sometimes by a red herring, and that's vy I take to both so naturally now; more especially to the former, vich is the support of my blessed existence. Here's luck."

Pipey poured out a bumper of his favourite beverage, and quaffed it to the very dregs; after which he heaved a great sigh, and appeared considerably relieved.

"And now to business," said Maydock.

"Have you told Pipey of the game Hammer?"

"I has."

"And he consents?"

"He's there."

"Well, that's all right."

"Ven is it to come off?" said Pipey.

"To-morrow night," said Maydock,

"Short notice," remarked Pipey.

"The shorter the better, said Maydock, "it admits of no funking."

"I 'aint a going to funk," continued Pipey; "I 'aint one of that sort,"

"Who said you were?" asked Hammer.

"Vell, nobody as I'm aweer of."

"Vell, then, what are you a talking of?"

"I 'aint a talkin' about nothink."

"Vell, then?"

"Vell, then?"

And here the matter dropped.

"Vot d'ye reckon the svag worth?" asked Hammer,

"What we may bring away is worth at least a thousand guineas," answered Maydock.

"And vot's to be our share?"

"Two thirds."

"Vell, that 'aint no dust," said Hammer, "but I think as how you might make it a leetle more, considerin' as how you has other work on hand at the place."

"Who said I had other work on hand?"

"I did," answered Hammer, "I did, and vill still say so. Do ye think I'm a fool and can't see and hear?"

"What have you seen—what have you heard?" asked Maydock, in an agony of excitement.

"Why, I have seen you in your sleep making grabs at a vill, and I've heerd you a talkin' of the vill, and vishing as how you could get into the vaults of the Dooke's house, and grab it; that's vot I've seed and heerd."

"Is that all?"

"Yes, that is all."

"You know no more. You do not know what will?"

"No."

"Then it's good for you. If you shared that secret, pal as you are, you would die by my hand, for it is fatal to all who know it."

"Nonsense."

"It is true. I tell you that that job is mine, and mine alone, and that I will not allow another to have a hand in it. It is a secret which concerns me alone, so don't interfere with it."

Oh, you may keep your secret," said Hammer, "I don't want to be bothered about dirty bits o' paper, give me the bright glittering svag, say I, and anybody may stick to bills. Howsomever, I don't see why you should stick out for a third ven you know as how you set such value on the vill. As long as you gets your precious vill you ought to be satisfied."

"Ought I?"

"Yes, yer ought."

"Well, I am not. Is not that sufficient? I am not satisfied, and will have my own way. Now, what do you say to that?"

"Oh, I aint got nothink to say, only that you've turned precious greedy all at vonce."

"And, if I have, you are no sufferer by it. Try and enter the Duke's villa without me, and see where you would be."

"Oh, pickles! Ve aint a going to try: you're the leader, and ve vill follow you. Isn't that enough?"

"It is. So let it be understood that we meet to-morrow at dusk for this expedition, and, further, let it be understood that I am master, and that my word is law."

"Oh, very well," said Hammer, "you needn't be so precious glum all at once."

"Then let the subject drop, and here's your healths in a bumper, with success to our mission.'

"Hear, hear," said Pipey. "I jines you in that ere noble sentiment. Our own healths, and success to our mission, and in particular the mission of Mr. Pipey."

"What a selfish dog that is," said Maydock, pointing out Pipey; "I never met his like. He thinks of no one but self."

"Oh, don't he though," said Pipey; "that is all you know about it. You don't know what a heap of people he's a thinkin' of benefiting at this ere present moment."

The conversation was here interrupted by the entrance of an old crone, who appeared to fill the position of Maydock's housekeeper.

"Here Maydock," she said; "the wench is in her tantrums again. I've tried to quiet her, but she wont cease her gab. You had best see what you——"

"Hist!" said Maydock. "Why do you come here troubling me? Could you not see that I am engaged?"

"Humph! What has your being engaged to do with me?"

"Everything."

"Nothing. I don't care about your engagements. All that I know is that the wench is at her hysterical fits agin, and that I can't stop here. If you don't choose to move, you may leave it alone."

With this the old woman slammed the door and walked away.

"Hillo, Maydock," said Hammer. "Vot's up? You seem to have a young 'un here on the sly. Suppose you introduce me and my friend Mr. Pipey."

"Yes, by all means," said Pipey, "introduce me. The gals, bless 'em, are awfully fond of me; she'll take to me directly she claps eyes on me.'

"Will she?" said Maydock; "perhaps she may, but at present she is not likely to clap eyes on you or anybody else; and so just keep your seats and be quiet, while I go and see what's up. I shan't be a moment."

Maydock rose and quitted the room.

"Vell,' said Pipey, "it strikes me that our friend has a bright game up in this quarter, aint he?"

"Oh, there's no knowing; he's such a deep 'un, no one gets at the bottom of his moves. But vot's the odds to us? let us drink his jolly good health."

"Vith all my heart," said Pipey; "it's most astonishing how much inclined I feel to drink people's jolly good health when the liquor's to my taste. I do believe I could keep going on drinking jolly good healths to everybody until I'd run through the whole human family." While he thus assumed an air of indifference, the mind of the boy was fully occupied by what he had just seen and heard; mentally he said, "I have the clue; she's here, but how am I to get at her?"

How indeed!

After an absence of a few minutes Maydock returned, but said nothing of the cause which took him from the room; finding it distasteful to him neither of his companions resumed the subject.

After a further carouse of an hour's duration, Hammer and Pipey rose to go.

"Good night," said Maydock; "good night to both. You had best get home and retire to rest, for you will be abroad to-morrow night."

"Good night," said Hammer. "I shall be here at dusk."

"And I," said Pipey, "shall be in the neighbourhood about that hour; if not, say I'm not to be trusted."

"Devil doubt you," said Maydock, "I don't; and so, once more, good night."

With this he led his guests to the door, and closed it on them.

"Now," said Hammer, "which road do you take?"

"Oh, I don't know," said Pipey, "vich vay is you going?"

"To the right."

"Oh, that'll be rather out of my road, so I'll say good night at vunce."

Had Mr. Hammer have said "to the left" it would have been all one to Pipey. His road did not lay with that of his companion, and he was most anxious to shake him off, so Pipey continued—

"It von't do to be seen standing about here, chattering, so let's take our hook at vunce. Neither of us can afford to run the risk of being nabbed vith to-morrow night's vork in view, so let's off at vunce."

"You're right, boy," said Hammer, "you're right, as you always are; so good night."

"Good," said Pipey, and they separated.

Hammer went away speedily to the right, and Pipey took to the left, but he did not go far. As soon as his friend was out of sight, he turned back, and took up a position opposite Maydock's house.

"I'm not a going till I've seen her," said Pipey. "If she's there I'll have a confab vith her, if I die for it; and so look out, Mr. Maydock."

Pipey had not long been in his position when he observed a light in the room on the first floor, and soon after he saw the shadow of a man flitting about.

"That aint the room," said Pipey, "that's the Yellow Boy going to bed."

He was right in his conjectures. A minute afterwards Maydock appeared at the window, the shutters of which he closed and fastened.

"He's off for the night," said Pipey; "and now vere can Liz be."

He looked at the upper window, but saw nothing.

He waited long and anxiously, but there was nothing to arrest his suspicions.

"Vell," he said, "I must try the back of the premises; it's evident she ain't in the front."

Casting a farewell glance at all the windows, to assure himself that he was right in his conjectures, he sped out of the street, and sought the back of the house.

It was but a short street, and he was soon out of it. He found that there were large courtyards at the back of the houses, secured by a tolerably high wall. Counting the doors, he at last passed before the one he desired to find, and then he once more scanned the premises.

There was a light in the attic.

"Now," said Pipey, "if that aint the old voman, it's Liz. I shall soon see."

With cat-like agility he clambered over the wall, and dropped into the court.

Again he watched, and this time his perseverance was rewarded. Gazing upward, he distinctly saw a female form flitting about in the attic.

"That aint the old 'un," he said, "consequently it must be Liz."

The person in the attic then came to the window, and appeared to be trying to force it open, but without effect.

"By gum," said Pipey, "that's Liz; she's a prisoner in that infernal old attic; and now to see vot's to be done for her."

He approached the house, and found no mode of entering it. Every window defied his skill and strength.

"There's nothing for it but the vatershoot," said Pipey; "so up ve goes."

Gathering up the rather voluminous skirts of his coat, Mr. Pipey applied himself to the old shoot which was fastened to the wall.

The boy had all the agility of a monkey with the strength of a lion, and, therefore, found no difficulty in making this dangerous ascent. In two minutes he was on a level with the attic window, but the shoot was a little too much to the left for him to look in from this position, so he looked about to see what could he done.

Fortunately for him in former times an ivy tree had been trained to the wall, and whilst the under part had either decayed or been cut away there remained a pretty solid trellis-work around the upper windows. Catching hold of this he swung himself from the shoot and found it easy work to get at the window.

He looked eagerly in, and was delighted to find that his labour had not been in vain.

Within the room was Liz.

The girl was disrobing for bed, and had divested herself of her outer garments, when Pipey appeared.

"Hillo!" said that individual; "vot's up?"

Liz was startled at the sound of the voice, and gazed about to see from whence it proceeded.

"Hillo!" said Pipey, again, "hillo, Liz, don't yer know me?" he tapped at the window.

"Open the vinder!" said that gentleman.

"I cannot," said Liz; "would to heaven that I could; had I been able to have done so, I should have precipitated myself therefrom long since."

"That vould a been a pity," said Pipey; "never say die, Liz; vile there's life there's hope. I'll see about this 'ere vinder."

Uttering those words, Mr. Pipey placed a hand in his pocket, and drew forth a knife, which he applied to the fastening of the window, and which, under his skilful touch, at once gave way.

As the window opened he threw himself into the apartment, and on the truckle bed which was prepared for Liz.

"Whew!" said Pipey, "perhaps this 'aint hot work, neither."

"How did you find me?" asked Liz.

"Oh, don't ask me that, my love," said Pipey. "I'm sure I don't know, only, I may say, that it's a been von of the heaviest jobs as ever I took in hand."

"But how did you know I occupied this chamber?"

"I didn't know it."

"Then how came you here?"

"I came up the shoot on a voyage of diskivery."

"But some one must have told you of my whereabouts."

"No, I smelt you out."

"I cannot understand your meaning. Nor can I comprehend why you have sought me, but from whatever motive you have, I pray that you will take me from this place."

"Vell, I vill, like a brick; only you don't think you could go down the shoot, do you?"

"No, no."

"I thought not; so you'll have to remain until I can get you out by some other way."

"Oh, do not leave me here, Pipey; you do not know how I am persecuted by that horrible man, and the still more horrible woman who waits upon me."

"You is!"

"Oh, I cannot speak the torture they make me undergo; threats—such terrible threats—are uttered night and day that I am half deprived of reason when I reflect upon them."

"What—what do they threaten you about."

"They want me to marry him."

"Who?"

"Maydock."

"They does?"

"Yes; to this end I am tortured night and day. Oh, friend, independent of the natural repugnance I feel to the man, how could I marry the husband of the woman who reared me. He told me she was not my mother, and that I was in no way related to her, consequently that I was to marry him; but I cannot bear his presence, and would rather die than marry him. Indeed, I—I——"

"Love some other feller; isn't that it?"

"Yes."

"I know all about it. He's a noble lord, aint he?"

"Yes, yes; his name is Lovelace. He was bearing me away from a persecutor when Maydock overtook us, and dragged me here. Oh, but find that gentleman, tell him where I am, and I shall be free."

"Oh, that vont do. You vouldn't be safe vith him."

"Yes, he would protect me."

"He vould try; but, lor, you're vanted too partic'ler for him to protect yer."

"I do not understand."

"No, and I mustn't explain, and so let the matter drop. Now, I tells yer, Liz, for the sake of old times, I'll see yer out of this crib."

"Thanks, thanks!"

"But it can't be to-night. To attempt an escape vould be only to make a mull of it. No, let me take my time over the matter, and if I don't pull you out of Maydock's clutches, hang me, that's all."

"But do not let me remain here long. Oh, I cannot bear the thought!"

"Put up vith it for a day or two, and then all vill be as straight as possible. Trust me, I won't desert yer. Listen: I know an old genleman as is in the legal line. He's under some obligations to me for saving his life. Now I'll tell him yer little story, and he's sich a soft-hearted old boy that he'll long to have yer under his protection, and vith him yer'll be as safe as the bank, and can set all the yellow vons in the vorld at defiance. D'ye understand?"

"Yes—that is, I can understand that you wish to do me a service, and that is sufficient for me to know. I shall trust in you."

"You can't do better, my lovely angel; ven yer trusts Pipey yer places yerself under the pertecting ving of the knowingest old hen as ever took care of a chick. I'm the von as can and vill see yer through the mess, and so take heart and vait till I comes again."

"But if you should never come—if your friend will not protect me?"

"Never come! vy I'd scorn the action. Vy, I'd come if they had me locked up in Newgate, and I had to find my vay out before I could get here. You don't know Pipey."

It was to be proved whether Pipey would keep his word; within four-and-twenty hours he was safe in one of the strongest cells of the prison he named!

"And as to my friend," pursued Pipey, "he'll only be too glad of the chance to do me a turn, and he's such a philanthropic old chick, that directly I tells him about yer he'll go ravin mad until he has yer under his own roof."

The latter part of this sentence was, as the reader may suppose, strictly correct.

"Well," said Liz, "you have relieved my oppressed heart, and I will not forget you in the future."

"Oh, lor!" said Pipey, "here's another who von't forget me. I never seed the like. No sooner do I do anybody a good turn than up they jumps, and says they'll never forget me, and that's all they does. Vy don't they give me such better proof that their precious memory von't fail 'em: vy don't they stump up?"

"You forget, Pipey, that I have not a penny in the world, nor the means of finding one," said Liz, bursting into tears.

"Oh come, I say, my Wenus, don't go on in that vay; yer know I vasn't a talkin about you. Vy, I'd sooner have my hand chopped off than take any money from you; I vos only a talkin' of the peculiarity of the vorld in general, and old Grimes in perticler. There's a man, Liz, as has taken a fancy to me; he's taken me avay from the pursuit of a beautiful perfession to which I was an acknowledged ornament; he's put me out of practice; he's reduced me to a sort o' respectable vagabond; and vot's my recompense? Vy, he coolly turns round, and says—'I vont forget you.' Vot do I care about his remembering me? that aint no manner o' use to me. But I do care about you thinking on me, Liz; for if you vosn't quite so good and beautiful, and if I vosn't quite so bad and confounded ugly; in fact, if I vos a sort o' Lord Lovelace feller, I should— Vell, never mind, that aint to be, and so ve'll say no more about it; but if I can't be anythink else, I'll be yer fast and firm friend; and if ever yer vonts me, yer've only got to say so, and you vill find I'm ready."

Liz stretched out her soft, white hand, and the boy pressed it affectionately.

"I believe you," said Liz: "I believe you, and I am grateful. Now go, or they may hear you, and frustrate your plans"

"Vell, they may, so I'll take another passage down the vater spout."

"When will you come—when will you release me?" cried Liz, as Pipey prepared to leave her.

"Vell," said Pipey, "it can't be to-morrow, I'm other vays engaged; but the following night I shall be here, and then you shall be free."

"You promise?"

"I'll keep my vord at any price."

"Then I shall trust in you. Hush, there is a footstep on the stairs. Quick, Pipey."

Pipey required no pressing; literally throwing himself from the window and on to the spout, he glided to the ground.

Liz pulled to the window, and awaited the approach of the person whose step had arrested her attention.

In another moment the old woman entered the room.

"I thought I heard voices," she said.

"Then you were deceived," said Liz.

"It appears so; but nothing like making sure. He! he! he! I'm one of the sure ones, I am. There's no deceiving me."

Liz replied not.

"No," continued the hag, "I'm not to be done, though I am seventy-five. I've my hearing and sight still, and I'm as nimble as many a chit of your own age."

"I desire not to hear of your abilities," said Liz, hastily; "they interest me not, so begone, your presence annoys me."

"Hoity toity, a fine outbreak, this is. What can have come over the wench? A few hours ago she was as demure as a strayed kitten, and as speechless as a mummy."

"There's such changes, and none can account for them. They come and go apparently without provocation. My demure fit, as you term it, is over, and I am now as fierce as the aroused tigress. I should advise you to get from my presence, lest I should do you an injury."

There was something in the bearing of Liz that the old woman did not like, and so she drew near the door, and held it in her hand whilst she took another glance at the girl.

"Mad!" said the crone, after a long stare at our heroine, "mad, clean mad. Hey, but she may do one an injury, if she has the chance. It is best to leave her until the fit has passed over."

"Are you not gone?" demanded Liz.

The woman required no further pressing. In another moment she had closed and locked the door, and left Liz to her own reflections.

CHAPTER XVII.

THE DUEL IN ST. JAMES'S PARK.

LORD LOVELACE contrived with the greatest difficulty to reach his chambers in St. James's-street, and admitting himself, he, in a short time, threw himself on his bed and was sound asleep; not even the terrible nature of his night's adventures could ward off for a moment the stupor which fell upon his senses

He slumbered deeply.

Before six o'clock, however, his servant entered his chamber and aroused him.

"Why am I disturbed at this hour?" he asked.

"I am sorry, my lord," said the man, "but there has been a gentleman beating at the door for more than an hour. He says he must see you immediately, for that his business is of vital importance and cannot be delayed."

"Show him in," said Lord Lovelace.

The servant withdrew.

"Some intelligence of the fair creature who was torn from me," said his lordship. "Yes, that must be it, for no other person could come here at such an hour."

The servant re-entered, and announced "Sir Mark Portland."

A middle aged man, of military bearing, entered the apartment.

"To what am I indebted for the honour of this early visit, Sir Mark?" asked Lovelace, looking considerably surprised at the unexpected intrusion.

"Order your servant to withdraw, my lord," said the baronet.

"You may retire, Morgan," said Lovelace.

The man instantly left the room.

"And, now that we are alone," continued Lovelace, "pray reveal your mission."

"It is soon done. But I really wish some other had been chosen for the task, for it is one for which I have little taste."

"Is it so unpleasant?"

"It is."

"I am more perplexed than ever."

"Doubtless," said the baronet. "But I will soon explain. You were at the ball last night."

"Yes."

"You were there introduced by the Prince to a lady living under his protection."

"I was introduced by his Highness to a lady whom he detained at Marlborough House against her will, against the law, and against all the promptings of manhood."

"Well," said Sir Mark, "on that point I will not argue. You admit the introduction?"

"Yes."

"Well, my lord, it appears that you took advantage of that introduction to bear the lady from Marlborough House, and thereby to convey a deliberate insult to the Prince."

"I did bear the lady from Marlborough House, and if the Prince feels insulted he may do so with all my heart. His feelings do not interest me."

"But they interest others, and his injured pride must receive some balm. There must be some satisfaction given."

"What! does the prince wish to fight me?"

"He has no such intention; but there is another who feels nearly interested in the matter, and that individual, as the friend of the Prince, claims satisfaction for him!"

"Am I to understand, then, that the Prince

feels insulted but dares not meet me himself, and so gets another to take up the quarrel for him ?"

"You can understand what you think proper."

"At eight o'clock, then," said Lord Lovelace, "behind Marlborough House."

"It shall be so," said Sir Mark, "and now I will take my leave."

"And I," said Lovelace, "will snatch another hour's rest; heigho ! it may be the last."

"That's very possible," said Sir Mark, "for Rooker is a devilish clever swordsman."

With this not over-consoling remark the baronet withdrew.

"Morgan," said Lovelace, when the street door had been closed upon the early visitor, "Morgan, what time is it ?"

"It's on the stroke of six, my lord."

"Very good; I will sleep till seven. Meanwhile, get some coffee prepared."

"Will you not breakfast as usual, my lord ?'

"No; I shall merely require a cup of coffee. I may return and breakfast at ten."

"Then your lordship is going out ?'

"Yes."

"Very good, my lord."

Morgan withdrew, and Lord Lovelace sank once more into a profound slumber.

We must now return to Marie.

On quitting Marlborough House, her first thought was of returning immediately to her father's roof, but before she had proceeded many paces she had changed her mind, and determined to seek out Lovelace and endeavour to obtain from him the information she had failed in eliciting from the Prince.

"Yes," she said, as she hurried across Pall Mall and into St. James'-street, "yes, I will see the nobleman, and obtain some information from him; he resides hard by, and I will have an interview before I go home."

She hurried on, and in a few moments stood at the door and knocked for admittance.

"Hillo!" said Morgan, who was busily engaged in the preparation of the coffee ordered by his master; "hillo! here is another visitor; why, all the town must have taken a fit this morning, or something is going wrong with the machinery of society. However, I suppose I must see into the business of this new arrival." He hastened to the door, and there found Marie.

"Is your master at home?" demanded the Italian.

"Yes, madame," said the valet.

"Can I see him?"

"His lordship has not risen yet, but will be prepared to see you very soon. He desired to be called at seven; it is now half-past six."

"Thanks," said Marie, "I will step within; I wish to see him particularly."

Morgan conducted her to an apartment, and then hastened to his master's chamber.

"My lord," he said, "may I beg a word?"

"Why, what is up now?" asked Lovelace, testily; "has the hour passed so soon?"

"No, my lord, but there is a lady in another apartment who desires to see you."

"Do I know her?"

"Yes, my lord; at least, your lordship must have seen her at the opera; it is the famous Italian, Marie Lavrouffe."

"Indeed!" said Lovelace; "I will see her immediately."

In a short time Lovelace entered the apartment wherein Marie sat awaiting him.

"Good morning, mademoiselle," said Lovelace; "to what am I indebted for this early visit?"

"I fear I have disturbed you," said Marie; "but my impatience, and the misery under which I suffer, must be my excuse."

"Pray offer no excuses; let me know your errand."

"You are, doubtless, aware of the—the—intimacy—which has of late existed between myself and—"

"The Prince; yes, alas! yes."

"Alas! indeed," said Marie, with a sigh; "well, my lord, not to weary you with a long story, you know, perhaps, that my appearance at the ball last night led to a *denouement* of a most undesirable character."

"You allude to a lady being placed under my protection by the Prince whilst he conversed with you, and the result of that act of his?"

"Yes."

"Well, I understand you so far."

"That lady, then, is the cause of my appearance here. That lady has robbed me of the love of the Prince; she stepped between me and him, and has made me miserable; she has done more:

she has wounded my self-love, and has made me a laughing-stock."

"She has done nothing of the kind; she was detained against her will at Marlborough House. She detested the very name of the man who brought her there, and she seized the first opportunity of ridding herself of his presence."

"She placed herself under your protection?"

"She did."

"And she is still with you?"

"No, alas! no. She is lost to me, I fear, for ever."

"How so?"

"She was torn from me as I was bearing her to a place of safety"

"By the Prince?"

"No."

"By whom, then? has she so many admirers?"

"This was no admirer; it was, I shrewdly suspect, by a common burglar—a cut-throat rascal, who saw her but once before."

"Who is this woman, who enslaves all upon whom she throws her glance?"

"She is poor and lowly born."

"Her name?"

"Elizabeth Maydock."

"Why do you ask it?"

"That I may store it up in my memory; that I may keep it there, borne with that of the Prince, that I may visit upon her my direst hate."

"Why should you do so? she never harmed you."

"She has."

"Never!"

"I repeat, she has. Is it not doing me a harm to rob me of the love of one for whom I have sacrificed so much? Is it not doing me an injury to have the finger of scorn pointed at me, and to hear people say, 'There goes the woman who was slighted at the ball for the new beauty; behold the deserted mistress!'—is not this an injury?"

"But if poor Liz has done this, you should reflect that she has been an unconscious instrument. This should be sufficient to quench your anger."

"Oh, my lord, there is such a passion as jealousy. Can I feel aught else but bitter hatred for the woman who has so humiliated me?"

"You should reflect that she does not deserve such an ebullition of feeling on your part. You should wipe away the memory of the whole affair."

"I am an Italian, my lord; let that answer suffice."

"I am sorry to find you so vindictive."

"Call me what you will, I care not, but you cannot cheat me out of my vengeance. I tell you it is ripening, and will, ere long, be felt."

"I regret that I cannot prolong the interview," said Lovelace, looking at a time-piece, "for I have an important engagement at eight, and, singular enough, it is in connection with the subject of your remarks."

"What do you mean?"

"Oh, nothing; Morgan, my sword and cloak. Will you remain here until I return, mademoiselle? I trust I shall not be long."

"Yes," said Marie, "I have more to say. I will await you here."

"Good. Shall Morgan send away your carriage?"

"I came here on foot."

"Indeed!"

"Yes, but I will not detain you with explanations now."

Morgan brought Lovelace his hat, sword, and cloak.

The young lord unsheathed the sword and hastily examined it.

"Not this one, Morgan, it is useless."

"It is the one you usually wear, my lord."

"Yes, but I will have some other this morning."

"There is but one other, and that has just been returned from the makers. It is the long Damascus blade."

"That will do."

This sword was brought and approved of. Lovelace then donned his cloak and stepped from the apartment, merely bowing to Marie.

Morgan was about to withdraw from the room, when Marie called him back.

"Where has your master gone?" she asked.

"I really do not know, madame."

"Is it not singular that he should go out thus?"

"Very singular, madame."

"And can you not guess his errand?"

"I can partly guess, madame."

"What is it, then?"

"I dare not say."

"I can be secret."

"In that case I may venture to tell you what I know."

"Yes, you may."

"Then, I must inform you that at six his lordship was waited on by Sir Mark Portland."

"The friend of General Rooker?"

"The same. There was a short interview between my lord and Sir Mark, and, as I had to remain without and the door was not quite closed, I heard sufficient to assure me that Sir Mark was the bearer of a challenge from the General on behalf of the Prince, in consequence of some real or imaginary insult put upon him by his lordship."

"Yes, yes," said Marie, "I see it all; there will be a duel and bloodshed. Oh, how can I prevent it?"

"I really do not see how you can interfere in such an affair."

"Nor I, nor I; but where will they fight? Perhaps there may be a delay, which may admit of some interposition."

"I really think not, madame, for they fight behind Marlborough House, and as the clock is striking eight there is every probability that before now they have measured weapons."

"And you knew all this and sought not to interfere?"

"How could I do so? The matter is simply an affair of honour, and I have no power to offer interference. You forget, madame, that I am only a servant."

"True, true; but still something must be done. You would not see your master murdered?"

"What can I do to prevent it?"

"Oh, what indeed! and yet something must be done, and I must do it; yes, I will endeavour to stop this bloodshed."

Marie hastily gathered her wrapper about her and hurried forth into the street, leaving the servant gazing at her in blank amazement.

When Lovelace quitted the house he turned into one of the streets leading into St. James's-square, and there he knocked at the door of the mansion of Lord William Maxwell, and inquired whether his lordship was within.

He was answered in the affirmative, and was speedily ushered into the sleeping apartment of the young nobleman. There was a brief conference, and then the two sallied forth together and made their way straight to St. James's Park, and paused not until they stood at the back of Marlborough House.

It was a miserable morning, and no one was abroad. They passed into the ground adjoining the house and leading into the park, unobserved, and there found awaiting them Sir Mark Portland and General Rooker.

There was a formal bow on either side; a brief whispering of the seconds, and then the combatants stripped off their coats and approached each other.

Rooker rolled up his sleeve and bared an arm of iron. He handled his weapon as if it were a toy, and by a few rapid movements tested its quality, and at the same time exhibited his skill as a swordsman. Another moment and the men were left together, the young lord looking but a puny foeman for the stalwart and sinewy old soldier.

Both were as cool and wary as can possibly be conceived of men placed in so terrible a position.

They knew that life hung upon a thread, and that a momentary tremble would perhaps prove fatal.

They looked into each other's eyes with an awful steadiness, and the blades of their weapons crossed and grated as the movements of the wrists set them in motion.

Neither seemed anxious to offer an opening, and so for a space of time, which to the seconds in the affair appeared an age, the foes stood with weapons crossed and but slightly moving. It was a terrible time, but neither appeared inclined to end its sickening monotony.

At length the General tested the wrist of his opponent by a pressure against his weapon.

It was as firm as iron.

Lovelace would not become the aggressor. He stood strictly on his guard, and attempted not to make a pass at his adversary.

Seeing with what pertinacity the young lord continued on the defensive, Rooker attempted to draw him by placing himself slightly open and throwing up his guard, but Lovelace would have none of this; he had determined on his course, and no effort on the part of the General could tempt him to alter it in any shape or form.

Well for him that he had so determined, as bad indeed would have been the result. Wearying of the inactivity of the affair Rooker assumed the aggressive, and made several desperate lounges at his opponent, but they were vain. Lovelace parried all successfully, and not attempting a retaliation, did not lay himself open. Thus the duel continued for some minutes, until at last both men grew hot with their work, and fought with the ferocity of tigers. Parry and thrust, parry and thrust, continued fiercely on both sides, and several wounds, which in a short space of time dyed the white shirts of the combatants with gore, were given and received.

It appeared that the skill of the General was fully balanced by the coolness and power of his opponent, and that the strongest man must prove the victor.

And thus the fight continued until, in an unlucky moment, Lovelace slipped his foot, and fell to the earth. In a moment the General stepped forward, and raised his sword over his face.

Glaring at him ferociously the old libertine was about to bury his weapon in the youth's heart when his arm was seized in a grip of iron, and, in a second, Lovelace raised himself on one knee, and passed his weapon through the old man's body.

So rapidly was all this done that the seconds had not an opportunity to advance and check it.

The opportune arrival of Marie had saved Lovelace!

So intent was the quartette on the deadly work in progress that they had not noticed the approach of Marie, who stole upon the combatants as noiselessly as a cat. She was within a few paces of the men when Lovelace fell.

Comprehending at a glance the state of affairs, she sprang forward, and seized the General's uplifted arm; and Lovelace, blinded by rage, and totally disregarding the helpless position of his antagonist, seized the moment for ending the strife.

In an instant the dishonourable advantage he had taken flashed upon his mind.

"Oh, God!" he exclaimed, "what have I done?"

"Coward!' cried Rooker, as he fell bleeding to the earth, "coward, this is a murder!"

"It is a just punishment," said Marie, "it is a just punishment, and an ample vengeance for me. Was he not down, and would not you have killed him? But, thank Heaven, I was at hand to prevent it."

"Devil," hissed the old man from between his closed teeth, "devil!"

"Oh," cried Marie, "this is but the commencement of my vengeance; it shall be reeked on all with equal force. Yes, writhe and die, and take with you to hell my imprecations. Fiend! did you not drag me from the arms of one who loved me? Did you not throw me into the power of a libertine? Did you not deprive me of honour, of virtue, of peace of mind? Yes; all this have you done, and now you are paid for your work."

"Wretch!" cried the General, "all this I did *not* do. Look into the recesses of your own black heart, and tell me if there lurks not there a devil, which tempted you into your path of evil? Ask yourself if you were not bad at heart long before I saw you. Question yourself and answer me, was not your mind full of ambition, of unholy passions, of dark and terrible pride and lascivious tastes before I knew you?"

"And if this were the case," said Marie, "did you not drag them forth, and make me their victim? Were they not still, and kept in check by a pure and holy affection, before you tempted me to arouse them? You not only tempted me but induced my parent to use force in thrusting me into shame and dishonour. My curse—the curse of a wronged woman be upon you."

"Fiend," cried the General, "I will not argue with thee. Oh, will no one help me? must I die thus?'

"For the love of Heaven!" cried Lovelace to Lord Maxwell, "make all speed for a surgeon, or I shall have murder on my head."

"It is too late," said Maxwell, stooping over the prostrate form of the General, "it is too late; he is dying."

Rooker gazed wildly at Marie and Lovelace. He raised himself as if in the act of giving utterance to a malediction, and then sank back a corpse.

"Bear him into Marlborough House," said Sir Mark, "come, Maxwell, help me to raise him. I see people in the park. There will be an awful stir here presently if we do not remove him."

Maxwell assisted the Baronet in raising the body, and they moved away with it in the direction of Marlborough House. Lovelace stood, sword in hand, like one suddenly paralysed or turned into a statue.

Marie regarded him fixedly for a few moments, and then, observing his almost helpless state, advanced and forced his cloak over his shoulders.

"Quick!" she cried, "you must fly; there is danger here. In a few moments they will return and arrest you."

"Arrest!" cried Lovelace, "yes, yes, they will; I never thought of that. Good God! must I be dragged away like a felon?"

"No," cried Marie; "I will save you. Come, collect your senses."

"I will, but the General—Rooker—"

"Is dead. Come, fly."

"Dead! Good God! yes, and I killed him—murdered him when he was defenceless. I am dishonoured."

"Folly," cried Marie, "rank folly. There is no dishonour in the matter. Was not his sword at your breast when I threw up his arm? Would he not have taken advantage of your defenceless situation, and have killed you?"

"Yes, yes; but that does not palliate my offence."

"It does; but it is idle to remain here. This is but a waste of words and precious moments. Come, fly with me."

"Whither? They will seek me at my house almost as soon as I could get there."

"They would, and you must not go there. Nay, trust to me. I said I would save you, and I will do so. Are you not satisfied with that, and will you not place yourself under my guidance?"

"Yes, yes, I will; for Heaven knows I am perfectly helpless."

"Come, then."

"Whither?"

"To the house of Phillipe Morlavine. For my sake he will protect you until you can escape from the country."

"I know not whither I go," cried Lovelace, "but I trust in you."

"You do well. Come, there is not a moment to be lost."

They hurried from the spot, and getting into Pall Mall, engaged a vehicle, and ordered the driver to hasten to a street in Soho.

CHAPTER XVIII.

A CONFESSION OF LOVE.

THE vehicle which Lord Lovelace and Marie entered in Pall Mall soon stopped at the given address in Soho.

"Remain in the coach for a few moments," said Marie, "I will step within and speak to Phillipe. Heaven knows how I am to meet him, but it must be done."

She knocked hastily at the door, and was soon admitted,

"Where is the Signor?" asked Marie.

"He has left London," said the servant.

"Indeed," said Marie. "Where has he gone?"

"He has retired into the country, madame, and given up his apartments here."

"Are they occupied?"

"No, madame."

"Then I will see the lady of the house. You know me?"

"Oh yes, madame."

"Good; then hasten to your mistress and say I would speak with her."

"Yes, madame."

And the servant withdrew.

The lady of the house soon appeared, and, after a hurried interview with Marie, Lovelace was summoned from the carriage.

"My acquaintance is gone," said Marie, "but you can occupy his apartments. This lady is a countrywoman of mine; you are safe here."

"Thanks," said Lovelace; "thanks, lady. I can never repay these kindnesses."

"Yes," said Marie, "yes, you can, Lord Lovelace."

"Oh, tell me how."

"On some other occasion; not now."

They were conducted into an apartment and there arrangements were made for Lovelace remaining until such time as he could depart from England, a course which was alone open to him after what had passed.

"I will return to your house," said Marie, "and send your servant to you at nightfall."

"Thanks," said Lovelace; "do so, and here are my keys. Give them to him and tell him to pack all such valuables as may be brought away without attracting observation."

"Yes," said Marie, "and I will also see how soon you can depart for the Continent. Depend upon it my arrangements shall be complete. And now adieu; I must go home."

She left him, and Lovelace speedily gave way to the crowd of dark thoughts which came upon him.

There he sat, a man-slayer hiding from justice, dependent for safety on a woman's tact, and alone in the world.

The house into which he had entered was but a third-rate one, and as his eye wandered over the apartment in which he sat, and lighted not on the elegancies and comforts of his own home, he could not fail to feel more dejected than he would otherwise have done.

His thoughts constantly reverted to the Italian girl.

"There is," he thought, "a something in her eye that alarms me; she looked upon me with mingled pity and passion, which I can scarce comprehend. It cannot be that she loves me. Psha! what a ridiculous idea—and yet it is impossible to mistake the meaning she conveyed when she said I could repay her kindness, but not now I trust, however, that I mistake, for truly I have no heart to give her. Besides, has she not been the mistress of the Prince? Is she not full of dark passions? Is she not imbued with evil? No, I never could love her, and Heaven grant she feels no such passion for me. No, my heart belongs to another, and that other is the sweet girl I saw last night. Yes, she, the poor Westminster ballad singer, the daughter of a beggar, perhaps, or thief, has my whole heart. Heigho! I have no thought for another." And then his thoughts turned on Liz and her probable fate in the hands of the burglar.

"What will become of her?" he cried, suddenly starting from his chair; "what will become of her, now that I am no longer able to help myself, much less to render her assistance? A few days, perhaps a few hours, may bear me from the land which possesses her. Yes, I may never see her more."

Occupying himself with these and similar gloomy reflections, Lord Lovelace continued to pass away many disagreeable hours.

We must now return to Marie.

Her father's house—her home, as she called it, was but a short distance from the place in which she had secured Lovelace, and so she approached it on foot.

She was instantly admitted on being recognised, and was conducted into her father's chamber.

The old Italian appeared strangely puzzled to see her, and at once demanded what had brought her there.

"I am come back to you," said Marie; "I have quarrelled with the man upon whom you threw me, and I am here in consequence."

"Oh, diavolo!" cried the Italian, "why did you quarrel with so generous a man?"

"Generous!" said Marie, mockingly.

"Yes, generous," continued her father. "Here, look around you; is it not generous of him to place me in this splendid house? Is it not generous of him to supply me with all the money I require? Is it not generous to give me a retinue of servants fit for any nobleman, and otherwise to provide comforts for my old age?"

"And what price has been paid for all this *generosity?*"

"Price? No price; nothing."

"Yes, man," cried Marie, fiercely, "a terrible ice; nothing less than my dishonour!"

pr

"Psha!" cried her father.

"Ah! you make so light of it, do you; it is well that you do so now, but a time will come when you will have to render up an account to one above, and then you will not so readily ' Psha!' at your crime."

"My crime?" cried the old man; "my crime? What do you mean by my crime?"

"My shame is your crime! Remember, you forced it upon me."

"Psha! you rave, diavolo. The girl is mad!"

"I am. Mistake me not; I am mad!"

"You rave! This is some fit of jealousy, and you will be better presently."

"If you mean by that that I shall be other than you now see me, you mistake me. Make not light of my words; I am mad with jealousy, and with a deep wrong, and I shall be avenged."

"This is folly; come, get back to your kind protector; if you have quarrelled with him ask his forgiveness, and all will be well again."

"I shall never return to him more."

"What?"

"I repeat, I shall never return to him more."

"What! deprive yourself of all the luxuries you enjoy? deprive me of my home, my money, and my servants?—But you jest."

"I am desperately in earnest."

The face of the old man darkened—he almost shook with anger as he turned upon his child.

"Hark ye," he cried; "I will not allow the folly to proceed. You will at once return to your protector or my curse shall be upon you, and I will drive you forth into the streets."

"I will never return."

"Mark me—I am in earnest."

"And so am I. I will never again return."

"Devil!" shouted the old man, "devil! get from my sight lest I tear thee to pieces. Get from me, or I shall comit murder."

"I will go," said Marie, calmly, "I will go; but you will yet be glad to seek me and bring me back again. When these fine things are stripped from you, as they will be, you will have no roof to cover you and no one to earn a crust for you; then you will seek me out."

"Begone, devil! devil! begone! Oh wretch—wretch! to deprive me of my comforts; oh fiend! to rob me of my home—my all."

"How obtained? Answer me that."

"Begone! do not madden me, or I shall plunge a knife into your black heart. Begone, and take with you my curses. May your remaining days prove but one long scene of torture, and may you end your life rotting, abandoned, accursed in the streets."

"I hurl back curse for curse;—old man, beware! I can foresee a terrible fate in store for thee. I shall be avenged, and you must participate in the vengeance now ripening."

She hastened from the room, and thence into the streets.

"I must return to Lovelace," she said.

In a few moments she was as calm as if nothing had transpired, and when she re-entered the house wherein the nobleman was secured she even smiled pleasantly and assumed an air of gaiety.

"You see," she said, as she appeared in the presence of Lovelace, "you see I have returned to you. My stay at home has been but a brief one."

"Why so?"

"Oh, a difference of opinion with my father; he thinks I should forego all feelings of my own and return to the Prince, in order that he may live in affluence, and I have thwarted him; and so we have parted."

"But you will return to him?"

"No."

"No!"

"Never more."

"But you are alone in the world, are you not?"

"I am."

"Then you will never think of leaving the only one who can protect you."

"I have done so. I would sacrifice anything—everything, rather than return to the Prince."

"Yes, but you must not sacrifice yourself; which you would be doing if you threw yourself upon the world without one hand to protect you."

"What should I get by the protection of a father who has already sacrificed me to his own avarice?"

"True."

"Ah, most true! I should be better without him."

"But you cannot be left in London without some one to guard you. It is too terrible to contemplate such a fate for one so young and beautiful."

"Its terrors do not daunt me, I am prepared for the worst. In all the wide world there is not one who has the least affection for me—there is not one who cares whether I fall or not; so what matters it?"

"It is of terrible import to all who possess one spark of humanity, I pray Heaven. I feel the greatest interest in your welfare. I should indeed be ungrateful were it not so."

"Yes, there may be many who, like yourself, may spring up in my path and feel interested in me, for a few short hours, but that is all. It appears to me that the whole world is set against me, and that the best thing that could befal me would be a speedy death, that I may end my accumulating woes in the grave."

"Oh speak not thus! There are many will love and cherish you; you will yet know happiness."

"Never."

"And why not?—your young heart will form other affections; change of scene and lapse of time will efface old recollections, and the past will be as a dream."

"Yesterday I might have echoed your words, but now, alas! I cannot.'

"And wherefore?"

"Because a something has occurred which shuts out all hope. I have indulged in a dream which will end in a few hours, and then life to me is a blank."

"What mean you."

"Oh, I cannot—dare not explain to you."

"And why not to me?"

"Ask me not!"

"Wherefore?"

"Oh, I dare not tell you."

"Your words are to me a mystery."

"Yes, I can readily conceive that they are so.

There is no sympathy in your heart which can divine what is passing in mine."

"I think I comprehend you. Poor girl!"

"Ah! Poor girl! you pity me, and that is all."

"What would you have?"

"What would I have? Heaven and earth! would I not have your love? Would I not have you love me as I love you?"

She threw her lovely white arms around his neck, and gazed up into his eyes.

"Oh," she cried, "do not cast me from you or I shall die! I have been cruelly treated, I have been brought up in total disregard for the conventionalities of society and in ignorance of the laws of strict morality. I have breathed an air of contagion. I have been thrust into the paths of vice. I have thought that I have loved, but I never knew the passion until now. Oh, teach me to forget the past—teach me to forget myself! Oh, make me a happier and a better woman! Horace Lovelace, I madly worship you!"

Was this the language of a true love, or was it the acting, the dissimulation, and the craftiness of a desperate woman clinging to one whom she thought would prove an acceptable protector and a ready tool for the consummation of a terrible vengeance?

It had the appearance of the former, but it was in reality the latter. Marie was acting a part. She calculated how deeply the Prince would be annoyed by her exhibiting her preference for Lovelace, and at the same time it was a blow at Liz who had unconsciously crossed her path and with whom she could see Lovelace was much smitten.

Truly she was a terrible woman! Never was mortal man placed on the brink of a more awful abyss than was Lovelace.

There he stood with a wondrously beautiful, highly gifted, universally admired woman clinging fondly about his neck, with her heart, which he presumed to be filled with pure love, palpitating against his, and with a fire burning in her uplifted eye against the power of which an angel might almost have battled in vain. He moreover took her to be ill-used, deserted, and afflicted. What did he do?

He did what ninety-nine in every hundred would have done; he forgot all except that one being in the wild rapture of the moment. He clasped her to his heart and he swore never again to leave her.

"I cannot marry you, sweet Marie," he said, "but will be a good and true protector. I will guard you fondly and truly, and I will forget all others and cling to thee."

A thrill of intense satisfaction ran through the frame of the Italian; a smile of triumph lighted up her dark eye. And was she happy? Yes, happy in her sin and wickedness. They sat before the blazing fire hand in hand, they lavished on each other the most tender caresses and then conversed on the future.

"Yes," said Marie, "we will fly together to my own bright land; under the warm sun and the clear blue sky we will wander in peace and happiness. We will live for each other in some sweet villa reposing beside a lake such as only can be seen in dear Italy; we will forget this cold, miserable clime and all we leave in it, and we will be happy."

"Yes, Marie," said Lovelace, quite enraptured at the picture the arch-deceiver was painting, "I have often dreamed of such a lot—I have often, in imagination, drawn upon my fancy such another lot. I never hoped that it could be realised."

"It shall be realised, and we shall be so happy."

"Yes," said Lovelace, " so happy."

But at that moment a vision of a fair girl with streams of waving golden hair flowing softly over a neck and bosom of marble whiteness and of velvet softness appeared before him. This creation of memory seated itself beside him, and told him a tale of long suffering, of poverty, of hunger, of temptation and persecution; and he listened, and felt a deep sympathy for the narrator. The sympathy grew into love, and he thought that from the fair figure his memory had brought before him came a deep responsive sympathy and then he took a deep oath of fidelity, of truth, of constancy.

And thus he kept it!

Four and twenty hours had not passed—one short day had not come and gone, and there he sat with another by his side—with his head pillowed on *her* bosom, with *her* arm around his neck, with *her* lips pressed to his; and so it came to pass that as he murmured—

"Yes, so happy!"

That a shade of sadness fell upon him, and that the words received a tone which spoke not of happiness, but, on the contrary of deep, dark, and unutterable misery.

But blame not Lovelace too harshly, he was but human; and far better than he have fallen before and since his day.

Oh manhood! where is thy boasted strength of mind, stability of purpose, constancy of heart? Is it not, after all, but a creation of the imagination—a dream of the enthusiasts—an unreal mockery?

Let us leave Lovelace to enjoy his brief dream of happiness with his new love.

CHAPTER XIX.

PIPEY'S FURTHER ADVENTURES IN COMPANY WITH MESSRS. MAYDOCK AND HAMMER.

THE clock had not struck eight on the morning of Pipey's interview with fair Liz when, after making a rather hasty toilet at a pump, and breakfasting on a glass of gin and milk at a tavern, he wended his way towards the chambers, or rather the office, of his patron Mr. Grimer.

That gentleman he met at the entrance to the place wherein his den was situated.

"Well, Pipey," said Grimer, "early astir, hey?"

"I ought to be," said Pipey, "I ain't a been to bed yet."

"Bad habits, bad habits," said Grimer.

"Oh wery," said Pipey, "wery, considering the game I've been on."

"Oh just so," said the lawyer, "just so; we must hunt our prey when it is abroad, hey, Pipey?"

"Yes, but what on old covey you are to talk about hunting and prey. Anybody would think you was a jolly old lion hunter of the desert, or an abominable North American Injun buffalo exterminator, to hear you a going on so, about hunting and that kind o' fun."

"Ah!" said Grimer, "the way to go through life is to think all mankind so many buffaloes, only to be hunted down and preyed upon. Depend upon it that is the precise feeling all mankind have towards you and I. We live—we feed upon each other, and unless we do so, we commit an error, and find ourselves inmates of jails or workhouses."

"Vell, that's a nice view to take of human natur, that is. Its wery evident that you ain't an elder of the methodist's chapel, you ain't. If ever I heard such an old brute!"

"Psha, you—a common thief—are a nice one to judge of Christian duties and the acts of others, arn't you."

"Vell, I don't know, but I've this to say, though: I never took from von as vasn't vell able to part vith it, and I've always shared the svag vith von as has been vus off nor myself; and it strikes me that there's a many going about under the mask of goodness who do vuss, and get applauded for their acts."

"Well, we will not argue the point."

"I dont think we had better," said Pipey.

And they walked on until they came to Mr. Grimer's office.

Step in, Pipey," said Grimer, "and relate your night's adventures."

"I'm with you," said Pipey.

They entered the passage, and Mr. Grimer had scarcely placed his hand upon the door of his office when it opened under his touch.

"What is this?" said Grimer; "why, I suppose I could not have locked the door last night."

Pipey stooped down and examined the lock.

"Vell," he said, "you may s'pose vot you like, but the door vos locked and has been forced. Yes, and by a regular artist too; look at the vay in vich the vork has been done—clean as a vistle—beautiful!"

The lawyer disregarded him and rushed into the chamber.

A glance sufficed to reveal the state of affairs.

"Robbed!" he cried, as his glance fell upon the open safe, "robbed—robbed!"

"That looks werry like the case," said Pipey, "hillo! here's the key in the safe, you must have left it there a purpose to oblige the cracksman."

"No, no," cried Grimer," in a perfect agony, "no, no; I remember locking my safe and securing the key in my drawer."

"Oh, this has been done by von as knows this here crib."

"It has," said Grimer, "it has; but my papers, my papers!"

He staggered to the safe, and immediately discovered that those belonging to the Duke's case were alone missing.

"It must be Maydock," said Grimer; "yes, he alone could have perpetrated this."

"He did not do it."

"How know you that?"

"Vosn't I vith him all night long? Didn't I see him safe in bed? And vosn't I down to his moves right and left? Vell I think as how I vos, and I tells yer it vosn't Maydock, think vot you vill of it."

"There was no other—yes—the Duke! He saw me hide the key of the safe. It must have been the Duke."

"Come now," said Pipey, "you must know a lot about the perfeshion to go on in that vay—a Duke open a crib in the artish manner in vich this von has been opened! Bah! It is impossible."

"It would appear so, but who could it have been if not he?"

"Vell, that's a mystery," said Pipey.

Grimer looked at him intently for a moment, and then said,

"There could be but three who would attempt this—Maydock, the Duke, and yourself! I am not sure that I am not protecting a double-dealer, a spy, and one in the pay of my opponents."

"Come, I say," said Pipey, "none of that, yer know, or else you are just likely to go down vithout expecting it. If yer the man to suspect me, the best thing ve can do is to part. Mind, I haven't sought to keep up the connection: vot's been done between us has been done by your vish, and not mine; and so let me have no more of yer humbug, but say I may go, and let me hook it, as I vonts to. I dessay I could make more out of Lord Lovelace than I could out of you, and so ve'll part, my friend."

"No, no!" cried Grimer, who at once comprehended that he wrongfully suspected the boy "no, no, Pipey, I ask your forgiveness; I wronged you by the suspicion; I am sorry."

"Oh, if so be as how you says you're sorry, vy that's enough for Pipey, he don't vont any more to say about the matter."

"Yes, I am sorry, Pipey, for I believe you are acting straight by me."

"Yes," said Pipey, "upright and down straight, like the fore leg of a dog, that's my motto."

"But is it not strange?" asked Grimer; "is it not peculiar? You say it could not have been done by the Duke."

"Take my oath it was done by a professional cracksman; never seed anything cleaner."

"And you know it could not be Maydock?"

"I'd svear to it vith my last breath."

"Nor by his emissaries?"

"He ain't got von as as he vould trust vith a vhisper of this job."

"How know you that?"

"Because his pal, Hammer, is in darkness on the subject."

"Are you sure?"

"Never vos more so."

"Then the mystery is impenetrable; but now to the affair of last night, for we must lose no

time in the discussion of the past, since, for the present, no light can be thrown upon it. No, let us rather look into the future; and what is there for us now—the will?"

"Is not in Maydock's grip."

"But he knows where to lay his hand upon it."

"I think so."

"And he will attempt to possess it?"

"Yes."

"Oh, when, when?"

"To night."

"Where is it, Pipey—where is it?"

"In the Duke's house at Kew."

"And he goes there to-night, does he?"

"Yes."

"And you go with him, Pipey; you go with him? Tell me, you go with him?"

"I am there."

"That is good. Lose not an opportunity, Pipey," cried the lawyer, in a perfect fever of excitement; "lose not the remotest chance of grabbing that will. Get it for me, and five hundred pounds are yours."

"Oh, I've spotted it," said Pipey, "and it vill be a rum go if I don't have it somehow or other, some time or other."

"Yes, Pipey; you are a clever boy, and you'll be sure to get it. Only strive for it, Pipey—only strive for it, and never despair. *Hunt him down*, Pipey. Ha! ha! that's a good motto, that is. *Hunt him down!* When you and I are rich, and roll about in our own carriages, Pipey, we will have for the motto on our crests—'Hunt him down.' Is'nt that a good conceit, Pipey?"

It may have been, but Pipey did not seem to appreciate it, and so said nothing in reply to the query.

"And now," said the lawyer, "what of the girl? Is there any news of her?"

"Yes," replied Pipey.

"You have heard of her?"

"I have seen her."

"You have! Was there ever such a boy! By Heaven, Pipey, you are a genius!"

"I vos alvays considered so," was Pipey's modest rejoinder.

"Well, Pipey," continued Grimer, "you have seen her, and where is she?"

"In the grip of Maydock."

"Where? where?"

"In his own crib, down in the very depths of the Minories."

"The devil!"

"Ah, he is a devil, and no mistake."

"But what are your plans, Pipey?—what will you do?"

"I aint made up my mind yet," said Pipey.

"But she must be rescued—we must have her."

"Yes," said Pipey, "so I suppose."

"Another five hundred for her," said Grimer.

"Oh," returned Pipey, "I shall vant a deuced sight more nor that, but ve'll talk o' that arter-vards."

"Yes," said Grimer "that's good policy; never count your chickens before they are hatched."

"I never do," said Pipey; "particulary ven you can't trust to the hen."

This was meant as a sly hit at Grimer, but he was far too excited to note it.

"And now," continued Pipey, "I'm off to bed; I've a long night's vork afore me."

"You have," said Grimer, "and a tedious one; to bed by all means. Nothing like sleep to cool the brain and make one fit for a desperate job. Yes, Pipey, go to sleep."

"I intend; so now good-bye. I have to find the vill and slope vith the gal, that's two jobs on hand; and now I'll go in for a third, and that's to trace who has stolen the missing papers, and it's much if I do that at the same time."

"Ah," said Grimer, "do that by all means. It shall go hard with one who has served me that trick."

Pipey withdrew, and Grimer set about his affairs, bewailing the loss of his papers, speculat-ing as to who could have stolen them, and arranging matters which were to form the business of the day.

Evening came at last, and with its appearance Mr. Pipey and the burglar Hammer appeared at the house of Maydock.

Their preparations were soon made, and after a draught of brandy all round, the trio set out on their errand to Kew. The journey was a long and tedious one to be performed on foot, but they dared not trust to a vehicle, and had no wish to run the risk of going up the river in a boat.

Hour after hour they plodded on through the snow-covered roads, keeping as near the river as possible throughout the journey. One after the other the little suburban villages were passed, the lights grew less, the open country was reached, and the march pursued with more safety. It was near midnight when Kew was reached. The villa of the Duke of Grasmount was situated near the bank of the river, and was not secured from intrusion by any walls; the grounds were large, and only divided from others and from the main road by a slight railing. A number of trees skirted the ground on either side.

Near at hand was the villa of the Prince of Wales, into which we have already penetrated.

"This is our crib," said Maydock, as he leaped over the rails which secured the grounds on the north side; "this is our crib, come on."

He found himself almost knee-deep in the long grass and snow-covered ferns on the other side.

"By George," he said, "this is cold work."

"Here we is," cried Hammer, as he came tumbling over the rails, "all right and tight at last."

"Yes," said Pipey, who was the last of the three to enter the grounds; "yes, but perhaps this ain't a nice place for coves as has got chil-blains."

"Hush!" cried Maydock, "you do not know who may be about; silently through the grass, boys."

It was a bitter task was that going through the grass, for in a few moments their feet and legs were saturated with snow, and, as it was freezing hard, their lower garments and shoes soon began to assume the peculiarities of wrappers of ice. It was as much as they could do to keep their feet.

"Vell," said Pipey, "if ve don't pull this ere off it'll be a nice thing, and no mistake; vy, it's worth all a thousand to valk over this ere in-fernal grass. Ugh! my legs are growing as stiff as two mop-sticks."

On they went, and at length reached the out-houses at the back of the premises.

"We must get round to the front," said May-dock, "for this won't do. I'll lay there's half a score of yelping dogs round those stables; but they never take the precaution to put 'em in the front."

"Come on," said Hammer, "any vere's you like, but no funking: that von't pay at no price."

"On ve goes again," said Pipey; and on they went.

It was a quaint old Elizabethan house, and was approached in front by a broad terrace, facing a lawn which sloped down to the bank of the river.

The moon shone upon it as the burglars ap-proached, and lighted up the grim masonry in a manner which gave it a very picturesque effect, but which was far from proving agreeable to those whose business it was to penetrate into the interior on their burglarious errand.

"Hang this moon," said Maydock; "give me darkness for such a job."

"Vere do ve get in?" asked Hammer.

"On the first window to the left of the hall door; that's the dining-room, there is plenty of plate there; but, after you have secured that, quit the room by the door on the right, and take the passage to the left; the fourth door on your right hand is the plate-cupboard. Do what you will, but silence."

"Vy, arn't you comin' vith us?" asked Hammer.

"No," said Maydock; "I've other work on hand. You mind your affairs, and I'll mind mine."

"All right, my chicken," said Hammer, "you can go arter vot you like, but give me good solid swag, like gold and silver plate, and plenty on it."

"Be careful," said Maydock, as they separated.

"Don't doubt us," said Pipey.

The two followed the instructions given them, and approached the window on the left of the hall door, whilst Maydock took to the right, and commenced operations on a window which opened into the library.

He was not long in effecting an entrance; a sharp saw of the finest tempered steel, and a large gimlet, were the implements he used, and in a few moments the fastenings of the window were cut away and the sash moved.

Then came the massive oak shutters, not hard to open before the little saw, whose teeth rushed through the wood almost noiseless, but with the greatest possible effect.

In a few minutes all obstructions were removed, and the burglar stepped into the apartment.

He cautiously opened his dark lanthorn, and then made an examination of the room, taking the precaution to bolt the door on the inside, thus securing himself from the sudden attack of any one attempting to fall upon him by that entrance. This done he reclosed the shutters and allowed the blaze of his powerful lanthorn to fall upon the room.

"Yes," he said, "this is the same old place I knew so many long years ago. This is the same place—nothing altered, nothing disturbed. The same books groan upon the shelves; the same busts decorate the cases, and the same grim old pictures frown from the walls. Yes, time hath not laid its destroying finger here, and whilst men and things have changed, this place keeps the same. It was here I had the interviews with the old Duke. It was here he bade me destroy his son's wife and daughter; it was here, when repentance came upon him, he made the will bequeathing this and much other valuable property to the family of the woman he had wronged. It was here that Liz was made a powerful heiress, and it was here that I was brought some three years afterwards, before the young Duke, to answer a charge of purloining plate. I knew not my power then. I thought the documents I placed in the hands of old Grimer but a blank sheet of paper. I thought my wife had destroyed the infant, and I found that I could not pitch upon any of the dead mother's family who could make the Duke tremble for his lands and titles, and so I submitted to degradation. In here I came, when having a hint that the child was not dead, to hide the will I had purloined from the office of Grimer; and now that years have passed, that the child has grown into a beautiful woman, and in my power, with all obstacles to her becoming mine removed, I now come to redeem the will, and end this life of misery,

of poverty, and crime. With Liz for my bride, and her property to back me, I will be a better man."

He cautiously felt the panneling of the room, and at length stopped before a square a little darker than the others: in one corner was a rather conspicuous knot in the wood.

"This is the place," cried Maydock, kneeling down, but he had no sooner uttered the words than he was startled by the report of several fire-arms.

"By Hell!" he cried, springing to his feet, "those burglars have alarmed the house; they are set upon and overpowered; not a moment must be lost."

He stooped again and placed his thumb on the knot in the panel. In a moment a piece of the skirting dropped down, and revealed an open space. Into this Maydock plunged his hand, and drew forth therefrom a small square case.

"It is here," he cried, "it is here! I must not lose a moment, or I am lost."

Already they were at the library door, but finding it closed the aroused servants shouted—

"To the hall door! to the hall door! they must escape by the window!"

There was a rush of feet, and then a rattling of the chains and bolts of the large door. Maydock heard it, and his heart sank within him; but nevertheless he ran to the window, and, dashing open the shutters, sprang through it, and on to the broad level terrace.

He had not gone many paces when the servants succeeded in opening the ponderous door. Catching sight of the fugitive, they raised their blunder-busses and fired after him, one of their shots striking him in his right arm, which immediately fell useless at his side.

On he ran, away to the left of the lawn, and in a few moments succeeded in reaching the shelter of the trees, but he stayed not his pace. On—on, was the only thought in his mind, and like a hunted buck he sprang wildly through furze and long grass, clearing every kind of obstruction with the greatest ease, and eventually reaching the park rails.

On the other side of these he paused to listen, but, save the distant yelping of the dogs, he heard nothing.

There was no pursuit, but still he ran madly onward, for he well knew that, as soon as circumstances permitted, he would have a whole pack of men and dogs at his heels.

Well for him was it that in the hurry of the moment the servants had not arrayed themselves in habiliments which would admit of chase being given, or he must have been captured; but as it was, before the people were ready to follow he was far from the spot, speeding towards London.

We must return to Hammer and Pipey, who were far less fortunate than their co-partner in the adventure. They opened the window of the dining-room with the greatest care, and in a few moments succeeded in getting a footing within. Hammer flashed his lanthorn about, and was not long in discovering a large quantity of plate in a recess in one corner of the room.

"Here's the stuff, Pipey," said Hammer; "bag it."

"Right you are," said Pipey, as they both drew forth from the depths of their capacious pockets a sack of sufficient size to hold as much plate as a man could well stand under.

"I say," said Pipey, "there can't be much more of this stuff in that infernal cupboard place Maydock spoke of. S'pose ve hook it vith this and leave the other for the good of the house."

"Psha!" said Hammer, "I never do things by halves. I want the whole of the stuff, and the whole I will have. Mark me, no funking, or I'll draw a knife across your throat; you're in for the whole thing, so stick to me."

"Oh, I'm right enough," said Pipey, "only it appears to me as how it's tempting Providence to attempt to grab any more; particularly as ve shall have as much as ve can do to stand under this."

"Silence, and follow me," cried Hammer, "this is no time for your sham, so shut up, and do your work."

They approached the door of the room, and found that it was locked on the outside.

In a moment Hammer's tools were out, and he was at work on the lock. Two minutes could not have elapsed when the impediment to their passage was removed, and the burglars found themselves in a fine hall, from which branched off such a number of passages as fairly confounded Hammer.

"Let me see," he said, "as he endeavoured to recall Maydock's instructions, "let me see—the passage to the left, and the fifth door—hang me if I haven't forgot! What did he say, Pipey?"

"Come along: I knows vere it is, if you must have it; only I varns yer to get out of it as soon as possible, for I thinks as how I hears a footstep somevere."

"Psha! it's only your fears. Now, then; if you know just show us the way to this here swag cupboard."

They went cautiously on, and in a short space of time came to the door of the supposed plate cupboard.

They tried it and found it locked.

This Hammer had expected, and his saw was in active service in less than no time.

He had, however, scarcely commenced his work, when a voice within shouted—

"Who is there?"

"Hist!" said Hammer, "some d—d mistake of yours. That's not the plate room."

"Who is there?" shouted the voice from within.

No answer was returned.

"Slope," said Pipey, "slope; or it vill be the vorse for yer."

But they were too late. A powerful bell sounded throughout the upper apartments of the house, and it was clear that all within it must be thoroughly awakened.

A man with a blunderbuss in his hand rushed from the room Hammer had attempted to open, and seeing the two burglars attempting to open a door on his right he fired at them. In their confusion the burglars had mistaked the door of the dining room and were trying all they approached in order to effect an escape.

The shot from the blunderbuss lodged in Hammer's shoulders and he fell to the earth bleeding badly.

"Curse it," he cried, "I'm shot like a dog: its all up."

"Yes," said Pipey, "and a good job too; I told yer how it would be, didn't I. Curse your greediness."

By this time the servants from the upper apartments had descended, and thinking it incumbent on themselves to do something they of course fired off their blunderbusses at random and otherwise distinguished themselves before the terrified women who had followed them down the stairs.

"Here," cried Pipey, deeming that one of the men who had not fired was about to favour him with the charge, "here, I say, don't go and blow the brains out of a poor kid as can't protect hisself. I'm only a young 'un, and ain't a going to make no resistance votsomever, so don't fire. I'll surrender myself immediately. I'm a perfect lamb, I am: and I vos brought here by this feller agin my vill, I vos."

Seeing what sort of an opponent was before them, the men lowered their pieces and approached.

The man who first fired was the foremost of the party. It appeared that Hammer had attempted to open his chamber instead of the plate closet, next which he slept in order to guard it.

"Well," said the servant, "you're a nice pair of visitors on a winter's night, arnt you?"

"Oh, please sir, it vos'nt me," cried Pipey, "I'm a poor innocent kid as they picked up and forced to come here agin his vill."

"They?—there are more of them?"

"Yes," said another of the servants, "I can see a light through the chink of the library door."

"My eyes!" said Pipey, "Maydock's in for it."

The library door was tried, but found to be secured on the inside.

It was then Maydock heard the men hasten to the hall door, but what followed is already known to the reader.

"Clear off," said Pipey, as he saw Maydock fly down the lawn, "clear off, and the vill vith him. A nice state of affairs this is. Oh, vot a fool I vos to have anythink to do vith it."

Finding that the fugitive was well out of their clutches, the servants began to pay their undivided attention to Pipey and Hammer.

The latter had fainted.

"I say," said Pipey, "you aint a going to let the cove die, are you? see how he's a bleeding."

"Oh no," said one of the servants, "he shan't die. It would be a pity the gibbet should be robbed of such an ornament. We'll keep him in order that he may be strung up with you, and a nice pair you'll make, wont you?"

"I ain't a got a doubt of it," said Pipey; "not a doubt of it. I alvays vos considered a handsome sort of kid."

"Ah, you're a nice innocent, you are," continued the servant; "why, you have already forgotten that you were forced here against your will, and what a poor, ill-used lad you were a few minutes ago."

"Oh, stow that!" said Pipey, "I aint a going to funk now; and if I showed the vite feather just now it vos only becos there vos a blunderbuss at my head. Just shove yerself in front of von, and see vether you'd enjoy yerself. I don't think yer vould if yer knew it."

"Run for a doctor, Tom," said one servant to another, "or this fellow will die. And as for you, Mr. Innocent, we'll just tie your legs, or you may be forgetting that you're a prisoner."

"That's werry likely," said Pipey; "I tells you plainly that, if I gets the chance to cut, I'm off."

Here Mr. Pipey winked affectionately at the servants, and said,

"Sorry to have disturbed you, my loves; it ain't our rule to break the rest of the fair sex."

Whereupon the servants all pretended that they were signally astonished, and placed up their hands and cried "Lawks!"

A proceeding which highly diverted Mr. Pipey, who submitted to be bound with the best possible grace; merely remarking that they had better not tie him too tight, as he vos delicate about the ancles and vosn't used to sich treatment."

The wounded man, Hammer, was raised in the arms of the servants and conveyed to a couch in one of the sitting apartments, whilst Pipey was placed in durance vile, in a small room, to await the arrival of the constables of Kew.

"Here's a nice game," said Pipey, "when left in solitude and darkness, "here's a nice game to be a playing of ven I should be a dodging May-dock and hitting on all sorts of plans for valking off Liz from his crib. My nerves! vot *vill* old Grimer say now, I vunder?"

As there was no one there to answer the question, Mr. Pipey, after a pause, replied to his own query in the following extraordinary words—

"He'll go ravin', he vill; he'll just throw his old vig at the cat, kick the cook, kiss his vife, commit suicide, and say he could'nt help it."

Why Mr. Grimer should do either one or the other of these extraordinary things we do not know, and we can only leave the reader to form his or her own opinion on the subject.

Mr. Pipey continued to talk to himself for about an hour, and then, tiring of the amusement, fell sound asleep.

The arrival of the doctor created quite a stir among the servants, for no sooner did he look at Hammer than he expressed his firm opinion that he would die.

The man who had shot him down felt slightly disturbed at this, for he never anticipated such a result. His mind was, however, afterwards relieved, for on a close examination of the wounds the doctor thought fit to alter his mind on the subject.

"Yes," he said, "there is a chance of his recovery if the charge can be extracted, and the fellow's previous course of life admits of his undergoing the terrible prostration which must ensue. He may recover, but he will never be a strong man again."

The constables next put in an appearance. They appeared but little pleased at being turned out of bed on such a bitterly cold night, and at once exhibited their Christian-like feelings towards mankind in general—and burglars in particular —by expressing their inclination to convey Hammer to the lock-up on the instant; but to this the Doctor objected.

"No, hang it, men," he said, "though the fellow is a vagabond burglar, let him have a chance of living, and ending his days in a proper manner on the scaffold he was born to grace. It would be a crying shame to rob the hangman of so promising a subject."

The officers murmured their objections, but retired, as they said, to take a squint at the other gallows bird.

When they entered the room in which Mr. Pipey was confined, they beheld that gentleman reposing in perfect ease on two chairs.

"Well, this is a cool one, anyhow," said one officer to the other.

"Yes," said the second limb of the law, "he don't appear particularly disturbed. Hillo! young scaffold mounter—wake up!"

The officer accompanied the latter part of his speech with such a severe shaking, as completely upset the equanimity and equilibrium of the recumbent Pipey.

"Hillo! young fellow," continued the officer, "what do you mean by going to sleep here?"

"And vot do you mean by disturbing a gentlemen a taking of his rest?"

"Well," exclaimed the officer, "of all the —— there!"

And he could not give vent to the indignation which stuck in his throat.

The other tried his hand at it, but with no better success.

"Now, you sir, don't be too imperent or you'll get it. You will be taught how to respect the law and treat its officers with consideration."

"Are you an officer?" asked Pipey.

"I am," returned the constable.

"You look more like a pickled baboon," said Pipey. But this was an assertion we fear he could hardly bear out, in consequence of his never having seen an animal of the class he mentioned in the condition he described."

"Well," said the second officer, equally as taken aback as the first, "if ever I did meet with such a—a—warmint!"

This was the very strongest term he could think of without sacrificing his dignity as an instrument of the law of the land.

"And now you've voke me up, vot are you going to treat me to?" demanded the outrageous Pipey.

"Treat you to!" repeated the constable, "treat you to! why a pair of handcuffs, you little rascal. Here, put these on, and see if you can't behave yourself."

"Oh," said Pipey, as his wrists slipped into the handcuffs, "this ain't the first time I've vorn bracelets."

"And it aint likely to be the last," said the officer, "unless they strings you up."

"Strings me up," said Pipey, "vy, they couldn't do it if they tried ever so hard. You don't know, I s'pose, that the king is a perticler friend of mine? and as to the Prince of Vales—vy, ve're bosom friends, and inseparable: and d'ye suppose they vould allow me to be strung up ? Bah ! they'd break their precious hearts."

The officers stared at one another in amazement. Itappeared that they had quite lost their breath with astonishment. It was some moments before they spoke again, and then not for the purpose of renewing the conversation, but to order Pipey to follow them to the lock-up.

"You will do very well there until it's time to take you to Newgate," said one.

"Yes," said the other, "you'll do there; and don't think as you'll get off, for we'll sit up and watch you. Such a slippery customer must be well looked after."

"You're as kind as an amiable old grandmother," said Pipey, "and twice as handsome, only I'm sorry I can't appreciate your care."

"Oh," said one of the officers, "Newgate will take all that brass out of you."

"Will it ?" said Pipey, "I doubt it; for I shan't be there long enough. The fact is, I've rather a particular appointment to-night, and I shall have to keep it, for there's a lady in the case."

"Keep it ! why, you don't think yourself capable of getting out of Newgate, do you ? Ha! ha! that's rather too good."

"You'll see," said Pipey, "I never break my word."

"Why, it was a tough job for Jack Sheppard, and he was about as clever a one as ever made the attempt."

"Jack Sheppard !" said Pipey, "Pooh ! He never did anything that the greatest duffer out couldn't have done. You will see what I'll do."

"Ah !" said one of the officers, "that's all idle talk; you're only a childish boaster."

"Boaster or not," said Pipey, "I'm out of Newgate afore to-morrow morning; so I give you varning. Mind what I says, I *always keeps my vord*."

Without more ado the constables untied the cords which bound their prisoner, and they walked him off to the lock-up house, where he was duly searched before being placed in his cell.

They forgot to remove the undersole of his shoe; had they done so they would have found concealed there as neat a little watch spring saw as ever mechanic manufactured.

CHAPTER XX.

MARIE PROCURES FROM THE PRINCE A PASSPORT FOR LOVELACE AND HIS VALET.—THE ESCAPE FROM ENGLAND.

SEVERAL days elapsed, and Marie had never quitted the house in which Lovelace was lodged.

The time had, however, now arrived when she had to appear at Covent Garden Theatre, to fulfil an engagement entered into some time previous.

She at first determined not to appear, but on reconsideration she agreed to sing for one night, and thus get an opportunity of meeting the Prince, from whom she sought to obtain passports for Lovelace and a servant, and also to stay the warrant which was out for the arrest of Lovelace for killing and slaying General Rooker.

"I do not like your meeting that man again," said Lovelace.

"Oh, fear nothing," replied Marie; "I shall deal cunningly with him, and shall procure the passports and stay the issue of the warrant. I have said it, and I will do it."

"But by what means ?" asked Lovelace.

"Oh," replied Marie, "that must be my secret."

It was evening, and the hour for the departure of Marie to the theatre had arrived.

"I shall be in an agony of doubt and fear until you return," said Lovelace; "and pray be careful how you come and go, for you may be tracked here, and then my arrest will be certain."

"You will not be arrested; the officer who enters here will not go forth again. I have taken every precaution."

"You are an angel, Marie; and I verily believe I should have undergone the terrible ignomy which my rash act would bring upon me if you had not watched over me so carefully."

"I am more than repaid by your love," said Marie. Whenever she uttered this word she fixed her dark, piercing eye upon Lovelace, for she could see him shudder as it was spoken. With a woman's penetration she discovered that, in spite of his caresses, his smiles, and his protestations, that his heart was elsewhere.

She saw this, but the only effect it had upon her was to arouse the tiger within her, but this she suppressed, for dissimulation was absolutely necessary for the successful issue of the dark projects of her brain.

"My love is but a poor gift," said Lovelace, "but you have it."

"Then I am more than repaid," said the Italian; "and now, Horace, I must go. It is the first time I have left you since the day on which we came here. I shall feel desolate when I quit you."

"But what shall I feel, in this dismal room, with no soul to speak to, and with only dark and disagreeable subjects to reflect upon ? Oh, I shall go crazed before you return."

"Bear up, sweet love," said Marie; "I shall leave my heart with you. Adieu."

"Adieu, Marie *mia*," said Lovelace, as he kissed her young cheek; "adieu, and for Heaven's sake be careful."

"You will have no cause to blame me," said Marie, and she took her departure.

The Italian quitted the house alone and on foot, first taking the precaution to see that there was no one at hand to recognise her. She walked some little distance and then entered a carriage which awaited her, and in a few minutes was safely conveyed to the door of the theatre.

Arrived there she hastened to her dressing-room, and soon arrayed herself for the part she was about to assume.

The theatre was very crowded that night, for,

independent of Marie's fame as an actress, her *liaison* with the Prince had got noised about until her name was literally in everybody's mouth.

All kind of rumours were afloat concerning her actions, and the tales told of her doings at Marlborough House and at Kew were more numerous than correct, and far more extraordinary than generous, for her conduct was at all times quiet and unassuming; but if the dog once obtains the ill name he had better be hung at once, for the world will magnify his fault and blaze up his errors until the public verdict will be that hanging is too good for him.

It was, then, more out of curiosity to see the mistress of a prince and the heroine of a desperate duel than to hear the singing of a popular vocalist that Covent Garden was so crowded on the night of Marie's re-appearance. Behind the scenes a crowd of fashionables had collected, and as the famous singer walked down the stage, all eyes were turned upon her.

But she bore the scrutiny without flinching, indeed she coolly murmured some of the airs she was about to sing, and appeared the least concerned of any one there present.

Seating herself at one of the wings, she entered into conversation with the other vocalists as they arrived, and calmly awaited the moment for her appearance on the stage. She had not been seated thus for a great length of time when a murmur on all sides of "The Prince, the Prince," told her of the arrival of that personage.

The Prince, accompanied by some of his companions, at once made their way towards Marie, but the vocalist took no notice of them. Others rose and bowed, but she sat quite still, and never as much as raised her eyes from the music she was pretending to read.

As if actuated by one feeling, and by common consent, all the parties in the neighbourhood of the great singer moved away, leaving the Prince in her immediate neighbourhood.

Comprehending that this had occurred, Marie arose from her chair and turned round, and her eyes, of course, fell upon the Prince, who stood bowing to her.

"Ah, my dear Prince," said Marie, extending her hand, "how do you do? You are really a stranger."

"Yes, Marie," said the Prince, "it is so; but whose fault is it that such is the case? you cannot say that I sought this long estrangement?"

"Oh!" said Marie, "you are referring to a slight misunderstanding we had when last we met. Have you not forgotten that yet?"

"How can I forget it," asked the Prince, "when it has been the means of depriving me of a sight of you for so many days."

"Why did you not seek me out?" asked Marie, with affected wonderment.

"Seek you out, Marie! What, after what escaped your lips when we parted?"

"Precisely."

"Why, you cannot remember what you then said."

"I do not. What was it?"

"Oh, if you have forgotten it that is proof sufficient that you could not have meant it, and so we will forget the matter."

"Gladly."

"Then we are friends again?"

"Do you wish that it should be so?"

"Can you ask it?"

"I do ask it."

"You cannot doubt it. Oh, if you could but know how dejected I have been since you left me."

"And I—do you think I have not suffered?"

"I wish I could flatter myself that such had been the case, although, Heaven knows, I would not have you undergo one pang."

"I have suffered many, but it is all over now."

She placed her hand affectionately within his, and her whole manner spoke of trust and love. She was indeed a consummate actress!

"And now, Marie, let me ask you to clear what appears to me a deep mystery. How came you engaged in that singular duel?"

"I heard of it, and determined to save Lovelace from Rooker, and at the same time to take an ample vengeance, for I hated Rooker."

"And yet it was Rooker who introduced you to me."

"I nevertheless hated him."

"That was cruel."

"It may have been so, but I could not help the feeling."

"But what has become of Lovelace? Do you know that?"

"I do."

"Then there is hope that we may get at him."

"Not through me."

"Will you not, then, deliver him up?"

"No."

"That is not only unkind, but directly illegal. Do you not know that you are liable to severe punishment for screening one who has offended the law?"

"I only know that he shall not be handed over to justice through me. In fact, dear Prince, I want you to obtain passports for him and another, and also to quash the warrant until he is gone."

"Marie!"

"I am quite in earnest."

"You cannot think that I would do so."

"I know you will, for I ask it as a favour."

"But I cannot do so; do you think that, powerful as I am, they would grant me passports for a man amenable to the laws for such an act as Lovelace has been guilty of."

"I do not ask it; you may obtain passports for whomsoever you please, but the description of the parties must correspond with that of Lovelace and a young valet of his whom he proposes to take with him to Italy."

"A young valet? Oh, Marie, I see how it is: there's a lady in the case."

"There may be; what then?"

"Oh, nothing, but I fear I cannot do your bidding."

"You must, indeed, Prince; so let us have no more argument on the matter. I shall never rest until Lovelace and his valet are out of England."

"Now," said the Prince, "I daresay you think yourself a very cunning little girl; but listen to me, and see how I can read you. This valet is no other than the lady of whom my little Marie was so unreasonably jealous at the ball at Marlborough House, and who left under the protection of this Lovelace. The fact is, you still think that her presence may shake your position in my affection, and you wish to troop her off out of England that you may have the field all to yourself. Am I not right?"

"You are very clever," said Marie, "but I shall not answer you."

"Ha! ha!" laughed the Prince, "but I am answered. Cunning as you are, I've sifted out the cream of your secret. Ah, Marie, you cannot deceive me!"

"I see I cannot," said Marie, with a smile, whilst in her heart she felt nothing but ineffable contempt for the self-satisfaction exhibited by the Prince. "I see I cannot, and so I will make no further attempt. But you will grant the favour I ask?"

"Well, I will see about it."

"But you will promise me to delay the warrant and procure the passport?'

"I will not quite promise."

"But I must have your word, my dear Prince. Ah, let your promise cement our hearts anew. Let this be the pledge by which our intimacy is again established."

"Oh!" cried the Prince, "I cannot resist you. Do as you will with me."

"That is a good Prince. Now I feel I love you dearly—you good, generous Prince!"

"Ah, that is flattery."

"No, it is truth. But hark! the bell rings for the commencement of the opera. When shall I see you again?"

"Will you not return with me to-night?"

"Not to-night, dear Prince. I must go to my own home, but I shall see you to-morrow."

"Are you sure you will not disappoint me?"

"Have the passports ready, and you may be assured I will call for them."

"Then I promise. To-morrow at mid-day."

"Adieu! You have made me happy."

* * * * *

The curtain rose on the performance, and Marie entered upon the scene. She was received by the audience with mingled applause and disapprobation.

By the gallants she was received with enthusiastic cheering, but there was a little prudish clique among the audience that viewed her past history with anything but approbation; and so, to herald their own virtue and show their detestation of vice in others, they thought it incumbent on themselves to hiss very loudly. But to all these manifestations of feeling Marie was deaf. She looked not on those in front of her, but, conscious of her own powers, applied herself to the business of the scene with a determination to excel which, perhaps, had never before possessed her.

A dead silence pervaded the vast body of people as the first notes of her full rich voice filled the house; and, as the air progressed, and as the volume of sound rang through the building, the coldest prude could not choose but listen attentively.

She gained their attention, and it did not take her long to win their hearts.

She played with a force and originality which carried all before it, and at the end of the scene in which she was engaged she received a rapturous recall but would not acknowledge it.

Without looking at the audience, and without exhibiting the slightest token of being engaged in singing for aught but her own amusement, Marie proceeded with her task, and from beginning to end secured a complete triumph.

At the end of the opera the applause was so boisterous that the manager stepped into her dressing-room and begged her to step before the curtain and acknowledge the marks of approval she had elicited.

"To oblige you," she said, "I will go; but I have no inclination to appear before people who have insulted me."

"Think not of it," said the manager, "think not of it, but step before the lamps, or they will tear the theatre down."

Marie complied with his wish, and stepped upon the stage once more.

Her appearance was heralded by the shouts and acclamation of the vast throng, and she crossed the stage amidst such a scene of excitement as is seldom seen within the walls of a theatre. Everyone appeared to be in ecstacies, and the manager was particularly jubilant, for he looked forward to reaping a rich harvest out of the engagement which he had renewed, and which had opened with such success.

But he was doomed to disappointment; Marie had taken her final leave of the British public in her capacity of vocalist. The many other characters she assumed in England thereafter we have yet to chronicle.

After all this wild excitement Marie retired to her private room.

"Where is the Prince?" she asked of an attendant.

"He is in the Duchess of B——'s box, signora," said the attendant; "shall I send word to him that you desire to see him?"

"Certainly not; is my carriage ready?"

"Yes, signora."

"Then tell no one that I am going; I wish to leave without interruption."

"Very good, signora."

The brief dialogue terminated. The attendant withdrew to order the coach to be held in readiness, and in a few moments Marie stepped unobserved from her room and into the street.

The carriage stood in readiness, and without molestation the Italian entered it and drove away.

In a short time she was at her lodgings and in the embrace of Lovelace, who had for hours been fretting for her arrival.

"I thought you would never come," he said; "I never found the time hang so heavily before."

"I have longed to return, dearest," she said, "but I could not get away a moment earlier."

"And how have you succeeded?"

"Remarkably well; by to-morrow night we shall be on our way to bright and sunny Italy."

"Anything, so that I am free from this terrible restraint. I think I should go mad if forced to remain here another week."

"And yet I am with you."

"You are, sweetest; and, believe me, when I say that, I feel grateful for your many kindnesses, and am deeply sensible of your love, but you cannot bring me liberty. Your presence is sunshine, but it cannot widen the limits of my prison. Your words are kind and soothing, but they cannot make me forget that I am a criminal, hiding from justice; and although you do all woman could do to lighten my durance vile, you cannot bring me fresh air and the incidents I have been wont to find in my previous mode of life. Forgive me if I speak peevishly; I mean nothing unkind, but the thought of regaining liberty has so aroused all the latent feelings within me, that not to give vent to them would be to impose on myself an agony which I can hardly endure."

"Think not of these things; to-morrow you are free."

"Yes, free; but how have you managed to procure this freedom?"

"I have seen the Prince."

The brow of Lovelace darkened.

"Nay, frown not," said Marie; "I have not purchased your liberty at the price of any personal sacrifices. I have been guarded."

"But you have had to promise ——"

"I have promised nothing but a visit to Marlborough House to-morrow."

Lovelace looked still more displeased.

"Fear nothing; I go but to secure the necessary passports."

"But the price?"

"Nothing more than the exertion of those theatrical abilities I am supposed to possess in so eminent a degree. Can you not trust me?"

Lovelace replied not.

"Can you not trust me?" repeated Marie, her eyes filling with that fire which ever lighted them when she was in the least annoyed or excited.

"You are but a woman," said Lovelace, gloomily.

"And, you would add, possessed of all those weaknesses which cling so pertinaciously to my sex; but you mistake me."

"Think of your former intimacy with this man," said Lovelace, "and then ask yourself if I am not right in hesitating to express approval of this intended visit."

"I do think of that intimacy, and the feelings aroused by the thought should be to you the best guarantee of my passing scatheless through the ordeal of the morrow. Let the hatred I bear the man be the guarantee of my safety."

"I see I must trust you."

"You cannot possibly do better."

The night passed, and the eventful morrow at length dawned.

Precisely at the appointed moment Marie presented herself for admission at Marlborough House.

She passed to the private apartments of the Prince, and was at once ushered into his presence.

"So, Marie," said the Prince, rising to receive her, "you are as punctual as you promised to be."

"Yes, I could not afford to delay a moment. I shall not rest until I have the promised documents and they are out of London."

"Ah, you women are so silly."

"We are."

"And so unreasonably jealous."

"Some of us."

"Yes, my little Marie in particular."

"Do you think so?"

"Yes, I am convinced of it."

"Ah, but the passports; you promised to have them prepared for me."

"Do you think I have forgotten?"

"I trust not."

"See here, I could not resist you. These are the passports, and I give you my word Lovelace and this same silly woman and *quondam* valet may leave England without fear of interruption."

"You are a good and generous man; I am under the deepest obligations to you."

She rose, and hastily prepared to withdraw.

"What!" said the Prince, looking with blank astonishment, "going again?"

"They must leave England before I can rest," said Marie.

"Psha!" cried the Prince; "what folly."

"It may appear so to you, but you know not the feelings which consume me. I must go and dispose of these people, and then—"

"And, then, Marie?"

"I am thine once more."

"But why leave me now? A messenger could take the paltry slips of paper, and you could stay with me."

"I will trust no messenger. I have said that I must see the departure of these people before I can rest, and it must be so. Let me be convinced that they have turned their back on England and I am happy."

"Well, I suppose you must have your own way; but promise me that you will not be long absent."

"I will return as soon as I have fulfilled my mission. Adieu, dear Prince!"

"Adieu, Marie," said the Prince, looking anything but pleased; "I shall be on thorns until you return."

"That is folly. Adieu, dearest."

Turning from the apartment Marie hastened away.

"Miserable dupe," she murmured; "blind fool! When you see me again be assured it will be to further my own ends."

She quitted the house with her precious documents, and in a short space of time presented them to Lovelace.

"And now," she cried, "for fair Italy and a life of joy."

The preparations were hastily made: Morgan, with all the luggage, went away many hours before his master. He procured his own passport, and, as a matter of course, made no sign of travelling with Lovelace.

Marie, wonderfully well disguised in the habit of a boy, quitted the lodgings of her protector as if in attendance on him, and thus quitted England.

Not a soul attempted to interrupt them, although it was quite apparent that Lovelace was recognised by more than one person, who, had not the hands of justice been tied, was possessed of the power to arrest his flight.

* * * * *

It is night, and a ship is beating down the channel in the teeth of a miserable wind. It is a gloomy, black, and terrible night, and the sea runs high, and the ship battles on with the greatest difficulty.

Lovelace and Marie are in that ship, and their miserable voyage is but in keeping with the dark and stormy course of their lives.

It is night in London, and at Marlborough House the Prince paces up and down his chamber, biting his nether lip, and giving vent to exclamations of bitter rage and disappointment.

The cause was apparent.

On a table before him lay the following scrawl:—

"Duped and wretched man, ere this reaches you I shall be beyond your power. I have played upon you with success and am now, *with Lovelace*, on my way to a far-off land. Think not that I have forgotten my oath of vengeance. I am now working it to the best of my power, and the time will come when it will fall upon you. Be assured of the undying hate of

"MARIE LAVROUFFE."

"Idiot that I am!" cried the Prince. "Idiot, idiot! not to have penetrated the designs of that devil. I feel I have loosed on the world a fiend that will haunt me to death, and against whose evil influences I struggle in vain."

CHAPTER XXI.

THE MYSTERIOUS HIGHWAYMAN AND MAYDOCK.

ON finding himself in comparative security, after his flight from the Duke's villa, Maydock abated his pace and went towards London at a brisk walk.

Congratulating himself upon the successful issue of his dark and dangerous mission, Maydock pursued his journey in a rather happy state of mind, notwithstanding many embarrassments which presented themselves to his view, on reflecting on the position he was occupying.

"I am not safe for a day," he said. "Who knows but that those fellows I have left captured at the villa may, to suit their own ends, turn round and peach. Should they come down on my crib they would find the girl, and then the game would be spoilt." Yes, he continued, "at all risks I must go far away with her and put beyond doubt the security of my prize. She without the will or the will without her would be useless, but with both I am a made man; and now that I have them it becomes me to secure them. Yes, yes, I must leave London with her."

He moved on; his pace increasing as the crowd of thoughts came upon him and disturbed his equanimity.

On—on towards London, and still without interruption.

Not far from Mortlake was a stretch of wild and, at that time, rather deserted country. It was a piece of land which the hand of man had not yet reduced to a state of cultivation.

It was the resort of gipsys and vagabonds of every description, and in the summer months their tents and fires might have been seen there during the hours of the night, but now that the snow was on the ground, and the wind howled over the spot, it was deserted; and when Maydock approached it on his return journey, there was not a soul to be seen in its neighbourhood.

It was not without a shudder that that bold, bad man, neared this place, for there was something so terrible about its weird aspect and loneliness that a tremble must involuntarily creep over the strongest at approaching it on such a night and at such an hour.

The place had a bad name too. It was near the high road to Kew, and people were forced to pass it as they journeyed to the fashionable little village on the Thames.

As a matter of course, those who most frequented the route were people of high position, and who were likely to carry considerable quantities of money and valuables about with them.

Kew was fashionable; a villa there, or near there, was an indispensible passport to gentility of the highest order; and therefore this little stretch of wild country tempted the visits of people of very doubtful character, and whose occupation may readily be guessed at. It had, about the time of which we write, gained a great notoriety as the chief *locale* of a mysterious and singularly brutal horseman, who plundered all who fell in his path, and very frequently destroyed his victims in the most remorseless manner.

Of this man little was known; the officers of justice declared they had never seen him, and in spite of continued watching and diligent inquiry could never catch the faintest glimpse of him.

But officers of justice didn't then, any more than they do now, confine themselves to the strictest rendering of the truth, and it was suspected by many who should have known something of the subject that the boldest of the limbs of the law shirked the possibility of coming into contact with a being who was known to be a remorseless blood-shedder, and who, moreover, had such a preternatural air about him as to gain for him a notoriety which was fast spreading throughout the length and breadth of the land.

These little circumstances, duly weighed and considered, will fully explain why Maydock hesitated in committing himself to crossing the haunt of a being of such startling peculiarities.

He had an alternative, however, and that was to take the high road, but this he dreaded more than the chance of meeting a highwayman.

"Bah!" he said, "there is honour among thieves; and even if I meet this fellow there won't be much harm done. The chances are ten to one that I know him and that he won't interfere with me, and at the worst, he will find I have nothing about me worth having—*except the will!* and if he wants that there will be a fight for it. I'm not without arms, and my chances are as good as his, although he is on horseback.

With this he felt in his pockets, and drew therefrom a couple of pistols, which he placed at half-cock and returned.

"There," he continued, "they never disappointed me on an emergency, and it isn't likely they will do so now."

He stalked on with a resolute air, and really looked a most formidable man to come in contact with. He was powerfully set, and there was an air of dogged courage about him which rendered him a most uninviting party to meet.

The moon, which for a while had been obscured, and which now burst out again in full radiance previous to its final disappearance behind the fogs which would roll up the river in another hour or two, lighted up the scene which extended before the gaze of the burglar. He could see the most distant objects, and the whole detail of the landscape was laid out before him.

"Psha!" he said, "devil a horseman is there in this neighbourhood, I take it."

He had scarcely uttered these words when, as if it had started out of the earth, the dark outline of a horseman appeared before him—standing out with almost miraculous boldness against the sheet of snow which stretched away as far as the eye could reach. The moonlight fell full upon the figures of man and horse. The animal was a wonderously beautiful black thoroughbred, and the rider was a tall and powerful man, clad in *a suit of black velvet, trimmed with bugles ;* he had a face which once seen, was never to be forgotten; it was of *ashy paleness,* and it was as expressionless as the chiseled semblance of humanity turned out from the studio of the sculptor.

"Hold !" cried this singular being, who, of course, will be recognised as the hero of the scene in Grimer's office on the occasion of the intended burglary by the Duke of Grasmount. "Hold! Maydock; we must have a word together."

"Oh, my God !" almost yelled Maydock, who had turned as white as the snow under his feet ; "oh, mercy ! mercy ! this is too horrible. Horrible thing !—ghost ! fiend ! whatever thou art —get thee hence. I freeze at the sight of thee ! Hence ! hence ! hence !"

The burglar writhed as if undergoing some awful torture, and which far excelled his horrors on beholding the being before him at the hop where he held his interview with Hammer and Pipey. Every nerve twitched, his eyes started from their sockets, his jaw fell as in death, and a cold, clammy perspiration saturated him from head to foot.

"You did not anticipate a meeting with me ?" asked the horseman, his awful face undergoing no change as he spoke.

"No,' cried Maydock, " no ; but speak not to me. I cannot bear your presence.'

"You remember me ?"

"My God ! shall I ever forget you ?"

"You remember the days long passed ?"

"Yes, yes."

"You do not forget when I first made your acquaintance ?"

"I forget nothing."

"What was I then ?"

"What mean you ?"

"I ask, what was I then ?"

"My master's companion and the ——'

"You hesitate; you would say—' and the partner of his guilt ?' "

"Yes."

"And my profession, have you ascertained that ?"

"I have heard that you were in reality the character you assumed to be on the occasion of a ceremony of marriage."

"Yes, you are right ; a ceremony of marriage between your master and a poor girl, whom he sought to ruin by fraud and deception. I was a minister of the Gospel !"

"So—so Grimer has told me," muttered Maydock, hoarsely.

"Yes ; and he told you further that I confessed all to him in a cell in Newgate, and that I was afterwards—"

"HANGED !"

"Yes, hanged. And he spoke the truth !"

"Oh, spare me !" cried Maydock, "spare me this horrible recital, and let me pass ; I shall go mad if I stay with thee another minute."

"Stay," cried the horseman, "I have not yet done with you. I have followed you from London, and have awaited you here for some hours in order that I may bring about this conversation, and I shall not allow you to move until I have quite finished with you.'

"What would you have ?"

"Listen : I have watched you for one whole month ; unseen I have dogged your steps : unheard I have listened to your plans, and fathomed your intentions. Not an incident in your life during the past month has escaped me, and, therefore you will understand why I have come after you tonight. Knowing your errand, I followed in order to avail myself of your knowledge and labour. You wanted to possess yourself of a will, and I required the same document. You knew where to find it, and *I know where to find you.* You have the will, and now must hand it to me."

"The will!" cried Maydock, " the will! I know of no will—I have no will. You are mistaken. I do not comprehend you."

"But I comprehend you. The will."

"I have no will."

"The will : another moment and I will take it from you. Beware!"

Maydock gazed up into the horrible white face, and he knew he was powerless. Terror had seized him, and an infant might have mastered him then.

"The will!" demanded the horseman, drawing forth a pistol.

"It—it is here," cried Maydock, and he drew forth the box, and handed it to the mysterious being who held such sway over him.

"It is well," cried the recipient, "it is well. I shall see you once more."

"Heaven forbid."

"I shall see you once more," continued the horseman, without noticing the interruption. "I know the child still lives, and as you know more of this matter than I do, I shall employ you in tracing the being I require."

With this he rode off.

A moment and Maydock collected his thoughts.

"Lost, lost!" he cried, "it is all lost now. The dead rise out of the grave to thwart me, and I am powerless to avert their influences. He has tracked me for a month—he knows everything, and I have struggled in vain ; and yet he said he knew the child still lived and that he should employ me in tracing it. Then he *does not* know all ! Ha! ha! He knows not who and where that child is. And yet his superhuman powers must defeat me. I am in his clutches. Oh horror ! in the powers of a spirit treading the earth in the shape of a hanged man !"

———

CHAPTER XXII.

PIPEY IN NEWGATE.—THE ESCAPE.

ACTING up to their promise, the village constables took the very earliest opportunity of conveying Pipey to London, for the purpose of lodging him in Newgate. The trio set out from Kew at about nine o'clock on the morning of the burglary and capture ; and, engaging a cart, they proceeded to town at a jog-trot, which did not conduce to the comfort of Pipey, who, being pinioned and seated on a very narrow board placed across the cart, found that he had all his work cut out for him in keeping himself upright.

"This may be pleasant travelling," said Pipey, "but if I had my choice I'd rather walk."

"No doubt of it," said one of the officers; "and I suppose it would be much more pleasant if we wern't here at all."

"Oh! I don't know that," continued Pipey. "I don't object to your company, as I knows of: and I may be doing vorse than taking this ere airing this morning,—it may have a marked effect on my constitution!"

"He's as hardened as a brute beast," said the constable. "No one who sees and hears him would think that he was a going to Newgate on a awful charge of burglary."

"Who, indeed?" said the other, in a contemplative mood, "who indeed?—but there, they're born in it. It comes nat'ral to them when they're in long clothes, and they keeps on getting worse and worse until they get so bad that they can't get no worser, and they gets lagged with pleasure and die with satisfaction at being the object of public interest through the mejium of 'The Newgate Calendar.' Ah! it's human natur'—it's human natur': we're all born and not buried."

After this outburst of eloquent soliloquy both officials lapsed into silence, and pursued the journey without further remark until they arrived at Newgate.

"Here we are," said the officers.

"Here we are," said Pipey; "and, now we are here, what are you going to stand?'

"Ah! you warmint," said one of the official Dogberrys, "you'll have standing enough before they've done with you here. This is the sort of place to take the imperence out o' yer."

The gates opened, and the little party entered.

The constables at the lodge at once recognised Pipey as an old acquaintance, and told him that they were proud to see him again, and hoped he had come to stop a little while, as his society was so agreeable. It was quite a pleasure to have him there.

Which bit of pleasantry was answered by Pipey assuring them that he was proud of their consideration, but that he was afraid pressing engagements would take him away very soon.

At which the officials laughed very heartily. It is astonishing how heartily officials will laugh even at the most remote sign of pleasantry.

"You'll find him a pretty child," said one of the officers from Kew; "he has cheek enough for twenty boys; and as to his contempt for the horrors of imprisonment it's awful to contemplate."

"What's he here for?" asked the chief constable, opening a ponderous record of crime of every description, to enter the charge against Pipey; "What's he here for?"

"Attempted burglary last night at the Duke of Grasmount's villa, at Kew."

"What! a youth like this attempt a burglary alone?"

"No; you see there were two others: one of 'em escaped, and the other is at the village badly wounded by a ball from a blunderbuss."

"What a pity they didn't blow his brains out, and have done with it," said the chief constable. "But somehow these fellows never do get killed until they get into the hands of the hangman. What's your name?" he continued, turning to Pipey.

"I don't think as how I ever had one," said Pipey, "that is, not in the reg'lar way. Mine's only a chance one, picked up anyhow, and vithout any perticler meaning."

"Well, such as it is, let us have it."

"Vell, it's Pipey."

"Pipey?"

"Yes, Pipey."

"Is that a Christian or a surname?"

"Vell, I don't know. I don't think it can be a Chistian name, 'cause no other Christian has von of the same kind; and I don't think as how it's a surname, 'cause it's not quite respectable enough to belong to a sir."

"Come, I say," said the officer, "this won't do. You can save your chaff for those who like it. I, for one, don't want any of it, so don't try it on, now. What's your name?"

"Pipey."

"Pipey what?"

"No it isn't Pipey Vot, at least not as I knows on, but only Pipey. I never vos called anythink else."

"But, curse the fellow, you had a father, what was his name?"

"Vell, I s'pose I did have a father, in fact I don't see how, in the course of natur, I could ha' been here if I hadn't had von, but vot his name vos I don't know."

"Don't you remember him?"

"No."

"Did he die before you were born?"

"I don't know that he's dead now; the fact is, I vos picked up by an old 'oman ven I vos a hinfant. You see she vos a trotting through the graveyard of the Abbey von night, and vot should she see in von of the precious doors but a small vite parcel, vich she picked up and opened, and to her no small gratification found me. Of course I vos a werry handsome baby, and took her taste immensely; and so she took me home and brought me up. She wern't a woman of werry good habits, d'ye see, and somehow or other I fell into her vay of thinking that it was a folly to vork ven it vos so easy to prig, and so I've gone on ever since I can remember. The name of Pipey vos given me by the fellows who hung about the public-houses in our neighbourhood vere I used to go and vistle of an evening in order to earn a few coppers to take home to the old 'oman, and I think that's all I know about myself and my name."

"Very good," said the officer; "then we will put you down as a rogue and a vagabond, name unknown, but recognised by thieves as 'Pipey.'"

"You can put down vot you like; Pipey's my name, and you'll find it on the books a good many times if you'll take the trouble to look 'em over, for they've done me the honour of keeping an account of wisits."

"Ah! I expect this will be about the last you will make, for if they commit on this charge you'll go for life, and so don't deceive yourself."

"I never do," said Pipey, "and so I inform yer that I aint agoing this time, and so don't deceive yourself."

"Well, if you get off you will have more luck than attends many."

"I shan't wait to see about it."

"What do you mean?"

"I mean that on the first oppertunity I'm off."

"Off where?"

"Out off this?"

"What! out of Newgate?"

"Yes," said Pipey, "and so I give you varning."

"Out of Newgate!" repeated the officer, "why, it couldn't be done."

"Oh, couldn't it?" said Pipey; "vell, ve shall see."

"Why, you couldn't escape from the weakest cell in the place."

"Try me."

"Well, I will. You get out! Bah! a brat of a boy to talk of getting out of Newgate, it's rank presumption."

"So I said," chimed in one of the officers from Kew; "so I said when he told us he should cut from it."

"Oh! its childish boasting," said the chief constable, "lock him up, and let it be in the old cell, at the end of the first passage to the right, No. 44—that's about the weakest cell in the place —and if he can get out of that I will forgive him."

"You vill see," said Pipey.

"So we shall; and now away with you, and try and get your folly out of your head."

"All right," said Pipey, walking away with one of the jailers, "we shall see. If I'm gone by to-morrow morning, don't say I did'nt give you fair warning of my intentions."

"Lock him up—lock him up! He's only a stupid boaster after all!"

Pipey was walked away, and conducted to the cell spoken of by the official in charge of the prison.

Newgate, at the time of which we are writing, was a different place to what it now is. It was then an over-crowded, ill-conducted place, where a few horrible drunkards and rascals filled the principal positions of trust, and where crime was augmented more than in any other place in London. It was a den of filth and misery, and those who had charge of it were no better than those sent there to receive the punishment of their crimes.

The cells were most obnoxious dens, and disease reigned over the whole place.

Pipey was conducted to the cell allotted him, and thrust in.

"There," said the jailer, "get out of that if you can."

"It don't look very much of a job," said Pipey.

"Don't it?" said the man, "then you had better try it on. Of course it wouldn't be a great go if you had the proper tools, but without anything to help you I think you will have all your work."

"Ah," said Pipey, "you are not supposed to know everything, clever as you are; so say nothing about it."

The door was closed and the key turned in the lock, and Pipey was alone.

The cell into which he had been thrown was a dark, noisome place, lighted only by a small grated window facing into the passage, at the end of which it was situated.

Age had done much for it, and it was in a state of extreme decay and dilapidation.

The door hung to its rusted hinges by a mere thread, and the woodwork which held the bolt of the old lock was worm-eaten and crumbling.

The floor was as filthy as could be imagined, and an almost intolerable stench pervaded the atmosphere of the place.

In one corner stood a heavy truckle couch, and a bundle of mouldy straw stood in another part of the place. On a small stone bench stood a small stone jug, which had evidently been left there since the last occupant had gone away.

Such was the cell into which Pipey was conducted.

"Vell," he said, when left alone, "vell, if I had'nt nothink to call me avay I'll be hanged if I'd stay here longer than I could help. Ugh! it's vorse than a grave."

It really was, for a more revolting place could never be conceived; vermin of every description abounded there, and the almost perceptible and overpowering effluvia served to make it entirely unbearable.

To Pipey the confinement was most distressing, for he was of a disposition which would not admit of solitude and inactivity being indulged in. He fretted and chafed like a caged hyena, and prayed for night to come in order that he might attempt what he contemplated doing.

Slowly the hours passed, each one seeming double the length of the others. Slowly the day waned, and slowly the night approached.

"It's awful," said Pipey, getting more and more excited each moment; "it's awful, and vot it 'll be if I don't get out on it afore to-morrow Heaven only knows. I should go mad to remain here and risk breaking my word to Liz; and she, poor girl, would turn up her heels if I didn't come. Poor Liz! even now that feller Maydock may be valking her off to some other place, and I mayn't see her again for nobody knows ven; and then there 'll be old Grimer a fretting away his fat like anythink about it, and altogether it von't bear thinking of. I only hope, by vay of consolation, that that Maydock has got scragged, that's all."

Murmuring such sentences as these, Pipey strode up and down his narrow cell for hours, and lost all his lightheartedness in the anxiety of the moment.

Eight o'clock at length came, and with it the jailer, who brought Pipey some bread and water, and told him to make himself comfortable for the night.

"There's some beautiful straw," he said, "and if you're tired you can sleep like a top."

"And if I ain't tired I can stop avake, I s'pose?"

"Well, I don't doubt but that you can observe your own opinion on the matter."

"I intend to do so."

"Well, no cheek to me. There's some water for yer, and there's bread, and you ought to be thankful for it yer young warmint; and so good night. By the bye, I suppose you've given up all thoughts of breaking out just now, haven't you?"

"Perhaps I have."

"Oh, I thought you would; it's one thing to talk and another thing to do. I thought the inside of the jug would take all the bounce out of you."

"Did you?"

"Yes."

"I suppose you've been taken in before now?"

"Well, I have."

"Just so; and, as people don't usually grow viser as they get old, it's quite possible that you may get licked vonce more; that's all, my friend."

"Oh, you're still on the high rope, are yer? Well, we shall see how plump you'll come down. By the bye, if you should chance to find some tools and force the lock, and if you should be passing my seat—it's just at the end of the passage—and I don't sleep very sound, just say you're off, will you, I should like to say good night to you?"

"I won't forget," said Pipey. "Ah! you make light of my vords just now, but wait a bit. There has been better than you deceived before now."

"Well, good night. I won't stand chattering with you any longer." The jailer left the cell and turned the key.

"There you are, my boy," he said, as he passed the grating, "get out if you can."

"All right," said Pipey, "and as I pass you I von't forget to vake you up and say good night. *Mind, you invited me.*"

"I did."

"Then I will oblige you."

The man walked up the passage fully convinced that Pipey was a lunatic.

"I must wait," said the boy, "I must wait full three hours more. It vill not do to run the risk too early, and as a little sleep never hurts anybody, I'll get forty winks before I commence proceedings."

He stretched himself upon the hard board, and very soon fell into a deep slumber. Over three hours elapsed before he again opened his eyes.

During that time the jailer had thrice turned his steps to the cell, and saw that the boy was sleeping. "Ah!" he said, as he walked away the last time, "ah! he's sound enough now, and I'm glad of it, for I really thought the young 'un did mean to get out if he could; but, as he has thought the better of it, I shall just dose off myself. Heigho! I'm mortal tired."

He soon ensconced himself in his seat at the end of the long passage he had under his special care, and proved how little care he had on his mind by immediately falling into a deep slumber.

Pipey awoke with a start.

A moment's reflection called to his mind his position, and what he had to do.

"Fool that I vos, to sleep so soundly," he said; "the devil knows vot time it is now, or vether there's a chance of getting off."

All was still as death, and the boy set about his task with a palpitating heart.

With infinite pain he squeezed his hands through the darbies.

Free from them, he pulled off his large and cumbersome coat, and slipped off his right shoe. Removing a screw from the heel, that part came off and revealed a hollow between the two soles. From this Pipey drew forth a fine saw, and then replaced his shoe. The coat, however, he abandoned.

"That's done," he said, "and now for the lock."

He felt his way to the door, and then inserted the little instrument in that part of the woodwork which held the bolt of the lock.

Rapidly, and with but little noise, the steel moved through the rotten old wood, but decayed as the wood was it took some time to cut round the piece which held the bolt. It was a long and tedious job, and was rendered all the more painful from the fact of the intense silence which reigned around.

At other times there would have been some stir in the other cells, but now there was nothing moving, and all that could be heard was the deep breathing of the prisoners.

At times Pipey thought he was detected and that footsteps were approaching, and he stopped to listen, but convincing himself of his error he applied himself to work anew, and at length succeeded in bringing away the piece of wood.

The door opened.

He had gained the passage.

The most dangerous part of the adventure was, however, to be gone through.

Softly he stole along the passage and at length reached the spot where the jailer slept.

There was a small lamp burning close by, and the lad could see the man distinctly.

His promise flashed across his brain. Should he awaken him and run the risk of detection, or should he fly?

He glanced uneasily at the man; he was of great strength, and by his side stood a bludgeon, one blow from which would have prostrated a bullock.

The thought was madness and at once abandoned.

"But," said Pipey to himself, "if it vasn't for Liz, I'd keep my vord; howsomever, I daren't endanger her to please myself, so here's off."

He turned from the sleeper and proceeded a few steps further.

Horror! what was that?

Before the fugitive was a door of immense strength.

To try it was the work of an instant. It was locked on the opposite side.

"The devil take the door," cried Pipey, "its all over now."

He turned again, and on his eye falling on the jailer he saw that worthy sitting half stupified, and with mouth wide open gazing upon him intently.

Acting upon the impulse of the moment, Pipey sprang towards him and catching up the bludgeon, before the man could well recover his self-possession, gave him two tremendous blows over the head.

The fellow staggered but did not fall, and Pipey again renewed the attack.

This time, however, the blow fell upon the man's open hand, and his fingers closed over the weapon with a grip of iron.

There was an awful struggle for the possession of the formidable weapon, during which Pipey was dragged from one end of the passage to the other. Fortunately, the blows received by the jailer began to tell upon him, and after one desperate struggle his strength began to fail him. Pipey repossessed himself of the stick, and seeing what plight the jailer was in he threw it away, and commenced an attack with his hands.

Griping one another they wrestled furiously, and at length Pipey caught his adversary by the throat and forced him to the earth.

"Hillo, my covey," he said, " you've got it this time, aint you? Aint you sorry you voke? My eye, but you are getting black in the face."

Seeing that Mr. Pipey held his throat in a vice of iron, it would really have been very extraordinary had it been otherwise with the unhappy man.

Every moment the boy tightened his hold, and after feebly struggling for a few more moments the jailer, entirely overcome, sank half strangled and wholly senseless to the earth.

Now that he had won this victory Pipey was in quite as bad a plight as before.

The first who entered the passage would see what had taken place, and he would be secured once more, and in a more effectual manner, besides incurring a severe punishment from the officials for the manner in which he had treated their companion.

"Vot's to be done?" said Pipey, " vot, in the name of all that's unhappy, *is* to be done?"

"Ah, I have it—a splendid thought, and the only von by vich I can get off. Now, if luck stands my friend I'm clean gone, and no mistake about it.

Stooping over the prostrate jailer he raised him in his arms and dragged him into his own cell.

"There you are, my old chump, and now I'll trouble you for your togs."

With this Mr. Pipey coolly pulled off the coat and waistcoat of the man, and also his scratch wig, in which articles he arrayed himself in the greatest possible haste.

He then tore from the fellow's belt his bunch of keys and closed the door upon him, quite convinced that he would not disturb anyone for a full hour.

The boy then retraced his steps along the passage until he arrived at the bench whereon the jailer had so recently sat in profound and peaceful slumber.

His next move was to extinguish the lamp.

This done he felt secure.

"Now," he said, "if some one don't soon come

I'll make a row and force 'em to come, for I shan't stay here much longer."

He had not long to wait, for the lamp had scarce been put out one minute when a footstep attracted Pipey's attention.

A clock without chimed the hour of midnight.

"Hillo!" said Pipey, "here comes another jailer to relieve my friend in the cell. Now let's see vot's to be done."

He was right. Another moment and the key turned in the lock, and the door swung open.

"Hillo!" said a voice, "Hillo! Pasco, where's your light?"

No reply.

"Why, Pascoe, I say, where the devil have you put the light?"

Pipey here thought it advisable to snore very loud.

"Oh, that's it, is it!" said the voice. "Asleep again. Hang the fellow, he's never awake."

Groping about, the owner of the voice soon came to the bench whereon Pipey reclined.

"Hillo! Pascoe, are you going to wake up?"

"Hillo!" said Pipey, mimicing the voice of the jailer to a great nicety; "hillo! vot's up now?"

"What's up?' Why, I'm come on, and you can get home to bed as soon as you like : that's what's up. Are you wide enough awake to understand that?"

"Oh! I know vell enough," said Pipey, "and I'm precious glad you're come, for I'm tired of this. Heigh-ho!"

"Come, wake up, man, and look here—hand over the keys."

"Where are you?"

"Here," said the jailer, placing his hand on Pipey's arm. "Here."

"And here are the keys," said Pipey, handing them over.

"And now be off: but, I say, as you put out the lamp, just go and light it again. I shan't take the trouble."

Pipey could fain have said, "And neither shall I," but he suppressed this, and replied—

"Oh, that's fair enough; where's the thing gone?"

The other felt about, and finding the lamp, placed it in Pipey's hand.

"There you are, and don't be long gone."

"I shan't hurry back."

"Won't you, sulky; then you had better give me the lamp and I'll go myself."

"No," said Pipey, "I made it go out, and I'll re-light it; that's only fair. Here goes."

"All right."

And Mr. Pipey was gone.

*   *   *   *   *

Pipey threaded a variety of passages, and at length reached the lodge. Fortunately it was but dimly lighted, and still more fortunate was it that those within were more than half asleep.

"Who's that?"

"Oh, it's only me," said Pipey, keeping up the voice of the unfortunate man he had so recently handled so roughly.

"Oh, it's only you, is it," mumbled the chief constable; "well, I wish I was you, and could go

off to bed instead of having to see the night out in this lively hole."

"Well," said Pipey, "I've no vish to vait here longer than I can help, so just stir a stump and let me pass through the wicket."

"Here," cried the chief constable, shaking the porter, "here! let that fellow out, and don't be long about it."

"Come on," said the porter, rubbing his eyes, "come on, old fellow; ugh! how cold it is." Pipey passed through the lodge, and into the court-yard in front of the gates.

It was an awful moment. On he went and the gate was reached.

"It's just the night one would like best for going home to a good bed," said the jailer.

"Yes," said Pipey, "just the night."

"How the wind roars; quick, get out and let me go in from this infernal draft."

"All right," said Pipey, stepping through the wicket; "I'm not the sort o' feller to detain yer. Good night, old never-sweat; remember me in yer prayers."

The wicket was caught by a sharp gust of wind, and slammed home. Pipey heard the bolts shot, and the man return to the innermost recesses of the prison, as he turned on his heel and fled.

Pipey had effected a triumphant escape from Newgate.

CHAPTER XXIII.

THE DUCHESS OF GRASMOUNT HAS HER SUSPI-
CIONS AROUSED—LINEY GOSMONT, THE IDIOT
SERVING-MAN—THE TETE-A-TETE OVERHEARD.

THE reader can now quite understand the cause
of the Duke's terror on seeing the mysterious intruder in Grimer's office on the night of his
attempt to possess himself of the papers there
secured.

The history of that singular character, who, by
a gesture, exercised such a terrible control over
the actions of the Duke of Grasmount and
Yellow Maydock, still remains to be told. At
present the reader knows sufficient of him to
comprehend the terror exhibited at his presence
by both the individuals we have mentioned.

It is difficult to tell at which incident the Duke
was most disconcerted—the appearance of Grimer,
with such startling proofs of the follies of his
earlier days, or the advent of this awful
witness, apparently rising out of the very grave
to bring about his disgrace and ruin.

The combined effects of the movements of these
men in connection with himself was, however,
quite sufficient to entirely unseat his equanimity,
and to dispossess him of the slight peace he
enjoyed in the retirement of his life up to the
very morning of Grimer's visit to his dueal residence.

At first the Duke thought he would trust all to
Grimer, and let him arrange matters as he best
could ; but reflection taught him that the crafty
lawyer would work only to serve his own
ends, without consideration for anything beyond
serving them.

This led him to the contemplation and ultimate
attempt to rob the lawyer. The signal failure of
this attempt, and the incident relative to it, had
almost deprived Grasmount of reason. For days
after the fatal night he kept his own apartments,
and refused to see any living soul with the single
exception of his own body servant ; even the
Duchess was refused admission to his quarter of
the house.

Day after day, and night after night, the Duke
lay in extreme mental torture, not knowing where
to turn for either consolation or advice.

The Duchess was a proud, passionate, overbear-
ing woman : he dared not unburthen himself to
her ; such an act could not be contemplated for
an instant.

He mentally ran over the whole list of his
acquaintances, but he failed to remember one who
would keep his secret, much more assist him in
ridding himself of the darkness which was gathering over him.

Not one ! not one to bite through the net and
set the lion free ! not one friendly soul to stretch
forth a hand and tender its services in the time of
need.

Verily, even dukes are made to feel what it is
to be alone, friendless, and unhappy. How
miserably absurd is the idea that wealth can purchase everything. Peace of mind, the first great
requisite of life, is beyond its power.

Let those who are dissatisfied with a humble,
useful, and happy sphere remember this, and strive
to be content.

After long and anxious thought the unfortunate Duke remembered that there *was* just one
person, and one only, to whom he could entrust
his secret.

His wife's sister, Lady Sophia Besgrove, a
widow, who had long since withdrawn from
society, but who had always been a particular
favourite with the Duke, had an only daughter,
Olivia by name, who resided with her parent at
Cobham, in Surrey, and gave every promise of
being an ornament to her sex.

She was beautiful, accomplished, and possessed
of a sweet and amiable disposition. Society had
frequently attempted to drag her into the vortex
of its gaieties, and more than a hundred exclusive
drawing-rooms had thrown open their doors to
her in vain ; she was content to share the comparatively humble retirement of her widowed
mother, and never appeared so happy as when
administering to her wants and engaging in the
simple pursuits of a country life. Olivia Besgrove was sighed for in vain ; she had no taste for
the dissipation and wild gaieties of the Court,
and London was only graced with her presence
on the occasions of her aunt's *réunions*, and
only then when the invites of her aunt were
of too pressing a nature to be declined without
giving offence.

Such was Olivia, and in this being the Duke
saw the only person to whom he could confide
the secret which was gnawing out his heart.

"Yes," he said, "I will confide my sorrows
to this child ; she is young, but thoughtful
beyond her years, and her advice may prove
worth taking ; at all events she will be some
one to repose my secret with, and if I do
not relieve myself of it I shall go mad."

Without further deliberation, Grasmount
sought out Olivia at her mother's home, and,
fortunately, meeting her precisely at the moment
of her parent's absence, he engaged her attention
and poured out the sad tale he had so long kept
within his breast.

"You see, Olivia, how I am placed," he said,
after he had concluded his narration ; " a syllable of this breathed to your aunt would bring
ruin and destruction to both. Moreover, should
this girl make good her claims, I am beggared
and irrevocably disgraced in the eyes of the
world. I could not bear the misery of the
separation from the Duchess, and the sneers of
the world at my downfall would drive me to an
act of which I dread to think. I am proud
and unused to troubles, and this heavy one dis-
tracts me."

"My poor uncle," said Olivia, "your tale
grieves me more than I can express, and more
particularly because I am unable to render you
the assistance of which you stand so much in
need. You appear to be on the very brink of a
dark precipice, into which one false movement
might instantly plunge you ; and you say truly
when you assert that there is not one in all the
world to whom you could confide that which you
have just related to me. It would appear that a
whisper from this Maydock could crush you,

whilst the man Grimer, although dispossessed of the papers, may know where to find the child, and might act in concert with those hold them, and thus crush you."

"It is so."

"And this horrible being who snatched the papers from you at the lawyer's office, he, too, is to be dreaded."

"More than all the rest. Great Heaven! they told me he had perished on the scaffold. I heard the vagabonds of the street cry out his dying speech and confession, I had the testimony of the lawyer that he had died by the hand of the hangman, and that he had given him up those very papers in the condemned hole of Newgate. And now he suddenly appears, and, with the other, concerts my ruin. It would appear that all the world has set its face against me now, and I am slowly and surely being dragged on to the very depths of shame and degradation."

"It is horrible," said Olivia, "horrible! but some effort must be made—something must be done to avert the impending ruin and desolation."

"Yes. But what effort can be made? who is to make it? Where is the individual who can and will assist me? I look around and I find I am alone."

"All hope has not yet fled, dear uncle. I know of *one* who will assist you."

"I know of none."

"Nay, there's one who would fly to the end of the earth to earn a smile from me; and if I tell him that assisting you is favouring me, he will strive to move heaven and earth in your behalf."

"To whom do you refer?"

"To Lewis Arndale."

"What! the famous King's Counsel?"

"Yes; for many months we have been engaged, and love each other as devotedly as two souls possibly could do. You know his talent is admitted on all hands, and he is spoken of as the most rising man at the bar. But his wealth has not yet increased in proportion to his fame, and, as he is too poor to give me the home he desires for me, and too proud to take me until his means will place me in the position he would select for me, our engagement has been kept a secret from every one but my mother, and now I only tell it you to convince you that I have some one who will act for you, and to whom you may safely entrust your secret."

"Could I believe that he would be silent."

"I would stake my life upon his discretion."

"Oh, Olivia," said the Duke, "but you know not the world; even Lewis Arndale might be tempted in such a matter."

"Never!"

"But if there is more to be gained by speaking than by silence?"

"Lewis loves me: is not that sufficient?"

"It is the best security for his serving me," said the Duke, "and I think—yes, I think, Olivia, that I could trust him."

"Oh, believe it. I would stake my life on his honour."

"Then let him act for me, Olivia; but I must trust you to tell him all. I could not bear the humiliation of relating again the tale I have this day told you."

"Fear nothing," said the lady, "I will give Lewis his instructions, and if there is aught to be done he will do it."

"Thanks, dear Olivia," said the Duke; "I leave you with a far lighter heart than the one with which I came."

"I trust in Lewis," said Olivia, and the Duke took his departure.

From the day of the foregoing interview the absence of the Duke from home grew more frequent.

He was constantly out at night, and the private manner in which he went forth, and the late hours at which he returned, at last excited the suspicions of the Duchess. Gradually the conviction grew upon her that the Duke had some secret which he was endeavouring to conceal from her; and knowing full well that it must be one of singular magnitude, or of a complexion which she should not know that the Duke should take so much trouble to hide, she grew singularly restless, and attempted by every means in her power to ascertain the why and wherefore of the Duke's conduct.

To this end she questioned the servants, and engaged emissaries to watch and report to her, but it was useless. The Duke baffled all attempts at detection, and the most that the Duchess could ascertain was that her lord had suddenly become more attentive to her sister and niece, and that his visits to Cobham were more frequent than they had ever been before. He had also been tracked to the Middle Temple, and had one evening been seen in the neighbourhood of the Old Bailey, but beyond this nothing transpired to set at rest the doubts which possessed the Duchess.

We have said that the Duke's lady was of a jealous and haughty temperament, and it was this that tempted her to play the spy on her lord. She could not conceive that anything but a secret amour could occasion such mysterious acts on the part of the Duke. She knew full well that money matters did not embarrass him, she was convinced that he was not a gamester, and she felt assured that he had no political passions that would tempt him into any secret work likely to occasion such conduct as the Duke had exhibited.

There was a secret, of this the Duchess felt convinced; and with the jealousy and curiosity of a woman she determined to ferret it out and possess herself of it. To this end she bribed the Duke's servants, but they could tell her little beyond the hours at which their master left the house and returned again. Even his coachman was bought over, but he only knew that the Duke would sometimes leave the carriage in some open thoroughfare, and walk away and not return again for lengthened periods. He declared he had never seen him speak to a second party, and never remembered anyone being taken into the carriage on any occasion.

The only satisfaction to be adduced from this was the confirmation of the suspicions of the Duke's secret. Had he had no cause for secrecy he would have never left the carriage and walked to his destination.

There was a secret, and that secret was to become the property of the Duchess. We shall see to what the knowledge led.

In the household of the Duchess there was a man named Liney Gosmont; a half wit, who was retained in the service of the lady in consequence of an accident he met with whilst endeavouring to stop a runaway horse on which she was mounted. This Gosmont was the servant of the Duchess previous to her marriage, and it was on an occasion when she was riding a spirited horse with Liney in attendance that the accident occurred which half deprived the fellow of reason, and which entitled him to her gratitude and care.

The horse was a spirited and ill-broken animal, but the Duchess was a good horsewoman and rode the brute without fear, but a time was at hand which was to teach her a lesson of which she little dreamt.

One day she was riding her fiery steed on a road in the immediate neighbourhood of some quarries, when he suddenly took fright and bolted with her. All her efforts to check his mad career were unavailing, and on he dashed with her, away in the direction of the quarries.

The ground leading to the quarries was an open moor or down, slightly inclining to the brow of the rugged masses of stone, which sank almost perpendicularly on the opposite side, a depth of full one hundred feet.

In length the quarry was at least a quarter of a mile, and the greatest portion of this distance the brow of the hill of stone was protected by walls and fences of sufficient strength and height to form a protection for the cattle grazing on the moorland.

Liney, who galloped hard after his mistress, saw to his satisfaction that her horse was rushing at the very best protected part of the quarry, but there was one spot where rails and walls had given way with a large mass of rock, and to this spot the servant, instead of following his mistress, as most would have done, rode as hard as his horse could carry him.

He had not calculated without thought and judgment. The horse, finding his career stopped in the direction he had taken, swerved, and, describing a half-circle, rushed madly on to the open spot in the quarry. The forethought of Liney had placed him in the only position in which he could render his mistress the slightest service.

He saw the horse come dashing on, and, dismounting from his own beast, stood prepared to check its mad career.

On—on he came, and the faithful servant stood firm, at some fifty yards from the brink of the awful chasm.

On came the terrified horse, and when he was within a yard of the servant he swerved, and, had not Liney sprang, with the agility of an antelope, at the bridle, all would have been over.

Using the strength of a giant he wrenched the bit so fiercely that the horse was staggered. He then embraced the neck of the beast and so entirely encumbered its movements that it moved only with the greatest difficulty and allowed the lady to dismount with comparative safety.

But Liney could not shake himself from the horse at the right moment, and was in an instant under its hoofs.

The off hind leg struck the poor wretch in the back of the head, and there he laid, stunned and bleeding, whilst the affrighted animal bounded off to destruction in the depths of the quarry.

Assistance was soon procured for the wounded man, and all that care and money could do for him was done; but although he recovered health, he rose from his bed a half idiot, of that description known as the rogue-fool. All the good in his composition was gone—all the evil remained. There was a great deal of cunning, and more dogged obstinacy about him, and his general contour made him most objectionable to all with whom he came in contact, but the lady would not, or could not, see harm in him.

She only remembered that the gratification of her idle whim in riding a horse on which she had no business had occasioned the mischief she beheld, and this she thought sufficient warranty for her protecting and gratifying the peculiarities of the man.

She wished him to be a pensioner on her bounty, and would have provided a good home for him during his life, but he would hear of nothing of the kind. He would wear her livery, and be in constant attendance on her; and as he served her well, and never offered her any of the annoyance his presence occasioned others, she was content to gratify him, and allow him much of his own way.

It was a common saying of the servants, Liney was not half the fool he looked, and there was certainly some justification for this, inasmuch as many of the fellow's acts savoured of strong common sense and judgment. The fact was he had periodical returns of sanity, and, when thus, thought proper to act the part which he played without effort when the darker period of his days came upon him. He, like many others, found it convenient to be a fool, and so he kept up his character to his own satisfaction and the disgust of all with whom he was associated, except the Duchess, into whose good graces he wound himself more and more every day.

This man always dressed in a very long brown coat, fastened tight across the chest and about the waist, and terminating in a long skirt, which clung about him like the garment of a woman. This coat was trimmed with the banding and silver buttons of the family in which he served, and formed his distinctive peculiarity. He further wore a hat of absurd proportions, and enormous white gloves. Taken in all, his appearance was most absurd.

His face wore that expressionless stare peculiar to semi-idiocy, his walk was quick and spasmodic, and he always carried his head on his left shoulder, and his mouth slightly open, and his eyes almost shut.

Such was Liney Gosmont, the body servant of the Duchess of Grasmount, and this was the man employed by her Grace to watch the Duke.

Liney had himself divined what was passing in the mind of the Duchess concerning the conduct of the Duke, and he had proffered his services to watch the proceedings of the suspected party.

"I fear I cannot trust you, Liney," said the Duchess.

The idiot replied by a grin, in which intelligence and animal cunning were strangely mixed.

"How did you comprehend that the conduct of the Duke was at all suspicious?" demanded the Duchess.

"Watched," said Liney, with another grin, more intensely disgusting than the previous one.

"And what have you discovered?" asked the Duchess.

Here the face of the idiot grew dark and expressionless.

"You know nothing?"

The fellow shook his head.

"Then what has made you suspicious?"

"I know;" and here there was another grin.

"Then you will tell me, will you not?"

"No!" replied the fellow, with some asperity; "no;" when Liney knows *all*, Liney tell, but not till Liney knows *all*."

"You know where the Duke goes?"

"I know."

"You know his errand?"

An expressionless stare was the answer to this question.

"But you guess something?"

"He! he! he!"

"You know the persons whom the Duke meets?"

"I know."

"Their names?"

"I know."

"Give me their names, I say."

"I won't! I know, I know, I know, but not *all*. I'll tell all or nothing. He! he! he!—Liney knows!"

"Oh!" cried the Duchess, "this is horrible. The humiliation—the disgrace of being placed in this position. But, my doubts once satisfied, I will have a great revenge for this torture. Liney!"

"Hey!"

"Keep your eye upon the Duke."

"Yes, yes," drawled the idiot.

"Let nothing escape you."

"No, no."

"And, above all, report what you hear to me, but to no other person. Do you comprehend?"

"I know."

"You will report to me everything that may occur on the instant; on the instant, remember."

Liney shook his head.

"Liney," he said, "only tell when he knows *all*. Liney not make fool of himself. Oh, Liney's cunning, Liney's clever, Liney knows; he! he!—Liney knows!"

"It is useless to endeavour to persuade him," said the Duchess; "he does not, or will not, comprehend. I must e'en wait his time. Heaven and earth! waiting on an idiot for confirmation of my husband's falsity!"

*   *   *   *   *

On the day on which the foregoing conversation between the Duchess of Grasmount and her servant took place the latter might have been seen journeying to Cobham on horseback.

His visits to that quarter had been frequent of late, and, singular enough, he always followed the Duke there, but never by the same path, nor within an hour of the time of the Duke's journey. Liney always followed him, and, so cleverly was the thing managed, that Grasmount never had the slightest idea that a spy was at his heels, although that spy happened to be a conspicuous idiot.

On the day of which we are now writing, however, the Duke had not made the journey, and Liney was going alone.

What was the occasion of this?

On the occasion of the last visit of the Duke, Liney had overheard Olivia say to him—

"Lewis will be here on Thursday, and, as Lady Besgrove will go to London, I shall have an opportunity of relating the whole tale to him, and of obtaining his advice thereon; so be with me on Friday, that you may know his opinion."

"I will, and Heaven grant that it will be favourable to me, although I confess I do not see how it can be so."

"Something to hear," said the idiot, "something to hear. Ah, Liney knows, and Liney will hear!"

Liney was, then, going to Cobham to endeavour to hear the promised secret, for he had no doubt that the tale referred to by Olivia was the *secret* of which he wished to become possessed.

So away he rode to the little Surrey village, to play the spy and endeavour to gain a knowledge of what passed between the lovers.

In time the village was reached, and the idiot sought the house wherein Olivia dwelt.

It was then a modern mansion, and was surrounded by a small park easily accessible from the road. Near the house was a garden and shrubbery, which even at that early season of the year presented a most attractive appearance from the number and variety of the well-kept evergreens, which were formed into little avenues, giving the place an air of extent which it did not in reality possess.

The gardens were arranged with an eye to seclusion, and it was easily comprehended at a glance that the inhabitants of the place were more pleased with its simple seclusion than with the glare and bustle of the more artificial world.

Liney placed his horse at bait in the village, and then strolled away in the direction of the house to which he was bound.

Avoiding notice as much as possible, he contrived to enter the park unobserved, and once within the precincts of the house he puzzled his head as to how he was to enter its doors and obtain the information he required.

It was to be done and it must be done; this he knew and felt, and, with a disregard of danger which a more sensible man would not have felt, he determined, at all risks, to stand at nothing in order to gratify himself and serve the only being he cared for on earth.

Pondering on the work on hand he stole into the garden, and, traversing its secluded walks, neared the house.

He had not been long engaged thus when the sound of voices arrested him.

He was behind some large shrubs, glancing at the windows of the house which opened into the garden, when the sound of a woman's voice fell upon his ear.

The shrubs were planted in a semicircle, and enclosed a rather open space at the meeting of two paths. In this spot, and under the shade of a large tree, was a garden-seat, on which he found reclining, and in deep converse, a man and woman.

A glance assured him that the woman was Olivia.

He readily guessed that the other was the Lewis he had heard mentioned as the being in whom the secret was to be reposed.

Grinning at his good fortune in dropping thus opportunely and with so little trouble on the very beings he sought, he prepared to listen.

He heard the man say,

"You will find it cold here, Olivia; had you not better return to the house?"

"No, Lewis," the girl replied, "not yet; I have brought you here in order that we might not be interrupted or overheard, for I have something to say to you which must be heard by no other soul."

"Indeed, Olivia?"

"Yes, Lewis; it is a secret which concerns my uncle, the Duke of Grasmount, so nearly that his whole property and his honour entirely depends upon its being kept most religiously: Lewis, he he is in trouble and in danger. He would ask your assistance : will you give it him?"

"Do you ask it?"

"Yes, Lewis, I ask it; and in assisting him you serve me, for I am deeply concerned for him."

"You have but to speak to be obliged."

"I knew it; but, Lewis, before I tell this secret, swear to me never to reveal it."

"I swear it, Olivia, by thy dear self. If ever I reveal a syllable of what you will say to me, let me be punished with the withdrawal of your favour : and that, Heaven knows, is the worst punishment man could conceive for me."

"It is well, Lewis; and now I will relate to thee this awful tale. Listen, and, when you have heard it, for my sake use your best energies to save him who is so nearly concerned."

The fair girl then related, almost in the same words as the Duke had used in telling it her, the secret of his early life and the more recent incidents which threatened to bring about so shocking an anti-climax.

The young lawyer listened with wrapt attention to every syllable, and when the girl had concluded he fell into a deep reverie, from which he did not arouse for many minutes.

At length he said:

"This is a bad case, Olivia, for it is one which cannot be approached by fair means, or handled with the instruments ordinarily used in my profession. It is a war of trickery and cunning, brute force, and underhand bribery. These men, Grimer and Maydock, and that other mysterious being described by your uncle as the priest who performed the ceremony of marriage, must either be bought over or outwitted; the girl must be sent far away, and every trace of the past blotted out. Until this is done your uncle is in extreme peril."

"But you will save him?"

"It is a case, Olivia, which pleases me not, for I am not one who has the slightest inclination for such practice; and believing your uncle to be justly punished for his heartless conduct in the past, I have still less taste for the work; but for you I would do my utmost in this or any other case in which you would enlist my services. I will endeavour to ward off the impending dangers."

"Thanks! thanks!"

"But do not rely too implicitly on me. I will not deceive you by holding out false hopes. The case is a desperate one, and one false step may wreck all the Duke's hopes—one ill-advised whisper may change the aspect of the whole case, and make the affair public. Be cautious, and speak to no one on the subject. The rest leave to me."

"I will, for I know I could not trust the task in better hands. Now let us return."

They walked slowly to the house, the young lawyer weighing the *pros* and *cons* of the case, and placing them vividly before Olivia, and she silent and dejected, for she had anticipated that Lewis would have held out some hope by which she could lighten the misery of her ducal relative.

But the unseen witness, idiot as he was, bore away such facts with him as was to place beyond the power of this most astute lawyer the chance of doing the Duke a single service.

CHAPTER XXIV.

REVEALS HOW PIPEY KEPT HIS APPOINTMENT, AND TRACES THE FURTHER VICISSITUDES OF FAIR LIZ.

IT may readily be imagined that Pipey loitered not on his mission to the Minories. In the hat, coat, and scratch wig of Pascoe, the jailer, he certainly cut a peculiar figure, and, used as he was to adopting a costume which, in the ordinary routine of things, would have been worn by a man of thrice his proportions, he certainly felt embarrassed in the garments he had now adopted, for they were even larger than any in which he had previously appeared in public.

"I never see sich togs," said Pipey, as he moved rapidly along and endeavoured to keep the skirts of his coat out of the mud. "It's awful, to be sure. I should like to know vy the feller could'nt vear things as vould fit a gemman of ordinary proportions. But I s'pose I shall get used to 'em. If I don't grow to fit them, they'll grow to fit me, and so ve shall accommodate vun another somehow. My eye, vot a row there vill be in College (he called Newgate the College) ven they find me missin'. I shouldn't be surprised if they didn't send out anxious inquiries arter me to-morrow, and give 'em earnest invites for me to return again, but I shall fight shy this time."

These were a few of the remarks murmured by Mr. Pipey as he strode along towards the east, dodging through the lanes and alleys, and ever and anon hiding from the observation of some late passer.

The clocks were chiming the three-quarters past midnight as he sped along Cheapside in the shadow of the houses.

He had scarcely got half way down this thoroughfare, when a man, habited in the usual costume adopted by the guardians of the night, came rushing out of one of the houses, and tumbled against him.

"Hillo!" cried the man.

"Hillo!" said Pipey.

"Why, I ought to know that wig and coat. Is it Pascoe?"

"It's that same indiwiddle," said Pipey, at once assuming the voice of his late jailer. "Vot's up?"

"Here, collar this."

The watchman tendered a small bag.

"Vot is it?"

"Gold—mizzle with it! Some cracksmen have entered the house here, and got nabbed by a dozen of us Charleys. Von of the coves is a tip-top good 'un, and handed over this bit o' swag on the quiet. He must take his hook; d'ye understand?"

"Oh, I'm up to a thing or two of that sort," said Pipey.

"Hush! here they come. You stick to me, and I'll take charge of my man—there must be two. To quash the suspicions of the others we'll share by and by. I ain't got no pockets, so you stand by the swag."

"I'll stick to it," said Pipey, and he meant to do so.

The door of the house was now thrown open, and some dozen of the watch, with three prisoners, stepped out into the street.

The watchman who had just mistaken Pipey for Pascoe, the jailer, at once stalked up to a tall man, habited in black, who was being dragged along by three of the constables.

"Here," said the well-bribed officer, "I'll handle this feller; my mate, Pascoe, will lend me a hand."

Pipey stepped up to the prisoner, and pretended to be busy in assisting the watchman in securing the burglar.

The others went off, and the trio were left alone.

"Turn into one of the back streets," said the watchman to Pipey.

Pipey did so.

"Now," he continued, "you two be off, and make good use of your legs before I spring the rattle."

"All right," said Pipey, "I twig the move; you're to be knocked over, and I'm off on the hunt. You're an old dodger, you are."

"You never mind, Pascoe; do what I tell you, and then meet me afore daylight, and stump up. On second thoughts, now they're gone, I'll take the purse."

"On second thoughts," said Pipey, smashing the hat over the eyes of the watchman, "I'll see you hanged first! Cut, long 'un!" he continued to the burglar; "go it for your life!"

The burglar required no second invite, and set off as fast as his legs could carry him, closely followed by Pipey, who, however, had some difficulty in keeping up with him, in consequence of the inconvenience occasioned by his borrowed clothes.

The watchman was singularly puzzled to account for the peculiar conduct of the supposed jailer, and therefore failed to give the alarm as quickly as he might have done, but at last he became convinced that he had been duped, and that Pascoe and the gentleman to whom he had entrusted his purse were two distinct individuals.

"Done!" cried the fellow; "done! and by my own foolery. Curse it!—it serves me right."

In a fit of frenzy the Charley commenced yelling and springing his rattle as if his life depended on the amount of din he could create.

"Help! help!" he cried; "help! to the rescue! —to the rescue!"

Three of the watchmen in charge of the burglars who had been secured, returned.

"What's the matter?" they cried, in a breath.

"Matter, why the prisoner has made a bloodthirsty attack on me, and has bolted."

"Where's your mate?"

"Gone after him."

"More fool he," cried one of the two who had returned. "He'll get a warm welcome in the Minories, if he ventures down there at this hour."

"After them!—after them! shouted the excited Charley.

"After them yourself, and be hanged to you!" cried the others; "those who lose may seek. We don't go into the Minories to-night."

They turned on their heel, and retraced their steps, and the disappointed Charley, seeing that his prisoner and purse were hopelessly gone, bundled after them, murmuring all manner of threats against the human family generally, and burglars in particular.

Pipey hurried on, and the faster he ran the more the individual he followed attempted to increase the distance between them.

At length Pipey, making a great effort, came up to the shoulder of the burglar, and shouted with his remaining breath—

"I say, stop it. I ain't a Charley. It's all square."

"What are you, then?" said the burglar, stopping suddenly, and looking at Pipey.

"Oh! I'm one of the right sort. You ought to be able to twig that vith half a eye."

They came to a spot where a lamp swung across the street, and stopped and viewed one another.

"Hillo!" said Pipey, "I've had the pleasure of seeing you afore. You're the Black Captain, and I've met yer at Mother Vistler's."

"Right," said the man, "I am the Black Captain."

"Then vot ever made you try on crib cracking. I thought you vos on the road."

"I am; but I do a little at either work when the occasion serves, all comes alike to me."

"Oh, you're von of the clever kind, I s'pose: you can come anythink, from the swallering the top brick o' the chimney down to preaching a charity sermon. There's lots like you about, but, like you, they comes to grief occasionally ven they tries on too much."

"Well," said the Black Captain, "you appear

to have a great amount of impertinence; my gang are not in the habit of speaking to me in the strain you use."

"My good fellow," said the outrageously impertinent Pipey, "its no odds to me vot your gang does, I ain't got much respect for persons, and I'd as lieve talk to you as anybody else I knows on, so make no mistake. It ain't your blood-stained hands nor your bloodless face as would make any impression on me, for ven I vos born my mother purchased a cast iron nerve, vich she made me swaller in some pap, and its done me good service ever since."

"Well," said the Captain, "it is not very often I take a fancy to individuals of any kind, but I must confess to a sudden and strong partiality to you. I like those who do not shun me. That my bloodless face, as you call it, should excite fear on the road is all well and good, but that it should also drive away every one nearly associated with me in terror is what I do not desire."

"I should think not," said Pipey.

"No, it is awful to be shunned by all mankind. I have known what it is to be alienated from every human being for years and years. All my fellow creatures have shunned me, and in return I have repaid them with bitter hatred."

"Oh, you look quite capable," said Pipey. Devil doubt you, I don't!"

"But this is idle talk; here we are at Whistler's: shall we enter?"

"You may, Captain," said Pipey, "but I've other fish in the pan?"

"Very good. When shall I see you again."

"I don't quite know. The fact is, I've only been out of Newgate a bare half hour, and as they may think I ought not to have gone without the leave of the judge, I shall have to make myself awfully scarce for a while. Yes, it vill take old Grimer all his time to pull me through this mess!"

"Grimer!"

"Yes, Grimer; do you know him?"

"Yes."

"Well, he'll have to get me out of this pickle, and no von else."

"Why should he?"

"Because he's got me specially in hand. I'm on his vork, and he has to look arter me in a proper manner."

"Humph! If you put your faith in lawyers you are very likely to get served out."

"P'raps," said Pipey; "but I aint much afraid."

"Very well. Good night!"

"Good night!" said Pipey, as the door of Mother Whistler's house closed upon the Black Captain; "good night, and good riddance to such company. And now for Liz!"

Leaving Pipey for a while, we will seek out the ady who engrossed his thoughts.

Liz passed the next day after Pipey's nocturnal visit in a perfect agony of excitement. The hours which must intervene between then and the time of his return appeared an age, and it was with anxious heart she counted them as they passed, one by one, and the gap of time lessened.

She feared, and not without reason, that the attempted rescue might be frustrated in a hundred ways; and her principal fear was that Maydock would remove her, and destroy all trace of her whereabouts before Pipey could possibly come.

It was, therefore, with no small degree of satisfaction that the day passed over without any occurrence calculated to excite her fears.

At nightfall on the night of the burglary she listened to the departure of Maydock from the house, and received the old crone who had charge of her.

"I shall stay here all night," said the old woman; "all night. Maydock has gone out, and nothing must occur in his absence. No, no, he shan't say that I let you slip through my fingers; he shan't say that I, in my old age, have lost any of the cunning of my younger days. No, no, I will watch you, my young lady. No doing me. No, no; no, no. I'm not to be done."

The presence of this ancient and obnoxious woman was far from pleasant to the young girl, but she could tolerate it, because it assured her of the absence of one she dreaded far more, and so she retired to rest with more satisfaction than she had felt since her introduction to that wretched place.

The night passed, and the eventful day dawned.

It was with difficulty Liz could suppress the feelings that agitated her.

If anything should happen now, she was lost.

Every sound made her start; every footfall sent a thrill through her frame.

She could not eat or drink, and she passed the hours away by pacing up and down her narrow chamber, praying for night and the return of Pipey.

If he should fail! But he would not fail. He had promised sincerely; yes, she would trust him; he would be sure to return.

Little did Liz dream of where her champion was, and what had befallen him. Had she had an idea of his position, the doubts as to the possibility of his coming would have been considerably increased; but being, happily, unconscious of all that had passed, the poor girl passed the day between hope and fear. Longing for, and yet dreading, the approaching darkness, hours thus passed away, and Maydock did not return. His absence was to her a mystery, more particularly so as the old hag had anticipated that he would return early in the morning.

What had befallen him they could not imagine.

The fact was that Maydock, when overtaken by daylight, had progressed no further in his homeward journey than Westminster, and, not knowing what information had preceded his advent in town, and not caring to risk anything, ensconced himself in the safe quarters of the "Smutty Quaker," preferring to wait there until night to running the risk of walking through the streets of London in the broad daylight.

At dusk, however, he set forth once more, and before eight o'clock arrived at his home.

He was met by the old hag who looked after his den for him.

"Well," he said, surlily, "what has happened, anything?"

"Nothing. What has kept you so long?"

FAIR LIZ.

"Bad luck."

"What! has the game been a failure?"

"Yes."

"And nothing come of it?"

"Nothing but dangers."

"What do you mean?"

"I mean that Hammer and the boy are taken, that no swag was secured, and that the will—"

"Well, the will—you have that?"

"No."

"Wasn't it there?"

"Yes."

"Well, couldn't you get at it?"

"Yes."

"And didn't?"

"I did."

"Go on."

"Well, it was stolen from me on the road home."

"What! Maydock allow himself to be robbed? Yellow Maydock let a prig empty his pockets? You were drunk!"

"You mistake; I was robbed on the highway."

"By whom?"

"By one against whom I should have struggled in vain. A phantom!"

"Pooh: you're either drunk or mad now; what do you mean by talking of phantoms to me?"

"I tell you, you old fool, I was met by a phantom, a thing in human form but in reality a spirit."

"I tell you, Maydock, you are mad or you would not talk of spirits and such like trash. I never saw you thus before."

"Because I was never before placed in a similar position; sneer at me as you may, I repeat my path was crossed by a being who was hanged at Newgate years and years ago. It was the person who married the Duke and the young girl he thought he was ruining, and who afterwards died through my instrumentality. I can see the eyes of the phantom now—glaring down at me out of that cold, expressionless face. I can hear its hollow voice demanding the will from me. I can even feel its icy touch. Ugh! it thrills through me now."

The old woman was becoming convinced that something serious had happened to Maydock.

His hand shook, and he appeared to be thoroughly unnerved.

"I don't know what ails you," cried the old woman, "but I can see it is something unusual; have some brandy."

"No," cried Maydock, "I have drunk enough brandy to day. I will have no more. It neither makes me drunk or drowns thought. It will neither nerve nor warm me. I will have no more of it."

"Then, what will you do?"

"I will see the girl: she is all left me now, and if I lose her I am worse off than ever I was, for I always had some hold on the Duke till this day."

"What do you want of her now?"

"I want to tell her what she is to expect."

"Well, you know where to join her. I'll stay here till you are sick of talking to her. For my part I hate the sight of her, with her puny face and long hair; she sickens me, and I would'nt seek her presence without occasion, I can tell you."

"You can do as you like," said Maydock, as he picked up a light and stalked up stairs."

The sound of his footstep was well known to the poor trembling girl, and as she heard the approach of the being she so dreaded, a shudder passed through her frame.

"He comes," she cried, "it may be to drag me from here. If that should be the case I am lost."

Maydock opened the door of the attic and entered. She shuddered and fell back on her couch almost stupified.

Maydock gazed at Liz fixedly.

She returned the stare.

There was a wild and terrible passion, which it would be folly to call love, but which was as much akin to it as the brutal nature of the man would admit of, exhibited on his part, and a fear and indefinite suspicion on hers.

He looked at her long and fixedly, and she, as if fascinated by his stare, allowed her gentle eyes to rest upon his repulsive face.

At length he spoke:

"You have been here long enough to know me," he said slowly, and with marked emphasis, " and I have seen you often enough to know you. I will speak the truth: I brought you here from sordid motives, and would have married you from similar promptings."

The girl shuddered.

"But," he continued, "that motive has long been merged in another. What I would have then done for gain I would now do from love. Yes, Liz, I love you!"

"Heaven save me!" muttered the poor, terrified girl.

"Do you love me?" continued the ruffian, without regarding the involuntary ejaculation which had escaped the poor prisoner.

"Do you love me?" he repeated.

Liz answered not.

"Am I to repeat the question?" he said; "do you love me?"

"No," said Liz, in a low voice, "no, I do not love you."

"I knew it," said Maydock, "I have seen it. In fact, I should have been an idiot not to have noticed it. Yes, I have seen you shudder at my approach; I have seen your eye speak the terror of your soul when I have spoken to you; I know you hate and fear me, but yet I asked the question."

"Oh, why?" cried Liz.

"Because," continued Maydock, "because you will have to marry me, and I thought it right to put the question in the usual form."

"But you would not marry one who—"

"Detests me, you would say. Speak on."

"Who—fears you?"

"Yes."

"You would not force me to the altar when I tell you that it would be my death?"

"Yes."

"You would force me there?"

"No."

"Bless you for that."

"Understand me," said Maydock, " I would not force you to an altar, for that would be an act of madness, but I would force you to marry me, nevertheless. Bah! no altar for me; a friend of mine—a poor, degraded priest—will come to me and perform the ceremony."

Liz turned as pale as death, and regarded Maydock with a look of horror.

"You would not do so foul a deed," she cried.

"I would marry you."

"But I will never consent to be your wife."

"You will."

"Never!"

"I repeat, you will."

"And I repeat, upon my soul, never! You may use threats and blows if you will, but you will not move me. You may starve me, but I will not consent. You may kill me, but you can never force me to an act against which my soul revolts!"

There was a dignity in her look, a queen-like command in her action which quite staggered the ruffian. The words were literally thrown at him, and with an intensity of expression which one who had seen her cower before him a few moments before would have deemed her incapable of using.

"Indeed!" said Maydock, after an effort to recover his composure, "indeed! but we shall see. You know not the effect of blows, and you have not suffered the pangs of hunger. They have a wonderful effect in bringing down a haughty spirit: and if you insist on maintaining yours I shall try them on you. Mark me, I am not a man to be trifled with. I am well known as one who, having set his mind on a task, never deserted it until it was accomplished; and I tell you I have set my mind on marrying you, and I will accomplish the fact."

"I would rather die."

"Oh, you can die after the ceremony; but you will live until then. But this is somewhat foreign to the matter which brought me here. I came not to talk of love, but to tell you that at daybreak you are to leave here. The place is too hot for us, and I am off out of it. Remember, at daybreak we start."

"I will never leave this place," cried Liz, "but to regain my freedom. I will go nowhere with you."

"You will go where I think proper."

"I will not leave this house in your company."

"You will."

"Never!"

"I say you will; and now that you know my determination you had better say no more on the subject. Mind, no attempts at escape; no shrieking, no alarming the neighbourhood. On the first sound of your voice I will drag you to a place where you may shriek yourself hoarse before the sound of your voice could reach a human being—I mean the cellars. There are several here, and they are deep enough to be effectual preventatives against opposition; and, moreover, they are well stocked with rats. If you care about them you can shriek for assistance; but take my advice and remain quiet—you would struggle against me in vain. I mean you no harm, but if you will resist you will find in me a fiend who would not hesitate to perform acts of which you could never dream. Mark this. I leave you to your reflections. Good night! Remember. at daybreak!"

Liz said nothing in reply to these words.

She saw that she was really with no ordinary ruffian, and the defiance which rose to her lips died away unuttered.

The poor girl was completely crushed.

"Oh," she said, "if he fails to come what a fate is in store for me."

She was alone once more, and her thoughts wandered from her brutal persecutor to Pipey.

"He will not come," she cried, "oh, he will never come. He is but a boy, and his words were idle promises of which he has not since thought. He will not come, and I shall be a victim to this awful man."

She paced the room wildly—she beat her bosom as if to keep down the emotions which overpowered her. She clasped her hands over her distracted brain and gave vent to her despair.

And the moments passed away fleetly enough with the happy and the gay, but how slowly to that poor girl.

The conflict of emotions which distracted her were sufficient to prostrate a far stronger being, and it was not to be wondered at that she sank under them and became for a while dead to all that was passing about her. She fell on her bed, and there lay, to all appearance lifeless, and beyond human aid.

How long she continued in this state she knew not, but in all probability some hours elapsed before she was again conscious.

On opening her eyes they fell on the grim visage of Maydock's housekeeper as she bent over her, engaged in bathing her temples with water and applying strong salts to her nose.

"At last," said the old crone, "at last! Well your tantrums get worse than ever. Before I'd be bothered with such a wench I'd cut my arm off. Faugh! I can't think what Maydock is dreaming off; he used not to do his work in this manner."

"Oh," cried Liz, "Maydock—I remember—where is he?"

"Where is he? Asleep, sound enough to be sleeping the sleep of death. I tried to rouse him when I heard you fall on the bed, but it was useless. Curse him, I don't think he can have slept for a month."

"Oh," thought Liz, "if Pipey would but come now."

"Are you recovered?" asked the old woman, after a pause.

"Yes," replied Liz, "quite recovered, I thank you."

"Oh, you have grace enough to thank me, have you? That's more than I gave you credit for; but it is idle to stand chattering here any longer: you have already kept me out of bed long enough."

"I am sorry," said Liz.

"Yes, I dare say you are, but I wouldn't give much for such sorrow. There, you'll do now."

She moved away.

"Good night," said Liz.

"Oh, good night. It's long past midnight, and as you are to go from here by daylight I should advise you to get some sleep."

"Do you know where they are about to take me," asked Liz, as her mind once more filled with the horrors aroused in her late interview with

Maydock. "Oh do you know where they would drag me?"

"No," said the old woman, "and if I did I would not say."

"Oh," said Liz, falling on her knees before the old hag, "there must be something of the woman left in you, and you must feel for one so young and lonely being thrust into so terrible a position. Let me entreat you, let me implore you—to look kindly on me and assist me to escape from this man's power."

"Not if you tempted me with gold enough to purchase an empire. I am entrusted with the care of you, and to that trust I will be true."

"You must have had children of your own," cried Liz, "oh, think on them, and tell me what you would do if they were placed as I am."

"My children," cried the old woman, "Oh, it is there you touch me, but the chord you strike only arouses the tiger within me. My children! hark ye, one of them fell a victim to the seducer, and was hung at Newgate for the murder of her child: a crime of which she was as innocent as myself; the other—my darling boy—they strung up for taking the vengeance to which he was entitled on the man who had destroyed his sister. When I think of this I am reminded of the vow of vengeance I swore against the whole human race and the hatred of mankind which the loss of my idolised children awoke in my bosom. Appeal not to me for aid in the name of my darlings, for it is useless trouble."

The old hag tottered away, and Liz attempted not to detain her: she saw that to hope for aid from that source was idle.

She was alone now, and the oil lamp was flickering feebly previous to going out, and threw great shadows over the old attic. The cold blast whistled through the chinks of the doors and came rushing in through the old windows.

Liz rose slowly: she was giddy and faint, and with difficulty reached the window.

"It grows late," she cried, piteously: "a few short hours and I am gone from here. He comes not—oh, he will not come."

She gazed out of the casement, and her eye fell upon the snow clad houses in the neighbourhood, and the deserted lane immediately under her.

"No sign of him—no sign of him; it is useless to hope."

Again she strained her eyes into the darkness and again she withdrew them.

"He will not come, and I am lost. Yes," she continued, "lost. My head swims round, my eyes will not keep open any longer; I must sleep, sleep! Oh God! if it so pleases Thee, let me not wake again."

Without removing her garments she threw herself on her hard couch and sank into a profound slumber.

Was she dreaming?

Could that voice be the creation of her fancy?

Was she really listening to the song? "Hush, let me hear."

She sat up in her bed and strained her ear. It was a reality; she was not dreaming. Distinctly from under her window came the strain:—

"I'm here, like a bird, I've risked life for thee;
  I'm here, in the cold, but vot's that to me?
  Oh, darbies and locks, all opened d'ye see,
  As I cracked the stone-jug with a fiddle-de-de,
  And got out o' Newgate without the pass-key.
      Fiddle-de-de—fiddle-de-de—
        Oh, a cracksman is he
  Who got out o' Newgate without the pass-key."

Mr. Pipey was evidently trying to extemporise a ballad in Maydock's back garden.

Liz sprang to her feet; the sound of that voice was indeed familiar to her, and in a second she opened the window and gazed down on the boy.

"Hillo!" said Pipey; "all square?"

"Yes," cried Liz.

"Vell, then, see me mount the shoot."

With the greatest agility Pipey caught the water-shoot in his hands and sprang from the ground.

In a few seconds he had mounted to a level with the window, and, catching the sill in the grasp of his right hand, he threw himself dexterously into the attic.

"Here ve are," said Pipey; "and how is ve?"

"Oh! thank Heaven you are come! I thought you had abandoned the task."

"Did yer?" said Pipey; "vell, now, that vosn't kind, considering the promise I made."

"True," said Liz; "but you know not the doubts and fears I have undergone since I last saw you, and you know not the agony I have endured in this prison."

"Oh," said Pipey, "but vot vos that to vot I've endured in mine."

"What do you mean?" asked Liz.

"Vot does I mean," said Pipey, "vy, I means that I've come here direct from Newgate."

"You have been imprisoned, then?"

"Vell, slightly; nothin' to mention, p'raps, but slightly."

"And they have released you?"

"Oh, no, they haven't, bless your innocence; you don't think to give 'em so much trouble, do you? No, Pipey isn't von of that sort; I released myself."

"Escaped from Newgate?"

"Yes, I told you Newgate shouldn't prevent me from coming here to-night; but then I hadn't the remotest idea that Newgate vould make the attempt, but it turned out that it did, and I had to keep my vord against long odds—but the game vill do served up cold. Now answer me a few questions—are you ready to cut it?"

"Oh, can you ask?"

"Vell, it vos a soft question."

"Hush! you speak too loudly; you will disturb them."

"Right. Vere's Maydock?"

"Below."

"And the old 'oman?"

"In the adjoining attic."

"Quiet's the vord, then. Now, are you ready?"

"Yes."

"Come on then."

"How am I to descend?"

"Whew! *I never thought of that.* Devil take

it! I only remembered my own talent at vater-shoot climbing."

"Lost! lost!"

"Oh, come I say," cried Pipey, "none o' that, it's rather too good. The cove as got out o' Newgate can get out o' this crib. I might have forgot that you vern't down to the vater-shoot business, but I'm not the von to sell you vithout a go in for a rescue. I've come to take yer off, and I'll do it in the face of fifty Maydocks. If I don't, kick me, that's all. Stay, is there anything the matter vith my 'ed; I do feel so precious queer and tight in the upper story."

"You have a wig on," said Liz, laughing, despite her fears.

"A vig!" said Pipey, pulling it off, "a vig! Vell, I'm blest if I could make it out. It's hurt me awful, but I'll pocket the affront for the sake of the poor unfortunate jailer."

With this he stuffed the wig into the capacious pocket of the jailer's coat. "There," said Pipey, "stop there. Vell that is a relief. Now, Liz, wrap yerself up and foller me, quiet as a mouse. Come on."

"The door—the door is locked," cried Liz.

"You don't say so," said Pipey, in pretended alarm. Dear me! Then ve shall have to perform the sorrowful dooty of spiling the Yaller Boy's lock."

He looked round the room, and picked up the fork given Liz to eat her meals with.

"My eyes," said Pipey, "vot a awful flat the yaller von must be to leave sich things as these about. Vy, he can't be right in his 'ed."

Mister Pipey seized the instrument which had come so opportunely to hand, and applied it to the wards of the lock.

"I could a' done it vith a nail," said Pipey, "but this is a beautiful tool."

A very little manœuvring forced the bolt of the lock back, and Pipey, with a mock grace, was showing Liz the way out, when an apparition appeared before him which put an end to his gaiety for a while.

Before them stood the old housekeeper, glaring at them with intense malignity and hatred.

Liz fell back in a fit of terror, but Pipey, with that presence of mind which always distinguished him in time of danger, sprang forward, and, seizing the old hag by the throat, pressed her to the wall, and rendered her speechless.

"I don't like throttling old vomen," said Pipey, "but I aint got no choice; besides, I aint possessed of no great amount of affection for you."

The hag struggled with all her power, but the strong hand of the youth was about her throat, and her senses left her as his grasp tightened.

"Do not hurt her," cried Liz, as she regained confidence and presence of mind.

"Hurt her," said Pipey, "I vouldn't hurt her for the vorld, only there's no help for giving her jist a slight squeeze."

"Oh, do not—do not grasp her throat thus. Her life may be lost."

"Yes, and so may your liberty."

"Think not of that, but let her go. I cannot bear to see her served thus."

"Don't look, then."

Pipey still tightened his grasp, and the old woman became black in the face.

"It's all right; she'll do now," said Pipey. "See here, how quiet she is."

He let go his hold, and the woman dropped back. Her head struck against the door, and she moved not.

"That's done in the proper style," said Mr. Pipey, viewing his handiwork with marked approval; "now Liz, down stairs."

Noiselessly they descended and gained the passage. In the room at the foot of the stairs lay Maydock.

The sound of the footsteps aroused him.

"Is that you Nan?"

"Yes," said Pipey.

"Is it time."

"Time! why it's not one o'clock yet," said Pipey.

"All right, call me at daylight, not before: I'm awfully tired: how's the girl?"

"Quiet."

"That's all right; call me at daylight."

He was sound asleep again.

"If she does call you at daylight," said Pipey, "her throat is a more vonderful piece of flesh and sinew than I take it to be."

They advanced to the street door, and found it well secured with bolts, bars, and locks of every description; but, as Pipey observed:

"They're on the wrong side to be good for much."

With the caution which distinguished him, he proceeded to withdraw all obstructions to his egress, and in a few moments the door opened, and they were in the street, hurrying in the direction of Mr. Grimer's.

Pipey was delighted, and Liz had as much as she could do to restrain his ebullitions of joy. He danced and capered about the streets, shouted and sang, and fairly hugged Liz in his frantic gladness.

"Bolted from Newgate and cracked Maydock's crib in one night! My eye! if that ain't vork it's a pity.

Oh, darbies and locks all opened d'ye see,
As I cracked the stone jug with a fiddle-de-dee;
And got out o' Newgate without the pass-key,
    Fiddle-de-dee, fiddle-de-dee.
    Oh, a crackaman is he,
Who'd get out o' Newgate without the pass-key."

"Hush!" said Liz; "hush! for Heaven's sake do not thus disturb the quiet of the night with that noise, we may be detected or overtaken."

"Detected! I'd like to see the cove as vould do it; and as to overtaken, who the deuce is there to do it?—not Maydock, he's safe for the next three hours; and not the old 'oman, for if she ever valks again it vont be this side of a veek."

They hastened on, Liz trembling with fear, and Pipey continuing his mirth with unabated vigour.

They hurried through the streets, and each step brought them nearer the promised place of refuge at Grimer's abode.

They were, however, unconscious that their footsteps were dogged by a tall figure clad in a suit of black velvet, spangled with bugles of the same sombre hue, and whose face, as the waning moonlight fell upon it, exhibited the expression and tint of death.

They were followed by the Black Captain.

CHAPTER XXV.

A CONJUGAL INTERVIEW—THE DUKE VISITS GRIMER—THE DUCHESS ON THE SCENT—PLOT AND COUNTERPLOT.

THE idiot serving-man lost no time in returning to town and seeking the Duchess, and, in an interview of considerable length, he imparted to her the secret of which he had in so singular a manner become possessed.

"Great Heaven!" she cried, when the tale was concluded, "to what a depth of degradation and shame have I not fallen through this man to whom I am tied. What is to be done? To continue to share his roof would be excruciatingly painful to me, but to expose him would not only be his ruin but my humiliation also. I will see him, and tax him with his perfidy."

The Duke was, as usual, in his study, and thither the Duchess hastened to confront him.

She entered. Grasmount had just read a letter from Grimer, requesting his attendance that evening at his office, as he had important matters to communicate. This had set the mind of the Duke on the rack, and he sat with the epistle in one hand, whilst with the other he clasped his throbbing brow.

In this position the Duchess found him. Hastily crumpling the letter, he thrust it into his breast, and rose to receive his wife.

She stood just within the chamber, one hand resting on the handle of the door, the other extended, motioning the Duke in an authoritative manner to keep his place.

"To what am I indebted for this visit?" asked Grasmount, inwardly suspecting some calamity.

"You will hear presently."

"You look and speak strangely. I do not comprehend you."

"But I comprehend you. Yes, Grasmount, at last I understand you thoroughly."

"You have taken sufficient time about it," said the Duke, whose imperious nature would not brook the insulting tone used by his wife. "I should have thought duty, if not inclination, would have prompted you to understand me years ago."

"Humph! you carry it proudly, but we shall see whether your haughty head will not bow before we have concluded this interview."

"If you come to upbraid me, you had best not waste words, for I am in no humour for quarrelling."

"Nor am I. I but come to demand explanations due to me. I came to ask what reparation you can offer for years of treachery and deceit, and for the position in which you have cast me?"

"How?"

"Listen."

"I am all attention."

"Our alliance has not been the happiest, for it was of mutual interests rather than of love, but nevertheless there were obligations entailed which are of a most serious nature to me. In the first place you offered yourself to me as a bachelor."

"I believed myself to be one."

"You should have assured yourself of the fact before you bound your lot so closely to mine. But to proceed: you were a widower, and the father of a child, whom you deserted—basely, cruelly deserted."

"No, no! I was taught to believe it dead."

"That may be so; but in our union many important considerations arose. I brought you enormous properties, and you were understood to possess others of equal magnitude, the amalgamation of which was to make our houses unrivalled in the proud list of English aristocrats. Well, it now appears that you are in reality but a pace before a beggar—that the estates you hold belong to another—and that for years you have been defrauding your child of all that was left to her by your father."

"This is true. But again I say I have done all this unconsciously."

"Indeed! And yet you have been moving Heaven and earth to keep the secret, and dispose of your unhappy child. Perhaps this has, also, been done unconsciously."

"It was done to spare you as much as myself. Remember your ruin is involved with mine. If one falls, both falls."

"Ah, there it is. Yours and yours alone is the crime, whilst I am called upon to share its punishment with you. Henceforth I may not walk the streets of London, or appear in public without having the finger of scorn pointed at me, accompanied by such sentences as 'See! there's the Duchess of Grasmount; the wife of the fraudulent Duke,' and 'Behold the partner of the man who has for years robbed and persecuted his own child.' Is not this so?"

"Oh, Heaven! it is, it is! But spare me, spare me! Believe me, I have suffered! You do not and never will comprehend how much I have suffered, for it is beyond human ken. Of the sleepless nights, of the days of waking agony, of dreams, of phantoms, of fears of detection and humiliation I will not speak, but they have formed part of the horrible punishment my evil-doings have brought upon me. Think of this, and spare me."

"It is not in my power to spare you; I come to ask what you have to propose to me. I want to comprehend your plans. If I am to share the reward of your guilt, it is but right that I should know how we are situated, that I may be prepared for any emergency that may present itself."

"I have no plans; nothing to reveal."

"I thought as much. You are in the hands of two villains."

"Yes, yes."

"One of these, a lawyer named Grimer, is in possession of certain papers which would throw a light on your former marriage, and a common burglar, named Maydock, is in possession of your father's will, and either has your child in his keeping or knows where she is to be found."

"True, true; but how knew you all this?"

"No matter now; suffice it to say that I have learnt all through those to whom you have entrusted your secret. Better, far better, had you kept it locked in your bosom. It might have eaten out your heart, but it would have, at least, spared you the pain of a scene like this."

The thoughts of the Duke instantly reverted to his niece, and the young king's counsel, her lover.

"Yes," he said to himself, "they have betrayed me. Fool! fool that I was to trust them."

"Again," said the Duchess, "again I ask you to tell me what you have to propose."

"I do not know what to do. Here is a letter from this Grimer, who bids me meet him to-night in order that I may hear some important revelation. After this, I shall be enabled to tell you my plans."

"Until then, my lord Duke, you had best dwell upon mine. They are as follow :—Should this terrible mystery come to light, I shall retire from England for ever, and shall never look upon you again. If, on the other hand, some arrangement can be made in private so as to effectually secure the secret within its present limits, I shall remain here, and to the world we shall remain as we ever were. Our tastes and habits have been very fortunately diametrically opposite, and we have seldom appeared in public together. This will now serve as a blind to the fact of our separation."

"Separation!"

"Yes, separation."

"You do not mean that we are to become estranged?"

"Irrevocably!"

"Great Heaven! reconsider your determination.

"I need not do so: it would be a waste of time; for I should not alter my resolve."

"Have pity upon me."

"You have had none on me."

"True; but still I ask you to spare me."

"Never. We are now separated for life—remember, for life. If we meet hereafter it will be as strangers."

"Stay."

The Duchess opened the door, and was gone.

"And it has come to this," cried the Duke; "I am exposed, ruined for ever, and by those I thought I could have entrusted with my life."

His head sank upon his breast, and he fell into a dark and gloomy reverie.

After he had lain in a state of semi-insensibility for over an hour, he was aroused by a light hand being laid on his shoulder.

He roused himself, and on looking up beheld his niece.

"I am come, dear uncle, to tell you that Lewis Arndale has a clue to the man, Maydock, and, as he thinks, to the young girl."

The Duke stared at her fixedly for some moments.

"It is not she," he murmured, "it is not she who has betrayed me."

"What do you speak of, uncle?—your look is wild and your language incoherent. I do not understand you."

"Oh, Olivia, we are betrayed; the Duchess knows all."

"Oh Heaven! how did she learn the secret?"

"At first I thought you had betrayed me."

"Uncle!"

"I know now that I was wrong; but there is another one who has done it, and that one is—"

"Oh, no, say not so, uncle, I am sure you are mistaken; he is incapable of such an act."

"He has done this. To whom, but to you and him, did I entrust the secret?"

"But Grimer—Maydock—they may have—"

"No, no; your aunt has told me that she heard it through those to whom I entrusted it. Believe me, Arndale has betrayed me."

"If that be the case," cried Olivia, "I will never see him more. My heart may break at the separation, but I will effect it. Never will Olivia give her hand to one who could act so basely."

"Do nothing hastily on my account; you know not how he may have been tempted. You know not the means by which this secret was extorted from him. It is I who am to blame, for trusting it to him."

"Nay, it is I; and I deserve all that can befall me for giving way to my heart's weaknesses. Mine is the fault, and on me let the punishment fall. I have loved Lewis Arndale, but I will never see him more. There, I renounce him for ever."

"Think, think!"

"I will think of nothing."

She seated herself at a desk and scrawled the following lines on a sheet of paper :—

"Lewis Arndale,

"You have betrayed my uncle and myself, and have thus ensured my detestation. Never see me more, for I should spurn you from me.

"Olivia Besgrove."

This she hastily sealed.

"Call a servant," she said.

The Duke obeyed her, and a servant entered.

"Take this to Mr. Arndale, at the Temple; there is no answer."

The servant withdrew.

"Thus," cried Olivia, "thus I serve those who would betray me or mine."

"But if he should be innocent."

"Innocent! Did you not say that to us alone you entrusted the secret?"

"Yes, yes."

"Then how can he be innocent?"

"True, true."

"No, uncle, I renounce him for ever. He is now no more to me than the veriest stranger on the face of the earth."

The proud girl bore it bravely for a while, but, the first outburst of passion over, she gave way to a fit of grief, and loudly bewailed her wretched fate.

"It is I, it is I," cried the Duke, "who have done all this. Where'er I turn I bring desolation and ruin with me. Those I love wither before me. My breath is a contamination and my presence a curse. Oh, that the Omnipotent would rid the earth of my detestable presence."

"Hush, hush! speak not thus. You are too severely tried. Whate'er your fault has been, your punishment has exceeded it. My poor—poor uncle."

The girl wept upon his breast, and he could not refrain from tears.

He had sinned, but he was punished.

* * * * * *

It was night, and Grimer sat in his dingy old office, awaiting a visitor.

He never remained so late in that dull old chamber unless some one who dared not approach him in the daylight was to pay him a visit.

On this particular night the face of Mr. Grimer was illumined with a grin of satisfaction which was but seldom observed there.

He paced the room nervously and rubbed his hands with a singular glee.

"Ha! ha!" he cried, "mine—mine at last. In my power—beautiful—beautiful as an angel. Mine—mine!—he! he!—that is grand. Ah! Pipey —Pipey is a genius. Oh! he's a great boy, is Pipey. I must make his fortune for him, some day or other. Ha! ha! Pipey is my darling. I love him: yes, I love him next to Liz and— myself. Yes, I will make Pipey's fortune."

Mumbling incoherently about Pipey and Liz, and matters in connection with them, he passed the time, varying the amusement by occasionally looking at his watch, and exclaiming—

"Not yet come!—not yet come!—how late it grows."

It was on the stroke of ten, and St. Paul's began to toll forth that hour, when a footstep was heard in the passage, followed by a knock at the door of the lawyer's office.

"Come in," said Grimer.

The door opened, and the Duke of Grasmount, muffled in a large cloak, entered the chamber.

"Ah, my lord Duke," said the old lawyer, "I began to fear my bait was not sufficiently tempting to draw you forth to-night, but I am glad you are come—very, very glad."

"You have news for me?"

"Yes—yes—glorious news."

"Indeed?"

"Yes, such news as you could scarcely expect to hear."

"What—what is it?"

"Oh! restrain your impatience: you will hear all in good time."

"The will—the will—you have not discovered that?"

"No, it is still out of my grasp, but I shall have it—I shall have it."

"The girl, then—you have discovered her?"

"Yes, I flatter myself I have."

"Where—oh, where is she?"

"Ah! that's *my* secret. No, no, my lord Duke, you must excuse me; I shall not reveal that. Why, where should I be if that secret was to go from me?"

"Oh, parley not with me. You know where she is to be found?"

"More than that."

"What?"

"Much more than that."

"It cannot be that—"

"I have her in my toils. Oh, yes, it can be so, and is so."

"Oh, I am thankful for that."

"And now to business. I have the girl: of her identity there is not a shadow of a doubt, and so no quibble can be raised on that score. She is under my protection, and now what do you propose?"

"Nay, it is for you to propose. What terms would you make with me?"

"Listen: if the girl marries me, I am, by law, the real possessor of the estates you have so long misappropriated, and I can at any moment turn you out, prosecute you, and take possession, but I am not inclined to go to such lengths. I love the girl, and care more for her than the wealth she possesses, and so I am inclined to deal generously by you. Give me forty thousand pounds, and I will relinquish all claim to your lands and titles, and swear never to reveal the secret of the birth and parentage of my wife. Refuse and—"

"Well, and if I refuse?"

"The world shall know of your illegal acts, and a felon's doom will be your lot! Moreover, this will not prevent my marrying your child, and taking possession of the property. You see our relative positions, and you will at once comprehend what a sacrifice I am making; but you have trusted in me, and I am anxious to prove that I never betray a trust."

"You are generous."

"You are doubtless grateful. Now, what have you to say?"

"I have to say that one part of your threat has already lost its strength. My crime is revealed, ah! to no other individual than the Duchess, who can at any moment betray me. As to the property, without documents, how could you prove your right?"

"Without documents?"

"Yes, without documents; *you know that you have not one!*"

"It *was* you, then, who stole my treasure."

"No, by Heaven, no; but I know who did."

"His name?"

"I shall never reveal it. I dare not think of it. You will know in good time."

"His name—will you not give it me?"

"No, it shall not pass my lips."

"Because it was you who stole them."

"No, I say again it was not I, but it was from no lack of inclination. If I had them in my possession I should only be too proud to acknowledge it, for then I should be free to deal with you and others as I pleased. The child and the will would be as nothing without those documents were forthcoming. One link missing the chain would be useless."

"Why, that is true."

"Now, Grimer, we meet as becomes us; we are equals; at least, equals until these terrible papers are forthcoming."

The lawyer hung his head. He was confounded at the sudden turn the conversation had taken.

In good truth he was for a time *non plussed*, but his habitual coolness soon came to his aid.

"Well," he said, "I own I am not so strong as I might be, but if the girl is not in your power, and the will and other documents should

again fall into mine—and that is not improbable, for he who brought me the girl can and will bring me the papers—where would you be? I am still inclined to treat with you, and I promise to marry the girl and make the terms I offered. Nothing can then annoy you. The will has lost its power; produce it who may, you have nought to dread but the *expose.* The girl is married, her husband is satisfied, and the world is silenced. As to the Duchess of Grasmount being acquainted with the case as it stands, I take leave, as a lawyer, to doubt that, crediting it to you as a trick of the enemy, deserving of credit for its cleverness,—as a weakness of my cause; but nothing more."

The door opened and in walked the Duchess.

"Then you are deceived, man," she cried, as she closed the door after her; "I know all."

"The Duchess!" said the Duke, quite confounded at her presence.

"The Duchess," said Grimer, "the devil!"

"Yes, the Duchess is here." Turning to the Duke she continued: "I followed you in order that I might see and hear this man. I have heard his propositions, and I advise you to agree to them in one part."

"I must have them agreed to *in toto*," said Grimer.

"In part," said the Duchess; "I advise that you hand him the sum he requires."

"That is very sensible of you," said Grimer.

"But," continued the Duchess, "I should impose one condition."

"Name it, madam," said Grimer.

"It is that you hand into my keeping the child whom you say is heir to the ducal property."

"Into your keeping?" said Grimer and the Duke in a breath.

"Yes, into my keeping."

"You forget that I have not the sum he requires. If I should raise it I should be committing a further wrong. I have not sufficient personal property wherewith to realise the amount."

"But I have, and I will pay it."

"Yes," said Grimer, "but you forget my affection for the girl. I love her, and it is only because I would marry her that I propose such easy terms to the Duke,"

"Psha!" said the Duchess, "the terms are exorbitant; and as to the proposition of matrimony, if the girl has eyes and sense she would turn from you with loathing and disgust."

"Be not too sure of that."

"I am certain of it."

"But she is in my power: I can use force."

"And I can use *finesse*. Now, listen to me. If you do not consent to accept my terms I will place the whole matter in the hands of the police. I will make known every particular of the case, and cause search to be made for the child and the documents. The *exposé* is alone all we have to dread. With our wealth and our power we should escape the punishment which would assuredly fall on those less exalted. The girl would not marry you, and when she found that she had a father ready to receive her, and try every means in his power to atone for the past, she would fly to him, and she would say, ' Father, take this wealth and use it as you think best; I will not touch it.' We could leave this country until the case died away from men's memories, and then return in peace. You see, Mr. Grimer, I am your equal. Now, what do you say to my proposition?"

Grimer was dumbfounded. He had never anticipated such a bold stroke, and he was forced to acknowledge to himself that he was beaten.

Secrecy was his great point, and if the Duchess made the affair public he was comparatively powerless.

He bit his nether lip until the blood trickled down his grizzled beard. Grimer was beaten by a woman.

"Now," continued the Duchess, "will you sell me this girl? It is a fancy of mine to have her. What say you?"

"I consent."

"You must do more," said the Duchess, "you must swear never to reveal to her nor to any living soul one word concerning her history."

The lawyer hesitated.

He reflected, but he saw no remedy for the blows dealt him. He could not retaliate, and he said,

"I will swear."

"One more condition."

"What, another?"

"Yes, it is the last." You must swear to use every effort to regain those documents. They are absolutely necessary, and I must have them."

"I will swear that also."

"And in consideration of your bringing them to me I will give you another five thousand pounds."

Grimer's eyes glistened.

"I will do my utmost," he said.

"I do not doubt you," continued the Duchess, "and now produce the girl and I will give you a banker's bill for the amount you have demanded."

"What—to night?"

"To-night; who knows what the morrow may bring forth?"

"True: to-night be it then. *Will you come to my house for her?*"

"Oh, she is at your house, is she?" said the Duchess; "good."

"Yes, yes," said the lawyer, "but you will not take advantage of my excitement; you promised me the money and you will give it me. I have dealt honourably by you."

"Oh, do not fear that I shall play the trickster so far. I have promised you the money and it shall be yours the moment the girl is in my presence."

"Will you come with me?"

"Yes; my carriage waits; we will all three go together."

They were about to start when a knock at the door of the office startled them.

"Who can this be?" cried the Duke, in great alarm.

"Conceal us," cried the Duchess.

"There is no occasion; it is only my emissary —the boy who found the child and brought her to me."

Grimer opened the door, and Pipey entered.

"Hillo, Grimer, svells here! I begs pardin, ladies and gemmen, at least, ma'am and sir; but I vosn't down to the fact that anybody vos here except the old 'un."

"Hush, Pipey," said Grimer, and then turning to the Duchess—for the Duke had become a nonentity in the scene, he continued, "If you would rather remain here, this lad will bring the girl to you. During his absence we could be arranging the necessary matters."

"Very well," said the Duchess; "if you can trust him, I would rather you adopted that course."

"I can trust him," said Grimer.

"Oh, yes," said Pipey, "you can trust me vith anythink, except cash and jewellery. I aint proof agin them; so I von't deny it."

"Begone," said Grimer, "to my house, as quickly as possible, and bring Liz here."

"Vot, bring Liz out at this time o' night? That's a good 'un."

"Begone, I say, and do my bidding."

"Oh, all right. Am I to valk it?"

"No," said the Duchess; "my carriage is without: use it, and do not spare the horses."

"Oh! I'll keep old powdered vig up to the scratch," said Pipey; "don't fear him. He'll go like vinking vith me behind him. My eyes, I'm coming to something at last, going for a gal in a real tip-top svell's turn-out."

Mr. Pipey could not contain his delight, and pranced out of the office in the most absurd fashion.

In a few minutes he was rolling away in the

direction of Mr. Grimer's abode, drawn by two magnificent horses, and attended by servants in the Duke's livery.

"If this ain't enjoyment," said Pipey, "I'd like to know vot is. If anythink vould tempt me to be so mean as to turn honest, it vould only be the life of a real svell."

"That boy found and brought your child to me," said Grimer, as soon as Pipey was gone, to snatch her from the man into whose power she had fallen. "He forced his way in the most desperate manner out of Newgate; for that and the crime for which he was sent to the prison, the the officers are after him. He must be saved : all the interest you may have must be exerted in his behalf."

"Wherefore ?" asked the Duchess. "Am I to protect every criminal who has been mixed up in this case ?"

"Perhaps not," said Grimer, "but you must protect as many as I may ask you to if you would have the will found. This lad is invaluable to me, and he must be permitted to be at liberty without the fear of the authorities at his heels. Without him I am almost powerless. Moreover, you owe him a debt of gratitude, for he became imprisoned in the service of the Duke. He was tracking the men who committed the burglary at your villa at Kew, when he fell into the hands of the constables."

"To what end was he tracking them? Was he making an attempt to save our property ?"

"No. He followed them to obtain possession of the will. It was concealed in the library of the house at Kew, and Maydock, who was one of the burglars, went there to bring it away."

"And he succeeded ?" asked the Duke.

"I've no reason to doubt it. He was in the library for some considerable time, and effected an escape. There cannot be two opinions as to his success. The boy knows this man's haunts : he can play upon him, as he is slightly in his confidence ; and if the will is to return into my possession it will only be through his instrumentality. Now, I ask, will you exert yourselves to save him ?"

"Yes," said the Duchess. "He is secure as long as he is in my service."

"That is well," continued Grimer ; "and now to business."

Pens, ink, and paper were produced. Writings were made and signed, and Grimer solemnly bound himself down to fulfil the obligations imposed on him by the Duchess.

The time occupied in these preliminaries had scarcely passed, when the rumble of the wheels of a carriage attracted the attention of the trio.

"They are come," said the Duchess, "and now we shall see what this child is like."

Pipey's voice was heard giving imperious orders to the servants, and the next moment the sound of a female's voice assured those present that he had fulfilled his mission.

The Duke trembled hard and fast. For the first time in his life he was to behold the child of his first, perhaps his only love. In spite of all, his heart yearned towards her from the moment her voice fell upon his ear.

It was his child, his first and only one, and that thought was sufficient to awaken emotions to which he had been an entire stranger.

"Where are you taking me," asked Liz. "Oh, you are leading me into some other trap."

"I'd scorn the action," said Pipey; "aint I yer real guardian and protector, and d'ye think I'd serve yer shabby ? No, not if I know'd it. Come along. Don't be afeard ; it's only a pair o' old svells, as is as proud as peacocks—twice as proud, and quite as harmless—as vants to look at yer."

The office door opened, and Liz stood face to face with her father.

An exclamation of surprise burst from the lips of the Duke and Duchess as they gazed upon her.

There she stood in all her wondrous beauty, rendering them speechless by her grace and charms. The night air had given a tinge to her hitherto pale cheek ; her eyes, filled with an expression of fear and surprise, wandered from one to the other, and struck all with admiration. The long, golden hair, which, in defiance of the fashion of the time, she wore unadorned, fell streaming over her white shoulders, shading her sweet face, and adding to her many charms. Her dress was the same in which she had been borne away from Marlborough House. It was rich and luxurious, but now somewhat soiled and creased by the dirt and narrow limits of Maydock's attic. Nevertheless, it served to show off her proportions, and lend her a noble grace, which certainly increased the surprise of those into whose presence she had come.

"She is extremely beautiful," said the Duchess, scarce conscious of what she uttered ; "I never saw one so fair."

"She is the counterpart of her mother ; poor murdered innocent," exclaimed the Duke.

"Silence," said the Duchess, "whate'er she is, she is nothing to thee."

"Why am I brought here ?" asked Liz of Grimer.

"To see your lawful protectors, my dear; this gentleman is the Duke of Grasmount ; this lady is his Duchess. Your parents were some distant relations of theirs, and it is to them you owe your deliverance from the toils of Maydock. They have sought you long and anxiously, and now through me you are restored to them."

"You speak in riddles," said Liz, "I do not comprehend you. My mother could not possibly have been related to those so nobly born. She was poor and lowly ; her every word and action denoted humble origin, and her way of life told the tale still more plainly. One born in a better sphere could not have lived so long and contentedly in the manner in which she passed her days."

"Ah," said Grimer "you are speaking of her whom you have been accustomed to look upon as your mother, but who in reality was only a servant of your real parents."

"Can I believe my ears ?" said Liz, amazed at what she heard.

"It is true," said the Duchess, taking Liz kindly by the hand, "it is true, fair maid ; to us alone you have now to look, for we are your only surviving relatives. Both your parents died when you were but an infant ; and the woman who has reared you, under the impression that by stealing you she would secure certain estates to which you were heiress, stole you, and has all these years effectually evaded all our attempts at recovering you; but, thanks to this gentleman, you are now with us again, and, believe me, we will love you dearly."

"I am so confused," said Liz, "that I scarce can believe my senses."

"Does not your heart bid you cling to us?" said the Duchess, affectionately.

"Yes," said Liz, "yes, it is so; I feel I love you." She threw herself into the open arms of the Duchess.

"And you, sir," she said, turning after a while to the Duke, "my heart yearns towards you. I know not how it is, but I feel a mysterious sympathy for you, the like of which never before agitated my bosom. It seems to me that I have looked upon you before. Your face is quite familiar to me, and if I have not heard your voice before, I have dreamt of something so like it that I am prone to blend the shadow with the reality."

"God bless you!" said Grasmount, deeply affected, and turning away to hide the tears which coursed down his cheek; "God bless you, my poor child!"

"Come," said the Duchess, handing her banker's bill to Grimer; "there is your fee, sir, and we are indebted to you for giving us this gem. Now there is nothing further to detain us."

"Am I to go with you both?" asked Liz.

"No," said the Duchess; "no, sweet girl, you are to go with me alone."

Liz gave her hand to Grimer, and the old wretch pressed it warmly. She then turned to Pipey, and that young gentleman, deeply moved said—

"Good-bye, Liz, you're a fine lady now. Think o' poor Pipey sometimes, and if ever yer get into trouble again send for the youth, and he'll fetch yer out of it. He's game to get out o' a condemned cell to do you a good turn."

"You are my best friend," said Liz, "and I will never forget you."

The Duchess opened the office door, and, wrapping her own cloak closely about the young girl, she led her to her carriage.

The Duke followed mechanically. He saw Liz seated in the carriage; he then caught the Duchess by the hand, and said hurriedly but under his breath—

"Forgive me, forgive me! Oh, God! do not cast me from you and my child."

"You have cast yourself from us," replied the Duchess. "Your acts be upon your own head. Remember our interview of this morning. We are now and for ever strangers. Your child is mine; attempt to dispute my right, and the world shall know all. I am desperately in earnest."

She sprang into the carriage, and it moved away.

The Duke, almost broken-hearted, stood looking after it in extreme anguish.

"Heaven and earth," he cried, "that it should have come to this."

He strode away to where his own carriage awaited him, and drove to his home, alone with his own dark thoughts; and thus, through a series

of desperate plots and counterplots, the Duchess won the first and best move.

She had secured the secret, and left unrevealed THE MYSTERY OF MARLBOROUGH HOUSE.

———

CHAPTER XXVI.

PIPEY'S GRIEF.—GRIMER RECEIVES YET ANOTHER LATE VISITOR. — THE MISSING PAPERS. — A FELON'S HISTORY.

PIPEY looked sorrowfully at Grimer for some moments, and then exclaimed—

"Vell, this ere's a rum go, isn't it? Vot's the meaning of the move, hey? I can't see through it?"

"Never you mind," said Grimer; "it does not concern you."

"Oh don't it," said Pipey. "Vell, I thought it did, considering that I've been a blubbering like a vater-spout for the last half hour. Poor gal! Vonder vether I shall ever see her agin. I'd sooner have had a double tooth out than have parted from her: and she's gone to be a svell, too. My eyes! She'll think no more of Pipey, now."

"Why, you don't suppose she ever thought of you, do you?"

"Vell, I don't know as how she did, and I can't say as she didn't. At all events, it vos pleasant to think that she cared for a cove a little bit, jist in a sisterly sort o' way; but now, I suppose, all low people 'll go out o' her head, and she'll think no more of a cove's getting out o' Newgate to serve her than she vould if he got out of his drawing-room, and came to her in a svell carriage, like the von in vich she's gone off. It's awful to think of."

"Nonsense! cease your folly. I am in no mood to stand it; and, mind, never speak to me of her going; I can't bear to think of it, for I had dreamt of calling her mine. I had hoped to have married her, and possessed her love."

"You! My eyes! Vot's come about that doves should go and live vith the ravens? *You* marry Liz! *you* have her love!"

"Yes, I. Is there anything so very wonderful in that?"

"Vell, vithout being too impressive, I should rather say there vos. You marry Liz!"

"Yes; and a good match it would have been for her."

"A good match! Oh, I like that. A good match! Vy, she'd shudder at yer touch; and, look here, old 'un. If I'd a thought as you had a notion of marrying her, yer vouldn't a caught me bringing her to yer, take my vord for it. I'd as soon take a sheep to a volf, that I vould."

"No impudence!"

"Vell, don't go on so. I can't bear to hear yer talk o' marrying her, it goes agin my grain."

"Let the subject drop. I do not want to hear of it until the first stings of disappointment have been worn down by time."

"Vith all my heart."

"Now—where are you going."

"Home."

"Are you sure?"

"Quite."

"I thought you would have made a night of it, as you called it, at some flash house or other."

"No, I'm not in the humour for that sort o' fun. I'm not partickler, but vith the look of Liz lingering in my head, I couldn't go to no such crib. I shall go home. Besides, it's not safe for me to be about. Those Newgate birds are arter me close, and I musn't go abroad too much, or I may have the trouble of making another escape, and I don't care about it."

"You do well to keep dark now, and may do so until after to-morrow. The Duchess will secure your liberty; she wants your services."

"Then she may vant 'em, for she vont have 'em."

"Why?"

"Because I don't care about vorking for her. I vosn't so much struck vith her personal beauty."

"But you will be serving Liz."

"That alters the case. Vot's to be done?"

"You must still dog Maydock. The will and the other documents are required. They must be found, and you must find them."

"You are sure its serving Liz?"

"Yes."

"Vell, then, I'll do it. But it's a ticklish job, for it's ten to von but the old 'oman recognised me ven I gived her the squeeze."

"You must be wary, and play you own cards as you best can. I will say no more."

"You've said enough. I'm on to him, and now good-night."

"Good-night."

"Had I better stay and see yer lock up? it's getting late, and it mayn't be pleasant for yer to stop here alone."

"You can go; I fear nothing."

"Good-night then."

"Good-night. Remember, keep dark until the day after to-morrow."

"I shan't show a sign," said Pipey, retiring from the office. "I'll go home and stop there. Lor, I shall have enough amusement in thinking o' the misfortune of Liz in having found people who are bad enough to want to make her respectable."

Pipey was gone.

Grimer, now that he was alone, drew forth the money he had received, and glanced at it.

"It is a large sum," he said, "and it is scarcely safe here, but better here than anywhere else. In the morning I will secure it. It is a great sum, but not enough for the priceless jewel. I sold her for it. Fool that I was to part with her! Fool, fool! she would have been a comfort—a joy. Her lightest touch sent a thrill of wild pleasure tingling through me. Her look aroused passions which I thought long since dead within me. Her voice enraptured my soul, and I have sold her—sold her for money. Bah! fool, fool! she would have been worth to me ten times this treasure, but they were too clever for me. They tricked me too cunningly, and I had no option but to give her up. She is gone, gone! and I may never see her more. She has left me alone and cheerless—alone without one comfort. No, there is my wealth; ah! I'll only think of

wedding myself to my gold. I love it, and will feast upon it. My gold, my precious gold, shall now be all in all to me."

He drew forth the key of his iron safe, and hastily secured the bill handed him by the Duchess.

"There," he said, "that is safe."

He was about to return the key to the drawer in which he usually secured it when a sudden thought struck him, and he placed it within his breast.

"It shall not go there," he said; "no, no, I had a lesson against that some time ago."

He spent a few more minutes in arranging his papers, and then put on his hat to depart.

His hand was on the lamp to put it out, when a shadow fell across the room, and on looking up Grimer beheld, standing in the doorway, the figure of a man, muffled in a cloak and closely masked.

"Silence," said the intruder, securing the door, "I mean you no harm, so do not create any disturbance."

"Who and what are you?" demanded Grimer, shaking with fright and mechanically grasping at the key hidden in his bosom.

"You will know presently; sufficient now to say that I mean you no harm."

"I do not know that."

"But I do. Had I wished to have fallen upon you I could have done so with ease whilst your back was turned upon me. I but come on a matter of business."

"I know your voice."

"You should do so; it was once familiar to you. Will you see my face?"

"As you please, but I have little time to spare now. You can call to-morrow."

"No; we must settle our affairs to-night. Look upon me.

The man removed his mask, and the light fell upon and revealed the never-to-be-forgotten features of the Black Captain.

"Great God!" cried Grimer; "has the grave given up its dead?"

"Yes."

"Avaunt!" cried the old man, in a fit of terror, "avaunt! let me pass."

"Psha! that is not the language Grimer was wont to use. That is not the tone in which he once spoke."

"True, and it is not the tone I now use; but with a being of so terrible a nature, how can I use other than scared tones."

"Psha! you talk folly. Do you believe me a supernatural?"

"Did I not see you hanged?"

"You did."

"What else then can I think?"

"Why, think that even the hangman could not deprive me of life?"

"You escaped from the gallows?"

"Yes."

"Great heaven! How could that be?"

"You shall hear anon; but first to business."

"What would you with me?"

"Listen. The girl born to those I married—where is she?"

"Why ask me?"

"Because she is in your keeping."

"It is not so."

"It is so."

"I repeat, it is not so. She is gone from me."

"You deceive me."

"Indeed I do not.

"Strange. She was with you this very evening. No denial. I saw her in your house."

"That may be so, for she has not left me more than an hour?"

"Whither has she gone?'

"To the house of those who had most right to her."

"Yo do not mean to say that you have handed her to the Duke."

"I do."

"I will not believe it."

"I cannot help that."

"Your love of gain would prevent your doing that, independent of other conditions, and so I take leave to doubt you."

"Nevertheless, it is the fact."

"We shall see. You would deceive me, but I shall be even with you."

"I have no cause to deceive you."

"You have. The will and other documents are out of your keeping, and you imagine, by hiding the girl, to keep some hold on the property; but you will not do it, save through me."

"Bah! how can you do aught in the matter?"

"How? With ease. I have the will and the remainder of the documents, and I am the chief witness of the marriage and other incidents in connection with the mystery. Do not mistake me. I am not to be choked off; so make no attempt."

"*You* have the will?"

"Yes; I have it. I stole it from Maydock on his return from the villa of the Duke at Kew."

"And the marriage certificate and the other papers?"

"Yes; those I took from the Duke himself in this very office on the night he made an attempt at burglary here for the purpose of carrying them off."

"This is strange."

"It is so. But it is true. Step by step I have gone on securing my proofs until I have them all. I now want the girl, and I demand her of you."

"Believe me, she is gone, and with those I have named."

Grimer then related the substance of his interview with the Duke and Duchess, concealing however the true amount of money he had received for delivering up Liz, and in consideration of the many services he had performed in her cause.

The highwayman was staggered.

"Fool that I was," he exclaimed, "not to have carried her off before. But there's no help for it now."

"No," said Grimer, "there is not; the game is up, and we must be content."

"You may be, but not I. Listen to me. I have set my mind on the girl. I have seen her, and love her, and I will have her."

"If you can get her."

"I am a desperate man, and do not stand on trifles. I have said, and I will do."

"We shall see. But you promised to tell me the secret of your re-appearance. As I did my best to serve you, I think I have a right to know your history. Will you tell me?"

"It has never yet passed my lips, but I do not mind telling thee. But you must swear secrecy."

"I swear it."

"On your soul!"

"On my soul."

"It is well. Now listen."

"To give you the history of a wayward childhood and an ill-spent youth would be but idle, and a waste of your time as well as my own. I will briefly say that I was the son of Silas Masters, a Yorkshire gentleman of considerable property, and that it was the great aim of my parent to educate me for the church. He was somewhat a fanatic in religious matters, and was inclined to sectarianism of the most absurd type. I, on the other hand, had no taste for the church, either as a profession or an institution. I could not bear the restraint placed upon me within its walls, and I would have shunned it but that my father forced me into it. My inclination led me to the sports of the field, and perhaps to the gaming-house. I loved the choice spirits who gloried in the hunt and the fight, and who were prepared to go to any length for women and wine. With feelings of this sort you will not wonder at my very soul revolting at the sombre livery of the profession I had embraced, and the stiff-necked habits entailed thereto. Well, I obtained a small living near my native village, and in a short time Robert Masters, the sporting pastor, was the scandal of the place. My father warned me that if I pursued my course of life he would banish me, and throw me on my own resources; but I heeded him not. At length he grew weary of me, and would have fulfilled his threat, had not an incident occurred which averted his thoughts in another way. It came to his ears that a girl, named Margaret Hather, the daughter of a near friend of his, had fallen madly in love with me, and this formed a diversion in my favour. He thought that if he could wed me to that good and virtuous girl, that I would amend my way of life, and become the man he wished to see me. Margaret was a pretty wench enough, but she was a poor, meek, soulless thing, whom I despised beyond measure, but at the time my father proposed that I should wed her I was in extreme monetary difficulties, and wishing to hide them, as they were mostly gambling debts, I consented to the match. It was the worst move I ever made. At the time there was living with me a woman after my own heart—a fine, dashing girl, who could pocket her virtue on an occasion, could ride any horse brought to her, shoot with the best shot of the place, and sing a love song with more sweetness than the mavis. She was all fire —all soul, and she loved me. I knew it, but I could not ward off the hateful union with Margaret Hatcher. My father would not be moved; my creditors were clamorous—exposure was certain. What could I do? I sent Lavinia to London, and promised to join her there, and in less than a week I led Margaret to the altar. With her I received a large sum of money, with which I satisfied my creditors and commenced anew.

"It did not take Margaret long to read me thoroughly: quiet, unassuming as she was, she was not altogether blind, and she found out my tastes and habits. The discovery almost broke her heart, but she struggled against the blow, and endeavoured to win me over to a course of life to which I had been a stranger. With her gentle eyes upon me, with her sobbing voice whispering in my ear, I combatted with the evil within me, and sought to drive it out. I foreswore my horse, and card and dice playing, and in a short time was in a fair way of becoming an altered man when, in an unfortunate hour, Lavinia returned to me. Tired of waiting for my arrival in London, she had again sought me out. She found me married. Instead of turning from me, as the majority of her sex would have done, with loathing and disgust, she clung to me, and used all her arts to wean me from my wife, compared with whom she was Cleopatra to a handmaiden. In her presence all my good resolutions forsook me, and I deserted my wife's arms for the embraces of my mistress. I drank to drown remembrance, and in my drunkenness I took Lavinia to my home, and introduced her to my wife as one whom I loved, and who loved me. Lavinia, delighted at this devilry, lavished all kinds of caresses on me, in the presence of my wife, and told her she had come to supplant her. This was an awful blow to the woman I had married. At first she staggered under it, and gave out signs of weakness and defeat. People said her heart was broken, but I heeded not them nor her. I thought only of Lavinia, and obstinately shut my eyes to the agony endured by my wife. After the first shock, however, Margaret recovered and bent herself to the task of winning me back from the path I was following. She submitted to the insults and injuries I heaped upon her in bringing my concubine under her roof, and installing her in her place: she upbraided me not, and by every means sought to hide my crime from the world, and induce me to become a better man.

"It was all without avail. It was beyond cure.

"Day by day, hour by hour, Lavinia persecuted her. I believe she went so far as to strike her, but I was so soddened with drink that I heeded it not. If she had battered the poor soul's brains out before my eyes I do not think it would have excited either indignation or horror in me. All that was human seemed to be dried up within my heart. I was a mere animal, crawling the earth to disgust mankind with my terrible deeds.

"Friends and relatives deserted me, and even my brutalised companions turned from me in horror. I was alone with Lavinia and my wife.

"Heaven and earth! how Margaret could have stood under the trials to which she was then subjected I know not, for now, as I review them in my mind's eye, I cannot but shudder at them.

"She, however, bore all with the meekness of a martyr, and ceased not in her attempts to recall me to some of the duties of life. Her prayers and entreaties were, however, rewarded with blows and curses, but she fell not under them; she had,

she said, a sacred duty to perform, and nothing could drive her from it.

"At last she became an eyesore to me: her presence haunted me like that of an accusing angel. I would have rid myself of her by any means.

"During my thoughts Lavinia one day said to me—

"'Why should this canting hypocrite haunt us longer?'

"'Why, indeed,' I replied, 'why, indeed. Heaven knows how heartily I wish to be rid of her.'

"'By any means?'

"'Aye, by any means.'

"'Poison?'"

"'What care I, so that she is gone for ever?'"

"'Enough!'" said the woman. "'Enough! she shall die.'"

"'Use care,'" I said; "'no bungling, or we are lost.'"

"'Never fear,'" was the reply. "'I will effect all without a chance of detection.'"

"What was done I know not; but one evening Lavinia came to me, and said,"

"'All is over with her. I have done it.'"

"'Done it?'" I repeated. "'What have you done?'"

"'Poisoned her.'"

"'Is she dead?'"

"'Not yet. Do you not hear her?'"

"I did hear some one stumbling about the passage outside the room in which I sat, and the sound frightened me."

"In another moment Margaret, ghastly pale, and staggering like a drunkard, fell into the room."

"Mechanically I raised her, and placed her on a couch."

"She turned her eyes upon me, and said—

"'Robert, I die. I am poisoned by the hand of the woman by your side. I have not deserved the cruelties you have heaped upon me. Heaven knows I have been good and true to you.'"

"'You have,' I cried, quite sobered at the spectacle she presented. 'You have. Heaven help me.'"

"'You call too late,' said my wife, 'it has deserted you for ever. I would have won you back to it, but you have prevented me. I die; and my death will prove to you a long, lingering curse which *the grave itself will not wholly obliterate.*'"

"With these words on her lips she died, and I and the guilty being at my side stood gazing on her fair corpse.

"'We shall be detected and punished,' I cried, as the terrible position in which I stood burst upon me.

"'Psha!' cried Lavinia, 'I have done my work too cleverly for that. Be true to yourself, and we can defy the world to fasten the guilt upon us.'

"The news of the death of my wife spread far and near, and the affair came under the notice of the authorities. My way of life, my relations to Lavinia, my horrible cruelties to my wife, were jotted down against me, and Lavinia and I were apprehended on a charge of murder.

"We stood the trial, but nothing could be proved against us. Lavinia had indeed done her work well, for on an examination of the body no trace of poison of any kind could be found.

"We were dismissed from custody; but, as may be supposed, we had to fly from that part of England where we had resided.

"We came to London, and as there was a considerable amount of the money I had received with my wife left to me, after all my extravagancies, we were enabled to live well and keep good society.

"As a matter of course I changed my name, and used my best endeavours to blot out all traces of my identity, and in this I succeeded remarkably well. No one in Wisbech could have possibly recognised in the gay and fashionable man on town, Robert Masters, the country parson, and so matters progressed satisfactorily.

"It was now that I formed an acquaintance with the Earl of Portville, afterwards Duke of Grasmount.

"He was then a mere youth, and fresh from his college. He wished to see life, and I showed it to him to the best of my ability.

"It was through me he became acquainted with Agnes Villiers. It was I who suggested the mock ceremony. It was I who performed it, and it was I who weaned him from the girl, on finding that, fool like, he had formed a real attachment for her; but with all the circumstances of that affair you are perfectly well acquainted. I told you every particular when I lay in the condemned cell at Newgate for—"

"The murder of Adelaide Lascells," broke in Grimer.

"No," continued Robert Masters, "not Adelaide Lascells, but Lavinia Hammond. Adelaide Lascells was but one of her many *aliases*."

"And why did you destroy her?" asked Grimer.

"You shall hear. Returning home one night, half drunk, half mad, I found her in the arms of some man whom I did not know. Under different circumstances I should have perhaps directed my anger against him, but in my then condition I fell upon her. She retaliated, and then ensued an awful struggle, which ended in my casting her to the earth. Whilst she lay there I seized from the table a heavy decanter, and with it beat out her brains."

"Horrible," said Grimer, shuddering at the words, " horrible! I never heard a more terrible narrative."

"You have heard nothing yet. Let me proceed. As you well know, I stoutly protested my innocence to the last, in spite of the direct evidence of the man who saw the crime committed. You know how desperately we attempted to fix the guilt upon him, and you know how signally he failed."

"Yes," said Grimer, "I remember it well."

"I was found guilty, and condemned to die," continued the Black Captain, "and I took leave of you in the condemned cell, at Newgate, entrusting to you the papers concerning the Grasmount case. The morning after our interview, I was to suffer on the scaffold, and, quickly, oh! how quickly the night passed, and the fatal morning came.

"I was pinioned and led forth by the hangman.

"I shall never forget the yells and execrations which greeted my appearance on the scaffold.

"Beneath me stretched a surging sea of human faces, all upturned, and with all the eyes fixed upon me.

"From a thousand throats uprose the roars of curses and hoarse screams of delight at the punishment my crime had brought upon me.

"In all that crowd, as I hastily scanned it over, I could not discern one look of sympathy, or one eye in which pity shone forth.

"All were wild with anger; all were lighted with fiendish passion.

"The sight almost made me sick.

"I can hear now the dull drawl of the minister as he read prayers to me, and exhorted me not to quit the world without confessing my guilt.

"I turned upon him, and bade him be silent, for that prayers were unavailing, as I hade determined to quit the world without satisfying the idle curiosity of a brutal crowd.

"It was in vain he appealed to me. It was unavailing that he poured forth a flood of words from his holy volume. I heeded him not, but, turning to the hangman, bade him do his office as soon as possible.

"He took me by the shoulder, and pushed me towards the drop. As he did so he whispered to me,

"'I say, you're highly honoured, old boy.'

"'Am I?' I asked, 'how so?'

"'Why,' said the hangman, 'Doctor Gascoyne, the famous anatomist, has taken a fancy to have you after you are cut down; and so, instead of being buried like a dog in the prison, you will be carried off to the doctor's, and cut up and lectured upon and examined, and all that sort of thing. Arn't that a comfort?'

"I answered not.

"Singular. Before the hangman had whispered these hurried words my mind had been full of death and the contemplation of the hereafter, but no sooner had he spoken than I became convinced that I was not then to die.

"Suddenly the last words of my wife rang in my ears—'*My death will prove to you a long, lingering curse, which the grave itself will not wholly obliterate.*' I heard them now as distinctly as when they were really uttered, and they served to convince me that my time was not yet come.

"The hangman came near me once more to adjust the rope and cap. As he drew the latter over my eyes, he again whispered,

"'The rope is not over long, and your end will be a painful one. I have orders *not to break your neck*. You will die by suffocation.'

"I felt the cord tighten about my throat, and for a few moments a terrible sensation came over me.

"I broke out into a cold perspiration, and gave way to an agony of indescribable fear.

"Gradually I ceased to hear the exhortations of the minister. My senses were leaving me. Every limb in my body grew stiff, and I went as cold as an icicle. More and more rigid became my limbs, and still less did I hear what was progressing about me.

"At length all was dark and oblivious. I knew no more.

*   *   *   *   *

"The next thing of which I was conscious was that some one was touching my neck, and that human beings were talking of me.

"I endeavoured to speak, but could make no sound. I sought to move, but the effort was futile.

"I could neither see, speak, nor move, and yet I heard distinctly.

"I felt no pain, I knew no other sensation than that of being touched by human hands; and, above all, I heard with a distinctnes which awoke feelings of great surprise within me.

"This is the conversation which fell upon my ear:

"'Well, he died game:'"

"'Yes, game enough.'"

"'Did he leave anything?'"

"'Nothing worth mentioning; there was his clothes and a few odd coins: that was all, nothing worth sharing.'"

"'Oh, that's always your yarn.'"

"'Well, never mind what my yarn is, don't stand grumbling there, lift the coffin down here.'

"'There you are. Mind I've no hand in sending him out, if anything comes of it. You say you are acting under the governor's orders, but that's more than I can answer for.'

"'Bah: hold your foolery. I tell you I have the governor's written orders for the delivery of the body to Dr. Gascoyne, who has taken a fancy to it for the purpose of chopping it up.'"

"'Who is to take it?'"

"'You and I, if you like. But if you're

afraid, I alone. I don't mind pocketing the whole fee, I can tell you.' "

"'Humph, I shall go. You ain't going to have everything your own way.' "

"'Oh, the sound of cash will very soon quash all your scruples.' "

"'Well, you can't say much; you're fond enough of it.' "

"'Well, if I am, I don't profess to have any false scruples, as you do ?' "

"'Don't you ?' "

"'No, I don't ?' "

"'Well, that's more than I'd like to take an oath to.' "

"'Oh curse your growling! now lend us a hand to get the body in.' "

"The next moment I felt myself lifted into a box, the narrow limits of which told me as plainly as possible that it was my coffin.

"'Are you going to nail down the lid ?' " asked the more surly of the two individuals who had held the conversation I have given.

"'No, where's the use ? he'll be out of it again in an hour.' "

"'True ; it's all right then.'"

"I could hear no longer and so I knew that the lid had been placed upon the coffin.'

"I had expected to experience some sensation of suffocation, but, strange to say, I felt nothing.

"I was next lifted up and knew that I had been placed in some vehicle. In another minute the jolting I received assured me that I was on the move.

"An hour's jolting assured me that I was making a tolerably long journey.

"At length the vehicle in which I had been placed drew up at the place where the doctor who had taken so violent a fancy to me resided.

"I was lifted out with some care, and carried up some steps. This I knew by the peculiar motion of the men who bore me.

"A few more jolts and I was deposited in the doctor's study.

"The sounds I now heard assured me that the lid of the box or coffin was again taken off, and that I was in the presence of human beings.

"'Umph,' I heard some one say, 'umph, a fine subject. A very fine subject, indeed. Here is your fee, my men, and tell the governor I am obliged to him—very much obliged to him indeed. Umph, a splendid subject. Perhaps you will lift the body on that board and cover it over. In the morning it will be dismembered, my young men. Umph, very satisfactory !'

"You may readily conceive that I could not endorse the opinion of the doctor.

"If there was any satisfaction in the matter it was all on the side of the professor of the healing art ; to me the sensations I underwent were horrible.

"I made what I conceived to be violent efforts to move my body and to speak.

"I thought I must have accomplished my purpose, but it was quite clear that to those in whose hands I lay I was but an inanimate lump of flesh.

"The men were dismissed and went their way, and I was alone with the doctor.

"'Umph,' I heard him say over and over, 'umph, very satisfactory ; quite delightful for my

young men, but I must reserve the head and neck for myself. The brain of such a criminal must be worth examining. Umph ! by the way—umph, I've nothing better to do—*I'll sever the head from the neck at once.*'

"Judge of the horror with which I listened to these words. Judge of the concentrated feelings of mental and physical agony I underwent, and pity me.

"I heard him unlock some piece of furniture, and draw therefrom a case of instruments. Distinctly I heard the clinking of the steel, and yet I could not move, could not speak, to save myself.

"On the terrors of that moment !"

Grimer shuddered, but waved his hand impatiently for the narrator to continue his tale.

"There was a sound," said the Captain ; "there was a sound of a knife sharpening ; the rasping of the steel seemed to tear through my very heart. The actual pain of a cut could not have been more terrible.

"In a few moments I felt the hand of the doctor on my throat. I knew that the other hand held a knife. Another moment, and I felt the keen steel on my neck.

"It was beyond endurance ; and yet I could not stir to save myself. At that moment Heaven, or Hell, interfered for me, and a knock at the door relieved me of the touch of the doctor.

"He left me, and from the conversation I heard I found that he was called away to attend some desperate case or other.

"My feelings of relief may be imagined ; but they were soon succeeded by a whole host of fears.

"If I did not recover during his absence, I knew I should have his knife across my throat on his return.

"Moments welded themselves into hours, and still I could neither move, see, nor speak.

"At length—oh, the delight of that moment ! —I became conscious that my limbs had lost their rigidity, and that I could move.

"Then a heavy film seemed lifted from my eyes, and the organs of vision resumed their functions.

"I gave vent to my delight in one wild scream, and then sat bolt upright on the bench on which I had been laid.

"Before me, clasping the door in terror, was a poor servant girl, who had been tempted to steal to the laboratory in the dead of the night to catch a glimpse of the mysterious box which had that day been brought to the house.

"She sank to the earth in a swoon, and I leaped from the bench. The whole force of my situation burst suddenly upon me, and I was appalled.

"There was I, a criminal, escaped from the hangman's hands. To be found there alive was to again face death.

"I cast a rapid glance around the apartment in search of clothing. There was none there.

"Without hesitation I left the place, locking the door on the servant, and rushed up the stairs toward the higher rooms.

"Clothes were my sole thought. Clothes I must have, and to obtain them I would have done aught that the human mind could conceive.

"I entered the first apartment I came to. It

chanced to be the doctor's own bed room, and therein I found many articles of dress, in some of which I arrayed myself. I then seized upon whatever articles of value I could find in a hasty search, and prepared to quit the house, but before going I cast one glance into a mirror which hung in the doctor's chamber. I saw the same ghastly white and impassable face upon which you now look. Years have passed, but there has come no change over those features. Nor sorrow nor anger can make them change—I know not why, save that they belong to a hanged man.

"To return. I made good my escape from the house, and soon found myself in haunts with which I was acquainted; but I dared not meet the gaze of those I encountered.

"The few who looked upon me turned away with feelings of horror, and I knew that to remain in England would be to become a marked character, and thus challenge the attention of those from whom I had, in so miraculous a manner, effected my escape.

"In a few days I was enabled to leave the country, and went to France.

"I have been in London again eighteen months, during which time I have placed myself at the head of a desperate gang of thieves, and am —"

"Going headlong back to the gallows, from which you have had so singular an escape," broke in Grimer. "There," he continued, "that will do. I have had enough of your story. The rest I can guess—all the moments of criminals of your class are so nearly of a piece."

"No matter," said Masters, "no matter, I have told you all; and I now tell you that I will win this girl upon whom I have set my heart. I am determined to have her, and nothing shall keep her from me."

"We shall see," said Grimer.

"Ah, we shall see; and now good night. I must be going."

"Night!" said Grimer, "why it's morning, and I should have been in bed hours ago, had it not been for this horrible tale of yours. Ugh! it will make me dream of terrible things for a month."

"I wonder you ever dream of aught else," said the Captain, stalking out of the lawyer's office.

"Oh! you're a bold bad one," said Grimer, locking his door, and stepping out of the house; "but bolder and worse have lived and died before you, and in the most prosaic manner too."

And thus terminated a night of singular interest to more than one of the personages of this history.

CHAPTER XXVII.

IN WHICH THE FIRST EPOCH OF OUR STORY TERMINATES.—A CHAPTER OF INCIDENTS.—LIZ IN DANGER, AND PIPEY TO THE RESCUE.

ROBERT MASTERS, village pastor, murderer, condemned felon, and mysterious highwayman, lost no time in assuring himself of the truth of Grimer's narrative. He set his agents to work, and in a short time discovered that all the lawyer had said was correct to the letter. Liz was under the protection of the powerful Duchess of Grasmount, and lived with her at the ducal villa at Kew.

"She must be torn from there at once," he said, on mastering these facts, "or it will be too late. I must get this fellow Maydock to assist in the task."

A resolution once formed was immediately acted on by the lawless captain of thieves, and he accordingly sought out the burglar, and, finding him one night at Mother Whistler's, he attracted his attention, and, drawing him into a recess, commenced his business. Maydock, who could not shake off his superstitious awe of the Captain, obeyed him like a dog in fear of punishment.

He would have sulked had he dared, but was forced to succumb to the superior will.

"I want you to execute a job for me," said the Captain.

"Name it, and if I can oblige you—"

"You will do so. I know you will, or I should not have broached the subject."

"Why should I not? we are old acquaintances."

"Just so; it is that fact alone which has induced me to seek your aid."

"What is to be done?"

"Listen: all the papers in connection with that Grasmount case are in my possession; you know how I possessed myself of the most important of them"

"I know, to my cost."

"Well, having the principal items to secure success, I am naturally anxious to secure the girl. She must be mine, and by your assistance."

"I feel no inclination to assist any man to the possession of a prize I so much covet."

"Nevertheless you will assist me?"

"I do not know."

"Do not play with me. I am a determined man. That I am your master you know—that you have only to stoop and obey me you must be assured."

"Well, then, since you are so hard upon a fellow I suppose I must."

"I am sure you must."

"But I have lost all trace of the girl, she was stolen from me by a young fiend whom I trusted."

"You mean the lad Pipey; a clever fellow—I know all about it."

"Indeed, and she is now —"

"With her mother-in-law at Kew."

"With the Duchess?'

"With no other."

"Then she knows all?"

"Everything."

"Then the game is up."

"Very nearly, and a fainter heart than mine would throw it up for ever, but I am not such a fool. One desperate move and she is mine."

"What do you propose?"

"I scarcely know. I have made two attempts to bear her from her nest, but they have been vain. Since your infernal attempt to rob the place it has been made so secure that all my arts have been defied; moreover, they guard their treasure so jealously that unless some bold *coup d'etat* is made nothing will drag her from her protectors."

" Nothing shall prevent me from getting at her. A tiger mad with hunger can as easily be kept from its prey as I from her. But give me the scent and I will secure the quarry."

" But to enter the house—there is the difficulty."

" It does not trouble me."

" No ?"

" No : look here."

Maydock drew forth an *antique key*. It was the one on which Mr. Pipey performed on the night when Grimer set him on the track of the burglar.

" Well," said Masters, " what of that?"

" That key will admit me to the villa. It is a relic of bygone days."

" Good. I see you are my man, and as I hate wasting time or words we will at once arrange preliminaries."

" With all my heart."

" Then to-morrow night meet me on the spot where I relieved you of the proceeds of your last journey to Kew. There a horse shall await you. We will at once to the villa, and if needs must be so—burn it down so that we can carry her off."

" That is my style," said Maydock, evidently pleased with the task in which he was to participate.

" I see we understand each other. Good night."

" Good night," said Masters, but in a tone which entirely checked the confidence and familiarity which had grown on his companion during the brief interview—" Good night ; I shall expect you."

" I will not fail."

" It will not be well for you if you do."

With this Masters waved his hand to signify that the interview was at an end, with his cold impassionate face fixed upon his subordinate. He made good his retreat from the room, all within it rising and respectfully saluting him as he passed.

" Curses on him," cried Maydock, " he holds me tightly in his grasp, and holds a spell over me against which I combat in vain. My nerves relax, my hand trembles, my will fails me, and I am forced to prostrate myself in his hateful presence. Is this cowardice? No. I am no craven, but I cannot combat with a being who sets death at defiance, and accosts one from the very grave. Since I cannot struggle with him, I must needs play into his hands, contenting myself with the stray favour he is pleased to cast upon me. Bah! I'll drown remembrance in drink. Care is a d——d bad bed-fellow, and once in his life killed a cat. I'll cut his company in the obliviousness of dissipation."

Maydock walked rapidly from the room in which the foregoing scene was enacted, and strode to a private crib in another part of Mrs. Whistler's hospitable establishment, where, in secret, he could brood over his sorrows and his wrongs, real or imaginary, and wipe out remembrance, burn out the small spark of humanity

yet within him, and sodden his mental parts with the fiery liquors of the respectable hostess.

As soon as he had quitted the room, something began to stir under a bench upon which he and Masters had sat. They had gone to a dark and unfrequented corner, but one, nevertheless, capable of giving those who frequented it a view of the entire room. It was a small niche, a recess in which the only window of the place was inserted. Around the window—a darkened, useless, and altogether dummy window, be it remembered, for the guests of Mrs. Whistler neither cared for having the light of Heaven thrown in upon them, nor their own light thrown out upon the streets—ran a bench, some two feet raised from the ground.

It was under this bench that the something alluded to began to stir. The something at first appeared very like a bundle of old clothes left there by mistake, and which had suddenly determined to roll itself off in search of its owner. The something next began to bear resemblance to a large dog, and finally assumed the parts and outline of a human form.

It was altogether a very comical human form, and one which, once seen, would not be easily forgotten.

It was the figure of a youngster, with a face expressive of all kinds of cunning, good humour, and devilry. This face was surmounted by a close-cropped head of hair, and possessed eyes of preternatural brilliancy and unlimited expression.

The body aforesaid was habited in a suit of clothes which was intended by its designer for a body of about four times the proportion of the body it encased, and this suit of clothes was, moreover, of very flashy colour and shape, the whole bespeaking the presence of no other individual than our friend Mr. Pipey.

On assuming an upright position on the bench, Mr. Pipey first of all shut his left eye; he then shut his right, and afterwards shut them both together, a proceeding which he immediately afterwards varied by shutting his eyes alternately with the rapidity of lightning.

After this peculiar performance had been extended over a space of a minute, Pipey drew up his mouth and whistled one long shrill note. Finding this did him good, he repeated it, and then exhibited some intention of re-commencing the eye-shutting entertainment, when he diversified the monotony of that proceeding by scratching his head.

How long he kept up these singular proceedings it is not for us to say ; suffice it that they were persevered in until the astonishment of the youth had subsided to an extent which admitted of his giving vent to his feelings in a soliloquy. " Vell," said Pipey (somehow he always did commence with that expressive syllable), " Vell, this here's another rum go, ain't it? Vite chops has got the vill arter all ! Maydock's licked out o' it, and I've been a throwing avay three precious veeks a dodging him about, and hiding avay under the most uncomfortablest of benches no end o' hours vithout any effect. The number o' times my hand has a been in that feller's pockets is alarming, and o' course all to no purpose, for the vill vos with old six foot o' lime-vash. But you've done a good thing this time, Pipey: you've come down on a good plot again this journey. Long Captain Lotts' vife wants Liz, does he? Vell, everybody vants her, and the misfortune is that everybody can't have her. I vos in the same line, but I gived it up, and gone in for the brotherly business; but of all who have had the cheek to go in for her, including Maydock and Grimer, Captain Marble Mug is about the very vust. Bolt vith her; I'd like to see him. Try to pull her out o' the villa, vill yer? Not if I'm avare of it, and it vill be queer if, after getting the note of vot's up, I'm not avare of it at the right time."

Running on in this strain Mr. Pipey reviewed the whole of his business, as it appeared to him. He weighed all chances, and struck a balance in favour of himself.

"I'll not drag in a dozen of 'em to help," said the boy; "von head's enough, and so I'll keep the know to myself, and do myself the pleasure of bringing the gal through it vithout assistance."

With his natural love of plotting and secrecy, the boy determined to have no second hand in the matter, although it was clear that his proper course would have been to have gone immediately to Kew, informed the Duchess of the intended plot, and allowed her to take the proper precautions to prevent a successful issue to the schemes under consideration; but this he would not for a moment contemplate. He had not half the faith in a whole army of duchesses as in his own power, and so he decided on pursuing his own course without interruption or deviation.

"Maydock has a key," he said; "and so have I. There's only von thing to do, and that is, to be at Kew before him and the Captain, vatch them in, then follow and floor 'em."

Pipey drew forth a key, which he had constructed from the mould he had taken when Maydock fell asleep at the public-house at Westminster.

"You're a good 'un, too," said Pipey, addressing the key; "it vos right to take your likeness, for yer see vot good I'm going to do now vith yer help. Oh, never lose a chance! that's my motto; and as an instance of the good got out o' not losing a chance, see, now, here—I am put on terms of equality vith these warmints by just taking a cast of you. Oh, I'll be down upon 'em."

We shall see whether Mr. Pipey will be as good as his word.

* * * * *

It is night, and two men meet at a lone spot not far from Mortlake, on the high road to Kew.

One of them is mounted on a charger, and leads a horse by the rein. The other is on foot.

"You are come," said he on horseback—who was, of course, no other than the Black Captain. "It is well. Here is your horse; mount and away as fast as possible. We have not a moment to lose."

"I'm with you." The speaker was Maydock, who vaulted into the vacant saddle, and set his horse in motion.

On went the two evil ones, side by side. On they flew over the wild tract of country in pursuit of their game.

And where was he who was to be at hand with the protection requisite to save the intended victim?

He *should have been* at the Duke's villa hours ago; but he is far from there.

A poor, jaded beast, carrying an excited rider, now appears on the scene.

The rider lashes the horse, and urges it forward; but all efforts are vain. The horse has fallen dead lame, and no effort can make it move beyond a walk.

"Devil take it!" cried the horseman; "this is awful work. Curse my folly for vaiting on Maydock, and attempting to follow him. Oh, curse me! curse me, for not being at my post hours ago! Get on, you brute! Hey on, on! Hey up! It's no use, rot you! I must run for it."

The horseman was Pipey, who, considering his best course would be not to lose sight of Maydock, in case any alterations of his plans should take place, had remained in London dodging his footsteps, and sticking to him with all the pertinacity of a bloodhound on a scent.

He had waited until the last moment, and had suddenly lost sight of the man he tracked.

In desperation he hired the horse which had served him so scurvily, and riding hard, he had just reached the spot indicated in time to see his men gallop off on two magnificent steeds, against whose powers he saw himself powerless to cope.

Pipey, uttering the bitterest curses, sprang to the ground, and in his passion struck the horse he had ridden most vindictively on the head. The poor brute uttered a neigh of pain, and being agonised in the leg which had broken down, sank to the earth, and lay there, whilst our young hero, maddened with excitement, flew over the ground in the direction taken by the horsemen.

Onward he sped; but he knew that the horses were making ten yards to his one.

On, on—still on; but with faltering heart and failing pace.

It is vain he strives to move in unison with the wild impulse which urges him on. It is all in vain! Nature is stretched to the utmost. It can do no more, and the poor boy rushes on, knowing that he races against hope, and that the chances are at least a thousand to one that on reaching the goal his lot will be despair.

It is a long race, but he still bursts forward. The skin is stretched to the utmost—the muscles swell, and the big blue veins stand out on the brow, and appear ready to crack. The brain seems to expand beneath the narrow limits of the skull, and lassitude conquers every limb, but still must he onward. Still must he strive and strive, for everything depends upon him.

No other shares his secret—no other hand can help him! The responsibility devolves on himself by his own willing, and so he has to strive on, and still without hope!

Let him pursue his terrible race, and turn we to those who have preceded him.

The distance the two horsemen had to traverse appeared but a span. A very brief space of time sufficed for covering it, and before midnight they were in the vicinity of the villa.

"There is a copse near at hand where we can secure the horses," said Maydock, as he led the way over a small hedge which divided the road from the park. Masters immediately followed, and in another minute their horses, trained to silence and obedience, stood motionless side by side in a small plantation, where they were tightly secured to a tree.

Maydock led his companion towards the house just as he had previously led Hammer and Pipey, but instead of advancing to the front and performing on the windows as he had previously done, he now assailed the back of the premises.

"There's a door here, which leads to the cellars. It has been closed for years, but the key I produced last night will open it to us. See there."

Maydock pointed to a small arched doorway, which stood in an angle of the building, and which bore traces of being opened but seldom.

"Be wary," continued Maydock, "there are many dogs in this neighbourhood."

They skulked along in the shadow of the wall and without the faintest noise until they reached the doorway indicated by the burglar.

There they paused.

Maydock soon produced his key, and clearing the wards of the lock inserted it.

In a moment the little entrance lay open, and the men hesitated not to descend, being careful to reclose the door after them.

They descended a number of stairs, and threaded a variety of passages, and soon found themselves in the vaults of the house.

"And now," said Maydock, "what is to be done?"

"We must think."

"Do you know the chamber wherein she sleeps?"

"Yes; I have watched it frequently. It is one of a suite of three—the centre one; in the first the Duchess sleeps; in the third, two or three attendants."

"Then the place must be approached through one or other of the two end apartments."

"Just so."

"The devil!"

"Ah, that is what I have said many times as I have contemplated the difficulty. The slightest alarm would bring such a host of servitors about us as would put escape beyond a possibility. But we must not hesitate now."

"There is nothing left, then, but to fire the house, and trust to the chances opening to us in the confusion which would follow."

"I agree with you, and, as it must be done, let it be done at once."

"Follow me," said Maydock.

He led the way through more passages, and at length ascended a flight of steps. Applying to the lock of a door the key he had previously used, Maydock now led his companion into the grand lobby of the house.

At the foot of the principal flight of stairs was a small apartment used by the butler as a pantry on all grand occasions.

The door of this room was temptingly open, and Maydock entered, followed by Masters.

"If it is to be done this is the place," said the former.

"Yes," replied Masters, taking a survey of the room, "this is the place. I see your drift; from this place the fire will at the same moment catch the upper apartments and the stairs."

"Yes."

"Proceed then."

To kindle a fire there was no real difficulty. Several wine bins, half filled with straw, lay about the room, and there was moreover a great quantity of paper, dry wood, cases of spirit, and other materials which tended to lighten the task.

Maydock instantly produced a light, and, applying it to a box containing straw, he had the satisfaction of beholding an immediate effect.

Cunningly he arranged the articles so that the fire should communicate from one to the other, and spread quickly.

With the greatest forethought, he raised the window a few inches to admit a draught of air, and, otherwise completing his arrangements, he and his companion withdrew, and retraced their steps to the cellars.

A fire so well devised did not, as may be supposed, take very long to spread. Everything assisted its progress, and in half an hour the house was in a fair way of being burnt to the ground

Seizing on the massive hangings and dry woodwork the flames extended, and it was not until the floor and wall of the butler's room had fallen in that any of the sleepers were awakened to a sense of the danger in which they stood.

As is usual, the servants were the first to discover the position in which they stood; and, as is still more usual, their first thought was of self-preservation. They rushed from their rooms, and flew over the staircase, leaving the Duchess and her ward alone in the upper apartments. Indeed, they were never thought of until the flames had half ascended the stairs, and entirely cut off their retreat.

The alarm was soon given, and the confusion became intense.

Maydock and Masters were without, anxiously watching the progress of their handiwork.

Concealed under the shadow of an adjoining office, they kept their eyes fixed on the house, and more particularly on that quarter where they knew the Duchess and Fair Liz slept.

Their interest soon grew into alarm; for they beheld no movement in the quarter from whence they were anxiously expecting it.

"H—ll's fury," cried Maydock, "what if the staircase should be on fire and they cannot escape."

They had calculated on the alarm being given sooner, and on the whole family rushing from the blazing pile into their arms, but they had made a miscalculation.

They saw but a crowd of half frantic servants rushing about in the greatest confusion; the object of their especial interest and the Duchess were nowhere to be seen.

"What is to be done?" cried Masters.

"Nothing can be done. We dare not expose ourselves, and must await the result from this spot."

"But she may burn to death."

"She may."

"And no one to lend a helping hand! Oh, it is horrible!"

"There is no help for it. It was a desperate chance. If it fails it cannot be helped. We have done all we could do."

"Yes, to burn her to death. But she must and shall be rescued! Look there—look there!"

Masters pointed to the house. At a window an immense height from the ground, stood a young and lovely girl, crying for help. There was a light behind her which plainly told that the apartment behind in which she stood was on fire.

"Heaven and earth!" cried Masters, "will no one attempt to save her?"

"All right, old Dover Cliff," said some one behind him, "all right. Ain't I here to save her?"

The speaker was Mr. Pipey, who, springing from his hiding-place with the agility for which he was so famous, cleared the intervening space between the office and the house at a few bounds, and then divested himself of his coat.

A crowd of servants collected about him.

"Some of you run for ladders," cried the boy, "and the others had best keep their eyes open in the shadow of yonder building, for that's vhere the fellers are who have lighted up this here blaze."

Maydock saw that the boy was pointing to the spot where he stood.

"Come," he cried to Masters, "come, the servants turn upon us; in another moment we shall be captured."

Self preservation was now the sole thought of the villains, and, turning their backs on their handiwork, they fled in the direction of the plantations, leaving Pipey to do the best he could to save Fair Liz.

The boy seemed to crawl up the side of the house, and, in a short time, had reached an overhanging ledge immediately under the window at which Liz stood.

With a shriek of joy the poor girl threw herself into his arms, and was dragged through the blazing mass of wood and drapery.

Pipey bore her in his arms along the ledge, but in doing so he passed a window at which he beheld the Duchess.

"All right, old lady," said Pipey, as he hurried on with his burden; "all right! your turn next."

By the time Pipey had reached the end of the ledge with his lovely burden the servants had returned from their hunt after a ladder. Placing this very requisite article against the house, they scaled it, and in a few moments received Pipey's rescued treasure.

"Mind you keep your eyes open," cried Pipey; "for there are those about who vill snap her from yer, if they get but the ghost of a chance."

"Oh, they wont do us," cried the servant who was topmost on the ladder.

"I don't know that," said Pipey, his facetiousness returning in all its glory; "I did hear of a gentleman, who vos in the habit of getting up much earlier than any of you, who lost his back teeth ven he chanced to doze in company of the same kind as is now honouring the willa vith their presence."

With this he placed Liz in the arms of the servants, and they bore her steadily down the ladder.

Pipey immediately returned along his perilous path, and dashing open the window of the apartment occupied by the Duchess, burst into the room, and found her insensible on the floor.

To snatch her up, and drag her through the aperture he had made, was but the work of an instant; yet, quick as he had been, he was but just in time, for as he stood on the ledge outside the window the floor of the room fell in, and the flames burst upwards.

"That's a narrow escape," said Pipey, looking back; "but better that than death."

He hurried on to the ladder, and this time dismounted from the ledge, and assisted in bearing the Duchess to the earth. His first impulse on reaching the ground was to rush away in the direction he had seen the servants take with Liz, but his progress was arrested by a sight which almost curdled his blood.

On the ground lay the men who had carried the insensible girl. They were bleeding from wounds on the head, and their treasure was gone.

"Devil take it," cried Pipey, "they are good ones, but I'll do 'em yet. Here, some of you run to the left, and get into the London road by the nearest cut you know. They will pass that way with the lady."

"Are they mounted?" cried a gamekeeper.

"Mounted!" cried Pipey, with contempt; "d'ye think I could see their horses a standing all ready to bolt at a moment's notice, *and not ham-string 'em?* Poor brutes, it vos a pity to do it, but I knew my men"

"Well," said the man, hurrying off, "if they ain't mounted I know a cut as will bring us into the London Road at least a quarter of a mile ahead of 'em."

"I'm with yer," said Pipey; "off we go."

And off they did go; rushing along the park, and darting off at angle which brought them near to the river, and consequently down to the London Road.

"Stand fast," said Pipey; "they must come this way, and they can't be far off."

He was right.

Very soon the hurried tread of men was heard in the distance, and a glance along the road revealed the figures of three persons—two men and a female, the latter laying unconscious on the shoulder of the tallest of the two villains, who had laid so devilish a scheme for her abduction.

"The flour merchant has her," whispered Pipey; "stand close, and be ready. They can fight like devils, and will do so when put to it."

"And so can and will we," said the men.

"That's yer sort," said Pipey; "yer game is

to beat 'em down afore they can get at their barkers. Don't give 'em a chance of putting their hands in their pockets."

Another minute and the trio approached opposite the ambush, and with a wild shout Pipey and his followers were upon the murderous incendiaries.

"Down with 'em," cried Pipey, and before Masters had time to defend himself, a blow on the shoulder from a stout bludgeon forced him to yield his burden.

Maydock was served in a similar manner but contrived to free himself from the attacking party and draw his pistols. Firing at those immediately attacking the Black Captain he freed him from restraint, and that worthy immediately followed the example set him and drew his pistols. Maydock had had his fire and had done some service, as two of the servants fell beneath his aim.

The Captain was about to try what he could do, and levelling his weapons, one at Pipey and the other at a man who was advancing upon him, he fired : both shots took effect.

But now the villains had done their worst, and there were yet six servants uninjured. Finding themselves beaten they turned and fled.

"They've given me a dose which, maybe, I shan't get over in a hurry," said Pipey, endeavouring to raise himself from the ground, " but I don't care much for that. So that Liz is safe I can die."

"Die, my man," said a servant, raising him gently from the ground, "die, why you are worth fifty dead men yet. Don't talk of dying. For what you've done to-night the Duchess will make a man of you."

"Yes, if Marble Head hasn't made a ghost of me."

Pipey smiled feebly, and sank back exhausted from pain and loss of blood. Liz and her boy-protector were picked up from the ground, and borne back to the villa.

By the time they reappeared there the fire had been somewhat suppressed, and the Duchess had recovered from the swoon into which fright had thrown her.

The first thought which crossed her brain was of Liz ; and on learning that she had been snatched from one dreadful fate only to fall a victim to another, her grief knew no bounds.

She was loudly lamenting for her lost darling when the group of servants advanced with Liz in their arms, laying side by side with her protector and humble friend.

"Who saved her ? " cried the Duchess; "tell me who saved her, and I will bless him a thousand times."

"It was this poor boy," said the butler, looking at the pale and motionless Pipey; "poor fellow, it was he who snatched her and your Grace from the house, and he has now fallen a victim to the villain who would have borne the lady away."

The Duchess, with Liz in her arms, stooped over poor Pipey, and, clasping his cold hand, gazed tenderly into his face.

"Brave, though misguided boy," she said, affectionately, " it is sad to see him die thus ; die? —no, no, he must be saved. Why do you all stand here ? A surgeon—a surgeon—some of you. A thousand pounds for the man who can save his life."

Several of the bye-standers rushed off in pursuit of surgeons, whilst the Duchess gave orders to convey Liz and Pipey to the residence of a gentleman in the immediate neighbourhood.

* * * * * *

Philippe Morlavine soon grew weary of his residence in Surrey. He panted for his native Italy, and hesitated not to accept the first excuse to return thereto ; it was not long coming. One day the grandmother of Marie, the grim old Zingari woman, sought him out and gave him the office to quit England.

"The time has come for action," she said.

"What do mean ?"

"What do I mean ? Did you not undertake the task of avenging my wrong ?"

"Yes."

"Then the task commences now. Marie is in Italy."

"Indeed."

"Aye, indeed ! She has sunk another step downwards."

"What do you mean ?"

"I mean she is now the mistress of another man. Great God ! The time may come when she will be the mistress of many."

"My poignard shall drink her heart's blood first."

"'Tis well. But there are others who must die first. Shall the betrayers live while the betrayed perish ?"

"Leave all to me. The fulness of time shall reveal my plans."

"I must, then. But I, too, must have a hand in the work. I will go with thee to Italy."

"Be it so. We will start without delay."

"We will waste not a day. Every moment is precious when vengeance is the work on hand."

END OF THE FIRST EPOCH.

THE SECOND EPOCH.

CHAPTER XXVIII.

CARLTON HOUSE.—THE COMING OF AGE.

THREE YEARS! How fraught with change is that brief period! Three years, and in the lapse of time the boy grows into the man, the man into second childhood, and thence to the grave. Great changes, wondrous movements and improvements grow and are perfected in the time. Old institutions decay and become forgotten, friends may become foes, and foes friends. The face of things change, and we find ourselves acting in new parts in new dramas of life, and we become conscious that we are not what we were.

Since the last chapter of this story we have advanced a period of three years, and we have now to see what time has done for those personages with which our readers are now familiar.

Let us first of all give a glance at that chief performer, whose name hovers over these pages as it does over those of the History of England, darkening them, and leaving behind a trail which can only excite the anger and disgust of those who follow it. We allude, of course, to the Prince of Wales. In this tale it is our aim to paint the manners and customs of the Court during the reigns of the Georges III. and IV., and in carrying out our intention we shall spare no one who deserves censure and opprobrium, nor shall we omit one particular which will tend to render imperfect the picture of life in England during the last century, or throw a light on the dark mystery which surrounded the life of the unhappy Queen Caroline.

With this brief preface to our second epoch we will at once see what the principal personages of our history are now doing.

The Prince of Wales—that sublime specimen of humanity, that burlesque on gentility, and that stain on manhood, whose very name cannot even now be uttered by Englishmen without a blush— is now in his twenty-first year, and has set up in life on his own account.

He no longer flits about Marlborough House, which for so long has been his town house, through the obliging disposition of its noble owner. Carlton House has now been furnished for the youthful heir to the throne, and the nation has paid for his luxuries with the most lavish hand. As Mr. Thackeray observes:—"His pockets were filled with money—he said it was not enough; he flung it out of window; he spent £10,000 a-year for the coats on his back. The nation gave him more money, and more, and more. The sum is past counting."

The Prince was undoubtedly a fool born, and those by whom he was surrounded strove as hard as possible to make him a confirmed lunatic for life.

They pandered to his lewd tastes; they flattered his vanity; they called him "the first gentleman in Europe"—he was the most confirmed bore in Christendom;— they said he was handsome—he was simply repulsive; they wrote his letters for him, and called him a patron of the arts, when, in reality, he had not a thought above the prize ring and the orgies of the night.

He was, in fact, a singularly objectionable man; but he was the Prince of Wales, and that title sufficed to cover a whole multitude of sins.

But, perhaps, these remarks are anticipatory; we had best allow our history to speak for itself.

It is the 10th of February, 1784, and the alterations at Carlton House are finished, and a grand entertainment marks the house-warming; the Prince gives a splendid ball to the nobility and gentry.

The scene was, perhaps, one of the most dazzling ever witnessed in England. The state chair was of gold, covered with crimson damask: on each corner of the feet was a lion's head, expressive of fortitude and strength (save the mark!); the feet of the chair had serpents twining round them, to denote wisdom (cruel mockery; the maker of that chair must have been a most able satirist). Facing the throne appeared the helmet of Minerva, and over the windows Glory was represented by Saint George, with a superb gloria.

But the saloon was the *chef d'œuvre;* it was hung with a figured lemon satin; the window-curtains, sofas, and chairs were of the same colour. The ceiling was ornamented with emblematical paintings, representing the Graces and Muses, together with Jupiter, Mercury, Apollo, and Paris.

Two ormolu chandeliers were placed there. The ornaments were truly beautiful, and the design was long the admiration of the town. It consisted of a palm, branching out in five directions, for the reception of lights.

A beautiful figure of a rural nymph was represented entwining the stems of the tree with wreaths of flowers. In the centre of the room was a rich chandelier.

The range of the apartments from the saloon to the ball room, when the doors were open, formed one of the grandest spectacles ever beheld. Through these glorious rooms, on the night of the ball, stole a sweet perfume, which filled the air and rendered it intoxicating to breathe.

The suite of apartments gradually filled with a crowd of gorgeously dressed people. They were the cream of English aristocracy. Seated on the chair of state is the Prince of Wales. He is not much altered, but appears stouter, and there is just a little more of the man about him. But still there is the same vacant expression of the face, and the unmistakable *animal* about the eye. He is, in fact, still the same man who met Fair Liz at the low beer house in Westminster on the night of the opening of this tale.

This ball night was supposed to be the entrance of the Prince into the world; but he had seen it, in many of its worst phases, long before. There he sat, dressed in his famous coat of pink silk, with white cuffs; a waistcoat of white silk, with various coloured foil, and *adorned* with a profusion of French paste; a hat ornamented with two rows of steel beads, five thousand in number, with a button and loop of the same metal, and cocked in a military style.

His shoes were adorned with an invention of his own (delightful piece of ingenuity and taste), in the shape of a buckle. It covered almost the whole instep, reaching down to the ground on either side of the foot; and on this the royal youth prided himself that he had made an important discovery, which was to benefit his generation. He was surrounded by a crowd of flatterers and toadies, and appeared highly delighted at the stream of fulsome compliments which was poured into his royal ears.

"Ah," said one, "I should not like to be answerable for the same amount of havoc as will be made by your Highness among the fair sex tonight. The result of the entertainment must be alarming—positively alarming."

The Prince giggled, and pretended that he was far from believing what he heard, but the delighted expression of his face proved that he thoroughly enjoyed the coarse flattery heaped upon him.

"Yes," said another, "his Highness will most assuredly create a great impression, but I think at the end of the night he will have to acknowledge himself a vanquished man."

"How so?"

"I mean there will be one present to whom he will have to deliver up his heart on demand, and to whom he will become a slave at first sight."

"Pooh! Why should I?" asked the Prince.

"Because the first and noblest in the world have done so, and have not been able to find an antidote for the spell this witch has the power of casting about her."

"Nonsense," said another of the by-standers, "this is one of Cavendish's pleasant fictions or extraordinary dreams. A glance at the charmer will dissipate all the expectations one may have formed from the description rendered. I really never knew Cavendish to look upon a tolerably pretty face without becoming enraptured with it, and dilating upon it as the lineaments of an angel. But he had better explain himself. It's as well to know who the new wonder is."

"Well, Everton," said Viscount Cavendish, a youth of extremely prepossessing appearance, but whose tastes and habits were of rather a low caste, "well, Everton, I will describe my wonder; and if, on seeing her, you accuse me of exaggeration in one particular, I will submit to be laughed at as long and as heartily as you may please. Know, then, that I have just returned from Rome, which place formed the culminating point of my Italian wanderings. I had no sooner taken up my quarters in the city than rumours of the wondrous English lady reached me. The very attendants at my hotel were enraptured about her, and I heard nothing else but a long-continued singing of her praises. Curiosity tempted me to seek out this enslaver of all hearts, and see if I could endorse the popular verdict. One day I encountered her in the Vatican. She was accompanied by the Duchess of Grasmount, whom I at once recognised and accosted. Being received with more than ordinary favour by the lovely duchess I fastened myself securely to her side, and she, I must say, with extreme reluctance introduced me to her charming companion. I was completely astonished. Such a miracle of loveliness never before presented itself before me, and I was at a loss even to acknowledge her slight but graceful bow. How shall I describe her? To a form as faultless as that of Venus de Medici add a face as glorious as ever looked from the canvas of an Italian *maestro*. Over her shoulders, uncontracted by the slightest fastening or ornament, fell, what I may with truth term a flood of golden hair; the only perfect shade of golden hair I ever looked upon. Her eyes were large and of the most heavenly blue; and such a hand and arm I never looked upon. The skin was of transparent whiteness, and the form as beautiful as was ever conceived by the most perfect painter and anatomist. The *tout ensemble* of this creature, your Highness, has never been equalled in my time; and I really doubt if, when she is gone, such another will ever present herself in the world."

"Bravo, Cavendish," said Lord Everton, "that is not at all bad; but really I must still doubt the absolute perfection of this lady until mine own eyes have looked upon her."

"As you will," replied Cavendish; "yet time will prove that I am right, and that my portrait is not flattered."

"That we shall be enabled to decide," said the Prince, "if, as you lead us to understand, she will be here to-night."

"She will."

"But who is she? You have, as yet, neglected to supply her name."

"Ah, your Highness, there you puzzle me. Her name is Elizabeth Balfour; but *who* she is is a mystery which no one can solve. There are many stories about her birth and parentage going the round of the saloons, but I believe the whole of them to be fictitious. They say the Duchess is quite silent on the subject."

"How mysterious."

"Yes," said Everton, "but quite in keeping with the whole movements of the family of late. For three years their establishments have been broken up, and whilst the Duke has lived in the comparative seclusion of his new villa at Kew, the Duchess has been wandering over Europe with no earthly aim that one can discover. I suppose this new beauty is some *protége*, whom she has been educating in Italy."

"I believe," said Cavendish, "that the mysterious one has been studying in Italy, and, if women can be belived, with excellent results, for she is reported a miracle of learning and accomplishments."

"Beautiful and learned!" said Everton, "if she should be but amiable, it appears that we have at last stumbled on that *rara avis*, a perfect woman."

"I am dying to see her," said the Prince; "I really was never before so much interested in any woman in the world."

This was a direct lie; he had been equally interested in a score or two of women of all denominations, from Princesses down to ballet dancers.

"Well, your Highness will soon be satisfied, for the Duchess is sure to come and as sure to bring her *protége*, for she is too fond of her to miss a single chance of exhibiting her."

"But I must caution your Highness," said Everton, "that Mrs. Fitz Herbert will be here to-night, and that she is readily jealous of every glance of your Highness which does not fall upon herself."

"Oh, true; poor Fitz-Herbert—I really think she is fond of me."

"Fond, your Highness! Why, the lady positively doats on the very ground on which you tread. Fondness!—call it rapturous love, or devouring passion, but do not apply the misnomer of fondness."

The Prince blushed,—he could blush,—and beat Everton with his pocket-hankerchief, and pretended to be very angry, and concluded by proposing to retire and refresh himself with wine. The task of bowing to the numbers that approached his state chair was too much for him.

During the absence of the Prince and his friends, we will take a glance at his guests. As we have already said, all the rank, wealth, and beauty of England was represented in those halls on that memorable night. There was a perfect blaze of beauty assembling, and the murmur of soft voices, the rustling of gorgeous dresses, mingling with the delicious music in the ballroom, rendered the scene enchanting. The fashion of the time made it pardonable for ladies to wear dresses which exposed far more of their persons than would be deemed consistent with modesty at the present day, and although a shrew or an amateur saint might enter a protest against such a mode of dressing, or rather leaving undressed the human figure, the effect was far from objectionable, and appeared quite in keeping with the character of the scene.

In spite of all that may be said or written on the subject, we trust it will be long before the brilliant white arm, and snowy swanlike throat shall be hidden in our theatres and ball-rooms.

The fashion has outlived the most virulent attacks of the bitterest satirists—amongst others that of the first Napoleon, who, at a grand entertainment bade the servant heap coals in the grate until the heat became quite suffocating, and on being questioned as to his reason for the act, replied, "I thought it would be requisite, for these ladies are half naked,"—and will survive as long as female charms remain unimpaired and sufficient vanity remains to prompt their due exhibition.

But this is somewhat foreign to our subject.

In such an assemblage as that we have been describing, it is only reasonable to expect to find some singular characters, and those who were present at that ball could have seen many.

There was one with whom the reader is already acquainted. He was a tall, powerfully built man, habited in a *suit of Genoa velvet of raven blackness.* The ornaments were black bugles of great beauty. The face of this man was ghastly pale, and lacked expression. At a glance it was easy to recognise the Black Captain, Robert Masters, but he was unknown as that individual in that assemblage. On his breast glittered a star and several foreign orders, and these trinkets were his passports to that place.

We can easily hear what was thought of him by listening to that group of ladies who scan him with so much interest:

"What a singular individual," said one, "does any person know him?"

"Oh, yes," said another, "I have met him twice at Lord Pardoe's; he is an Austrian, and his name is Count Carlo Paskewich; he is, as you say, a singular individual, for he is always habited as you see him, and ever assumes the same expression of countenance which you now see.

"How pale he is."

"Ghastly pale: but he never has any other. I sat near him when there was a wild dispute between him and Lord Overmore at the card table at Lord Pardoe's. Words ran high, and Overmore became most insulting, but there was no change in the demeanour of the Count; and the singularity of his countenance then attracted universal attention. How I should like to touch his face; it really appears to me to be marble.

"It certainly doos not appear to have any warm blood coursing through it."

"Well, I would not marry such a man for the possession of an empire. Ugh! think of waking in the night and looking at that face on the pillow by your side."

"Fancy it on your heart, chilling it to stone!"

What singular fancies will possess the ladies when once they give the rein to their imaginations.

"He appears to know no one," said another of the ladies to whose conversation we are rude enough to listen.

"He is a comparative stranger," said the lady who had the honour of the captain's acquaintance; "and were it otherwise, I doubt if he would have much to say, for he is of a somewhat morose disposition, and does not care to make acquaintances."

"He is indeed a character, but one I should not claim acquaintance with."

"Dear me!" suddenly exclaimed one of our party of gossips, "dear me! there is that funny little Captain de Pipes, who made us all laugh so at Wilmott's the other evening; how I wish he would come this way."

"To what regiment does he belong?" asked another.

"That is a secret. He, too, is somewhat of a mystery, for no one knows him and no one can guess at his regiment."

"Does he not say what corps is honoured with his quaint figure?"

"No; he always passes the subject off with a jest, but he is accredited by the Duchess of Grasmount, and many ministers, members of parliament, and judges of the supreme courts; so I presume he is worth knowing."

"He is at all events a complete droll: the other evening some one asked him the number of his regiment and he replied 'The 107th Wild Whistlers of the Wilderness,' an answer which threw us all into convulsions."

"Oh, I do not believe he belongs to the army at all."

"You are perfectly right," said a gentleman who approached our group, and joined in the conversation, "your are decidedly right: your humorous hero is no more a soldier than myself."

"Then who and what is he?"

"A gentleman, I believe: and one to whom we are much indebted for the security we are now enjoying in this metropolis."

"What do you mean?"

"Can you keep a secret?"

"Oh yes," cried all the ladies in a breath.

"Well then: your hero is no other than the government spy and thief taker—Kilworth."

"What! the man whose name is now in the mouth of all London."

"Yes."

"Good heavens! But what is he doing here?"

"I can but guess, but my impression is that he is paying particular attention to that Austrian Count, Paskewich."

The astonishment of the ladies at this revelation may readily be conceived: but we must leave them to discuss the subject, and meanwhile we must pay more attention to Captain de Pipes, in whom the reader has of course recognised his acquaintance, Mr. Pipey. But his doings since we last saw him must be told in a fresh chapter.

CHAPTER XXIX.

CONCERNS PIPEY AND REVEALS WHY HE WAS AT CARLTON HOUSE, TOGETHER WITH THE MEETING OF THE PRINCE WITH FAIR LIZ.

MR. PIPEY soon recovered from the effects of the wound given him in his encounter with the Black Captain and Maydock on the occasion of the fire at the villa at Kew.

Naturally hardy he suffered but small inconvenience from the wound, and having youth on his side he soon recovered health and strength.

It was the determination of the Duchess of Grasmount that he should not return to his former mode of life, and by dint of much coaxing, backed by the arguments of Liz, he promised to throw up thieving and seek a more honest mode of passing through the world.

The Duchess had him educated and then purchased a commission in the army for him, but in a very few months he came to her and told her it was beyond him to settle down into the routine of military life.

"There is no excitement in it," he said, "I must have something more lively, or I shall give up the ghost."

There was a long consultation as to what could be done with him, when a friend of the Duchess came to the rescue.

Divining the bent of the youth, and discovering in him a natural aptitude for plotting and intrigue, he procured for him an office in the Secret Service of the Government, and then Pipey, or, as he was called by the Duchess, Captain de Pipes, found himself in his right position.

He soon became invaluable to the Home Office, and was at times employed on missions of the utmost importance at foreign courts.

Never was there a nose for smelling out a plot equal to that owned by Pipey, and never was there an inclination so capable of appreciating the gift of the nose. Pipey was always on some scent or other, and was always equal to the occasion; but however emergent the case, however laborious the task before him, he could always find time to watch over and protect Fair Liz.

To this might be attributed the fact of her having passed over a period of three years in safety.

Knowing well her enemies she kept them in view, and on the departure of his pet from England he knew that she was safe as long as he had those who could injure her under his special care.

Thus he had been her guardian angel for three years, and the task had been a light one : but now it was to begin again in earnest. Liz, still more fatally beautiful, was in England, and Masters had found her out. He was powerful and clever, and Pipey had to play his cards with care, to escape the chance of losing the game.

"He is deep," said Pipey (we shall never be enabled to call him De Pipes), "but I am deeper. If he gets over me I shall be mistaken. It is not under the mask of Count Paskewich he is likely to take me in. I'm down upon him."

And he was !

He had followed him day and night, and now in the course of things tracked him to the Prince's ball.

"And a very good thing it is too," said the secret agent of his Majesty's Government, viewing his Royal Highness with evident satisfaction.

The arrival of the Duchess of Grasmount was the signal for a general commotion throughout the assemblage.

The reputation of the mysterious beauty had preceded her, and all the fashionable host was literally on tip-toe to get a sight of the new belle.

They had some time to wait, however, for the Duchess was late. But when, at length, she did appear, the scene was one of intense excitement.

She entered the grand saloon surrounded by a perfect galaxy of fashion and beauty ; but dazzling as was her set it was eclipsed by the being who formed the central figure.

It was our old acquaintance, Fair Liz : beautiful as she always was, her loveliness was now transcendent, and as the eyes of the gazers became rivetted on her, murmurs of enthusiastic admiration were buzzed about the vast hall.

Fair Liz now became convinced that she was the centre of all this attraction, and at first her natural modesty made her a little awkward, but a slight pressure of her arm by the Duchess entirely reassured her, and she trod the apartment as proudly as a queen and yet with the most womanly grace.

The Prince and his friends left their elevated position and advanced towards the new comers : a condescension of the most marked character.

"Be firm," whispered the Duchess to her as the royal libertine advanced, "remember it is beyond his power to harm you now."

"Do not fear," said our heroine.

In another moment she was face to face with her late persecutor.

As his eyes encountered her's a look of blank astonishment spread over his countenance, and he was too confounded to speak for some moments.

At length he muttered forth some vague compliment, which was almost inaudible.

The Duchess soon placed the Prince at ease.

"I see your Royal Highness recognises an old acquaintance. The re-union is quite charming."

"I have great pleasure in saluting an old acquaintance—dare I say friend ?"

"Undoubtedly," the Duchess assumed for Liz, "undoubtedly; my gentle friend has informed me of your former intimacy, and I see no reason why the title of friend should be dropped."

The Prince looked at the Duchess. There was that in her glance which assured him that she comprehended the nature of the former intimacy alluded to, and that it was not distasteful to her. He observed this with satisfaction, and taking the hand of Liz pressed it warmly.

It was not without a shudder that the poor girl underwent this ordeal; but she contrived to hide her feelings as well as she possibly could, and submitted with a better grace than might have been anticipated.

On the buzz of admiration subsiding, and the introductions having been completed, the majority of those who had surrounded the Prince and Fair Liz moved away, and left them together.

Even the Duchess turned her attention to another part of the room, and, as if by predetermined arrangement, the Prince was left to hold converse with Liz.

Ah ! fair Duchess, your plans are far deeper than would appear at the first glance.

Liz was seated on a lounge, and the Prince hung over her and gazed with a kind of wild rapture into her eyes. The poor girl shrank back under the burning glance, but it was useless to evade it. She felt, when she did not see, the fiery eyes so filled with dark passions piercing her very heart.

She wondered why the Duchess did not return to her. She could not comprehend her position, but she was compelled to endure all that was most distasteful to her pure mind.

"The words of the Duchess," said the Prince, "somewhat reassures me, fair lady; but I would learn from your own lips whether the past is forgiven and forgot. Believe me, I never dreamt of your position in society when in the height of my youthful ardour and indiscretion, and I therefore claim your pardon."

"You have it," said Liz. "I have long since ceased to think of the matter. I pray you, do not recal it to memory, for its details may engender a feeling within me which I would rather smother that permit to kindle."

"I will say no more. Indeed I, too, would fain forget that past which reflects so little credit on myself."

"Your Highness had best not pursue the theme," said Liz, becoming annoyed with the forced apologies elicited from the Prince.

"True, let us change it. I hear you have but recently returned from Italy. Did you admire the country?"

"Much," replied Liz, vacantly.

"I do not wonder at it. Land of poetry and of song! true home of soul! I, too, should enjoy Italy. I think I should have been tempted there had I but known that I should have met thee."

"How so," demanded Liz.

"Can you ask? Would it not be rapture, would it not be bliss, to spend one's days beneath Italia's clear blue sky with thee to gaze upon, with thee to hold converse with! Would it not be the quintessence of enjoyment to compare thee with olive beauties of that land, and admire all the more the delicate lily because it was intermixed with the full blown damask roses? Should I not have been supremely happy had this been my good fortune?"

"I do not know by what right you address me thus," said Liz, indignantly. "Surely there is nothing in the past to induce you to think that such compliments are welcome to me, and undoubtedly no word or action of mine this night can have emboldened you to think that your companionship would ever be tolerated by me."

"What!" said the Prince, not in the least disconcerted, "what! the same haughty beauty as of old, the same fire, the same uncontrollable spirit! Ah, me! It is hard to encounter its fury, but I would far rather see you thus excited than so impassable—so calm and placid."

"Your Highness is insulting."

"Nay, by heaven! Nothing could be further from my thoughts!"

"Then you are annoying. Will not that induce you to desist?"

"Indeed! I cannot desist talking to you, fair lady; and to talk to you and not speak of admiration and love is impossible."

"I tell you such language is distasteful to me."

"Ah, me! ah, me! I am born to meet your scorn. Will nothing soften your heart towards me?"

"Yes. Remember that I am a lady, and that I dare not listen to such language as that which you use."

"And wherefore not?"

"Do you ask me?"

"But I must persist. Wherefore not?"

"Because it is language to which every honourable woman should be a stranger, although a Prince be the utterer."

"But I swear, dear lady, I love you! I swear I have never ceased to wear your image in my heart, and to cherish it there as the dearest treasure it ever possessed. Is not that sufficient excuse for any warm language I may use?"

This conversation had begun to excite attention, and more than a score pair of eyes were fixed upon those who held it.

Liz was much confused, and failed to reply to the question of the Prince, a proceeding which he chose to interpret into a passive acquiescence to his query.

He was therefore about to follow up the advantage he supposed himself to have obtained, when Captain de Pipes, ever watchful—ever ready to assist his fair friend, stalked boldly up to the spot, and throwing himself carelessly on the lounge beside Liz, exclaimed—

"Well, here we are again. And how do we like the new apartments, and what do we think of the company?"

This was a bold stroke, but the interruption was acceptable to Liz, who at once turned her attention to Pipey, and assured him that she was enjoying herself amazingly.

"Yes, you were," said Pipey to himself, "about as much as would the lamb in the jaws of the famished wolf."

"I am not aware, sir," said the Prince, boiling over with anger, "by what right you interrupt my conversation with that lady!"

"And I," said Pipey, "am not aware by what right you force your conversation on that lady when it is palpable to the whole assembly that it is distasteful to her. Your Highness would do well to retire."

This brief conversation was carried on in so low a tone that it was quite impossible for the bystanders to catch a word of it, but it was quite palpable that the singular scene which had been progressing between the Prince and Liz had attracted universal attention; and seeing that this was the case his Highness thought it best to accept Pipey's advice and retire.

He did so with a smile, but under it worked a tumult of feelings which rendered the "first gentleman of Europe" very uncomfortable.

"He is a nice youth," said Pipey, "but he musn't show off any of his monkey tricks with me or he will hear of something he would rather have kept dark. I know something of his proceedings which will scarcely bear the light, and if he does not mind his youthful eye it will be made public."

"Oh, Pipey," cried Liz, "you should not have interfered; you have made an enemy of the Prince, and he will never forgive you."

"Then he may leave it alone. But don't fear

for me. The Prince can't harm me. I'll singe his fingers for him soon, and then you know I shall be safe. 'Burnt children will not play with the fire.' But here is the Duchess. I will leave you in her company. Beware of her! I am afraid she does not mean well by you."

"How?"

"Hush—not another word!"

The Duchess now approached Liz, and Captain de Pipes, bowing slightly to her, stalked away.

CHAPTER XXX.

THE SCARLET RIBBON.—A BAND OF DESPERADOES. —THE DISCOVERY OF A PLOT.

THE Black Captain wandered through the rooms of Carlton House without bestowing any particular attention on those with whom he came in contact.

The few whom he knew he passed with a slight nod of recognition, declining many invites to enter into conversation, and apparently endeavouring to be as much alone with his thoughts as the distracting character of the scene in which he moved would admit of.

An interested observer might, however, have noticed that from time to time he cast most searching glances amongst several groups of men, apparently searching for some person or persons with an earnestness approaching anxiety.

What was most singular on the part of the Captain was, that ever and anon he would dive his hand deep into his pocket, and on producing it would exhibit, bound tightly over his white glove, *a narrow scarlet ribbon*. With this on his hand, he would pass his fingers over his eyes, so that the ribbon could be distinctly seen by those who were sufficiently interested in him to take particular note of his actions.

This proceeding on the part of Masters excited no marked attention, but as he passed on it could be observed that some score or two of gentlemen, and a few ladies also, exhibited on their gloves a band of the same coloured ribbon.

It was evident that this was some signal, and that Carlton House was besieged by some mysterious band of men who had met there for the practice of purposes which would not well bear the light let in upon them.

Masters at length reached a small retiring room, which was tenantless. Entering the apartment, he evidently awaited with feverish anxiety the arrival of some one whose advent he expected with more alacrity than was realised.

In a few minutes, however, a second individual, a young man of remarkably prepossessing appearance, dressed very elegantly in full costume, entered the retiring room and confronted the Captain.

"You are here at last," said Masters, with some petulance.

"I am here now that it suits me to be here. What have you to say?"

"Beware, Lewis Arndale; do not trifle with me, for I will not brook your insulting tone." It

was Lewis Arndale, the young King's Counsel, who faced Masters. "Beware," continued Masters, "I am master, and my orders must be obeyed."

"Yes, by those who fear you; by me only when they suit me. Understand me, I am as disinclined to be trifled with as yourself; and as I do not admit your authority, I shall hesitate before I obey any of your commands that may prove distasteful to me."

"Indeed."

"Yes, indeed."

"Are you not a member of the Scarlet Brethren?"

"Yes."

"And am I not their master?"

"Yes."

"And have you not taken the oaths to conform to all the rules of the secret association?"

"Yes."

"Then how dare you disobey me?"

"Because I am proud, and do not fear you. Because I detest you, and will not bow to your will."

"Bold words."

"True words; and I fear not the uttering of them. Mark me, you and I had best come to an understanding. We must be equals, or something bad will come of it. You use this society of criminals for your own purposes, and I for mine. We are both men of the world, and play with these puppets as we please; but we must pull the string between us, or there is an end to the game."

"You would not betray us—you would not dare?"

"You do not know what I would not dare do if put to it, so do not trifle with me."

"Well, I see the one way in which we can go on amicably together is as you propose. Let us be friends."

"I say rather let us be equals—there can be no friendship between us."

"Be it so; we now understand each other."

"Yes; and now you will perhaps explain why you gave the signal?"

"Certainly: I have had a brief interview with the Duchess."

"Well?"

"She wishes us to lay violent hands on the Duke's daughter to-night."

"To what end?"

"Can you not guess?"

"No."

"Have you not watched the girl to-night?"

"I have but barely set eyes upon her."

"Had you done so you would have seen that she was deeply engaged with the Prince, and that a long interview between his Highness and the girl was planned and encouraged by the Duchess, who purposely left them together."

"Still, I ask to what end is the girl to be carried off?"

"To gratify the passion of the Prince—to what other end do you suppose?"

"Is it possible the Duchess would act so base a part?"

"She would do anything in the world to further her own interests, and at present she would make good use of his sapient Highness, and the price is to be—"

"The honour of the girl she professes to love."

"Yes. But do not mistake her. I believe the profession of affection to be real to the extent to which such a nature as that of the Duchess could sink, but self-interest would swallow up all minor considerations, and the honour of a young girl would be, to her, but a slight price to pay for the advancement of her lightest wish."

"And what may be her present aim, that one she loves must be sacrificed to gratify it?"

"That, time will reveal. I do not know for certain at what she aims, or I would tell you. I can but guess."

"She is a bold, bad woman."

"She is a sister of our association, and, therefore, must not be abused by one of us. By our oath we are bound to assist and protect each other, and, therefore, we must obey her orders now that she is pleased to demand our services. There must be no murmuring, no hesitation. Our awful oath forbids such ebullitions of private feeling. We assist all round. The Duchess, through us, brings to a successful issue her plots and schemes, and hides her failings and frailties. You, through us, have increased your renown, and made yourself powerful; I have accumulated wealth, and our brethren have, under our care, become rich and formidable. Shall we not, therefore, make sacrifices one for the other. Heaven knows this task of the Duchess's goes more against my will than it can against your's, for I had hoped to possess the girl myself."

"You?"

"Yes, and it was not until the Duchess became one of us that I abandoned the plan."

Lewis Arndale reflected a few moments, and then, turning to Masters, said:

"Well, what do you propose?"

"This is the plan:—The Duchess will suddenly disappear from the rooms; a rumour will be buzzed about to the effect that she has been taken suddenly ill, and forced to return home. You will then advance to the girl and offer to see her home. She, knowing you, will have no suspicions, and will readily accompany you."

"Whither?"

"Into a remote part of the grounds, where she will be surrounded and brought back."

"To the arms of the Prince?"

"Just so."

"A terrible scheme!"

"Call it what you will, but play your part expertly."

"Heaven protect the poor girl!"

"So say I. And now that we understand each other we may separate. Adieu!"

Arndale replied not, but walked away in a mood anything but happy.

"Heaven and earth," he muttered, "this is my reward for straying from the straight path! I joined this band of desperadoes that I might track this white-faced hound, and try to secure the proofs of my entire innocence of the terrible baseness imputed to me by Olivia, and here I find myself assisting in the very business I should of all things have prevented. Oh! would that I had died ere I had taken that terrible oath which binds me down to such a terrible course as that which opens to me this night. It is terrible—terrible! and I cannot struggle against it. For three years I have struggled and suffered to win back the good name which was filched from me, I know not how. For three years I have yearned for my Olivia, and now that I had begun to think she would soon return to my embrace she is torn from me for ever. What can I do?"

He turned, and before him stood Olivia Besgrove.

She had entered the retiring room without the slightest suspicion of Arndale being there, and had not even noticed his presence until he turned from the spot where he had been standing, and came face to face with her.

For a few moments neither spoke. The meeting was a most awkward one, and each was equally confounded at it.

"I beg pardon, Miss Besgrove," stammered Arndale, "I will withdraw."

Olivia spoke not, but there was that in her manner which held out an inducement to the young man to stay.

"This meeting," continued Arndale, "is most distressing to me. I would have avoided it at any risk."

"Am I then grown hateful to you?"

"God forbid! But to meet thus is more than I can bear."

The poor young man bowed his head upon his breast and a tear fell from his eye.

Another moment and Olivia had entwined her white arms about his neck and pillowed the drooping head on her bosom.

"Nay: my own Lewis," she cried, "I cannot bear to see you suffer thus. I will forgive and forget the past. I will cease to think on that terrible affair that separated us. You were indiscreet and betrayed a trust, but I can forget it all and take you back to my heart again."

"As Heaven is my judge, Olivia, you accused me wrongfully. I never even contemplated the betrayal of your secret."

"Then it is I who should ask your forgiveness. Oh, why did you not contradict my bold thoughtless assertion; your word would have sufficed."

"Yes, Olivia, but my pride forbade such a course. I should have left it to time to vindicate my honour. I could not stoop to the denial of so cruel, so unjust an accusation."

"True, true; I alone have been to blame. Forgive me, and take me back to your heart. Say that I am once more dear to you."

"You are—you are, my sweetest one; but do not ask me to renew our intimacy; do not tempt me too far, lest I should prove weak, and grasp at the bliss of which I am for ever deprived."

"What mean you, Lewis? Your words are to me a deep and unfathomable mystery."

"Oh, do not seek explanations, Olivia; do not ask me to speak, for my lips are sealed. Suffice it to say that there is an insurmountable barrier between us. Know that I, and not you, have placed it there, and with that knowledge let us part for ever."

"Enough, Lewis; I understand you. Since our separation you have formed fresh ties, and have outlived the love you once bore me. It is so,

it is so—but I cannot upbraid you. The fault has been on my side. I have dashed the cup of bliss from my own lips, and have only myself to blame. It is right we part. God bless you!"

Lewis was speechless. He clasped his hands over his brow, and staggered against the wall. Olivia approached him, and imprinted a long and fervent kiss upon his lips, and the next moment was gone from the chamber.

Lewis remained half stupified for some moments, and on looking up found that Olivia's place was supplied by a little, bearded man, who wore the dress of an officer of some foreign service; in his hand, however, was the badge of the brotherhood.

This fearful token at once recalled Lewis to his senses, and reminded him of the task he had to perform.

"Yah!" said the little officer, "*Monsieur es treiste*, have ze *malade*, vot you call ze melancholies. Yah! that is sad, ver sad"

Lewis, in his then frame of mind, would have escaped from this person, but the scarlet ribbon prevented his stirring hand or foot. This was a brother, and he was bound to listen to him.

"Vell, Monseiur, vot is ze ordaire? I see ze Captaine Noir, or vot you call him Black Captaine, and he tell me zere is von letle job to do straightway, and he say, seek out Monsieur l'Avocat, and him say to you in vot particular you can render ze assistance. And I am here, Monsieur."

"Yes," said Lewis, "I had almost forgotten. There is a task for at least a dozen of the brethren to-night. Can you assemble them?"

"My eye, yes, twenty dozens if Monsieur did vish."

"A dozen will be sufficient."

"And vot are they to do?"

"Take them to the most secluded part of the garden and let them lie in ambush."

"My eye, yes, they shall be ver close, so close that not von shall see them, I take my oath."

"There they must await my coming. I shall bring with me a lady."

"Oh, I see: it von case of abduction. Yah, yah, it is very good."

"I wish I could bring myself to think so," said Lewis, "but no matter, assemble the men and let them be prepared to bring the girl back to the house as quietly as possible."

"Oh, I sal see. This is von amour of ze gay Prince."

"Yes."

"I shall think so. Ah, it vos von shrewd guess of me.

"You have no time to lose," said Arndale, cutting short the conversation, which the little foreigner evidently wished to prolong.

"But before I sal go," said the little officer, it is right you sal tell me who is ze lady."

"Just so," said Lewis; "it is the fair girl brought here by—"

"Madame la Duchesse?—*oui, oui.* I should guess so. Oh, but she is *la belle femme. Diable!* Vat von lucky man is zat Prince!"

"Curses on them!" said Lewis, walking away, "curses on them! They all jump at the work as readily as crows do at carrion. And now for the signal."

Singular as it may appear, the little foreigner burst into a most uncontrollable fit of laughter as soon as Lewis Arndale had turned his back.

His mirth was for a time excessive, and then recovering himself he gave vent to expressions of delight in far better English than might have been expected of a native of another country.

Recovering from his unaccountable mirth he left the retiring room and mingled with the crowd in the saloons. A few minutes afterwards a report spread throughout the rooms that the Duchess of Grasmount had been taken suddenly and dangerously ill, and had been driven home with all speed.

This was the signal for Lewis Arndale, and with a sickening at the heart he hurried through the rooms in search of his victim.

The search was in vain.

Fair Liz was nowhere to be found.

The consternation of the Black Captain may readily be imagined.

CHAPTER XXXI.

THE BARGAIN AND THE DISAPPOINTMENT.— ANOTHER CHANGE IN THE FORTUNES OF FAIR LIZ.

LET us turn back for a while, as the latter part of the preceding chapter has led us somewhat in advance of our tale without explaining the intricacy into which we have so suddenly fallen. We have now to turn our attention to the Duchess. It might have appeared singular to most of our readers that the Duchess of Grasmount should have taken so sudden and so violent a liking to the child of her husband's first wife and first love.

Those who are capable of reading the mysteries of the human heart and diving into the secret springs of a woman's likes and dislikes, must have seen as plainly as we had written out the facts that the Duchess of Grasmount was not actuated by any motives of affection when she so suddenly determined to take her husband's child under her protection with the avowed intention of cherishing her and guarding her against the evils which beset her in her most perilous journey through life.

Such an act as that which the Duchess proffered to do could only emanate from a fool or one whose angelic nature could raise her above the ordinary standard of humanity by blotting out all the darker passions of the heart, and deepening all those which raise us nearer and make us more worthy heaven.

The milk of human kindness did not, however, flow freely through the bosom of the proud and vindictive Duchess. She had strong likes and dislikes, and over all her acts pride held full sway, and governed with a rod of iron.

One of her pet fancies had been that she was the first and only love of the Duke. She considered herself far above him in every particular, and had always imagined that it had been a deep condescension on her part to walk to the matrimonial altar with him. It was only the bare supposition that he was wholly and solely devoted to her, and that no other image had ever been impressed upon his heart, that tempted her to do so.

Judge, then, of the feelings with which she listened to that romance which her serving man, Liney Gosmont, had overhead and revealed to her. There was a blow to her pride! There was a fall for her imagined greatness! The obedient, retiring, devoted Duke had loved another, had married her, and the offspring of the woman lived in the person of a young and miraculously beautiful girl— the breathing counterpart of the one whose image was doubtless indelibly imprinted on the heart of her lord.

Pride had sealed her lips, but nothing could seal up the dark passions to which the discovery gave rise.

The only thought was of vengeance—on whom?

The Duke was invulnerable, for by aiming her shafts at him they struck a rock of adamant, from which they glanced back and planted themselves in her own bosom.

The rival had long since mouldered in the grave.

Who, then, was there but her living image on whom vengeance could be wreaked?

Not one!

The Duchess saw at a glance her plans.

She could not permit the girl to be thrown on the world. There were too many who knew her history ready to pounce upon her and bear her to the altar for the sake of the wealth to which she was entitled, and of which she had been defrauded.

She could not entrust her to her father. In his glance she read a love which maddened her.

In his embraces there was happiness for both, and so she withheld her.

"No, no!" she cried, "there is no revenge—no vengeance in either of these courses. I must have her under my own care. I will make her love and trust me, and when I have completed my plans I will strike a blow which shall send consternation to all their hearts, and make a complete triumph for me!"

Her triumph was the ruin of the poor girl.

She increased her charms. She gave her education and accomplishments which had made her the delight and envy of European society, and now she contemplated bringing her back to the scenes in which she had suffered so much, and thrusting her into the clutches of that terrible libertine whom she dreaded so much. The plan was diabolical, but it did not appear half terrible enough to satisfy the promoter.

Dragging down a young and beautiful girl to the very depths of perdition was to her but a slight revenge for her wounded pride.

And so Fair Liz was dragged to the Prince's first ball at Carlton House.

* * * *

On his Royal Highness leaving the side of Fair Liz, after being so rudely ejected, as it were, by Captain de Pipes, he tried to soothe his ruffled spirits by a slight conversation with the Duchess.

That lady was quite prepared to receive him.

"Well," she said, as the Prince approached and offered his arm, "and what is the opinion of your Highness on our new English *belle?*"

"She is charming," said the Prince, "but she is stone."

"Insensible to your charms?—impossible!"

This was said with a sneer, but his sapient Highness had been sneered at for years with impunity, and so he, of course, passed over that of the Duchess without noticing it.

"Impossible as it may appear," said his Highness, "it is a fact of which I am very painfully aware."

"Ah!" said the Duchess, "you alone are to blame in the matter. You once *stole her* instead of trying to *win her*. Do you think a woman's vanity could withstand that?"

"Perhaps not. But at the time I thought I was dealing with a street ballad singer instead of—"

"A relative of mine."

"Just so. But, by the bye, you have not yet informed me in what manner you stand related. There is a mystery about this which fairly puzzles me."

"Oh, it is quite a romance. The fair enslaver is the child of a distant relative, who, giving way to some Quixotic feeling, chose to work for a living instead of receiving it from his elder brother. By the way, he was the youngest son. He started forth into the world; attempted to work, as he termed it; failed, of course; and equally as a matter of course married below himself; fell into the deepest poverty, became beggared, starved, and died, leaving his wife and child to beg for bread. Do you not now comprehend?"

"Perfectly."

The Duchess was glad of this, for she did not. Nevertheless, she continued—

"Ah, it was a sad history; but no more of it—it makes me wretched to think of it."

"I should suppose so," said his Highness.

"And she is still hard-hearted?" continued the Duchess, leading the conversation back to its original channel.

"Still the same," said the Prince, with a sigh.

He was quite an adept at sighing. He had a perfect well of melancholy, from which he could pump up sighs and tears without number, when he thought there was anything to be gained by it. Some one had told him that women were to be won by these artifices; his dense brain had, after a while, comprehended the fact, and he lost no opportunity of exhibiting his ready-made stock of sorrow.

"Dear me," said the Duchess; "how perverse and hypocritical we women are! To think, now, of the sly baggage assuming such airs when an hour or two ago she assured me she was dying to behold you again, and was wondering whether, amongst the hosts of beauties who courted your love, you had still reserved a small corner of your heart for her."

Oh, woman, woman! what an adept art thou at lying!

"And she said that?" asked the Prince, his eyes fairly glistening with delight.

"Yes," was the unhesitating answer of the Duchess.

"You send me into rapture," cried the expectant Prince; "I am positively in a fever of delight. And she loves me?"

"Yes; as dearly as ——"

"You love Sir Roderick."

"Hush! Hush—for the sake of Heaven! What are you saying?"

"Oh, it's all right, my dear Duchess, there is no one to hear."

"But if a whisper should get abroad! I thought my secret—"

"Was safe with me?"

"Yes."

"It is as safely locked in my bosom as in your own,' said the Prince, with his hand on his heart.

"But the slightest indiscretion—the least word—"

"Would be your ruin. I know all that, and so you can trust me all the more. But we wander from the subject of our interview — your relative. She loves me, and yet shuns me so; I cannot understand her."

"My dear Prince, if you live a thousand years you will not understand the sex. They are far beyond your comprehension, close student as you are."

"I begin to believe so."

"But do not fear: this coy one will be yours before long."

"How long? Oh, give me some hope!"

"Well, say a month."

"A month!—intolerable period! I shall expire in a fortnight."

"Well, anything to oblige you—let us say a fortnight."

"My dear Duchess, it is beyond me to wait. It must be sooner."

"Then have your own way, you wilful man, and name your own time."

"May I?—may I?"

"Yes."

"Then I name to-night."

The Duchess opened her eyes in the greatest astonishment. She professed to be dumbfounded, and yet, as the reader has seen, she had made all arrangements for the due carrying out of the plan now proposed by the Prince.

"To-night!" said the Duchess—oh, absurd!"

"Not at all."

"But my dear Prince—"

"But my dear Duchess—"

"But consider, the girl—"

"I have considered; she is by far too slippery to permit of a chance being thrown away. She has served me ill enough before; I must insist."

"Oh, you presume upon the knowledge of my secret."

"I believe I am too much of a gentleman for that," said the Prince, with pretended anger.

"Well, I do not mean to offend," said the Duchess; "but really you are so unreasonable."

"Is it unreasonable to love so desperately as to refuse to allow the possibility of disappointment?"

"Well, I admit there is some reason in that."

"And I shall be made happy?"

"If I have any power, yes. There is my hand upon it."

They had walked into the garden and were now unobserved. The answer of the Duchess gave the Prince so much delight that he favoured her with a very warm embrace, accompanied by such kisses as were not quite warranted under the circumstances: more particularly as they came from a youth who was dying in love for another lady.

"Now what do you think our young friend would say if she saw that?" asked the Duchess, but without much anger in her tone.

"Say? why, she would say that you were an angel, and that too many kisses could not be lavished upon you."

"I very much doubt whether she would make any such silly observation," said the Duchess, "but now I must return to the saloon. I have a little farce to act, and one in which I shall require your assistance."

"I will do aught in the world for you."

"Perhaps so : I have already had a very warm proof of your regard, but I require no further assurances."

"Tantalizer!"

"Cruel deceiver!"

"Bewitching beauty!"

"Frail Adonis!"

More of this deliciously insipid conversation we shall not report, lest it sicken the reader. They say "there is no fool like an old fool."

But if any one had chanced to have overheard the foregoing, we believe they would have been tempted to add—"unless it be a young one."

*   *   *   *   *

The Prince and the Duchess returned to the ball room, where in a short time the Duchess pretended to be overcome with the heat.

"It is very hot here," she said; "I think I had best retire."

"Pray do not think of going yet," said the Prince; "you will recover presently."

"No," said the Duchess; "it is a touch of my old illness, caught in Italy; I think I had best retire."

"In that case I will order your carriage," said the Prince.

"Do."

"Pray permit me," said a splendidly dressed and very handsome man, moving in the scene.

"Oh," said the Prince, "I will allow you, Sir Roderick, to deprive me of the pleasure."

The gentleman addressed as Sir Roderick ran off in great haste, and on returning the Duchess placed her arm within his and walked away with him.

*   *   *   *   *   *

By another mode of egress, and almost at the same moment, Fair Liz might have been seen quitting Carlton House under the protection of a very little and very peculiar foreign officer.

She was again saved, and, as usual, by the never-losing Pipey, for he was the foreign officer.

———

CHAPTER XXXII.

A VERY FRAIL WOMAN—A PROMISE OF MARRIAGE —THE RESULT—WHERE AND HOW FAIR LIZ PASSED HER FIRST NIGHT UNDER THE PROTECTION OF PIPEY.

LET the disappointment of his royal Highness of Wales be conceived; it certainly baffles description, and therefore we will not attempt it.

Fair Liz—the beautiful, the long-coveted—had again slipped through his fingers, and he was for the space of two whole hours beyond the power of his toadies and consolers. A kind of imbecile desperation took possession of him, and he—no, he did *not* attempt his life, he—got drunk !

Wine was his remedy for all evils, and he flew to it on all pressing occasions.

Wine the foe—wine the friend—wine the magician, that was his comforter; and the quantities he took under emergencies certainly proved that he had one claim at least to the title of the "first gentleman in Europe," since one of the paramount qualifications for the distinction was, at that period, the large number of bottles a man could boast of being capable of drinking at a sitting. Enough on that head. The Prince became as drunk as a pot-house sot at midnight.

In his cups he told his grief. He was not a young man who would allow sorrow, like a worm i' the bud, to feed on *his* damask cheek.

He certainly preferred talking. He told Cavendish he was "v'ry mish'rable," and illustrated the fact with a wholesale pumping from the well of tears before alluded to.

The toady was grieved to hear of his master's sorrow.

"Nay," he said, "it is not worth speaking of. A woman is but a woman after all, and if this one is gone there is at least a score of others as chaste and beautiful left to fill her place."

"Not like her," murmured the Prince, looking

affectionately at his miraculous shoe buckles, and doubtless cogitating on the absurdity of a woman rushing from a man who could invent such beautiful things as those; "not like her."

"Fifty like her," continued Cavendish, "and fifty better. There is, for instance, Mrs. Fitz Herbert. Is she not lovely?"

"Fitch—bert is a fine woman—dev'lish fine woman."

"And loves you sincerely."

"Sure?"

"Positive."

"Then I love her. Where is she?"

"She is and has been here during the whole night, pining away to think that you had taken no notice of her."

"Poor thing, poor thing!" At this point there was another flow of tears."

"I see you are pained at having slighted her. Why not make amends?"

"How?"

"Why, retire with her; and by every means in your power convince her that you have some affection for her."

"I will, I will," said the Prince.

"That is well. Let me lead you to your chamber, and there Mrs. FitzHerbert shall come to you."

"And stay with me?"

"I do not know. That will depend upon yourself."

This conversation took place in one of the many small rooms attached to the grand *suite*, and on its termination Cavendish, having first ascertained that the road was clear, led the Prince out of the room, and assisted him, by a private flight of stairs, to his chamber.

The inebriated and amorous Prince had contrived to locate himself in a very beautiful set of chambers in his new home.

They consisted of three apartments, leading from one into the other. The first was used as breakfasting-room and private sanctum; the second was a dining-room: the third a bed-chamber.

Into the second of this suit of rooms the Prince was led and duly deposited on a lounge.

Restoratives were applied, and in a short time he somewhat recovered his senses.

Excuses were made for him in the ball room, and the company began to depart.

Finding herself rather isolated, Mrs. FitzHerbert, a remarkably beautiful woman who had entered upon the prime of life, but whose every charm was unimpaired, was making a move towards the doors when Cavendish caught her by the arm and drew her on one side.

"Whither away?" asked the courtier.

"Home," was the response; "is it not time?"

"For the majority, yes: for you, no."

"What can you possibly mean?"

"The Prince desires an interview in his private apartments."

"The Prince!—why he has never noticed me for the night."

"He has been indisposed. You will not refuse to see him?"

"No. If he desires my presence I will go to him."

"Allow me to escort you," said Cavendish.

He offered his arm, and then bore his victim off in triumph.

At the door of the Prince's apartments he left her.

"My mission is fulfilled," he said. "The Prince commands that no one enters here with you, and further that no interruption to your interview shall take place."

He left her.

The heart of the woman sank within her as she stood at the door of the apartment she was expected to enter.

It was a peculiar position, and she had not expected to be similarly placed. No wonder she hesitated.

Unless we may be mistaken, let us at once say that we believe that the failings of this woman found their origin in a true affection for the man she was about to visit.

She was not led by mere ambitious motives or love of position: the head was not strong enough to guide the heart, and — the result is before the public. After a few moments of hesitation, the lady knocked a trembling little knock at the door.

"Enter."

And she stood in the presence of the man she loved.

He was certainly not a very lovable picture.

The famous pink coloured silk coat was very much creased. The elaborate frills were crumpled, and soddened with water. The face was yet wet with spirits, and strong perfumes applied to the brow and nostrils. The hair was soddened and disordered, and the *tout ensemble* of the right royal gentleman was damp and clammy.

He looked as if he had been boiled, and the cook had neglected to properly strain him off.

He was, however, surrounded by everything that was beautiful and entrancing.

The hangings of the room were of Utrecht velvet and blue silk, relieved by gold and white.

A bright fire sparkled in the bright steel grate, and was reflected in the numerous mirrors which hung around the walls.

The lamps were well shaded with blue transparencies, which softened the light, and lent an air of repose and still beauty, strictly in keeping with the whole scene.

It was here that Mrs. FitzHerbert found the Prince.

He raised his eyes on her entrance, and partly rose to receive her.

He certainly would have waited some time before a more elegant creature would have obeyed his summons.

She was tall and commanding. Her face was exquisitely chiselled, and her eyes were of the deepest, softest blue. Over her head and snowy shoulders fell a cloud of raven hair, and the outline of her form was exceedingly lovely.

There was more of the queen than the sylph about her, but her beauty was undeniable.

If she had one weak point about her it was her mouth, and this, though well-shaped, was indicative of that weakness of mind which characterised her.

She was as beautiful as an angel, but she was

as weak as—well, she was a very ordinary kind of woman!

Around her she clasped a massive mantle of pure ermine, which she had assumed on intending to leave the ball room. It lent additional beauty to her majestic form.

The Prince was enraptured. He held out his arms, and in another moment that regal form was clasped to the heart of that anything but regal heir to the throne of England.

"Do you love me?" asked the Prince.

"Can you ask? Am I not here?"

"True; it is the best proof of your affection."

"I fear I have done wrong. I know I shall forfeit your esteem."

"Nothing of the kind. You would assuredly have done so, however, had you not come."

"Then you really desired my presence. You were ill, and you wished me near you?"

Poor dear Prince—how pathetic!

What a pity it was that some good angel had not whispered into the ear of the deluded woman that the beloved one had but a few minutes recovered from a fit of drunkenness brought about by disappointment in the possession of another heart. There was no good angel there. We doubt if any ever approached the place during the whole period it was occupied by his Royal Highness. And so poor Mrs. Fitzherbert was quite prepared to believe her darling when he said,

"Yes, dearest; yes. To whom should I look for comfort if not from you?"

There was more embracing and more kissing, and finally the lady threw off her ermine, and consented to remain there the night.

She would, in all probability, have done so under any circumstances, but the bait which tempted her to throw off her virtue with the ermine was a *promise of marriage*.

She was really to be Princess of Wales!

He had promised—nay, he had sworn, to marry her. He, of course, loved no other. He should die if he did not possess her, and she, equally as a matter of course, loved him; and she would die if she did not become his. But she had scruples of conscience.

"Could they not be removed?"

"I do not see how."

"Does no plan present itself to you?"

"None: you are a Prince."

"What matter. That will not prevent my marrying you. In the eyes of men such an union will not be binding, but will it not be registered in Heaven? Will it not be binding between us?"

"And you will marry me—you will promise to love and cherish me, and I shall be the sole, the lawful mistress of your heart?"

"As firmly as the rites of the Roman Catholic Church can bind us."

"Enough!"

We will draw a veil over the scene.

*   *   *   *   *

Pipey hurried the trembling girl he had snatched from ruin through the streets, and away into the neighbourhood of Lincoln's-inn.

He had chambers in the square; and, on arriving there, produced a key, with which he admitted himself to the house he inhabited. It was dark and gloomy, but he held Liz affec-

tionately by the arm, and led her up the stairs as tenderly as if she had been a helpless child.

In a few moments they stood within his chambers.

They were two, not over elegantly furnished, not very commodious, but comfortable and clean. Pipey struck a light, and spread over his table a light and plain repast.

"Eat," he said, "it will do you good."

"I cannot eat. Oh, if you but knew how wretched I am."

"I can guess," said Pipey, "I can guess. Heaven bless you."

He threw off his assumed beard, and his own old roguish, smiling face beamed down upon that of Liz.

"God bless you," said the poor girl, seizing his hand and covering it with kisses, "you have been a good and true friend to me. Without you I should have been——I dare not think what I should have been."

"Well, then, don't think anything at all about it. I'm sure it's not worth while. Am I not your brother?"

"You are indeed, my more than brother."

"Hush, hush," said Pipey, "do not say so. I have long struggled to keep down a feeling which will rise here"—he laid his hand on his heart—"in spite of myself. I know it is useless, hopeless, and I fight it down. But it is in vain, all in vain. I repeat to myself over and over again, she is too good, too beautiful for me—a poor half-reclaimed thief; I know she loves another, I feel that she cannot love me, so I will be her brother, and if ever brother struggles more for sister than I will for her, I'll suffer death. There, that's what I say when I get foolish, you know; and if you don't want to see me foolish now, don't go talking of 'your more than brother.' Bah!" cried the young man, brightening, "let us have no more of this—pitch into that pie, its first class."

"Indeed I cannot eat," said Liz, watching her protector, "indeed I cannot eat; do not regard me, I shall recover my spirits by the morning."

"Well, if you will not eat, go to bed like a good girl, and sleep away the remembrances of this night's perils. There," said Pipey, pointing to the door of his chamber, "there is my humble dormitory, get into it."

Liz cast her eyes about the room in which she sat. "But you," she said, "where will you sleep?—there is not as much as a couch here."

"Here!" said Pipey, "oh, of course not. I shall sleep with a friend on the next floor. Don't bother about me, for I shall be all right."

"In that case I will retire to bed."

She rose and extended her hand, Pipey grasped it tenderly and pressed it to his lips.

"Nay," said Liz, kissing her brave little friend affectionately on the cheek, "it is not thus brother and sister should part."

Pipey blushed a deep crimson.

"I say," he said, "if you do that again, I shall not dream of washing that side of my face again, and a pretty spectacle I shall soon look."

With this forced bit of humour, Pipey handed Liz her chamber candle and he closed the door on her.

"Bless her," he murmured, "bless her! Not a

hair of her head shall they touch, without first laying me in the grave. Then I can only commend her to the care of Heaven."

*   *   *   *   *

The dreams of Liz were pleasant ones.

She was happier now than she had been for many a long day. Despite all the apparent kindness and the luxuries heaped upon her by the Duchess, there was a something that whispered to her that all was forced and unnatural, and that she was amongst enemies.

Her father she saw but seldom, and when she did the interview was a stolen one and generally of a sombre character.

Now she felt free from restraint — she knew that there was one good and true heart beating near her and for her: she trusted in him who owned it for protection, and she felt that she sheltered in the shadow of a giant. Her dreams, we said, were happy ones; in them flitted a face she had not gazed upon since the night she had been taken to Marlborough House. Once she woke, and could have sworn, that, standing over her bed was the figure of a tall and beautiful woman whom she felt was her mother.

So real did this appear that she was for a moment quite startled and uttered a slight cry.

In a moment a hand was on the door of her chamber, and a voice inquired what ailed her?

"It is nothing, I was startled by a dream—no more. What is the hour? Why are you not in bed, Pipey?"

"Oh, I'm going now," said that individual, I'm going; but I have had some work to do."

He had had work to do, and the task was not yet fulfilled. It was to watch faithfully at that door until the light of day broke in upon the scene.

CHAPTER XXXIII.

A LETTER FROM MARIE LAVROUFFE, VENICE, TO SIGNORA PELATANA, LONDON.

IT was about this period of our story that the following letter from Marie was received by the Italian who owned the house in Soho where Lovelace lay concealed after his duel:—

"Villa of Calato, near Venice.
"Carlotta mia,

"It is three years ago that I last saw you. You will doubtless remember the occasion; it was when I quitted England with my Lord Lovelace. Shall I trouble you with an outline of all my doings since then, or shall I pass them over, and come at once to the subject that leads to the writing of this letter? You would, perhaps, think it a tax upon your friendship to wade through the history I could write, so I will spare details and pen such facts as will lead up to the primary object of this letter. Know then, my only friend, that we reached this place without incident worth recording, and that soon afterwards my love purchased and furnished the villa in which I am still residing. It is a sweet place, seemingly built for lovers true; there is an air of poetry about it to which you in England are a comparative stranger, for such scenes are rare there; but you know the style of home to which I allude. Situated on the bosom of a gentle stream, imbedded in a forest of flowers, secluded from the rude gaze of obtrusive people.

"Was I happy?

"I think I must have been; my design in cohabiting with Lord Lovelace was the furtherance of a deep vengeance. For months and months I lost sight of my purpose, so I presume that I must have been happy!

"Alas! for such happiness, how short lived it was.

"Looking back I can only regard it as a dream.

"Lovelace seemed to forget old ties and old associations. The coldness which I could not fail to mark in his bearing towards me died away, and he became fervent and even demonstrative in his affection.

"There was nothing too good for me. There was nothing I could dream of but what was mine; my lightest thought was attended to, and it appeared that Lovelace was all devotion.

"Oh! if he did not love me I am well assured that the passion which consumed me was that of true and firm devotion.

"My vengeance slumbered. I thought its every ember was crushed out, but no; it is not so.

"Eighteen months, Carlotta mia, eighteen brief months fled, and I became a mother.

"A little bright-eyed girl was born to me, and brought my joy to a culminating point.

"Morn, noon, and night I felt unutterable bliss with my little one; Lovelace appeared in ecstacies.

"He even proposed that when I was enabled to go forth, we should be united.

"'Cara mia,' he said, 'I will think no more of the past, I will let it die away from my memory. If another image ever had a place in this heart of mine and shared its love with thee, I will tear it out, and thou shalt in the future see only thine own therein.'

"'I love you, I love you,' I cried, 'father of my babe, Marie lives for you alone. Bitter is her hate, deep, unutterable is her love: Marie is yours for ever; she loves you with all the strength of her nature. She will be true, and you shall never regret your act.'

"He clasped me to his heart, and whispered—

"'Bliss of my existence—only joy of my soul— I swear to love and cherish thee for ever!'

"Another month of bliss!

"Oh, my child—my child, what a blessing it was to me: one month of true happiness — such happiness as I had never known before — such happiness as I had never dreamt of!

"But only one short month: the joy died out as suddenly as it came.

"My infant was one month old, and health and strength were fast returning to me.

"'In a week,' I said to Lovelace, 'in a week I shall be thine for ever!'

"'Yes,' he said, 'in a week;' but there was that in his tone which jarred upon me, and, with my woman's instinct, I at once divined that the thought of the fulfilment of his promise did not delight him as it had done.

"The thought struck a chill to my very heart.

"Lovelace now absented himself more frequently from home, and when he was in my society he was dull and thoughtful.

"I would fain have persuaded myself that this was only some temporary gloom, and I eagerly accepted his laboured excuses.

"'Business annoys me,' he said; 'I have news from England that distresses me; it will be all well before long.'

"But it did not become well. Week by week matters went worse and worse, and I could not shut out the conviction that an awful change had come over the father of my child.

"I communicated to my physician the fear and suspicions that agitated me, and he consented to watch my lord and search into the causes of his altered bearing towards me.

"The physician loved me: he never told me so, but there was that in his eye, in his voice, in his bearing, that told of the fact as plainly as if he had communicated it to me.

"I knew I had a trusty emissary; but, at the same time, I was on my guard against him, for I knew to what extremes jealousy will tempt me.

"For a whole week I learnt nothing.

"The physician was indefatigable, but he discovered nothing.

"He saw Lovelace lounging about with brow clouded and look abstracted, but he saw no more.

"'I have failed to note anything,' he said, 'but I do not yet despair.'

"'You do not despair of what?'

"'Of tracing to its source this melancholy and altered bearing observable in Lord Lovelace.'

"'You do not despair,' said I, scornfully. 'You have watched for a whole week and have discovered nothing, and yet you talk of not despairing. Had he been false your cunning would have traced the source ere this. I believe him now: it is business of a painful nature, with which he will not distress me, that keeps him away from home and makes him thus changed towards me. I will not doubt him more.'

"I said this, but I did not mean a word of it. The bolt had entered my heart and stuck there still. The physician had not withdrawn it by his report.

"I liked his honesty, however; men, as men go, do not frequently exhibit such candour.

"He had failed to make a discovery, and he scorned to invent one. How many in his position would have had recourse to their faculties of invention?

"My words were only spoken to whet his appetite, and urge him on in his work.

"I saw that they had the desired effect.

"He winced under them, and his eyes flashed fire. I saw that he had no intention of abandoning the game.

"'Trust me,' he said, 'men are not thus agitated by mere business matters, and English nobles have but little to trouble them. Love, disappointed love, is at the bottom of this, and I will drag the secrets of his heart to light.'

"He left me writhing under the smart of his words, but I did not exhibit a trace of my emotion before him.

"I was too proud for that.

"These were days of suspense and mental torture.

"The physician came again.

"There was that in his manner which told me he had been successful.

"Oh the agony with which I viewed his look of triumph.

"'At last,' he said, 'at last.'

"'What do you know?' I cried, 'Oh, what have you discovered?'

"'Precisely that which I anticipated. Lord Lovelace is false.'

"'It is a lie,' I cried, with the frenzy of an enraged tigress, 'it is a base lie! I know better.'

"'It is true,' he said, with a coldness which chilled me, 'it is as true as sacred writ.'

"'Speak!' I said, almost choking, 'speak! What have you discovered. This suspense is madness!'"

"'Five weeks ago two ladies arrived in Venice. One was in the prime of life, the other young and beautiful to a degree—so beautiful that all Venice raved of her. Soon after her arrival Lord Lovelace was seen following her in her daily walks and rides, and by his bearing excited the attention of all observers. It was plain he loved her. Daily, hourly, he has been seen following her, but was never once observed addressing her. It seemed to content him to follow in her path, to gaze upon her from a distance, to see and not be seen. Yesterday the ladies departed for Rome, and I was a witness to the agony displayed by Lovelace when their carriage left the door of their hotel. He stood at a distance and watched the ladies unseen and unnoticed. As the horses dashed away I heard him exclaim—

"'Gone once more—gone from me for ever! Oh, God! that I should be bound—irrevocably bound down thus, and she still alive, still as beautiful as ever, and perhaps still loving me.'

"I touched his elbow, and he turned.

"'A lovely girl,' I said, pointing to the carriage just disappearing.

"'Beautiful as an angel,' he returned. 'Oh, is she not beautiful?'

"And then he appeared to remember to whom he was speaking, and with a distant bow walked away, leaving me convinced that I had discovered the secret in which I have so long been in search.

"'Well,' I exclaimed with all the fortitude I was capable of mustering; 'well, and who was this—this woman? you have not yet told me that.'

"'She was an English lady, and I must do her the justice to say that one more beautiful I never looked upon.'

"'English!' I cried. 'Stay, she was tall and fair, had large and languishing blue eyes, and a quantity of golden hair flowing unrestrainedly about her shoulders; a face of singular beauty, but shadowed by an expression of melancholy. Is not this the picture?'

"'Yes,' he answered, 'painted to a nicety.'

"'It is she, then. She has forgotten him.'

"'You know her?'

"'Know her? Heaven and earth! have I not cause to remember her?'

"'An old acquaintance of my lord's?'

"'Yes, yes. Oh, Heaven! that she should again cross my path, and at such a moment. It is maddening!'

"'It is vexatious,' he said, with a sneer.

MARIE.

" 'Mock me not' I cried, 'for you know not the anguish I endure. Oh, for revenge! some sure and sudden revenge!'

" 'On her or on him?' he asked.

" 'On both,' I replied.

" 'It would not be easy to find her,' he continued; 'but your lord is at hand, what is to prevent you wreaking vengeance on him?'

" 'True,' I said; 'true; but the means?'

" 'What would be the reward of the one who provided them?'

" I knew at what he aimed, and I replied,

" 'Myself.'

" 'Enough,' he said; 'enough. You shall have revenge.'

" He went away, but came again next day.

" Placing in my hand a small phial, he said,

" 'This will serve your time, but remember its price.'

" 'You need not remind me,' I said; 'I shall not forget.'

" 'I love you,' he continued, bending over me until I felt his feverish breath on my cheek; 'I love you with a passion with which only an Italian can love; when *he* is gone, will you be mine?'

" 'Yes,' I answered; 'yours.'

" 'It is enough.'

" I submitted to his scalding kisses and his warm embrace, and he went away.

" He loved me! I felt that. It is easy to discern the fact. I knew he loved me, and I was somewhat grateful to him. There was an inexpressible satisfaction in feeling that there was some one who loved me in that terrible moment.

" The bruised heart, even such a heart as mine, heals with kind words and words of affection. It clings to kindness as does the clinging plant to the stalwart tree. What wonder, then, that I felt something like love for one who, beyond a doubt, passionately loved me?

" Long and anxiously I gazed upon the little phial. I removed the stopper: a faint perfume greeted me and I reclosed the orifice in dread. Mine was a dark and terrible business, and I feared lest the very air should breathe the secret of my intents.

" Lovelace returned home towards night: he was as absent and melancholy as he had ever been, but I fought down the terrible impulses of my heart, and received him with a show of affection which I had the greatest difficulty in assuming.

" He would neither eat nor drink, and the contents of my phial remained intact.

" 'No matter,' I thought, 'the time must come.'

" Before retiring to rest that night, Lovelace came to my side, and taking my hand, said to me—

" 'Marie, you have been good and true to me since I have known you, and I am grateful. You ...., when first we met, I had no heart to give you; but your fatal beauty overcame my scruples of conscience, and I could not withstand the temptation you threw in my path. Some months have passed, and you have borne me a child. At first I deemed the little stranger a blessing, and its advent aroused within me a feeling such as I had never before experienced. I thought it was a deep and holy passion, and under its temporary influence I promised you marriage. I find now that I was mistaken, and that I do not love you so devotedly as a wife should be loved; and therefore I would wish to retract my promise. God knows, I am deeply grieved to have to say this; but I feel I ought. Feelings over which I have no control induce me to move from your side. I find I am no longer happy there, and I must go.'

" 'What!' I said; 'you have used me as your toy as long as I pleased you, but now you wish to cast me off, and lavish your affection on another.'

" 'No,' he said, 'such is not the case.'

" 'Do not lie,' I replied; 'I know better; but we will not quarrel.'

" 'It were best not; we will part in peace, for, believe me, I have no wish to interchange an unkind word with the mother of my child.'

" 'Well, what do you propose?' I asked.

" 'You shall see; my arrangements are all made. Here is a document which secures to you during your life, and your babe at your death, the sum of two thousand pounds per annum. If ever you wish for more, or if I can at any time do aught to augment your happiness, do not fail to let me know, and I will not fail you.'

" 'You are generous,' I said.

" 'No,' he returned, 'only just, perhaps scarcely that.'

" We retired to rest.

" He slept soundly, but I never closed my eye throughout the night; my brain was working and my heart was on fire.

" There was no love left in it then. No trace of affection. I was cast off! Was not that enough to madden me.

" Morn came at last, although I thought it would never come.

" Lovelace awoke.

" 'I shall quit you to day, Marie,' he said 'I think it best we should part at once.'

" 'With all my heart,' I said.

" 'And you will not grieve—you promise to forget me and be happy?'

" 'Grieve,' I said, with a sardonic laugh, 'why should I grieve?'

" 'True,' he replied, 'true; why should you grieve?'

" 'You will be kind to the child, will you not?

" 'It is my child; is not that sufficient?'

" 'I believe you will do all that is requisite for it. Be good to it and teach it—'

" 'To avoid the path followed by its infamous mother. Is not that what you would say?'

" 'I would not have been so cruel.'

" 'No: you would have used other words, but you would have conveyed the same meaning. I thank you, but I do not require any instructions in the art of rearing my child.'

" 'You will not teach it to hate me.'

" 'I will teach it the story of its mother, and let it have its own effect. If she could hear it and not hate her father, she is no child of mine.'

" I saw he was hurt by my words, for he replied not, but turning from me bowed his face in his hands, and I think wept.

" I dressed and descended to the breakfast room.

"It was my habit to make a cup of chocolate and send it to Lovelace before he left his room by his valet.

"This was the only opportunity I should perhaps have of using the contents of the physician's phial.

"I determined not to allow the opportunity to slip, and making the chocolate, poured into it a few drops of the poison.

"Summoning the valet—the one you will remember to have seen in London—I gave him the cup, and bade him take it to his master.

"'It is the last I shall ever make for him,' I said.

"He fixed his eye upon me, and mine fell to the earth. There was something in the gaze of this man I could not understand, and as he took the cup from me I thought he penetrated into the very depths of my soul and read all that was there concealed.

"He, however, quitted the apartment without a word, and, clutching the wall for support, I awaited the issue of my work. Oh, terrible were my feelings!

"The minutes passed, and I heard only the hurrying to and fro of the servants.

"No sound from the upper apartments.

"No shriek of pain, no cries of terror! But still I waited, and still I clung to the wall for support.

"The valet has set down the cup and left his master, I thought: when he returns he will find him dead!

"Two hours!

"Yes, I had been awaiting the issue two whole hours, and still no sounds from above! What could it mean?

"At length my own servants came to me.

"'Signora did not ring, so they came to see if anything was required?'

"'Nothing,' I said; 'where is my lord's servant?'

"They had not seen him for more than two hours. Did the Signora require him; should they search for him?

"'No, no,' I cried, 'I will find him myself. He is doubtless in my lord's room.'

"I went up the stairs, but my heart sickened at each step, and I dreaded to advance into that room. I expected to face a corpse.

"Long I hesitated on the threshold, but at last advanced, passed through the dressing room, and into the bed chamber.

"It was without a tenant!

"As soon as I had recovered from my surprise, I commenced gazing about me in search of some explanation of this singular business.

"The first thing on which my eye rested was the cup of chocolate, cold and untasted as I had sent it to him.

"Laying beside it was a strip of paper, on which was scrawled the following words:—

"'Wretched woman,—You are but an amateur in crime, or you would have adopted a less transparent device to rid yourself of me. *Had not my valet seen you* poison the chocolate, I should have at once detected the presence of the drug you have used. I could punish you for your crime, but I will not do so. I will not even deprive you of the allowance I have made you. At first I thought of seeing you, and taxing you with your crime, but I think it were best not. I am gone for ever, and my last words to you are: Seek to reform yourself, and curb your horrible passions, but, above all, teach your child (I will use your own words) "to avoid the path followed by its infamous mother." You are infamous now, Marie, and God have mercy on you.

"'LOVELACE.'

"I held this note in my hand, and seated myself on the bed. At first it stupified me, and I could neither move nor speak, but at last I shook off this weakness, and gazed once more about the room.

"He had taken with him the greatest portion of his wardrobe, but, in the disordered state of the apartment, the haste with which he had made his preparations was very visible.

"On the dressing table I found the following letter:—

"'London, 15th ———, 1780.

"'Dear Lovelace,

"'I have much satisfaction in informing you that the last traces of that unhappy affair with the old General have been wiped out, and that you may once more appear in England with safety. We have induced the Prince to laugh at the little rivalry that existed between you, and he is now anxious to resume his former intimacy with you. So tear yourself away from the fascinating inamorata, and fly back to those who are so anxiously awaiting your appearance in England. By the way, what a deuce of a stir your advent will make!

"'Yours ever,

"'CAVENDISH.'

"From the above I gleaned that Lovelace is in all probability once more in England.

"You will say, 'more probably in Rome,' but I know better.

"My first thoughts were that he would fly there after this wax doll who has so fascinated him, but my emissaries have convinced me that he fled not there. Had they found him you can readily guess what kind of fate he would have met with.

"The physician I have before alluded to, Antonio Bartolo by name, has made me fulfil my promise, and I am now his mistress.

"Oh God! how I hate and fear him! He is terrible! Shall I describe him to you?

"Tall and ungainly, with a slight stoop; habited with a slovenliness inexcusable in one of his high standing in society. His face is dull and sallow, and he wears a long and rigid black beard. He is, however, wonderfully clever, and has an enormous practice. I do not hate him as an enemy. I do not fear him as a man.

"I cannot describe to you the feeling with which I regard him.

"My soul revolts at his touch, and his kisses are to me the sting of a serpent, but I dare not show this. He is so dark and terrible that I should dread his discovering my feelings. I am no craven, but the ascendancy he has obtained over me leaves me powerless, and I am obliged to submit to his embraces with the best possible grace I can assume. I am assured he hates my child, and I dread lest he should kill it.

"I love my little one, and I would not have a hair of its head hurt for the world. So much for Antonio. I think I can hear you exclaim as you read this, 'Heavens! how has she fallen!' I have fallen, and the depths to which I have sunk are such as to place beyond a possibility the chance of a reform. I live for revenge now. Believe me, if it were not for that I would enter Bartolo's laboratory and at once end this miserable career.

"One more subject before I close. I have again met my grandmother. She came to my house not many days ago: she looked more terrible than ever. I shuddered at the sight of her. She told me she had hunted for me from one end of Italy to the other, and that she had sworn a great oath, in which she was joined by Philippe, to encompass the ruin of those to whom my ruin was due. Bartolo was at first included among the number, but a sight of him was sufficient to make her dismiss all thought of interference with him. She is, moreover, a member of the Scarlet Brethren, to which both Bartolo and I belong. The rules and oaths of the Association will admit of no interference with each other; and, on Bartolo exhibiting the ribbon, she at once altered her tone towards him. I do not know which I fear most—this terrible old woman or Bartolo; they are both so hideous, so powerful, and so unnatural!

"And now to the motive which induced me to trouble you with this voluminous epistle.

"Independent of our long intimacy, I have learnt that you are a sister of our Association, and therefore the one most likely to render me the assistance I require.

"I would have you seek out this Lovelace and the woman he loves, who ere this will have returned to London.

"Watch them closely, and keep me informed of their movements. I shall wreak a terrible vengeance on them both, and I call you to aid me in my task. I know you will not fail me.

"Do not my wrongs cry for vengeance?

"Am I not an object for your pity and assistance?

"Remember your long friendship and the ties of our order. Around this is the scarlet ribbon —the badge of sisterhood—the sign that assistance is required. Obey the signal, and secure the love of

    "Yours in the bond of sisterhood,
      "MARIE LAVROUFFE."

CHAPTER XXXIV.

PIPEY HAS AN INTERVIEW WITH A DUCHESS, AND MEETS A LORD WHO IS KNOWN TO HIM.

WHEN Liz awoke, after her first night's rest in the chambers of Captain de Pipes, she found the bright sun streaming in upon her; and springing from her couch, soon arrayed herself, and went into the adjoining room.

There she found the gallant ex-Captain busily engaged, in conjunction with a fussy old lady, in preparing the morning meal.

"Hillo!" cried Pipey, "this is against the rules. Mrs. Boodles was about to bring you your breakfast in bed."

"Which I was," said Mrs. Boodles—who, we need scarcely explain, was the housekeeper of out friend's establishment; "and it's a pity, it is, that a young lady of a delicate constitution— which such was my poor dear daughter, who died of an inflammation of the lungs; and her father, my good man, says to me, 'Sarah,' said he—which my name is Sarah Boodles, at your service—'that girl,' says he, 'is a far too good for this world, and will die as sure as eggs is eggs'—should not have her breakfast in bed, which perwents the cold a striking in to her precious lungs, and makes her comfortable and nice all day long."

Liz, as may be supposed, was somewhat surprised at this singular rhodomontade, and it was some moments before she found words to thank the old lady for her kindness, and to assure her that breakfasting in bed was against her rules.

"I prefer rising early, rushing into the pure air, and having a long walk before breakfast; but I have somewhat overslept myself this morning, in consequence of the fatigue I underwent at the ball last night."

"Ah," said Mrs. Boodles, "which them balls is nice things sure-li. I never went to but one of 'em, and that was with the late Mr. Boodles, and he said to me when he was down in Oxfordshire, said he, 'Sarah, there's a county ball at Oxford town all this 'ere blessed night, and will you go?' said he. 'Go!' said I, 'and what am I to go in, without a rag to my precious back?' 'and,' said he, 'what the devil,' said he—he were addicted to swearing, as he were to cock-fighting and malt lickers—'what the devil,' said he, 'do you mean by having nothing to go in, when there's that booti- ful dress I bought you to be married in, which is a Irish poplin, and cost four-pun-ten, without the lining.' And I remember how tight they made it at the waist, which was nigh fit to burst, and gave me the spasims for a week—which for spasims fourteen drops of brandy on a piece of sugar is a excellent cure, and one to recommend. 'Well,' said I, in answer to Boodles, 'that 'ere dress was made for me nine year ago, and when I was a maiden fair to see; and how I'm to get it about me, bein' the mother of four sons and two darters, which finer was never seen, though I says it, is to me a mystery not to be revealed. 'Howsomever,' said he, 'to that ball we goes, and that dress you wears, as I'm a livin' sinner.' And then, mum, I had to go to my box, which was a hair one, with brass nails all druv in beautiful to behold, and out comes the dress, and with it sich a heap of lavender, which was folded up with it so that it should keep sweet and wholesome. Would you believe it, mum, it took some three whole hours to lace up that precious dress, and there I did't dare draw my breath for fear of splitting it up somewheres. At last, mum, to that ball I went, and there was the Lord Left-tenant of the county, the mayor and the corporashun, and the town crier and the beadle, and all the other great people, and all a looking bright and dazzlin', and like lovely fairies, only what hadn't got no wings, which fairies and cherry- bims has—the cherrybims perticklerly so; which it puzzles me what they sit down upon, and what they eat, seeing as how they are all wings and no body. In the happiness which came over me I forgot even my tight dress, and savin' an occasional spasim was quite comfortable, and the Lord Left-tenant, quite condescendin' like, he says to me, 'And how do you do, mum?' says he; to which I says, 'Sir,' says I, 'the enjiment is great, but my dress is tight, and its pothery hot, and I'm all over in a muck sweat,' at which he laughed as if I'd said something funny, but I s'pose that were his high breedin'. Well, mum, to make a long story short, the time passed, and at last the supper was served up, and we all sat down to it. 'Joe,' said I to Boodles, which his name was Joseph, and only Joe for short, 'Joe,' said I, 'I should like the wing of that fowl,' and I got it. The next minute I seed a turkey and I took a fancy to the leg and a part of the breast with the sassage meat attached. 'Joe,' said I, 'I must have some of that turkey.' 'It's too far off,' said Joe to me. 'I can't help it,' said I, 'you know how I am at this moment—which I was in the interesting way, mum, and had only five months to go—'I can't help it,' said I, 'and that turkey I must have, if you don't want to see your own offspring marked from head to heel with a roast turkey covered with sassages.' After a while I got the turkey, and much I enjied it; but would you believe it, mum, just as I had bolted the last mossel, that dreadful dress went off with a crack like the report of a gun, and there was I a sittin' at that table before all that company in a state dreadful to behold.'

Liz and Pipey strived hard to suppress their laughter, but in spite of their endeavours they at last gave way to their mirth, and enjoyed as hearty a roar as if they had no cares, and that all the world lay before them strewed with flowers for them to tread on.

"Ah," said the old lady, "I've laughed myself since then, but I'm sure it were no laughing matter to me at that time. But here's the breakfast ready, and now sit down and enjoy it."

"As you did the turkey, hey, Mrs. Boodles!"

"Which I hope you might, barrin' the accident which follered."

"A quaint old soul," said Liz, as the garrulous old lady withdrew and left the young pair to their morning meal; "but does she not think it strange to find me here in the position in which I am now placed."

"Fear nothing," said Pipey, "I have told her sufficient of your history to allay suspicion and stop her tongue. She is a good old soul, but too fond of talk."

The breakfast was discussed and thoroughly enjoyed, and then Liz asked Pipey what he intended doing for her, as it was impossible she could remain in the position in which she was then placed.

"True," said Pipey, "very true. I have thought of that myself, and will soon devise some plans for your safety and happiness. I must see the Duke and Duchess this morning."

"To what end? Surely you will not let those terrible people know of my whereabouts? Oh, they would drag me back to the infamy I so much dread."

"Do not fear me," said Pipey; "I will protect you from them. You can trust yourself with me, can you not?"

"Oh, yes," cried Liz. "I feel that while I am under your care I am safe."

"You are; so have no fears. My errand to the Duke and Duchess does not concern your present whereabouts, but simply your future welfare. They must make some provision for you."

"Why should they?"

"Because they have so deeply wronged you. But ask me nothing on that head, for at present my tongue is sealed. One day you will know why the Grasmounts should provide for you; at present the secret would only be a curse to you."

"I do not understand you."

"No, but you will at some future time."

Pipey assumed his walking gear, and calling in the assistance of Mrs. Boodles to clear away the breakfast things and keep Liz company until his return, he set out on his journey to St. James's Square.

He was well known at the residence of the Grasmounts, and entered the mansion without difficulty.

"Where is the Duke?"

"In his study. Shall I announce you?"

"No; I will take the liberty of walking in unannounced."

Pipey ascended to the Duke's study, and had his hand on the door when the sound of voices within arrested him.

It was the Duchess whose voice he heard.

"Yes, Grasmount," she cried, "I triumph now. For three years I have plotted and planned the ruin I have now brought upon your child. At the moment when her name was in the mouths of every one—when all the world is speaking of her as the good, beautiful, and accomplished belle of the new season, she falls into the clutches of the libertine and is ruined."

"Oh, where is my child — my poor, innocent child? What have you done with her?"

"Where is she?—in Carlton House! Yes, in the arms of the Prince. Ha! ha! you would wrong me, and think I would submit tamely. You have mistaken me, and now I can afford to pity you."

"Oh heartless, cruel, unnatural woman, to ruin one so good and beautiful—a poor unoffending girl, who never did you harm! It was the act of a fiend."

"It was the act of an outraged woman—I glory in it."

"That woman," thought Pipey, "has been enjoying herself quite long enough; it's time to put a period to her satisfaction."

Without knocking he entered the chamber in which husband and wife confronted one another.

"Who bade you enter here?" demanded the Duchess.

"No one, that I am aware of," answered Pipey, saucily; "I heard some misunderstanding going on, and I took the liberty of entering to set things straight."

"What mean you?" demanded the Duchess.

"Have you heard? Have you heard?" groaned the Duke.

"Oh, yes; I have heard the Duchess striving hard to make a fool of herself."

"What?"

"Well," said Pipey, "you have been making a fool of yourself, beyond a doubt."

The Duchess looked confused.

"I believe you made an assertion to the purpose that the child of the Duke had met her ruin at Carlton House?"

"I did; I rejoice thereat."

"Well, on that assertion I say you have made a fool of yourself."

"What mean you?"

"I mean that you are an extremely bad general, for you have out-manoeuvred yourself."

"Do you mean to assert that my scheme of vengeance has failed?"

"Most signally."

"In what particular?"

"In every particular."

"Did they dare fail me?"

"Oh no, they did their best; but I put a stop to their game."

"You?"

"Yes, I."

"What did you do?"

"I snatched Liz from Carlton House, instead of abandoning her to her fate; that's all."

"And she is—?"

"Beyond your power."

"Oh, thank God for that!" said the Duke— "thank God for that!"

"Villain!" cried the Duchess, almost foaming with anger, "you shall suffer for this!"

"Oh, don't trouble yourself," said Pipey, "I've had quite enough suffering in my time, and do not wish for any more; so spare yourself any pains on my account."

"I will drag you to the scaffold yet."

"If I do not anticipate you, and do the same good office for you," said Pipey.

"You talk thus to me! How dare you!"

"Oh, I dare do a great many things; the least of them is confronting a poor weak woman, such as you are now."

"I will yet prove my power!"

"Will you allow me to prove mine?"

"I defy you."

"Do not tempt me. It would not take me a moment to humble you; but I would rather spare you."

"Boaster!"

"Fool!"

"Heaven save us!" cried the Duke, "to what are we not come, that such language should be used here with impunity!"

"And whose the fault?" demanded the Duchess.

"Mine—mine—all mine," said the poor man, almost grovelling before his wife.

"Yours the fault," said Pipey, "but most bitterly have you atoned it. I now come to you to do the crowning act, and settle upon your child an allowance that will keep her as she has been used to live, until she finds a protector and provider in a husband."

"I forbid it," said the Duchess; "she shall have nothing from you; and moreover I command that she be returned into my keeping immediately. It is the price I demand for my silence."

"I am awaiting your answer," said Pipey to the Duke, without heeding the Duchess.

"I know not what to say," said the Duke.

"You are quite at liberty to use your own discretion," said Pipey, "I will answer for the silence of the Duchess."

"Insolent wretch!" almost screamed the Duchess; "but I will pay you for this in full. I have set you up, and I will drag you down."

"Pshaw!"

"Seek not to carry it off with this bravado. I will be even with you in spite of your insolent assurance."

"I am waiting to hear what you propose," said Pipey, still confining his attention to the Duke. "What allowance do you propose to make?"

"Not a penny," cried the Duchess. "I swear to reveal all I know if the Duke consents to make the slightest allowance to that girl."

"And I again and again repeat that you will be silent as the grave."

"We shall see."

"Now, my lord Duke, what is your proposition?"

"You have heard what the Duchess has said?"

"Yes; and I suppose you would add that her will is your law?"

"What alternative have I?"

"Very good. That is your answer. I would have spared the Duchess, but she forbids it. Since I cannot persuade I must force her. Madam, you *must* acquiesce in all that is said and done in this matter."

"Must?"

"Yes, must."

"Hell itself cannot force me."

"Perhaps not, but I can."

Pipey dived his right hand into his pocket, and on withdrawing it exhibited on his glove the badge *of the scarlet ribbon !*

He placed his hand on his knee, and the eye of the Duchess at once caught sight of the fatal sign.

Her cheek blanched, and she staggered back into a chair.

"What says the Duchess now?—is my charm potent enough to move her?"

"Spare me! spare me!" cried the woman in a frenzy.

"Do you consent to my bargaining with the Duke?"

"I will consent to anything but the degradation of an exposure. Spare me!"

"I have yet another charm. Who saw you to your carriage on quitting Carlton House last night?"

"Oh, God! oh, God! Spare me! spare me!"

"Dear me," said Pipey, "I had not the slightest intention of making such a great stir about trifles. Why should I spare you? What do you mean?"

Pipey looked at the Duchess with an air of extreme simplicity; but in his face there was that which plainly told his victim that she was powerless.

"This is to me a deep and terrible mystery," said the Duke. "Explain by what means you gained this ascendancy over the Duchess."

"I'd rather not."

"I insist."

"Oh, if you insist—"

"No, no," cried the Duchess. "Seek to know

nothing. I am convinced that this man means well by us. Consent to what he will propose; it were better for us all that you do so."

"Ah, now you talk like a sensible woman. I told you it would be all right with the Duchess," said Pipey, turning to the Duke; "and now, let us turn to business matters. The girl is still in danger in this country. She can be trusted to no one—no, not even to her considerate friend the Duchess; so that I propose to send her abroad."

"Whither ?"

"Into some continental nunnery, if no other asylum can be found for her."

"Well ?"

"For this purpose it is necessary that an annual income be settled upon her—say, a couple of thousands of pounds—in order that she may continue to live as becomes one of her birth and education."

The Duke glanced at the Duchess. She waved her hand in token that he should consent.

"Really, the Duchess is most obliging to-day; I'm quite charmed with her."

"No badinage," said the Duchess; "let this matter be concluded."

"Very good," continued Pipey; "I am glad to see the business humour so strong upon you. What I propose is that an adequate sum, say the one I before mentioned, be given me quarterly for her use, and that with it I dispose of her as I think fit, and place her beyond the reach of her foes until the will and other documents of which I am in search come into my possession. When she is beyond the malice and designs of all men, and may be left to herself, her course I cannot determine, she may think proper to leave you unmolested in the enjoyment of the property which is hers, or she may lay claim to it—I cannot say which, but in any case you must not attempt to interfere with her. If these terms be complied with I will be silent and keep her secret; if not, I speak. The result be upon your own head."

"I consent," said the Duke, "I consent; but how am I to know that you will apply this money to her uses? What security have I for your honesty?"

"The best possible. For every penny I receive from you I will produce your daughter's receipt. Is not that satisfactory enough?"

"Yes, yes, that will do; I am content."

"Then produce a thousand pounds for present expenses. The girl must at once leave England."

The Duke gave Pipey a banker's order for the sum he claimed.

"It is well," said Pipey, folding up the paper. "For this you shall be furnished with the receipt of your daughter; and now my business is over I have only to take my leave. Adieu! I trust this interview has been as satisfactory to you as it has been to me."

There was no answer, and Pipey left the closet. He had only descended a very few stairs, when a hand was laid upon his shoulders, and the Duchess, pale and trembling. stood before him.

"I am in your power," she said.

"Oh, don't mention it," said Pipey, "it's nothing."

"Make no jest of it. I feel the position in which I am placed. I am no longer blind to the horrible fate in store for me if my secrets should be revealed."

"Fear nothing on my account. As long as you are true to Liz I am with you, but attempt to injure her, and I speak."

"'Tis well. I know I can trust you."

"Yes, as long as I can trust you."

"That will be for ever."

"I hope it may. Adieu!"

"One moment !"

"What now ?"

"Answer me. By what means have you become possessed of my secrets? You are not a member of the brotherhood, and I thought there was but one who knew of my intimacy with that gentleman who led me to my carriage last night. Have Masters and the Prince betrayed me?"

"Not to me."

"Then how did you become possessed of the facts which I see you are able to reveal ?"

"I dare not tell you! In my capacity of a secret agent I become acquainted with strange facts concerning all manner of persons. Amongst others, your secret, fell into my possession; but, rely upon it, they are both safe. With that assurance I will leave you."

"But the brotherhood! You will not betray them ?"

"Not until it suits me to do so, which will not in all probability be for some considerable time. By the way, that reminds me, this brotherhood, as you term them, know nothing of my acquaintance with their secret. You must not reveal the fact to them."

"But I have an oath —"

"And I have a will of my own. You inform your friends of my acquaintance with their secrets and I will crush them and you; and so once more adieu."

"Adieu.'"

Pipey was gone.

"There is nothing for it but his death," said the Duchess, "nothing—nothing. Ah, he must die; but the means, the means."

* * * * *

Pipey went briskly along Pall Mall, quietly congratulating himself on the success of hi mission.

"I flatter myself no diplomatist could have managed matters better. Poor Duke, poor Duchess. They are both my tools now. Ha! ha! what a scene there will be between them. The Duchess will be maddened at her defeat, the Duke triumphant and suspicious. Well, they will lead a happy life, I'm thinking."

A few more paces and Pipey ran against a gentleman, with his head turned away, who had not noticed his approach.

"I really beg your pardon," said the gentleman, "it was really very careless of me."

"I think the fault was all on my side—good Heaven!"

Pipey glanced upon the face of the person whom he addressed, and started back uttering the exclamation we have given.

"You seem astonished. Do you know me ?"

"I think I do."

"I have been absent from England three years, and I had thought that time had so changed me that my best friend or my worst enemy would not know me."

"Perhaps not; but still I should know you among a thousand. I never forget a face I have once seen, and I have seen yours but once before. Lord Lovelace, I believe?"

"That is my name. Where have we met?"

"Just below this spot—outside the gates of Marlborough House."

"When?"

"On the occasion of a certain ball given by the Prince. Do you not remember the occasion?"

"Perfectly."

"You had a lady with you."

"Yes, yes! Do you know her?—do you know where she is to be found?"

"Perhaps I do."

"Then this meeting is most fortunate. Oh, you do not know how I long to meet her. Is she well? Is she in safety?"

"Well, and in safety."

"Heaven be praised for that!"

"So say I."

"But you have not told me where I shall find her."

"No, and am not likely to until I first of all ascertain whether she would be pleased to meet you again. Three years may have made some changes in her feelings, more particularly as she only met you once."

"True, true. I see that you are right."

"All I can do for you is to promise that, should she desire to see you, I will communicate with you. Give me your address."

"It is here."

Lovelace drew forth his case, and handed Pipey his card.

"That will do. I shall lay this before her, and will communicate the result to you as early as possible."

"Many thanks. But to whom am I indebted for this secret kindness?"

"My name is Captain de Pipes."

"Then allow me to shake you by the hand and call you friend."

"With all my heart. Her friends must be mine. Adieu."

Pipey strode away.

"Yes," he said to himself, "the hand of fate is in this matter. He loved her—loves her still; and she—ah, I can see it—has never ceased to love him. It is as well they should come together. Their happiness may break my heart, for with their union my occupation, and the great object of my life, is ended. But it is for her good, and I will bear the trial."

He hastened home, and found Liz in company with the ancient Boodles, anxiously expecting his arrival.

"You are come at last," she cried. "Oh, how glad I am! I began to fear that you had quite deserted me. How pale and anxious you look! Has anything occurred to distress you?"

"Nothing; everything has gone better than I could have even dreamed of."

"Why, then, those anxious looks? They are strangers to your kindly face."

"Which a sweeter-tempered milingtary gentleman never lived," chimed in the Boodles.

"All is well, excellent well," said Pipey, with a smile; "and see here; I found an old friend for you—one who will prove a better and more worthy guardian than I have been."

"That would be impossible," said Liz; "quite impossible."

"I do not know that. Glance at the name."

As the eye of the young girl fell upon the card she had taken between her fingers, she started in amazement, and turned pale as death.

"Now, am I not right?" asked Pipey.

"Where did you see him?—did he ask for me?—did he look much altered?"

Pipey gave the substance of his interview.

"And now," he added, "I have but to bring him to your feet, and my task is ended."

"Are you, then, tired of it?"

"That is an unkind question. Could I ever tire of guarding you? No, no, Liz; love where you will—marry whom you please—you shall still feel that I am near you to protect and guard you. The task will be a light and agreeable one if you but bid me continue it."

"Until death!"

"I accept the charge, and you shall never have to complain of infidelity."

"Which she wouldn't," said the Boodles, "for a sweeter tempered and more lovely young lady I never met, though I says it to her face and should'nt. Ah, she reminds me of poor Lady Gotawnyboy's eldest, which was brought into this world when I was head housekeeper at Gotawnyboy Hall. She were a dear soul, she were; and fell desperate in love with a real Earl, all covered with strawberry-leaves—which they says is a true sign of nobility; though I don't see how that could be, only strawberries is a nice fruit—and well I knows it, having eat five gallons when my third girl was about to be brought into the world, which they made me ill, and brought on an internal disorder, wus than spasims. The young lady were called Angelica, and the real Earl would have married her, only she went ill of the small-pox, and got out of bed pitted all over—which, as I said, shouldn't a made a bit of difference, only men is so fickle, and earls is so pertcikler—which it is a shame, and well I knows it."

Pipey here sent the old lady into the lower regions to see after the dinner.

"And mind we have something nice."

"Which it's a pheasant," said the Boodles, "and as fine a one as ever I see in all my days."

Mrs. Boodles had no sooner retired than Liz burst into a flood of tears, and, throwing herself into Pipey's arms, said,

"Generous, noble friend, how long is the debt to go on accumulating? When am I to be enabled to repay you for all your goodness to me? This last act outdoes all others, for I well know the secret of your heart and the struggle it must have been to have conquered all feelings but the one of devotion to me. You are all goodness. Oh, would that fate had willed it that I could have repaid you according to your deserts. Would that I could —"

"Love me?"

"I do love you, but —"

"The love is not of the kind that would induce you to marry me."

"Alas! yes."

"I know it, and it is perhaps well that it is so. In Lovelace you will find one whose worth and education makes him a more suitable companion for you than I could possibly be. He will make a good husband. And if he does not —"

"If he does not?"

"I shall know how to make him."

"What do you mean?"

"I mean that it will be as bad for him as it has been for others who have persecuted you; but, psha! this is idleness; Lovelace idolises you, and will treat you as devotedly as I would have done had you loved me."

"Would that I could do so."

After this they were silent.

CHAPTER XXXV.

THE MEETING OF THE SCARLET BRETHREN.

It was night, and the streets of London were becoming deserted.

We have to take the reader once more to the neighbourhood of Soho, and to that very street in which Lord Lovelace lodged before quitting England after his fatal duel.

The night air was murky, and the sky clouded and heavy.

It was after ten, and most of the houses were closed and exhibited no lights.

The residence of the Signora Relatana, the Italian boarding-house keeper, was, however, ablaze with lights, as it usually was at that hour.

There is a saying that the most public places

are oft the most private, and the members of the society of Scarlet Brethren were evidently strong believers in this theory, for they chose the residence of Signora Relatana as their place of meeting in nine instances out of ten.

Being a boarding-house it was only natural to suppose that it would be constantly full of people; and as the majority of the boarders were pleasure-loving foreigners, but little notice was taken of the number of persons who thronged to the house once or twice a week.

The Signora's establishment had, moreover, the reputation of being a gaming house, and this doubtless assisted in blinding people to the real motive which brought so many visitors under her roof.

On this particular night a number of persons might have been seen entering the house of the Italian.

Men and women flocked there from all directions.

The majority of them came alone. But few came in parties of more than three.

They were all apparently anxious to avoid notice, for they were well muffled in cloaks, and hid their faces as much as possible.

They thrust open the partly closed street door and entered without ceremony.

In the passage they were met by a servant who to each fresh comer, raised his hand and made a, curious sign and uttered the word

"*Mort.*"

To which the visitors replied with a counter-sign—

"*Patrie.*"

They now passed along the lobby until they reached the extreme end, where they passed through a door into a small darkened chamber; here they were challenged by some one unseen.

"*Patrie,*" uttered a voice, to which the comer answered

"*Mort.*"

Then a trap opened in the floor, and the persons descended a flight of stairs into an underground apartment.

It will be seen that the lighting up of the apartments exposed to the street was a *ruse* to divert attention from the place of meeting used by this London branch of the Secret Society of Scarlet Brethren.

The underground apartment alluded to had evidently been constructed for the special purpose for which it was used. It was a spacious place, running under the garden of the house supported by arches; from which descended brilliant candelabra, in which were placed a large number of wax lights. Although the walls were uncovered; various attempts had been made to deprive them of the appearance of bareness.

The floor was covered with a soft Turkey carpeting, and about the place were scattered magnificent lounges and easy chairs covered with scarlet velvet.

In the centre of the apartment stood a long massive table, at the head of which was a chair, evidently placed for the president of the meeting. Notwithstanding all the glitter and luxury of the place, it could not be deprived of the air of a vault.

At the foot of the flight of stairs was placed a large screen, behind which was laid a table covered with long scarlet gowns, one of which was assumed by every person who descended into the vault. Thus every one in the place was enveloped in scarlet, and a very curious picture it made. After a while the place became very full, and it was evident that the throng was made up of almost every branch of the society.

At the head of the vault, seated in the large chair before alluded to, was Masters, to whom every fresh comer tendered his obedience before taking his seat.

Near him was the Duchess of Grasmount, Lewis Arndale, and Signora Relatana.

For some time the assemblage was divided into little groups, carrying on a desultory conversation, but at length attention became centralised in the Black Captain, who, on rising, addressed himself particularly to the Duchess of Grasmount:

"Sister of our band," he said, "we failed you when you bade us execute your commands: say, is the task yet to do, for by our oaths we are forced to continue our work till you bid us stop. But were it not so we would all gladly render you assistance in consideration of the love and respect we bear for you."

"We would."

The Duchess rose.

"I thank you," she said, "the task is ended. My scheme has failed, and I have no longer any occasion to monopolise your time or engage your attention."

"But you will explain to us how your scheme failed?"

"No."

"We should demand to know it."

"I know you have the right, but I pray you to forego it. Enough that there was an error on my part, by which your services were rendered useless."

"Indeed! That surprises me, for Lewis Arndale half suspected that you were outwitted by some one who accosted him in a retiring room at Carlton House."

"What is that?"

"A very singular matter — Arndale was addressed by a man having a slight foreign accent and who exhibited to him the badge of brotherhood, but whose description does not correspond with that of any member of the band."

The Duchess turned pale.

Masters fixed his eye upon her, and seemed to read her very thoughts.

"Do you think it possible that we are betrayed?" he cried.

The Duchess remembered the words of Pipey:

"Inform your friends of my acquaintance with your secrets, and I will crush them and you."

What was to be done?

"Listen," said Masters, "your cheek blanches, and you are silent. I ask you again: Do you think it possible that we are betrayed?"

After some hesitation the Duchess replied:

"Yes!"

A thrill of amazement ran through the assemblage.

"I have weighed all the chances," she said, "and I have concluded to tell you all I know, but," she continued with deeply impressive voice, "beware, for the person you have to deal with is no ordinary man."

"No matter, he must die."

"To that conclusion I have come, and would have done the task without exciting the alarm of the brotherhood had you not forced me to speak."

"Who is it that possesses our secret?"

"One I have befriended and raised from the dregs — a snake I have warmed in my bosom until it has stung me."

"His name?"

"It is well known to you. It is the boy whom they nicknamed Pipey."

"Indeed!" cried Masters, "how could he have learnt our secret?"

"I do not know, but it is certain that some one has divulged it, or that it has leaked out from some unsuspected source. Remember, he is in the service of the Government, and has numberless sources of information open to him of which we know nothing—of which we cannot even dream."

"True; but it is very strange."

"It is, and immediate action must be taken to silence him for ever."

"Yes," said Masters, "for ever, or we are lost."

"Of that I am well assured. He will be silent as long as it suits his purposes, but no longer. Rely upon it, he will effect our ruin sometime or other."

"Is it possible that others can share his knowledge?" asked the Signora.

"I think not," said the Duchess. "He is far too cunning to whisper such a secret until he cared no longer for it; and I know that time has not yet arrived. To what end he has so far spared us I do not know; but he must have urgent reasons."

"No matter," said Masters, "he must die; and to you, Duchess and sister, we entrust the task of ridding us of him."

"To me?"

"Yes. Did you not say that you purposed doing so without alarming us?"

"Yes, yes; and I will still undertake the task."

"It is a difficult one. I know this boy full well, and believe he is a match for the best of us. He must, therefore, have no quarter; and although to you, individually, we consign the office of ridding us of him, we must all be engaged in the same game, and never release a nerve in attempting his destruction. On his death depends our safety."

"Then he must die!" said the whole of the assemblage, with one voice.

"Meanwhile," said Masters, "we are unsafe even here. We must meet no more for some time, and all trace of us in London must perforce disappear. Remember, let no one use the signs until he has permission. No personal danger must tempt him into claiming the assistance of his brothers. All must progress as if we were no longer a body, or we shall fall into some unforeseen trap, and rush upon our destruction. Am I understood?"

"Yes."

"Then let me be obeyed."

"And now to business in earnest," said Arndale; "it appears that we shall not meet again for some time, so let our arrangements be perfect."

One by one the members of the band came to the table, and stating their cases, revealing their wants, or describing their gains, deposited before the president, or received from him, quantities of gold, according to the manner in which they were situated. After this a general movement of departure was made, and one by one the people cleared away.

There was no rush, no unseemly haste.

As if pre-arranged there was rather a long wait between the departure of the various persons, and so rapidly did they disappear on reaching the street that there was nothing suspicious about the movement; and no one took more notice of the departures than would be excited by a score or two of guests quitting an ordinary party, perhaps not so much.

"Shall I see you through the streets?" asked Arndale of the Duchess.

"No," said the Duchess, "I am well muffled, and have nothing to fear. I would rather be alone."

Arndale bowed and left the lady.

She hastily quitted the house, but was closely followed by a man who had watched her departure from the vault, and had quitted it immediately after her.

He permitted her to get some distance in advance of him, and then, casting a glance about him, to assure himself that he was not watched, set off after the retreating figure.

By the less frequented route the Duchess sped on towards St. James's-square, and unmolested she reached her own door.

Here the person following her came suddenly upon her, and, catching her by the arm, cried,

"Well, madam, you prefer war to peace. You have revealed my secret to-night, and your precious brotherhood already thirst for my blood. You are to murder me, are you? Good! Try it on. Oh, foolhardy woman! what have you not done? I would have spared you, bad as you are, but you court war, and you must have it. Remember my words—I will crush them and you—and I will do what I promised. Keep on, and be convinced that I shall be as good as my word."

He dropped her arm, turned, and hastened away.

It was Pipey!

"Alas!" cried the Duchess, when she had partially recovered from her stupor, "alas! I am beaten, for I cannot cope with a devil."

Gloomily she turned to her door, and was admitted by her serving man Liney.

"Come to my apartment as soon as possible," she said; "I have much to say to you."

"I know, I know," said the idiot, "trouble again. Liney can see. He knows."

"Silence, and obey me."

"Yes, yes, Liney will obey you; even if you tell him *to commit a murder!*"

"I may do that," said the Duchess, as she walked to her private apartment."

CHAPTER XXXVI.

THE MEETING OF LIZ AND LORD LOVELACE.

DID he love her?

Who shall say? Love is so strange a thing, and the shapes it assumes so numerous and quaint, that it is hard to trace it when it lurks in the human breast; but in the case of Lovelace it may be supposed that he did really love since he never ceased to remember her whom he had met but that memorable once, but who then unreservedly gave her heart to him.

With Marie he had never been happy, although he certainly grew more fond of her after the birth of her child.

It may be urged that no man who had done as he had done could really and truly have loved.

It might have been so, but the sequel will prove that.

Meanwhile we must assume that there was a passion burning in the breast of the young nobleman that led him on in the pursuit of her who had kindled it. Whatever it was, it had proved lasting; for three long years it had smouldered, and at last burst forth anew and apparently with more force than had originally been the case.

And Liz loved Lovelace.

There could be no doubt on the subject, for had it not been so she would have turned more favourably towards him who had been so long her devoted slave.

She could not love Pipey, and therefore she must have loved Lovelace.

These, or very similar thoughts flitted through the mind of Pipey himself as he watched his fair charge after the revelations he made to her.

He saw her eye brighten and her cheek flush.

There was a smile on her lips, and he knew she was happier now than she had been for years.

"Yes," he said, "she is happy. She has not seen him, but the thought of his being near her fills her with joy. She shall see him."

He would hesitate no longer.

Why should he delay their happiness? It would be cruel.

It must not be.

Coming to this conclusion Pipey soon sought out the favoured one.

"Well," cried Lovelace, as he saw Pipey entering his chamber, "she has not forgotten me. She has sent for me?"

"She has not forgotten you. She will see you."

"Oh, thanks, thanks! Blessings on you for those words! They charm me."

Pipey did not answer.

Lovelace was in a few moments prepared to set out, and he was soon hastening with Pipey to his home.

Pipey conducted him to the presence of Liz, and in a moment they were locked in each other's arms.

Mrs. Boodles was present, and was deeply affected.

Moving herself violently into a chair she exhibited marked indications of choking.

"Which it's spasims," she said to Pipey, "and fourteen drops of brandy on a lump of sugar I must have if you wouldn't see me a blessed corpse at your feet."

Despite the torture he was undergoing, and perhaps glad of any excuse for bustling about, Pipey procured Mrs. Boodles' infallible specific and administered it with alacrity.

"Beautiful as ever!" whispered Lovelace. "Oh, how beautiful! and you have never forgotten me?"

Of course she had not, and of course he knew it, but he wanted to hear her say so: just as if he could not have spared her the trouble.

But lovers are so unreasonable.

Why should we detail all that Lovelace and Liz said to each other?

The tale would be flat and uninteresting as lovers' talk usually is, and we should not be thanked for reporting it.

To them it was doubtless full of interest and pleasure.

To them it was a rapture—to others, we have a shrewd suspicion, it would prove tiresome, not to say idiotic.

The opinion of Mrs. Boodles was, however, different.

"It's beautiful," she said to Pipey as they looked on the happy lovers; "it's beautiful to see 'em a billing and cooing like them precious turtle doves; and it reminds me, it does, of the time when Boodles came a courting of me, only he did not dress so fine, nor talk so pretty, for he were but a common man, though he stood over six foot in his stockings; but as I used to say, what can you expect of a man who is fond of cock-fighting, and gives way to drink? Yet to give the man his due he was very good to me for a month or two, but after that he took to pitching things at me, which his favrits was brickbats, sometimes varied by stone bottles, and they did hurt when they hit, perticlerly on the head and small of the back."

"I should say so," said Pipey, with his eyes fixed on Liz, whose back was towards him. "I should say so—what were you saying, Mrs. Boodles? Let me see, you said that some one stole your pickles, and you felt hurt at their offering you stone bottles. Oh, ah; very funny. Yes."

"Which I didn't," said Mrs. Boodles, much annoyed at finding Pipey had not paid any heed to what she had said; "my observations was that brickbats and stone bottles *did* hurt when they hit one on the head, or in the small of the back; which the proof of the pudding is in the eating. But lor', how ill you do look! What ever is the matter?"

"Nothing," said Pipey, "nothing; a sudden pain."

"A spasim? Do try the fourteen drops of brandy on the lump sugar."

Liz turned round, and at a glance saw what ailed Pipey.

She therefore ceased to confine her attention to Lovelace, and commenced a conversation with the poor dejected Pipey.

But Pipey was not easily consoled, and would have given his hand to have started off, and be alone.

Not so the Boodles. She seemed thoroughly to enjoy the scene progressing before her, and in spite of many hints of the most palpable character, obstinately refused to move an inch. She heard that Lovelace had been abroad, and " on that hint she spake."

" Ah, sir—that is, my lord," she said—" it's a mercy, and so it is, that you have come home with your right number of legs and arms, which it isn't often them does who goes out among the savages and Injins of the praries—which cannibals they are, and nobody can deny it."

" Why, my good woman," said Lovelace, " you do not suppose that *all* foreigners are ' savages and Indians ?' "

" Which I certainly do," said Mrs. Boodles, " every one of 'em ; and well I knows it ; for Mrs. Milkworth's husband, who was a soldier bred and born, and as fine a man as ever walked, he went foreign, and got his arm knocked off by one savage, and his leg knocked off by another, and which they roasted 'em before a fire, and eat 'em before his very eyes—which is the truth, as I am a living woman, and here to tell it."

Lovelace laughed heartily, but fidgetted about, and appeared very anxious to get rid of the garrulous old soul ; and Pipey, observing this, carried her off forcibly to the lower regions, glad of any excuse for quitting a presence in which he felt anything but comfortable.

" You have not yet told me who your kind friends are, nor have you explained the mystery of your appearance at Venice with the Duchess of Grasmount," said Lord Lovelace to Liz, as soon as they were alone.

" It is a singular story," said Liz, " and as mysterious to me as it must appear to you. I have told you that I fell into the hands of Maydock on being torn from your side on the night of our meeting. After that I lived for some considerable time a prisoner in the burglar's attic. From that fate I was rescued by the man who has just left us. I then resided for a short period with one Grimer, a lawyer, of the city, who treated me with the utmost consideration, but from whom I was taken by the Duke and Duchess of Grasmount, both of whom appeared to take the utmost interest in my welfare, claiming relationship with me. With the Duchess I left England, and with her I travelled over the greater part of the Continent, receiving all the care I could desire, studying, by her direction, under the best professors France and Italy could afford. My long-neglected education was thoroughly looked to, and I was soon made a proficient in all the accomplishments most acceptable to woman. Then we returned to England, and our first public appearance was at the ball given by the Prince of Wales. Oh, how can I tell it ! The woman who had so long and so tenderly regarded me thrust me upon the loathed Prince, and to his evil passions I should have fallen a victim had not my good and generous friend promptly rescued me, and brought me here, where I have enjoyed the only hours of real happiness I have known since last we parted."

" A strange and eventful tale," said Lovelace. " But why should the Duchess have acted so fiendish a part ?"

" I cannot conceive, but there is some mystery still enveloping my history with which I am not acquainted. I do not know why I think so, but something tells me that the Duke of Grasmount is my father !"

" Indeed !"

" Yes. Very frequently, when I have looked into his eyes, it appeared to me that I had some vague recollection of having seen him before, and my heart has yearned towards him mysteriously. Then, again, I have heard words pass between the Duke and Duchess which have tended to strengthen my opinion, but I know nothing definite."

" Do you think your friend knows aught of your affairs ?"

" I sometimes think he could reveal the whole secret of my life, but he is always silent on the point."

" No matter, dearest," said Lovelace. " As my wife all your troubles must end ; give me, then, the right to protect you. Become mine, and whoever may be your parents, and whatever their value, I will recompense you for their loss by true love and devotion. You shall know no care, and never have a cause for sorrow. Let me call you mine."

" I am not skilled in the artifices of the world," said Liz, " and therefore cannot dissemble as others could, and as, according to the fashion of the times in which we live, I ought to do, and therefore I will at once say that I have never ceased to love you, and that I would gladly be your wife, but that I fear you have not known me long enough to assure yourself that you love me sufficiently well to make me your wife. Therefore, let us wait."

" No, no," said Lovelace ; " I have tested my passion by three long years of probation, and I find it strong as ever. Let me implore you not to hesitate. Consider the dangers by which you are surrounded."

" Let me have a few days—a few hours—"

She looked up, and saw that Pipey had entered the room.

" If you love him—and you do love him," he said, " do not hesitate, for he is right ; your best protector is a husband."

What could Liz say after that ? She hung her head, and was silent.

" Consent !" cried Lovelace, " consent, dear one. You hear what your best friend advises. Let me be happy, and thus secure your own happiness."

Pipey took their hands and joined them.

" For years," he said, " I have watched over and protected her. We were both friendless orphans together, and I was her brother. We have become man and woman together, and I have been brother—a good and true one. How good, how true, you will perhaps learn from her own lips. I have loved her with more than a brother's love, but I saw that her heart was yours, and I have never once paraded my passion or presumed upon my position. I have watched over her, protected her, and striven for her welfare that she might be happy. Pure, also, as I knew her first, I return her to your arms. You have a priceless gem, so guard and learn to know her as the treasure she is. Take her, and God bless you."

The latter part of this speech was almost inaudible, for the choking voice in which it was uttered. There had been a great struggle, an immense effort of self sacrifice, but he had conquered and fulfilled his duty.

"He is all goodness—all greatness," cried Liz, "he is my brother, and as such I shall ever regard him."

"He is then my brother likewise," said Lovelace, grasping the young man's hand. "I shall learn to love him as much as I now honour and respect him."

During this scene Mrs. Boodles, freed from the restraint placed upon her by Pipey, had again ascended from the lower regions, and established herself in the sitting room, as she said,

"To see it out; for them love makings is so sweet and so reminds me of early days; which memry's a blessed thing and brings back feelings which lies deep in the heart and will come out in spite of age and an accumulation of fat."

The interruption was this time very acceptable to all parties, for they had come to an awkward pause, and were glad of any chance of changing the subject.

Finding herself encouraged by the smiles of her auditors Mrs Boodles seated herself and commenced the story of her love.

"Ah, my dear," she said to Pipey, "I did think, for you, and you alone, that blessed creetur" pointing to Liz, "was brought into the world, but it seems it isn't to be after all, because human natur can't be governed, and the heart's a wilful thing and like a warm plaister you stick it against a thing quite unconscious like and there it'll hold, and if you attempts to move it you tear away the flesh and leave a wound, which is as much as to say that a young lady's heart is a plaister and that she's stuck it again' my lord there, and can't pull it off again no way, which it was my own case and well I knows it. There was two of 'em, my lord, as wanted my hand at the altar, which one was a grocer and the other a gardener, and it was the latter as had me, which Joseph Boodles was his name, and in his Bible said in poetry beautiful to read :—

> 'Joseph Boodles is my name,
> And humble is my station;
> Oxford is my dwelling place,
> And England is my nation.'

Which I always says is very pretty, and ought to be writ in every book as is printed. Well Boodles was as fine a man as ever trod in shoe leather, whilst the grocer, whose name was Winkles, was rather undersized, but with good looks, a fine business, and plenty of money, which Boodles hadn't—as I soon found out for myself. All he had in the world was four terrible game cocks and a badger, to which he was addicted, as likewise to malt lickers. Well, my dear, I didn't know what was to be done, for whilst my heart pleaded for Boodles something else told me that Winkles was the man, for he could give me all the comforts I could desire. So there was a dreadful struggle between love and selfishness; and proud I am to say it, love was the victor, although much I've suffered for it ever since, in consequence of Boodles turning out such a brute, which brute he was, although he's dead and gone, and I didn't ought to say it of him now. The upshot was that Winkles and Boodles had a meeting in the

back yard, and after a desperate fight, which lasted five minutes, Winkles was pitched into the water-butt and the cover put down, which it was sat upon by Boodles until the unfortunate grocer was as near drowned as possible."

"An unfortunate little grocer," laughed Lovelace.

"So he were, sir; he was unfortunate in losing me, which a good wife I should have been to him, though I say it myself—but a poor, lone woman hasn't anybody to speak for her, which she doesn't want to be a worm and crushed to death, she has to speak for herself, regardless of opinions; which I wish you every joy, and a blessed family, to be the pride of their mother and father, and all the comforts of life, which one of 'em if you has spasims is brandy, fourteen drops on a lump of sugar, and many times I've proved it."

Having ran herself out of breath, Mrs. Boodles retired, and Lovelace prepared to follow her example.

"To-morrow," he said, "at my own house in St. James's, we will become one. Till then, adieu."

He kissed her tenderly, and withdrew.

"To-morrow," thought Pipey, "to-morrow the dream ends, and life loses its charm."

"To-morrow," thought Lovelace, "I shall be happy; yes, happy beyond my deserts, for I have sinned. Oh! if I but dared tell her all!"

He did not dare, and so went on his way.

Had he been less occupied with his thoughts he would have been conscious that he was followed by a woman, who clung to his steps with a doggedness which proved the seriousness of her purpose.

It was the Italian boarding-house keeper, fulfilling the mission of the deserted Marie.

CHAPTER XXXVII.

THE DUCHESS AND SERVING-MAN. — GRIMER AGAIN AT WORK.

"You want me?" said Liney, entering the apartment of the Duchess soon after her return from the secret meeting. "What do you require?"

"There is work for you to do, and it must be done. People may call me fool for trusting you, but I would rather trust you than one half of those who express great cleverness, and boast a mind stronger than your own. You have proved faithful to me heretofore, but I have never yet tried you to the extent to which I am now forced. The work in hand is of a terrible nature. Do you understand?"

"I know, I know. You can't give me too much to do. I gloat over your work, and will do it faithfully. Try me!—try me!"

"I must try you, for I am at bay, and danger threatens from which you alone can save me."

"Danger!"—the eye of the softy gleamed fire —"Danger! Show me—let me tear it away! I will save you at the risk of my life. You know I will. You know—you know."

"Yes, I know."

"Then I'll do it. Tell me—tell."

"Listen, then. A man is hunting me down. He threatens exposure—ruin—perhaps death! What must be done with him?"

"He must be driven away."

"That will not do. He is a bloodhound, and will not be driven off. You know how to deal with such a man."

"Yes, he must die."

"Ah, you are right now."

"Yes, he must die."

"And you will do it, Liney?—I have only to look to you."

"I hate blood. There must be no blood."

"As you will, but he must die."

"But no blood, I say; I sicken at it—I faint, and it kills me. Let me get my fingers on his throat, and I will do it, but—faugh!—the sight, the smell of blood!"

"Silence, fool! you speak too loudly. All the house will hear your mad ravings of blood. I say, do as you will, so that it is done."

"Faugh!" cried the idiot, writhing as if in pain; "let me not see his blood and he dies; but blood—blood—blood!—oh, do not let me see that!"

He spoke loudly, and the Duchess, in extreme fright, sprang from her couch, and clutched him by the throat.

"Silence!" she cried, "silence, or *your* blood shall flow."

The sudden action of the Duchess brought the poor fool to his senses, and he was silent.

He stood trembling in front of his mistress.

"Yes," he said, meekly, "I know, I know. What more?—what more?"

"Only this—I must put you on the track, and leave you to do the rest. I will show you your victim—"

"And I will do the rest."

"Are you sure?'

"Quite sure. You must be saved, and I must save you. That is enough. Liney knows, and he never forgets."

"That is well; and now I must think how we are to meet this man. He is cunning, and difficult to trap. Even now he may be far away, and out of danger."

"Not out of danger, for I'm after him," said the idiot; "let me but sight him, and night and day, day and night I'll hunt after him until I have him in my clutch, and then—"

"And then?"

"He shall die."

"At any risk?"

"Yes."

"But you must use care. If you should be detected."

"I see—I see. You fear for yourself; but no matter—no matter. Let them take me. Let them cut me into pieces and they shall not make me speak. Liney is too devoted a dog for that."

"Good. I believe you are to be trusted. I do not doubt you."

"Do not, for Liney knows."

"Good night. Let us speak no more. To-morrow evening I shall have more to say to you; now to bed."

The man walked away without uttering another word.

* * * * *

The morning following this interview the Duchess was breakfasting alone, when a servant entered her room and informed her that some one wished to see her."

"Who is it?"

"The man gave no name, but said his business was of the utmost importance."

"I am engaged."

"So I told him, but he would not be denied. He assured me again and again that he must see your Grace.

"Well," said the Duchess, languidly, "admit him."

In another moment an old man, weather-beaten, and clad in a rusty suit of black, stepped into the chamber.

His eye was as sharp and bright as that of the fox, and was filled with deep cunning and intense penetration.

There was no mistaking him.

It was the old lawyer, Grimer.

"Good morning," he said to the Duchess; "good morning, your Grace. Tell your man he may withdraw."

The Duchess obeyed.

"Now," she said, as the door closed, "why are you here? I thought I had done with you for ever."

"I thought you had, but such is not the case."

"How so? Ah! the will—have you found it?"

"Alas! no. Wish I had. My errand is unfortunately of no such pleasant character.

"What do you mean?"

"Mean! Why, I mean that we are all beaten now. Lord Lovelace, the man whom the girl Liz loves, has returned to England, and has seen her. I see you look surprised to think I know aught of the girl and her movements, but I know all—all. The trap laid for her at Carlton House—the rescue by Pipey—the disappointment and the *denouement*. Ha! ha! No one can beat me! I'm always down to the game, I am."

"Speak. I have heard of this Lovelace. You say he has returned to England, and has seen the girl. You must, then, know where she is."

"Of course I do; and I also know the result of the interview."

"Speak on."

"All in good time. I have never heard a word, but I have been on the watch, and have seen things which speak as plainly as words. What do you suppose, now?"

"Oh, do not torture me with idle questions; what have you to say to me? What is there to reveal?"

"A secret of great importance."

"Then let me hear it."

"Well, I see no objection. Lord Lovelace marries the girl to-night."

"What do I hear?"

"Facts. I have seen the arrangements, I have bribed the servants, and I can even name the priest who is to officiate."

"Good Heaven!"

"Well you may be astonished; so was I, for,

after all, I never thought that the boy Pipey would be fool enough to sanction such a proceeding."

"He is in the secret, then?"

"I should think so. It is all his planning, and if something is not done, and done at once, the wedding will take place. Lovelace will demand explanations and restitution, and such things will be revealed as will set the town talking for the next six months. Pleasant, isn't it?"

"Oh, horror—horror! But something must be done."

"So I think."

"Will you undertake the task?"

"What task?"

"That of staying this wedding; of snatching away the girl, and of effectually disposing of her. What other task do you suppose there is to do?"

"Is that all?"

"Do not mock me. Will you undertake this?"

"And the consideration?"

"Your own price. I care not as long as you effect the work.'

"That's business-like, but there is much to do, nd a deep one in Pipey to fight against.'

"True.'

"But there is a chance of doing him yet, if I can but get the assistance of Maydock, though he's but little to be trusted."

"Do you rely upon him?"

"No, but he's the best hand on such a job; and, although I owe him one for attempting my life at Blackfriars, I would smother ill-will for a time, and engage his services."

"But you remember that he carried off the girl, professed some passion for her, and would have married her had he had the chance."

"Yes, but that was three years ago, and out of that he has been in prison fully two years. It should have been hanging with him had I had my way, but there was a flaw in the evidence, and for a matter that, in nine cases out ten, would have been a gallows' job, he got off with two years' imprisonment. But all that must be forgotten, and he must be held."

"As you will; but act with care."

"Trust me."

"I will do so. Would to heaven I could trust you a step further!"

"What do you mean?"

"Dare I speak?"

"I am to be trusted."

"Well, then, I will speak. I am guilty of that which would perhaps transport me, and cover me and mine with eternal shame. Ask me not what, for I cannot speak. My secret is in the hands of this fellow whom you call Pipey, and he threatens to betray it."

"Well?"

"Do you not understand what I would have?"

"No."

"To be plain, then, I want his life."

"Pipey's life? And you want me to take it?"

"No; I want you to put one on the scent who will do my turn; that is all."

"That is all! And you would ask me to become an accomplice in taking the life of my old friend and pal—my own boy, Pipey! Dear me—dear me!"

"No matter; I can do without you. Do not think of the matter."

"Oh, I didn't say I couldn't do it."

"You hesitated."

"Yes; but consider my feelings. He was like my own boy, he was."

"Psha! But no matter. I say again, I can do without you."

"Stay—stay. Not so hastily. I might be tempted, you know; but really it's very sad."

"No more than you do every day. Will you assist—in a word, yes or no?"

"But the reward?"

"Oh, if it is only money you require you shall have that in plenty, so do not hesitate."

"Well, I'll throw on one side my feelings to oblige you, and I'll put your people on the track; and after all there's no such harm in it, for Pipey has turned his back upon me ever since he has grown honest, and a great man. Ha! that was a good man spoiled, that was."

"Would to Heaven I had died ere I so befriended him! This is my reward. He holds the sword over me, and I know not when it will fall."

"It won't fall if you get away from under it quickly; and to that end I'll assist you all in my power."

"And you will be silent?"

"Oh, yes, as silent as the grave—as the grave."

"Good! Now what are your plans?"

"They are too elaborate to detail now, for I must away. Time is precious, and there is much to be done before nightfall."

"True. When shall we meet again?"

"Can I come here to-night after the work is over?"

"No—no; tell me where I can meet you, for you must not be seen here again to-day."

"Very good. Here is an address: come there, and bring with you this person whom you would put on the boy. I will take him to his roost to-night, if we but secure the girl."

"If! There must be no if! It must and shall be done."

"Do not be over sanguine. I would not answer for success when Pipey is pitted against one."

"My ruin depends upon you; remember that.'

"I will; and I promise to do all that man can do; but there is a point at which human ingenuity fails and we are thrown upon chance. That may be our fate to-night.'

"Heaven forbid it!"

"Oh, Duchess; it is bad when we are reduced to such straits as to have to appeal to Heaven in cases like this!"

————

CHAPTER XXXVIII.

GREEK MEETS GREEK.

EVEN while Grimer was yet holding his secret interview with the Duchess an emissary of Pipey's was at the side of that worthy, explaining to him the aim and mission of the lawyer.

"Indeed," said Pipey, as he listened to the relation of the plots and schemes of the old lawyer, "if he means business we must be on the look-out for storms, for, to give Grimer his due, he is no mean enemy."

"He is not; and, if I am not deceived, he will use every means to be conceived in order to frustrate this marriage and carry off the girl."

"He will have a tough task."

"He may; but when determined he is not the man to be baulked. Who, think you, will be in the affair with him?"

"I have no idea: it is so long since I had dealings with him that I am now entirely unacquainted with his set of tools."

"There's an old acquaintance of yours on the scent."

"Of mine?"

"Yes, of your's; a very old friend."

"Not the Black Captain?"

"No."

"Hammer, perhaps."

"No."

"Then I can think of no other."

"What do you say to the Yellow Boy?"

"Maydock?"

"The same."

"A gross absurdity."

"Is it?"

"Yes; worse than absurd."

"Bah! wise as you are, you don't know what men will do when they are reduced to want."

"It strikes me, friend Palmer, that no amount of want and privation would ever induce Maydock to work with Grimer."

"We shall see. I am inclined to think otherwise."

"You would think as I think had you seen them struggling together on Blackfriars Bridge the night of the Marlborough House ball."

"No matter. Our people have been on the watch, and they find that Grimer has already made some slight advances to the burglar, which have been favourably received. This job is a paying one, and the Yellow one will jump at it, as sure as we are here, living men."

"Well, to be fore-warned is to be fore-armed, and so I will not slight your words, although they bear absurdity on the face of them. Now, have you any insight into the plans of the enemy?"

"No."

"What?"

"They have baffled me."

"Pshaw! You jest."

"I never was more in earnest."

"Why, Palmer, you surely cannot be at fault?"

"I am, most thoroughly."

"Then you know —"

"About nothing. At least very little more than I have told you, and that, in a rough calculation, amounts to be about an entire blank."

"But you know of Grimer's scenting out the return of Lovelace. You know that the old fox has been on the watch and discovered our roost. You have traced him to the house of the Duchess, and you guess his errand; and moreover, you know the men with whom he will work, and yet have no clue to the manner he intends commencing his operations?"

"Just so."

"Then, for once you're beaten."

"I don't say that."

"No, and I will not say it. If you have failed, I will not. I must away myself, and worm out these hidden secrets."

"You will do no such thing."

"Indeed, but I will."

"I say you will not—nor shall you."

"And why?"

"Because danger threatens you at every turn. You know not who dogs your footsteps; death lurks behind every post, ready to pounce upon you; your enemies are all unseen—most of them unknown; and, therefore, I say you shall not go."

"But you have failed, and therefore something must be done."

"Something shall be done."

"But what?"

"We must play on the same tack as themselves; and although we do not know the movements proposed, we can yet checkmate them."

"We must; my heart is set on this marriage, and it shall be solemnised. My honour is also concerned in it; for if anything should happen now they would impute the failure to motives which I could not bear to have assigned to me. Now, what is to be done?"

"I have had but little time to think. Where is the girl?"

"Safe in the upper rooms."

"Are you sure?"

"Yes."

"Then keep her there."

"I mean to do so."

"Is the house secure?"

"Perfectly so."

"Can you trust that old woman of yours?"

"Yes, with my life."

"Good; you know the motive I have for asking."

"Perfectly well."

"Have you given her instructions to admit no one to the house?"

"Yes."

"And she will have sense enough to obey you?"

"To the letter."

"Then so far so well. Too many precautions cannot be taken. I tell you this: if the house be not already surrounded by those in the pay of the lawyer, it soon will be; so keep a smart look out."

"I suppose we shall have to meet an open attack?"

"Doubtless; for if scheming fails they will resort to violence. You can trust no one in this matter. The very man you have engaged to convey the girl to St. James's-street may be tampered with, and prove in the service of the lawyer."

"By Jove! A glorious idea!"

"What is it?"

"I've not yet engaged a carriage."

"Well, that's not a very glorious idea. What are you driving at?"

"Ha! ha! Splendid!"

"You're as mad as a March hare."

"Am I? You will see."

"Now, if you have any idea, just give expression to it without all that laughing. Clever as you are, there are times when your abominable hilarity gets the better of you and reduces you to idiocy."

"Oh, hang it, Palmer, that's not complimentary"

"I didn't intend it to be. I'm not complimentary—never was; always had a preference for strict truth and bluntness; so don't expect anything else from me. And now, what about the idea—for I see by the twinkle of your eye that something is running in your head?"

"Yes; and this is it: You say you believe the house to be surrounded?"

"Yes; I should say that every house in the street contains one or more of old Grimer's agents."

"Well, that's a blessing."

"Is it? I fail to see it."

"Yes; but you will open your eyes in a few moments."

"Go on, for heaven's sake."

"Well; we must send at once and order a carriage."

"What, in the face of being watched?"

"Just so."

"Why, we should be followed."

" Just so."

" And ten minutes after we leave the job-master he will be bought over by the opposite party."

" Precisely my opinion."

" Then what the —"

" Now don't excite yourself, but listen. We will suppose just what you say. In a few moments you will go and order the carriage. You will be followed, and after you have selected your conveyance and given your orders, the coach proprietor will be tampered with, and the vehicle made unsafe for the conveyance of the lady. Well, at the given time the coach comes here, and we place a lady and gentleman in it, and they are driven off."

" Yes, into the net spread for them by Grimer."

" Yes, *a* lady and gentleman, but not *the* lady and gentleman."

" Hey ? By Jove, I begin to understand you."

" I should think it was time."

" You would place substitutes in the carriage, and while the whole troop of vagabonds rush away with their supposed prey —"

" The real parties, well disguised, will step quietly out of the house, and walk off to St. James's-street."

" Hurra ! It must be a clever man to beat the bold Captain de Pipes, after all."

CHAPTER XXXIX.

"ROGUES ALL, MY LORD."

THE afternnon was far advanced when two men of anything but prepossessing appearance wended their way towards the office of Grimer, the Old Bailey lawyer.

They were both past the meridian of life, and both bore, distinctly marked upon their brows, the stamp of crime and the deep marks of dissipation.

Advanced as they were in years, they still looked older in villany, and the veriest stranger to the ways of the world would at a glance have pronounced them both criminals of the deepest dye.

It was Maydock and Roger Allerton.

The former the reader knows. The latter was a half burglar, half pirate and smuggler—a man of bold actions and bad repute.

He chiefly preyed upon seafaring men when on shore, and when on the high seas it was usually with the black flag flapping over his head.

He had recently had some peculiar dealings with the old lawyer, Grimer, and being a fellow of extreme penetration, and one capable of thinking as well as of acting, he had been entrusted by the old lawyer with many delicate missions—not the least of which was the providing of a gang of desperadoes for the carrying off of Fair Liz.

Roger Allerton had just been in the Minories to seek out Maydock, and induce him to act in concert with the old lawyer once more.

He had, after a long and tedious search, found the burglar, who, as usual, was out of the way, and not best pleased at being inquired after, in consequence of pressing engagements to appear before those entrusted with the commission of the peace.

Mr. Maydock was much wanted by the authorities. He was well aware that his next appearance at Newgate would, in all probability, lead to a life job, and so he was careful to be found absent when inquired after.

But Roger Allerton was not the man to give up such a case in despair, and so after a while he lighted upon his man.

He had a hard task before him, for Maydock could not forgive the lawyer the many tricks he had played him ; and it required a great deal of coaxing, and a great number of threats, to induce the fellow to even listen to the proposals made.

When he heard the plans revealed he at first absolutely and positively declined to take part in their execution.

" No," he said ; " go back and tell the old hound that I'd rot before he should, through me, get possession of the girl."

But Allerton did not choose to do anything of the kind, and after a great deal of talking, swearing, and brandy drinking, the agent of Grimer triumphed, and walked off his man to the presence of his employer.

The meeting between the old enemies was anything but a display of mutual forgiveness and amity.

" Well," said Grimer, " you are come, are you ? I thought you would."

" Did you, then ? I thought I wouldn't, and your friend here will tell you that I didn't much relish the job."

" I suppose not, but necessity forced you."

" Ah ! necessity. You can put the hounds off the scent when it suits you, and it's pleasant to be able to smell the fresh air without the feeling that there's some one at your heels ready to pounce down upon you, and carry you back to a loathsome dungeon. It was that, and that only, that tempted me to come."

" Well, since you are here, I suppose you mean business ?"

" It all depends."

" You know the nature of the job ?"

" Yes ; I've been told."

" And you agree to take part in the affair ?"

" I can't say, for I can't forget a certain night, when you and I had an awful struggle on a bridge over this very girl. I can't forget that you afterwards, by the aid of your cursed boy, tore her from me when she was in my power ; and, above all, I can't forget that you did your best to hang me, and that it was only owing to a flaw in your evidence that I escaped, and got imprisoned. All these things rankle in the heart, and make one feel that he would rather injure than serve the man who caused them."

" Psha ! We, who live by preying on one another, should have no such feelings," said the lawyer.

" So I say," said Allerton ; " never mind who you take by the hand now-a-days ; your enemy yesterday is your friend to-day, and so on the *per contra*. Money is everything. Smother all personal feelings when cash is floating about, and you see a chance of grabbing it ; even though the hand that holds it out to you be the same that held a pistol to your head the moment before."

"Good," said the lawyer, "that's prime advice. I like your style of doing things, Allerton; you'll go through the world the right way I see."

Mr. Grimer had peculiar notions of going through the world the right way.

His "right way" meant *hunting down* the weaker enemy and fawning on the stronger.

His right way meant any mode of making money without coming in contact with the hangman.

"Well," said Maydock, after a pause, "time has deadened the feelings I had towards the girl, and I'm no longer able to fight for her on my own account; so, for the nonce, I will give up the lead and play second fiddle, provided the money's forthcoming."

"Fear nothing; there's lots in this job."

"Then we understand each other. I'm with you."

"I thought you would be. Now to business."

There was a long discussion of plots and plans. There was talk of abduction, and even murder. All the chances and dangers of the case were reviewed, and at length a distinct mode of action was settled upon.

It was bold and intricate enough, but as it was fated that it was never to stand the test of development, we will not trouble the reader with it.

Suffice it to say that, just as the three plotters had matured their designs, a messenger rushed into the office, and delivered himself of information which entirely changed their course of action.

"Now, then," said Grimer, "where are you from?"

"Soho."

"And what has brought you away? Has anything happened?"

"Yes."

"They have left the house?"

"No, no."

"Then what has been done?"

"Simply this: one of those fellows in the pay of that Captain de Pipes, or whatever his cursed name is, has been to engage a carriage."

"Well?"

"Roberts and I followed him, traced him to Millhurst's yard, and found out that he had engaged a close travelling carriage and pair to be at the house of the Captain in Soho at nine o'clock to-night, for the purpose of conveying a lady and gentleman to St. James's-street, and thence to Kew."

Maydock uttered a long and piercing whistle.

"Hillo," he said, "this is simplifying affairs with a vengeance. Why, the job is as easy as turning your hand now."

"So it is," said Grimer. "Millhurst will oblige me in any way, and once let me get my pair of beauties into one of his carriages, and there shall be no private wedding in St. James's-street to-night."

"Ha, ha," roared Maydock; "to think they should have gone to the very man Grimer can buy up at his own price! Ho! I thought Pipey had more sense."

"The cleverest sometimes outwit themselves. You ought to know that, Maydock."

The burglar made no reply. He did not relish any of the old lawyer's personal pleasantries.

"Well," said Allerton, "everything is clear enough now. Instead of St. James's-street you must treat the young couple to a ride below London Bridge, where we'll dispose of the swain and take the girl for a trip on board the Laura.

"My eye!—won't that be an astonishment to her!"

"No doubt," said Grimer, "but be careful."

"Yes," said Maydock, now thoroughly entering into the spirit of the affair; "be careful, for though they've played into our hands, so nicely, they may yet shuffle through our fingers, if there's any mistakes made."

"Let your party be strong enough, and use all precaution to avoid alarm, and all will go well. I must see Millhurst. He, he! I'll take care that he supplies a carriage like a vault. No screams, no struggles will do in the one I select. Moreover, it shall be quite big enough to hold two fine fellows under the seats, who will take care to be so very attentive, and keep the young pair so fully occupied, that they won't attempt to open their mouths and engage the attention of those passers-by whom they may meet in their journey due east. He, he, he! This is luck. It's beautiful—beautiful!"

So thought the others; for they all laughed, and seemed to enjoy the affair immensely.

The bait had taken, and there was every chance that Pipey would successfully prosecute his scheme.

CHAPTER XL.

THE TRIAL OF THE PLOT AND THE ISSUE.

AT nightfall three persons entered the house of Captain de Pipes.

One of them was Lord Lovelace; the other two were apparently domestics—a man and a woman, dressed in the ordinary costume of the class to which it seemed they belonged.

Their advent was hailed with delight by the watchers in Grimer's interest, and preparations were instantly made for a movement and immediate action.

"So," said Pipey, as from his window he looked down upon some dark forms flitting about the streets, "all is well; they have taken our bait, and will be guided where we will. The hook is in their jaws, and we can drag them where we please."

"Are you sure you have baffled them?" inquired Lovelace. "Are you certain that your plan will succeed?"

"Yes, yes; trust to me. An hour after my man had left the stables of Millhurst old Grimer was there, and doubtless bought him over. You have only to follow my instructions, and all will be well."

"I trust so."

"I am assured of it. Now assume your disguise; there is but a short time to spare, and there must be no waiting, or suspicions may be aroused."

" Where is Liz ?"

" With my people, assuming her disguise."

" 'Tis well. I will soon follow her example."

Lovelace entered Pipey's dressing-room, and in a few minutes reappeared in the costume of the man who had entered the house with the female before alluded to.

His own clothes he handed to Pipey, and that worthy started off with them to the lower regions sacred to the Boodles' interest.

In a few moments Liz entered the room in the costume of a serving-girl.

Pipey and Mrs. Boodles followed her.

" This is a strange style of costume for such an occasion, dearest," said Lovelace, " but our friend knows what is best for us, and we have only to obey his orders."

" He will prove right," said Liz.

The lovers seated themselves at a table, and commenced a conversation, while Pipey and Mrs. Boodles withdrew and contemplated—the former with a cloud on his brow, for he could not see them together without becoming wretched, strongly as he battled against the feeling.

Mrs. Boodles was all astonishment.

" Which," she said, " I never dreamt of seeing so sweet a young lady put on the 'umble raiments of my niece Selina—which it's a honour to her, and well they fits her, and pretty they looks upon her handsome figer ; and it's only the great as looks well in rags, good clothes been lost on them ; and true nobility, though clothed in gold and velvets, will show up in spite of their 'umble dress been cast side."

Finding that she had not *quite* conveyed her meaning in this strange speech, the old lady continued :—

" Which it's a mistake I made, meaning all the while to say that good birth will show itself, although dressed in sackcloth and ashes—which a a plainer dressing angel that was Lady Gotawny-boy's eldest never was seen ; and pity for her it was that she should have come to so bad a fate—which small-pox it was, as I'm a livin' woman. But it do strike me as strange to see a lady as is going to be married all dressed up like a dairy-maid, whilst the dairymaid and the footman are a putting on the beautiful clothes of the gentlefolk."

" Ah, never mind, Mrs. Boodles ; there are more things in heaven and earth than you ever dreamt of in *your* philosophy."

" Which I was always good at," said Mrs. Boodles, jumping off on a new tack, " as my poor man, Joseph Boodles, used to say to me : ' Ah, my dear,' said he, ' they may talk of ferlosophers, if they like,' said he, ' and of their House of Parliament men, as talk for hours,' said he ; but they should hear *you* talk, and *you'd* astonish some of 'em '—which, if it is'nt saying too much, I *would*, sir ; for I can see as far as most people—which nobody can see through stone walls or deal boards, save ghosts and goblins, from which heaven preserve us ! But, as I was a sayin' of the sweet young lady ; to see her dress in that 'umble costume do puzzle me, and make me stare—for I can't tell why she should wear it, although people now-a-days do some peculiar things, and I suppose the fashion changes—which it's all owing to furringers, and I'd have 'em all hung, if I had my

way—which is saying a good deal, but I assure you I mean it."

What foreigners could have to do with the change in the style of costume adopted by Liz and Lord Lovelace did not appear quite apparent to the listeners to Mrs. Boodles, and that lady, for a short time, indulged in her own reflections, but without coming to any satisfactory solution of the mystery which presented itself to her gaze.

In a few minutes the two domestics entered the room, attired in costume befitting those whose characters they were assuming.

" That will do," said Pipey, shaking off his gloomy feeling ; " that will do ; a thick veil and a slouched hat, and you would pass muster before more critical judges than those who will be likely to see you, Fear nothing," he continued, " you will be followed by those who will protect you, and rescue you from the danger which may threaten you."

" I fear nothing," said the man.

" Above all," continued Pipey, " do not, by word or motion, betray your secret until you get to the end of your journey. We must have them entirely off our scent at all risks."

" I understand you."

" It is well ; there are no other arrangements that I know of, and now we have only to await the arrival of the carriage."

Punctual to the very moment a vehicle drove up to the door, and without delay the masquerading parties descended the stairs, and entered it.

The door was closed on them with a crash, and the horses were started at a great pace.

" Well, I never did see sich hurry," said Mrs. Boodles, who had lighted the parties to the door ; " poor dears ! the've carried 'em off as if they was mail-bags, instead of good Christians."

Pipey, from behind some curtains, saw the haste with which the vehicle was despatched, and smiled with satisfaction at the result of his ingenuity.

" In two minutes we shall be clear of the whole party ; but should any remain, your costumes will deceive them this dark night ; so all will be well."

He then turned to Mrs. Boodles, and ordered her to hurry on her things for the purpose of accompanying Lovelace and Liz.

" It will give more reality to the assumption of the parts you are to enact," he said to his lordship and intended bride.

Whilst Mrs. Boodles was adjusting her walking gear, Pipey carefully loaded and handed to Lovelace a pair of pistols.

" Take these," he said ; " I do not anticipate an attack, but it is well to be prepared for the worst."

" I know how to use them," said Lovelace, placing the weapons in his pocket.

In a short time Mrs. Boodles was ready for her walk, and Lovelace and Liz left the house with her.

It was well that all the precautions taken for success were so well observed, for the trio had not walked far when Grimer encountered them.

He peered at them anxiously, but failing to recognise them, turned away abruptly, and with a grunt.

It was not, however, Liz and Lovelace that he

had anticipated meeting, but Pipey; for turning to a doorway, he addressed himself to Liney Gosmont, who was concealed under the shadow of the portal.

"Servants, I suppose," he said to the idiot; "not your man yet. But he will be out; keep your eyes open."

"Liney knows," murmured the fool, "Liney knows."

"Yes," thought Grimer, "and a nice know it will be for some parties. The idea of setting such a softy to do such a task! I foresee ruin to both the instigator and the tool."

It was some time before Pipey could nerve himself to going forth on that night.

Not that he had any fears for himself—not he; it was the ordeal he had to go through that he dreaded.

"To see her married," he said to himself; "to see her tied to another; to behold their joy!—it's that which unmans me. But the task must be done. I have promised them I will come, and I must keep my word, though my heart breaks."

Time slipped away until he found he could wait no longer, and with an effort he threw his cloak over his shoulders, covering the military uniform he wore, and strode away into the street.

"Hillo!" said the lawyer to the fool; "hillo! I say—keep your eyes open. This is your man. I should know his walk though he marched in the centre of an army."

Another moment and Pipey passed the spot where the lawyer and Liney were concealed.

Well sheltered though they were, and dark though the night was, Pipey caught sight of their forms. Placing his hand on the pistols he wore beneath his cloak, he held himself prepared for any movement on the part of the enemy, but he had nothing to dread. They were in ambush merely for the purpose of watching, and not for action.

Pipey passed on without the slightest show of having noticed the watchers, and it was not until he was some distance away that the lawyer ventured to move or speak

At length he turned to the serving-man, and asked,

"Did you see him?"

"Yes."

"Distinctly?"

"Yes."

"But his face. Should you know him again?"

"Yes. But I will not lose sight of him; I am on the track now."

"Very well. Then my business is over. I must now back to the office and await the coming of Maydock and the others."

The lawyer took one road, and the idiot followed Pipey.

Alive though our hero was to the importance of being wary, and though he continually turned to see if he was followed, the serving-man managed to escape his notice, and kept at his heels unobserved.

*   *   *   *   *

When Pipey arrived at the house of Lord Lovelace he found Liz, her destined husband, and Mrs. Boodles, together with the clergyman who was to officiate, awaiting him in a magnificent drawing-room.

The poor fellow felt sick and faint, but he struggled against the sensations that overpowered him, and advanced to the little group anxiously awaiting him.

Liz saw at a glance all that was passing in the breast of her humble admirer, and a pang of deep agony shot through her heart.

At that moment, perhaps, for the first time, a doubt as to the strength of her love for Lovelace crossed her mind.

It was then she asked herself if the feelings she possessed towards the nobleman were not those of gratitude and admiration rather than those of deep and unchanging love, and it was also then that she questioned herself as to the real nature of her love for the poor fellow who for years had devoted himself to her interests.

But it was too late now to think: it was too late to draw back.

She closed her eyes, as if to shut out thought, and feeling some one grasp her hand she moved mechanically towards the gorgeous but temporary altar erected for the occasion.

It was Pipey who had grasped her. Seeing that some *contretemps* would inevitably ensue if something were not immediately done, he motioned to the clergyman to take his position and commence the ceremony. It was like a dream to the poor girl.

It may be doubted whether she had a distinct idea of the part she was playing in that scene.

The words of the clergyman rang in her ears, but they were indistinct, and sounded like the murmuring of voices heard between sleeping and waking, or like the murmuring of the sea, or dull wail of the wind at night. At length came the fatal words:

"Wilt thou take this man to be thy wedded husband? To love and to cherish," &c. &c.

And there was a pause.

No answer!

A touch on the arm, and a wild stare, and the answer:

"Yes!"

All was over.

The poor, nameless girl was now Lady Lovelace, and clasped in the arms of her husband.

"God bless you!" said Pipey, as he stalked away with his old housekeeper, back to the now desolate roof. "God bless you. Your mother's blessings be upon you."

The door closed upon him, and he hurried out.

No pace could be too quick for his wild thoughts.

On, on.

Still on. Still unconscious of the poor old woman who strove in vain to keep by his side.

Back to the lone chamber; back to the cheerless hearth.

Back to desolation and despair.

*   *   *   *   *

Let us change the scene.

The hour is the same, and Grimer sat in his cold, damp office, listening to the clocks chiming the quarters, and anxiously awaiting the return of his emissaries.

Would they never come?

It appeared so to the lone and anxious watcher as he paced the limits of his den, and waited with increasing impatience.

At length there was a sound of hurried footsteps.

The outer door opened, and some one staggered through the passage. A hand was on the lock of his door, and he sprang forward to open it.

Next moment Maydock, smeared in blood, which flowed from a gash in his head, fell across the floor of the room.

For a long time he remained entirely unconscious of what was passing. He was dead to the voice of his employer, and to the rough efforts used to bring back consciousness. At length he opened his eyes and gazed about him. Before him he saw the pale and distorted face of the old lawyer.

"What has happened?" cried Grimer. "What is the meaning of this?"

"Sold," cried the burglar; "sold—they have beaten us."

"You lie," screamed the old man. "You lie. It is not so. It could not be so. It is a mistake. It cannot be so."

"It is so," said Maydock, wiping the blood from his brow, and showing it to his employer; "look at that and convince yourself."

"But what has occurred? How have they escaped? Did I not see them in the carriage? Did I not see all prepared, and the vehicle move away?"

"No."

"You lie. I saw—I saw all this, and there is some vile plot to defraud me."

"I say you did not see *them* into the carriage, for they never got in. We were tricked—beaten with our own weapons. A pair of servants were substituted for the real parties, and thus we were all driven off the scent, and they, doubtless, escaped by some device about as clever as that paid off on us."

"Fooled! fooled! Beaten by a mere boy! Oh, it is too much to bear!"

"Ah, but you don't know all. The carriage was followed by some of the clever thief-takers, and the pair of dummies rescued from us before we knew where we were."

"It is maddening."

"So you would say had you been beaten as we have been. I have got off the lightest of the gang; the others were frightfully punished, and I have left two of them for dead."

"Oh, but I'll have revenge for this."

"And so will I—I swear it; such a revenge as will shock the whole world by its terrible character."

"'Tis well; such words soothe me—soothe me. Revenge! It is the only thing left for us now, for all is lost."

"Yes, all is lost."

CHAPTER XLI.

BY THE WATER SIDE—LOW LIFE—THE PRINCE AMONG THE BEGGARS—ARRANGEMENTS FOR QUITTING ENGLAND.

DOWN by the river, below London Bridge, stood an old house well known as the resort of the most notorious beggars of the metropolis.

The house was called "The Blind Fiddler," and was one of the worst dens to be found in England.

The orgies practised there were notorious throughout London, and the dandies of the day, disguised to suit the company of the tavern, often rushed there to ensure that excitement which the west end of the town could not furnish.

The notoriety of this house at length reached the ears of the Prince of Wales, and that worthy at once determined to fathom its mysteries. He was now married, after the rites of the Roman Catholic church, to the unhappy Mrs. Fitz-Herbert, of whom he was already heartily tired— not finding, after the first burst of passion had exhausted itself, the kind of woman he had anticipated, and moreover, not being capable of experiencing a love genuine enough to last after his sensual promptings were gratified.

Leaving her to her own resources, the Prince wandered forth as usual in quest of fresh excitement; and getting too well known in the neighbourhood of Westminster, he determined to try his fortunes in the east. "The Blind Fiddler" held out to him unlimited attraction, promising new excitement and fresh sensation; so calling into play the services of Laurence and Portman, the men with whom we first met him at Westminster, he one evening determined to set forth on his new venture.

It was a dark and murky night when the three adventurers entered the portal of "The Blind Fiddler."

They were but indifferently well received, as strangers were always looked upon with suspicion.

"Now," cried the landlord, as the three strangers entered the principal drinking room, or "kitchen," as it was called, "now, the footing."

"Right, my friend," said Laurence, who knew the ways of his new acquaintances; "say what."

"A gallon of beer each," said the landlord.

"And moderate enough too," observed Portman; "and as we have had a tolerable good haul lately we'll come down handsome: make it a half-guinea, Tom."

"Hurrah!" shouted the motley crew of beggars, on hearing this liberality.

"What line?" asked the landlord, alluding to the style of business practised by the new comers.

"Oh, sometimes skittles, sometimes cards," said Laurence; "we're not particular."

"Sharpers," said the landlord. "Well, when you west-end blades come east, we like to bleed you. Now what do you say to a guinea?"

"Oh, with all my heart," said Portman; "I'm not at all particular."

This further liberality elicited more cheering.

"A rum lot," said the landlord, who had taken a great fancy to his new guests, finding that they were not without money.

"Yes," said the Prince; "as peculiar a set as ever I cast eyes upon."

"You don't know any of 'em, I suppose?"

"Not one."

"Then I'll point out a few to you. That little fellow in the go-cart is the king of the beggars—one of the most drunken little scamps in all London. He is only two feet eight inches in height, thirty-one inches round the body, twenty-two inches round the head, and fourteen inches from the crown to the chin. He is double-jointed, and is possessed of terrific strength, particularly in the hand. He always sleeps on the floor, and has done so ever since he was eight years old."

"A peculiar character," said the Prince.

"Yes; and there's another," pointing to a cripple in a tub. "That's Phil-in-the-tub, a fellow who attends weddings, and has been made notorious by Hogarth, who has sketched him in his picture of the 'Industrious Apprentice.'"

"I recognise him now," said Laurence.

"Yes," continued the landlord, "and there's another I should say you had seen in the west."

"What, the woman dancing?"

"Yes; she's known as the *Barker*, and gets her living by pretending to be in fits, and barking like a dog. She's well known about Holborn. When she's tired of the fit trade, she regularly goes about London early in the morning to strike out the teeth of dead dogs that have been stolen and killed for the sake of the skins. These teeth she sells to bookbinders, carvers, and gilders, as burnishing tools. At times she frequents Thames-street, and the adjoining lanes, inhabited by orange merchants, and picks up from the kennels the refuse of lemons and rotten oranges. These she sells to the Jew distillers, who use them in making acid and lemon drops for the poor confectioners."

"Pleasant eating," observed the Prince.

"Oh, bless you, sir," continued the landlord, "you don't know one half the dodges they're down to. Well, the Barker likewise begs vials, pretending to have an order for medicines at the dispensary, for her dear husband, or poor sick child, but cannot get the physic without a bottle; and when she can she begs some white linen rags to dress the wounds with. These she turns into money at the old iron shops. Her pal is that fellow near her. He is scarcely out of prison three months in the year. He scratches his legs about the ankles to make them bleed, and he never goes out with shoes to his feet. He generally does the naked dodge, and thus gets the soft ones to give him clothes. That man at the back part of the room has been in the medical line; he's an Irishman. He writes well, and get's a living by drawing out petitions and begging letters, for which they stump up a shilling or more, according to their length."

The host had now to move away and his three strange guests were thrown on their own resources for amusement.

As yet they had not been long enough in their company to enter into the spirit of the fun, and so contented themselves with observing their singular companions, until at last the chairman of the meeting rose, and, pointing to the Prince, said,

"I call upon that 'ere gentleman with a shirt for a song."*

The Prince was quite confounded; he had not anticipated such a movement, and stammered out the best apology he could.

"Indeed," he said, "singing isn't in my line."

"Vell," said the chairman, "that's as may be, but it's either sing or find a substitute."

"All right," said Laurence, coming to the rescue, "I'll sing for my friend. I'm used to get up a squall on an emergency, so here goes."

"Now for it," cried the chairman, endeavouring to obtain order; "listen to the swell's ditty."

Knowing his company, Laurence, without further preface, sang the following ballad, called

THE BEGGAR'S WEDDING.

"Then Tom of Bedlam winds his horn at best;
Their trumpet was to bring away their feast;
Pick'd many bones they had found in the street,
Carrots kicked out of kennels with their feet;
Crusts gathered up for bisket, twice so dried,
Alms—tubs, and *olla podidas* beside;
Many such dishes more, but I would cumber
Any to name them, more than I could number.
Then comes the banquet, which must never fail,
That the town gave, of Whitbread and strong ale.
All was so tipsy that they could not go,
And yet would dance and cry for music hoe.
With tongues and gridirons they were played unto,
And blind men such as they are used to do.
Some whistled, and some hollow sticks did sound,
And so melodiously they play around.
Lame men, lame women, manfully cry advance,
And so all limping jovially did dance."

This wretched doggrel, manufactured for the occasion, seemed to give immense satisfaction to the beggars, who applauded it to the echo.

After the song more drink was called for, and paid for by the three strangers, and then the landlord returned and entertained his guests with a few more descriptions of those by whom he was surrounded. One of these characters was a notorious fresh-water sailor, who never saw a ship but from London Bridge, but who, nevertheless, imposed on vast numbers of people by representing the poor distressed sea-faring man.

"His name is Jack Stuart," said the landlord, "and he travels about London led by his dog 'Tippoo.' This dog will lead him to any part of the town, and is one of the most extraordinary instances of docility and sagacity I ever met with; and I assure you I've seen some clever specimens of the canine race. His business is to make a response to his master's 'Pray pity the blind,' by an impressive whine, accompanied by uplifted eyes and an importunate turn of the head; and when his eyes have not caught those of the passers by he has been seen to rub the tin box against their knees, to enforce their attention. When money is thrown into the box he'll put it down, take out the contents with his mouth, and carry it to his master."

"You've quite a collection of characters," said Laurence.

"Yes," replied the landlord, "quite; and there are many whose stories you'd like to hear, but I've no time to tell them now, for there's a rough lot of customers come into the bar, and I must look after them."

With this he stalked away once more.

---

* A well known fact.

"There's a fine wench," said the Prince to Laurence; "ragged and dirty though she is I shouldn't mind a kiss from her."

"Shall I call her?"

"Ah, do.   She's deuced pretty."

Laurence attracted the attention of the girl to whom the Prince pointed, and she immediately approached him.

"Here, my love," said Laurence.   "Here's a gentleman in the respectable line who's taken quite a fancy for you.   Sit down here and talk to him."

The girl immediately complied with this request, and seated herself close to the Prince.

"What's your name?" asked that worthy.

"Lola," replied the girl, in sweet Italian accents.

"Lola's a sweet name.   Where are you from?"

"Venice."

"Have you been long in England?"

"A few months."

"You speak the language very well."

"I lived with an English lady for three years at Venice."

"But what made you take to this peculiar mode of livelihood.   One so pretty and well-behaved might do better."

"Perhaps so."

"Ah," said Laurence, "you don't know how well these foreign gipsies do.   Are you a ballad-singer?"

"Yes."

"I thought so.   In her line they make heaps of money; that's the motive she has for keeping this society."

"There may be other motives."

"I can't see them."

"But I can."

"Well, then, name them."

"I could name a score, but that of prosecuting a *revenge* will suffice."

"Ah," said the Prince, "you Italians think of nothing else. Hang the dreadful word. I can't bear it."

"Have you, then, felt the vengeance of an Italian woman?"

"Well, no; but I was once threatened with it, and in spite of lapse of time, and many changes, I can't forget it, although the poor little threatener may have done so."

"And she may not."

"As you say—and she may not, but I trust she has, for the memory of that voice and those terrible eyes still trouble me, and were it not that I persuade myself of her death or forgetfulness I should be miserable, for I believe my little tormentor was, in her fury, quite capable of perpetrating any mischief."

"If she was a true Italian, and you awake her vengeance, be assured it will follow you until you or she drop into the grave."

"Oh, nonsense," said the Prince, who, however felt far from feeling that it *was* nonsense; "such stuff is only fit for children to speak of; let us dismiss the subject."

"With all my heart," said the dark-eyed Lola.

"And now will you take some wine with me?" asked the Prince, becoming more and more enamoured of the Italian beggar as he gazed into the depths of her dark liquid eyes.

"Yes," said the Italian, "bright sparkling wine is more to my taste than the heavy and stupifying ales of England. Let me have wine."

The Prince immediately ordered some for his new flame.

"Don't show your money," whisperer Laurence, "you know not what you do."

The Prince, who was pulling out a handful of coins, replaced them and produced two or three shillings, which he placed on the table in payment of the newly-furnished stoop of wine.

"Your friend is more cautious than yourself," said the Italian, who had observed the movement and advice of Laurence, "this is no place for the display of gold."

"You are quick to observe," said the Prince.

"Yes; or else *I should not be fit to fulfil my mission.*"

"What mission?"

"No matter."

"What a singular girl," thought the Prince.

At this moment the door of the room was thrown open, and several seafaring men entered and took their places at an occupied table.

They were a rough set of fellows, and their appearance did not seem to give any satisfaction to t he majority of those assembled, for their mirth and jollity suddenly ceased, and they applied themselves to talking in whispers, dividing themselves into little groups, and eyeing the intruders with extreme uneasiness.

"Our new friends do not appear very welcome," said the Prince.

"No," said one of the beggars, who overhead him; "we are not so strong and hard as they,

and in their cups they beat and ill-use us badly All mirth is over for this night."

He was right.

One by one the beggars took themselves off, and after a while the seamen, one or two women, and the Prince and his friend were the only ones left.

"I don't like the look of those fellows," said Laurence; "we had better go."

"Wherefore?"

"I don't know, but they are not the sort of men I desire to be in company with. We had much better begone."

"Oh, nonsense," said the Prince, "they are rough, hearty fellows enough, and I don't care about leaving our little friend here."

"Perhaps she will come west with us."

"I will if you will wait another half hour. I cannot leave just now."

"Do not wait," whispered Lawrence, "she may be in league with some of these fellows, and danger may lurk in this place. It is a sad neighbourhood after nightfall."

"Psha," cried the Prince, "what nonsense you talk. I shall wait."

"Your friends suspect without occasion," said the pretty Italian, divining by a single glance the purport of Lawrence's whispered words. "I know no one here, and am by all unknown. But I expect to find one here presently of whose whereabouts and plans for the future I must possess myself to-night. Remain or go, as you think proper. I do not wish to detain you."

"I choose to remain," said the Prince. "Such pretty lips were never formed for the utterance of falsehood, and I will be their owner, even with my life."

Had the Prince noticed the expression of the woman's mouth and the glance of her eye as he uttered these words, he would have recalled them instantly, and entertained very different opinions, but he was now under the influence of drink and a new passion, and consequently could see nothing which interfered with the gratification of his pleasure.

Seeing that remonstrances were in vain, the two companions of the Prince seated themselves by his side and awaited any further movements that might come.

A half hour elapsed; at the expiration of which two men, closely enveloped in long travelling cloaks, entered the room and joined the party of sailors.

At first their appearance attracted the attention of the Prince and his friends, but their notice was of but short duration. The cups had more attractions for them than watching strange personages.

Not so the Italian girl, Lota.

She fixed her eyes upon the new comers the moment they entered the room, and never took them off until they quitted it.

The new comers avoided turning their faces towards the Prince and his party, and conversed with the men at the table in low tones.

"Well, my lord," said one of the seamen to one of the new comers, "you want us to take you off as soon as possible."

"Yes," said Lord Lovelace, for it was he, "as soon as possible."

"It can be done to-morrow, if you will post down to Deal."

"I will do so."

"And the terms?"

"You have not named them."

"Well, let me. Will five hundred be too much?"

"No. That is reasonable."

"Very, well, then. The lugger shall be entirely at your service for the trip."

"I will be at Deal to-morrow. Here is an earnest of a hundred pounds for you."

"Thanks. Conceal your face as you pass the table at the other end of the room. Do you note who sits there?"

"No."

"It is the Prince."

"Indeed."

"Yes; and there is a peculiar looking girl eyeing you very attentively; so, look out. Who's your friend?"

"He is no friend. He is my servant, an Italian, and a trustworthy fellow."

"I hope so."

"I am assured of it. And now, good night. Come, Pedro."

Lovelace rose, and, muffling his face, hurried from the room, followed by his servant.

They had no sooner gone than the girl sprang to her feet, and, assuring the Prince that she would return in a few moments, ran from the room.

As the landlord closed the door on the two late visitors, the servant Pedro contrived to catch his cloak in the door, which was slammed home, and thus held him fast.

"Open the door," shouted Pedro.

"What is the matter?" asked his master.

"See, I have caught my cloak."

"Ugh!" ejaculated Lovelace, walking on; "be quick, and follow close."

It took several moments to open the door again, and, by the time this was effected, Lord Lovelace had got many yards from the house. As the door opened, the Italian girl came forth.

"Well," she asked of the servant, "what news?"

"He goes to-morrow."

"Whither?"

"To Naples."

"And hence?"

"To Venice."

"Good. Farewell."

"Farewell. Who are your companions?"

"The Prince of Wales, and two court gallants."

"Keep with them."

"I will take care to do so."

"And now I must fly to rejoin the Lord Lovelace."

CHAPTER XLII.

A LETTER FROM CARLOTTA TO MARIE, AND WHAT FOLLOWED ITS RECEIPT.

"MARIE MIA,—He is here! He had not been in England twelve hours before I knew of his presence, and was dogging his footsteps. Night and day I have followed him as his shadow, and there has been no act of his that has escaped me.

"Will you be enabled to bear the shock of the news I have to relate?

"Are you sure you have ceased to love him?

"Ask yourself this question when you have read thus far, and if you find a vestige of the old flame yet lingering in your bosom, thrust this letter into the fire, or it will make your poor heart bleed anew.

"Lovelace had not been in England long enough for his most intimate friends to know of his return, when he met a fellow who is known here under a variety of *aliases*, but who in reality is a Government spy and thieftaker.

"This fellow has for years been the guardian angel of your rival; and only the night previous to his meeting Lovelace had rescued her once more from the Prince, into whose clutches the Duchess of Grasmount had thrown her.

"This fellow—whom I will call De Pipes, that being the most popular of his *aliases*—revealed to Lovelace the position of the girl, and procured an interview for him with her.

"What passed at that interview may easily be divined, when I tell you that instant preparations were made for a marriage.

"The Duchess of Grasmount, for reasons only known to herself and those in her confidence, thought proper to make an attempt at thwarting the union; but it signally failed, mainly through the exertions of this De Pipes—who is a fiend incarnate.

"They are married, Marie. That is all I can now tell you. They are married, and will, by to-morrow have sailed for the Continent.

"All that could be done has been done; but they have escaped us here.

"You must now play out the drama yourself, for your enemies will soon be near you.

"Beware of what you write home concerning the Brethren. We are suspected—perhaps betrayed. There has been no meeting for many nights, and I fear there will not be one for many more.

"All your English admirers appear to be marrying. The rumour of the town now is, that the Prince has married a Mrs. Fitz-Herbert—a woman who passionately loves him, and who long sighed for his favour in vain.

"What think you of that?

"I am but a poor letter-writer, Marie, and have thus soon expended all my topics.

"Let me hear from you soon, and believe me ever "Your affectionate,

"CARLOTTA."

Marie was seated one evening in her chamber, gazing out at the clear bright star-lit heavens, when the above letter reached her.

She had grown paler, and was more woe-begone than we have previously seen her. Her husband all but conquered her terrible temper, and she was humbled in his presence—for he was a man of dark and terrible passion, and one capable of exercising unlimited power over woman.

He was, as Marie described him, a tall, ungainly man, with a slight stoop. His face was dull and sallow, and to it was appended a long and ragged black beard, which only made him ten times more repulsive.

He was habited in very old and ill-fitting garments, and was always dirty.

His talents as a physician were, however, enormous, and the demand for his services was greater than he could attend to.

All Venice spoke of him as a man of vast talents : some of his cures having been sufficiently miraculous to gain for him—among the superstitious and easily excited people in whose midst he lived—the reputation of a wizard.

Such was the man to whom the once-beautiful mistress of the Prince had bound herself.

Marie hated and feared him, but dared not show it. A glance of his wild, dark eye was sufficient to crush out the rebellious spirit which rose within her. Bartolo had gone to Venice to attend a case of some importance, and Marie was alone.

Her thoughts were running on the absent Bartolo.

"Would to Heaven," she said within herself; "would to Heaven that I could rid myself of him, for I grow more weary of this life every day. I sicken and pine, and shall one day kill myself if I am not relieved of this awful monotony, and the terrors inspired by his presence. Then, there is my poor child ! He hates it bitterly, and would murder it did I not keep watch over it day and night. Oh, I must do something; but what, I know not. I would poison him, but that his great skill would detect the presence of a drug if I administered one. What else I can do I know not."

A servant entered the room.

"A letter, signora."

"Place it on the table, and go."

The servant did as he was desired.

Marie did not look towards the letter for some moments.

"A note from Bartolo," she said to herself, "telling me not to await his coming. As if I cared for *his* coming !"

At length her eye fell upon the epistle, and discovering her error she sprang from her seat, and snatching the letter, tore it open, and anxiously devoured its contents.

"Married !" she cried, as her eye ran over the words ; "Married, and happy, and I—oh ! my God ! And I—"

She buried her face in her hands and wept.

"The is no peace for me," she cried : "there is no rest for me on earth. Would that I could die."

She read the letter over and over, and then again spoke aloud,

"They are married, and I am tied to this fiendish man. A despised and crushed mistress ! But I will not endure it. Something shall be done. They coming here," she continued, fixing her eyes again on the paper ; "they are coming to Italy, and I shall have no power to reach them whilst Bartolo keeps me thus secluded and powerless. They are coming, and I shall miss my opportunity. But, no ! That cannot—must not—be. I will kill him."

She bent her head on her bosom and fell into a deep and uninterrupted reverie.

She remained thus for several minutes, and then gazed out of the window once more. She started back with a shriek.

Before her was the old Zingari woman, her grandmother.

"Unhappy," cried the old woman ; "still unhappy. Ah ! yes, and thus it must be until the grave receives you."

"You say truly. Until the grave receives me I shall know no peace."

"What new trouble is it now ?"

"Come in, and I will tell you."

The window was only a foot from the ground, and the old crone stepped into the apartment.

"Now, if I am to be made your confidant, speak."

"I will read you a letter I have just received from England."

Marie drew Carlotta's letter from her bosom, and read it to the old woman.

"Well," said the crone, as the last words fell from the lips of Marie, "what of it ?"

"What of it ? Is it not enough to madden me ?"

"I do not see it thus ! What have the marriages of the Prince and the Lord Lovelace to do with you now ?"

"True ! but still I have some feeling left within me, and I cannot submit to the torture with resignation and silence."

"Indeed !"

"Oh, indeed. Do you think I can look upon my babe and calmly think that its father is the husband of her who has again and again crossed my path, and reduced me to despair ? I tell you it has driven me mad, and I must and will be avenged."

"*You shall.* I am at work for you now. In time ample vengeance shall be yours."

"In time ! You speak of an indefinite period ; I must have a speedy revenge. They are coming, and I must be free to battle with, and crush them. Their happiness must be nipped in the bud, and I must triumph over them speedily. The first joys of their wedded life over the blow will lose half its force."

"True."

"Yes ; I will act, but I must act with freedom. I am fettered now, Will you break the chain ?"

"What do you mean ?"

"I mean that there must be one out of the way before I can proceed with my vengeance."

"I understand. You mean your child ?"

"Yes."

"That is easily done. I will kill it."

"No, no. If it is to die, it shall be killed by no other hand than mine."

"Well, then, you shall kill it."

"The means ?"

"I have it with me."

The old crone felt in a pouch she wore at her side, and drew forth a small sealed packet.

"That contains a potent poison," she said ; "it cannot be traced, and its effect is slow, but certain death. Ten drops given to an infant will suffice."

"I understand you."

"And you will do the deed ?"

"I will do *that which I have determined to do.*"

"Good. I am glad of this resolve, for I detest the sight of your brat. It is an eye-sore, and best out of the world."

"Yes."

"I am glad you at length think so, and now adieu! Be assured that I shall be on the path of this Lovelace. I have something to avenge, and I think I have a surer hand than yours. Now I go."

The old woman stepped out at the window, and walked away.

"She thinks I would kill my child," said Marie, "but that shall never be!"

"It is for him!—it is for him!"

* * * * *

At the time Marie and her grandmother held the interview just given, another scene was being enacted in another part of the house.

Estelle, the nurse of Marie's child, had crept stealthily to the door of the room in which Marie sat.

She listened.

Voices fell upon her ear, and she knew that there was no fear of interruption.

"Now," cried the girl, "now to execute the task of my master!"

She stole back to the chamber in which she had left the child sleeping, and hurriedly snatching it up, enveloped it in her mantilla, and ran with it from the room.

Watching her opportunity she stole from the house, and rushed away in the direction of Venice.

She sped along the road at a great pace, and at length reached that city.

She had not proceeded far before she was joined by a man.

It was Dr. Bartolo.

"Well," he said, "have you seized the brat?"

"Yes. I have it here."

"It is well. You know what you have to do?"

"You have told me."

"And you will do it?"

"I dare not refuse to do that which you tell me must be done."

"'Tis well. I have ordered that the child should be thrown into the canal, and you agree to do it."

"You say you love me?"

"Yes."

"And that in order to ensure a continuance of your love I am to drown the babe?"

"Yes."

"Then I will do it."

"You are a brave girl."

"I am a fiend, but I would do aught in the world for you, because I love you. I know not why, for you are not one calculated by appearance and manner to attract the love of a young and untutored girl as I am, but you have thrown a spell over me, and I madly worship you. I am your slave, and you have only to hint at a work in order to have it obeyed."

"It is well. I see I can trust you, therefore I will now leave you, for we must not be seen together. Remember, to secure my love the child must perish!"

"I am not likely to forget."

"Adieu, then. Meet me on this spot in an hour."

"In an hour I will be here."

The girl left her master and rushed madly along the streets in the direction of the Grand Canal.

After a while she reached it, and selecting a spot she deemed favourable, unmindful in her wild excitement that she was watched, she took the infant from under her mantilla, and holding it aloft for a moment, dashed it into the canal.

She turned and fled.

* * * * *

After sitting an hour at the open window through which the old crone had disappeared, Marie rose with the intention of seeking her chamber.

"I will go to my child," she said; and taking up the lamp she went towards her chamber.

"Estelle," she called, as she opened the door; "Estelle, I am about to retire."

No answer.

"Estelle, are you asleep?"

Still no answer.

"Estelle, I say—where are you?"

Not a sound—not a movement.

"She has left the child," thought Marie, "and gone to the servants' room for something. She will return."

The child's cot was before her, and Marie gazed upon it from the chair in which she had seated herself.

"Poor innocent!" she said; "they all thirst for your blood, although you have wronged none of them. They would have you dead and in your grave; but I love you, and will shield you from them all."

She rose, and went to the cot.

Uttering a cry of terror she started back.

The child was gone!

Staggering to the wall, Marie seized the bell-rope, and pulled it violently.

In a few moments the chamber was filled with the servants.

"What ails the signora?" asked the foremost of them.

Marie was speechless, but she pointed to the empty cot.

"The child is gone," said the servant.

"Where is Estelle?" demanded the half-frenzied mother; "where is the nurse?"

Estelle had not been seen for some hours. The servants all thought she was watching the child, as was her custom during the hours it slept, before its mother retired to rest.

"She has stolen my child," cried Marie; "she has stolen my babe, and killed it!"

"It is impossible."

"It is true. They have tempted her, and she has fallen a victim to their wiles."

The servants answered not. It was palpable that the child was gone, and all were dumbfounded.

"Leave me," said Marie; "leave me—I would be alone."

The servants were about to withdraw, when one of them turned, and asked if Marie would order a search to be made.

"It is useless," said the mother; "it is useless. The precautions have been too well taken—all is over with my poor innocent babe!"

The servants now retired, with traces of deep sorrow depicted in their faces.

On being left alone the poor distracted mother burst into a flood of tears, and wept for full an hour as though her heart were breaking.

At length the storm was calmed, and she strove to shake off the traces of her emotion.

"They have stolen my treasure," she cried, "and I have to punish them for their work. They have stolen my child, and I must avenge the act. Let me be calm. Let me meet him as I should do. Him! Yes, it was to him I owe this last and greatest blow. It is to him I have to look for the vengeance that is my due."

It was morning now.

Bright, serene morning, and Marie stripped off her robes, and substituted for them a loose wrapper.

She used cold water freely over her face and head, and at length divested herself of all traces of her grief and excitement.

She appeared as if she had just arisen, and, saving that she was pale, no one would have suspected the storm of grief that had so recently agitated her. But she was an excellent actress, and knew how to govern her facial expression.

Descending the stairs, she ordered the servants to prepare breakfast, for she expected the immediate return of the doctor, who would, doubtless, require some refreshment after his night's labour.

She went forth into the garden, ordering the servants to call her as soon as the morning meal was prepared.

In an hour she was summoned into the house.

Everything was prepared for the meal. Chocolate and coffee steamed in the urns, and the light viands of an Italian breakfast were arranged around.

"You may go," she said to the servants, "and when the doctor comes tell him this meal is awaiting him here."

As soon as they were gone, Marie made a cup of chocolate for herself and drank it.

She then soiled one or two plates with the food on the table, and carefully prepared all the signs of having made a meal.

She then drew forth the phial, entrusted to her by her grandmother, and poured its contents over every article of food, and into the coffee and chocolate.

"He can't escape," she said, "it has no smell, and is quite tasteless. He must die."

Almost immediately after this the doctor entered the room.

His surprise at seeing the calm demeanour of his mistress was indeed great.

"He cannot conceal his secret," said Marie, "he will assuredly betray himself. It is well, he shall have plenty of chances."

"You are up early, Marie."

"Yes. I rose refreshed, and was not so much of a dullard as to lay abed after having had sufficient sleep. You see, I know how to follow your advice."

"She cannot yet have missed the child," thought the doctor. "And you have already breakfasted," he said, aloud.

"Yes," she replied, "I was hungry."

"She *cannot* have missed her infant," the doctor said to himself once more.

"Did you have a very bad case last night?"

"Yes, a very bad case."

"And how is your patient?"

"Very patient. Is no more."

"You do not say so! Did your skill, then, fail to save him?"

"I never exerted myself."

He sat himself down to the breakfast table, and prepared to eat his meal. Marie could scarce conceal her emotion; but she knew what depended on her tact, and she battled over the storm, and sat passive and collected in her chair.

"By the way," she said, as if a sudden but trivial thought had just struck her, "there has been a mystery here to-night."

"A mystery, in what way?"

"Estelle has disappeared, and with her the child."

"You do not mean it?"

"Indeed, I do."

"Estelle disappeared—and with her your child? Oh! it is absurd."

"It is a fact."

"You can't mean it—because you are calm and passionless. Had you lost your child, you would have been full of grief, for you loved it."

"I did."

"Well, then, why attempt to deceive me?"

"There is no deception."

"Then, you assert that you have lost your child?"

"Yes."

"And that you do not grieve for it?"

"You behold me! Judge for yourself."

"You are calmness itself."

"Then I do not grieve."

"It would appear so."

"It is so. I am no fool to weep my eyes because my servant should think proper to adopt and run away with my nameless, fatherless brat."

"That is well. I love to hear you say that. Now you are, indeed, my own bravest Marie."

Considerably relieved in mind Doctor Bartolo applied himself vigorously to his breakfast, and swallowed his chocolate with much gusto.

Marie watched him narrowly, and rejoiced to see that he ate and drank unsuspectingly.

After a few moments of silence the doctor broke out into a loud laugh.

"Why do you laugh?" demanded Marie.

"Because I am so pleased about the disappearance of your child."

"Indeed."

"Yes, Marie, indeed; and to think that you should take it so calmly. Why I anticipated a storm."

"You *anticipated* a storm?"

"Yes."

"Then *you knew of the disappearance of the maid and the child?*"

"Hey? No! That is—Psha! Why should I conceal the affair now that I find you thus? Yes, Marie, I did know of the stealing of the child, for it was I who directed it."

"Suspected as much."

"You did?"

"Yes. My heart told me you were at the bottom of it."

"Well, I was. The fact is, I was miserably jealous of the brat, as who would not be in my position, and so I determined to destroy it."

"It is dead then?"

"I hope so."

"Dead?"

"Yes; but you do not care?"

"No, no. I am indifferent to its fate."

"Of course you are. But, would to Heaven that I had known that before; it would have saved me a world of trouble."

"Would it?"

"Yes, Marie, it would; why I had to make violent love to your maid in order to win her over into my service. Weeks and weeks I have been tempting her, and it was only yesterday morn that she fell into my way of thinking, and consented to execute my commands."

"Indeed!"

"Yes, Marie; you have no idea of the world of trouble I had with her, and, even after I had her word pledged, I dared not trust her, and had to manufacture an important case at Venice, in order to account for my absence last night—"

"That you might assist in the murder?"

"Just so. But there was no occasion. The girl was true as steel, and met me with the child in her arms, quite prepared to execute her task. She left me, and in an hour returned without the child."

"She had destroyed it?"

"Yes; she threw it into the canal."

"It is well."

"I thought you would say so; you have no longer a care, and are as free as ever."

"Perfectly free."

"Ah! you are a perfect heroine. Would that all women resembled you!"

"You flatter me. But Estelle! what has become of her?"

"She is buried in an obscure house near the church of St. Andrew, fearful lest she should be detected, and anxiously awaiting my return for the purpose of shipping her off to England."

"Poor girl!"

"Yes, poor girl! The Signora Lafonté will have a sad time of it with her if she continues moaning and groaning as she did while I remained with her."

"She is, then, in the house of the Signora Lafonté?"

"Yes."

"And this house is near the church of St. Andrew?"

"Yes."

"Good. I will go to her."

"Go to her? Wherefore?"

"To dispel her fears, and provide her with the means of quitting this place."

"You will not, then, permit her to return?"

"She loves you!"

"Ah! I forgot. It would not do for her to come here. No, no; give her the means of flight, and let her go. The further away the better."

"Oh, never fear. She shall go far enough."

"That is right; and now I will retire to rest, for I feel unaccountably moody to-day."

"Are you unwell?"

"Within the last few minutes I have felt uneasy. I have a pain as if something were gnawing away my heart."

"Indeed!" cried Marie; "then I am not deceived. My vengeance will be complete!"

"What do you say?" cried the Doctor, in terror.

"I say that you are poisoned! Aye, poisoned by so potent a drug that even your skill cannot counteract its effects. Now, Bartolo, I am even with you. A life for a life!"

"Fiend! Oh, that I should have fallen into such a damnable trap!"

"You are defeated at last, and now I can tell you of all the bitter hatred I have long borne towards you. Now I may speak of the abhorrence and detestation I have ever felt for you, and of the loathing I have experienced at the very sight of your ungainly form. You are dying, and I can speak fearlessly—you are helpless, and must hear me. The spell is broken, and I am free. Your eye has now no terrors for me; your voice can arouse no fears within me, and I will speak. Yes, Bartolo, from the hour you first dared to speak to me of love I have hated you. What sympathy could I have for such a being as you? What was there in common between us? Nothing, nothing. I despised you, but I am wayward and strange, and do singular acts. One of them was binding myself down to thee. But if I hated you before, that hatred grew into something more terrible when I marked that you had set your heart on destroying my child. I kept watch over its couch, and I engaged the girl of all others I thought I could trust the most, and I left her unsuspectingly in charge of my child for a few short hours, but you had tampered with her. It was you that had made her false to me, and she stole my child. I missed it but a few short hours ago! What did I do then? I raged, as all women would do in my position. I wept and wept, and my heart broke; but in the midst of my grief I remembered you. Your image crossed my mind like a thing of fire, scorching up my grief, and rendering me callous. It was then I determined to trick you, and learn the fate of my child. It was then I dressed myself thus, and prepared the trap into which you have fallen, and it now remains to me to take ample vengeance on the murderess. You have furnished me with the place where I shall find her, and I will go there and kill her. Now, Bartolo. what think you of your mistress?"

"Oh, horrible, horrible, most horrible! Something eats out my vitals. I cannot speak."

"I rejoice in your anguish; I gloat over your pain. Ha, ha! It is a rare sight!—a rare sight!" and the frantic woman clapped her hands.

"The servants," cried Bartolo; "the servants!"

He staggered to the bell-rope, and, in his violence, tore it down.

In a moment the room was filled with domestics.

"Assist me, assist me, to my laboratory. It may not yet be too late."

"Stir not," cried Marie; "you are my servants, not his, and he shall have no assistance from me."

"I am poisoned," screamed the doctor; "for the love of the Virgin take me to my laboratory."

"Do not move. He has murdered my poor innocent babe. Is it not just that he should die?"

The men uttered a yell of rage, and stood glaring at the doctor without moving to assist him.

"Let him die alone, and in this place. Retire, and leave him to his fate."

Marie and the servants left the room, and the doctor was alone.

"Good God! I shall die, and no one will lend me any assistance. They lock the door, and I am a prisoner."

He staggered about the room, and at length approached the window. It looked into the garden.

"If I can struggle to the window of the laboratory I may yet be saved."

He staggered on, and was about to throw open the window, when the hag, Vendeta, appeared before him.

"What ails you?" she demanded.

"That you should best know. I am poisoned?"

"Poisoned? How, and by whom?"

"How, I know not, for I could neither smell nor taste the drug which I have swallowed. By whom you may readily guess. Oh! I am in an agony of pain."

"Marie, then, has done this?"

"Yes."

"And wherefore?"

"Do not ask me; and quit my sight, for you but mock me. The poison must have been given to her by you."

"It was."

"You, was it? And you have forgotten your oath?"

"No, no; I gave her the poison for her infant. She told me she wished to destroy it."

"Cunning devil. She blamed it on me."

"It may not be too late to save you, and I will do so if I can for my oath's sake, and that alone, because I hate you."

"Here," she said, drawing a dried herb from her pocket, "chew this."

The doctor did as he was desired, and in a few moments fell into a profound slumber.

CHAPTER XLIII.

THE DEED OF VENGEANCE IN THE OLD HOUSE NEAR THE CHURCH.

As soon as Marie quitted the presence of the doctor, she flew to her chamber, and hurried on her walking attire.

"Are you going out, signora?" demanded her servant.

"Yes," replied the mistress.

"Shall I order your horse?"

"No; I shall walk."

"Shall I order your servant to be in attendance?"

"No. I go alone."

"Can I assist the signora?"

"No. Begone! and let me not be disturbed."

"The signora shall be obeyed."

As soon as Marie was alone, she hastily opened all her drawers and cupboards, and, snatching therefrom every article of value that came in her way, she concealed them about her person, and then went to a small box at the further end of the room.

This she opened, and, after a long search, drew from among a heap of laces and other articles of female attire, a small and beautifully wrought dagger, mounted in gold and elaborately jewelled.

"This," she said, "must never leave me again until I am lowered into the grave."

She placed it in her bosom, and then fled down the private staircase of the house, out of the garden door, and was soon out of sight. She sped towards Venice.

*   *   *   *

In the top most room of a miserable old house, situated near the church of St. Andrew, was concealed the nurse-girl Estelle.

She sat in the room with the curtains drawn, as if she feared to allow even the light of Heaven to enter and fall upon herself. She was seated in a large chair, and kept rocking herself to-and-fro violently, accompanying the motion with hysterical sobbing.

"Oh! why did he tempt me to do it? why did I kill the babe? Why did I listen to him? Oh! holy Virgin, do not blast me. Let me get from this place and suffer alone and unknown for my crime. But let him I love come with me. Do not separate me from the man for whom I have sinned so deeply, or I shall die—I shall die."

The woman to whom the house belonged here tapped at the door.

Estelle rushed towards it, and admitted her.

"Come in," she said; "I wish you would never leave me, your presence is such a comfort to me."

"I am glad of that, for I am come to stay with you some time. Do you feel more calm now?"

"Yes, more calm, but do not feel less acutely. Heaven forbid that I should."

"Why, to hear you talk, my poor child, one would think you had been guilty of *murder*.

"Hush," cried the girl, turning ghastly pale —"not that word—not that word. I cannot bear to hear it."

"And why not?"

"Because it is a terrible one, and it disconcerts me."

"Oh, in your nervous state trifles do great things. Let us talk of pleasanter subjects. When did the fever leave you?"

"What fever?"

"The fever from which you have been suffering. The fever of which good Doctor Bartolo cured you. Ah! I forgot. People who have been deliverers have no recollection of their sufferings."

"Did the Doctor tell you he had cured me of a fever?"

"Yes, to be sure he did, and also that you had a sad time of it, and that you raved dreadfully, and was under the delusion that you had *killed a little child*."

"Did he tell you this?"

"Yes."

"*I understand him now.*"

"And he also told me that he was afraid that in your sleep, or in a slight relapse, you would again refer to the painful subject; and bade me beware what heed I paid to your talk."

"He was good to say that."

"Yes; it was thoughtful of him; but there was no occasion for his telling me. Oh, I tell you, I am well acquainted with the ideas people take into their heads when they suffer from fever, and so am prepared for anything."

"What else did the doctor tell you?"

"He told me that you were a poor orphan, and that your mistress behaved unkindly to you, and would have thrust you from the house while the fever was at its height, but for his interference. And he also told me that, having related your case to his good wife, she immediately ordered that you should be removed from the service of your cruel mistress, and kept here with me until you gained sufficient strength to enable you to undertake the charge of her infant."

"Yes; I see the doctor has told you all."

"He has; and one cannot but admire him for his goodness of heart."

"What a well-devised tale," thought the girl; but she only said, "His heart is a very kind and generous one."

They conversed in this strain for upwards of an hour, and then their conversation was interrupted by a loud knocking at the street door.

"That is the doctor," said the girl; "it is just the hour at which he promised to call."

"I will admit him."

The old lady left the room and descended the stairs for the purpose of admitting the person at the street door.

To her surprise, instead of finding the doctor she came face to face with a lady.

" What is your pleasure, signora ?" said the old woman, with a deep curtsey.

" You have a young girl here who was brought to you by Doctor Bartolo ?"

" Yes, signora, a poor young thing, who has suffered much from a fever, and who, by his kindness, was rescued from a cruel mistress. Is not that the one you inquire after ?"

" The one I seek is a servant, named Estelle."

" That is the same, signora."

" She was brought last night by the doctor."

" Yes, yes."

" And a very good, quiet, poor creature she is, signora."

" I have no doubt. Can I see her ?"

" Oh, yes, signora."

" You say she has been ill."

" Yes, signora, very—very ill."

" Did the doctor leave her any wine ?"

" No, signora."

" Then be good enough to step out and purchase a bottle."

" I will do so with pleasure ; but the wine-shop is some distance off, and I shall be gone some time. Will you excuse that ?"

" Yes."

" Then I will make all the haste I can."

" Do not hurry. I have much to say to this young girl, therefore I would rather be alone than otherwise. Is there any other person in the house ?"

" Not a soul, signora ; all my other lodgers are young men engaged in business, who seldom return home till night."

" It is well. There is money for you—get the wine."

" I will execute your commission, signora. May I presume to ask if the signora is the doctor's lady ?"

" The same."

" I thought so," said the old woman, " I thought so. Blessings on you for your kindness, and blessings on him for his."

" Thanks. Now hasten."

" I will fly. You will find poor Estelle in the top room. She is very, very wretched. The sight of you will cheer her."

The landlady turned and left the house.

As soon as she was gone, Marie—for, as may be supposed, it was Marie, locked and bolted the door after her.

" Now," she cried, " I am alone with her, and we can settle accounts in peace."

She turned back, and walked slowly up the stairs.

At the door of the top room she paused, and beating her bosom to keep down the palpitation of her heart, she prepared to enter.

The door was not closed, and she stepped within the chamber and stood face to face with the destroyer of her child.

Who can pourtray that terrible tableau?

There stood the mother, face to face with the murderer of her innocent child.

Estelle shrieked, and turning ghastly pale, fell on her knees before the woman she had so deeply injured.

Marie stood calm and immovable. There was a terrible fire in her eye, and her lips were compressed firmly together.

Beyond this there was no sign of the raging passion which consumed her.

" You know why I am here," she slowly uttered. Estelle spoke not.

" You know why I come ?"

A faint, almost inaudible, " Yes."

" I want from you my child."

" Oh, spare me—spare me !"

" The child you took from its cradle last night and bore away with you."

" Spare me ! For the love of Heaven spare me !"

" It was my first, my only infant, and I loved it deeply, fondly—and I cannot lose it. What have you done with my child ?"

" Oh, God of Heaven ! you know—you know !"

" I want the answer from your own lips. Where is my child ?"

" Destroyed—destroyed."

" By whom ?"

" By me."

" And wherefore ?"

" Because I was mad—because I listened to temptation, and knew not what I did. Do not stand there gazing on me like that, for your eyes scorch up my hair, and drive me mad !—mad !—mad ! Leave me, leave me ! or, if you will, hand me over to justice—but do not, do not, stand over me thus, like an accusing angel, demanding the list of my evil deeds. I cannot bear it—I cannot bear it !"

" You have destroyed my darling child."

" I have."

" You have taken from me every joy I had on earth."

" Yes—yes !"

" You have sinned against the laws of God and man."

" Yes—yes ! And I know the punishment."

" You do not."

" I do, signora, I do. I will not ask you to forgive me. I only beg of you to give me over to the officers of the Inquisition, and let me suffer. I can bear all their torture, but not yours—not yours !"

" I have said you do not know your punishment, and now I will prove it. You are to die."

" Yes—yes !"

" But not by the hand of the executioner."

" By whose ?"

" By mine ! I am the avenger of my child."

" Oh, say not so."

" I am. Prepare to die."

" Oh, give me time—give me a day, an hour. I am not fit to die."

" I will not give you a moment. You are mine, body and soul. By murdering my babe, you have become mine. The hand of man cannot rescue thee now. We are alone, and my vengeance cannot be interrupted."

The victim shrieked, but it was of no avail.

Marie caught her by the hair of her head, and swung her to the earth.

" Miserable wretch !" cried Marie, placing her hand in her bosom, and drawing forth the small dagger we have already described. She raised it above her head, and tightened her hold on the hair of the girl until she bent her neck across her knee, and left the white throat unprotected. "Miserable wretch, meet your fate!"

"Horror! horror!" shrieked the girl. "Oh! horror! God stay your hand, and save you from this crime. Let me—let me rise."

"No more. Say 'God receive my soul.'"

"I cannot."

"I give you a second."

"I cannot."

"Then go and stand before 'the seat of judgment side by side with my child!"

The eyes of the girl started from her head.

She held up her little white hands and attempted to stay the dagger, but it was a vain attempt.

The little weapon was torn by the frenzied mother from her feeble grasp, cutting her fingers to the very bone, and then it was raised once more.

It fell.

Who shall describe to the full the terrors that followed?

The weapon was buried to the hilt in the snowy neck.

A moment, and it was drawn out. There was a convulsive shudder of the body, and a loud shriek, which died away into a dull, gurgling moan. Then the body fell to the ground with a dull thud.

It lay there for a moment, and then a final effort was made by the dying wretch to rise once more to her feet.

She started up, and stared at the murderess, who stood with the bloody weapon in her hand regarding her fixedly.

She made one attempt to start forward and grapple with her assailant, but her eyes became glazed, her strength failed her, and she fell prostrate, deluged in her own blood.

Marie for some moments stood as one in a trance.

Her face blanched, and a sickness came over her heart.

She gazed at her red hand, and then with a shudder buried it in the fold of her dress.

She was a bold woman—a fiendess in human form; but it was the first time she had shed human blood, and the ordeal she went through almost proved more than her strength would admit of.

It was some minutes before she recovered herself, but at length she became conscious that there was a loud knocking at the street door.

Starting from her trance she hastily gathered up her dress, and rushed from the room.

Down the stairs she flew, and then went to the street door.

The old woman at once saw that the visitor was disconcerted.

"You are ill," she said; "let me assist you back to the house."

"No, no—I want air—air—fresh air! I am faint and sick."

"Let me beg of you not to go forth until you are better."

"Away!" said Marie; "let me pass, for I must fly."

"Indeed, signora —"

"Away!"

Marie unconsciously drew forth her bloodstained hand, and waved the old woman away from the door.

In a moment she saw the fatal error she had committed, and strove to remedy it by instant flight.

Dashing past the keeper of the house, she flew like mad down the street, and was in a moment out of sight.

The old woman clasped her brow, as if to recal some thought or fading vision; and then suddenly started forward, and sped with all the haste she could make up the stairs to the room where she had left her lodger.

She burst open the door, and a loud shriek told that she had discovered the deed which had been perpetrated in her absence.

CHAPTER XLIV.

ALARM OF THE POPULACE.—THE FLIGHT AND PURSUIT.—THE OFFICERS OF THE INQUISITION.—TRACKING THE MURDERESS.—WHERE MARIE FOUND A REFUGE.

THE old lodging-house keeper, as soon as she recovered from the first shock the tragedy upon which she gazed had occassioned, at once attempted to staunch the blood which oozed from the wound in the girl's throat.

She placed her hand over the heart; but it had ceased to beat.

The jaws fell, and the eyes were glazed and fixed in death.

"Poor thing," cried the keeper of the house; "poor thing! this is sad—very, very sad. Oh, Santa Maria, why was this terrible deed done? But the murderess—she is escaping while I stand here idly moaning. Let me fly into the street, and call in the aid of the Inquisition."

She rushed from the chamber of death, and hastened into the street.

Standing close by her own door, she cried aloud:

"Help! help! Murder! murder! A bloody deed has been done in my house! Arouse! Call up the officers of the Inquisition! Quick! track the murderess!"

These cries, again and again reiterated, soon attracted a large crowd of people to the door of the house.

"What is the matter?" asked a man of the frantic woman; "what has occurred?"

"Go in and see for yourselves; there has been murder done."

A large number of men crowded into the house, and hastened up the stairs.

Meanwhile the old woman never ceased screaming for the officers of the Inquisition, and lamenting the murder of her lodger.

"Sweet girl!" she cried; "it was a cruel, cruel deed! Oh, why was it done? Who could find the heart to kill one so young and beautiful?"

While she yet cried thus, the party that had entered the house returned, and added their cries to those of the woman, and in a few minutes the whole neighbourhood was in arms.

Bells tolled and cries rang through the streets; and in a short time a party of officers of the Inquisition came to the spot.

"What is the matter here?" demanded the officer in command.

"A deed of violence has been done in this woman's house."

"Indeed! Let us enter and see what has occurred. Come with us," he said, catching the lodging-house keeper by the shoulder, and thrusting her in.

"Close the door," he continued to his men, "and let none enter."

His order was obeyed.

In a few moments he stood beside the corpse.

"A young girl," he said, "and stabbed through the throat."

"Yes; is it not horrible?"

"What do you know of this?" said the officer, without heeding the woman's remark.

The woman briefly told the history of the girl, as it had been told her, and then added the episode of the visit of the lady, her return from purchasing the wine, and what then occurred.

"A strange story," said the officer; "were not your suspicions aroused in any way?"

"No; I thought the lady was the doctor's wife."

"Do you not know that the doctor has no wife?"

"I always understood that he was unmarried."

"What kind of woman was this?"

"She was dark, and had long raven tresses; she was rather under the ordinary stature, but so perfect was her form that this defect would pass unnoticed."

"Truly. I think I know to whom you allude; but until something more satisfactory is ascertained you must be made a prisoner. The case is a most suspicious one, and you must not be permitted to be at large until matters have been thoroughly investigated."

"I a prisoner?"

"Yes, you; painful as it is to us to serve you thus, we have no alternative; but you will doubtless be enabled to clear yourself easily. Your arrest is a matter of form."

"But I at once rushed into the street and gave the alarm; and see, here is the bottle of wine I fetched."

"My good signora, I have no doubt of your innocence, but for awhile I must leave you under the care of one of my men; and now we must proceed after this person. Which road did she take?"

"The right."

"Good; the city is alarmed, and if there be such a person as you have described flying from the consequences of her own rash act, she must soon be overtaken. Come men; to the right, and let us not waste a moment."

They left the room and the house, locking the door after them, and leaving the old woman in the charge of one of the officers.

Making hasty inquiries as they ran through the streets the officers, like blood-hounds on a scent, rushed madly after their prey.

"Which way?—which way?" they cried in answer to the inquiring shouts of—

"Whom seek ye?"

"To the right."

"To the left."

"Straight on."

"Cross the bridge, cross the bridge—on, on—she took the left road."

There was a perfect Babel of voices, amid which the officers ran on.

Through the streets, over the canal bridges—by the water-side—through the churches, down long and dark passages, and away—away into the depths of the city.

Onward they flew. Onward—still onward, but never obtaining a glimpse of her they sought, and still the people shouted as they passed,

"Whom seek ye?—whom seek ye?"

And still rang out the counter question, "Which way? which way?"

"To the right."

"To the left."

"Straight on."

*   *   *   *   *

Marie, with the speed of a startled fawn, rushed wildly through the streets, attracting universal attention as she passed.

People stood in the roads and looked after her; many sighting her red hand, and reading thereon the history of her deed of vengeance.

She flew onward until at length, by a strange coincidence, she came to the very spot where her victim had, a few hours before, launched her child into the canal.

The first thought which possessed her was to fling herself into the water, and end all cares and sorrows in death.

But thoughts of Liz, Lovelace, the Prince, and the Doctor, crossed her brain and she muttered,—

"No, no; the time is not yet come. But whither shall I fly? Where can I hide this terrible hand."

A figure darted forth from behind one of the pillars by which she stood, and, standing in her path, bade her stay.

"Who are you?"

"Do you not know me?"

"Phillipe!"

"Aye, Phillipe, the forsaken—the despised. Come with me. I know what occurred last night. I *guess* what has occurred to-day."

Marie uncovered her hand.

"Ah," said Phillipe, starting back, "I see my suspicions are confirmed. Come, quickly."

He caught her by the hand, and dragged her towards a house not far off. And as he hurried on the voices of the crowd of officers of the Inquisition and their followers fell upon their ears.

"Another moment," cried Phillipe, as he dashed open the door of the house, and sprang into the passage; "another moment, and all would have been over with you. The hounds are now off the scent; let them stand at bay."

He led her up the stairs of the house, and seated her in a strong but indifferently furnished chamber.

They now regarded each other fixedly. The same thought occurred to both simultaneously.

"How wonderfully changed!"

"Had not my love survived my memory," said Phillipe, "I should not have known you."

"And I should have passed you without recognition had you not spoken; but that voice, to which I have so often listened, recalled the features now so changed."

"It is right that you should forget," said Phillipe, "but it is strange that I should fail, for you have never quitted my thoughts since we parted, and when chance threw me in the way of the Zingari woman, who has joined me in an oath of vengeance on your betrayers. Oh! the memory of that terrible night when I saw you in the clutches of those English devils—when I was thrust from your presence with scoffs and gibes! It has dwelt with me till now, and I feel the torture as acutely as ever. It will never leave me until I have requited them. Scoff for scoff—gibe for gibe—honour for honour!"

"Oh, bring not back the memory of that dark past—I cannot bear to think of it. It is too terrible for contemplation, as has been my whole life since then. Oh! you know not how much I have suffered."

"I know all."

"Not all."

"Yes, everything. I have learnt every movement of your life since we parted, and could recite the tale as well as yourself."

"Aye, but the darkest scenes lay unrevealed to you. You do not know how the man with whom I have lived has thirsted for my babe's blood; how, last night, the poor innocent was stolen from me, and cruelly drowned; and—oh! how can I tell it?—the vengeance I have taken."

"I can imagine what has been done."

"This morning I poisoned the doctor, and an hour ago I spilled the blood of the murderess of my babe."

"That is the vengeance you should have taken on those dogs of Englishmen."

"No! For them is slower, more intense torture. They shall have their doom, but it shall not be the speedy one which has fallen to the lot of Bartolo and his concubine. Oh! my child, my child—shall I never see thee more?"

"Do you regret it."

"Regret it! Heaven and earth! do I not regret it! My darling!—my little innocent! Should I have done what I have done had I not proudly, madly loved it?"

"True. But now that it is dead do you wish it to be alive again? Remember what would be its fate; remember your own, and think what would befal it did it live. Nameless, dishonoured, spurned! Such a life is not that which it would thank you for."

"True. But my great love should have reconciled it to life. My devotion should have blunted the sting of the world's scorn, and have made it happy. Oh! my child, my child! I shall never see thee more!"

"Marie, listen to me. *You shall see your child again!*"

"What do you mean? Do you mock my anguish?"

"No! Heaven forbid it! But I say you shall see the babe once more."

"I do not understand you."

"Then learn that the babe did not die last night."

"Ah! ah! what do I hear? No, no, I could not have been deceived; I heard her declare that she killed my babe."

"She thought she did. Look out at that window, just below. As the girl came with the infant in her arms, I was abroad, and, judging by her air that some dark deed was to be done, and recognising her as your servant, I watched and saw her toss the baby into the canal. Without alarming her, I dropped into the water, and, ere a minute had elapsed, brought your child to the land. I knew it to be yours by the crest and initials on its clothing, and I determined to adopt it as my own."

"Oh, good, generous Phillipe, take me to my child—let me see it once more!"

"No, no; it was not for that purpose I saved it. The child is mine, and must be brought up in ignorance of you and yours. In the future you shall look upon its face again, as I have promised you, but now you shall not see it."

"Cruel! cruel!"

"Not so. By this act I am doing a kindness of which you cannot now dream, but which will one day become more palpable."

Their conversation was now interrupted by the angry shouting of the mob outside the house.

They had tracked the murderess to this spot, but here all trace of her ended. No one could give any further clue to her route, and all eyes were turned to the water.

"It must be so," said one of the officers; "she has evaded the Inquisition by taking her own life. Ah! to-morrow will reveal the mystery—a corpse floating on the canal will tell the tale of the woman's doom."

The excitement of the pursuit over, the officers took but little further heed of the affair.

Leisurely they turned their backs on the canal, and retraced their steps.

"We must have a prisoner," said the officer in command.

"Ah! well, how fortunate that we have secured the lodging-house keeper."

CHAPTER XLV.

THE PREPARATIONS CONCLUDED—LEAVE-TAKING—THE BILLET—SUSPICIONS AND FEARS—FAREWELL TO ENGLAND.

"At length, dearest," said Lovelace to Liz, the night after his visit to the inn by the water side, "at length preparations are concluded, and we may fly from the scenes that have grown so painful to you."

"I am so glad," said Lady Lovelace; "so glad; for every moment I have passed here of late has been one of anguish and misery. Until time has changed us and those who make our lives so unendurable, we will return here no more."

"You wish it, my love; I am the slave of your lightest thought." He kissed her affectionately, and, putting on his hat, left the house. He had no sooner gone than a servant entered the room, and announced Mrs. Boodles.

The affectionate old soul had come to take a farewell of the young girl who, during her stay with Pipey, treated her with so much kindness and consideration.

"Which you're a going to furrin parts," said Mrs. Boodles, rushing into the presence of Lady Lovelace. "Ah, my dear, it's an awful place; and if they *do* let you come back alive, it's just possible that it will be with one arm and one leg, and your precious face a tattooed all over like a savage of the wilderness."

"No fear of that," said Liz. "You forget I have been abroad before."

"Which you escaped by a miracle, my dear. It is'nt one in a thousand as ever comes back as they go, for them cannibals are such critters; there's no trusting 'em with a bit of flesh without they gobble it up—which it's no difference to 'em whether it's an old horse, a dromedary, or a soldier's leg! It all comes one to them."

Lady Lovelace laughed at the innocent old woman's exposition of foreign cannibalism, and assured her that she should not trust herself among those whose tastes led them to consume human flesh as a delicacy.

"But it's no odds," said Boodles, " it's no odds; you're a going away from us, and it's no matter where. Near or far, it's all one if you go. Ah! as long as the sea lays between you and those who love you the hearts left behind can only bleed for you—which hearts do bleed, and well I knows it."

"I shall leave no one in England to grieve so much after me."

"Oh, won't you! Ah, my dear! then you little knows the heart as beats in the bosom of the Captain—which it's all a bustin' with love for you, although you're a married woman, and it's so very wrong."

The lady blushed.

"Pray do not mention the subject," said Lady Lovelace; "I dare not listen to it."

"No, you're married, and a great lady now, and it isn't for a poor honest gentleman like my dear master to think of you or your likes, but this I'll say and stick to it if I die for it, there isn't a better man in the world, and not one which would have proved a better husband to you, had you looked kindly on him instead of the lord."

"True—true, every word; but we can't tutor the heart to love against its own inclinations."

"That's precisely what I've always said. 'The heart ain't to be taught,' says I, ' and it's no use a trying to make it,' which is well known and a fact, though I says it, as is only a poor widow, which I've not had much book learning in my time. But I musn't take up much of your precious time, my darling, which you'll excuse me calling you, only it's more natural than my lady. I know you must have plenty to do, and the dear Captain said he'd follow me here and take leave of you, which I don't want to be present, for, as I said before, you were meant for one another, and it's a mistake you didn't come together, which the parting would be more than my nerves could bear, and might bring on spasims, and I don't suppose you have any brandy at hand, which I answer for

it, fourteen drops on a piece of loaf sugar, is the only remedy."

The parting was an affecting one. The lady had grown to love the garrulous old soul, and she, in her turn, clung to the love of the lady as a thing but to be too dearly prized.

Tears were shed, and promises of mutual remembrance interchanged, and/then they separated.

Pipey came next.

Tears were in his eyes as he said farewell, and his heart was in his mouth.

He kissed the hand extended to him, and with but a few words, rushed from the house brokenhearted and desolate.

Long and bitterly did Liz sit and weep over this parting.

She could not at first realise that he was gone, and that she was to see him no more for years— perhaps never to see him again; but, as the bitter truth became more and more palpable, so her heart sank, and so she became more and more desolate.

But there was her husband.

Alas! thus early she began to doubt if he would prove the watchful, generous, self-sacrificing protector Pipey had been; and so his image did not bring to her any consolation when her old and tried friend had left her.

At length she mastered her grief, and walking to her chamber, began to busy herself in preparing for her voyage.

Under her direction her maid opened and repacked boxes and drawers without number.

Wardrobes were opened and dresses selected, folded, and packed.

Articles of the toilet were arranged, and at last Lady Lovelace had almost completed her task.

Going to an old and unused escretoire, she drew from it several bundles of papers, and carelessly examining them, threw them in again.

"Will you not take any of these papers?" asked her maid.

"No," said Lady Lovelace, " they appear to be old and useless papers belonging to his lordship. It is a pity they should encumber these drawers; I will examine and burn them."

"Can I render your ladyship any assistance?"

"No, I shall not want you until I ring. You may go."

Lady Lovelace was alone.

"Yes," she repeated to herself, " these papers should not lay about thus, they accumulate dust, and serve no purpose. But it is as well to examine them all before I destroy them, in case any may prove of service."

The lady seated herself at the escretoire, and commenced turning over the bundles of papers.

They all belonged to Lord Lovelace, and proved to be a batch of careless correspondence, which had been thrown on one side, and which had accumulated for years.

At length she came to a small note, written on foreign paper, and addressed in a peculiarly delicate hand to his lordship.

Lady Lovelace hesitated some time before she opened this letter.

An unaccountable dread came over her as she touched the paper, and something whispered her that she had best not read it.

Twice she threw it down among the heap she had perused, but she took it up again, and gazed upon it.

At length her curiosity got the mastery of her fears, and she unfolded the dreaded paper.

As one in a dream she read the following words:—

"Darling of my heart, you are lingering still, and more than a week has passed. Ha! the lake and your fishing has more charms for you than Marie; but I will not upbraid. You must want a change, and shall have it, although I wish you could only look at my child—our child: it grows so beautiful every day, and I think I can see your loved smile in its face—but that you will say is my stupid imagination. Come to me, my own Lovelace, I long to see you—oh! how much I cannot say, for our home—our sweet sunny home — appears desolate without you. There, I have finished, and not one mis-spelt word or Italian sentence! Am I not an apt pupil in the English tongue? But who could fail to learn with such a master.

"Thine, thine own,

"MARIE."

"Good God!" cried Lady Lovelace, as she perused these words, "what can this mean? Her own Lovelace! *his* child! My brain reels, and I do not know whether I dream or not! Oh, horror! what a fate is mine!"

She read and re-read the words until she could have repeated every line without perusing the paper.

She could not reflect on what she had read; her mind was too much unsettled for that. All she knew was that she had married one who had loved another.

"Oh, God!" she cried, "if he should be married to another!—some poor, confiding Italian girl, whom he has now deserted. But no, that is impossible; he would not be so vile. What shall I do? I must have all explained — he must answer all! I will produce this letter, and make him explain it."

She placed it in her bosom, and returned to the lower apartments.

It was almost the hour for dinner, and Lovelace was expected every moment.

At length he came.

He rushed into the room as buoyantly and full of spirits as ever, and approaching his wife, without noticing her gloomy looks, he cast himself at her feet and said—

"Well, darling, I've been absent some time. I hope our friends have not called yet, for I hope to be able to say farewell to them."

"They have been here."

"And have said 'adieu?'"

"Yes."

"Why, how ill you look. What has happened? Oh, I suppose you are grieved at parting with those who have been so good to you during so long a time. Ha! I do not wonder at it, girl; I, a comparative stranger, have grown very proud of them, particularly of that fine fellow De Pipes, whom I positively admire. But you are still depressed. I fear something more serious has happened."

"Something serious has happened, my lord."

"Indeed! you alarm me. Pray explain."

"That is what I shall ask you to do."

"Your words are very mysterious, and there is a coldness in your manner that chills me. What have I done to merit this?"

"I shall ask you that question, but first answer me another. Do you know any female of the name of Marie?"

Lovelace turned pale.

"Oh," said his wife, "your looks answer me. You do know some one of the name."

"It is not so uncommon a name."

"No."

"Then why ask me?"

"Because I believe you have been intimately —too intimately—acquainted with one of that name."

"Lady Lovelace," said his lordship, rising, and assuming the air of an injured man, "I am not answerable to you for any intimacy I may have formed before I knew you."

"True," said Lady Lovelace; "but if you wronged another by a marriage with me, or if I am wronged by your leading me to the altar having plighted vows of love to another, you are answerable to me, and therefore I demand that you will explain this."

Lady Lovelace drew forth the epistle of Marie, and placed it in the hand of her husband.

"You recognise it?" she said; "and now explain it."

"Oh! ask me not to do so," cried Lovelace, throwing himself at her feet, and clasping both her hands in his. "Pray ask me not to do so."

"I must know: without prevarication—without hesitation—or I quit this roof at once and for ever."

"Listen to me, and I will tell you all."

Lovelace, without rising from his knees, poured out the whole story of his amour with Marie Lavrouffe, from the moment of their meeting to the hour of their parting.

"Now," he said, "now that you know all, will you forgive me?"

There were many extenuating circumstances in the case, and Lady Lovelace could not but acknowledge them; yet in the parting of her husband and his former mistress she recognised a trait of character which she could not contemplate without disgust.

"Am I forgiven?" said Lovelace again, "do not keep me in an agony of suspense. Oh! say you will pardon me!"

"I do pardon you."

"Oh, thanks, thanks! And you will forget?"

"I will strive to do so. I regret that we ever met. It was an evil hour that brought us together, and, had I but dreamt of this amour, not all the love I had for you should have tempted me to accept your hand. But it is too late to talk thus; we are one, and I will keep the vow I have taken. I will try to forget, but ask me not to do so now, for it is a work of time."

No more was spoken.

The spell was broken, and the dream—the short feverish dream—was ended.

"Fool that I was to marry her," said Lovelace; "I might have known that it would come to this."

"I am punished," said Liz, "fearfully punished, for obstinately shutting my eyes to the merits of one who so dearly loved me."

A few hours of misery passed, and then the travelling chariot of Lord Lovelace drew up to the door of the house, and husband and wife were, a moment afterwards, speeding towards the ship that was to bear them from England.

CHAPTER XLVI.

LINEY TRACKS PIPEY. — THE DUKE'S VISIT.— PIPEY'S EXPLANATIONS.—FOREBODINGS.—THE FIGURE BEHIND THE CHAIR.—THE DEATH-DEALING BLOW.

MORN, noon, and night did Liney Gosmont keep upon the track of Pipey; and so cunningly, so stealthily was this performed, that Pipey was unconscious of being dogged.

Even the many agents he had in his employ, and who constantly kept near him, had no suspicion of the watchful presence of the idiot; and so the shadow of death constantly hovered near our hero, and threatened to fall on him at every turn.

Liney had continually attempted to effect an entrance into Pipey's home, but without avail; Mrs. Boodles was too well tutored in her master's business to admit strangers without his consent, and so Liney met with nothing but rebuffs from this quarter.

One night, however, Mrs. Boodles left the house, on an errand, and as she passed the spot where Liney lay watching the premises he so longed to enter, the housekeeper dropped the pass-key, and walked on, unconscious of her loss.

The quick ears of the idiot detected the sound of the falling key, and as soon as the woman was out of sight, he sprang into the road, and seized it.

His eyes glistened as he looked upon his prize, for in a moment he knew its value.

Awaiting his opportunity, he leaped across the road, and inserted the key in the lock, and Pipey's door was at length opened to him.

Stealing with cat-like steps through the passage, the idiot hid himself in a closet near the foot of the stairs.

Thus the first step was gained.

The house was open to him to roam about it until he came across his intended victim.

He had not been thus secreted many minutes when a loud knock was heard at the door, and Pipey ran down the stairs to see who summoned him.

Before opening the door he eyed his visitor from a small window in the fan-light, and then, finding that all was right, drew the bolt of the lock.

Before him stood the Duke of Grasmount.

"To what am I indebted for this visit?" said Pipey.

"I will tell you anon," said the duke; "but will you allow me to enter? It rains very fast, and I am now wet to the skin."

"Enter and welcome. This way."

Pipey led the duke up the stairs, and introduced him into his sitting-room.

"You are, indeed, very wet," said Pipey; "let me lend you a coat, and put your own before the fire."

He tendered a garment as he spoke, and the duke immediately accepted it, throwing off his own.

"You may think this visit strange," said Grasmount, "but I could not rest until I knew more of my child. I am more interested in her than you may give me credit for, and I should like to know what you have done with her?"

"Is it possible you have not heard?—and yet how should you!"

"Heard! What?"

"That your daughter is married."

"Married! To whom?"

"To one who loves her—Lord Lovelace."

"Indeed! You astound me."

"Doubtless; but in the excitement I forgot to make you acquainted with the fact. The duchess was, however, well acquainted with it."

"The duchess!"

"Yes, the duchess; and to do her every justice, she did her best to prevent the consummation of the union."

"I cannot understand her."

"I should say not, indeed. She can beat me, and I think I know more of the world than your grace."

"Of a sudden she appears to be changed into a perfect tigress."

"Not changed into one—she always was one, but it's only now that the act has come to light. Ah! if you but knew all! But no matter."

"No matter," said the duke; "you are right, her conduct does not trouble me now. But my child—I long to know something of her."

"You now know all that I can tell you, save that by this she has sailed for Italy."

"Why Italy?"

"It was the choice of her husband."

"Tell me. Did she love him?"

"I have every reason to believe so," said Pipey gloomily.

"That is well. I would have her happy. But Lovelace, does he know aught of her birth and parentage?"

"He knows nothing; and I did not deem it right to tell him aught."

"You did well. But should he institute inquiries?"

"He is not likely to know much, unless he fell into the society of your enemies; and that he is not likely to do. Lady Lovelace herself is in ignorance of her birth."

"True; a miserable truth, and one which maddens me when I reflect on it."

At this point there was a loud whistle in the street, just beneath the window where the Duke and Pipey sat.

"Ah!" said Pipey, starting to his feet, "it is the whistle of one of my men. Will you await my return?"

"I will gladly do so."

"You will find some books on the shelves that

will amuse you for a few minutes. I do not expect to be detained."

"Pray do not hurry on my account. My time is my own, and I have no better way to pass it than in sitting here."

"Very good," said Pipey, taking up his hat and leaving the room.

The door was closed on the Duke, and the next moment Pipey was in the street.

"What is it?" he demanded of the man who awaited him.

"I have just found out that there is some one about the place who is, and has been, dogging you. Come with me. Mortlake will tell you more."

Pipey closed the door of his house and started off—locking up the man he was invited to search for under his own roof.

Gosmont heard the door open when the Duke entered, and also when Pipey made his exit.

"Now," thought the idiot, as he crawled from his lurking-place, "now I will search. He must be once more alone, and if I find him— if I find him —"

He grinned maliciously, and, drawing a knife from the recesses of his great pockets, he stole up the stairs, and quietly entered the room in which the Duke was sitting.

It chanced that Grasmount sat with his back to the door, and being absorbed in the book he had taken from Pipey's little library, he heeded not the arrival of the idiot.

Liney at once recognised the coat worn by the Duke as that in which he had frequently seen Pipey, and therefore concluded that his victim was in his power.

Stealthily he crawled towards the chair, holding his breath as he stopped.

The next moment he completely covered his

victim, who still read on, unconscious of the awful position in which he stood. Thus the two remained for the space of a second, and then the idiot raised his great arm.

"Die!" shrieked the idiot; and the knife fell, and was buried in the throat of the Duke.

"Oh, God!" shrieked the poor man, springing to his feet and staring wildly at the assassin; "oh, God, I am killed!"

The blood saturated the garment the Duke wore, and he fell to the floor.

Liney stared at the fallen man as one petrified with fear.

"Not the man!" screamed the idiot; "not the man! I have killed the Duke! I have killed the Duke!"

"Oh, I die, I die!"

The murdered man rolled over and over and over, in extreme agony, and still the idiot continued crying, "Not the man! not the man!"

This scene continued until the last breath escaped from the Duke's body.

It was an awful sight, and one at which the stoutest heart might have quaked.

At length came a silence.

The horror of the deed he had committed having become allayed, the next thought of the idiot was to effect his escape.

Self-preservation was now his only thought; and with the rapidity of lightning he flew down the stairs, dreading at each step to see the door open, and some one come to arrest his flight.

Through the passage he rushed, and scrambling for the lock, he opened the door, and fell over—Mrs. Boodles.

Gathering himself up, he rushed on, and in a moment was out of sight.

"Which it was that awful man as always was a trying to get into the house," said the old lady, rising to her feet.

She was about to enter the house, when the wind blew the door to, and her entrance was thus stopped.

"Which it's cold," she said, "very cold and dreary; and I wishes I knew how to get in, I do! Mr. Pipey is sure to be out, he is; and here I must stop until he comes back."

Liney had not progressed in his flight many hundred yards when he was violently arrested.

A well-known voice rang in his ear, and he stirred not.

Before him stood the Duchess.

She had been watching the house.

"Well," she said, "what is done?"

"Oh! blood! blood! blood!"

"Ah; it is done, then?"

"He is dead! he is dead!"

"'Tis well; fly, or you may be seen."

"He is dead; alas! the Duke, the Duke!"

"What mean you by the Duke?"

"Let me speak — let me tell you. Liney watched the house, and at last found an entrance. The woman dropped the key, and I used it. I had not been in many minutes, when a knock came to the door. It must have been the Duke who came."

"Well?"

"He was admitted, and went up the stairs to an upper room."

"Yes, yes."

"I waited, and at last I heard the door open again, and some one quit the house."

"Well?"

"I thought it was the Duke."

"And was it not the Duke?"

"No; it must have been the man I had to kill."

"Great God, what do I hear?"

"I stole up stairs, and silently entered an apartment, in which a light was burning."

"Yes."

"Well—well—I forget."

The idiot was growing confused.

"Proceed with your tale. What then occurred?"

"Let me think—let me think. A light was burning."

"Yes."

"And at a table sat a man. He wore the coat in which I had seen him I was to kill."

"Yes; I listen."

"His back was towards me, and being satisfied that he was the man, I struck him down; and then—the blood—the blood!"

"Think not of it. What then occurred?"

"He turned his face upon me."

"Yes?"

"And instead of my man I saw the features of *the Duke!*"

"The Duke!"

"Yes. I have missed the right man, and killed my master."

The Duchess was stunned at what she heard.

"Can I believe my senses?" she said.

"It is true. Liney knows it it is true."

"He appears certain. If he should be right."

"I am right. Liney knows."

"Then all is over with me!"

"No, no! Don't say that."

"Fool!" cried the maddened woman; "fool, fool—what have you done?"

"I don't know. What has Liney done?"

"You have destroyed me. They will hunt me down for this. The deed *must* come to light, and it *will* be traced to me."

"No—no."

"I say yes. But I must give up all without a struggle. Listen, and answer my questions. Who was in the house besides the Duke?"

"Not a soul."

"You are sure?"

"Liney is sure."

"And when you came to the street were you seen?"

"No!"

"Are you sure?"

"Yes—but stay. Liney fell over some one in the doorway. Yes, Liney knows that now."

"Oh, agony! What do I hear? And even now you may be followed."

"No, no."

"Yes, yes, I say. But I must think on what to do. The carriage is in the street yonder. We had best fly. And yet to be in doubt. No! I will go to the house and see what has been done and who is there. I must satisfy myself or I shall go mad—mad—mad!"

She clasped her brow and stamped her feet heavily on the stones.

" Liney will take you away. Come, come."

" No, no; I will go to the house. Stay you here."

" And if you do not return——"

" Go away, where you will; but fly from this place."

" I will, I will. If they take you all is over, for you cannot hold your peace."

" I will tear out my tongue for you."

" Speak not thus, but obey me. Remain here."

" I will, I will."

The Duchess moved stealthily towards Pipey's house, and Liney hiding in the shadow of a door-way gazed after her until he could see her no longer.

The rain and wind that had for a time died away now commenced again with redoubled fury, but the Duchess heeded it not.

CHAPTER XLVII.

LOLA AT CARLTON HOUSE—MRS. FITZ-HERBERT'S SUSPICIONS—THE STORY OF LOUISE.

MRS. FITZ-HERBERT had had a tolerably long reign.

His Royal Highness had been her devoted slave for a period of six weeks.

This was for him an enormous stretch of constancy, and people began to wonder whether the amour was a lasting one, and if Mrs. Fitz-Herbert had in reality inspired a true passion in the bosom of the most inconstant man in the world.

Speculation was soon set at rest.

His Highness began to hunt up his old companions, and to absent himself of an evening from Carlton House; leaving poor Mrs. Fitz-Herbert to pine and grieve in solitude.

The Marlborough House band of beauties, to whom our readers were introduced early in the story, had long ago been disbanded.

Some of them were pensioned, others married to insipid court hangers-on, and one or two sent adrift in the world, without friends, money, or protectors.

They were very pretty poppets to dress up and play with, but children of all growths tire of their toys, and His Royal Highness grew sick of his.

He was disgusted with the mummery he had instituted, and, like Frankenstein with his monster, his own creations had become a terror to him.

He had made those girls the bad, dissolute beings they had become.

By forcing them to adopt the costumes and the manners of the opposite sex he had crushed all the womanhood out of them, and made them a something only calculated to excite loathing and terror.

By the agency of Laurence all these women were disbanded and got rid of, and, as we have said, for a time the Prince devoted himself solely to the beautiful Mrs. Fitz-Herbert.

At length came his adventure among the beggars, and his meeting with Lola.

The voluptuous form and large speaking eyes of the Italian at once fascinated him, and then—farewell to Mrs. Fitz-Herbert !

With brutal indifference the voluptuary un-hesitatingly brought his new flame to the house in which the old one yet remained.

What did he care ?

He confessed himself sick of the poor, devoted woman, who, although she had stifled the cry of conscience by the catholic marriage ceremony, was still conscious that she had sacrificed all to him.

Her pangs of remorse—her sufferings on finding herself discarded—did not interest him.

Here was a new passion.

Here was a new and still more beautiful toy, so the old one was to be thrust aside for ever—never to be thought of more. There was no compunction : she had served her turn, and was thrust away with as much indifference as if she had been a soiled glove !

Expostulation with him was vain.

Laurence endeavoured to persuade him from so suddenly casting off Mrs. Fitz-Herbert.

It was the night of the meeting with Lola.

" Your Highness had best not so suddenly introduce this girl into Carlton House," he said.

" Wherefore ?"

" It may pain Mrs. Fitz-Herbert."

" Nonsense."

" But she is so very sensitive."

" What matter ! Has she not been served well ?"

" The very reason she should feel the more grieved now."

" I can't see it ; so say no more on the subject."

" Then you are determined ?"

" Yes ; and the best thing you can do is to get rid of Fitz-Herbert as soon as possible."

" I shall be glad to obey you, but how am I to proceed about the task ?"

" As you will, so that you rid me of her."

" At once ?"

" Without delay."

" I must think of some scheme."

" Think of no scheme : go to her, and say I'm tired of her ;—say what you will, only get rid of her."

" Very good."

They spoke in a chamber on the ground floor of Carlton House.

Above was Mrs. Fitz-Herbert. In the next apartment was Lolo, in the company of Portman. Laurence went to the chamber of Mrs. Fitz-Herbert, and the Prince sought his little Italian.

We shall now see how Laurence executed his mission.

He found Mrs. Fitz-Herbert seated before the girl in *deshabille*. Her tiny foot rested on an ottoman, and her morocco slipper was being torn to pieces by a pet spaniel.

She was employed in glancing over the leaves of some vapid French novel.

We have hinted that she was not a woman of very strong mind, and the stupid, and in many cases revolting, *materielle* of the French romancist was about the most substantial literary dish she was capable of digesting.

" Where is the Prince ?" she asked of Laurence, on his *entre*, " it is two o'clock, and I have not seen him since last evening."

" His Highness is—"

" Well ?"

" I scarcely know how to tell you."

" Why not ?"

" Because my information will grieve you."

Mrs. Fitz-Herbert fidgetted in her chair.

" Speak on," she said, " I am prepared to listen."

" Well, His Highness is engaged with a lady."

The eye of Laurence wandered from the pretty face of the lady to the little foot so provokingly displayed on the ottoman.

" She's very pretty, and a fine woman," he said. " I wonder whether she would fancy me."

He had thought her a pretty and a fine woman before, but while his master entertained that opinion he dared not turn his eyes longingly on her daintyness. Now he saw his opportunity.

Mrs. Fitz-Herbert looked puzzled.

" What do you mean ?" she asked.

" Ask me not to pain you by explanations. I have not the courage."

" What *do* you mean?—pain me—have not the courage—what dreadful thing am I to hear ?"

" It is dreadful, that such love—such devotion —should be discarded."

" Discarded !"

" Alas !"

" Speak out, man, and let me know the worst, I am prepared to hear all you have to tell me."

" Then I have to say that the Prince has fixed his attention — can I say his love ? — upon another."

" Powerful Heaven !"

" Alas ! alas ! it is too true."

" I cannot think it."

" I can convince you. The new favourite is even now beneath this roof—even now locked in his embrace."

" Oh ! Heaven !—and I his wife !"

" You forget—"

" Yes—yes, I have forgotten. I have been kind, but I am so no longer! I see all now most clearly. He loves me not, and I have deceived myself into thinking that the ceremony we went through was binding."

" In the eyes of Heaven it was so, but in the opinion of man—"

" Ah ! there it is. He is a prince and I—"

" An angel ; too good to be linked with such a man."

This was uttered passionately, and Mrs. Fitz-Herbert raised her eyes in astonishment.

Laurence hung his head, as if he had been betrayed into an expression of thought which he would fain have concealed.

" Tell me," said the lady, after a pause, " tell me ; who is this woman ?"

" An Italian girl."

" Where and when did he meet her ?"

" This night, at a low house by the side of the Thames."

" And she is—"

" A taproom ballad singer."

" Is she beautiful ?"

" An ordinary Italian peasant."

This was a lie ; but Laurence knew the game he was playing, and sought to add to the loathing and disgust for the Prince already rising in the breast of the woman before him.

He well knew that the more her self-pride was wounded the better chance there would be of her regarding him with favour.

" And he has left *me* for such a woman ?" said Mrs. Fitz-Herbert.

" For *such* a woman," repeated Laurence.

" It is too dreadful."

" It is disgusting."

" But it proves the man unworthy a woman's love."

" Yes ; unworthy indeed."

" Oh ! that I had cast my affections on one who would have appreciated them ! Oh ! that Fate had thrown me in the path of one who would have loved me as I have loved this man ! But, alas ! it was not to be, and all has been but a dream. The future is a barren waste, on which I dare not look."

" And wherefore ?"

" Can you, who know all, ask me that ?"

" I can and do."

" And know that henceforth, in the eyes of men, I am a discarded, worthless object. I have been used, and thrown aside. Few would stop to pluck the faded flower ; few, indeed, would regard me with other feelings than those of contempt."

" You know not the heart of man if you think thus. There are many who would not only feel a joy in possessing your love but be proud to link their fates to yours *at the altar.*"

" I know not one."

" I know one."

" Indeed ! Who is he ?"

" He kneels at your feet."

Laurence dropped on his knees, and snatching the hand of Mrs. Fitz-Herbert, imprinted on it a passionate kiss.

It was not withdrawn.

" I triumph !" said Laurence to himself ; " she is mine."

" Rise," said the lady, " rise, I beg. This is absurd. You do but jest."

" Indeed, I am serious. Oh ! how serious."

" Pray leave me !"

" No. Hear me."

" I dare not."

" You must. Oh, sweetest, since I first saw you I have madly worshipped you, but I saw that your heart was given to another, and that that other was my prince, my future king. My devotion to him was sufficient to make me hide my passion successfully. I could have been content to have allowed it to eat my heart out had not this event transpired to-night. I saw that you were not loved. I saw an unworthy, low bred, nameless foreigner lifted to your place, and to me was intrusted the mission of informing you of the dreadful termination of your dream of love and happiness. To me ! the man who would die for one smile of yours ; who would follow you to the end of the earth and be content if you bade me not leave your path ! Oh, Heaven ! that I should tell you that you are discarded. That mine should be the lips that bring you as it were face to face with your doom ! What can I do ? What can I say ; save that I am your slave and that I madly, fondly love you ! Let me then strive to heal up the wound a bad fearless man has made in your heart. I ask not for your love.

I shall be repaid if you can give me toleration. But I will do all man can do to make you forget the past and find happiness in the future."

"Pray, pray rise. I dare not listen to you."

"But give me one word of comfort; let me have one ray of hope."

"Oh, sir, sir, I cannot say I love you, and without love ——"

"Speak not of it! I ask you not to love me until I prove worthy such honour. I only ask you to be mine for your *own* sake and mine.'"

"Give me but an hour."

"A moment were an age. Let me ask you to decide."

"My position is a terrible one."

"It is. Think of it Let not the world say you left this house discarded and thrown aside. Better let it brand you with fickle mindedness. If you will but make me happy I will put such reports floating about the surface of society that not one shall dream of the real secret of your quitting the Prince, and your pride will have no fall."

"You are good, and I am grateful to you."

"Then you will make me happy ? You will be mine ?"

"What shall I say ?"

"Only one little word ?—Yes !"

"Then if it must be so—Yes !"

Lawrence sprang to his feet and clasped the lady to his heart.

Their lips met and for a moment they were silent.

After all, Mrs. Fitz-Herbert did not appear to be dissatisfied at the change she had made.

"In an hour be prepared to leave this terrible roof," said Laurence.

"Yes," she said, "in an hour."

"Till then, adieu.'"

"Adieu."

"I shall think the hour an age. Dearest, adieu."

He kissed her passionately, and quitted the room.

She retired to her bed-chamber, and summoned her maid.

The girl, half asleep, answered the bell.

"Be prepared to leave here in an hour."

"In an hour, madam ?"

"Yes, in one hour. Assist me to dress, and then pack up my jewels, and those dresses I shall most require."

"Is madam going on a journey !"

"No, I return to my own house."

"Has anything serious occurred ?"

"Nothing whatever."

The girl looked completely puzzled, but busied herself about obeying the commands of her mistress.

*　*　*　*　*

Laurence descended to the lower apartments, and to the chamber to which Lolo had been conducted, where he found his royal master, half drunk, and with the Italian girl on his knee, carrolling a ballad in his greedy ear.

Portman had left.

"Well," said the Prince, on the entrance of his slavish follower, "what cheer ? Have you rid me of Mother Fitz-Herbert ?"

"Of whom do you speak ?" asked the Italian.

"An old fool that's mad after me, darling, but whom I detest. Say, is she gone ?"

"She will be in a comparatively short time, if you lend me a carriage to bear her away."

"Take six, if you like ! State coaches and all !"

"One will suffice, I am obliged to your Highness."

"Well, how did she take her dismissal ? Did she grieve ?"

"Bitterly !"

"I thought she would."

"Ah, your Highness, she loved you well."

"Of course she did. She couldn't help it, could she, you little rogue ?" he asked the Italian, chuckling her under the chin. "Ah," he said, "she's bundled off to make room for you! Are you not proud ?"

"Very proud !"

"That's right. You ought to be."

"Oh! I am."

"Well, she cried, I suppose ?"

"I thought she would never cease weeping."

"And she called me all manner of hard names."

"No. She was more hurt than enraged."

"Oh! I see ; just what that fellow the poet says—'she was more in sorrow than in anger,' hey ?"

"Just so, your Highness."

"Poor soul ! Well, I'm sorry for her."

"She bade me say she would never cease to think of you."

"But she must."

"You cannot control her thoughts."

"But I say she shan't think of me. I want to be free from her. I don't want to feel that she even thinks of me."

"What then is to be done ?"

"I don't know. Why don't you marry her ?"

"Your Highness !"

"Well, what is there so wonderful in that ? Why not ?"

"It is an honour of which I dared not dream."

"Oh! nonsense. Marry her and be happy."

"But you forget the lady has to be consulted in the matter."

"Nonsense, talk her into it. I say you *must* marry her; so let me not have to hear of the matter again."

"I will do my best."

"Then you will succeed ; and if you do succeed, I'll not upset your devotion—and now get out."

"I will obey your Highness."

"I mean to lock the door until that woman is gone. Tell Portman to acquaint me with her departure."

"Yes, your Highness."

Laurence, laughing in his sleeve, withdrew from the royal presence.

"And now, wench," said the Prince, as he turned the key in the lock, "sing me another of these songs."

He seated himself on a luxurious lounge, and then encircled the girl with his arms.

She pillowed her head on his bosom, and warbled forth another melody.

*　*　*　*　*

Lolo was now at home in her new quarters.

She was one who cared but little for adopting a moral tone which she did not feel.

The only passions that nature had developed in her to any extent were those that characterise the animal.

She was the slave of her wild will; and, to gratify that and the fierce flames that burnt in her bosom, she would stop at nothing.

It is only right we should now tell the reader that she was in the employ of the woman whom Marie had made her friend and *confidante*.

Acting in this position she had been set upon the track of the Prince : her employer well knowing that, should she meet his gaze, she would find no difficulty in fastening herself on to him.

The day after her introduction to Carlton House she was formally installed as its mistress.

There was an immense outlay for new robes and jewels, and a staff of servants was selected for her.

But there was one serious hitch.

She could not satisfy herself in the selection of a lady's-maid. All the girls that were inspected by her for that office fell short of her standard, and were discarded accordingly.

At length the Prince had to accede to her demands, and go forth to find the all-important servant.

In his emergency he called in the aid of Portman.

"Here," he said, meeting the favourite on the stairs, after quitting the presence of Lolo, "here! that little Italian devil can't be satisfied with the servants of the house, and wants something superior in the shape of a maid. Can you recommend one?"

"I do not think I can."

"Don't say no, for I know not where to look for one."

"There is but one that I know of; but, I suppose she would scarcely suit."

"To whom do you refer?"

"I mean your quasi-page of Marlborough House—Louise."

"Why will she not do?"

"I did not think you would have cared to have her near you again."

"And prythee wherefore?"

"I can give no sufficient reason for the supposition."

"Well, then, I think she will do very well. Will you find her?"

"Yes; there will be little difficulty in so doing."

"How?"

"The fact is, I always had a penchant for the little wench, and when she left Marlborough House—"

"You took her to your own house—yes?"

"You have made a correct guess. I did so."

"Well, and then you tired of her, and packed her off; and lately you have found her again in poverty, and wish to do something for her?"

"That is the history, as graphically related as I could myself have done it."

"Good. Let her come, and if she won't suit I'm afraid *ma petite ami* will have to do without

a maid, for I'll trouble no further in the matter."

"She shall be with the lady in the course of an hour."

In the course of an hour Louise came, and was conducted to the presence of the Italian.

Lolo gave a glance at the new comer, and finding her first impression favourable, bade her advance.

"What is your name?" she asked.

"Louise," replied the girl.

"Ah! a pretty name. Have you ever filled a position similar to the one you now seek to hold?"

"Never."

"You have, if I mistake not, seen better days?"

"Yes, far better."

"Do you think you would like to fill a servant's office?"

"I have no choice."

"Indeed—are you so poor?"

"Yes, very poor."

"Ah, that is sad. Well, Louise, I like you, and, if you choose, will engage you."

"Thanks, madam."

The engagement was soon effected, and the ex-mistress became the servant of the reigning favourite.

Poor Louise: her's was a sad tale, and its interest will make it worthy of being related at length.

We will give it :—

She was the daughter of a minister, who resided in a little village some fifty miles from London.

She was an only child, and was petted until her disposition was ruined.

A sweet child, she grew to be a lovely woman; but all her beauty was on the surface. Her mind was a dark and unsightly thing, and her passions unwomanly in the extreme.

At the age of seventeen she formed an attachment to a young man who resided near her father's home.

He was a free-hearted, generous youth, and loved Louise devotedly, but he soon discovered her worthlessness, and weaned himself from her.

Near the incumbent's house was a large mansion, the property of a nobleman of great wealth and influence.

He seldom used this residence save during the hunting season, and then it was filled with guests.

One season there came to Mallbrook a young baronet, whose only recommendations were his good breeding and good looks.

In town he was known as a drunkard, a libertine, and a gambler.

He, nevertheless, possessed many showy attractions, and was just the man to engage the attention of a young and giddy girl, unused to the world and its ways.

Louise was invited to stay a few weeks at the Hall, and there she encountered Sir Arthur Darrell.

He saw in her an unsuspecting victim, and she in him the *beau ideal* of the man of whom she had dreamed, but never before met.

She loved him ; but he cared nothing whatever

for her beyond the gratification of his passions, and the pleasant passing away of a few monotonous days.

She threw herself in his path, and he took advantage of her want of caution, and deficiency of moral strength.

After a late stroll through the gardens adjoining the Hall, Sir Arthur and Louise were returning to the house, when Sir Arthur dropped a hint to the effect that he should like to see her again that night.

"Where can we meet?" she asked.

"Can you not come to my chamber?"

"Sir Arthur!"

"What harm in that?"

"Much! You forget you speak to a lady. If you have aught to say to me, you can surely say it now."

"Indeed I cannot."

"Then we cannot meet again to night."

"Adieu, then. I thought you loved me."

"I *do* love you."

"And you prove it by refusing the first request I ever made."

"But it is so wrong."

"If you think so it is as well we part now and for ever. I hate the cold conventionalities of the world. I am one who discards the rules of a straight-laced hypocritical society, and I thought I had found in you a kindred soul, but I see I have made a fatal error."

"Stay! I, too, think but little of the world, and care not for its ways; for they are not my ways. I would, however, observe something like decency: you have asked that of me which the savage would not do."

"Ah, you mistake, fair Louise. I know more of savages than you imagined, for I have lived among them. Ah, there was once an Indian maiden—"

"Who loved you?"

"Who loved me to madness. I was her father's captive, but she made my imprisonment light and easy to bear by her presence and her love."

"And did you love her?"

"Not as I love you."

"But you did love her?"

"I should be a liar if I said no; but let us dismiss the theme, it is too trivial to dwell upon."

"No, no! Tell me more of this Indian girl."

"Well, Louise, she loved me; but dared not show it, or the vengeance of her tribe would have fallen upon her, and the result would have been too terrible for contemplation, more especially as she was the betrothed of another. A young warrior, the favourite of her father, was to be her future lord, but she loved me. She was mine, mine own, and in the dead of the night, when the pale moon would look down upon the Indian village, even as the moon above our heads now looks down upon us, she would steal to my tent. A slight touch would awaken me, and on opening my eyes they would fall upon a marvellous vision of loveliness. There would stand my Indian maiden, gazing down upon me with true fondness in her lustrous eyes. Ah, she was indeed beautiful! From her sweet head fell a stream of raven black hair, enveloping her shoulders, and falling gracefully down her back. Across one shoulder

she wore a slight scarf, of a golden texture, which barely hid her heaving bosom. A fantastic skirt scarce reached her knee, and her tiny feet were encased in shoes, worked in the rarest beads. Her arm and shoulders were bare, and at her back hung her bow and case of arrows. I would hold out my arms to her, and she would come to me; and the nights would pass as visions of joy. If nature had not intended that man and woman should love thus, would it have brought that lovely girl, unacquainted with crime, and knowing no other guidance but that of the heart, to my tent night after night, if it was wrong for her to be there? I cannot think so."

The tale of the Indian maiden was an entire creation of Sir Arthur's brain; but he knew his game, and saw at a glance the best mode of securing it.

Louise had listened to him attentively, and as he spoke had crept insensibly nearer to him, and when he ceased her head was pillowed on his arm, and her eyes were fixed upon his.

He looked down, and kissed her.

"Will you be my Indian maiden?" he asked.

And she returned his kiss and murmured—

"Yes."

From that night Louise dated her downfall.

Night after night she shared Sir Arthur's couch, and at last all the household grew to know of the intimacy that existed between the baronet and the rector's daughter.

In the course of time the shame of his child reached the old man's ears, and he went to the Hall to ascertain the facts of the case.

There was no attempt made at secrecy; both the Baronet and Louise shamelessly avowed their unholy intimacy, and declined to separate.

"To you," said the old man to Sir Arthur, "I speak not: you are answerable to God for my child's ruin; but I appeal to her, before she takes another step in the downward path, to return to her old father, and try to amend her ways. His home is still her home, his heart will still warm towards her, and his tongue shall make no mention of the awful past. In the name of God, then, my child, I bid you leave your betrayer and cling unto me!"

The cold heart of the girl heeded not the beautiful and Christian-like words of the father, and she turned from him and clung to her seducer.

Again and again the old man begged and prayed his erring child to heed him, but it was in vain. She turned her back upon him, and bade him go.

He imprinted a solemn kiss upon her forehead, commended her to the care of God, and then went home.

His heart was broken, and he laid down and died.

Sir Arthur supplied the unhappy Louise with money, gave her jewels, and then sent her off to London to await his coming.

He gave her an address and a letter of introduction, and told her to wait for him at the house of the lady to whom he recommended her.

She left for London, and the Baronet packed up his trunks, arranged his affairs, and flew to the Continent.

He cared no more for Louise, and had thus rid himself of her.

She reached London, and sought out the house at which she was to take up her abode.

She found it to be a fashionable mansion in the West-end, its owner being a Mrs. St. Jermaine, a lady whose reputation was none of the best, and whose house bore no enviable character.

But this Louise knew nothing of for some time.

She delivered her letter of introduction, and found Mrs. St. Germaine a lady so entirely after her own heart that she immediately struck up a warm friendship with her, and entered into the style of living for which the house was famous—or, rather, infamous.

Besides herself, there were three other young ladies in the house, all of whom were introduced to her as the neices of Mrs. St. Jermaine.

With these ladies also she grew on intimate terms, and soon delivered herself up to the *abandon* of the establishment.

After she had been in this house a fortnight, and began to have some idea of its character, Mrs. St. Jermaine came to her and asked if she was not tired of waiting for Sir Arthur.

"Indeed, I am not," she said, "for the fact is, I have been so happy here that I have never troubled to think about him."

"And suppose he should never come?"

"Well, my heart would not break."

"You would not grieve after him?"

"No."

"You are sure?"

"Quite sure."

"Well, then, I will tell you something. Sir Arthur will *not* come here."

"What do you say?"

"Read his letter—the one you brought with you."

Mrs. St. Jermaine drew forth Sir Arthur's letter and placed it in the girl's hand.

"Read it," she said.

Louise took it, and read as follows:—

"DEAR ST. JERMAINE,—The bearer is a silly little country girl whom I wish to commend to your care. We have enjoyed each other's society for some weeks, and have been remarkably happy. It would be a pity for us to be together longer and eventually part in anger, so pray find another and more worthy lover for her, and receive the blessing of   "Your distressed
                    "ARTHUR."

Louise bit her lip, and was silent.

"What say you to that?" asked Mrs. St. Jermain! "Why I thought you would not grieve about the man?"

"Neither will I. It is not the man I care about, but the indignity of being turned off in this provoking manner."

"Psha! It is nothing. There is no accounting for the tastes of these gay young bloods; so think no more of him."

"You may depend I will not."

"Well, now come to the window, and let us see who passes."

Mrs. St. Jermaine and her young friend seated themselves at the window—not to *see* who passed, but to *be seen* by the passers.

Louise knew it not, but she was sitting at that window to undergo the scrutiny of the youthful scions of the nobility who supported Mrs. St. Jermaine and her establishment.

It was afternoon, and the young bloods had just come from the Fives' Court, or the horse bazaars, and were returning home for dinner.

Just as we should say, "Let us drop in at Tattersall's, and see if there's anything new in the stables," they would say—"Before dining let us look at Mother St. Jermaine's, and see if she has any fresh face worth gazing upon."

Her house was a well-known institution, and one to which more respectable girls owed their downfall than any other in London.

So it came to pass that, whilst sitting in the window of this house, Louise was undergoing a close inspection, and was being put up at a kind of auction.

Each passer made a mental bid for her, and each nod they received from Mrs. St. Jermaine was a sort of auctioneer's recognition thereof.

At length the Prince of Wales passed.

As a matter of course *he* scanned the window very closely. He was a great admirer of Mrs. St. Jermaine. He had a thorough appreciation of her establishment; her line of policy suited him, and the wares in which she dealt were those in which he principally speculated.

He looked up, and eyed Louise attentively.

As he passed he bowed to her, and lifted his hat twice before he disappeared from her sight.

"Who was that gentleman?" she asked.

"Who, but the Prince of Wales?" replied Mrs. St. Jermaine.

"Ah; then he mistook me for some one else."

"No, no."

"Why then did he bow to me?"

"Because he always pays homage to beauty. You have smitten him."

"Indeed!"

"Yes, indeed; and if I mistake not we shall soon have a visit from his Highness."

"He is not well favoured."

"Most ladies would think him so. His rank should hide all personal defects."

"It would not do so with me."

"It should do so, if you wish to get on in the world."

"Ah—I am not worldly."

"Then learn to be so."

"I could not *sell* my love."

"You would be foolish to give it away; it is of too much value."

"Love is not a ware that I care to traffic in."

"Oh, child, you will learn to think differently after a residence of two or three years in this metropolis."

"I think not."

"We shall see."

The gallants grew fewer now, and the street was quiet again.

The business of the afternoon was, therefore, over, and Mrs. St. Jermaine drew her young charge from the window and bade her dress for dinner.

"Take as much pains with yourself as possible

No. 22.

for be assured you will this evening be honoured with a visit from the Prince."

Louise laughed as if she doubted the truth of Mrs. St. Jermaine's prophecy, but inwardly she determined to excel herself that evening both in her dress and manner.

To fascinate a prince was, indeed, a triumph; and although it must be confessed he was a very uninteresting specimen of the species, still it was a triumph, and Louise determined, if possible, to effect it.

CHAPTER XLVIII.

THE ABDUCTION OF MRS. BOODLES.

WITH cat-like stealth the Duchess approached the door of Pipey's house.

From the opposite side of the road she caught sight of the occupant of the doorway.

From information she had received from some of the brotherhood concerning Pipey's household, she had no difficulty in determining that the woman she beheld was the old housekeeper.

"It is she, then, who obstructed the flight of Liney—what can be done?"

It was at once apparent to the Duchess that this woman must be removed. But how?

No thought of her murdered husband crossed her mind.

For his fate she had no care. Self-preservation engrossed her whole attention.

A thought struck her.

She crossed the road, and assuming a faintiness she staggered against the steps of the door.

"Lawks!" cried Mrs. Boodles; "which, if it was the last words I should utter, she's a woman."

"Help me! he'p me !" said the Duchess feebly.

"Which I will, my poor soul," said the unsuspecting Boodles. "And what's the matter with you, is what I asks?"

"I am overcome with terror at the lightning—that is all."

"And what might have brought a lady—which a lady I see you are—out in such weather?"

"My carriage is at the bottom of the street. I left it that I might unseen and stealthily enter the house of an old servant, who lives not far from here, and who is now lying on a bed of sickness. She was no favourite with my husband, and I dared not let my visit become known to him. This, you see, is the result."

"And a very bad result, too. You are wet to the skin, and half-frightened to death; and to think that I've lost my key, and can't ask you inside."

"Never mind," said the Duchess, "it is of no importance, and the faintness has passed. If you will lend me your arm as far as the place where my carriage waits, I should esteem it a great favour."

"I will gladly assist you so far, my poor dear; which sorry I am that the key is lost, for I could offer you such a nice cup of tea—and good it is to warm the heart and cheer the sperets of the weak. Now I'm at your service."

Mrs. Boodles re-adjusted the mantle of the Duchess, and placing her arm within her arm walked away with her in the direction pointed out by the pretended sufferer.

Liney stole stealthily after them, watching them in bewilderment.

A walk of two minutes brought the two women to the spot where the carriage of the Duchess waited.

"I must use no force," thought the Duchess, "or it may awaken the suspicions of the servants."

The steps of the carriage were lowered, and the Duchess was about to step in, when she once more assumed a faintness, and staggered back.

"Which it's a coming on again," said Mrs Boodles; "and what is to be done I'm sure I can't say."

"Oh, do not leave me," said the lady; "do not quit me, or I shall die."

"Which I wouldn't for all the world, my dear. But what shall I do ?"

"Pray ride home with me. I can send you back in the same carriage. But I fear I am giving you more trouble than you care to take."

"Not at all, not at all, my dear. If good I can do for you, it's with pleasure I'll do it. So get into the carriage, and I'll follow, with all the pleasure in life; and a brute I should be if I didn't—which I well know what fainting fits is, having been a martyr to 'em for I don't know how long."

Without a suspicion the good old creature followed the crafty Duchess into the carriage, and in a few seconds was being borne away towards St. James's-square.

The Duchess still assumed a faintness, and thus had time to reflect on the course she should pursue with respect to the woman she had entrapped.

Maintaining a strict silence, she revolved in her mind a number of schemes for the disposal of the old lady; but the majority of them were dismissed as soon as formed, being either too dangerous to risk, or altogether impracticable.

As will be seen hereafter, she might have saved herself all this trouble; for at her house was awaiting her a man with more power to frame schemes of this kind, and to execute them, too, than twenty such as herself.

A short drive brought the Duchess to the door of her mansion, and entering, she bade Mrs. Boodles follow her and accept of some refreshment.

Refreshments were Mrs. Boodles' weakness. She was always prepared to attack them, and to dispose of a sufficient quantity, too. So she hesitated not to follow the Duchess at the first hint.

"Which it's a cold night, and a little something warm won't hurt."

Immediately afterwards she found herself in a luxuriously furnished room, seated before a roaring fire, and warming her feet on the fender with as much ease as if she had been at home.

The Duchess begged to be excused for a few minutes whilst she went to her chamber, and changed her attire—an excuse for getting away, in order that she might think on what was to be done in order to dispose of her victim.

She quitted her room, and was about to ascend the stairs, when her own servant approached, and informed her that there was some one in her boudoir who awaited her coming.

"A lady or gentleman?" she asked.

"A gentleman your grace."

"How inopportune; well, say I cannot see him to night."

"I think your grace will see him. It is the solicitor from the City."

"Indeed."

"Yes, your grace, he has been here a full hour, and has expressed so earnest a wish to see you that I bade him wait until your return."

"You did well; I will at once see him. Take refreshments to the lady, I have just left, and let me not be disturbed."

"Your grace shall be obeyed."

The Duchess went to the apartment indicated by the servant, and on opening the door, found Grimer awaiting her.

"At last," said the lawyer, "I was beginning to despair."

"What brought you here ?"

"I came to warn you."

"To warn me of what ?"

"Of the fact that my old friend Pipey is by this time aware of the fact that your confounded idiot is dodging him."

"Indeed !"

"Aye, indeed, and if you will take my humble advice, you will at once draw him off the scent, and put on a better man, or evil will come of it."

"He is off the scent."

"What! You don't mean to say that he has disposed of Pipey ?"

"No."

"I thought not. It would take a deal to make me believe that such a thing ever could kill so clever a lad. But why is he withdrawn from the work."

"Listen, man, listen. Strange things have been done to night. Very strange and terrible things. But I will tell you all I know, and then form your own opinions."

The Duchess then gave Grimer as accurate an account as she was able of the incidents of the night.

"Whew," whistled Grimer, "there is much in this; I say, you've the whole in your hands now."

"I know that."

"Have you thought of anything?"

"No; my brain is too bewildered, and I want you to think for me."

"I see a spendid field for action now; we must get rid of this old woman, and then to work. By Jove, you made a master stroke in securing her."

"Yes; but what do you propose doing?"

"I don't know yet, but it seems clear that this job of to night's is the making of you, if its properly worked."

"I don't see to what you allude."

"Don't you, then I do. You are now the owner of the Duke's money and property. There is no fear of any exposure, and you can get rid of Nipes without having murder to answer for.

The Duchess looked up enquiringly.

"Leave all to me. I'll so bring things about that before long Pipey shall stand at the Old Bailey on the charge of murdering the Duke. I have the ideas, but they are—yet—too crude to place before you. Leave all to me, and with time and good fortune I'll make the most out of this, and you shall call me a genius."

"But this woman?"

"Have no fear, I will dispose of her."

"What do you purpose doing with her?"

"I'll put her under the care of Yellow Maydock, and she will be all safe. In the morning I'll commence my plans for the disposal of Pipey.

"And what part am I exeected to play?"

"A simple one. Assume the deepest distress at the absence of the Duke, make every inquiry after him; sit up to-night, as if in momentary expectation of his return; send messengers to the House of Lords and his club to know what has become of him, and threaten or coax that idiot of yours into silence. Curse the dog, I dread him, for he has no command over himself."

"Have no fears for him. He has become embued with a sense of the danger in which I stand, and so will keep his tongue still. You might tear him limb from limb without getting a word from him."

"I'm glad you've such confidence in him; for my part I'd as soon trust the city crier."

"We shall see if my confidence be misplaced."

"Well, if it is, you have only yourself to blame, for I have warned you sufficiently. Folly—and, will stand to it that it was an unpardonable folly —to trust your secret and such work as you have done to the keeping of such a fool."

"Heed it not. Leave me to manage him, and do you do your part well."

"You can rely upon me. Now for a carriage."

"What do you intend doing?"

"I shall take this old woman to Maydock's place immediately. In the dark she will not know whither she is going, and when I've accomplished the greater part of the distance I'll dismiss your servants, and do the remainder on foot, so that they may be in ignorance of our designs."

"A good plan."

"Trust to me for work of this kind. It is, you know, in my line, and I like it. I don't think I could live without it. Besides, it pays better than any other."

The lawyer extended his hand.

The Duchess took the hint, and dropped a heavy purse into it.

"Now," continued Grimer, pocketing the cash, "now for this old woman."

"Will you see her?"

"No, I shall act the part of servant, and wait for her within."

"It is the best plan."

"Adieu. I shall see you again to-morrow."

The lawyer left the room, and waited in the lobby umtil the Duchess had given her orders, and prepared Mrs. Boodles for her journey.

Re-entering the room where she had left our good old friend, the Duchess approached her, and inquired whether the servants had attended to her demands.

"Oh! yes, ma'am," said the Boodles, with her mouth full of pheasant, "them young men o' yours do know how to behave to an old widow, and well I knows it, for this bird is the most lovely tastedest, and this brandy is the full flavouredest speret as ever passed my lips—and in my time it's much good victuals I've a eat and enjied, 'um. Which, my Boodles used to say, 'you do seem to have a appetite,' said he, 'and good feeding ain't a lost upon you, for them gowns of yours, what with letting 'em out,' said he, 'and having pieces put in, and one thing and the other,' he said, 'it's a lot of money they runs away with, and it's a long pull against a man with a family.' 'Well, Boodles,' said I, which his name was Boodles, and he was as fine a man as ever I seen, 'well,' I said, says I, 'if you are a Christian you won't begrudge your own wife animal ailments,' said I, 'for you've got this to think of· What I eats isn't for myself alone,' said I, 'but goes to support your own off-spring at my buzzum, and your own offspring what's yet unborn, and not acquainted with the light of day.' And I always said this with such a frown as used to shut him up; and I could see by the sheepish manner in which he'd bend his 'ed how ashamed he was of hisself for a uttering of them words. But there, I'm a running on and never asking of you how you feel?"

"Thanks. I am better now — better — far better."

"And it's cruel bad you look, for all that. What I'd recommend you to do would be to eat a leg of this pheasant, and take a hot and strong glass of this 'ere brandy, and then put your feet in hot water, with a teaspoonful of mustard— which your nose should be first well tallowed, and then go to bed—which an old stocking round the throat, and your flannel petticoat about your legs, will be found a improvement."

The Duchess thanked her new acquaintance for these hints, and then gave her a hint that she had best think of returning home, as it grew late, and she may be expected.

"What that blessed lamb, the Captain, of whom I've never been thinking, so taken up have I been with this pleasant and lovely speret, will be expecting of me, and wondering where I've got to."

Mrs. Boodles sprang to her feet and adjusted her cloak.

"Which my feet is now as warm as toast, and comfortable I shall be for the rest of the night."

"My carriage awaits you at the door, and is at your entire service. Pray receive my thanks for the great kindness you have done me in coming here."

"Oh, my dear, don't mention it, for all the obligation is on my part; for well with any trouble would it be to come and taste that pheasant and that speret—which a woman at my time of life has an eye to her comforts, and can't help it."

The Boodles followed the Duchess into the hall, and was then harded over to the care of Grimer, who placed her in the carriage that awaited her, and was about to follow, when Mrs. Boodles shouted—

"Which my directions is 42, Great Pitman-street, Soho."

"All right," said Grimer; "I am aware of that."

"Where to?" asked the driver.

"Go towards the Minories until I tell you to stop."

Grimer sprang into the carriage beside the unsuspecting woman, and the vehicle rolled off towards the quarter indicated by the lawyer.

CHAPTER XLIX.

THE STORY OF LOUISE CONTINUED—THE PRINCE AND HIS TASTES—THE ORGIES OF MARLBOROUGH HOUSE—THE DISMISSAL OF THE FEMALE PAGES, AND THE DESCENT FROM MASTER TO MAN.

MRS. ST. JERMAINE had a very select company at dinner that evening. There were her four or five "nieces," some two or three noble young officers of the King's Guard, and last, but not least, there was his Royal Highness of Wales!

He could not withstand the temptation of the new face, and so came to pay his *devoirs*.

As yet no one had paid Louise any marked attention, and she had yet to learn the manner in which a "niece" of Mrs. St. Jermaine's was treated by the supporters of that lady's establishment.

Louise had visited the theatre, had supped at all hours with the dissolute frequenters of her new home, but as yet she had been more of a spectator than actor in the scenes which characterised the house.

The fact was, St. Jermaine had strictly forbidden any of her patrons to cast their eyes upon her, as she was intended for a superior position than that they could offer her.

The fashionable procuress had quite made up her mind that Louise should grace the establishment of the Prince, or, at least, of some one equally powerful and capable of paying for her, so the ordinary frequenters had to take their eyes off the new beauty, and be content with the old ones.

At length the all-important moment arrived.

The Prince came, saw, and was smitten.

During the dinner he scarcely ever took his eyes from her, and directly it was over he followed Mrs. St. Jermaine from the room, and inquired into the girl's antecedents.

As a matter of course the wily woman did not tell him the exact truth.

"Who is she?" demanded his Highness.

"The daughter of a very much respected gentleman in Hertfordshire."

"And how came she here?"

"She quarrelled with her friends and ran away, receiving from one who knows me well an introduction to my house. Ah! it was a clever rascal that sent her to me. I have heard from Louise that he had tempted her again and again, but had failed to effect his purpose, and then you see how he took advantage of the girl's quarrel with her friends. He introduced her to me in order that I might give her that worldly tone, and show her so much of gay life as would make her more willing to lend a ready ear to him when he seeks her."

"And he has not yet sought her?"

"No."

"I am glad of that."

"Wherefore?"

"Because I am smitten desperately."

"Well."

"Well, she must be mine."

"Indeed! I'd have you know she has a will of her own."

"No matter; you can manage matters for me."

"Well, my sweet Prince, I dare say I could have done so had there been an occasion, but the fact is, there is none."

"What do you mean?"

"Simply that Louise has seen you and loves you."

"You jest."

"I am not in the habit of doing so, and am now in sober seriousness. She saw you pass, and was at once enslaved."

"Ah! it was the prince that enslaved her, I presume."

"No, the man! How was Louise, a poor little country girl, to know anything of you?"

"Was she never in London before?"

"Never."

"Was it, then, a genuine conquest?"

"Yes, but I have been singing your praises until the spell has become perfect."

"For which you must be handsomely rewarded."

"I must, indeed. Why, half the nobles in

town have already addressed her. My desk is filled with offers for her."

"Well, well, put them all in the fire. She must be mine, and mine alone.'

"But you have already half a dozen mistresses. Louise will not tolerate them."

"I will dispose of them all until she becomes used to my ways.'

"That is to say, you will confine your sole attention to her until you tire of her, and then she will have to fall in with the ruck, and take her chance with the others. Am I not right?"

"Think what you will."

"And you may do as you please; only remember I do not often offer you such a gem as this, and must, therefore, be well remunerated for handing her over."

"You shall have no reason to find fault with my munificence."

"Very well, we now understand each other, and I will send Louise to you."

Mrs. St. Jermaine left the Prince and sought Louise.

"Now," she said to the young girl, "is your time. If you think the Prince worth gaining you must not spare your caresses."

Louise smiled confidently, and walked to the apartment where his Highness awaited her.

He received her awkwardly, but she, by easy carriage and genial smile, soon reassured him.

They spoke first of London, and its sights and attractions.

The conversation then turned to individuals, and Louise told her companion of those she had met at the theatres, and at Mrs. St. Jermaine's table.

"Why," said the Prince, "you have seen the majority of our London *beaux*, and what think you of them."

"In truth, I think but very little of them."

"And yet they are deemed attractive and gallant men."

"That may be the case, but my taste is a peculiar one, different from that of the majority of my sex."

"And they all failed to inspire the gentle passion within your bosom?"

"Everyone."

"Alas!"

"Why that sad expression?"

I cannot help reflecting that if all others have failed to win your affections, how little chance I hold of being in receipt of the least possible portion of them.'

"I said not that."

"You did not. But I cannot conceal from myself my own inferiority."

"You forget, the failings of some persons are virtues in the eyes of those who look not with the casual glance, and feel not with the ordinary passions."

"Would that I could flatter myself that my failings were thus recognised."

"They may be."

"By whom?"

"Why ask me?"

"Because I love you!"

"And I love you!"

The next moment they were locked in a long and rapturous embrace.

His Highness pillowed his head on the bosom of the young girl, and was supremely happy. She reflected that, as his mistress, she would enjoy unlimited luxury, and hold power beyond the limits of her wildest dreams, and she too was happy, if happiness was the wild and feverish sensation that agitated her.

That night Louise changed her quarters, and was conducted to Marlborough House, where for a few days she lived in comparative secrecy.

Gradually, however, she was brought into contact with the friends of the Prince at those midnight revels of which we have before written.

After the theatres or the balls and card parties each evening, the fashionable beauties and leading men of the town, with the favourite opera singers, and ballet dancers, would find their way into Marlborough House, and there would hold such revels as at first confounded the young girl.

Glorious music from unseen sources would float upon the air: perfumes would be wafted from orange plants and exotics in every variety. The apartments would be brilliant with lights shaded by lustres of every hue, which toned down the glare, and shed a soft and sweet radiance around.

Wines of the richest vintage would be quaffed, and fruits from every clime eaten.

Women of wondrous beauty, but of anything but moral character, dressed in costumes which but barely hid those charms which virtue would blush to expose, crowded the velvet covered lounges and held in their embrace the young bloods who were the personal friends of the Prince.

Wild revelry was indulged in without intermission, and scenes of intoxicating brilliancy kept up night after night until all sense of delicacy was drowned in the fierce delights provided.

These scenes bore more resemblance to the incidents of an Eastern romance than anything transpiring in cold, worldly, impassionate London.

From deeming them revolting, Louise grew to tolerate them, and then by easy stages to take delight in them.

And thus time passed, until a new mistress took the place of first favourite, and she had to look for her pleasure in some other direction than that taken by the Prince.

At length his Highness conceived the idea of forming his corps of female pages, and for a time this little band served to please him vastly.

The pages were his cast-off favourites, but in their new characters they were once more looked upon with longing eye, and in turn, reinstalled to the position in his Highness's affections.

For a considerable time these pages were his delight, and he took a vast pleasure in increasing their number, and selecting the most fascinating girls of London to enter the ranks. But when this peculiar man came of age, and had to take up his quarters at Carlton House, he thought that it was time to disband his little regiment of fair pages and dispose of them as he best could.

He was now coming prominently before the world; his every act was to be observed and chronicled, and he rightly imagined that what might be tolerated as the wild freaks of a high-spirited boy, might disgust and beget unqualified condemnation when viewed as the acts of a responsible man.

And so the pages were sent adrift, pell mell.

Some returned to their homes, some became the mistresses of the favourites of the Prince, and others entered the receiving houses of the procuresses.

Louise, as we have said, became the mistress of Portman—a low, drunken rascal, who existed solely on the bounty of the Prince, by whom he was tolerated in consequence of his intimate acquaintance with the low haunts of London, in which his Highness took delight.

It was in a fit of wild desperation and rage that the girl gave herself up to Portman—one which she long regretted.

From the first moment they quarrelled, and as time progressed, they grew more and more opposed to each other, and at last separated; but this was not until Portman had forced from her the whole of her money and jewels.

Almost penniless, and with only one dress to her back, Louise left the house of Portman.

"I must needs seek Mrs. St. Jermaine once more," she said; and with tearful eyes and heavy heart she bent her steps in the direction of the house of the fashionable procuress.

CHAPTER L.

THE STORY OF LOUISE CONTINUED—MRS. ST. JERMAINE'S RECEPTION OF AN OLD FRIEND—DOWN INTO THE DEPTHS OF DEGRADATION.

A WALK of a very few minutes brought the girl to the door of Mrs. St. Jermaine.

She knocked, and was immediately admitted.

"Whom do you require?" asked the servant.

"Mrs. St. Jermaine," replied Louise.

"I will see if you can have an interview."

The man walked away, and in a few minutes returned, and conducted the girl to the dressing-room of her old acquaintance.

She found Mrs. St. Jermaine sipping her chocolate before the fire.

She glanced up languidly, and recognising Louise, nodded coldly, and motioned her into a chair.

"Well, darling," she said, "what brings you here?"

"I have come to see whether you will receive me once more."

"Hey?"

"You have heard of the break up of the establishment at Marlborough House?"

"Yes; and I heard you had found a wealthy protector."

"Would that I had."

"Then you found no protector?"

"Yes; but, alas! it was one with whom I had best not have met."

"How so?"

"Because he has squandered my money, pawned my jewels and wardrobe, and turned me adrift on the world."

"Indeed! That is sad. Who was it?"

"Portman."

"What! you the mistress of that low hound?"

"Yes, I was mad, I know, but I am terribly punished for my folly."

"Folly, indeed! Why, who do you suppose would care to look upon you after hearing that you were the mistress of Portman—a man who spends most of his time with the women of the low gin houses of Westminster?"

"Alas! alas!"

"Ah, it is too late to cry alas; you should have thought of that before."

"What shall I do?"

"Well, if you ask my advice, I should recommend you to seek one of the receiving houses in Soho; you may there fall in the way of some substantial tradesman who will not mind your antecedents."

"What! am I, then, fallen so low? Will *you*, *too*, send me away?"

"I cannot assist you. The path you have chosen you may walk in. I can have nothing to do with the cast-off mistress of Portman."

Louise burst into tears at this treatment, and rose to depart.

"I pity you," said Mrs. St. Jermaine, "and as a proof thereof accept these ten guineas. They will serve you until you find a friend."

Louise would have fain thrown the proffered gold at her who offered it, but the thought of her position crossed her mind, and she allowed the money to drop into her palm.

With breaking heart, she left the house and, almost unconsciously, walked away in the direction indicated by the procuress, viz., that of Soho.

Houseless—penniless—she had no alternative; and so had to bend to the circumstances that oppressed her.

Chance led her to the house of a notorious old hag, known as Mother Matthews.

Here she was well received, and made welcome.

She was shown to a chamber that was henceforth to be *hers*.

It was a panneled room, and, as the girl looked about her, she could not help suspecting that in that room many deeds of violence had been committed.

She had heard of robberies committed in these panneled chambers, and as she reflected that she might soon become one of the infamous things whose trade was to decoy men to this place, she shuddered, and for the first time for years thought sorrowfully of her old home in the little country village.

As sad memories crowded upon her, she heard the voice of a female in the room next her own, chaunting the following beautiful Scotch ballad, that was at that time most popular in London:—

"Wae's me, for my heart is breaking!
　I think on my brithers sma',
And on my sisters' grief,
　When I came fra' hame awa'.
And oh! how my mither sobbit,
　As she took from me my hand,
When I left the door o' our ould house,
　To come to this stranger land.

" There's na place like our ain hame—
    Oh ! I wish that I was there—
There's na hame like our ain hame,
    To be met we ony whae.
And oh ! that I was back again,
    To our farm and fields so green,
And heard the tongues o' my ain folk,
    And *was what I hae' been.*"

Louise gave way to a passionate flood of tears, and cried :—

" Oh, God ! what have I come to—what has befallen me !"

She might well ask that, for she was now on the lowest ring of the ladder, and sunk into the depths of misery and degradation.

She had not been many hours in this house before she was witness to the following scene :—

A poor old couple came to the door of the house and asked for their child, whom they knew to be harboured in the house.

Mother Mathews went to the door and told the old people that their child was not there.

The poor old woman protested that she knew of her being in the house, and plaintively begged that the erring one might be allowed to return to her own roof.

The infamous old woman still persisted in asserting that the girl was not there, and ended by taking the mother by the shoulders and thrusting her out at the door.

The poor woman fell on the door steps, and one of her legs was caught in the door and nearly broken.

Her shrieks of agony were terrible to hear.

The husband ran up and forced open the door, and released his wife.

They went away, but Mother Matthews had not yet done with them.

She indicted them for committing a riot, and had them apprehended ; but, on the case being investigated, the magistrate dismissed it.

Health and spirits gave way under participation in such scenes as these, and in a short time Louise become a perfect wreck.

She did not attempt to quit the house, and ere long her ten guineas were expended.

It was then she began to feel her true position.

The old hag of the house refused her food and drink, and told her that if she did not go forth into the streets to ply her trade she would turn her from the house and let her rot in the streets.

Louise was very ill and knew not what to do.

" Give me a few days," she said, " only a few days to get strength, and I will do all you can desire of me. But indeed I am too ill now, I am wretched—wretched ; and if I do not have food another day of starving will about kill me."

" Well, I will feed you another day," said the crone, " but after that look out."

That very night Louise heard sounds of mirth in the house. A half-drunk mate of a Indiaman had entered the house, and was spending his money freely, and holding high revelry.

Louise sat in her room and listened, and shuddered as the sounds of merriment fell upon her ears. At length she heard sounds of footsteps on the stairs, and the next moment the sailor burst into her room.

He was a fine fresh-coloured young man, of a jovial disposition, and with a face full of mirth and frolic.

He rolled up to the chair on which Louise was sitting, and placing his arms about her neck, kissed her, and seated himself by her side.

" What cheer, lass ?" he cried, looking into her face. " Old Mother Skinflint below told me you were the prettiest craft in the fleet, and so I've come to judge for myself."

" Don't distress me," said Louise, " I am ill, and in no humour for romping."

" Hey, my heart ; but you do look washy about the gills. Where's the pain ? and what's the complaint ?"

" I am weak and sick at heart, that is all."

" Is that all ? Well, lass, we'll soon find a remedy for that. Hang it ! a taut little girl like you mus'nt hang out signals of distress and not get 'em answered. Hey up, my pretty one ! We'll soon see you righted in no time."

The sailor left the room, and soon returned with a bottle of wine and glasses.

" Now, I'll shut up this door," he said, " and then we shall be all alone, and have nobody to disturb us. Weak, and sick at heart ! By George ! that's a complaint soon cured."

The girl could not but feel pleased at her new acquaintance.

He was every inch a man, and although she had never before met on terms of equality one so far beneath her in education and station, she took pleasure in his society, and spoke to him kindly.

" Nay, my lass," said the mate, " you're not used to this sort of thing—hey ?"

" Alas ! no."

" Well, you don't look like one of the class. What brought you to such a place ?"

" I cannot tell you, sir. My history is too sad for rehearsing now. It would give you no pleasure to hear it, and it would cause me utter pain to tell it."

" Well, then, my lass, say nothing about it."

He seated himself still nearer the unfortunate girl, and they spoke of things of a more congenial tone.

Louise felt better after she had partaken of the sailor's good cheer, and her spirits, in some measure, returned.

At length it waxed late, and the mate rose to depart

" I suppose you do not want my company," he said, " and I'm too much of a man to press myself where I'm not required."

Louise looked astonished.

She had anticipated no such generous feeling.

What could she do ?

Was she to turn the man who treated her so kindly out of the house at that hour ?

Was that just ?

Echo should have answered—

" Yes."

But there was the old evil spirit working within her.

There were the old evil passions rising and swaying her, and instead of sending her generous friend from her chamber, she bade him remain.

They passed the night together.

It was about four o'clock in the morning that

one of the panels of the chamber moved from its place, and the old wretch who owned the house, accompanied by a stalwart ruffian, entered and glided to the bed side.

They first of all rifled the pockets of the man of all he possessed, and then awoke Louise.

The old hag placed her hand over the mouth of the young girl to enforce silence, and then whispered her to leave the room.

Scarce comprehending what was meant, the girl complied, and all three glided silently from the chamber.

They descended into the lower apartments, and there the old woman commanded Louise to dress herself and go out for a few hours.

"I do not understand your meaning," said the girl.

"Then you may reflect upon it in the streets," replied the woman. "Out with you."

"Why should I go into the streets at this hour?"

"Because if you remain here your bed-fellow will, in all probability, give you into custody."

"Why should he do so?"

"Because he has been robbed."

"But not by me."

"No matter by whom—you slept with him. He locked the door of the room, and no one but you could have done this."

"Ah! A light breaks in upon me; you have robbed him."

"You had better not say so. Now, wench, leave the place directly, or I will call the watch, and give you in charge myself."

Poor Louise knew not what to do.

She never dreamed of being placed in such a position, and it almost maddened her.

"Come," cried the old woman, "on with your cloak, and off with you as fast as you can go."

She assisted in arraying the girl, and then forced her into the street.

It was a cold morning, and she knew not where to go.

At first she thought of running far from the spot, and hiding from the danger that threatened her.

But this thought was soon dismissed, and after walking a little way she turned back, and lingered about the house.

Meanwhile the sailor had awoke, and, missing his companion, sprang from the bed and dressed himself.

Unsuspicious of being robbed, he never thought of searching for his money, and imagining that Louise had descended to the lower apartments, he opened the door, and went after her.

In the kitchen he met the old woman.

"Well, mother," he said; "where's Louise?"

"Where's who?"

"Louise."

"I don't know who you mean, my man."

"Not know who I mean! Why the young woman with whom I passed the night."

"I did'nt know you had passed the night here. I am not responsible for the doings, or the comings and goings of my lodgers; and so I can't tell you where your Louise is."

"You don't mean to say she's gone?"

"How should I know?"

"Hillo," said the sailor, "I begin to suspect something."

He now searched his pockets, and, as a matter of course, found all his money, his watch, and rings gone.

"Well," he said, "this is a nice piece of business. I've been robbed."

"Robbed, have you? Well, it serves you right. You ought to know with whom you pass the night."

"What! why you infernal old hag, it was you who sent me to the girl's chamber."

"Your lie in your teeth! I never saw you before, and if you are not out of my house in a minute I'll have the watch and lock you up."

The sailor saw that he was beaten, and that he only had to submit, not having any inclination for a sojourn in the lock-up for creating a riot.

He knew too much of the world to run his head against such a stone wall as he saw before him.

"Well," he said, "I've been nicely fleeced, but never mind, I'll be even with all concerned. And to think that that smooth-tongued jade should be such a bad 'un, after all. Well, there's no trusting to appearances, after that."

He left the house, the old woman following and laughing in her sleeve at the success of her plan.

She closed the door after the man, and he strolled leisurely out of the street.

Just as he reached its end he saw, walking leisurely along, a figure he thought he recognised.

"Hillo!" said, "I know the rig of that craft, or my eyes mistake me. Where have I seen her?"

It was a woman he was observing.

"Hey?" he cried, "why yes. It's the very girl. Hillo! Miss Modesty, I've found you, have I? Well, I'll make you pay dearly for your whistle."

At this moment a watchman came up to the spot where he stood, and was passing him when the sailor stopped him.

"Hillo, governor!" he said, "where are you sailing? Bring yourself up and recounter that craft going before the wind yonder."

"What d'ye mean?" asked the watchman, not quite understanding the technicalities of the seaman.

"What do I mean? Why, I mean for you to observe that girl hanging about yonder course."

"Well."

"Well, old boy, we've laid yard-arm and yard-arm together all night, and, somehow, she parted company without a sound, and then—"

"You found all your cash gone, hey?"

"That's the state of the poll, old boy."

"Well, will you charge her?"

"Charge her? d——e, yes. It's not the cash I care about, but it's the way in which I was served after treating her so well."

"Ah! you don't know 'em; they would cut the throats of their brothers for a guinea, any hour of the day. However, it's no use talking; I'll take her into custody."

They approached the girl, and the watchman, before she could turn round, seized her by the shoulder, and told her she was his prisoner.

"Your prisoner!" said the girl; "oh, sir, I have done nothing wrong—indeed, indeed, I have not!"

"Oh, of course not," said the man; "of course not! That's the old cry. You devils never do anything wrong; it's the men that are the bad 'uns. I know all about it."

"And, you, sir," she said, turning to the seaman, "you do not think me guilty. Do you?"

"Guilty of what?" said the watchman.

"Of robbing him," said Louise.

"Hold! That's a confession. You wern't charged with robbing him. But you've put your foot into it now, and no mistake."

"I did not rob you," cried Louise. "I did not indeed."

"Ah, my lass," said the sailor, "I wish I could think so, but you see I can't believe you, for nobody else could have done it. As I said to my friend, the Charley, here, it wasn't the money I cared about, but it was the artful way in which you served me out. If you had said, I want money, you might have had the last penny, as long as all was fair and above board, but to be robbed as I have been, I can't stand that."

"I see it is useless to plead innocence, you will not believe me; but God knows I never wronged you."

"Would that I could think so."

"Oh, come along," said the watchman; "that's enough gab about it."

The sailor no sooner saw the rough handling the watchman gave the unfortunate girl, than he deeply regretted giving her into custody.

"Hang it!" he said, "I didn't mean to serve the girl bad, after all. There is no knowing what might have tempted her to take the money, and it's hard to judge in these matters."

It was too late now to think of releasing her.

He had of his own free will given her into custody, and he had now only to follow out the directions of the officer, into whose hands he had placed his case.

They walked to the nearest station-house, the poor girl sobbing bitterly all the way, and ever and anon protesting her innocence in the most touching manner.

At length she was placed under lock and key, in a cell of the lock-up, there to await the hour at which the magistrate came to deal out justice.

The watchman did not allow the sailor to depart from the station-house, and there was nothing but to await the opening of the court in the room set apart for the use of the watchmen.

At length the hour of eleven struck, and the sailor was told to go into court.

He found his way into the hall of justice, which, in appearance, very much resembled a deserted barrack. There was a raised platform, on which the magistrate sat, in a chair much too large for him. There were benches for the accommodation of the public, and two or three boxes for the cooping up of prisoners, prosecutors, and witnesses.

As soon as the magistrate took his seat he bellowed out to the clerk—"Call the first case."

The clerk did so, and the "first case" proved to be that of a gentleman who had indulged too freely in malt liquors the night before, and had mistaken the gutter for his couch; and, on being called to a consciousness of the fact, paid the Charley for his kindness by punching his head.

This individual was fined and bundled off, and the second, and third, and fourth cases called and disposed of.

Then came that of the mate and Louise.

The officer in charge of the case stepped forward and explained to the clerk that this was a case of robbery by a prostitute.

Poor Louise stepped into the box, and, covering her face with her hands, wept bitterly.

Whereupon the magistrate shouted,—

"Don't make that row."

And the clerk echoed,—

"Don't make that row."

And the officer in charge of the case reiterated, "His worship says you ain't to make that row."

"Now, then," said the magistrate, "who is the prosecutor?"

No one moved.

"Isn't there any prosecutor?"

The officer the in charge of the case here rushed from his box, and catching the sailor by the collar, pulled him into the position usually occupied by prosecutors in that court.

"This is him," said the officer.

"That's the man," said the clerk, rising, and pointing out the sailor to the magistrate, as if the mate had been some minute object, which he had just discovered.

"Oh," said the magistrate, "you are the prosecutor, are you? Why didn't you answer to your name?"

"I never heard my name called," said the seaman.

"Never heard your name? Perhaps, sir, you will say your name was not called."

"I don't see how it could have been, considering nobody here knows it."

"Nobody knows it," repeated the magistrate; "and do you suppose, sir, anybody wants to know it? Answer me that. Do you consider that you are a person of so much importance that this court is dying of curiosity to know your name? Hey?"

The magistrate was in a passion.

He suddenly remembered that the prosecutor had been called, and that no name had been used; he, therefore, hid his error by blustering. He usually did this: in fact, it was, and still is, a common proceeding with a vast number of his brethren.

"Now then, prosecutor, what is your name?" asked the clerk.

"Harry Lanyard."

"Harry Longyarn," repeated the clerk.

"No; Harry Lanyard."

"Why didn't you say so at first?" said the official.

"I did."

"You did not, sir. You said it was Longyarn. I've gotten it written down, and how do you suppose I could have it written down if you hadn't said it?"

Lanyard did not see his way clear to answer this question, and so he held his peace.

"Well, now, sir," continued the clerk, "what are you?"

"Second mate of the Sea Gull."

"Second mate of the sea gull? What's a sea gull?" asked the magistrate.

"Do you hear, sir? His honour asks you what's a sea gull."

"Well, your honour, a sea gull is a jolly great bird as hangs about the coast and feeds on fishes."

"And do you mean to say, sir," said the magistrate, looking awfully important, "do you mean to assert, on your oath, that you are mate of a bird that feeds on fishes?"

The sailor roared outright.

"How dare you laugh, sir? How dare you smile in my presence?"

"Well, I ask your honour's pardon, but there's something so droll in being mate of a bird that feeds on fishes."

"Then, sir, how dare you make such a barefaced, impudent assertion?"

"I never said anything of the kind. I only said I was mate of the Sea Gull."

"Yes, sir; and when asked what was the sea gull, you replied, 'a jolly great bird as hangs about the coast and feeds on fishes.' You have that answer down?"

"Yes," said the clerk.

"Very good," continued the magistrate; "perhaps you will again contradict me? You had better."

"I ask your honour's pardon; I never meant any offence. I should have said that the Sea Gull was a merchant sloop, trading between London and Lisbon."

"Very good, sir; you've taken quite time enough to give that answer. I should advise you to be more careful, or I'll commit you for contempt of court. I will, as true as I sit here!"

"Now," said the clerk, "what name does the prisoner give?"

Louise did not reply.

"What name?" repeated the clerk.

"What name?" cried the officer in charge of the case, roughly shaking the poor girl by the shoulder.

"Louise Graham," sobbed the unhappy woman.

"Never mind, my lass," said the sailor, looking up to the prisoner, "never mind; it will all come right by and bye.'

"What's that?" cried the magistrate; "what's that the prosecutor remarked to the prisoner?"

"He said it would all come right by and bye."

"What does he mean by that?"

"What do you mean by that?"

"I mean nothing, only I don't care about seeing the poor wench take it so much to heart."

"Hold your tongue, sir; what has her taking it to heart to do with you, sir? I'll commit you if you don't mind."

"What are you?" continued the clerk to Louise.

"I have no occupation."

"Yes you have, a very bad one," said the magistrate, looking as if he thought he had said a good thing.

"Where do you live?" continued the clerk.

"I have no home."

"She has no home, your worship."

"Of course she hasn't," said his worship; "they never have."

"Does anybody know her?" continued the clerk.

No one appeared to know her.

"Has she been here before?"

"Never heard of her before," said the chief constable.

"And a good job for her," said the magistrate.

"Now, prosecutor, we will hear your story. You say you are second mate of the Sea Gull, and that you trade between London and Lisbon. Are you married, or single?"

"*Single.*"

"And where does your wife reside?"

"I have no wife."

"What!" said the magistrate, "no wife. How dare you tell me that you are married, and have no wife!"

"I answered, single."

"Married, your worship," cried the clerk, "decidedly married. I have it written down."

"Of course you have. I distinctly heard him say married."

Lanyard really believed that he had committed an error, and again apologised, and once more received a warning.

"Well," continued the clerk, "you say you are single, do you?"

"Yes."

"And where is your home?"

"I have no home."

"No home! That's very important. And now, what do you know of the prisoner at the bar?"

"Nothing."

"Then why did you give her in charge?"

"Because she robbed me."

"You know nothing of her, and yet she robbed you. A very neat contradictory statement. Perhaps you will explain."

"I mean that I know nothing of her beyond the fact of meeting her at a house I entered last night."

"Oh! you know nothing of her beyond the fact of meeting her at a house you entered last night. Where was that house?"

"Somewhere in Soho."

"Somewhere in Soho—a very definite description. Are you aware of the fact that there are a number of houses in Soho?"

"Yes, sir," repeated the magistrate; "are you aware of the fact that there are more houses than one in Soho—streets full of houses? More than one house—more than a thousand houses."

"So I suppose."

"Oh, you suppose so, do you! Well, sir, being aware that there are more than a thousand houses, you will now tell us which of the thousand houses it was."

"I really do not know; I am a stranger to the neighbourhood."

"A stranger to the neighbourhood; ah! we can believe that if we think proper. Now, proceed with your tale."

"Well, the yarn ain't a long 'un, and I can spin it out in no time. Just look here. I was on the loose, and I went to a house of entertainment, and there saw the craft as is brought to anchor in the dry dock above. She appeared to be in trouble, and I ordered something for her, and she seemed as grateful as possible, and I took a downright fancy to her. Well, we passed the night together, and when I opened my eyes in the morning, the craft had sailed, and taken with her all my money and my watch. That's the long and short of it."

"Oh, that's your yarn, is it! Well, where did you find her again?"

"In the streets, where I met her hanging about the corner of a street near the house where I had passed the night."

"Yes," said the clerk; "you saw her in the street and gave her into custody."

"That's the state of the case," said Lanyard.

"Now, officer," continued the clerk, evidently anxious to get the affair over, "what do you know about it?"

"I met the prosecutor at the corner of Great Francis-street, your yourship, and he was a examining of a female that was a walking down another street, and he says to me—"

"Never mind what he said, just confine yourself to what you did."

"Well, he said—"

"Didn't I tell you that we don't want to know

anything about what he said. If he said anything it was his duty to have told us what it was, not yours. Now, in consequence of what the prosecutor communicated to you, you went after the woman, and took her into custody on the charge of robbing him?"

"That's it, your worship," said the officer.

"Very well, you could have said it without any bother, only you officers will be so long-winded."

"Now," said the clerk, "is that the prosecutor's case?"

"That's the case," said the officer.

"What did you find on her?" asked the clerk.

"Nothing."

"Of course not; she had made away with it."

"Perhaps the prosecutor had best ask for a remand," suggested the officer, "in order that we might try and trace the property."

"Trace the property! Trace money—how absurd. No, officer, it's gone—it's gone, and the prosecutor must be content to lose it."

"Now," said the clerk to Louise, "what have you to say in answer to this charge?"

"I can only say that I am innocent."

"Oh; of course. We fully expected you would say that; but what we want to know is whether you can say anything to disprove what has been urged against you?"

"I only know that early this morning I was aroused by parties in the room in which I slept. They were the proprietor of the house and another. They bade me get up and leave the chamber, and this I did; but indeed, indeed, I know nothing more. I never saw the money belonging to the man who now accuses me. Indeed, indeed, I am innocent. I would not have robbed him to save myself from starvation, for his was the first kind face I had looked upon; his were the first words of comfort I had heard for many a long day. He was good to me, sir—oh! I cannot tell you how good! I was perishing for want of food, and he gave me plenty; I was dying for words of sympathy and consolation, and he lavished them upon me. Could I—could I—rob this man?"

The hard-headed, hard-hearted dispenser of justice was moved by this pathetic outburst, and he could not refrain from uttering a word or two of sympathy.

"You appear to be a well educated girl," he said, "a very well educated and well bred girl. How comes it that we find you in this position?"

"I have gone astray, sir; I have left a good home, and have fallen upon a pitiless world. At first I found the life I led all pleasure—all gladness, for then I was associated with only the rich and powerful. But misfortune fell upon me, and I was reduced in circumstances, and had to descend to the house in which I saw the prosecutor. Step by step I have descended downward, until I came here and appear before you, sunk in the very depths of degradation and shame."

"A sad tale—a very sad tale, and I sincerely pity you; but I have a stern duty to perform here, and I am bound to dismiss from my mind all that will prejudice the justice of the case. I am sorry that you do not say anything to clear yourself. Yours is a very slight defence, and I cannot see that it will serve you in the least."

"May I be allowed to say a word?" said Lanyard, "you see, your honour, I did this without thought, and after all I might be wrong and she right. It's just possible that the old shark might have got in in the night and walked off with my money, so it may be as well to set the little craft adrift once more, and may be she'll not get into such queer anchorage again."

"I cannot comply with your request, but I can commit the prisoner to take her trial at the Old Bailey, if you like, that will give you time to search into the case."

"When would she be tried, your honour?"

"In about three weeks."

"And in three days I shall have sailed for Lisbon."

"Then I must deal summarily with the case. Taking the case as it stands I can only see that the prisoner is implicated in this robbery and must not escape justice; but in consideration of this being her first offence, and finding the evidence against her so slight, I think the justice of the case will be met if I commit her to prison for the space of one calendar month."

"Why you don't mean to say you're going to send the girl to gaol?" asked Lanyard, looking in amazement at the magistrate.

"The case is disposed of. Remove the prisoner. What is the next charge?"

Lanyard was about to offer some further indignant protest against the decision of the magistrate, when the officers of the court hustled him from the witness-box, and out of court, before he had the power of saying another word.

"Hillo," he said, when he was in the street, "a pretty d——d mess I've made of this. What did I want to send the poor wench to prison for? Curse me; but I've got her into a nice strait, I have—and she innocent too. I'll stake my life on it. There was'nt a bit of guilt in her face."

He re-entered the court-house, and demanded to know if he could see the girl.

"No," said the officer on duty; "you can't speak to any of the prisoners."

"Then there's nothing for it but to go away," said the man; "but, by Jove, this morning's work will be a thorn in my side for many a long day to come."

Meanwhile Louise was removed half-fainting from the dock, and carried to the lock-up, there to await the arrival of the prison van.

CHAPTER LI.

THE STORY OF LOUISE CONCLUDED—THE PRISON TAINT—THE MEETING WITH PORTMAN.

ONE month in prison!

Louise left the gaol in which she had been

incarcerated a changed woman. Little or nothing of her former self remained.

Her face wore a settled expression of melancholy. Her eye was sunk, and her features were pinched and haggard.

She was a mere wreck.

The month passed slowly and painfully, but at length it came to an end, and she was free.

They dismissed her from prison, ragged, dirty, and penniless.

What was she to do?

There was but one thing—she must beg.

Terrible was the thought to her. How could she ask for alms? No! she could die, but she could not beg.

Adhering to this resolution, she passed two whole days and nights in the streets of London without breaking her fast.

On the third day chance led her into the West-end of London, and passing through the Green Park she found herself in the neighbourhood of St. James's Palace, the place where she had entered at will, but which she could not hope to enter again.

She stood gazing at the grim old pile for some time, watching the guards pace to and fro in the courtyard and at the gates, and then she turned to walk away, when a horseman came out from under one of the arches, and rode slowly towards Pall Mall.

She recognised him—it was Portman.

Actuated by some ungovernable impulse, she ran into the road and stood before the horse.

"Out of the way, woman!" cried Portman, "out of the way! What possesses you to stand there?"

"Do you not know me?" she asked.

"Know you—how should I?"

"And yet we have met very often."

"There is that in your voice methinks I should remember; but I cannot call your face to mind. What is your name?"

"Louise."

"Good God! reduced to this state? What can have befallen you?"

"Listen, and I will tell you. When we parted, after you had robbed me of all I possessed in the world, they spurned me because I had been your mistress; they drove me from the circle in which I had before walked, and sent me to a low den for prostitutes somewhere away in Soho. I was ill, and the few pounds my former patrons gave me were soon expended, and I was threatened with the streets when chance brought to the house a man with whom I passed a night, and who, next morning, accused me of robbing him, and had me imprisoned for a month. Three days ago they released me, as you see me, filthy and penniless. Since I quitted the prison I have not known the taste of food. I am dying of starvation, or I should not have crossed your path."

"What a terrible tale! Take this guinea, and come to my house—here is the address—by-and-bye. I have wronged you, and I will do all I possibly can for you. Stand aside now, and let me pass."

"Go," said Louise, "I will call upon you, as you say you have wronged me, and to you, therefore, I have most right to look for help."

"This evening at eight."

"I will be there."

Portman rode away, and Louise hastened through the park into Westminster."

She entered a dingy-looking shop where second-hand clothes were exhibited for sale, and having purchased a clean dress, she left and sought some house where she could change the one she wore for it.

One of the low lodging houses of the neighbourhood presented the most likely place she could light upon, and entering, she sought and obtained the accommodation she required.

Having broken her long fast she sallied forth again, looking brighter and cleaner, and in St. James's Park passed the time until eight o'clock.

At this hour she hastened to the lodgings of Portman, which were situated within a short distance of St. James's Palace.

Knocking at the door, she asked if Portman was within.

She was instantly admitted.

"Mr. Portman expected a lady to call at eight. Are you the person?"

"Yes."

"Then I will instantly tell him of your arrival."

Next moment Louise was in the presence of the man who had served her so disgracefully.

"Sit down, Louise," he said, "sit down and let us talk. Why, you look a thousand pounds better now than you did when I met you a few hours ago."

"Yes," said the girl, "food tells a wondrous tale. Although what I have eaten has been but coarse and scant fare, it has done me great service."

Portman now demanded to hear the girl's history in full; and, after partaking of a glass of wine, she detailed all those incidents at which she slightly hinted on meeting him a few hours previous.

"A very sad, sad story," said Portman, "when she had concluded her brief history; "a very sad story, indeed. But now let me know how I may serve you. I am better off now than I was, and anything I can do for you I will do with pleasure, for I owe reparation of no slight nature. Shall I find you a good protector?"

The girl started to her feet.

"Not the best in all the world," she cried. "No, no, Heaven knows I have had enough of that life."

"Then what am I to do for you?"

"Find me employment, I care not what the nature; but give me a chance of earning a honest living."

"What! the gay and brilliant Louise work for a living? You must surely jest."

"I never was more serious. I want to earn my bread honestly. I care not if the office I fill be that of a menial, as long as it is not attended by the dishonour I have been so long accustomed to."

"Well, Louisa, the matter will require some consideration. I do not at present know of any situation you require; perchance, I may hear of something to suit you. At all events, I will make every inquiry about the Court, and will grasp at the first opportunity."

"I thank you. Hesitate not to accept for me the first thing that offers. If the employment be that of a scullery wench, I care not."

"I will see that you are better cared for than that. Meanwhile, accept this purse: you will require money."

"No, no," said Louise; "I dare not."

"I will take no denial. Remember, the money is your own."

Louise replied not, and taking the purse from the man's extended hand, dropped it silently into her pocket.

"There is nothing more to say," said Portman, "and so I will bid you good night. In the morning, let me know where I may find you in case I should require you speedily.

Louise bade him good-night, and left the house.

She took lodgings in the immediate neighbourhood, and for a few days saw no more of Portman, who occupied himself in searching for some manner of employment for her.

At length came the advent of Lola at Carlton House, and then Portman hastened to Louise with the offer of the employment about which the Prince had spoken to him.

"I would rather not have gone near him again," she said, "but I have no choice. I will undertake this employment."

The result of this determination is before the reader.

Louise was approved of by the imperious Lola, and gladly assumed the domestic duties entailed upon her position.

The further events of her history will now run in connection with the other characters of our tale.

CHAPTER LII.

MR. GRIMER MEANS BUSINESS — MRS. BOODLES DISPOSED OF—INFORMATION OF A MURDER—WHO WAS SUSPECTED AND ACCUSED—A TERRIBLE BLOW FOR PIPEY.

GRIMER had anticipated some trouble in conveying Mrs. Boodles to the residence of Yellow Maydock in the Minories, for she was a woman of considerable strength, and one who evidently would not mind trying conclusions with those who attempted to molest her.

Fortunately for the plans of the lawyer, the pheasant and the spirits had a very soothing effect on the lady he was bearing away, and she had not been very long in the carriage before she fell into a profound slumber.

The carriage rolled on through the streets, down into the city, past the Fleet Prison, and away in the direction of the Minories.

During the whole of the ride the Boodles moved not, and even when Grimer pulled the check-string, and brought the carriage to a standstill, the slumbers of the good lady continued.

"Now for it," said the lawyer, shaking the old soul, and rousing her out of her sound nap; "now then, my good woman; get out."

"Which I do believe as how I was sound asleep," said the Boodles, rubbing her eyes.

"Well," said the lawyer, "it certainly looked very much like it."

"Which how it came about, if not through the pheasant and them nice sperets, I can't think."

"Come," said the lawyer, "I have stopped the carriage some little distance from your house, and we must walk the remainder of the way."

"With all my heart, sir; but I don't know why I should trouble you to go any further, seeing that I well know my way, which good you are to have come all this distance with me."

Mrs. Boodles now stepped out of the carriage, and gazed wildly about her.

"Which of this is Soho," she said; "I must be dreaming."

Grimer dismissed the carriage, and turned his attention to Mrs. Boodles.

"This is a by-lane known to but few people," he said; "come, I will take you to your house in no time."

"Well," said Mrs. Boodles, "I suppose you know more about it than I do, but I must say that after all the years I have lived in the neighbourhood it does appear strange I should not know where I am."

"You are, perhaps, a little confused," said Grimer; "but come along, I will soon put you right."

"I dare say you will sir; for whether it's the pheasant or whether it's the sperets—which beautiful they was as ever I tasted—my poor head do seem so confused you can't think."

They hurried on.

Grimer took the unsuspecting woman by various turns into that street in which was situated the house of Maydock.

He hurried her towards the door of this disreputable place of abode, and then asked her if she had any objection to wait while he made a short call on a friend of his.

"No," said Mrs. Boodles, "not as long a it is a short call. But I can't wait long, for the poor captain will be expecting me, which where I'm gone to must be a puzzle to him of the darkest dye."

"I will not detain you long if you will step in, but the visit is one of some importance."

He knocked at the door, and next moment it was opened by Maydock in person.

"What brings you here?" he asked of Grimer.

Grimer, by a signal, gave him to understand that he was to hold his peace; and next moment the victim was within the portal, and caught in a trap.

The lawyer could not suppress a chuckle of satisfaction at his own cleverness.

"Show the lady into a room for a few minutes," he said; "I wish to speak with you alone."

"Very well," said Maydock, opening the door of his front room, and admitting Mrs. Boodles, who looked about her in amazement; for the scene was one to which she was unaccustomed, and the appearance of Maydock, which was the reverse of prepossessing.

The door was closed on the woman, and the two men went into an adjoining apartment.

"Now, then," said Maydock; "what's in the wind now?"

"Listen to me, and be sure and act upon my words."

Grimer briefly related the story of the death of the Duke of Grasmount, and exposed the plan he intended pursuing in order to implicate Pipey in the deed.

"I see," said Maydock! "I see. You want this old bird well looked after. By Jove! she would be a dangerous witness to have in the box."

"She would; and therefore must be kept as close as possible."

"Then she musn't stop here."

"Where do you mean to take her?"

"To a house I know down the river, below Purfleet. She will be safe there, if I can only get her down."

"Heed not the expense; here is money for you. She must be got out of the way, and kept dark."

"The best way to keep her dark would be to cut her throat."

"That would do if it was our own job, but, you see, it is that of the Duchess. If this woman is not kept hanging over her as a terror, she might turn round upon us—and I have seen such a thing done before now."

"You are right. I know my work, and you may trust me to do it."

"I think I may. Ha! ha! we were rivals once, and wanted to cut each other's throats, but we know better—we know better now."

"Yes," said Maydock, "we know better now."

Inwardly, however, he muttered a deep curse, and smarted under the memory of that fearful encounter on the bridge, on the night of the Marlborough House ball.

"Well," said Grimer, "now that we understand each other, I will go. You will see me to-morrow."

"Where shall we meet?"

"At my office."

"I will be there."

"Aye, come and report what you have done, and I may have news for you. I am now going to Newgate; I have some friends there, and I must give them a hint of what has been done to-night, and put them on the scent of this boy, who has so long and successfully baffled us."

"I wish you all success."

"Aye, fear nothing, I shall succeed. Good-night, and be careful!"

"Good-night!"

The lawyer left the house.

"Well, now, for this old woman. Deuce take it! I don't know what to do with her. I suppose, though, the best thing to do is to give her some of this."

He poured from a small phial a few drops of a white liquid on a cloth, and folding it carefully walked into the front room.

"Well," he said to Mrs. Boodles, "how are you feeling now?"

"Which I'm obliged to you for the asking, but I'm rayther uncomfortable, having a wish to get home as soon as possible, and not quite understanding where I am, and what the meaning of all this is."

"So I should suppose."

"And where is my friend the old gentleman is what I would like to know?"

"If you mean the man who brought you here, he's gone."

"Gone!"

"Yes, gone."

"Then all I have to say is, that if he calls himself a gentleman I never seed one."

"You're about right, old girl; there's not much of the gentleman about old Grimer; of that you may take your oath. However, it's no use talking on that score. D'ye know where you are?"

"Which I believe, sir, I am in the neighbourhood of Soho."

"No you arn't."

"Then perhaps you will have the goodness to tell me *where* I am."

"With all my heart. You are in that well-known resort of the thieves of London, known as the Minories."

"In the Minories? Why, how did I come here?"

"That you ought to know. I didn't bring you, you may be sure of that."

"Oh!" said Mrs. Boodles, a light suddenly breaking in upon her, "oh! mercy me, what a fool I was to to fall asleep in that carriage. I'm a lost woman! I've been deceived by a gang of robbers, and they've brought me here to murder me."

"Not quite so bad as that."

"Oh! sir," said the Boodles, "you ain't a going to rob and murder me, are you? which it ain't much good, for except two two-penny pieces, a nutmeg, a thimbles, and a knuckle bone, which good it is for the rheumatics, I haven't anything at all about me."

"Bah!" cried Maydock: "we want nothing of you but silence."

"Which I'm proud to hold my tongue and take my leave," said the old lady, rising and making for the door.

"No you don't," said the robber, rising, and standing in her path.

"Murder!" cried the old woman.

"Silence!" said Maydock, fiercely, "silence! or it may be the worse for you. Hark ye! You are my prisoner. You know that which you have no right to know, and therefore must remain under my safe keeping."

"I don't understand," said the good old soul, terrified beyond measure, "I don't understand you. I know nothing—I never did you or anybody else any harm. For God's sake let me go."

"Do not deceive yourself," said Maydock; "you pass not the threshold of this door to-night."

"I'll scream the house down."

"You had best not try, or I'll knock your brains out against the wall."

The old woman staggered back aghast.

Maydock hereupon advanced towards her, and drawing from his pocket the cloth on which he had poured the drug, bound it closely over her mouth rnd nostrils.

For a few seconds she struggled violently. and then her head drooped, and she sank back passively into a chair, insensible.

"That's over," said Maydock, "and now to place her in the old attic. They won't hear her there if she chooses to cry out, which I scarcely think she will do."

Mrs. Boodles was a woman of great weight, and Maydock had great difficulty in moving her, but he was a man of immense power, and although he staggered under his burthen, he contrived at length to reach the attic.

He threw the unconscious woman on the rough couch once occupied by Liz, and there left her.

The old attic appeared more gloomy than ever; during the periods of Maydock's incarceration and long absences the house had been solely looked after by the old crone who acted as his housekeeper, and since the night of Pipey's attack upon her throat she had been little better than an imbecile.

Four years had told sadly upon her.

The few teeth she had had fallen from her head, her eyes were bleared, her hand was palsied, her memory and powers of hearing had gone, and her form was a mere shadow.

She lay night and day in her attic, seldom crawling over the stairs for food, and contenting herself with what Maydock chose to bring her.

She was filthy, and an object of disgust; and it was sad that the grave did not open to receive her.

On earth she was but an eye-sore.

Maydock, however, took but little heed of her. If she died she died, and if she lived she might shift for herself.

She was nothing to him but a dead weight about his neck, and he heartily wished her numbered with the dead.

Such was now the house and household of the thief.

*   *   *   *   *

Grimer bent his steps towards Newgate.

Arrived at the prison, he found means to effect an entrance, and straightway sought the house of one of the officials—a thieftaker of great note.

This worthy had retired to rest, but Grimer took the liberty of awaking him.

He entered his chamber without ceremony, and shaking him roughly by the shoulder, called to him to wake.

"Hillo ! Dan Haggis," he cried; "hillo, here ! wake up!"

"What's the matter?" asked Dan, rising up in his bed, and looking at the lawyer.

"Matter enough, my boy, as you will find out, by and by. Here, while you are asleep in your bed, murder is committed, and the perpetrators escaping."

"Murder ! What d'ye mean, Grimer ?"

"As I came through Soho I heard some sounds of a murder being done in the house of Pipey, the Government spy."

"Indeed ! What does this mean, hey ?"

"You're dark ?"

"Yes, we can trust one another."

"Well, then, as yet no one knows of this but myself. I shan't say who told me about it—suffice it I know the circumstance ; and, thought I, this is a rare opportunity for Dan, for Dan hates this pet of the Government, who grabs all the big rewards, and shoulders better and more deserving men out of 'em."

"So he does, so he does."

"Well, then, when the little bird whispered to me that this murder had been done in his house, and that neither he nor his housekeeper were to be found, I thought my old friend Dan might like to be made aware of the circumstance, so that he can make his name, and gratify his spite against Pipey at the same time."

"Good, old boy ; I see your drift. You know more of this than you mean to tell ; but never fear me, I'll keep your secret for you, and am only too much obliged to you for your kindness in coming here."

"I knew you would be—I knew you would be."

"But I say, between ourselves, is this fellow Pipey really in it ?"

"Hang me if I don't believe he's the real culprit."

"Honour ?"

"Honour ; and you will see that there's something very suspicious about it when I tell you that the victim is no less a person than the Duke of Grasmount."

"My eyes ! the Duke of Grasmount found murdered in Pipey's house: that is a go."

"It is ; but now I must leave you, and have only to caution you to act with care. You're playing against a clever hand."

"I know I am, but you shall see I'm as good as he at a pinch."

"Very well, I trust in you; so now, good night."

"Good night, and be assured I'm on the *qui vive*."

Grimer left his friend, and ere long the thief-taker was dressed, and selecting one of his men to accompany him, set out in the direction of Pipey's abode.

*   *   *   *   *

It is now necessary that we look after Pipey, who, it will be remembered, we left in the street in which his own house was situated, receiving a communication from one of his own men.

"Where is Mortlake ?" asked Pipey, as he walked away in company with the man.

"At his own house."

"Let us hurry, then; for I have important business at home."

"What is up ?"

"Nothing in which you are concerned."

"All right," said the man ; but he did not much relish this answer, and for the remainder of the distance—Mortlake lived in Holborn—they maintained a perfect silence.

Pipey heard from his assistant that a serving man of the Duchess was dogging him night and day, and the subordinate wished to receive the orders of the superior in reference to it.

Pipey treated the affair very coolly, and told his men to keep sharp watch.

After giving some orders of a miscellaneous character, he quitted the house, and proceeded to retrace his steps towards his home.

He had arrived within two hundred yards of his own door, when two figures darted from under the shadow of some houses, and throwing a cloak over his head, bore him to the earth.

A carriage here readily drove up from a bye street, and into this Pipey was thrust.

"Release me," he cried: "Release me! What have I done to be treated thus?"

"You will know all in good time."

"At least tell me into whose hands I have fallen."

"I am the Black Captain, whom you have so often braved!"

CHAPTER LIII.

A MEETING AND RECOGNITION—SUSPICIONS—THE WIFE'S TEARS—THE AVENGER.

VENICE!

At length Lord and Lady Lovelace were once more enjoying the delights to be found in the far-famed "City of Song."

Venice! With what different feelings did husband and wife regard its familiar scenes.

Lovelace could only think of the hours of wretchedness he had passed there with Marie.

His wife could only call to mind the happiness she experienced in believing herself the well-loved relative of the Duchess.

Lovelace pointed out to his wife the spots from

which he had watched her leave and enter her hotel. He told her of all the agony he had endured whilst she was in the city, and of the impracticability of his remaining there after she had quitted it. He spoke of love, and in unmistakeable loving tones; but they fell all but unheeded on the ear of her who listened to them.

She could only think that he had loved and had lived with another. That there was a child springing from that intimacy, and that he had deceived her.

It was the deceit that galled!

Lovelace could not fail to see that his wife regarded him coldly.

He could not shut his eyes to the fact that she regretted the union she had formed, and this preyed upon his mind.

Did he love her?

He asked himself this question very frequently, and would have persuaded himself that his heart answered in the affirmative: but there were moments when doubts crossed his mind, and he thought that, after all, admiration was the only passion with which he was inspired.

He seemed to regard her as a beautiful picture or statue that he had desired to possess, because all men thought it so rare.

But having it, the same feelings failed to agitate him.

He pressed her to his bosom, but there was no sympathetic beating of the heart.

He kissed her lips, but felt not a return. There she was! His! His own—with him day and night. His by law; his by the sacred tie—but not his in heart.

No love seemed to bind them together.

Lovelace thought of the deep passion and wild raptures of Marie.

And Liz thought of the persevering devotedness of her early friend.

"I must have loved Marie," Lovelace would say to himself. "Yes, that was love, but I mistook the passion."

"I never loved this man," was the constant thought of Liz; "or, if I did, it was love without respect. Ah! he is so different to the man who, for years and years, has devoted his whole life and energies to my welfare. It is he I should have married."

Two beings, bound together till parted by death—feeling as they felt, actuated by the thoughts and impulses that swayed them—were not likely to live in any peace or happiness; and, truth to tell, the shadow had already seemed to fall upon them, and their lives were darkened by a cloud.

Pity 'twas they ever met.

Lovelace engaged, in the most fashionable quarter of the city, the best house he could procure, and herein he took up his quarters.

As soon as possible he made inquiries in the neighbourhood of his old villa concerning Marie, and satisfying himself that she was no longer likely to molest him, he began to enjoy something like peace of mind.

He was a man whose tastes led him frequently into society, and enjoyment was the first thought of his life.

He soon formed a circle of acquaintances, and his time was principally passed out of doors.

He would have induced his wife to accompany him, but she declined, feeling, as she said, no inclination for the gaieties of the city.

"But," urged the husband, on the occasion of his presenting her with an invitation to a fashionable dinner party, "but you must conquer this indifference to society. As Lady Lovelace you must appear more frequently in public, and live as becomes the lady I have married."

"I shall follow my own inclinings," replied the wife, "and shall endeavour to judge for myself what best becomes your wife. It is not my will and pleasure to go abroad; therefore press me not on the subject."

"But you cannot always continue thus. You must act as becomes your position first or last, and why not now?"

"I have yet to learn that I am doing aught unbecoming my position."

"I did not say you were; I merely ask you to go into society with me."

"And I wish to be left in retirement, as my health and spirits will not admit of my enduring any excitement."

"Your spirits were not used to be so low?"

"No."

"You are then dissatisfied with your lot?"

"No."

"I am not what you imagine me to be. By some means I have forfeited your esteem."

"Have you forfeited your own?"

Lovelace replied not.

"At all events," he said, after a pause, "you will oblige me by coming with me this evening?"

"Not this evening."

"But a great musician—the first of the Italian school of vocalists—has promised to be present. You would like to hear her."

"Perhaps so; but in an hour I shall be listening to a voice as sweet as that of any Italian that ever warbled."

"What do you mean?"

"Simply that, as soon as the stars rise in the clear blue vault of Heaven, a young girl, in the garb of an Italian peasant, comes under my window and sings to me."

"Indeed!"

"Yes, such a beautiful voice I have seldom listened to, even in the best of our theatres."

"No uncommon occurrence here. The best singers of the country are found among the itinerant musicians. Well, you are not to be tempted to-night?"

"No, I prefer remaining at home."

"Oh! Then I will remain as well, for I care not to go without you."

He threw off his hat, and sat in his chair near the window.

"You had best go," said Liz; "let not my disinclination for company interfere with you."

"I care not to go without you. Besides, I feel some curiosity to hear the singer of whom you speak so highly."

"You will soon be satisfied, for it is now near the hour at which she usually comes."

Lord Lovelace took up a book and commenced reading, and Liz occupied herself with her own thoughts.

Night stole on them unawares, and ere Lovelace

dropped his book the firmament was filled with stars.

They were aroused by the notes of a guitar.

"Hark!" said Liz. "Hark! my mistress is here."

"Ah! then I shall have a treat, no doubt."

"Indeed you will. Bring chairs into the balcony and listen to her."

Lovelace took two chairs from the room and placed them on the balcony.

Liz threw a shawl over her shoulders, and stepped out into the air. Lovelace followed her.

They seated themselves, and Liz hung over the balcony to get a glimpse of her songstress. Lovelace leaned back in his chair, and awaited the song of the strolling musician.

In a few moments a voice of extreme sweetness filled the air.

No sooner did the first notes reach the ear of Lovelace than he sprang to his feet and uttered the word

"Marie!"

The movement and the voice reached the girl below the balcony, and ceasing, she threw her instrument over her shoulder, and, uttering "It is he—it is Lovelace!" rushed from the spot.

Liz looked on in amazement, and for some minutes spoke not.

After a while she rose to her feet and re-entered the apartment.

Lovelace followed.

"I see," said the wife, "I see you have discovered an old acquaintance."

"Oh! speak not of her. I cannot bear to hear her mentioned. Have I not suffered enough through her?"

"Had you not best follow her, and ascertain how fares your child?"

"Oh, do not drive me mad!"

"Drive you mad!—heaven and earth! You mad! Is it not I who have most cause to talk thus?"

"Spare me!—spare me!"

"Have you spared me?"

"I dare not listen to you!"

Lovelace caught up his hat and rushed into the street.

"Oh, Heaven!" he cried, "why, oh, why am I thus persecuted?"

He walked rapidly through the street, and, turning a sharp angle, came full against the strolling musician.

"Marie!" he cried, "why are you here?—why have we again met?"

"Ask yourself that question. I did not seek our meeting, you may be well assured."

"You have ruined me."

"I understand. The lady on the balcony was your wife."

"Yes."

"Ah! It is well I know it."

"Wherefore?"

"Because she is my victim. I shall wreak my revenge upon her."

"Upon the innocent! Heaven forbid!"

"I trace my misery to her. Had she not come to Venice, you would not have dreamed of leaving me, and I—and I should not have come to what I am."

"What mean you?"

"I mean that I am a hunted criminal—a blood-stained woman hiding from the Inquisition; I mean that the only mode I have of seeing the world, of breathing the air of Heaven, of hearing my own voice—is by adopting this guise, and stealing forth at nightfal as you have seen me. And to think—to think that chance should have led me to your door."

"Marie! Marie! you are mad! You cannot mean what you say; or, if there be truth in your words, I pray you reflect, and govern your dark passions. What do you here, being in such extreme danger? Why do you not fly?"

"Fly! Whither?"

"Anywhere beyond the reach of justice."

"Shall I tell you?—I will! It is because my child is here. Ah, they have taken my babe from me, and I know not where to find it. They told me I should see it no more, and they would have had me wander over the face of the earth without it, alone and uncared for. I could not do it. Day and night I pray of them to restore my child to me, but they only mock my anguish, and bid me begone without it—and I cannot, I cannot!"

"Poor girl!"

"Poor girl. Ah, you pity me! you, who have brought me to this—for you have brought me to this: you dare not deny it. I was better when my child was born to me. My whole nature changed; I was at peace, and then you turned from me. I saw that you loved me not, and that your whole soul was devoted to another. It drove me mad. It made me the fiend I have become."

"But, Marie, I will do all I can to atone."

"What atonement can you make? They want to drag me to death. They have stolen my darling—my only treasure—from me, and you are married to another. What, I ask—what atonement can you now make?"

"I will see you properly cared for."

"You mean you will give me more money. What use to me has been all I have received from you? How can I expend it? All I require is peace of mind, and that you cannot purchase with money. Your gold will not cleanse my soul of its guilt—it will not bring back to me my little child."

"Oh, merciful Heaven, that I should have lived for this moment."

"You feel it, and I am glad of it; but you have not yet felt all. Wait, and experience the fate that is in store for you!"

"What mean you?"

"Mean that I have registered an oath of vengeance, that is now working against thee, and all those of your cold land who have been instrumental in my ruin. I mean that your hour of bitter trial is not yet come."

"Pursue this fiend-like vengeance no further. Let me entreat—let me implore!"

"What you will, but I listen not."

"Marie, Marie!"

He called upon her in vain.

She was gone.

He returned moodily to his house.

"Yes," he said, "I must quit this place at once. I was mad to have returned to it. Mad—mad—mad."

He entered his home, and sought the apartment of his wife.

He found her bathed in tears.

"Lady Lovelace," he said, as soon as he could find words to utter, "Lady Lovelace, I am come to bid you prepare to leave this place at once."

"Wherefore?"

"After what has passed I dare no longer remain here."

"Must I, then, fly from my rival?"

"You must fly from your *enemy* and mine. If we remain here danger will come of it."

"You may go. I shall remain."

"Go without you?"

"Without me!"

"I could not dream of such a thing."

"But you will have to reconcile yourself to do this. I remain."

"For what purpose?"

"To learn the history of the past; to learn the character of the man I have tied myself to."

"You are mad to do this, and I pray of you not to persist in such a course."

"I shall do as I have said."

"In that case, naught will induce me to leave you. I have warned you of your danger; and if you will not fly from it, I must remain and protect you."

"As you will. I care not whether you go or stay, for henceforth we are nothing to each other."

"Lady Lovelace!"

"I have spoken."

"But you will not thus cast me from you."

"I am not to blame. For what has transpired you have only yourself to blame."

"I know it; but you need not make my torture so great by your cruel words and acts."

"I can never again use other words to you, and my acts must be governed by yours."

"Oh! have you no mercy? What have I done to you that you will not spare me?"

"What have you not done?"

"I cannot speak."

"Then I have no desire to prolong the interview. Good night."

"Whither go you?"

"To cool my fevered brow in the night air."

"There is danger in the streets."

"No matter."

"I pray you, do not quit the house."

"I cannot hear your objections to my going; I presume you fear my meeting with your concubine?"

"Oh, Lady Lovelace! such words do not become you."

She stopped not to reply. Running down the stairs, she left the house.

CHAPTER LIV.

"THERE IS A DIVINITY THAT DOTH SHAPE OUR ENDS, ROUGH HEW THEM AS WE MAY."

IN a wretched hovel, near a spot we will call the Angelo Bridge of the Canal, lived the old gitana, the granddam of Marie.

She was seated before a scant fire, flickering feebly in an old and rusty stove, when a knock was heard at her door, and a man entered.

"Ah! it is you, Phillipe, is it?"

"Yes, it is."

"Well, have you determined?"

"Yes. Behold!"

He drew aside his cloak, and in his arms was discovered a little child.

"You see I have at last taken your advice, and brought the brat."

"Ah! you have done well; but you would do better if, instead of forcing me to take it to Carlshoof, the chief of our tribe, you would consent to my dashing it into the canal."

"Never! The child is innocent, and not answerable for the sins of the parent. I will, therefore, suffer death before any harm shall befal it. I risked my life to save it from a watery grave, and I would have it live to years of maturity—"

"That the blood coursing through its veins may lead it into the sins in which its mother has been steeped, in which I have seen my own child dyed, and into which it must inevitably sink if it lives."

"I do not agree with you."

"But I know I am right. The curse of Heaven is upon it, and against that it will struggle in vain. It were an act of vengeance and a deed of kindness to put it out of the world."

"But I forbid it. The child *shall* be taken to Carlshoof."

"Very well, very well, leave it with me."

Phillipe stripped off his cloak, and, throwing it on the dirty board of the hovel, contrived to make a tolerably comfortable bed for the little one.

He laid down his burthen carefully, and stood gazing at it with every sign of affection.

"Poor little one?" he said; "poor bird! you little know what the future has in store for you. It may be that it were best you died now; but that shall not be with my consent. Through life those pale blue eyes would haunt me, and drive me mad. To the grave I should bear with me the memory of thy little voice and cheering smile. Oh! powers of mercy guard and protect thee!"

"Psha!" said the gitana, rising, and looking with disdain upon the young man; "is this your vengeance—is this the way your anger falls upon those who have robbed you of the treasure you professed to value so much? Your's is the passion of the school-boy, who talks of vengeance as if it were a toy, until he comes face to face with it, and then the aspect of affairs changes, and he slinks away, affrighted to think that he had taken so many liberties with the name of a thing so terrible."

"Put me before a man," cried Phillipe, "let

me have an enemy worthy my prowess, equal to me in position and strength, and then see if I slink away from my oath. But if vengeance means shedding the blood of little children, I must own that I both dread and fear it."

"You are a fool to talk thus. Vengeance means the extermination of one whole race of foes—men, women, and children, are alike included. Sweep the whole race from the earth—leave no trace behind—and then thou shalt say thou hast had vengeance!"

"I never listened to words so terrible coming from a woman."

"I do not doubt you, for there are but few women who have had such occasion as I have to use such words. Oh! I am at war with the whole human family! I have been robbed of all that could make life tolerable to me; and all who are but a shade happier than myself I can only look upon with hatred."

"I fear I do wrong in leaving the child with you. I will take it with me."

"No, no; I will see your wish is obeyed. It shall go to Carlshoof."

"You speak earnestly, and I cannot but believe you. I will leave the child."

"Do so. I will start with it to the mountains an hour after midnight."

"Adieu, then. We shall meet in the camp?"

"Aye! in the camp."

*   *   *   *   *

Phillipe walked rapidly over the Angelo Bridge, to gain the opposite side of the canal, in the neighbourhood of which was situated his own house.

He had not reached the door when a female hurried from under the shadow of some houses near at hand, and seized him by the arm.

"It is I, Marie," said the woman.

"What madness is this? Are you not afraid of the fate in store for you should you fall into the hands of the Inquisitors?"

"Yes; but I could not longer remain in the old house. I felt as if I were going mad. I wanted air, and I adopted this means of getting it."

"It is a means that will place your life at the disposal of the officers of justice."

"No matter; I care not."

"Care not. What! are your hopes of vengeance burnt out? Are you no longer actuated by the hatred you so recently bore your enemies?"

"Aye, and more fiercely than ever. It is on that theme I would talk with you. It is that subject I have waited here to canvas with you."

"What have you to say?"

"Much. They are here."

"To whom do you refer?"

"To whom but Lovelace and his wife."

"Indeed!"

"Aye, indeed."

"What do you propose doing?"

"Is it for me to propose aught?"

"You are right, it is I who must act. They must both die."

"And is this the vengeance you contemplate? Oh, fool! death to them would be happiness.

Torture, torture! That is the vengeance I must have."

"Do they love each other?"

"How am I to tell you that? I presume such to be the case."

"Then the first movement must be to separate them."

"Aye, that is sure. Let them yearn for each other; and let their hearts bleed in solitude and separation. I know the agony, and can wish them no more punishment."

"She must be carried off."

"Whither?"

"To the mountains. I can induce Carlshoff, the gipsy, to receive her."

"And he."

"Fear not for him. I will be upon his track night and day."

Marie told Phillipe in what place he could find Lovelace and his lady, and promising to meet again on the morrow at the same time, they separated, Phillipe urging her to seek her own home, and not to quit it again under any pretence.

*   *   *   *   *

Lady Lovelace, distracted in mind, and sick at heart, wandered about the streets of Venice as one in a dream.

Chance guided her footsteps, and after walking for more than two hours, she found herself in the neighbourhood of the Angelo Bridge.

For some time she occupied herself in looking into the clear sky above and the silent stream beneath her.

From the reverie into which she had fallen she was aroused by what appeared to her to be the faint cry of an infant.

She started, and gazed about her.

It was very light, and she could see for a considerable distance.

Approaching her was an old woman, who held something in her arms.

Lady Lovelace drew into a niche of the bridge, and stood so as to conceal herself from view.

It would have been difficult for her to have explained her act, but instinctively she felt that something wrong was afoot.

Slowly the old woman hobbled on, and at last came to a standstill just by the spot where Lady Lovelace lay concealed.

"I cannot do it," said the woman, who was no other than the gitana; "I cannot obey him. I would as soon protect the young of the tigress that had torn me."

"It must and shall die. There is no one at hand: all is still as death. No better opportunity will occur. Nay, then, let it down in the dark waters beneath."

She held up the mewling babe she carried, and advanced to the parapet of the bridge.

"In!" she cried, "in, and die with the curse of the gitana upon thee!"

The infant was sprawling above her head, and in another moment would have been struggling for life in the canal, when Lady Lovelace sprang forward, and snatched the innocent victim from her grasp.

The hag started back; and, then, finding herself opposed only by a woman, drew her knife, and made a rush at the young girl.

"Back," cried Lady Lovelace, "back, or I will call for aid, and have you arrested for attempt at murder."

"Fool!" cried the hag, incapable of governing her wrath; "fool, I will have your heart's blood before the hand of man can rescue thee."

She sprang forward with the leap of a tigress; and, nimble as Liz was, she could not avoid the blow aimed at her.

The knife fell upon her arm, and inflicted a severe wound.

Thinking more of the safety of the infant than of herself, she turned and fled, crying loudly for help.

The old hag hobbled after her; but she was not sufficiently nimble to catch the younger woman, wounded as she was.

At the foot of the bridge Liz ran into the arms of a woman, who was advancing.

"Take the child," she said; "take the child. See! she comes—she comes! She will murder it."

The woman was Marie!

She did not recognise Lady Lovelace nor the infant; but, prompted by some feelings of humanity, she did as she was told.

"What has happened?" she asked.

"I know not—I know not. The old hag who advances attempted to drown the infant. I snatched it from her and fled, but not before she had stabbed me. Fly with the child. Fly!"

"But I cannot leave you thus; you faint."

"Yes, yes! but it matters little for me. Oh! for the love of Heaven, save the infant."

"And thee, too. Summon a little strength, my house is close at hand. Quick, or she will be upon thee!"

Thus urged, the lady staggered after Marie, and was soon in the house with her.

The hag, seeing that her intended victim was joined by some one, stopped short, and watched them from a distance.

Her sight failed her, and, not being able to distinguish that the new comer was a woman, and her own grandchild, she thought it wise to stand at bay rather than advance.

Meanwhile, the two women closed and locked the door of the house they had entered.

"Be not afraid," said the Italian, "the house is old and deserted, but no harm will befall you here."

"I am not afraid."

"Follow me, then. Hold my dress, we must mount the stairs—they are old, and unsafe to one who knows them not."

"Thanks."

"Come, come, it is only a short distance to the top, and there I will find a light. Poor babe! poor babe! do not weep!"

They mounted the stairs, and, opening a door, Marie led the lady into a chamber.

"Stand there," she continued, "stand there a moment, and I will find a light."

By the aid of a tinder a light was obtained, and in a few seconds an oil lamp was blazing on the table.

Simultaneous the two women confronted each other.

They started back in mutual astonishment.

"His wife," cried Marie!

"It is the singer," said Lady Lovelace, dropping into a chair.

"Powers of mercy!" cried Marie; "what could have directed me to your aid?"

Lady Lovelace spoke not.

Turning for an instant from her rival, the eye of Marie lighted upon the babe she held in her arms.

With a wild shriek she held up the child close to her eyes.

She then passed her hand over its features, and cried—

"Yes, yes; it is real—it is no dream—my own babe!"

"Your child."

"Yes, yes; my child. Tell me, tell me, how you came by it."

"I have already said I snatched it from an old hag, who was about to toss it into the canal."

"Yes, yes. What was she like? How was she dressed?"

"She was very aged and hideous, and wore the costume of the Zingari."

"Oh, Heaven! My own granddam."

"Powers of goodness, forgive her."

"Hell take her, say I, unfeeling hag that she is. My own babe," said the mother, tenderly regarding her offspring, with eyes brimming over with love and joy, "my own darling babe. Do I hold thee to my heart once more?"

The child seemed to remember its parent, for it ceased crying, and nestled close to her bosom.

"Ah, my child knows me. Look, look; see how it clings to me; is it not love, is it not love?"

"Yes," said Liz, faintly, "yes; but I faint for want of air—I drop to the earth. Oh! the blood is still flowing from my wound. I must seek aid."

For a moment the Italian regarded the poor English girl with a fixed stare, in which hatred was strongly marked, but then a better feeling possessed her. The feeling that the woman before her had not even wronged her in thought, would present itself to her, and, above all, she could not forget that to her she owed the life of her child.

"I will aid you," she said, laying the child on a couch; "I will aid you, although till this moment I regarded you as my bitterest foe, and thirsted for your blood."

Liz fell back fainting, and the Italian busied herself in restoring her to life.

"Poor girl," she said, regarding her rival with a look of commiseration; "the knife of the Zingara has done its work; the wound is deep and dangerous. And to think it was in rescuing my child from death! *His* child! How inscrutable are the ways of Heaven!"

The wound was bound up, and in a short time Lady Lovelace opened her eyes again.

" You are better?" asked Marie.

" Yes, much better."

" I am glad of that."

" I think I can walk home now. I wish you a good night!"

She rose from her seat, but immediately fell back again in a complete state of exhaustion.

" Oh!" she continued, " this is dreadful. I cannot walk—I cannot move."

" No matter, you are safe here. I will attend to you. You saved my child—can I do too much for you ?"

" The child—is it uninjured ?"

" Yes."

" Thank Heaven for that !"

" You thank Heaven! Do you know whose child you have saved ?"

" Yes, too well."

" And you thank Heaven that you have been the means of rescuing it ?"

" Why should I not do so ?"

" Because its mother was your rival."

" I know it."

" And you do not hate me ?"

" Heaven forbid !"

The Italian looked at her rival in utter astonishment.

" Oh!" she cried, " oh, that I had been thus good. Oh! that I could feel towards her as she feels towards me."

" And why should you have other feelings towards me than those I hold towards you. I never wronged you."

" True. But you have twice crossed my path, and were it not for you I should not be the thing you behold me. As soon as the Prince saw you I was discarded. I then found Lovelace. I saved his life, and I grew to love him. We lived here happily together. This dear child was born to us, and very fast all the evil in my nature was disappearing when you once more came in my way. You know your spell around the father of my child, and he cared for me no longer. He cruelly deserted me for you. Is not this sufficient cause to make me hate you ?"

" But I tell you that, not until after I was tied to Lovelace was I aware of his intimacy with you. Oh! would to God I had known it. I should then have been spared many many hours of wretchedness."

" You do not love him, then ?"

" I fear not."

" Strange !"

" It is. But the heart often leads us astray. He came to me when I was poor, nameless, persecuted; his voice was full of sympathy and love, and I listened to him with a rapture to which I had heretofore been a stranger. Before I had time to know him I loved him. Then came a long separation, and when I saw him again, I found that the same feeling possessed me, and I formed a hasty union. Oh, that Heaven had prevented it, for it was a fatal error! It was gratitude and admiration I felt for him — not love, not love. Now that I am bound to him for life, I am painfully conscious of my mistake."

" Then you love another ?"

Lady Lovelace blushed crimson and replied not.

" I know that such must be the case, for gratitude and admiration are so akin to love that one who had never felt the true passion would not know the difference between them."

" You may speak truly."

" I know I speak the truth, for I am skilled in the mysteries of the human heart, and can read them easily. But you are too ill to talk; in the next room you will find a couch; rest until the morrow; you cannot quit this house to-night—it would be unsafe."

Liz would have attempted to go, but when she stood upon her feet her head swam round, and she fell back into her seat.

Seeing her helpless condition, Marie placed her arms about her waist, and carried her to the sleeping-room.

She gently laid her upon the couch, and regarded her attentively.

" I never wronged you," she said, repeating the words of Lady Lovelace; " I never wronged you. No lady, no, it is true. Your wounds have been inflicted unintentionally, and one less vicious than myself, would imprint a sisters' kiss upon your fair brow, but I am all evil. There is no spark of goodness in me, and I turn from you with the old fire burning in my bosom. Heaven help me! I never before knew how terrible a being I am. Sleep on, sleep the sleep of peace and innocence. Would that I could!—would that I could!"

She turned away, and burst into tears.

" No comfort for me," she said, " no comfort for me. Oh! would that I was dead."

She entered the room she had just quitted, and snatching up her child, she hugged it to her bosom.

" At least, you will love me; at least, you do not shudder at me; but the day may come when you will do so."

A sudden thought flashed across her brain.

" If they should come," she cried, " oh! if they should come, and snatch thee from me. I dare not stay here. No, no. This is no place for me. I must fly, or they will tear thee even from my bosom, and slaughter thee before my eyes. Oh! cling to me, and we will go far away. Far away, and never return. But his wife!" She tore from a drawer a piece of paper, and wrote these lines upon it.

" To Phillipe Mourlavife.

" Heaven has restored my babe to me. I fly to save it from thee. Beneath this roof sleeps the wife of Lovelace. Spare her! I do not hate her as I thought I did. She has softened my heart towards her by rescuing from the zingari my babe, and restoring it to me.

" Do not seek me. I shall fly the country, and I hope to forget it and all connected with it.

" Farewell!

" MARIE."

Leaving this on the table, she threw a mantilla out her shoulders, and clasping her babe to her art, hastened from the house.

*　　*　　*　　*　　*

The Zingara woman hesitated on what course she could pursue.

"It is best to tell him all, and at once," she said, after some reflection. "Aye, let him know the worst, and at once."

Crawling along the bridge, she darted away in the direction where Phillipe lived.

In a few minutes she was at his door. Giving a peculiar knock at the shutter of the window, she was instantly admitted.

"What has brought you here?" demanded Phillipe, as soon as the door was closed.

"A dire misfortune."

"What mean you?"

"Simply that the child is gone."

"The child gone!"

"Yes, lost."

She then related all that had occurred at the bridge of Angelo.

"Devil!" said Phillipe; "to think I could not trust thee thus far. My curse upon you!"

"Ah, curse on! but that is useless. I tell you the hand of fate was in it, and I could not struggle against its power."

"No matter. We will settle scores another time—we have now to act. This child must be recovered."

"How?"

"I will seek it from one end of the world to the other."

"Where will you commence?"

"At the house of its mother."

"Why there?"

"Because I cannot but believe that she it was who rescued it."

"Do you think I do not know Marie?"

"You may know what you will, I *feel* that the child is with its parent, and under the parent's roof I will seek it."

"I will follow you."

"Come then, let us hasten, or we may be too late."

They left the house, and went by the nearest roads to the lone house wherein Marie lived.

"See; there is a light in the upper window," said Phillipe; "she is there."

"Can you enter?"

"Yes; I have a pass key."

He applied a key to the lock, and the door opened.

"All is still," she said; "let us make no noise, and we may surprise her. Should she hear footsteps she may conceal the child."

She stole with the stealth of a cat up the stairs of the house, and soon reached the landing-place.

Phillipe applied his ear to the door.

"There is no sound from within," he said; "we will enter."

They turned the handle of the door, and stood in the apartment.

It was empty.

On the table burned the light that had attracted their attention, and led them to suppose that Marie was there.

"Not here!" said Phillipe; "she must then be in the next chamber. Give me the lamp."

He advanced to the table, and was about to take up the lamp, when his eye fell upon the note addressed to him by Marie.

He snatched it up and read it over and over again.

"Great Heaven!" he cried, "it is as I thought—she has the infant, and has fled with it. Rescued by the wife of Lovelace, who is now under this roof! This is a surprise!"

He took the lamp, and went towards the next room.

The Zingari woman followed him closely.

Next moment they were gazing upon the form of Fair Liz.

"Oh! it was she, indeed, who took the babe from me. See, I left the mark of my knife upon her arm. Would that it had been upon her heart; but it is not yet too late."

"Back," cried Philipe, "I am the avenger; not you."

"What will you do?"

"Go you and engage a gondola, while I keep watch here."

"What do you mean to do?"

"I shall bear her away to the haunt of Carlshoof, and then reflect upon what I shall do with her."

"I will obey you," said the hag.

"Mind you find a man who is in our pay."

"I shall be careful."

"Quick as lightning; there is not a moment to be lost."

The hag hobbled away, and Phillipe was left alone in the chamber.

CHAPTER LV.

WHERE PIPEY WAS TAKEN BY THE BLACK CAPTAIN—THE UNKNOWN FRIEND.

AFTER a long drive over the London roads, Pipey, by the easier motion of the carriage, knew that he was in the country.

A few minutes only seemed to pass in rolling over the easy roads beyond the metropolis.

The carriage stopped, and the Black Captain ordered his captive to alight.

He caught him by the arm, and assisted him to dismount. The cloak was not removed from his head, and he had to move under the guidance of the man who had made a prisoner of him.

He mounted some steps, and then became conscious of having entered a house.

"Mind how you go," said the Captain. "We are going down stairs, so I won't release your arm."

They descended a great number of steep stairs, and, as it appeared to Pipey, traversed a long stone passage, which resounded again as they passed through it.

"Now," said the Captain, "we may venture to take off the cloak."

The heavy covering was taken from the prisoner, and he found himself in a small apartment, vault-like and close in smell. It was well illuminated, and the furniture was covered with red cloth and velvet.

"Welcome to the new hall of the Scarlet Brethren," said the Captain, bowing with mock civility to his captor.

"Don't mention it," said Pipey, whose imperturbable gravity and transcendant impudence returned the moment he found himself in any difficulty.

"How are ye all?"

He bowed slightly and familiarly to about half-a-dozen cloaked and masked figures who surrounded him, and then continued,—

"This isn't so fine a place as you used to have; not so extensive in size—not so elegant in fittings—and by no means adapted to the accommodation of large parties."

"What know you of our late meeting place?"

"Oh, had the pleasure of visiting it on several a sions."

"You had? It was well for you that you were not detected, or you would not have quitted the place alive."

"I presume it amounts to much the same thing since I am here now."

"You are right. You have had but a little longer lease of liberty. Your day has, however, come at last."

"Very well. There's no help for it now, as the lady said when the parrot bit her nose off."

"It is well you can take it so coolly. All men cannot look death in the face without flinching."

"So I should say, or you would not have removed your delightful establishment so far out of London."

"No matter. You were not brought here to argue, but to know your fate. To-morrow you die."

" Why not to-night ?" asked Pipey. Better get it over at once, if it must be. I'm quite indifferent."

" I have said to-morrow. Away with him."

Two of the Brethren here advanced, and taking Pipey by the arms, forced him towards the end of the apartment.

Here a door was opened, and Pipey pushed through.

Only one of his guards followed him.

The passage into which he was thrust was narrow and dark.

After advancing a few yards, his guide touched his right arm, and pulled him gently into what appeared to be a small stone cell.

" You will remain here," he said.

" Thanks," said Pipey; " I haven't any idea as to the kind of place I am in, but what the eye don't see, the heart cannot grieve after ; and so if this place is not furnished in the first style of elegance I shan't know the difference."

" Do you know why you were told you were not to die till to-morrow."

" No."

" It was in order that you might be brought here without a struggle. You are in a niche in a wall. When I quit you a door will be closed upon you, and you will be entombed alive !"

" What a miserable fate."

" Now you know why the Captain spoke of death to-morrow."

" Yes, and he did right ; for if I had suspected this I should have certainly kicked against it, and I do not know but what I will do so now."

" Try."

Pipey tried to move his arms, but he found them fastened to his side.

" You can neither move hand nor foot," said the attendant. " You see we take good precautions here."

" Oh, hang it !" said Pipey, " this is too shocking a death even for me to bear. Why not slit my throat at once ?"

" Because this is the death awarded to all who pry into the secret of this band. You now regret your curiosity, I should say ?"

" No, I regret nothing. Serve me as you will, you shall not say that I flinched."

" I like your spirit, and regret your position."

" I wish that your regrets could release me from my position ; and then I should ask you to keep on regretting until I was beyond your reach."

" I see you are not yet inclined to die."

" Not quite."

" And you would thank me for releasing you ?"

" I certainly should consider myself under a direct personal obligation."

" Listen to me. I know you well, and I believe you would befriend those whose interests I have at heart, although I am now incapable of showing it. In a word, you have been a true friend to the daughter of the Duke of Grasmount ?"

" I trust I have."

" That is sufficient reason for my serving you. In an hour I will attempt your release, but in a great measure you will owe that to your arm and valour. All I can do for you is to free your arms, and give you this weapon."

The speaker groped about in the dark, and placed a dagger in the hand of Pipey.

" In one hour," he continued, " some one will visit you for the purpose of seeing that I have done my work."

" I must, then, drag him in, plunge this dagger into his heart, and leave him to the fate marked out for me ?"

" You are right. Dare you do this ?"

" I dare save my life at any price—at any risk."

" 'Tis well ; but, before I go, you must listen to my further instructions, and make me a promise to fulfil my orders."

" Speak on."

" In the first place, you must strip the man who will visit you of his scarlet gown and mask, and assume them yourself."

" The very thing I should have done without instructions to that effect."

" The next point will be to fasten this entrance carefully. You will find the spring in the wall to the left—a brass knob, which must be pushed in with some force ; once closed, it will open no more until the walls are torn down."

" A pleasant prospect !"

" Listen to me, and speak not. You will thread the passages to the left, and they will lead you to the hall you recently entered."

" Yes."

" The Black Captain will utter the word ' Silent !' and you will reply, ' As the grave !' "

" ' As the grave,' " repeated Pipey. " I shall make no error."

" You will then mingle with the Brethren, and conduct yourself as one of them until the meeting breaks up, and then you must quit the place."

" With all the pleasure in life."

" Mind, no bungle. Not only your life, but mine, depends upon your discretion."

" You may rely upon me. It is a description of business to which I am accustomed."

" I know it, and therefore have but few fears for you."

" And now, what promises do you require from me ?"

" First, that you will never seek to betray this band until I unseal your lips."

" How shall I know you again ?"

" I shall remind you of this night's work when next we meet. Will not that be sufficient to establish my identity ?"

" Yes."

" Do you, then, promise ?"

" I promise."

" You must swear it."

" I swear it, by my soul."

" Enough. In the second instance you must never allude to the mode of your escape from this dungeon."

" I swear that too."

" And, lastly, you must swear to quit the country at once."

" Quit the country ?"

" Yes."

" Wherefore ?"

" Because your life and mine are at stake while you remain here."

"Oh, very well—I will go."

"You swear it?"

"I swear."

"And at once?"

"At once."

"'Tis well. I must now leave you. Adieu! you are once more at liberty."

Pipey raised his arms and moved his legs, and found that the bondage in which they had been placed was entirely removed.

"Well," he said, "you are a brick! I shall never forget you, whoever you may be, and if I ever have it in my power to do you a good turn, depend upon me."

There was no reply.

"Hillo," said Pipey, "one more word."

Still no reply.

"Why, I suppose he's gone."

Pipey stretched forth his hands and found that he was shut in. There was no aperture above, below, or about him. He was entombed!

At first he feared that the voice to which he had listened had only mocked him, and then again, as his hand closed over the weapon that had been placed in his hands, hope returned.

"He must mean well by me, or he would not have given me this," he said to himself.

"Well, well, if the worst comes to the worst I can at least plunge this into my heart and be at rest. Death by starvation does not stare me in the face!"

*   *   *   *   *

We will follow the unknown friend of our hero. He groped his way through the passages, and returned to the vaulted saloon, where a few of the Brethren—conspicuous among them the Black Captain—sat conversing.

"Well," cried the Captain, "is all well?"

"Yes."

"He is safe?"

"He is safe."

"Ha, ha! It's a sad death for so brave a boy, but thus must perish all who seek to pry into the secrets of the Brethren."

"You are right."

"How did he conduct himself? Was he at all broken at last?"

"Not in the least."

"Wonderful spirit. But that dungeon will crush it, or I am much mistaken."

"He will eat his heart out before he exhibits a sign of fear, or asks for the slightest commutation of the terrible sentence."

"I believe you; in one hour from this," he said, addressing himself to a little man who stood near him, "in one hour from this you will go to the tomb in which the prisoner is confined, and there give him his last look at a human face. You have been a minister, and therefore it devolves upon you to say the last words he will ever hear. In an hour he will be in a fit frame of mind to hear them. Do you mark my words?"

"I do."

"As you fasten the fatal spring, murmur a prayer for his soul's rest. It is all we can do for him."

CHAPTER LVI.

THE DISCOVERY AND IDENTITY OF THE BODY OF THE DUKE.

THE thief-taker from Newgate, with his two assistants, were soon at the door of Pipey's house.

It had been whispered about that murder had been done in the house, and a crowd of people had assembled at the door, and were conversing in low tones as to the truth and nature of the reports that were fast spreading.

They had been knocking at the door.

None dared to burst it open for fear that, in case the whispers should be verified, they would be implicated in the affair.

There was an immense excitement on the arrival of the officers, and a passage was made in the crowd for their entrance.

They came to the spot with a show of authority, and elbowed the people back with more roughness than was called for; but that was a common practice, and so great was the respect for those in authority, that such rudenesses were passed by without being marked.

The men at length reached the door.

They tried it, but it refused to open.

"Produce the pick-locks," said the thief-taker, and his men at once proceeded to insert the instruments of their trade into the key-hole of the door.

After a while it yielded to their skill and strength, and the door swung on its hinges.

As a matter of course there was instantly a rush of the mob to obtain admittance.

"Keep back," cried the thief-taker; "keep back. None of you must enter here."

One of his men was left at the door to keep the people at bay, whilst the other two searched the rooms.

On the ground floor they, of course, saw nothing. They then mounted the stairs, and on entering the sitting-room of Pipey, discovered the body of the Duke, stretched upon the floor.

"By George, Grimer was right," said the Newgate official; "here's a nice bit of business, and no mistake. Well, young Mr. Pipey is in for it this time, if he never was before."

"Stabbed in the back," said his man, turning over the body. "What a rum way to put a fellow out of the world! Well, you may say what you like, but nothing would make me believe that such a clumsy job as this was done by the Captain."

"Just stow that gab, can't you. Whatever you may think about it say nothing. It will suit our book to fasten this upon Pipey, and if he don't turn up with a good account of himself, it's a certain thing that he'll be in for it."

"Well," said the man; "it don't much matter to me whether you fasten it upon him or not. I don't suppose I shall be any the better off, whoever it may be fastened upon."

"Won't you, spooney; then I do. If we could get rid of this Captain and his gang, we should be the better off for it! All the work he monopolises would fall to our share, and we should make our fortunes in no time."

"Whew !" whistled the man, "I never saw it in that light before ; but you're right however, and nothing will give me greater pleasure than to see you have your will in the matter."

"Enough about it ! Just you run off to the house of the Duchess of Grasmount, and break the matter there. You must bring her back with you, if possible."

"I understand you, and will obey."

"Quick, then. I will await your return."

"I'm gone."

"And, here, drop a hint to those boobies hanging about the door that the thing's a sell, and let them get away home. We don't want any more alarm made than we can possibly help."

The man obeyed these instructions to the letter.

He flew to St. James's-square, and broke his intelligence to the servants, desiring that they would at once procure for him an interview with the Duchess.

"That is easily done. Her Grace has not retired to rest. Being anxious about the duke's return, messengers have been sent to the clubs, and to every point where he would be likely to have gone, but, of course, without avail."

The man left the officer in the hall whilst he sought the apartment of the Duchess.

"There is a man in the hall who desires to speak with you concerning his Grace," said the servant.

"What man is it ?"

"An officer, as I think, your Grace," said the servant, hesitatingly.

"Oh !" cried the Duchess, in well feigned alarm, "oh, my heart tells me something dreadful has happened. Tell me—tell me what it is ? Let me hear the worst ?"

"So please your Grace, I would rather you heard the man himself."

"Admit him—admit him. What am I to hear ?"

The officer was led to the apartment.

"Break it as gently as possible," whispered the servant. "Poor, dear lady ! she appears to be sadly cut up, and the shock may kill her."

The man had no liking for his task, but he was bound to fulfil it ; and so he walked nervously into the presence of the lady.

"Oh, sir !" cried the Duchess, on seeing him, " oh ! sir, sir ! tell me what has happened to the Duke—let me know the worst. He is ill · he has met with some terrible accident—I see by your face that something serious has befallen him."

"Madam," said the man, "I grieve to say that something serious has happened."

"I knew it—I knew it ! Oh ! tell me what it is ?"

"Are you strong enough to bear a great—a terrible shock ? Can you trust yourself to hear bad—very bad news of the Duke ?"

"Yes, yes, let me know all ; the worst cannot be so bad as the torture I now endure."

"Then I grieve to tell you that the Duke is—"

"Dead ! I read the word in your face. Tell me, is it not so ?"

"It is, madam."

The Duchess threw herself into an arm chair, and gave way to a burst of hysterical sobbing, which lasted some minutes. At length she raised her eyes, and told the officer to proceed.

"We found him murdered in a house in Soho."

"Murdered ! Oh ! who could have done so vile a deed ?"

"That we have not yet ascertained."

"Murdered ! So good—so true—so generous a man ; who would have turned aside rather than tread upon a worm ! Murdered ! It is too cruel—too sad to believe !"

Wretched hypocrite ! She played her part to perfection.

So well was it done that the officer, used as he was to such scenes, deeply sympathised with her distress and bereavement, and was filled with sorrow that she should endure an agony apparently so deep and bitter.

"I must tax your strength to the utmost, madam. You will find this a sad trial to bear, but you must struggle against it as you best can."

"What have you now to say to me ? After what I have heard I can bear anything."

"I want you to come to the house with me. It is necessary that you should identify the body there. You may also be enabled to point out some things that may lead to the detection of the murderer."

"I will accompany you," she said.

"It will be a sad trial for you," said the man. " I trust you will have strength to bear it."

"I trust so," she said ; " oh, how sincerely I trust so !"

The carriage was ordered, and in a few minutes the widowed Duchess, attended by several servants and the officer, drove off in the direction of the house wherein the crime was committed.

They reached the spot, and the Duchess was carried from her carriage into the house, and assisted up the stairs.

By this time more officers had arrived, and the body of the Duke was lifted on a table, and covered with a large cloak.

The Duchess, now overcome with real feeling, fainted as she was borne into the room ; but this was more occasioned by the tumult of sensations that oppressed her than by any grief the sight of the corse brought to her.

After a while she recovered, and the Newgate official related to her in what manner the body had been discovered. He then asked her to identify it.

The cloak was removed, and she gazed upon the well-known features of the Duke.

"There is no doubt," said the officer, "there is no doubt as to the identity of the body, your Grace."

"Not the least," she answered.

"And now I must question you for a few minutes, in order that we may, if possible, find some clue to the detection of the perpetrator of this deed. When did the Duke leave his home ?"

"Early last night."

"Did he tell you, or any of the household, that he was coming to this house ?"

"No."

"Are you aware whether or not he was in the habit of coming here?"

"I have long suspected that he has had some dealings with the man who lives in this house."

"You know the man to whom you allude?"

"Yes, I once befriended him."

"He was, then, intimate with the Duke?"

"Tolerably so."

"Do you know whether or not there was any enmity between them?"

"I do not know of any. They rather appeared to be sociable together—too sociable when their relative positions is taken into consideration."

"Then they had secret dealings together?"

"I suspect as much."

"I must now tell you that we have searched the body, and found that there is no money or valuables about it. Can you say whether the Duke left his house with either about him?"

This was clearly a leading question.

The Duchess saw what would be the result of her answer, should she assert that he had valuables about him. There would at once be a reason for the murder.

"The Duke always wore diamonds of great value, and I have reason to believe that late last evening he left the house with a great sum of money about him."

"Indeed, madam! Your words give us a clue to the murderer. The man who owns this house, and the old housekeeper who resided here with him, are nowhere to be found. It is only reasonable, therefore, to suppose—"

"That they committed the murder. Oh, Heaven! what a vile deed; and so little provocation!"

"Ah, madam; you know not what may be at the bottom of this. Money may not have been the motive power in this instance, although it may have been a consideration. It is, however, too sad a subject wherewith to engage your attention, and I gladly permit your immediate return to your own home."

"No, no," she cried; "I will remain here—I will not leave his side!"

"You can do no good, madam; and you must have a care of yourself. Let me beg of you to return to your home without delay."

After many entreaties the Duchess gave what appeared to be a reluctant consent to the proposition of the officer, and suffered herself to be led from the house.

To all outward appearances she was deeply stricken with grief too great for expression. Inwardly she rejoiced. Her plans appeared to be working admirably, and she was more at peace than she had been for many a long day.

Only one thought agitated her, and that was, what had become of Pipey?"

CHAPTER LVII.

THE ESCAPE FROM THE TOMB—AN ORDEAL—WHERE PIPEY FLED—WHOM HE SAW AND FOLLOWED, AND THE RESULT OF HIS EXPEDITION.

AN hour—it appeared an age to Pipey—passed over, and then he who had been a minister came to the tomb in the wall to fulfil his dread mission.

Pipey heard not his approach. and he was not anticipating his coming, when the door of the little dungeon flew open, and a light burst in upon him.

Before the captive stood one of the Brethren, habited in his scarlet cloak, and with his face concealed by a mask.

To fall upon him, and thrust him into the hole, was but the work of a second.

The man would have called for help, but before he could speak Pipey's hand was upon his mouth, and he was within the cell.

"I will be more merciful to you than you would be to me," said the prisoner—"you would leave me to die of starvation—you would entomb me alive, but I free you from life before I leave you."

With the hand that was free Pipey smote the man to the heart with his dagger, and he fell forward with a death wound, from which the blood flowed in a crimson stream.

Until he was dead Pipey held him, and prevented him crying for help.

At length the head dropped forward, and Pipey relinquished his hold.

"It is all over with him," he said; "and now to effect my escape."

He tore off the scarlet gown and mask from the man appointed to seal him up in his tomb, and, adopting them, he picked up his lantern and closed the ponderous door.

In the wall, and in the place indicated by his unknown friend, Pipey found the brass knob referred to, and, thrusting it inward with his whole strength, he heard the spring, that closed the door for ever, go forward into its place."

"Thank Heaven," he said, "it does not entomb me."

Cautiously he threaded the labyrinth of narrow passages, keeping to the left, as he was told.

At length he reached a small flight of steps, at the top of which was a door.

"Now for it," said Pipey, as he dashed boldly into the vault.

"*Silent!*" said the Captain.

"*As the grave,*" answered the liberated man.

"'Tis well."

The Brethren then resumed the business in which they were engaged, and no further heed was paid to him who had just quitted the tomb for the living, save by one man, who advanced towards him, and whispered in his ear—

"All's well?"

"Yes," said Pipey; "as right as a trivet."

The man then walked away again.

Some few moments elapsed, and a messenger

arrived, and reported to the Captain the death of the Duke of Grasmount at Pipey's house.

Pipey, well as he could guard himself against exhibiting any impression of sudden surprise, started as he heard the intelligence communicated.

"Well," said the Captain, "what does it mean?" Who has killed him?"

"It is suspected that the Captain himself has done the deed, for nothing can be heard of him."

"The Captain himself? Ho, ho! so they suspect him, do they?"

"Yes, and all the hounds of Newgate are upon his track; and it's hard if, before another hour passes over, he's not within his old quarters, the cells of the prison."

"Don't fear; nothing of the kind will happen, for happily the Captain is in a cell from which the hand of man will never rescue him. He is below!"

"In the tomb?"

"Yes, in the tomb; fast sealed."

"Then the thief-takers will experience a sad disappointment, for they hope to lodge him in Newgate."

"He is better cared for, and we are well rid of a dangerous enemy."

"Just so," thought Pipey.

In a few minutes the assemblage broke up, and the members of the mysterious band threw off their cloaks and masks, and silently left the house.

Pipey contrived to be left until the last, and he then threw off his cloak and unmasked; pulling his hat tightly over his brows, and burying his face as much as possible in his cravat.

No one heeded him, and, quitting the vault, he found his way through the passage, and up the many steps he encountered in his journey, and at last stood in the open air.

"Oh," he cried, "oh, if I but dared to let them know I had escaped! If I could but return for a moment and throw them into a fever of consternation! It would be splendid fun, but I have taken an oath, and I must not break it."

He gave one glance at the house he had quitted.

It was an old fashioned mansion, of the Elizabethan school of architecture, and stood in the centre of a little park, approached by a lodge, at which he beheld an old man leaning against the gate, and gazing into the road.

The place had the appearance of the mansion of a well-to-do gentleman, and there was not, within or without, a sign of the real purpose for which the building was used.

"I should know the place," said Pipey, reflecting a moment; "I should know the place, for it seems quite familiar to me."

"Yes," he continued, "it is Highbury, and this house belongs to the Duchess of Grasmount. Good, charitable soul; I suppose she has given it to her amiable Brethren for their use and entertainment. Well, I must do them the credit to say that their *internal arrangements* are as *snug* as could be."

With these words he turned his back upon the building in which he had run so narrow a chance of losing his life in the horrible manner we have detailed, and set out at a quick pace towards Islington, on his way back to London.

* * * * *

Pipey made his way as speedily as possible, and by the least frequented roads, into the Minories; and there, entering the shop of a dealer in second-hand wearing apparel, he exchanged his clothes for that of a seafaring man, and purchasing a large beard, he effected a complete metamorphos in himself.

"Now," he said, "I can walk about in comparative safety, and may venture westward."

He walked to the house of one of his own men, who resided in Holborn, and entering, made himself known.

His men wondered what had become of him, and began to have grave doubts about him, when the report that he had murdered the Duke got wind, and he came not forward to dispute it.

"Come," said his assistant, "we will set ourselves to work to clear up this affair, and I think I already have a clue to it."

"Indeed! in what manner?"

"You remember the idiot of the Duchess, against whom I last night warned you?"

"Yes."

"Well, what so reasonable as to suppose that he mistook the Duke for you, and dealt him the blow meant for you. He had, they say one of your coats on, and it appears to me that we can soon get at the bottom of the case."

"You may, but I cannot. This very day—almost at once—I must quit England."

"How?"

Pipey here related to his lieutenant the whole of his adventure, suppressing only the nature of the Scarlet Brethren, and the names of those he knew to be connected with it.

He told of his capture, imprisonment, and escape, and then repeated the oath of secrecy he had taken.

"So you see," he said, as he brought the relation of his tale to a conclusion, "I cannot remain here, and I dare not return until I receive the consent of my unknown preserver."

"Stuff," said the man, "I should not consider an oath binding under such circumstances."

"But I do. Had you been placed in the position I was, you would know the full obligation which I am under to that man; and I will never break oath with him."

"As you will; but when you go I will do my best to ferret out the mystery."

"Do so. I know my case could not be in better hands."

"I'll give you cause to say so before I have finished with it."

Pipey drew from his friend all the money he could scrape together, and then bade him adieu, promising to write to him as soon as he reached a place of safety.

They parted, and Pipey retraced his steps towards the Minories.

Arrived there, he sought a public-house frequented by seafaring men, and, entering the public room, called for some ale and tobacco.

So well was he disguised, and so admirably did he act his part, that no one would have taken him for aught but the man he was representing.

His aim in coming here was to get some intelligence of the ships leaving port for the Continent, and to this end kept his ears open, but without much effect, for conversation did not chance to run in the channel he desired.

At length two men entered the room, and at once rivetted his attention. One was a seafaring man, the other was Yellow Maydock.

They kept together, and conversed in a low tone, and Pipey never took his eyes from their faces.

"What game is up now?" he asked himself. "No good, I'll warrant, but I should like to know what it is."

The room gradually filled, and the men became interrupted in their conversation.

They then walked to the end of thee room, where Pipey was sitting.

It was less crowded, and consequently more to their taste.

They seated themselves near the watcher, and re-commenced their talk in the same low tone.

They at length called for some spirits, and commenced drinking.

After a while the sailor passed a glass to Pipey, saying,—

"Drink, mate."

"My respects," said Pipey, tossing off the spirit after the approved fashion of old tipplers.

"You look one of the right sort," said the sailor, after a pause, and pushing another glass towards Pipey.

"I'm as well as most people, as people go," said Pipey.

"Out of a berth?" inquired Maydock.

"Hillo," said Pipey, to himself, "this fellow is getting inquisitive; "he wants something done. I know my man. Then he said aloud, 'Yes, I'm doing nothing now, thanks to the Preventive Service.'"

"Oh! you're that line?" said the seafaring man.

"Yes," replied Pipey, "I've done something after that fashion."

"And now you're hard up?" asked Maydock.

"Yes," said Pipey; "clean thrown upon my beam-ends."

"And want a job?" asked the sailor.

"That I do, badly enough."

"And you're not particular about the style of living?"

"Fellows with no money in their pocket are not too particular."

The men winked at one another.

"I told you that was our man as soon as I entered the room," said the sailor.

"Yes," said Maydock; "and I put him down as one of the right sort."

"Did you, though," said Pipey, in affected simplicity.

"Yes," said the sailor; "that we did."

"And now," said Maydock, "we want a little quiet work done. Are you game to earn a ten-pound note?"

"I just am."

"Well, it's to be done in this way. I've an old woman under my charge that must be taken, to-night, as far as Purfleet."

"And then tossed overboard?"

"Devil a bit," said Maydock; "we only want to keep her dark for a few days, until the ship in which my friend here has an interest, comes round from Deal."

"Oh, is that all?"

"Yes, a ten pound note easily earned, isn't it?"

"It is, and I'm with you. Where does your ship go, mate, on leaving the river?"

"Sometimes to Spain and sometimes to Italy. It's Italy the next voyage, I believe."

"Well, if you could make it convenient, I should like to book a voyage with you, for I'm tired of hanging about here."

"I'll see about that, my lad. At present we must stick to matters in hand. There's work to do, and it had best be done at once."

"Yes, at once," said Maydock; "so if you're ready come along."

"I'm both ready and willing."

"You can pull well, I suppose?"

"Yes, tolerably well."

"That will do."

They rose, and beckoned Pipey to follow them.

It was now quite dark, and a slight breeze had sprung up.

"My eyes!" said the sailor; "but if this breeze keeps up we shall have a tough job to get down the river, as the tide will turn before we have been pulling an hour."

They walked along, and very soon Pipey saw that the men were leading him in the direction of Maydock's house.

"No matter," he said; "I'm well up in the neighbourhood."

They walked on, and at length came to the door.

"Enter," said Maydock. "I want to look after a carriage, and will rejoin you in a few minutes."

The sailor and Pipey entered the house. It was evident that the former knew the spot well, for, catching Pipey by the button-hole, he said—

"Come along, mate. I know the ropes of this ship, and can take you about. Here, come into the Yellow Boy's fore cabin; he keeps some good stuff somewhere."

They entered the front room, which will at once be remembered by our reader.

"Stand easy, mate," said the sailor, "I'll find a glim here somewhere."

He groped about for a while, and then found a flint and steel, with which, and the aid of a tinder, he struck a light.

"Here we are," he said, quite smart and jolly, my boy. Make yourself at home,"

"All right," said Pipey, "I'm one of the easy going ones, I am."

The sailor went to a cupboard, and found a bottle of spirits, which he produced and made free with.

"Drink," he said to Pipey, "drink, mate. You'll want all the pluck it'll give you before the night is over, for there's a devil of a wind up, and going down that river against it will be tough work."

Pipey drank of the proffered stimulant, and returned the bottle.

"A rum fellow is our friend," said the seaman.

"Is he ?" asked Pipey.

"Ah, that he is," continued the seaman ; "I've known him many a long year, and many's the bright pound he's put in my way ; but it's always through some dark business like this. You can't get to the bottom of him. There's no worming things out of him."

"He appears to be a downy one."

"You're right. And now what's your name, mate ; I like to have something to hail a fellow by, it's more sociable than mate or master."

"So it is. My name's Harry Bedlow, and I don't care who knows it."

"And mine's Tom Shattler, and ditto, ditto."

"Well, now we know each other, and I hope that the acquaintance will be a long 'un.'

"I hope so too. Have another pull at the bottle. Here's the Yellow One coming, and if he gets hold of it he'll drain the lot."

Pipey thought he had taken quite enough of the fiery liquor, and refused to drink again.

Then Maydock entered the room,

"All's right," he said ; " the carriage is outside, and all's ready. Hillo ! you seem to have dipped pretty freely into that rum."

"Of course we have. D'ye think we could sit here and do nothing ?"

"All right. But bear a hand now ; not a moment is to be lost."

They rose from their seats, and Maydock seized the light, and led the way np the ricketty old stairs.

"Mind how you come," he said. "You ain't used to this place, and may topple over and break your neck."

"¡No fear of me,' said Pipey to himself. "But I wonder who this old woman is."

They soon reached the attic, and Maydock, drawing the key of the door from his pocket, inserted it into the lock, and entered the room.

Imagine the astonishment of Pipey when he found that Mrs. Boodles was the party he was engaged to carry off.

He started back in amazement.

"Hillo !" said Maydock, marking the action, 'What's your game ? What made you jump ?"

"Nothing," said Pipey, "beyond the astonishment of finding that this is the party we are to have all this fuss about. Do you know I thought you had an Eastern princess, or a dowager duchess stowed away up here."

"Did you though ? Well, you see I havn't."

He turned his attention to Mrs. Boodles. That good lady was seated on the edge of the little truckle bedstead Pipey remembered so well, and which brought back to him recollections of one he dearly loved.

"Now then," said Maydock, "get up, old woman, you're to go."

"Which I hope it's to my home you mean, seeing as how that place I have not seen for four-and-twenty hours, and never tasted a bit of food, nor quenched my thirst with as much as a drop of water, since them pheasants and that speret passed my lips, which no lady she was, and wus than that gentleman, to faint in that manner, and get a poor lone woman to see her home, and give her pheasant, and then serve her like this— which a wus attic I never beheld in my born days, and a disgrace it is to humanity, and no broom has been over it for years if I die for it !"

The old lady sat bolt upright, and spoke the foregoing words in tones the most indignant.

She was now thoroughly roused, and seemed indifferent to her position.

"Come," said Maydock, as she ceased to speak, "come, that's enough of your jaw. I want you to move. Are you coming ?"

"Which I want to know where I am going to, before I stir another step."

"That is our business. Come along."

"I shall not move a foot of mine until I know where I am going."

"Going to the devil!" roared Maydock, "if you don't shut up, and move. Hark ye, I've no wish to harm ye, but if ye won't move I'll serve ye just as I did last night, and then you'll go easily enough."

Recollections of the drugged handkerchief came across the old lady's mind, and bursting into tears, she rose and followed the brutal fellow without further resistance.

"What that poor dear Captain will do without me, I can't think for the life of me," said Mrs. Boodles ; " so fond as he was of having his breakfast ready when he got up of a morning, and in such low spirits as he is, and wanting some one to cheer him up, is awful to contemplate, and nearly breaks my heart. And surprised he will be when he finds me gone, and no fault of mine, for I couldn't help losing my key, and standing under the doorway in that dreadful storm —which well I know that the man who ran out of the house had no business in it, and nearly broke my leg. And then that artful woman to pretend to faint, and get me to go home with her, and eat them pheasants and drink that speret, and fall asleep and carried off—and it's grieve his life out he will, as sure as I'm a living woman."

"Oh, oh !" thought Pipey, "here, then, rests the secret of your being carried off. The murderer of the Duke tripped over you on the steps, and fearing you would be able to recognise him, the Duchess carried you off. I can see my way before me now. This is, indeed, a lucky chance !"

They quitted the attic, and were about to descend the stairs, Maydock leading the way, Mrs. Boodles next, the sailor following, and Pipey last, when the door of the second attic was pushed gently open, and the terrible old hag who had once been Maydock's housekeeper crawled out and caught Pipey by the leg. He turned round and started back in extreme fright.

"God of Heaven !" he cried, " what is this?"

She was disgustingly filthy, almost starved to death, and half naked, and had more the appearance of some hideous animal than a human being.

"Hillo !" cried Maydock, "what brought that old devil out of her hole, I wonder? Get in, I

say, or I'll kill you"—and Maydock raised his hand threateningly.

"Ha, ha!" screamed the old woman; "I don't forget, I don't forget. *He tried to kill me*, he did; but he didn't do it, he didn't do it. He couldn't, though he tried so hard, and his fingers were so strong!"

The recollection of his flight with Fair Liz flashed across the mind of Pipey, and he thought himself betrayed.

"Bah!" cried Maydock, lifting the old woman with his foot, and kicking her back into her den; "Bah! she raves still. Some time ago she was nearly killed by a fellow who got in here one night, and from that time to this she has done nothing but talk of it. But it's strange, young fellow, that she should seize upon you, like that. I never saw her do such a thing before."

"And I hope she'll never do such a thing again," said Pipey, with assumed jocularity, "at least with me; for she gave me such a fright as will live in my memory some time to come."

"Don't heed it, but come along."

"Which, if I was asked my opinion," said Mrs. Boodles, "I should say it was a baboon, and not a human being; and thankful I am that I'm not as I was very often when my poor Boodles was alive, or for certain the blessed infant would have such marks as no Christian infant ought to have, if it didn't happen to come into the world altogether a monkey, a crawling upon all fours! which terrible it is, and well I knows it, being well up in all domestic affairs; which a ladder would be much easier to get down than these old stairs, being corkscrew-like, and narrer at the corners, which a mercy it is if I don't fall."

Maydock was not over well pleased with the loquacity of Mrs. Boodles, and bade her "hold her jaw" in a tone which convinced the poor old soul that her best course would be to shut her mouth at once ; and this she did.

They left the house, and jumped into the coach in waiting for them.

A smack of the driver's whip and they were off.

The direction taken was towards the river, and running along as near its bank as was possible, they reached a little pier at Blackwall.

On this pier or quay was a boat house, and this place was entered by the sailor, who soon came out with an old man, who produced a small and old boat, into which the whole party was to get, and pursue their journey down the dark and dismal river.

The sailor and the old man launched the frail boat, and the latter returned to the boat-house, in order to find the oars to propel it to its destination.

"It's a queer night," said the old man, "and if you ain't quick about it you will find getting down the river a tough piece of work. As far as I'm concerned, I wouldn't try it myself."

"We must," said Maydock, "there is no help for it."

"Well, all I have to tell you is to pull fast and keep near the shore. It's the best thing you can do under any circumstances, but to-night in particler."

"All right," said the sailor, " I've been down too many times not to know something about it. Go ahead."

"Which, if I'm to get into that awful boat," said Mrs. Boodles, "the bottom will come out, and we shall be *propogated* into the water."

"Hold your infernal tongue, and get in," was the response of Maydock.

It was all very good to say "get in," but how to do it was a sort of mystery not easily explained.

Mrs. Boodles, assisted by Pipey, got down the steep flight of steps leading to the river, but no sooner did she put her foot on the boat, and lean her by no means moderate weight upon it, than it careened over, and she was remarkably agile in landing it again.

"As I'm a living woman, it's never to be done,' said the poor old soul, trembling violently, "and what it's to be done for is to me a puzzle which cannot be explained, seeing that I am not so young as I used to be, and the mother of a large family, and only a poor widow, which nobody can make not the worth of a pin's point, and fourteen stone in weight if an ounce, and it's a sad thing ; and if that dear Captain were only here what a blessing it would be, and me all alone, looking into the great river, and he wondering where I am all the while, and nobody to give him as much as a cup of coffee of a morning, and he used to having his breakfast ready as soon as his eyes were open."

Maydock sprang into the boat, and, drawing it close against the steps, held out his arms, and taking the old lady in them, with as much ease as if she had been a child, he lifted her from her feet, and seated her in the stern without any difficulty.

"Now then," he said to the other two, " jump in, and let us be off ; this won't pay any longer."

The men did as they were desired, and next moment the boat was pushed off, and floating down the river.

Maydock seated himself by the side of Mrs. Boodles, and the others took to the oars, and pulled strongly against the still rising tide.

"If it should come on to rain," said the sailor, " we should be nicely in for it."

"We should be drowned," said Mrs. Boodles— "we should be drowned, and there would be an awful end for us."

"There would, indeed," said Maydock ; " but there ain't much chance of it, old 'un, so hold that tongue of yours."

"But let me ask of you, sir, in the mildest manner possible, and with all due respect, where you are going to take me ? because I know I shall be sea-sick very soon, and never a drop of brandy to prevent it, and my poor head is distracted. I wish I was dead, I do !"

"Oh, you'll be right enough, you will, so don't fret about it."

"Which I don't ; but I can't help saying that I think it is ungentlemanly, and not to be endured ; and if I'm to go to furrin parts, I know I shall be eaten up by them cannibals, which they live on human flesh, and prefer it fat, if travellers' books are to be believed—more especially Robinson Crusoe, who dressed in skins, and carried an umbrella when he didn't want it— which my belief is that he was a madman, and under the impression that it was always raining."

In such conversation as this the time passed.

Meanwhile the wind rose, and the sky became dark and threatening.

"Pull away," said the sailor to Pipey—" pull away, and let us get more in-shore, or we shall make a miserable mess of it. Devil take it—how it begins to blow !"

"And me as cold as any frog I ever see'd," said Mrs. Boodles.

"We shall catch it now," said Pipey, " for I felt a drop of rain."

"The deuce you did."

"Yes, and there's another.'

"I feel it now. The drops are as big as half-crowns."

And now the rain came down heavily, and the wind fairly screamed.

"Keep in shore—keep in shore," was the constant cry of the sailor, and Pipey would answer with—

"All right."

And then both pulled more vigorously, and the little craft went slowly on.

Once or twice Mrs. Boodles, in the excess of her fear, tried to rise to her feet, and it was as much as Maydock could do to keep her down.

"If the tide turns," said the sailor, " we shall have to put in somewhere, for it would be madness to go on."

"Hadn't we better put in at once."

"By all manner o' means," said Mrs. Boodles.

"By no means," shouted Maydock. "Go on, we must not stop."

"Well, I think the young feller is right?" said the sailor, "but as you're cap'n, you can do as you like, only don't say you wasn't told about this, that's all."

"Nonsense, nonsense," said Maydock; "there's no manner of danger, and we must get down, and by water. I cannot risk going on shore now."

"All right—all right."

The river was now a dreary sight.

Here and there lay a ship or barge, tossed by the turbulent waters.

On shore, on either side, twinkled lights from the houses; and, at length, these disappeared, and the voyagers could see nothing.

They kept on and on, the little boat tossing about fearfully, and becoming more dangerous each moment.

Woolwich was at length passed, and then the storm broke out in all its violence.

The wind was fearful to hear, and, blowing against the tide, made the water doubly turbulent, and it was with the greatest difficulty that the oarmen could ply the blades in their hands.

They tried their best, using all their strength and skill; but nothing could stand against such weather, and the progress was small indeed.

In a short time they were all drenched to the skin, and had but faint hopes of their lives remaining to them.

Maydock sat in gloomy silence, and Mrs. Boodles continued uttering snatches of prayer and groans of anguish.

"Mind," cried Pipey to the sailor, "mind how you go, and pull hard, or we shall be aground. Don't you feel how we drift in?"

"Aye, aye, you are right; back water! back water!"

Pipey did as desired, and they gradually crept out from the shore; but they could make no more way than heretofore, every moment increasing their peril; and they saw that, unless the storm ceased, the little craft would fill and go down.

As it was, she had shipped over a foot of water.

When it was at its worst, and when hope had departed from all in the boat, there came a sudden return of joy.

The elements had spent their fury, and all was still in little less than half an hour.

The summer storm blew over as suddenly as summer storms generally do, and save for the wetting they got, no one of the four was the worse from being exposed to its fury.

They had hard work to reach Purfleet, however.

The tide had turned, and as the breeze was still stiff, the work continued extremely hard, and the perspiration streamed out of every pore in the skin of the rowers.

Still the work continued.

It was almost morning when they ran into a little creek at their destination.

There was the same difficulty to land Mrs. Boodles as there had been to embark her; but once more the great strength of the robber was brought into play, and the old lady was lifted from the boat.

They walked some little distance from the bank of the river, and at last reached a house which stood on the road side, commanding a view of the water.

It was an old-fashioned country inn, and here they entered without difficulty for the door was open, and they had but to walk in.

In the passage they were greeted by an old fellow in the garb of a half waterman half landsman, who on recognising Maydock, held out his hand, and said—

"Shake a paw, old fellow. Who's your mates and the petticoat?"

Maydock briefly introduced his companions, and then caught the old man by the collar, and dragging him on one side, held a whispered conversation with him.

"Oh!" said the old fellow, on hearing Maydock, "I see—I see. I'm right: mum, you know," and then, turning to the dripping and intensely cold Mrs. Boodles, said—

"How d'ye do, marm? Had a wetting, I suppose? That's bad—very bad. Not used to the water?"

"No; only in the shape of tea, or when strengthened by a drop of brandy, which it would be a very acceptable thing just now."

"And that you shall have if you follow me. I've a nice, snug room upstairs, and you can rest there capitally."

"Which I should be grateful to you to my dying day," said Mrs. Boodles.

She attempted to move, but her limbs were numbed with the cold, and she could not stir without the greatest difficulty.

"There, young un," said the host, to Pipey; "first catch her by the arm, and follow me."

"I'll hand her up stairs to you," said Pipey, hastening to assist, as desired.

The landlord led the way, and Pipey followed, bearing most of the weight of Mrs. Boodles on his arm.

They with difficulty ascended the stairs, and then entered a little room, in which was a tolerably clean bed, and which also had a bright fire burning in the grate.

It was snug and clean, and Mrs. Boodles drew a sigh of relief as she looked about her.

"Which it is a relief to sit in a decent place after being shut up in the dungeon I have come from, and worth a wetting, although it did frighten me, and how the wind did howl, and hoping you'll not forget that drop of brandy, for which my poor heart will be grateful.

"I'll get it for you," said the man, and as he passed Pipey, he whispered—

"Stop with her."

Pipey winked, and the landlord withdrew.

As soon as he was gone Pipey closed the door, and walking up in front of Mrs. Boodles, removed the false hair from his head and face, and stared at her with a broad grin on his countenance.

"Which it is himself," said the old lady in

astonishment, "and only to think that I didn't know you."

"Hush! there is danger in letting them see you know me, for to them I am only a sailor out of work."

"I know! But what does it all mean?"

"It is a long story."

"But why did they carry me off?"

"Because you saw a man quit my house, who perpetrated a murder there!"

"A murder! my goodness!"

"Yes; a myrmidon of the Duchess of Grasmount killed the Duke—mistaking him for me."

"Which it's best as it is," said Mrs. Boodles, with evident satisfaction. "Now I can go home and clear up the mystery, and pay out that woman who made me drink the brandy, and then sent me home in a carriage which never took me there."

"I am sorry to say that we cannot go home. I must quit England; I have sworn to do so, and I cannot break my oath."

"And must I be left with these dreadful men, or go back alone, which is wus: seeing that I should p'raps fall into the power of that woman with the brandy and the pheasants again?"

"Fear nothing, I will never leave you. Where you go I shall go. Take no notice of what you see and hear; think always that I am with you, and watching over you."

"Which I will do, as sure as fate. Oh! I don't care for 'em now; they can do their worst, and I'd snap my fingers at 'em, a nasty set of rapscallions!"

"Hush! some one comes."

Mrs Boodles, with a smile of perfect contentment on her face, looked towards the door, and saw the landlord enter, bearing with him a glass of hot spirits.

"Which you are a kind good soul," said the old lady, "and much good may it do you."

"Seeing that you are going to drink it, I should say that to you—but no matter; drink it, and be content."

Mrs. Boodles required no second invite: seizing the tumbler with avidity, she placed it to her lips, and quitted not her hold of it until she had sipped it all away.

"There," she said, "I think I shall do better now."

"I'm glad of that," said the landlord, winking at Pipey; "and now I'll leave you to dry your togs. I'll bring you some supper in a few minutes, and after that you can go to bed."

"And glad I shall be to do it."

Mrs. Boodles neither looked at nor spoke to Pipey, and he quitted the room with the old man.

Directly they got outside the landlord closed and locked the door, and, turning to Pipey, said—

"That's a rum 'un, that is; she seems to take things cool."

"Yes," said Pipey, "she looks to be in the habit of doing so."

"There's some fellows below as wouldn't mind having her in their hands."

"Indeed!"

"Aye, indeed."

"And why?"

"Because they imagine she had a hand in a murder done in London a day or two ago."

"Oh! and that's why Maydock has brought her down here?"

"Yes. If she but opened her mouth, the complexion the case now bears would be entirely changed, and a very different state of things come about."

"And what brings the officers here?"

"Oh, they're everywhere. There isn't a spot for twenty miles round but what they've visited and searched."

"For whom?—this woman?"

"Yes; and her master, who is supposed to be the principal in the affair."

"And they've no trace of them?"

"Not the least."

"It was fortunate they searched this place before our arrival."

"By Jove, it was! Maydock gave me quite a start when he came in and gave the whisper who his party was, but it's all neatly managed."

"And who is this fellow who they suspect to have done the murder?"

"His name is Pipes, and he is a noted thief-taker, and secret agent of the Government."

"I've heard of him."

"Of course you have; however, mum now! A word dropped below would play the devil; and I've only told you this at the request of the Yellow Boy, who tipped me the wink to put you on the fly, so that you mayn't drop a word below and blow the gaff."

"I'm right now."

"Yes, you'll do; I see you're one of the right sort."

"I hope so."

"Come on, then, and let us have a good stiff drink together, it will do you good."

"It certainly won't harm me."

They went down the stairs and entered the bar-parlour, wherein was seated about a dozen fellows, three of whom Pipey at once recognised as officers.

Pipey assumed the gait and manner of a sailor to perfection, and entered the room without inducing the officers to give him anything but the most casual of glances.

He sat down and heard himself talked of in the most absorbing manner by the officers, who detailed his career, gave his most extraordinary adventures, and invented others in which he never took part, with a facility that proved them good story tellers, if not particularly mirthful men.

Pipey could have fain laughed aloud many a time and oft, but he suppressed his mirth, and listened with a face which betokened the utmost indifference to all that was said.

His appearance was that of a stupid, boorish seaman, and no one took the slightest notice of him save his own companion, who ever and anon pushed some spirits and tobacco towards him, but paid nothing.

———

CHAPTER LVIII.

SHOWS HOW LOLA AND THE PRINCE HAD A

QUARREL.—THE RESULT.

LOLA led a tolerably comfortable life in the splendid home of the Prince.

She had everything her heart could desire, or her fancy give birth to.

She loved not the Prince, and took but little notice of his flirtations, so that they agreed very well.

Lola was capricious and passionate, and completely mastered her master.

Her will was law, not to be disputed, and she exercised sovereign sway, like a little despot as she was.

The only person she treated with any degree of consideration was Louise, who was her prime favourite, and was petted accordingly.

The Prince feared her!

The power of woman is certainly extraordinary.

Here was a tolerably stalwart, muscular, and hot-tempered man subdued and brought to the feet of a little dark-eyed Italian peasant, whose caprices were those of a sick monkey, and who had as much brain as could about be stowed away in the head of a sparrow.

Such things are certainly extraordinary, and would form a splendid subject for the consideration of the learned in human nature.

For our own parts we would give much to have it explained; but we fear we shall have to wait a long time for the man who can clear up the mystery.

We have seen many attempt it, but we have generally found that they have been miserable imposters, who, whilst giving birth to numbers of high-flown theories in their closets, go into the drawing-room to be delightfully hen-pecked by little ladies of no particular pretentions to mind or beauty, and have their hair in curl papers, and who wear shoes down at the heel·

Shall we then blame the Prince for submitting to the petty tyrannies of Lola?

We had best not: passing over the matter as a thing which we must be content to despise—until we love!

There came an open rupture between them at last, however.

It was on the occasion of the young girl's receiving a letter from Italy.

How she got it no one knew.

The Prince saw it lying open on her dressing-table, when she on one occasion left the room in haste."

With that gentlemanly feeling which always distinguished him, according to unprejudiced historians, he immediately took up the letter and devoured its contents.

They were as follows:—

"Do not leave him, day or night—your mission is to torture. Fortune has favoured you, and you have him in your power. The oath you swore to me was to facilitate my vengeance on all who had a hand in the downfall of my poor Marie. Are you sure you are keeping your word? Remember! Must I remind you that you are to leave no stone unturned in effecting the purpose you have been despatched to execute. As you value my friendship, and that something else that I will not mention, persevere.

"I am, yours,

"PHILLIPE."

Lola entered the room.

On seeing the Prince with the letter in his hand, she started forward, and snatched it from him.

"How dare you?" she cried.

"How dare you receive this, and what does it mean?"

"No matter to you."

"I does matter to me. I am the person alluded to in that letter."

"Well?"

"Well, you have tricked me."

"It is a lie. I never sought you, you found me, and induced me to come here with you."

"That is true, but you have planned some schemes against me—you have played upon me, and now you would do as you are desired to do by the writer of that letter."

"Remember that letter has been written by one who is ignorant of the manner in which I have lived here with you. He thinks I still feel as I felt before I saw you. Am I, then, to blame?"

"Yes."

"Psha—you are unreasonable."

"No; I am barely just. Were I to do as I should do I should take you by the shoulders and thrust you from the house."

"Dare you thus address me?"

The first gentleman in Europe said he dared.

"And," he continued, fiercely, "I give you three hours to be gone; if you have not taken your departure at that time, I shall make my servants thrust you from the doors."

The Italian bit her lips, but said nothing.

"Mark my words," said the Prince, "for I mean them. Begone! or take the consequences. I should place you in a prison, but I have too much respect for your sex to do that, so get from my sight. You may take your baubles and dresses with you; they may serve to get you another keeper."

He hissed the last words through his teeth, and left the room.

As soon as he was gone the little Italian gave vent to her rage in a flood of tears.

* * * *

In the corridor, advancing to the room of her mistress, the Prince met Louise.

He had seen her but seldom, and had almost forgotten her.

She was now looking in perfect health, and, dressed in the costume of an upper domestic, looked as beautiful as she had ever done.

There was a modesty and grace in her simple

attire that lent her additional charms. As the Prince advanced she curtsied low and bent her eyes upon the ground.

He passed her and she was about to move on when he turned and opening a door close at hand, bade her follow him into the room.

Louise tremblingly obeyed.

As soon as the young girl was in the room he took her hand and, seating her in a chair, looked into her face and said:

"You look wonderfully beautiful, to-day, Louise; even more beautiful than on the day when I first saw you."

"Your Highness is pleased to compliment."

"I speak the simple truth, by Heaven!"

"I have suffered much since then," said the girl.

"Ah, you remind me that I have behaved ill towards you. I swear I shall never forgive myself for my cruelty."

"You have nought to forgive yourself," said Louise," all that has befallen me has been the result of my own indiscretion. I do not even owe my first false step to you."

"Well, that relieves me of a great care," said the Prince; "but this is not exactly the subject on which I would have spoken to you. I want to make amends for my past neglect."

"Your highness is really very good, but I desire nothing. I am well cared for, and happy in my position with Madame Lola."

"I do not doubt you; but that position is no longer suitable for you. In fact, it no longer exists!"

"Indeed! am I dismissed?"

"No; but she is."

"I do not understand your highness."

"Can I speak any plainer? Lola is packed off —dismissed from the house, from my love."

"And wherefore?"

"Because she has proved a traitor."

"I am deeply grieved that she should have offended your highness."

"But I am not, since it gives me the opportunity of raising one more beautiful—one more worthy to her position."

Louise was silent.

"Do you not guess to whom I allude?"

"I do not."

"Then know it is yourself."

"To me?"

"Yes, loveliest, to you."

"Your Highness is surely jesting?"

"I never was more in earnest. I swear it upon these lips."

Louise started back.

"Hillo! What means that?"

"Oh, sir! sir! pray speak not thus to me. I cannot listen to such words."

"How now?"

"I have sinned once, and I know the penalty; try me not again. Take from me the temptation you would now offer."

"Hey-day! Is the girl mad?"

"No, but I have been mad, and have now recovered my senses."

"You forget the splendour—the power I offer you."

"I do not forget them; neither do I forget the suffering, the misery, that follows when that splendour and that power is taken from them, as you have now taken them from Lola. I have gone through the ordeal, and I know all its phases; and I have resolved to risk no more."

"Psha! you are a fool."

With this neatly turned compliment the Prince turned on his heel and went to the door.

As he held the handle in his hand he turned and said—

"Help your mistress to pack up her boxes, and then do the same service for yourself, and leave here. I desire to see no more of either one or the other."

CHAPTER LIX.

MARIE AND HER CHILD—WHAT BECAME OF THEM —LOVELACE AND HIS CHILD.

ON quitting her lone house Marie rushed madly through the streets, bearing her child pressed to her heart.

She knew not whither she was flying, and her whole aim was to leave behind her the city of Venice.

With the rapidity of wind she flew onward, and chance carried her away in the direction of the villa in which she had lived so long with Lovelace.

She had walked for upwards of an hour when she found herself in the neighbourhood of the well-known house.

Coming there so unexpectedly she was struck to find herself in the vicinity of a place so well known to her, and, forgetting the feeling that had urged her onward, she paused and gazed about her.

"A flood of recollections crowded upon her, and she sat down, and looking at her child, wept bitterly.

Some minutes passed, and then, conquering her emotion, she sprang to her feet, with the purpose of continuing her journey.

In her path stood a form she well knew.

It was that of Bartolo, the physician.

She screamed aloud, and would have fled, but he blocked up the path she wished to take, and told her to pause.

"No, no," she cried, "let me pass—let me fly. I never wished to see you again! A curse upon myself for coming here. I meant it not, but I had no control over myself. I came without heeding whither I was flying. I pray you let me pass— let me pass!"

"No; you must hear me."

"I pray you spare me."

"What is that on your bosom?"

"It is the child you would have destroyed."

"Would have destroyed! Was it not drowned?"

"No, no; God's will was that it should be saved, and saved it was—saved to be restored to my arms."

"Indeed! This is new to me."

"Oh, do not longer detain me; I have no wish to speak another word to you. Let us separate."

"Not till I have spoken—not till you have answered my questions."

"Quick, then, and let me continue my flight."

"Whither?"

"Anywhere out of Venice—out of Italy."

"First hear me. I have some right to your attention. Had it not been for your grandmother you would have had my life."

"No, no!"

"I say yes! I was found dying. You gloried in your terrible act, and I should have been in my grave had not a timely restorative been brought to me."

"Speak not of this!"

"I will speak of it."

"Oh! had you but one spark of feeling, you would spare me."

"I have no feeling for you. To torture you is the greatest gratification I can have."

"Spare me."

"No—listen! After leaving me for dead, you sped to Venice, and there murdered a poor girl—"

"Your mistress, and the would-be murderess of my child."

"No matter—you attempted her life."

"I did, and I glory in the deed."

"Wretch!"

"What were you to attempt the life of my innocent babe?"

"Pah! it would have been well for you—well for it—had I succeeded in destroying it."

"Fiend, you are baffled! The will of God is against you, and your acts are frustrated—your intents set at defiance!"

"Not yet."

"What mean you?"

"This: Chance has again thrown you in my path to-night, and chance, or, as you have it, the will of God, has sent thy child with you. The possibility is that after all it is marked out for me to kill it!"

"No, no, you are jesting—that cannot be your intent. We are nought to each other now: you can have no animosity against this poor babe."

"I have."

"It is impossible."

"I have."

"It never harmed thee."

No matter. I detest it, and through it I can touch thee. Ah! Do you fancy I have forgotten the poison? Do you fancy I ever can forget it if I live to be a hundred years old? it will dwell in my memory for ever."

"But you will not harm the babe. Do what you will to me, but spare—oh, spare, my poor innocent child."

"Ah! Your words do but increase the desire I have to kill the thing. Through it, and through it only, I can touch your heart, and I will wring it now."

"Ah, Bartolo, I see you do but jest. I see you wish but to frighten me. Well, well, you have done so, and now let me go my ways; let us part."

"You mistake me. I have no intention to part with you thus. I want that child."

"You shall not have it.!"

"If I have it not I will seize you, and hand you over to the officers of the Inquisition. I will declare the child mine, and they will give it me; then I shall be doubly avenged. Both you and the brat will be in your graves."

"Oh, do what you will with me, but pray spare my child. Do not, do not harm the innocent that never harmed thee."

"The child."

"I will not spare it."

"The child."

"I swear you shall not have it."

"I swear I will have it. Give it me."

"Beware! I will struggle with you to the death for my child. Advance to lay hand upon me, and I will plunge this into your heart."

She drew from a fold in her dress the little stiletto with which she killed the servant girl, and held it threatening with her right hand, whilst the left clutched her darling infant.

"Psha! do you think to frighten me with such a toy? I will wrest it from you with the ease I could take a spoon from the hand of your brat."

"Do not come near me. I am a desperate woman, and, if I use this weapon, it will be to find a sheath for it in your heart."

"Fool! it is useless to you. See how I will pluck it from your grasp."

She stepped back to have a better chance of using the weapon, and she clutched it firmly as the doctor advanced.

"Back!" she cried; "back! or Heaven have mercy upon you,"

Without a word he came within reach of her arm. He raised his hand, and she made a blow at his heart with the weapon.

He stepped on one side quickly, and as the blow descended, grasped the wrist of the woman, and quickly disarmed her

"I told you how it would be," he said, throwing the stiletto into the road, "now for the child!"

"You shall tear me limb from limb before you shall take from me my child!"

"Come, let me have it, or I will beat you to the earth!"

He laid violent hands on the child, who shrieked piteously.

Its cries aroused within the breast of the mother the fury of a tigress, and she bit and tore the hands of her persecutor with her nails.

Nevertheless he contrived to take from her the precious burthen she carried.

"See!" he cried, "the child is in my power. I triumph now, and be assured I will not bungle as did the nurse."

"Oh! spare my child. Give it back to me—give it back! I will pray for you, night and day I will bless your name, if you will but spare my poor unoffending child."

"I want neither your prayers nor your blessing. It is this brat I want, and I have it. Go! and know that within an hour it will cease to exist."

"Oh, God! have mercy upon my babe; spare it—spare it! Oh! is there no help?"

There was help for her. At the moment she spoke, a dark form sprang over the low wall which fenced in the gardens of the house, and advancing upon Bartolo, the new-comer raised his arm, and dealt him a blow that stretched him on the ground in a state of insensibility

The child was torn from his hold and replaced in its mother's arms.

"Oh, God bless you!" cried Marie, "God bless you, whoever you may be!"

"Marie, do you not know me?"

It was the voice of Lovelace.

"Come," he cried, "come away from this spot, and tell me how this happened."

He turned towards the city, but Marie caught his arm, and crying, "not that way—not that way," drew him towards the country.

They walked for some time without speaking a word, and then Lovelace broke the silence:

"Who was that man who attacked you?" he asked.

Marie told him the history of her intimacy with him.

Lovelace sighed, and bowed his head.

"It is a wretched fate," he said; "it is a wretched fate to live thus. Day and night—night and day—same token of my evil career will burst forth and stare me in the face. Turn where I will violence and bloodshed will present themselves to me, and threaten me with perdition."

"It is sad," said Marie; "it is sad. I know what it is to feel thus."

"Crime and bloodshed everywhere, and I the instigator."

"It is an awful fate."

"It is."

"Tell me, Marie, tell me why you are leaving Venice thus!"

"It is because I dare stay there no longer."

"Why?"

"Pain—in danger of my life from the Inquisitors. They still thirst for my blood to avenge the death of the woman I slayed. Where I go I know not. My aim is to leave Venice far behind."

"But how did you recover this child?"

"By a miracle, at the very moment I thought it gone for ever; and when for the second time its life was threatened, a good angel, in the form of a woman, interfered for it and brought it back to me."

"Tell me her name, that I may bless and pray for her."

"I will do so. It was your wife."

"My wife!"

"No other."

"Explain, Marie."

"It is an easily-told tale. The child was taken from its protector, my grandmother, who was to take it to some person, or place, in order that it might be concealed from me, and the woman, filled with bitterness towards the helpless infant, was about to thrust it into the canal, when your wife passed, and she snatched it from her grasp and brought it to me, receiving from the hag a wound that will trouble her for many a long day."

"My wife wounded! Oh, God! oh, God! When will this terrible strife end?"

"I know not. But the drama of bloodshed is not yet played out. There must be more and more ere the curtain falls."

"I trust not, I trust not. But my wife, tell me of her."

"Wherefore should I speak of her?"

"Has she not saved your child?"

"Has she not robbed me of you?"

"Forget that, and think only of her act this night."

"You may be assured that it was that—and that alone—I remembered when I had her senseless in my power. Had any other thought been uppermost, should I have spared her? No! the life I had sworn to take would have been then forfeited to my revenge."

"That should be forgotten now."

"It is forgotten—at least as far as this is concerned. I will not take her life; I will never injure her."

"That is well."

"But the other—the others I can never forgive."

"It is a wicked thought."

"It may be, but it is one I cannot dismiss. I hope I never shall dismiss it."

Instinctively she put her hand on that part of the dress in which she had been in the habit of keeping her weapon.

She missed it!

"Heavens!" she cried; "it is gone!"

"What?"

"No matter. Ah! I remember he threw it into the road when he tore it from me."

"Of what do you speak?"

"Of nothing that I can tell you *now*. I must go back."

"Wherefore?"

"To find what I have lost."

"I will accompany you."

"You may do so; indeed, it is best you should do so. If he be still there I am powerless, and at his mercy again."

They retraced their steps.

In a few moments they were on the spot where the desperate struggle had taken place.

Marie stooped, and began to search diligently.

Lovelace, without knowing why, did the same.

At length his eye detected something glistening on the gravel.

He stooped and picked it up.

"I have found a stiletto," he said.

In a moment Marie was at his side.

"Give it me," she cried; and she tore the little weapon from the grasp of her former lover. "See! it is that I lost!"

"And wherefore all this trouble about such a toy?"

"It is the toy that shed the life blood of the would-be destroyer of my child—of your child. It is the weapon with which I have now to avenge myself. Do you fly from me, for I feel the old thirst for blood creeping over me as I touch this weapon. Begone, for I am desperate now."

"Marie! Marie! govern that passion. Oh, govern it, or it will be your ruin."

"It *has been* my ruin!"

"Then throw it away. Do not touch it, Marie, I pray you."

"Begone!"

"Marie, listen to me."

"Begone, I say. I wish for no further converse with you."

"You are mad, and I will not leave you thus."

"Follow me at your peril. Our roads are different: take yours, and let me seek mine. I will hear no more—begone."

"But not thus. You will require money."

"Not yours."

"But my wife—you will tell me where I may find her?"

"Yes; or at least I will tell you where I left her. If she be still there, it is by a miracle."

"Speak—speak!"

"Seek her at the old house near the bridge of St. Angelo."

"Before we part let me have one kind word. Do not let us separate thus."

"Yes, even thus. Begone, and if you can avoid it, cross not my path again."

With this she sprang away from him, and he watched her form until it disappeared in the darkness.

CHAPTER LX.

A NOBLE WIDOW AND HER ADMIRERS—RIVALS—PECULIAR POSITION OF A LADY OF QUALITY.

THE news of the Duke's death spread rapidly throughout the city of London.

It was the theme of universal conversation, and the position of the widow was canvassed in all the best circles of London society by those who had an eye to sharing with her her reputed wealth, and possessing such full-blown charms.

At every club the marriageable men "talked the thing over," and at least half a-hundred determined on laying immediate seige to her heart.

One there was who received the news of the Duke's death with more delight than all the others; for if report spoke truth he was the most likely to be elevated to the lordship of the mansion in St. James's-square, seeing that he had already more than half the heart of the Duchess in his keeping.

This individual was no other than Sir Roderick Cashley, a penniless but remarkably handsome baronet of middle age, but whose acquaintance with the mysteries of the toilette gave him the power of adorning himself so as to eclipse the majority of his youthful associates.

He was well formed, well favoured, and well spoken; and had easily got the ear of the Duchess, who was remarkably susceptible to soft words when addressed to her by good-looking men under her own age.

Under those circumstances it may reasonably be supposed that our Baronet felt a degree of pleasure approaching the indescribable when the tidings of the shocking murder reached his ears.

He had no thought of the poor dead man—no vision of the gaping wound, the stark body, and the glazed eyes, came not across his mind. No recollection of the warm pressure of the hand, now cold and stiff in death, oppressed him.

He was a thorough man of the world, and could only see in the melancholy catastrophe his own elevation to a most enviable position.

There were very few real mourners for the Duke; indeed, except his neice, Olivia, and one or two old servants, no one shed a tear over his fate.

Many were "sorry," after a fashionable standard of sorrow, but there was no real grief.

The Prince of Wales "was sorry," and being in that frame of mind, thought it right to say so to the Duchess; and so ordered his carriage to do her Grace the honour of paying a visit of condolence.

"It's very soon to intrude," he said to himself, "but I suppose there is not a very large amount of grief to suppress before an interview can be had; besides, I want to open my heart to her on my own loneliness and desolation. She could always lend a ready ear to my woes."

So the carriage was ordered, and the royal friend drove off to the mansion in St. James's Square.

Arrived there he was instantly admitted.

"Is the Duchess to be seen?" he asked.

"If your Royal Highness will remain here, I will ascertain," said the servant, ushering the Prince into an elegant apartment near at hand.

He had not been gone many moments before he returned, and stated that her Grace would receive the Prince in her own apartment, if he would do her the favour of visiting her there.

Of course he would.

When he made calls on ladies, he had a very great partiality for visiting them in their own apartments.

Perhaps it was because he did not like giving ladies the trouble of receiving him in state, and felt a pleasure in waiving all manner of ceremony.

Be that as it may, he always chose the dressing-room and *boudoirs* to the drawing-rooms.

The ladies seemed to know it, too; and, peculiar as it may appear, they generally received him in extreme *dishabille*.

It would appear that such a course gave him most delight, for it was universally adopted.

As the Prince mounted the stairs in search of the apartment of the Duchess, he saw a man, bearing with him a large box of crapes and silks; and the appearnce of this individual bespoke him a mercer and draper.

His exit was speedy, and the Prince entered the room as he departed.

The Duchess was alone, and in the most bewitching state of undress in the world.

The probability was that she had been trying on some widow's weeds, for her own dress lay on a soft velvet couch beside her, and the Duchess was lacing what, if we knew anything of the mystery of female attire, we should call stays.

On seeing the Prince the Duchess started, and pretended to be extremely shocked, but she did not blush in the least.

"How stupid of my servant," said the Duchess; "I told him I would receive you in a few moments."

"Not at all foolish, since he has given me the pleasure of looking upon such loveliness."

"Oh, Prince."

"Pardon me, your Grace; but thoughts will find expression in words when one's admiration is so much excited."

The Duchess moved to the couch on which lay her wrapper, but the Prince placed his hand upon her fair shoulder, and bade her not hurry for him.

'We are old friends, you know;" he said.

The Duchess smiled.

It was rather a gay smile, too, for one so lately bereaved of so good and well-beloved a husband. But, perhaps, duchesses are differently constituted to the common run of humanity.

It is, perhaps, right that they should be so.

But we are wandering from our lady, who has been all this time attempting to lace those awkward—peculiarities.

The holes were, however, too small, or the tapes too large, or something was out of the way, for the more she attempted to do them up the more obstinately they refused to be done up, so at last the lady gave it up in disgust, and, flinging an Indian shawl over her shoulder, took her seat beside the Prince.

He gazed upon her with marked admiration.

She was not at all a bad-looking woman to gaze upon, despite her years, and the Prince seemed to know it.

She was tall, symmetrical, and displayed all that beauty of proportions and dazzling perfection of physical development which characterise the most attractive period of woman.

Her posture upon that sofa might have shown that her limbs were full and tapering, and that her contours were firm in their rich modelling; while the fineness of her hands and feet, as well as the proud, yet graceful carriage of the head, showed her patrician breeding. Her hair was a dark brown; her eyes were of a liquid clear blue; her features were faultlessly outlined; her complexion was beautifully clear, and the skin seemed to be of a velvet smoothness. As she now sat, half reclining upon that sofa, the beautifully formed lips, moist and red, were slightly apart; and fitting portals did they seem, with their contrasting ranges of ivory inside, for the fragrant breath. The white arms, bare to the shoulder, were admirably rounded; and upon the brow, high and polished, the tracery of blue veins were delicately defined. The *corsage* was cut very low; but the costly white lace which trimmed it ascended over the richly moulded bosom, yet hiding those glowing contours only as much as the foam conceals the swelling wave.

Altogether she was a beautiful specimen of the gentler sex, and the longer that fair being was contemplated, the more completely would all delicate, refined, and æsthetic impressions rise dominant over, or rather, we should say, subdue and absorb, whatsoever sensuous thoughts might, in the first instance, have been engendered by a beauty so rich and softly seductive. But nothing was capable of crushing out the animal in the Prince, and as he glanced at all this loveliness, it was easy to comprehend what was passing in his mind; but he was in the presense of one who would admit of no liberties —from him; he had attempted them before, and the repulse he had met with now kept him completely in check.

"Ah, madam," said the royal visitor at last, "I presume you can guess the object of my visit at this sad time?"

"Yes," said the Duchess, "yes, dear Prince, and I am highly honoured. Ah! I have had a sad loss."

"You have, madam, but it is not irreparable; you must not shut yourself up from us and give way to your grief as some do: such a course would deprive us of the greatest beauty and the most estimable lady of the land, and we cannot afford to lose her."

"Oh, Prince, you still flatter. How am I to receive such compliments?"

"In the same vein in which they are uttered. Believe them all your due."

"I should be the greatest fool in Christendom to do so."

"Pardon me, the epithet you have used would be more applicable if you were not to do so."

"Psha."

"May I ask if there be any trace of the murderers of the Duke?"

"Not the slightest, and I fear they are now far away."

"That is sad, very sad; it is a pity that such wretches should escape the gallows."

"It is, indeed."

And here ended the fashionable display of sympathy.

Conversation next turned to the Court.

The Duchess was all anxiety to know what was doing there, but the Prince was unable to furnish information. He had not seen the interior of St. James's for a week.

"And how is that?" asked the Duchess, on hearing the assertion of the Prince.

"I have been in bad health and worse spirits," he replied.

"Indeed; have you lost a friend or a mistress; or, are disgusting tradespeople troubling for money?"

"Not the latter, or I should have applied to you for assistance."

"The friend, then?"

"No."

"Well the mistress?"

"Ah, you are right, Duchess, I am miserably, disgustingly, alone and forsaken."

"How sad."

"It is sad."

"And of all the beauties in the world there is not one who is happy in being called your mistress."

"It is so."

"And what do you purpose doing!"

"I know not."

"You must not be left alone."

"True? can you assist me to one who will love me?"

"Prince; in my position; in my grief."

"True; I forgot. I should not talk of such things at such a time. Pardon me."

"Nay if you are pleased to talk of love I cannot stay you. It is not because I am alone that others should not mate."

"You will then think of me?"

"Yes."

"I confess myself under the deepest obligations for I am quite forsaken, and know not where to turn for the desired one."

"I have one in my eye."

"Would it were yourself."

He threw his arms around her, and drew her towards him.

She did not resist very much, and his arms were not removed.

"Nonsense, Prince," she said, with a smile that exhibited something like gratification. "How can you talk so?"

"How can I look upon you and talk otherwise?"

"Now, do be quiet, and listen. I say, I think I have one in my eye."

"And I repeat, I would it were yourself."

He imprinted a kiss on her snowy shoulder, and the voluptuous woman threw herself back resignedly into his arms.

"Well," she said; "if you insist upon holding me in this absurd position, I cannot help it, but you will grow sadly tired."

"Never!"

"We shall see. And now, to continue, you have seen Oliva Besgrove?"

"Who, that has eyes, has not seen her?"

"Well! How do you like her?"

"She is the counterpart of yourself, an angel!"

"Will she make you happy?"

"Could you doubt it?"

"I do not know; there are such diversities of taste!"

"On such a point there could be but one opinion—she is perfection!"

"Well, her mother has recently died, and I shall now take her to live with me. You will have frequent opportunities of seeing her, and if you but press your suit, I do not see how you can fail to win her."

"Say you so? Then I am happy once more."

"Do not be too hasty."

"How am I to be otherwise than hasty? I am dying for love; you offer it me, then withhold it, and next bid me be not too hasty. That is direct cruelty."

"Poor Prince! he is sadly il-lused."

"I am, indeed."

"And now you have been here long enough; so pray rise and leave me."

"How am I to do so? Will a needle leave a magnet until it is torn from it? You are my magnet, and I cannot stir. I am spell-bound."

Well might he say so.

With that splendid form reposing in his arms; with that bosom heaving under his touch; with those eyes fixed wickedly upon his own, he was in the power of an enchantress, from whom he in vain sought to move.

"Since you will not go, I must," said the Duchess, playfully kissing her royal admirer, and springing from his side; "so, adieu, *mon chere* Prince!"

"Not so. I pray you do not dismiss me thus."

"What more would you have? I am sure I have been a very good and patient woman to submit to your bear-like hugging so long. Adieu, adieu! Let me see you again soon, and I will show you Olivia."

With this she sprang into the adjoining apartment, and was out of sight.

The prince knew her too well to follow. His dismissal was peremptory and decided, and he well knew that all he had to do was to retreat as soon as possible.

"Devil take it!" he said; "I believe the woman is as true as steel to that bescented and powdered Sir Roderick; but no matter—the beautiful niece is more to my taste, after all; but it will be an age until I see her; meanwhile, I shall have nought to do but be on my good behaviour and wait."

He turned and left the house.

*   *   *   *   *

The Duchess was doomed to receive many visitors that day.

The next comer was the favoured admirer, Sir Roderick, the penniless but handsome baronet.

He, too, was received in the dressing-room, but not in the agreeable *dishabille*.

Perhaps his taste differed from that of the Prince.

Be it as it may, when her Grace appeared before him she was majestically arrayed in a gorgeous dress of black velvet, with ermine trimmings. She wore a number of splendid diamond ornaments; and one would have imagined she had been dressed for a ball rather than the reception of an ordinary visitor, and an old and favoured friend, too.

But, as we have said, tastes differ, and maybe the Duchess well knew that the way to the heart of the Baronet was in the exhibition of her magnificence and enormous wealth of jewels.

His taste inclined to the glitter of fashion—the Prince preferred beauty unadorned.

Who shall say that the Prince exhibited the inferior taste? We should be the last to do so.

The handsome Baronet advanced to meet the lady, and, taking her white hand within his own, pressed it respectfully to his lips.

"You are most welcome," said her Grace. "I have expected you since yesterday."

"I feared to intrude, or I should have flown hither."

"How could *you* intrude?"

He seized the white hand again, and kissed it for a reply. He then took heart, and kissed the pouting coral lips.

"Am I, then, welcome?" he asked.

"Most welcome."

"And you have not forgotten me—I have been in your thoughts during all this period of anguish?"

"You have, indeed."

"You make me happy. It is the wrong time to talk of joy, but I cannot help expressing mine, though the revelation pain or shock you. Imagine how happy—how unspeakably happy—I must be now that I may see you—may love you—without restraint. I who have been so long compelled to admire in silence, and at a distance. Oh, picture my joy!"

"I can—I do."

"Ah, you know how deeply I love you?"

"I think I do."

"I am delighted to hear you say so; such words make me delirious with joy, for I madly worship you. That which to others has appeared a cruel murder has created no horror in me. I could bless—I could worship the hand that inflicted the blow."

"Hush! I must not listen to such words."

"True, you must not, and I am mad to utter them; oh, forgive me."

"I do."

"Then I will speak no more; but say you love me—say that I may hope—"

"Roderick, this is not the time—not the place."

"Yes, yes, it is both time and place. Confirm my bliss or I shall go mad."

"I do love you, Roderick, and at some future time—"

"Do not banish me. Delay the happy day if you will, but do not—oh, do not tell me to keep away from your presence."

"I will not do so. You are at liberty to come and go when you will."

"At all seasons—at all times?"

"Yes, yes; in all but the name you shall be my husband, and that title shall be yours in time, but you must wait. Society claims something like a show of grief from me, and I must not defy the laws of propriety. We can be all in all to each other without the world knowing ought."

"We can—we will."

They embraced warmly, and the Baronet was smothering the Duchess with kisses, when the door of the apartment opened, and the Black Captain, habited, as usual, in his sable suit, stepped into the apartment.

His ghastly white face exhibited no sign of intelligence. He might have been a painted statue standing there, for ought of life that was discernable in him, until he opened his lips.

After a pause he said,—

"I fear I intrude; your are careless of your servants, I presume. I knocked twice, but you could not have heard me. It is unfortunate; shall I withdraw?"

He asked this question, but showed no sign of retreating.

In fact, as he spoke he took a step further into the apartment, and glanced about as if for a chair.

The Duchess was for a moment surprised and confused, but she soon recovered her equanimity, and introduced the intruder.

"Do not go. Sir Roderick Cashley, allow me to introduce an old friend in the person of Count Carlo Paskewich; you will be delighted to know each other."

They might be in the course of time, and had circumstances been conducive to that end, but, unhappily, the gentlemen did not at the first blush appear in the least inclined even to be commonly civil to each other.

They bowed somewhat coldly to each other, and then the Captain took a chair and seated himself.

"I had business to communicate to your grace," he said; "or I should not have intruded myself upon you at such a time."

"Pray make no apologies."

"I should utter a thousand, if my business were of less importance; but knowing you will feel the deepest interest in what I have to communicate, I must ask you to grant me as early an opportunity as possible for its revelation."

He spoke in a tone of command rather than of intreaty, and the tone of his voice at once annoyed Sir Roderick, who rose suddenly, and said—

"Perhaps, as the *business* of this gentleman is of so much importance, I had best withdraw."

"Oh, no," said the Duchess.

"Pardon me," said the Captain; "I think the gentleman adopts the wisest course. Pray sanction his going, for we *must* speak in private."

Sir Roderick blushed crimson with suppressed rage.

He would fain have flown at the supposed Count, and torn him limb from limb, for his cool exhibition of effrontery; but the presence of the lady restrained him.

"Since it must be so," said the Duchess, with an attempt at a smile, "I must ask you to retire, Sir Roderick. I shall see you again to-morrow."

"Perhaps," said the offended Baronet. "For the time, madam, adieu. We *shall* meet again, but I am unable to say when."

With this attempt at an awfully grand outburst of spleen and indignation, the Baronet stalked out of the apartment.

"I fear I have somewhat discomposed your friend," said the Captain, as the Baronet disappeared. "He is one of those hot, spirited people who take offence at a very little."

"Your arrival was most inopportune."

"So I perceived."

"It would have been but gentlemanly on your part to have allowed a servant to announce you."

"I presume so."

"Then why break through the usages of society, and intrude yourself as you have done?"

"Because the news I bear is of so vital a nature to both you and I, that it drove the usages of society clean out of my head."

"What, then, is this all important communication?"

"It is but a word; Pipey is dead!"

"Dead! how? Explain."

"With all his cleverness, I proved one too many for him; and catching him on the hop, made a kidnapping case of it, and bore him to a new retreat."

"Yes, yes—"

"Being there, you may readily guess what became of him."

"The living tomb?"

"Yes, the living tomb was his doom! He died in the place my ingenuity and your wealth constructed for those who betrayed us, or those who had a more than desirable knowledge of our existence."

"It was a terrible fate."

"Was it not deserved?"

"Yes, yes; think not that I regret it. On the contrary, your work deserves and has my best thanks. You relieve me of a great burthen, and I know not how to reward—to repay you."

"Have you any desire to do so?"

"Can you ask such a question?"

"I not only can, but do ask it."

"Then know that I would do aught in the world that was within my power to repay the service you have rendered me."

"I have a boon to ask that I fear will be refused."

"I do not think that you could ask aught that I would refuse."

"I am sure I shall. I did not think so when I entered this room, but since I have been here I am doomed to disappointment."

"I do not comprehend—"

"So I presume, but I will soon make all clear to you. Three magic words dispel the mystery. They are—*I love you!*"

The Duchess started as if stung by a viper.

She gazed into the face of the man before her, but it was white, unimpassioned, and expressionless, as usual.

Soon she recovered her equanimity.

"Psha!" she cried, "you jest with me."

"I am in too serious a mood for jesting, madam. I repeat the words—'I love you;' and by giving me your hand you may repay the service I have rendered you."

"It is impossible!"

"Indeed! I must confess that I thought it improbable, but I have to learn how it is impossible."

"Oh, sir, sir; consider?"

"I have no right to consider. I am a gentleman by birth—my misfortune is that which has also been yours. Evil passions have made me an outcast and a branded man. There is only this difference between us: My acts are known, and I am amenable to the laws for them; yours are, *as yet*, unknown; and, in the eyes of the world, are spotless; but a breath could crush you."

"But that breath will not escape human lips."

"Why so?"

"Because, if you speak truth, the only man who *could* speak of my dark deeds is no more."

"How do you make him out the only man? There are a hundred more—myself for instance."

"You, and the others of that fraternity to which I have the misfortune to belong, are silenced. You dare not speak."

"Psha, lady! You know not what men will do when put to it."

"What! Would you dare break the terrible oaths you have taken?"

"It would entirely depend upon circumstances."

"But think of the nature of your oath. Does not the very thought of breaking it freeze the very blood in your veins?"

"Nothing of the kind."

"Then you must be the worst of villains."

"That is a very harsh term to apply to a gentleman; but I excuse it, lady. I love you, and as all is fair either in love or war, you must pardon the means I may use to ensure a return of my passion."

The Duchess was completely dumbfounded at this terrible avowal on the part of the Captain, and sank into a chair, completely crushed.

"After all," said the Captain, "what is there so very objectionable in me? in education and behaviour I am your equal. I am the supposed owner of a very high-sounding and altogether eligible title; and if you do not reveal that I have no right to it, the world will be none the wiser, and I shall pass muster in the fashionable throng without bringing discredit upon you. Added to this, you know me to be powerful, resolute, and brave; qualifications that render me a very fitting mate for a lady who stands in a position so precarious as that which you occupy. Reflect upon this."

"I cannot reflect upon it! If I think upon it I shall go mad."

"Wherefore?"

"Do not ask me."

"Ah! There is no occasion; I divine your secret. You love the man I saw here when I entered!"

"Sir!"

"Oh, do not attempt to deny it. I knew it, or rather suspected it, some time ago, but I did not think it worth mentioning until now."

"Supposing you are right?"

"I trust I am wrong, for it will be a painful thing for you to wean yourself from the affection."

"Do you dare insinuate that I must renounce Sir Roderick?"

"I never insinuate—I order! You must renounce this man."

"I tell you I will *not* do so."

"You mean warfare with me. Umph! as you will. I am prepared for battle."

"You think to terrify me by your threats of revealing my acts, but that will not do. I am not so weak and disreputable a thing as you imagine me to be. I am not shaken by your words, and I tell you to your teeth you dare not speak—for in ruining me you do the same for yourself, and a hundred others."

"I have thought of all this."

"You have? And you still hold the threat over my head?"

"The sword is still there, madam; it hangs by a thread! A touch will bring it down."

"I am still unmoved. The Prince shall protect me against you."

"I defy him and all his myrmidons as I have a thousand times before."

"Wretch, villain, quit my presence. I will inform the brethren of this, and their vengeance will be swayed by me."

"I am absolute master, and they are but my slaves. As I lead they will follow, so be not deceived."

"Begone, I say—I will listen no further."

"Am I then dismissed?"

"Yes."

"Finally?"

"Begone!"

"Well, I will go; but I see you are somewhat disconcerted, and will not take your answer while you remain in this humour. I will see you to-morrow, and then you may be in a better frame of mind to talk on this theme."

"Will you dare intrude yourself here again?"

"I most certainly shall, and I advise you not to refuse me admittance."

"Begone, I say, for I cannot speak with thee."

"For a lady so dumb, I think you have said a very great deal; but a truce to this badinage, I will call again, as I have promised, and I know, after due reflection, you will be inclined to receive me better."

"You will never receive a better reception from me while Sir Roderick lives. He has my heart, and he shall have it in spite of you. Go, and *bear that in mind*."

"I assure you *I will not forget it*."

"Are you not gone?"

"Adieu! or, rather, *au revoir*; our separation will not be long enough for the utterance of an adieu."

With this the Captain saluted the Duchess with profound respect, and withdrew.

As soon as he was gone, the Duchess went into a flood of hysterical tears.

She had held up bravely in the presence of her torturer, but as soon as he was gone she could restrain herself no longer.

CHAPTER LXI

THE REFLECTIONS OF THE DUCHESS—THE NOTE TO SIR RODERICK—HIS APPREHENSIONS—THE MEETING AT THE CLUB—TAUNTS AND JEERS— A MEETING ARRANGED—THE RESULT THEREOF.

WITHIN an hour after the departure of the Black Captain the Duchess had dried her eyes and began to reflect calmly on the position in which she stood.

She reflected on the character of the man with whom she had to deal, and at once saw that it would not be wise to enter into open warfare with him.

"Such a desperate villain," she said, "will make any sacrifice to gain a darling object, and it will not therefore be wise to enter the lists with him. I may come off scathless, but I cannot prevent the *expose*. I should be banished from society—from England; and that would be death to me. No! I must dissemble—I must use cunning, and get the assistance of Grimer. He has done me good service before now, and I know he has no affection for this man, and would not hesitate to rid me of him, if I could but show him the way. Yes; it is as well to act under a mask for a while. But how to proceed? The first step must be the temporary dismissal of Sir Roderick. I cannot reveal ought to him, or he will learn more than it is desirable to reveal. Ah; I must let him suppose me fickle, capricious and exacting. His love will not cool during the short time of his banishment; and if it does, it will not be worth the having; so I shall have nothing to regret. Yes, yes; my course of action is marked out, and I must commence at once, for there is not a moment to lose."

Her Grace produced writing materials, and in a short time had penned a note which she sealed and addressed to Sir Roderick.

Calling a servant, the missive was placed in his hand, with orders to deliver it without delay.

This was the commencement of the scheme of her Grace to rid herself of her too attentive *brother.*

* * * * *

There was a very aristocratic club in Pall-Mall, known as "Wightley's," thither, on leaving the Duchess, hastened Sir Roderick.

This was the most exclusive club in London, and its vouchers were passports into the best society.

By some chance Sir Roderick had been elected a member, and, by gaming and scheming, contrived to keep up his subscriptions with something like regularity.

He was somewhat of a favourite with the young nobles who frequented the place, for he was a man of the world, and a man of fashion, and was an excellent *chaperon* for them as long as they had plenty of money to throw away upon him.

"Wightley's" was an income to the *roue,*
and he was oftener to be found there than at any other place.

On this particular morning the Club was rather full, and the principal saloon was crowded with fashionable loungers, busily employed in reading the morning journals and the new magazines.

"By Jove," said one, who had the *Times* in his hand: "by Jove, it's a perfect bore to wade through these papers now, for there's nothing in them but reports of this murder of the Duke of Grasmount.

"Horrible!" said another. "I wonder when they intend leaving off, and letting the old boy lay at peace in the grave?"

"Not until they discover the murderer," said another.

"Then it strikes me that it will go on for ever, for there's no sign of his turning up as yet."

"What do you think of it, Cashley?" said one, appealing to the Baronet.

"What should I know of beyond that which is patent to you all?"

"Oh, by Jove, that's all stuff, you know, for everybody says that you are so sweet with the widow that you ought to be the oracle of the affair."

"This is an affair, Dartford, on which I do not allow anyone to jest, or even utter a light word, so, if we are to be friends, pray do not speak of the matter in my presence."

"Oh, I meant no offence whatever; but you really reveal the truth of the rumours by your snappish behaviour. Ah! ere twelve months are over we shall have another phase of the sensation, and the newspapers will be enabled to make capital out of another 'approaching marriage in high life.' It is rumoured that Sir Roderick Cashley, Bart., will soon lead to the altar the beautiful Duchess of Grasmount, widow of the late Duke, who, it will be remembered, was barbarously murdered, some months ago, in a house in the neighbourhood of Soho; ha! ha!"

"Dartford," cried Cashley, much incensed at his levity, "I must, once for all, warn you against such badinage. If you continue it, we shall exchange something more tangible than words on the subject."

"Hillo!" said Dartford; "it's getting desperate. Here, I shall have a challenge, and be forced into a duel with the most accomplished swordsman of the day, if I go on; but I've done. If you are so touchy on the point, I will not again touch it. No offence, I trust."

"None in the least, if matters end here."

"As far as I am concerned, they do."

"Very good."

"Hillo!—look here! Our Austrian friend, Count Carlo Paskewich, is with us. What a sombre-looking bird it is, to be sure! Who has seen him smile?"

It would appear that not one had had that pleasure, for there was a dead silence, and the Count approached.

The group exchanged greetings, and the Count, taking up a newspaper, seated himself in an easy chair, and busied himself with the news of the day.

A few minutes passed, during which the gossip of the day circulated from lip to lip, and all the *petite* scandals duly canvassed.

The next stir was made by the entrance of a servant, who approached Sir Roderick, and handed him a note, enclosed in an envelope bordered by an edge of black.

"From the Duchess of Grasmount," said the man.

"Does the bearer wait?"

"No, Sir Roderick."

"Thanks."

The man withdrew.

At the words, "From the Duchess of Grasmount," the Captain lowered his paper, and fixed his eyes upon the Baronet, who slowly broke the seal, and read as follows:—

"DEAR SIR RODERICK,—

"Circumstances, over which I have no earthly control, have occurred since our meeting, and necessitate our estrangement and separation for a few months. As you love me, do not seek me. Think what you will of this. Let me seem as unkind and fickle as you will; but know that I love you, and if you have for me one iota of the passion you profess, you will obey me, and not necessitate my closing the door upon you, as I shall have to do, if you persevere against my express commands. Farewell.

"Believe me,
"Yours only,
"A. G."

"Devil take her!" cried the Baronet, in a boiling rage, as he finished the perusal of the note.

"Hillo, Sir Roderick!" cried the incorrigible Dartford. "I hope that was not meant for our friend the Duchess."

"What?"

"Why, that emphatic wish."

"What did I say?"

"You said devil take her."

"Psha! I am annoyed—heed me not."

"Something distressing occurred? Can we share your trouble?"

"No, no."

"It must be something serious to make you so far forget yourself."

The Baronet was about to reply, when the Captain, who had not taken his eyes from the face of his rival, said, in a sneering tone—

"Yes, very serious. Nothing short of a dismissal."

"What say you?" demanded the Baronet.

"I merely hazarded a guess."

"Then pray do not make guesses on my affairs. They are offensive."

The Baronet failed not to mark the tone of satisfaction used by the Captain, and, despite himself, he could not divest himself of the idea that to him he owed the missive he had just received.

"You are easily annoyed," said the Captain, still more pointedly. "I could not have been far out, or you would not have heeded my words."

"I propose that we settle the matter by reading the note," said Dartford. "That would be jolly fun."

"He does not dare give you the opportunity you desire," said the Captain.

"Sir," said Roderick, "who and what you are I know not, but if you persist in interfering in my private matters I shall chastise you."

"What!" cried the Captain, springing from his chair.

"Gentlemen, gentlemen," cried the others, "really there is no occasion for this."

"There is the greatest occasion," said Cashley. "Am I to submit to be talked at in this most offensive manner by a man coming we know not whence, and who, for aught we can tell to the contrary, is some penniless adventurer intruding himself into London society under a borrowed title, and for purposes the very opposite to honest."

Like an enraged tiger the Captain flew towards Sir Roderick.

In his hand he carried a light cane, and with this he smote his rival across the face with a severity that brought the blood on the instant.

Maddened by the smart and indignity put upon him, Cashley attempted to draw his sword, but the gentlemen threw themselves between the rivals, and dragged them away by different doors.

This scene created quite a consternation in the club, and very soon it became the all absorbing topic of conversation.

"They must fight," said one.

"Oh, yes; no fellow could submit to such a welting as that without calling out his man."

"True; devilish pity for the foreigner, though, for Cashley's the best swordsman out."

"Yes, Carlo will get it now, if ever he did, and Cashley is not likely to let him off lightly, for the affront was mortal."

"It was, and I pity the poor devil, but certainly the Baronet provoked him to it."

"I don't know that. The provocation seemed to come from the other side."

"Well, we differ, than's all."

In this fashion the affair was canvassed.

Let us see in what manner the principals were acting.

The mutual friends of the parties drew them from the club house, and walked them away in different directions.

They both retired to their own homes, the Baronet in a fever of excitement—the Captain highly delighted; for, as may be supposed, he had planned all that had taken place.

On leaving the Duchess, he had firmly determined on ridding himself of a troublesome rival.

The lady had told him that she would not be his wife while Sir Roderick lived, and he firmly believed her; but at once determined upon the removal of the impediment.

With this view he sought the club-house, and had not the opportune arrival of the note from the Duchess furnished the opportunity, he would have found other cause of quarrel, and attained his end.

The Captain, for the sake of appearances, had taken chambers in the neighbourhood of the Palace of St. James's, but beyond an hour or two during the day, he seldom occupied his expensive apartments. Now, however, he determined to remain in them until he had seen the result of the *fracas*.

It was four o'clock, and he knew that, before the dinner hour, he would receive a friend from his rival.

The coming of this individual he ca mly awaited.

Time passed, and at six o'clock the servant of the house brought up a card, on which the Captain read—

"MAJOR HECTOR PARRY."

"Hem!" he said, as his eye fell upon the name, "he means business, I see; for this Parry is the most bloodthirsty old villain in al London, and never acts without men mean fighting. Well, let him fight. I would rather kill him with a weapon in his hand than commit a murder; and I should not hesitate to do that had I no other mode of ridding myself of him."

The servant now ushered in the sanguinary Major.

"I'm proud to make your acquaintance, Count," said the fire-eater; "although under such painful circumstances. I presume that you guess the nature of my errand?"

"I have no difficulty in doing so. You represent Sir Roderick Cashley, whom I chastised this morning?"

"I represent the gentleman whom you assaulted, Count. We cannot admit the word 'chastisement.'"

"Well, I care but little what word you use; it is a matter of no moment to me."

"I presume so—I presume so. But we are not here to argue that point. As a man of honour, sir, may I infer that you will give my friend the satisfaction of a meeting; for such an indignity can only be wiped out with the sword."

"I imagine so."

"I trust, sir, you will not be mean enough to offer the humble and abject apology which i can alone accept, and it must be *most* humble, *most* abject, I assure you."

"My dear sir," said the Captain, "be under no alarm. I have not the remotest idea of offering the veriest particle of an apology, I do assure you."

"I am glad to hear it, Count; very glad to hear it, because, as a man of honour, my friend must cross swords with you over the affair."

"Just so."

"And now as to the preliminaries; will you refer me to your friend?"

"My dear Major, I will save you all that trouble; act as you will. I place myself in your hands, being assured that the arrangements that will suit your friend will be found quite acceptable to me. Name your own time and place, and bring your own weapons, and I shall be content."

"Count, you speak like a true gentleman, and although I may not take your hand until this unhappy business is over, I respect you, Count—I respect you."

The Major was quite in his element.

He saw before him a man whose coolness promised well for his actions on the day of battle, and he began to entertain high expectations of an excellent duel.

"Dismiss all formalities," said the Captain, "and let the matter come to a speedy end. I detest being bored about such matters."

"My dear Count," said the Major, "if it is left to me, you need be under no apprehension of delay. I will make a point of getting the affair off as early as possible. I think to-morrow morning would be the most convenient time. Eh?"

"With all my heart."

"To-morrow morning be it then."

"Have you a choice of place?"

"Oh, no."

"Well, then, Battersea-fields will serve the purpose very well. I object to the parks now; they are too common."

"As you will."

"Oh, this is bringing it to an amicable conclusion," said the Major; "this *is* satisfactory. I declare, sir, you have given me more pleasure than I have experienced for many a long day. After it is over, Count, if all should end happily, I shall have great pleasure in taking your hand. You're a man after my own heart, and I respect you—I do, upon my soul. You're even a superior individual to my friend Cashley; and I always took him to be the most gentlemanly fellow in the world. It is a pity you disagreed, it is upon my life; but as it is, there can be no retraction—it must come off. Any disappoint-

ment now would be the death of me—I'm sure it would."

"You need have no fears, as far as I am concerned."

"I feel assured of that."

"Well, then, all is arranged?"

"Except the time, and that is a most important item in the affair."

"Ah? ah? yes, to be sure. Well, Major, I must leave that to you, as well as other preliminaries."

"Then I say seven o'clock on the instant. Seven, sir, is the most gentlemanly hour, I do assure you."

"Well, then, seven. I shall be with you as punctually as if my engagement were with a lady."

"That is right. Punctuality is the very essence of a duel. Both at the spot to the very instant—that's my rule. No waiting about in the cold; no delay, in order that a gaping crowd of rustics may gather about. Sharp there—preliminaries promptly settled—men at work—all over in five minutes—carriages ready—off again. Splendid sight, sir!"

"I quite agree with you. I rather enjoy it."

"Sir, you're the first *principal* I ever heard make use of that remark; but I respect you all the more for it. Now I must go, or my admiration for your character will become so profound that I shall forget our relative positions, and grow too warm. Sir, I wish you good-day! Remember, in the morning—sharp seven—Battersea-fields, and mind that your friend knows his business; I hate acting with men who do not know their duties."

"I shall satisfy you even on that point."

"And now, adieu, my dear Count. I must hasten to my friend, and tell him how charmingly everything has been settled."

The little Major withdrew, highly delighted at the issue of his mission, and the Captain, after dining, took himself off to a meeting of the Scarlet Brethren.

*　　*　　*　　*　　*

The next day broke clear and bright, and at an early hour whole crowds of people were astir.

Had they suspected what was progressing, or about to progress, in Battersea Fields, the possibility would have been that they would have found their way to that then little-frequented spot, but as they had no intimation of what was on the *tapis*, they, as a matter of course, went their several ways, and left the Black Captain and his friend, and Sir Roderick and the Major, with a military surgeon, to wend their way to the scene of action undisturbed—in fact, unnoticed.

As a matter of course, a great number of the immediate friend and acquaintances of the parties knew of the meeting, but they religiously kept the secret, it being very unfashionable to prevent, or even attempt to witness, two men, bearing each other deadly enmity, attempt to cut each other's throats.

Almost at the same moment the two carriages

of the rivals reached a point form which Battersea Fields were accessible.

Springing lightly from the conveyances, they walked to a secluded spot, and here the Major paused.

He eyed the ground critically, and then turned to the man who accompanied the Captain.

"This will do, I think?"

"I'm satisfied. Allow me to see the weapons."

The surgeon took from under his cloak several swords, evidently suited for the purpose to which they were about to be put.

They were lithe and well-tempered blades, and a slight examination sufficed to assure the gentleman who inspected them that they were perfection.

"I see no reason for further delay," said the Major, appealing again to the friend of the Captain.

"Not the slightest."

"I presume there is to be no retraction?"

"Nothing of the kind."

"Very good."

The Captain and Sir Roderick now threw off their outer garments, and stood in their shirts; their arms were bared, and then the seconds stepped back, leaving them to confront each other.

Both looked fierce and determined, and both exhibited, by the manner in which they handled their weapons, that they had a perfect mastery over them.

Across the left cheek of the Baronet's face was a livid welt, and, on facing his antagonist, he placed his hand upon it, and said,—

"The memory of that cut can only be wiped out with blood!"

"Psha!" cried the Count, "this is play-acting, and I want none of it here—*En garde!*"

"*En garde!*"

"I shall kill you," was the remark of the Captain, as his weapon crossed that of the Baronet.

The fencing was very admirable on both sides, and for many minutes it appeared as if it would be impossible for either to receive a scratch, so well did they defend themselves.

"Every art, every trick, was put in force, but neither would be drawn off his guard.

"It is just a question of strength," said the Major, looking on composedly. "The strongest wrist must have it."

They continued thrusting and parrying until, by mutual consent, there was a cessation of hostilities.

"What think you of him?" asked the Major of his friend, as he drew apart with him.

"He is the very devil; I cannot make a point."

"How is your wrist?"

"Badly twisted, and stiff; it gives me pain to use it."

"Then your course is clear; you must make a savage onslaught, and trust to chance. If you continue this play your hand will soon be useless, and you are at his mercy."

"Yes, yes; I know and I feel I am already in his power. He is the best swordsman I ever met."

"Do not wait. Come, come; have heart, man, and do as I tell you."

"I will, but you will note the result. Did you hear what he said to me as we crossed swords?"

"Yes, he said he would kill you."

"And he will do so! Do not be deceived, my friend. You will see that I am right."

"Oh, nonsense. Can anything be done? Can the affair be ended? Are you satisfied?"

"No? It must go on, and if I die, you will report of me that I died like a man."

"Psha! Do as I tell you, and fear nothing."

The rivals once more met and the fight recommenced; from the outset of the bout Roderick acted on the aggressive.

"He made the most furious lounges at the Captain, and appeared to be bearing him down, but he was very wild in his aim, and each thrust was parried with most consummate skill.

Maddened at the calmness and marvellous tact of his adversary, Sir Roderick redoubled his thrusts, and fought as fiercely as man could fight.

At length fortune seemed to favour him.

He broke through the Captain's guard, and his weapon appeared to be going straight to the heart of his adversary, when, by a skilful movement, the Captain caught the weapon under his left arm and, shortening his own, glared wildly into the eyes of his victim, and sent it through his heart.

With a yell of agony the poor wretch fell quivering to the earth.

The surgeon and the second were at his side in a moment.

"What do you make of it?" asked the Major.

"It's all over with him: he's pierced through the heart, and has not many seconds to live."

"Roderick, old boy," said the Major, "look up. Have you anything to say?"

In a moment the eye of the dying man was lifted to the face of his friend.

"Tell her—tell her," he said, "that I died for her."

"Of whom do you speak?"

"The Duchess."

"Ah!" remarked the Captain, coolly; "I will take that message myself."

Sir Roderick glared at him fiercely.

"Villain!" he cried, "I owe more than death to you."

He sank back and spoke no more, whilst the Captain drew on his coat and sash, and, touching his hat gaily to the Major, left the field.

* * * * *

Some hours later in the day, the Captain was once more in the drawing-room of the Duchess.

"I am here, according to promise," he said.

"I see you are here," said the lady; "would that you were far away!"

"That is unkind, after all I have done to win your smiles."

"What mean you?"

"I mean that I have killed the man who stood in my path, and kept from me your love."

"You do not tell me so," screamed the Duchess.

"Oh, yes I do," said the Captain. "You remember you told me you could not be mine while he lived; and so I took the first opportunity of ridding myself of him."

"By murder?"

' No: according to the laws of the duello. We' met like gentlemen, and he died like a man. By the way, he sent a message to you. 'Tell her,' he said, 'tell her I died for her'—which I thought a very stupid remark; but as I intended coming here, I brought it, as a matter of course. Now, my dear Duchess, I should hope that your eyes are opening to the kind of man with whom you have to deal."

The Duchess replied not.

Her eyes were indeed opening, and she saw that she would have to play a deep game to rid herself of so desperate a suitor.

She subdued the torrent of abuse she felt inclined to heap upon him, and merely said—

"You are, indeed, a determined man."

"I would sweep away twenty such fellows, if you but told me you loved them, and that they stood in my path, and I know you would think none the worse of me for so doing. Women love the men who hesitate not to shed blood, and go through fire and water for them. I know the peculiarities of the sex."

"I can say nothing to you. I am too confounded. For Heaven's sake leave me!"

"I will do so, and you will see me no more."

The Duchess looked immensely delighted at this avowal.

"At least," continued the Captain, "not as the Count Paskewich. For some time, if not for ever, that noble Austrian must be *non est*, or he will be in danger of transportation for this morning's work. But fear not that I shall desert you. No, madam, we shall meet frequently. In disguise I shall come here, and in the ordinary course of business you must come to our meetings, so that we shall have many opportunities of practising courtship. And now I must say adieu. In another hour I shall be kindly inquired after by all his Majesty's officers in the city of London. Within one week we meet again."

He took his departure, and left the Duchess to weep over the fate of her long-favoured suitor.

CHAPTER LXII.

THE RECEPTION OF LADY LOVELACE BY THE GIPSIES—THE HUSBAND'S VISIT IN SEARCH OF HIS WIFE—THE INTERVIEW AND THE DISCOVERY.

WHEN Lady Lovelace recovered consciousness she was being rowed along the great canal in a large gondola.

She gazed about her, and, to her horror, found that one of her companions was the woman who had inflicted the wound upon her arm.

"Powers of mercy!" she cried, "whither am I being taken, and who are you?"

"Speak not," said Philippe; "you are in good hands, and we are friends."

"You speak my own tongue," she said, "are you an Englishman?"

"No."

"Why am I here? What do you intend doing with me?"

"No matter; keep quiet, and all will be well."

"I will not hold my peace," cried Liz, "some evil is intended, I am sure. I will cry for help and alarm the people on the shore."

"You had best not," said the old woman, drawing a stiletto, "you know the taste of this and will again if you are at all unruly."

"Sheathe the weapon; the lady will be quiet enough."

Poor Liz saw that it was useless to struggle against such force, and, hiding her face in her hands, gave way to a flood of tears.

They journeyed on in the gondola a few hours and then they were put on shore, and a long and tedious walk ensued.

They reached the open country and made for the mountains, and it was not until late in the day that they halted.

They were then far away from Venice, on the bright blue hills, and no trace of the City of Palaces was to be seen.

The region they were now in was known as the haunt of the Zingari and several daring brigands, whose lawless bands preyed upon the travellers to and from the city.

Several of these parties did they meet in their journey, but they passed without molestation.

There appeared to be a freemasonry among them, known to Philippe, who, on a word or a sign, received food and wine, and was passed on or directed, as he desired.

The halt was made in a glorious hollow between two large hills. At a glance, the lady saw that she was approaching a gipsey's encampment.

"Here we are," cried the Italian, with something like delight in his voice: "there are the tents, and there's the wreaths of smoke rising from the fires of the wanderers. So hasten—hasten."

In his excitement he caught Liz by the shoulders and almost dragged her along, until she was in the midst of the camp.

The appearance of the new comers caused a stir in the encampment, and in a few moments they were surrounded by as desperate a band of villains as could be met in a day's walk.

They were all habited in fanciful costumes, decked out with pieces of ribbon and gold and silver lace.

In their belts they wore large, glittering knives, and many of them had pistols studded with silver-headed nails, and all were conspicuous by a display of soiled finery.

In a few moments a string of women came tripping to the spot; and then the appearance of Liz underwent a great deal of criticism an remark.

They seemed to regard her as some strange animal, for they crowded about her, and gazed at her with singular interest.

They had, in all probability, never seen any one like her before.

Her fair skin and golden hair certainly presented a marked contrast to their own olive complexions and raven locks.

Her dress, too, was rich, though soiled from exposure to the damp air, and then to the dust and dirt met with in their long walk to the mountains.

Altogether, she seemed to amuse, as much as she surprised, the Zingari women.

While yet they were engaged in their inspection, a cry of " The Chief! the Chief!" disturbed them, and they drew back to make way for a tall and powerful man of middle age, who came to the spot.

He was habited somewhat after the style of the others, but the texture of his clothes was finer, and his ornaments of more value than those they wore.

In his belt was a knife, the handle of which was closely studded with precious stones; and the handkerchief about his head, as well as the sash around his waist, were of the finest and most delicately-tinted silk.

The face of this man was of a better type than that of either of his band. It was strikingly Italian in all its characteristics; but there was an intelligence about it that was missed in the countenances of the major portion of the lower order of his countrymen.

Such was Carlshoff, the chief or king of the Zingari, to whom we have introduced the reader.

" Who have we here?" he said, as he advanced towards Philippe.

" A captive of mine," answered that individual.

" A captive to be ransomed, eh?"

" No; a captive to be detained."

" For what purpose?"

" Vengeance."

" Explain."

" This is the wife of Lord Lovelace, one of the betrayers of she whom I am proud to avenge."

" I understand you now. But this fair lady must not be sacrificed."

" That is as you shall determine. It will be sufficient for me that she is detained here. Separated from him, it will wring both their hearts, even as mine has been wrung, and that is sweet revenge for me!"

" You are a Brother, and we cannot refuse thee aught; but we may ask thee, in charity, to spare the feelings of this lady as much as possible. She is too young—too good and pure—to be tortured. I would fain make her captivity as light to bear as possible."

" As you will. I am content, so that she be kept here."

" In that you shall have your own way, but no further. Madam," he continued, turning to Liz, " be under no apprehension. We receive you as a sister, not as a prisoner."

Liz would have thanked the chief for his kindness, but her tongue refused its office, and she could but bow her head in reply.

Orders were given for her reception into the tents of the women, and then the gathering dispersed.

" You were a fool to bring her here," said the old hag to Phillippe, when they were alone. " Better that I had despatched her in the chamber, as she lay sleeping."

" I think so—I think so."

" You have acted like a chicken-hearted fool, and this is your reward. Can you not see that Carlshoof looked upon the girl with loving eyes even from the moment he first looked upon her? We shall have this chit raised to be queen of the tribe, ere long, if we do not take some steps to rid ourselves of her."

" What do you propose?"

" Poison."

" Psha! Carlshoof would suspect you on the instant, and his knife would be drawn across your throat for your pains."

" I fear him not."

" But I do. I have no wish to die the death of a dog by the hand of a wandering gipsy. Mind, I forbid violence. Chance may soon do that which we desire to see done, and then we shall have naught to answer for."

They separated, both longing for, but neither daring to shed the blood of the girl they had brought to the encampment.

*   *   *   *   *

Meanwhile, Lady Lovelace had been taken to the tents of the unmarried women of the tribe, and there treated with all the rough kindnesses the poor women could show her.

She was looked upon as some pretty toy, and the poor Italians could not cease acting the child and playing with her.

They heaped caresses upon her, and would have killed her with kindnesses had not one or two exhibited a little compassion, and released her from their tender mercies.

On the whole Lady Lovelace was not unhappy among those rough gipsies.

Since her departure from England she had known but very little peace, and it was relief for her to be rid of the man to whom she was tied, and whom she now found, to her sorrow, she loved so little.

Freed from the restraint of his presence, and enlivened by the pure air she breathed, and the genial influence of the bright blue sky over her head, together with the simple pattering of the unsophisticated creatures among whom she was thrust, her almost broken spirits revived, and, day by day, she became more cheerful, and her health grew stronger.

Daily she saw Carlshoof, the Chief, and in every way in his power he exhibited his marked preference for her over others.

Truly, there was occasion for the suspicions of the old hag; it was just possible that the Chief was in love.

As the hag walked about, his eyes were upon her.

He seemed but to live in her presence, and to receive happiness only in her smile.

The choicest fruit that the clime could produce was daily gathered—perhaps stolen would be the better word—for her use.

The finest wines, the choicest delicacies, were her's, and she reigned supreme, to the discomfiture of Philippe, the old woman, and one Biondella, a glorious specimen of the Italian Zingara.

Biondella was a gipsy of the purest Italian type. Her face was that of the Roman women of old, and her form boasted of the matchless perfection of a Venus.

She was of the most delicate olive complexion, and her hair, traced and plaited with ribbons with common pearl, was of a deep blue-black, that fairly glittered in the sunshine.

Until the arrival of Liz she had been the pet of the tribe, and there was not a man or woman who would not have laid down his life for her.

It was presumed that the Chief loved her; but, be that as it may, she certainly loved the Chief, and hesitated not to show it.

Since the arrival of Liz, Biondella had been absent from the camp; she now returned to find that she had a rival.

In years she was little over sixteen, but in appearance she was a full-grown woman. The Italian sun is a quick ripener of female charms.

Now, although Biondella found that in Liz she had a formidable rival, she did not, as may be supposed, entertain for her a direct and fiery hatred.

There was some charm in the presence of Liz that softened down such feelings, if it did not entirely quench them.

Still Biondella regretted the presence of the young English girl, and would not have paused at a trifle in ridding the camp of her presence, but yet she did not hate her with that absolute hatred that Marie had felt towards her up to the moment when she rescued her child from its cruel grand-dame.

Nevertheless, the three we have named quickly consorted to rid themselves of the intruder.

Whether they succeeded will transpire in the course of this history.

A week passed.

In that time Liz had become, as it were, completely naturalised in her new home.

The camp seemed to her to be her natural element, and into its unrestrained mirth and festivities she entered with all her soul.

At times, however, the dark cloud that ever and anon fell over her life, would blot out the sunshine, and then she would leave the camp and wander forth among the trees, and weep and think of one face that haunted her day and night—it was *not* that of Lord Lovelace!

During one of those temporary fits of gloom, Liz resorted to her favourite haunt under a group of trees, from which a view of the camp could be had.

Here she sauntered to and fro, thinking of the days gone by, when a voice near at hand startled her from her reverie.

"Liz—Liz," it said, "fly,—fly with me. Not a moment is to be lost."

Had a thunderbolt stricken her to the earth, she could not have received a greater shock.

She could not move. She dared not speak; but in a moment her hand was clasped, and she felt herself drawn away from the spot on which she stood. Then she roused herself, and turning, faced her husband!

'Come, dearest!" he cried "come, fly. I have stolen here unobserved. I have watched you throughout the day, and it is only now that I have been able to approach you."

"Why, did you come hither? Fly, fly, I beseech you! There is danger for you here. Should they see you, they would have no mercy."

"I know, I know; but I will not fly without you, my wife—my darling."

"Talk not thus, Lord Lovelace, for there is deceit upon your tongue. Those words have been uttered before, and to other listeners. Seek her you have wronged, and try to atone for the injuries you have heaped upon her. Leave me to my fate. I am happy here—happier than I have ever been before, so leave me, leave me."

"I will not—I cannot. I have sought you day and night since you left home. I know of the attempted murder, of your interference, and the wound you received in rescuing my child. I traced you from the house of Marie, and lighting upon the very gondolier who bore you from the Angelo Bridge, I was enabled to track you to this spot, and now tell me not that I have found you to part thus suddenly and for ever."

"I do tell you so. I must tell you so, Lovelace. You have wronged me, and you have wronged another! Seek her—own you owe her all your love—and your child claims all your care. I tell you that I am happy, so leave me. I pray you, leave me and save yourself. The grandmother and lover of the girl you deserted are here. They bear you the bitterest enmity, and, should they meet you, death would be your doom. I beg, I pray of you to leave this place, and for ever."

"Will you not fly with me?"

"No, No; it is best we part."

"Liz, Liz; you will break my heart. I shall die if you leave me thus."

"You mistake, Lord Lovelace, your heart is not so much affected as you think. I thank you for seeking me; I am grateful for all your care; but, depend upon it, I judge rightly when I say that it is best we separate and meet no more."

"Stony-hearted woman," cried the husband, "you love me not. You have never loved me, and now, at the first opportunity, fly me."

"It is true. Lovelace, I could never have loved you. It was but a dream of love, that faded away almost as soon as engendered. You know full well that those feelings are yours also. Attempt not to deny it—I know I am right; and in your cooler judgment you will acknowledge the truth of what I now assert. Should I return with you, it will be but to enjoy the briefest of blissful dreams. Your love of society will draw you again from me, as it has done before, and I will not wreck my new-found happiness by pandering to your pleasure. Once for all, leave me, and seek me not again. '

"Cruel, cruel !"

"I am not deserving that appellation, as you will see anon."

"Your coolness wounds me to the quick. I shall go mad.'

"It is your self-pride I wound—nothing more."

"Bah ! I was a fool to seek you at all; but I will play the cringing ass no longer. Adieu, and may you live to repent your act."

"May you live to regret your crimes. Adieu !"

Lovelace seized the hat that had fallen from his head, and, readjusting it, was stalking from the spot, when Philippe, followed by a band of Zingari, sprang from behind some bushes, to which they had crawled during the progress of the above conversation, and, catching Lord Lovelace by the arm, at once made him a prisoner.

"At length," cried the Italian—"at length I have thee, and my vengeance is about to be wreaked !"

"Who and what art thou ?"

"He who was the loved of the woman you wronged, and whom you cruelly deserted. He who is her avenger, and who has now to shed your heart's blood—and who would do so, did not the laws of this tribe forbid the taking of a life, save in self-defence, without the express sanction of the Chief. Now you know me."

"I do, and can afford to despise you."

"No insolence! or I brave the laws of the Zingari, and strike thee dead at my feet."

He partly drew a knife as he spoke, but Liz was at his side, and held his arm.

"Why not strike !" taunted Lovelace : "it is but manly to strike a defenceless foe. You will only act up to the traditions of your country—I advise you to do it."

"Dog ! you shall not tempt me to forget myself, although I could fain tear thee limb from limb. Bear him to the camp ; I will hear him speak no more !"

"Do not harm him !" cried the infuriated Italian ; "do not harm him, I pray thee !"

"Silence, woman !" and think yourself lucky to have escaped the doom that shall be his."

"You hear," said Lovelace, "you hear how courteously your new-found friends treat you. I wonder not at your choosing to remain with them."

"This was spoken in a tone of bitter irony, and the Italian was stung by it; but he still withheld his hand, and merely motioned to the band to move on with their prisoner.

Dragging Lovelace with them, the gipsies hastened towards the tents, Liz following behind in an agony of doubt and fear.

* * * * *

The appearance of the new prisoner again brought forth the whole of the gipsy band, and a semicircle was formed about the tent of the chief, to which Lovelace was dragged.

Carlshoof soon appeared.

He seemed disturbed at the sight of the prisoners—perhaps, in consequence of Liz clinging to him, and weeping so bitterly.

"Who is this ?" he demanded.

"It is my enemy," said Philippe.

"The Englishman who so wronged thy love ?"

"The same."

"We will hear what thou hast to urge against him. Speak !"

Philippe advanced, and told the whole history of his love, from the moment he first met Marie, to that in which he last saw her—the murderess, the homeless outcast from society, and the heartbroken mother of a deserted child.

The relation of the story was listened to with indignation by the men, and with sobs and tears by the women ; and at its conclusion there was raised one wild chorus of—

"His life is yours,—take his life."

"Stay !" said the Chief,—" we have heard but one side of the tale ; the other may be different. Englishmen, we will hear what thou mayst have to urge."

"I have naught to say, save that I was enveigled into a detestable connection with a consummate courtesan. That I am the father of the child I own ; that I left her I own, but I provided amply for both her and her child."

"Think your money could heal a broken heart ?"

"No ! But you have not been told the whole story. I left this woman because she attempted to poison me, and I was in fear of my life."

"That is, indeed, a different version of the tale."

"It is," said Philippe ; "but there is yet another. Marie was tempted to her crime by his desertion. If he had not absolutely left her, he took from her his heart—his love—and gave them to the lady who now stands trembling by his side. He deserted one for the other ?"

"How say you ?"

"I will speak no more," answered Lovelace ; "I do not acknowledge your power to try this question. If I am amenable to any law of the land, I will answer to that law, but not to a band of desperadoes."

"Unfortunately for you," said the Chief, "the desperadoes, as you call us, are absolute in these mountains ; and you will be amenable to such laws as they lay down."

"I repeat, I will say no more."

"Then I shall ask the tribe for their decision. What say ye—does this man merit death ?"

"Yes."

"You hear their verdict ?" said the Chief ; "you are to die."

"No, no," cried Liz ; you will spare him—you will save him !"

"Ask it not," said Lovelace, proudly. " Rise, Lady Lovelace, I command you ; your place is not grovelling at the feet of a cut-throat and a thief."

"Those words to me !" cried the chief.

"Heed him not," said Liz, "he knows not how he speaks. Forgive him — let him depart. He will go hence ; he will return to his own land, and come amongst you no more. Let him depart uninjured, and I will bless you !"

"Lady," said the Chief, "his life is in the hands of our brother Philippe; to him we give his life, and it is he alone who can spare it."

"To you, then," cried Liz, "to you, I appeal. Have mercy, and spare him as you hope to be spared when called upon to answer the sins registered against you. He never knowingly did you harm, therefore let him depart, and stain not your hand with his blood."

"You ask me that which I must refuse. I have sworn to have his life, and must take it."

"It is, then, yours," said Carlshoof. "Do with it as you will."

"I will have it at once."

"Not until after midnight."

"Wherefore?"

"It is a law of our tribe. Blood shall only be shed in the day from after midnight until midday, except in self-defence. There is a tradition amongst us that binds us to this course, and we must pursue it."

"There is," shouted the men.

"Evil would come of a departure from the rule, and it shall not be done with my consent."

"So be it, then," said Philippe, "I will wait until after midnight."

"Meanwhile," said the Chief, "convey the English Lord to a tent, and let two of the tribe remain sentries over him."

CHAPTER LXIII.

THE CHIEF AND LADY LOVELACE—A DECLARA-TION OF LOVE—THE OFFER OF RELEASE—THE REFUSAL — THE RIVALS — A BARGAIN—THE POWER OF LOVE.

Liz was completely distracted at the awful termination of a day which had opened in merriment and happiness.

She was not allowed to approach the tent in which her husband was confined, and, therefore, took herself of to the quarter of the women, and remained there in moody silence.

At length, as night gathered about her, she sank into a deep reverie, from which she was aroused by a light touch on the shoulder.

She looked up and beheld Biondella.

"You love the prisoner in the tent yonder?" said the Italian.

"He is my husband," was the reply of Liz.

"Ah! and you would fain save him?"

"I would, indeed."

"Does he love you?"

"Oh, God! I would that I were certain on that point."

"I see; would you be content to be with him, and think of no other if he could be saved?"

"I would give my life to save his, whether he loves me or not."

"I understand you. We shall meet before midnight."

With this Biondella vanished from the tent.

There was again a gloomy pause, and then Liz was once more awakened to a knowledge of the presence of some one in the tent.

She looked up and beheld the Chief.

"Lady," he said, "I am come to speak of the prisoner."

"Oh, speak not of him, speak not of him, unless you will save him; you could do so, but you will not."

"Lady, why should I betray our brother for the stranger? The tribe has adjudged him the life of your husband, and I have confirmed their decision, for it was a just decision. Why should I, therefore, save the life justly forfeited?"

"Is it justly forfeited?"

"The tribe have spoken."

"But what says your heart?"

"It is silent."

"Then you own the injustice of the award, and you will save him? I see, you will do so. You are all goodness, and will not let him die."

"He has injured you."

"I forgive him."

"Then I ought to do so?"

"Yes, yes; you ought, indeed."

"But why should I offend Philippe, and incur the anger of the whole tribe? What is to be my reward?"

"The consciousness of having done a good act."

"That will not suffice."

"Then I know of no other reward. Stay! Money!—money in galore shall be yours, only save Lovelace. I promise—I swear—to enrich you for life if you will set him free, and allow him to make his escape from this unhappy country."

"I am rich; I require not gold."

Liz hung her head.

"Then," she said, "I do not know what will tempt you, for I have nought else to offer."

"You have, lady."

"What is it? Name it!—name it! and it shall be yours!"

"If I have aught to give it shall be yours."

"Give me, then, your love."

Liz started.

"Do you refuse me that?" continued the Chief.

"Ask it not," said Liz; "I have no love to give thee."

"Art sure?"

"I am sure."

"Then Heaven save your husband—I will not."

"Oh, say not so. Hear my prayers. I will do aught in the world for thee; I will work for thee—will be your slave—only spare the life of my husband."

"Be my bride, and it is done."

"I cannot!—I cannot! It would be sinful!"

"Have you determined?"

"I have determined."

"Must he, then, die?"

"His life is in your hands."

"Then he dies. If you would have heeded me, I would have spared him and risked all. But you have decided for me—you have pronounced his doom."

"You cannot mean it—you would not be so cruel!"

"I shall see that he dies within an hour after midnight."

"Cruel, cruel man."

"I could apply the same word to thee, but will not do so. Hereafter you may repent of your act."

The Chief left the tent.

"He is gone!" cried Liz—"he is gone, and no one will save him."

"Yes, I will!"

Liz looked up, and saw Biondella.

"I have heard all," she said—"I have heard all, and have marked how nobly you have acted. Make me but one promise, and I will keep my word, and save your husband."

"What do you desire of me?"

"It is that you quit this spot with your husband, and never return to it more."

"Why must I go?"

"Because the Chief loves you, and I love the Chief."

"I understand you."

"And you will accept the terms!"

"Gladly."

"It is well, then. Follow me to the tent. Alessandro is sentry, and through him I will release your husband, But heed me. On escaping from the camp, fly rapidly towards the east, and throw yourself on the protection of the brigands you will encounter. They are at enmity with Carlshoof, and will protect you against him. If you hasten you will be saved; for they will not discover that you are gone until after midnight, and it is not yet ten o'clock."

The girl seized a gourd that lay in the corner of the tent, and drawing from her bosom a small phial, she poured its contents into the gourd.

"If Alessandro loves me as he has said he does, he will drink that draught, and then he will know nothing of the escape of his prisoner."

Biondella caught the hand of Liz, and drew her from the tent.

They threaded their way through the labyrinth of bright canvass, gleaming in the silver light of the moon, and were soon at the tent of the prisoner.

Arrived here, Biondella warbled in a sweet low voice a verse of an Italian melody, and in a moment a head, followed by the whole of a man's body, presented itself from under the tent.

"Is that you, Alessandro?"

"It is I."

"I am come to sing to you, and have brought the poor English lady with me, in order that she may be near her husband."

"You have grown kind of a sudden," thought Alessandro, but he was far too pleased with the presence of the lady of his love to give breath to any such offensive remark. He merely said—

"I am pleased that you are come. The prisoner is asleep, and I may talk to you."

"Will you drink of my wine, Alessandro?"

"Nay, I dare not; it is against orders."

"But my wine."

"I must not drink."

"Then you love me not."

"Heaven only knows how much I love thee."

"And yet you refuse to drink of my wine?"

"Supposing it should contain a potion that would send me to sleep, and that during my sleep the prisoner should escape?"

"And supposing that is precisely what I willed, would you hesitate to drink?"

"Biondella, do not tempt me."

"Will you drink?"

"I dare not."

"Then I swear to speak to thee no more."

"Biondella, swear not that."

"Wilt drink, then?"

"I will drink."

"Now thou art more reasonable."

"But promise me that it is not drugged."

"I promise thee nothing. I will not even assure thee that it does not contain a deadly poison; and now, if you love me, I shall see you drink."

The Italian hesitated a moment, and then applied the gourd to his lips.

"It is good wine," he said, "but methinks it has a bad taste."

"Or does the bad taste lay with thee?"

"Nay, my taste is good enough."

"Then drink again, and tell me if the wine is not better than thou dost at first take it to be."

Alessandro did as desired, and then threw down the wine.

"It is drugged," he said. "Biondella, you have deceived me. It is drugged, and I am disgraced."

"Fool, speak not! Do you not value my love?"

"Yes, yes; but what am I to do? The prisoner——"

"Leave him to me."

"I—I must—I die!"

"No, no; you will but sleep and rest."

"Treacherous—treacherous Biondella!"

The man rose to his feet and tried to shake off the drowsiness that was creeping over him, but the drug proved too powerful, and after staggering about for a few seconds he fell to the earth in a deep sleep.

"He is safe now," said the gipsy girl, "free your husband and begone."

Lady Lovelace required no further inducement.

Dashing aside the canvas, she entered the tent and rushed towards her husband.

"Come!" she cried, "come with me, you are free."

Lovelace held out his hands.

They were bound.

He then pointed to his feet. A stout rope was also observable about his ancles.

"What shall I do?" cried the wife.

Biondella had entered the tent at the same moment, and now advanced and, drawing a small dagger from her girdle, she freed the prisoner. Stretching forth her hand imperiously, she motioned the Englishman and his wife to fly.

"Begone," she said, "begone! In a few moments you may be deprived of the chance."

Lovelace moved forward, but Liz paused, caught the hand of the Italian girl in hers, and pressed it to her lips.

"I shall be indebted to you for ever," she said. "Believe me, I am deeply grateful."

The girl replied not.

Her hand was still extended and she motioned them forth.

Suddenly she started back and her face turned a ghastly white.

Her eyes were fixed upon the opening of the tent.

Instinctively Lovelace and his wife turned their glance in the same direction, and there, gazing fiercely upon them, stood Carlshoof.

Liz uttered a shriek and was about to start forward, when Lovelace drew himself up for an attack.

"Stay," said Carlshoof, "hold your hand or I shall send this to your heart."

As he spoke he drew forth a small dagger and presented it at the unarmed man.

"Stay," he continued, "I am not your enemy."

"Will you attempt to delay my flight?"

"Do you take her with you?"

"Yes."

The face of the chief darkened, and the dagger was clutched convulsively.

Biondella then darted forward and threw herself at his feet.

"Do not stay them; let them begone!" she cried.

"Wherefore should I let them begone? and why have you proved a traitress to your tribe?"

"Speak not to me—ask me not."

"I will ask thee. Why are you a traitress?"

"I will tell," said Liz; "it is because she loves thee."

In a moment the truth flashed across the brain of the Chief, and stooping, he raised the girl from the earth.

Placing one hand over his eyes, he with the other waved the others away.

"Begone!" he said, "begone! I have been weak. Let me not look upon you again, and I may forget the dream that has been so full of mingled happiness and pleasure to me."

Lovelace and his wife started away before he had finished speaking, and Carlshoof and the devoted Biondella were left to confront each other.

CHAPTER LXIV.

RETURNS TO PIPEY—THE OLD INN AT PURFLEET —THE DETECTIVE'S TALE.

WE left our hero seated with the landlord of the inn, his friends, and the officers who were in search of the supposed murderer of the Duke, and quietly listening to their conversation.

It is now time we return to this scene, and take up the thread of our narrative at that point.

Perhaps an hour passed in ordinary conversation, and then one of the officers growing loquacious with the brandy he drank, volunteered to tell the company a tale of one of his own adventures.

The proposal was hailed with tokens of satisfaction, although, truth to tell, every one wished him and his friend far away. But seeing that he was not to be cheated out of his story, they all settled down to listen.

"My name is Greys," said the officer, "and I'm pretty well known in London. I've done a great deal, first and last, in the cause of justice, and I could tell you tales of my experience that would take me a month to relate. However, I shan't trouble you with more than one just now, and if you're prepared to listen, just draw up close to the fire, and I'll tell you how I tracked and brought to the gallows Simon Haskitt, of whom you've all heard.

"Well, lads, it was just four years ago that he danced on nothing, and this is how it came about.

"There was a little shop at the corner of Boswell-court—the old court I mean—and here lived an old woman called Bentley. She was his aunt, on the mother's side.

"You may have seen the little shop in your time.

"It was small, dirty, and rather repulsive in appearance.

"In the window was a small collection of sweets, a few dried oranges, some children's dolls, and little picture books.

"Oh, I remember the dolls well. They all hung on a line, and of a night, when the oil lamp was put in the window to light up the wares, and the wind blew in through the cracks in the windows, they all set to dancing on their lines, and threw great quaint shadows over the room inside; and this, aided by the light from the fire, served to make the place look anything but enticing.

"Here, too, sat the old woman, and with her was a young and beautiful girl—Clara they called her. Her other name nobody ever knew, because, you see, she was an orphan; and Mother Bentley had picked her up when she was but a baby, and reared her as her own child, without ever enquiring who her parents might have been.

"Well, as I said, Clara was a beautiful girl. Notwithstanding the filth and odd ways of the old woman, she grew up neat and clean, and took a pride in her herself, and was always the talk of the people in the neighbourhood.

"Her hair was a bright golden colour, and her eyes bright blue. I ain't much of a hand at doing justice to female beauty, so I shan't attempt to describe her any further. You can, perhaps, better imagine than I can describe what she was really like.

"The old woman was peculiar in her ways, and was an awful temper. People said she led the poor girl an awful life, but no one ever heard her complain; on the contrary, she was always excusing faults that others condemned, and ready to smooth down the rough points they were always finding out and exhibiting relentlessly.

"She wasn't happy, though. The careworn expression of the face would tell you that well enough. But still she was ready to hide her sorrows from the world, and do her best to make all think that the old woman was one of the best of God's created beings.

"So time passed.

"Simon Haskitt, as I have said, was the old woman's nephew; and a greater scamp never lived.

"He lost his mother early in life, and went to live with his aunt, who brought him up as her own boy.

"He was a coward and a bully, and from the first led the poor little Clara an awful life.

"He beat her mercilessly, and continually taunted her with her misfortune in having no parents, and living on the charity of his aunt— as if she could help that!

"Well, I suppose you wonder how I know all this? You see it came out in evidence at the trial; but I'm going to tell the story straight forward, without any beating about, and that's how it is.

"To resume—

"Mother Bentley put Haskitt to a trade; and for two years he stuck to it pretty well. Then came a break out. He ran from his master, and, after scamping about for some weeks, joined the merchant service and went to sea.

"They saw nothing of him for years, but at last he came back—a man.

"He appeared to be quite altered in every respect.

"All the wilfulness appeared to be quite gone

out of him, and he was kind and generous to Clara.

"He even brought her home presents from foreign parts, and made as much of her as if she had been a pet dove.

"Well, this pleased his aunt, who always wished him to take a fancy to Clara and marry her.

"The old woman was as delighted at his preference for Clara as she was at his turning up after his long absence and silence; and one night, as the three were seated in the little old shop, stooping over the fire, she turned suddenly on Haskitt and said to him—

"'Did they ever tell you I had money, Simon?'

"The young fellow was somewhat puzzled at this direct question: coming too in so unexpected a manner, and hesitated before he replied to it, but at last he answered ·

"'Yes, aunt, I've heard folks say that you've saved up a little.'

"'Well,' said the woman, 'it's true, and for once rumour doesn't lie. I have saved a little, and it's for you—that is—for you and Clara. You must marry her, and when I'm gone you'll have all—all.'

"The girl hung her head and blushed, and Simon put his great brawny arm about her, and drew her towards him, and said:

"'But supposing she won't have me.'

"'She will,' said the aunt, 'she will, I know that well enough, she will. Ask her.'

"'What d'ye say, Clara,' he said, looking straight into her eyes, 'is aunt right?'

"And she dropped her head still lower, and then replied:

"'Yes.'

"So he kissed her, and they all appeared very happy.

"'We'll be married at once,' he said, 'there's no occasion for waiting.'

"'Marry her when you will,' said the old woman, 'but no taking her away from me, she must stay here, and you must go to sea again, for not a penny of my money will you touch 'till I'm gone. Work, work, and save, as I've worked and saved, and then you'll do well enough: your little added to mine will be sufficient to keep you well for life, but if you had it now, and sought not to increase the store by your own exertions, it would dwindle away to nothing; so go to sea again, and come not back until you have something to bring your wife, besides a few paltry presents.'

"Simon pretended to see the force of this, and readily consented to act in obedience to the will of his aunt.

"'But,' he said, 'I must have a wife to work for, and so will marry at once.'

"He looked at Clara as he spoke, and as she did not offer any opposition the affair was settled, and in the course of a week they entered the church of St. Clement's, and came out man and wife.

"It was now time for Simon to seek another ship, and go away again; but day after day,

week after week passed over, and there was no attempt made at going.

"He appeared to grow more and more indolent each hour.

"The pot-house and the skittle-alley were his constant resort, and when he came home to his aunt it was only for more money.

"After a week or two Clara was forgotten.

"He seldom gave her a look, and her beauty seemed to fade away under the chill of his cruelty and neglect, and she grew in a few months to look a pale, haggard, and care-worn woman.

"At length Simon entirely exhausted the patience of his aunt, and she ordered him to come to her house no more.

"'If you do not go now and carry out the plan proposed,' she said, 'I will cut you off without a penny, without a penny mind!'

"'Oh, nonsense,' said Simon, who was at this time half drunk, 'what should you cut up so rough about. Havn't I been away long enough? Can't I stay in England a few months now that I am come home?'

"'Not with my consent.'

"'Well, then, I shall stop without it.'

"'As you will, but mind you don't come here. My door is closed against you.'

"'Psha! Look here — listen to something like reason. Give Clara and I a few pounds, and let us set up for ourselves. I can take a boathouse, and get some work that will keep us very well; and as I'm sick of the sea, that will be more preferable than getting another ship. Now, what d'ye say?'

"'I say the same as I have said before; you have no money of mine, and I tell you that you shall not take Clara from me. She shall stay here—here with me; and I'll have my way in the matter.'

"'Oh, you will? Well, now I'll show you that I'll have mine. Where's Clara?'

"'I don't know.'

"'Well, I'll wait till she comes.'

"'To what purpose?'

"'To take her away with me.'

"'You would not dare.'

"'You'll see.'

"'She won't go—mark me. I'll forbid her, and she will stay.'

"'I'll command her, and she will go. She's my wife, and I'm her master. My word is law, and I will be obeyed—by her, at least.'

"'Simon, Simon—you are a villain! I thought you had grown better, but I see the badness of your youth is still in you, and you are the same wretch you were as a child.'

"'The same,' said Simon, 'the same. I'm not altered, and I hope I never shall.'

"At this moment Clara entered the room, and Simon rose to his feet, and bade her follow him.

"'Stay with me,' cried the frantic old woman; 'stay with me—leave me not! He would drag you from me to possess my gold. Don't let him! don't let him!'

"Clara glanced uneasily from one to the other, and appeared confounded.

"'You have heard what she says,' continued her husband, 'and you must hear what I say. You are my lawful wife, and I tell you that I am forbidden this house, and that you must seek another with me. Will you come quietly, or will you force me to drag you away?'

"'Do not tear me from her,' cried the poor girl; 'let me stay with her, and I will pray for you. She is old, and would die without me to help her, and attend to her wants. Let me stay with her.'

"'You have heard me. Come, or I shall use force.'

"'You would not be so cruel.'

"'Don't tempt me, or you'll see.'

"'But something can be done—something *must* be done. Do not drive him away,' she said, kneeling at the feet of the old woman; 'do not forbid him your house, and all will be well.'

"'He knows my determination. Let him fulfil his promise, and go to sea again, and we are friends. If he insists upon remaining here, and spending his days in idleness and drunkenness, we part now, and for ever.'

"'You hear, Simon,' cried the agonized wife; 'you hear. Pray, pray do as she wishes, and all will be well.'

"'I'll go to sea no more,' was the reply. 'You want to get rid of me, I suppose; but you shan't—you shan't. I'll stay, if only to worry you.'

"'God forbid that I should wish to be rid of you,' said Clara, 'although you have not treated me as you should have done, Simon.'

"'That's right! You upbraid me, now. It's quite right, I suppose, that you should do so. It's the duty you owe your husband. But I'll have no more of this farce; put on your shawl, and follow me.'

"'Oh, Simon, Simon! let me stay! For Heaven's sake, let me stay!'

"'You have heard. Will you come, or shall I drag you forth by the hair of the head?'

"'You hear him,' cried the wife; 'you hear him—what can I do?'

"'Remain.'

"'I dare not.'

"'I should say not,' said Simon; 'I should say not, indeed. Come along.'

"'Will you go? will you leave me for that villain?' screamed the old woman.

"'I cannot help it,' said poor Clara; 'he is my husband, and his will is my law.'

"'Go then,' cried Mother Bentley, 'and never let me see either of you again. Ungrateful hounds that you are, begone! and I'll look to strangers for comfort and assistance, and, what's more, I'll give them my money—every penny—and you shall have none. Go and starve.'

"With these words ringing in her ears, Clara left the home of her childhood and followed the footsteps of the man she called husband.

"It was a sorry day for her, and she knew it, but what was she to do? Simon's was a will of iron, and she could not disobey it; so she followed him without a murmur, but with a bleeding heart.

"He led her to a wretched den in the East-end of London, and took her into a miserable cellar.

"'There,' he said, 'this is your home; I can afford no better. You'll get none of the comforts you've been used to, but you'll have to put up with the inconvenience.'

"'I will do so, Simon,' she said.

"And so he left her, and went his way.

"For forty-eight hours he returned not, and during all that time she neither tasted food nor drink.

"Then he came back, and gave her some coarse meat and bread and a few pence.

"'You see what you've got by marrying me.' he said. 'This is how I'm forced to live. and you will have to put up with the same fate.'

"'I know it, Simon,' she replied, 'and I'm not going to complain.'

"'No,' he said—'d——n!—it's that I don't like. If you'd only turn upon me I wouldn't care; I should know what to do then; but I'm beaten by your pitiful looks and smooth tongue—beaten all to nothing!'

"Once more he left her, and this time he was absent four days.

"He returned, and found her fainting for want of food.

"Again he served her as he had previously done, and again he left her.

"This system went on for a month, and at the end of that time it appeared that Clara was fast sinking into the grave.

"No one approached her—no one descended to her miserable cellar. Poor and wretched as were the people who occupied the upper part of the house, they were as princes compared with the poor occupant of the damp, naked cellar, and consequently they left her to her fate.

"I've found there is a great amount of aristocracy and pride in rags.

"Here was a specimen of it.

"Well, time passed, and a month had slipped over.

"Then Simon came again to his poor, forlorn wife.

"He was flushed in the face—his utterance was thick—his breathing hard and quick; altogether, he appeared to be under the influence of excitement and drink.

"He threw some gold at the feet of the poor woman, and said—

"'There, make the best use you can of that. I've had hard work to earn it for you.'

"When he was gone she picked up the gold, but shuddered as she touched it, for something told her that it was not honestly come by.

"She attempted not to use it for two days, but at the end of that time she was so weak and ill that she felt that death must come then if she did not purchase food and stimulants, so she went forth and changed some of the money.

"As she re-entered the house, for the purpose of seeking her cellar, she was accosted by one of the tenants.

"'Good day to you, ma'am,' said the woman. 'It's a fine morning.'

" ' Very.'

" ' Have you heard the news to-day ?'

" ' No,' said the poor girl, ' no; I seldom hear any news.'

" ' I did'nt know whether you might have heard it at the tavern, I saw you come out.'

" ' Yes; I've been for a little wine. I have felt so ill and low lately.'

" ' Ah, indeed, ma'am ? And to think you didn't hear of the murder.'

" ' Murder !'

" ' A terrible suspicion flashed like lightning across the brain of the poor woman.

" ' Yes, ma'am,' continued the gossip ; ' of the awful murder in Boswell-court.'

" ' Boswell-court !'

" ' Yes, ma'am. An old woman, who kept a little shop there, was found this morning with her brains knocked out against the edge of a trunk, which——My God ! the woman's dead.'

" Clara had swooned away.

" There was no occasion for her to hear more. The appearance of her husband—the gold he brought her—all convinced her, on the instant, that to him could be traced the crime of which the woman spoke ; and thus it came about that she fell senseless at the words to which she had listened.

" As she sank to the earth, the food and wine she had purchased, together with the gold she had in her hand, fell to the ground.

" The woman picked up the money, and looked at it in astonishment.

" She then summoned some of the neighbours, and Clara was carried to her cellar.

*　　*　　*　　*　　*

" There was a great deal of talk about the mysterious fainting of the woman of the cellar during that day, and people looked very blank as they canvassed her conduct, and reflected on the money found in her hand when she fell.

" The gossips had enough to occupy them fully, and over their gin the subject was freely canvassed.

" Clara was not visited by many people, for there was little sympathy to be found in that quarter.

" They let her lie on her rough couch, and come to as she best could.

" The day passed ; night came—and with it Simon.

" The peculiarities that distinguished him in the morning were now more apparent than ever.

" There was a horrible expression on his face ; and weak and ill as she was, the wretched wife could not fail to remark it.

" ' Well,' he said, as he entered the cellar, ' how have you got on to-day ? What did you do with the gold ?'

" It lay on the ricketty table before her, and she stretched forth her hand, and pointed to it.

" ' There is what remains.'

" ' And have you eaten and drank well ?'

" ' No,' she said. ' No : I have touched nothing.'

" ' Why ?'

" ' Because I know how that money was obtained.'

" Simon sprang to his feet.

" ' What d'ye mean !'

" ' Simon ! Simon !' cried the poor woman ; ' they have told me that she is dead—that she was murdered. I guess by whom.'

" ' Oh, you do, do you ?' said Simon : ' and what d'ye mean to do ?'

" ' God help me ! What can I do ?'

" ' Much, and I believe you would do, if you had the chance.'

" ' Do you think I would reveal your guilt ?'

" ' I know you would.'

" ' No, no,' she cried ; ' bad as you are I would not do that.'

" ' I doubt you.'

" ' Simon,' she cried, ' there is a terrible meaning in your eye. I read there trouble—deep, dark trouble for myself.'

" ' Oh, you do, do you ? Well, what of it ?'

" ' Simon ! Simon !' shrieked the woman : ' what are you contemplating ? For the sake of your own soul, get from me ere you commit a second deed of blood.'

" ' Oh, you see my game, do you ?'

" ' I see you mean not well by me.'

" ' I do not. By God ! I don't mean to let you live and split upon me. I'm suspected already ; they're after me now, and there's only one way to save myself.'

" ' And that way is—'

" ' By killing you, and letting you bear the guilt.'

" ' You will not do this ! Simon, you cannot act so cruelly by one who never harmed you—by one who has grown up by your side—who has been your sister, playmate, and friend, and who is now your poor, dying wife—I say, you could not do this ?'

" ' And I say I can, and must ! My safety is more to me than your life, so, you may depend upon it, you will die.'

" ' No, no ! you do not mean it ! Let me live : oh, let me live, and I will never betray you.'

" ' I don't doubt it ; but, if you live, they will accuse me ! By your death I see a way to escape the punishment in store for me, so expect no mercy.'

" ' I will shriek for aid.'

" ' Do so, and no one will heed you ; they are too used to such cries here to heed them when they hear them. If you were to cry for a month there's not one in the house who would come to your assistance.'

" ' Then God help me !'

" ' You have need of his help.'

" As he spoke he drew from his pocket a long clasp knife, and opened its glittering blade.

" The poor woman, pale and motionless with horror, slunk into a corner, and with eyes dilated and mouth open, contemplated her fearful husband.

" ' I must do it,' he said ' I must do it. There's no help for it. I must kill you, but it's to save myself.'

" Still no word escaped her. Still no sound —no movement told that aught but a terrible sculptured thing, bearing a semblance of humanity, lay huddled in that corner, and fixed its great unmeaning eyes on the man before it.

"Gradually, and with a step tottering with fear, but with a mind steadfastly bent on the awful purpose that occupied it, the man advanced.

"At length he stooped over his victim.

"She moved not.

"Her eyes closed and her limbs fell motionless.

"He then placed his fatal hand upon her head and drew her forth.

"With but little effort he caught her in his arms and threw her on the wretched bed.

"He then glanced at the knife, and, drawing a long breath, clutched the shaft more tightly.

"An instant, the glittering blade was drawn sharply across the poor white throat.

"There was a convulsive shudder of the body and the blood poured out in a crimson stream, and ere long there was no movement, and the form that lay on the bed was an inanimate lump of clay.

"He contemplated his work in silence; he was calm now—awfully calm—and assuring himself that the door of the cellar was fast locked, he drew from his pocket a short crowbar, and with this commenced to dig up the stones of the floor.

"They were large flags, and as time had worked upon them, and made the gaps between them many and great, he had no difficulty in performing his task.

"In half an hour he had removed four of the great stones, and there was room for the admission of a human body.

"From the hearth he took the great iron shovel, and cleared away the earth, leaving a hole two feet deep.

"Here, then, was a grave.

"His next act was to take the body, wrapped in its blood-stained shroud, and lay it in the grave.

"This was done without trouble or hitch, and then the earth was replaced, stamped down, and otherwise disposed of, and the flags replaced.

"Another hour was occupied in clearing away all traces of the bloody tragedy.

"The task was no difficult one; but it was an adept who performed it, and ere long it was done—done in the most perfect manner.

"There was no trace left.

"The surplus earth was carefully picked up and folded in a cloth, and then the murderer blew out the light and, taking his burthen of clay with him, left the cellar and walked away.

"Well, we fellows got scent of the murder as soon as anybody, and at once set about the discovery of the murderer.

"Knowing the family, I at once settled in my own mind who was the guilty party. But there was no proof, and I was powerless to act.

"After searching the house again and again, after going from top to bottom and examining everything, there was no trace to be found.

"I was upon the track of Simon. I clung to him day and night, but I discovered nothing.

"He did not appear even to be flush of money.

"To make matters more intricate I learnt that, on the night of the murder he was not in London.

"Having a job in the country, he had left the previous day, and twenty people could prove an alibi.

"I was almost in despair, and was about to give up the chase, in common with most of the other officers engaged in it, when one morning I saw Simon enter a low beer house.

"I could not resist following him, and on entering I found that he had gone to the bar.

"I went there too.

"He called for some brandy, and I did the same.

"Receiving his spirit, he tendered a coin in payment.

"It was a very old spade guinea.

"This determined me. My suspicions were at once confirmed. That guinea could have only come out of the strong box of his aunt.

"That very day I heard of the disappearance of his wife.

"Chance led some of our fellows into the neighbourhood where she had lived, and there heard the tale of the money, the fainting, and then of the mysterious disappearance.

"This induced him to think that the murder could be traced to the woman; it only confirmed my suspicions of the guilt of Simon.

"I said nothing, but determined to watch closely, and at the first opportunity to enter the house in which poor Clara lived.

"I did so. My inquiries led to nothing; I could not hear of Simon's coming or Clara's going; but still I was not dispirited.

"'Where did she live?' I asked.

"'In the cellar.'

"'Who occupies it now?'

"'No one.'

"'Is it locked?'

"'Yes; it is still in the possession of Simon Haskitt.'

"'Ah, I see. And where is he to be found? Does he come here?'

"No one had ever seen him.

"I dismissed my informant, and then descended to the cellar.

"I found it locked, but it was no trouble to me to open it, and the lock fell under the wrench I put upon it.

"I entered, and a faint, sickening smell assailed me.

"It was a smell I knew well, although others less skilled in such matters would have set it down to age and damp. I knew it to be that of a decomposed body.

"I carefully examined every spot, hoping to find some trace of a struggle; but none presented itself.

"I went on my hands and knees and examined the flag stones.

"I tested them, and found, as I anticipated, that they had been recently moved.

"I then took the shovel from the grate and removed a large stone.

"I wanted no further evidence.

"Springing up, I replaced the stone, and, closing the door, left the house to seek assistance.

"I found two of my mates, and then we returned.

"You, of course, guess that we found the body of the murdered woman.

"I will not give you the details of all the horrors of that scene. Suffice it to say, that we removed the body and bore it away, to the amazement and horror of the people of the house.

"In unfolding the clothing from the bed which encircled the corpse we found a great *clasp knife*, On the handle were the initials 'S. H.'; but it needed not this striking evidence to convince us who was the perpetrator of the deed.

"I at once set out in search of the murderer. I knew his haunts, and after a slight search I found him in a beer house.

"He was seated in a public room, and was more than half drunk.

"He was surrounded by men and women, whom he had been treating to drink.

"I walked up to him and caught him by the hands.

"In a second the darbies were on his wrists, and he stood looking me in the face.

"'Well,' he said, 'what's this for?'

"'Can't you guess?'

"'No.'

"'Well then, I'll tell you. It's for the murder of Mrs. Bentley and your wife, Clara Haskitt.'

"'For the murder of Mrs. Bentley," he gasped, "You must be mistaken, I know nothing of the affair."

"Oh, it's no use pretending to be so green, my lad. Do you see this?" at the same time showing him a something which had been found that was known to have belonged to him.

"He staggered back in great alarm, but instantly recovered hisself-possession, and, with a sneering laugh, asked me what proof there was against him.

"'Oh,' I said, 'we've lots of evidence. There's everything been done to accommodate you, my fine fellow, so don't be under any alarm for safety.'

"The people looked aghast but did not attempt to interfere with me, and I caught my prisoner by the collar and dragged him away.

"'I say,' he said, this is a joke, isn't it? and if so its' gone far enough.'

"'It's a joke that will go just as far as the gallows and no farther,' I said, at which he pretended to laugh again.

"'Tell me,' he said, 'what's against me; it will ease my mind.

"'Well, then,' I replied, 'we've found the body of your wife, and we've found the knife by which the deed was committed. Is'nt that enough?'

"'It's strong as far as it goes; but what's that to do with the old woman?'

"'Plenty; the chain of evidence doesn't want a link—but I shan't say another word on the subject, or I may lead you to convict yourself, and that's against the law.'

"After this he was silent and moody, and hung his head in deepest dejection.

"Next week he was tried.

"A whole batch of evidence came up against him, and he was found guilty on both charges, and condemned to death.

"To the last day he protested his innocence; but then he confessed, and gave, in nearly the same words as I have related it, the story I have told.

"You may depend upon it; and I got plenty of praise for the part I played in this affair, besides a handsome reward offered by the Government.

"That's the tale, boys."

*   *   *   *   *

It was now broad daylight, and the officers rose to take their departure.

"Good bye, governor," they said to the host, as they pulled on their overcoats; "good bye, and many thanks for sitting up with us. If ever you come to London, we'll do as much for you."

"Never mind him, my boy," said the first speaker, "he's green in the profession yet; wait a while, he'll know better by and by. But, as I was a going to say, if ever you should be in want of a friend, I'm your man, for you've acted a trump to-night, and there is no mistake. Thanks."

"Thanks," said the old landlord; "thanks: I shan't forget you."

"Nor I you, old boy—that's certain. So good night."

"Good night," replied the landlord.

They shook hands all round, and then the officers went out of the house, and the doors were closed upon them.

"Whew!" cried Maydock, as they turned their back upon him, "I thought they would never go. Devil take them, what a deal of jaw they have."

"Ah, that they have," said the sailor, "they're like parrots; they like to hear themselves talk, and are always harping on the same string; but blessings on 'em for going."

"Yes, blessings on 'em," said Pipey, "they're a useful lot sometimes, but cursed nuisances at others."

"And now," said Maydock, "let us see about business."

CHAPTER LXV.

THE FORTUNES OF MARIE—PARIS—SINGING IN
THE WINE SHOPS—A CHANGE OF LUCK.

IT was the aim of Marie to reach France, and
in its gay capital to commence life anew, and
under another name.

As Marie Lavrouffe she would have been
welcomed there, for her fame as a singer was
European.

But, unhappily, there was another reputation
hanging to that name which she wished buried
for ever, and so it was discarded.

"I can begin over again," she said to herself.
"I can commence once more: there is still
sufficient of the old voice and the old beauty left
to insure me a welcome wherever I go, and so
Paris shall be the next starting place."

Had she, at the same time, resolved to strike
out a path of virtue with her new enterprise it
would have been as well, but, unhappily, no such
thought entered her brain.

The sole aim of her life now was revenge, self-
aggrandisement, and the preservation of her
child from the ills that were threatening it.

Its honour she would have guarded with her
life, but there was no thought of self.

"My child shall be virtuous," she said, but at
the same time she took no step towards placing
before the little one any laudable example.

The same resolves had been made by her
mother, and her mother's mother, but with a like
result.

Marie's funds were but low, and travelling in those days was not accomplished with the facility and at the cheap rates at which it is now done, and Marie's task was one of pain and trial, but she bore with it cheerfully.

She sang at every town and village through which she passed, and her pretty face and marvellous voice gained for her numbers of admirers, many of whom marked their appreciation of her charms in the most substantial manner.

When this occurred, Marie rode on her journey; but the sums expended, she was obliged to pause and use her voice, and if she failed to receive any sum by which she could afford to ride, she would again pursue her journey on foot; but never despairing—never daunted.

So after many weeks she entered the great city of Paris.

She was ragged, footsore, and weary, but undaunted.

"A time will come," she said, as she was passing the magnificent Hotel de Ville, "when even the portals of such a palace as this will open to receive me."

Her plan was already laid out.

She would inquire her way to the Opera, and having once made herself conversant with its whereabouts, she would seek some humble lodging, and then return day by day to the vicinity of the Grand Theatre, and by singing in the streets, and in the houses of entertainment where she would be most likely to be heard by those connected with the establishment in which she hoped to enter, to call attention to her powers, and get talked about.

But, meanwhile, she was penniless, and without a home.

Entering Paris at dusk, and with only a meagre stock of money in her pocket, she sought out that part of the city most suitable to her means.

She retired early to bed in a hotel of the humblest pretensions, and then slept until the coming day.

She was early astir, and having taken a slight repast in a neighbouring *cafe*, set out to commence life in Paris.

Day after day passed over her head, and found her persevering in the task she had set herself.

Week after week went on, and still Marie appeared to be as far off as ever from the desired effect.

True, she succeeded well in obtaining a livelihood.

Among such gay and music-loving people as the French, she could not fail to be appreciated, and in the wine-shops and on the Boulevards she could always command an audience and a shower of sous.

But this was not her object.

Day by day she came regularly to the Opera, and set herself down to the work she had undertaken.

She looked at the great building towering above her, and said,

"It is there I will be heard; nothing but death shall prevent me."

*   *   *   *   *

She had been five weeks in Paris, and one afternoon was as usual singing the gay airs of the sunny South in the neighbourhood of the Opera, having for an audience a crowd of idlers who lingered in the bright sunshine, to listen to the pretty vocalist, when an old gentleman hurried past on his way to the theatre.

Marie had previously noticed that he was connected with the establishment, but whenever he approached her he appeared too much distracted by thought to listen to her.

As he now came towards her, however, she noted that there was an idleness in his gait, and a sharp, penetrating expression in his eye, that spoke well for his not being for once preoccupied.

"Now," she thought, "is my time."

Pausing in the simple song with which she had been delighting her song audience, she broke out into a splendid *cavatina* from an opera then enchanting all Paris.

But ere the first bars had been sung, hope forsook her—the gentleman was passing on without noticing her.

Her voice trembled and fell, and the notes were dying away upon her lips, when the man by whom she wished to be heard turned, and as if he had suddenly determined to waste a few moments in listening to her, approached, and looked into her face.

Once more hope revived, and the singer poured forth a whole flood of melody of the most brilliant description.

As he listened, the old gentleman grew more enraptured, and when Marie finished, he clapped his hands with enthusiasm and cried—

"Bravo! bravo!" with so much vehemence that Marie's face flushed with triumph, and her eyes sparkled with gladness.

"Here, ma'amselle," said the old man, tendering a piece of money, "you are a beautiful singer. I have been delighted, entranced! Are you, *Italiano?*"

"*Si, signor.*"

"My own country," continued the old gentleman, speaking in Italian, "although it was so long ago I saw it that I have grown to forget it, and to believe myself a Frenchman. But, with such a voice, why sing in the streets?"

"Alas, I am poor, very poor," said Marie, "and have no friends."

"Ah! that is sad. I am not rich, and I have but very little influence, for I am only chorus master yonder, but what I can use is at the service of my countrywoman."

"Oh, signor; how can I thank you."

"No thanks to me, fair one; I have done nothing for you as yet, but I will try. Ah! these boors look very inquisitive, get you into the wine shop yonder, and await my coming. I think I can find something for you in the chorus."

"You are good, signor. Oh! how good."

"Bah! It is nothing," said the old man,

"who would not do as much for a fair compatriot in trouble?"

With this they separated, the old gentleman entered the theatre, and Marie sought the wine shop he pointed out.

In the drinking-room, or saloon, were a number of men, many of whom recognised her, for she had sung there frequently.

As she entered, they got up a loud chorus of "bravos," and demanded a song.

But Marie was in no frame of mind to comply with their request.

Her heart was too full, and her mind too distracted for singing, and so she put them off with some slight excuse, and, sitting down, anxiously awaited the coming of the old chorus master.

One hour passed, and Marie was almost despairing of his coming, when he suddenly presented himself before her.

"You were growing impatient," he said, "and I have to apologise for keeping you waiting: but they will not excuse one at the *Opera*. And now to business. What is your name?"

"Marie Laporte."

"Marie Laporte; good. Mine is Albertini—and now we know each other. And now—excuse the question—how comes one so skilled in music, so graceful in bearing, and so well born as you appear to be, in this position?"

"A misfortune. Excuse my answering further."

"Ah! I see; and will ask no further question on that score. Have you been long in Paris?"

"Five weeks."

"And why have you not sought employment at the theatres or concerts?"

"Look at my dress," said Marie, exhibiting the simple and travel-stained garments of an Italian peasant; "is this a costume that would insure me an engagement at even the meanest of the theatres!"

"True; dress goes a long way; but with your voice—*mon Dieu!* you could force an entrance as *prima donna* into the *Opera* itself."

"You jest with me."

"Not I," said the enthusiastic chorus-master, "I never was more in earnest. Have you never sung on the stage?"

"Oh, yes, frequently—in England."

"And made no success?"

"I never had the opportunity."

"Ah! that is sad. These English will not see talent until it is thrust under their noses by the French. Ah, but the next time they hear you they shall believe in you."

Marie could have contradicted this, but held her peace.

"Now," said the old man, "I must make my revelation. I can introduce a soprano into the chorus at once—will you accept the offer?"

"Oh, gladly," cried Marie, catching the hand of Albertini, and kissing it rapturously; oh, how gladly, signor!"

"Well, it shall be so arranged. Where do you reside?"

"I am ashamed to say, my lodging is so poor."

"Then you must leave it. Here are a few

francs; owe them to me until you draw your salary."

"Oh, how shall I ever repay such goodness?"

"By singing as you sang in the streets to-day, and, above all, by avoiding the temptations thrown in the path of a young *debutante* at the Opera."

Marie hung her head, and blushed scarlet.

"Yes," she said, "your advice is good, and I will try to follow it. I know how true you speak, for I have had bitter experience of the temptations to which a poor girl is subjected who seeks the stage as a mode of livelihood."

"How say you?"

"Will you despise me if I should tell you all?"

"Why should I?"

"Then know that at home, in the humble lodging I have taken, is a little one who depends upon me for bread. That poor child is the offspring of sin."

"Hush, hush! I comprehend."

"And you do not hate me?"

"Heaven forbid."

"Thanks. You are, indeed, a friend. Each moment my obligation to you increases tenfold."

"That must not be. I cannot consent to be the recipient of so much gratitude with so little pretension to assume the character you would have me play. To what I have done for you you are most welcome. It is but a trifle of the most insignificant kind. Besides that, am I not doing myself honour by finding such a member for the chorus? But ah, me! They will not leave you to me long. I shall see you taken from the ruck and placed in the foremost position."

"I fear you are too sanguine of my success."

"Not at all—not at all. Time will show that I am right. I seldom make false estimates, and now get you home, and be at the theatre at twelve to-morrow. We rehearse an opera of some importance, and you will have to go through the chorus music with us."

"I shall do so with immense satisfaction."

They then separated.

The old man was delighted at serving his countrywoman, and Marie felt herself already on the upward path. She saw herself on the first wing of the ladder. To advance would not be so difficult.

But the satisfaction she felt was not of the most pleasing kind. She saw the way to gratify her ambition—to satisfy her longing for admiration and applause, and this was all she cared for.

CHAPTER LXVI.

THE PRINCE IS AT LENGTH INTRODUCED TO OLIVIA—THE INTERVIEW—TRIAL AND TEMPTATION.

POOR Olivia Besgrove was very lonely after the death of her mother, and when the Duchess of Grasmount importuned her to take up her residence with her, pleading her own solitude and misery, it is not to be wondered at that the young girl very readily consented to change her residence, and take up her abode under the care of her aunt.

Had she known what was passing in the brain of that designing woman who sought her society with such strong expressions of never-dying affection, she would have turned away and blessed her solitude rather than have exposed herself to the designs laid for her; but unhappily, she was ignorant of the fate which was marked out for her by her wretched aunt, and unsuspectingly transferred herself to St. James's-square.

Her betrayal was not to be accomplished by a *coup d'état*.

The Duchess had marked out a plan by which the Prince was to worm himself into her good grace, and effect his cruel purpose.

There was to be no rash proposals and attempts, such as had been tried and had failed in the instance of Fair Liz.

The ruin of the unsuspecting girl was rather to appear her own act, and to this end her Grace exerted all her cunning.

She cordially detested the young girl, in consequence of the late Duke having taken her into his favour, and entrusted her with the awful secret of his life.

This act on the part of the Duke was sufficient to raise the ire of the bad woman against her niece.

She looked upon Olivia as filled with deceit and cunning, and to effect her downfall would be the darling aim of her life.

As a matter of course, the young girl was literally smothered with affection as soon as she presented herself under the roof of her aunt.

The deceitful Duchess protested that they had been separated too long, and professed the deepest regret that any misunderstanding should have ever arisen between them.

Poor Olivia, unacquainted with the arts of the worldly, listened delightedly to all she heard, and blamed herself for having thought ill of a woman so filled with virtues, and whose heart could expand so wide to admit at once one who had been a comparative stranger to her.

Had not an occasional thought of Lewis darkened her happiness Olivia would have speedily become the gayest of the gay.

Gradually, but by almost imperceptible degrees, the Duchess drew her niece from her retirement, and introduced her to the fashionable world.

Without, apparently, aiming at giving her a taste for pleasure, she allowed no opportunity to escape whereby she could dazzle her into admiration of a town life, and the unsuspecting victim was led on by the hidden chain, step by step, until she found herself taking a positive pleasure in a course of existence which she had heretofore despised.

Pleasure is a fatal fascinator. Once fix your eyes upon it, and it will draw you on into a vortex from which it will cost you an immense effort to escape.

Olivia found it so.

She made the effort, but failed, and in a very short time after the death of her mother it was whispered that she was becoming too fond of the brilliant dissipations for which her aunt was famous.

She dressed extravagantly, rode and drove the most magnificent horses, and saw more of the world than would have been deemed discreet by the majority of her sex.

Of course this change in her disposition was noted by Lewis, and deeply regretted; for, in spite of all, he loved her as devotedly as man could love, although his passion was hopeless.

A crowd of the gay young blood of the town was constantly at the side of the fashionable *belle*, and at length people began to ask why the Prince was not to be found among them.

It was a most unusual thing for a lady of any pretensions to personal beauty to appear in the fashionable hemisphere without his Highness of Wales being immediately reckoned among the most ardent of her adorers, but in this instance he was an absentee, and people would talk about it.

But the nine days' wonder was soon to explode.

One day the Duchess entered the *boudoir* of Olivia, and, throwing herself on an ottoman, commenced a vapid and uninteresting discussion on the merits of the principal leaders of fashion.

Olivia had her favourites, and the Duchess had hers; and at length the dispute waxed warm.

They could not at all agree, and at last the matter appeared likely to drop without being settled, when the Duchess suddenly broke out with the following :—

"Well," she cried, gaily, "since neither one nor the other of my *proteges* please you, what say you to the Prince of Wales?"

"I have seen but very little of his Highness, and know but little of him."

"But what say you to his appearance?"

"It is well enough."

"Is it not *very* well?"

"For aught I know to the contrary."

"Do you not think he merits the title of the First Gentleman in Europe?"

"How can I possibly tell?"

"Ah me! Have you no ambition to form his acquaintance?"

"Not the least."

"Most ladies have."

"That is possible, but I am not like most ladies."

"But conceive the pleasure of having such a man at your feet."

"If all is true that I have been told there would not be much gained by that."

"It is not well to pay much heed to all we hear said against great men."

"That is true; I do not."

"Then you should not judge the Prince of Wales by report."

"I do not. I have never yet taken sufficient interest in his Highness to form any judgment at all."

"But would you like to know him?"

"I should not run after the chance."

"Perhaps not; but would you accept it if it were thrown in your way."

"Perhaps I would — perhaps I should not. It would much depend upon the humour I was in."

"But if he desired it; nay, if he was positively dying for the honour."

"What honour?"

"Of an introduction to you."

"Of an introduction to me! Absurd!"

"It is not all absurd; in fact, it's a positive certainty."

"You must be jesting with me."

"Indeed I am not. Lord —— tells me that he does nothing but talk of the new belle, and regularly importunes his friends to introduce him; but they, cunning wretches, refuse the poor man the pleasure."

"Oh, this is an impossibility."

"Indeed, it is nothing of the kind. What so reasonable as that the Prince, a man of taste, should seek to know the lady whose name is now in the mouth of every one? What absurdity is there in the first gentleman in Europe wishing to know the first lady, for such they have named you?"

"I cannot credit it."

"It is nevertheless a fact. Each day your reputation spreads, and, ere long, you will be acknowledged as the leader of English fashion, and the most admired lady of any time. Why, thousands are already dying for you."

"And amongst them the poor Prince, I presume?"

"Yes, amongst them the poor Prince."

"Make me believe that if you can."

"I can readily do so. I will bring the Prince himself to you, and make him repeat my words."

Olivia now looked really interested.

"You surely do not mean what you say?"

"I do. You will not object to receive his Highness?"

"Why should I?"

"Just so; I thought there may be some silly scruples, but I am glad there are not."

"And I shall really be introduced to the Prince?"

"Yes, and hear from his own lips how strong is his admiration for you."

"That I would rather not do."

"And wherefor?"

"Because I do not care to be made a jest of to my face."

"Made a jest of! Forsooth, there is but little jesting in the matter."

"Then I think it best he should not come."

"Psha! you have given me your promise."

"Well, as you will."

"Then I will that he comes. And if I may offer a word of advice, it is that you receive him with the best possible grace. His influence at Court will advance you to the foremost position and make you the most enviable of your sex."

Here the conversation veered round again to other topics, and after a while the Duchess left Olivia alone.

Light and frivolous as the conversation with the Duchess had been it nevertheless left a lasting impression on Olivia.

The thought that the Prince was devoted to her was not at all distasteful to her.

To be admired by a man in his position was a compliment to her woman's vanity.

And then there was the prestige attached to him at the court. His influence could, as the Duchess had said, raise her to the foremost position, and, therefore, it would be as well to cultivate his acquaintance.

With these thoughts in her mind she glanced into her mirror and saw there a face which she knew to be beautiful, and which she had no doubt was quite capable of doing all the execution the Duchess attributed to it.

"Let him come," she thought, "he will not waste his time."

Was all thought of Lewis gone then?

Did not her mind revolt to his old and true love?

It did.

But had he not voluntarily thrown her off when she made all the advances towards reconciliation that it was possible for a woman to make?

He had.

And then there was a Prince ready to fall at her feet.

Why should she think of the struggling young lawyer?

Psha! he should be banished from her thoughts for ever.

* * * * *

The Duchess made good her word next day.

She and Olivia were engaged to dine with Lord Belmore, and the Prince was coming to escort them.

At an early hour he was there.

His equipage was to take them to his lordship's, and the ladies were dressed as became the occasion.

Olivia looked her best.

Never had she so far surpassed herself.

Over a white silk petticoat she wore a pale blue velvet train, looped back with sprays of silvered flowers.

Her magnificent arms and rounded shoulders were bare, and her raven hair was fastened loosely with the simplest of flowers.

Radiant in her beauty she awaited the coming of the Prince.

The Duchess was no less magnificently, though somewhat more sombrely, dressed, as became a widow of so recent date.

"Here is his Highness," said the Duchess, as the sound of wheels fell upon her ears, "now let me see you look your best."

Olivia smiled.

In another moment the Prince entered the apartment.

They rose, and he advanced to meet them.

A glance at the Duchess assured her that he was delighted at the appearance of his new acquaintance.

Of course this was unnoticed by Olivia, who hung her head and silently went through the ceremony of introduction.

Then came a short conversation.

The Duchess was all smiles, all pleasantry, and the Prince was equally delighted.

He seated himself by the side of Olivia, and conversed with her in a manner that soon put her at her ease ; and while they were thus engaged, the Duchess found an opportunity for leaving the room.

"You have been too much of a recluse, Miss Besgrove," said his Highness, "and we really owe the Duchess a great deal for bringing you into society."

"She is very good to me."

"Ah, and well might she be, for where could she again find so lovely a companion ?"

"You flatter me."

"That would be an impossibility."

"I fear not."

"I fear no language I could use would do you justice."

He drew nearer to her and passed his arm behind her, and allowed it to rest on the back of the lounge on which they sat.

He looked into her eyes, and she bowed them to the ground.

There was that in his gaze which brought the crimson to her cheeks.

But still she moved not.

"How is it possible," he continued, "that one so beautiful could have so long lain in retirement without being dragged forth to glad the world ? To look into your face and think that such has been the case seems to be almost an impossibility."

"Why so ?"

"Because the world has too few such beauties to gladden it to permit one to voluntarily hide herself from its admiring gaze."

"Ah, that is rank flattering."

"Indeed, it is honest truth."

"I cannot believe it."

"Allow me to assure you of the fact. But is it possible that you have never heard this before ? Is it possible that no one has as yet told you as much ?"

Olivia blushed, and hung her head. A shadow of pain passed over her face, but it was of but a moment's duration.

"No," she said, "no ! Such words were never before addressed to me."

"Ah ! then you have been kept among savages who have not known how to appreciate beauty. Would that it had been my fate to have met you before !"

"Wherefor ?"

"Because each day that I have not known you has been a day lost. A blank in my life ! I begin to live from this hour only."

"Your Highness confuses me."

"I would not do so for the world."

As if by accident the arm that had lain on the back of the lounge now dropped on the shoulder of the lady, and again did the eyes of the Prince seek her's.

Still she moved not.

Emboldened by this the Prince took her hand in his and pressed it warmly.

"Do you not believe me ?" he asked.

Olivia hesitated a moment and then answered softly—

"Yes."

"Thanks," he said, and he raised the little hand to his lips.

Each moment the hand on her shoulder was tightened, and then it fell upon her snowy bosom.

At the touch she started to her feet and darted forward.

Fortunately, at this moment, the Duchess returned to the room, and prevented that confusion that must otherwise have ensued.

"Come," said her Grace, "we must hasten. I am sorry to have kept you waiting, but an important matter has detained me."

She glanced at her niece, and read in her face that something awkward had occurred.

Guessing how matters stood, she whispered to the Prince, as they quitted the apartment.

"Be careful," she said ; "there is no trusting you for an instant."

He understood her, and, during the remainder of the evening, behaved very differently to the fair Olivia.

CHAPTER LXVII

THE LANDLORD'S YARN ABOUT THE GREAT CAPTAIN ENGLAND.

PIPEY thought the proceedings of his companions were becoming rather tiresome, as another twenty-four hours passed in inactivity and without any further movement being made towards getting away.

Although they were constantly breaking out with

"Now, let us get to business," they certainly made no attempt to do so.

A few incoherent words about what was to be done were uttered, and then the old landlord and his guests turned to drinking again with redoubled ardour, and long rambling tales told all round was the mode adopted for killing time.

Towards night, and after the little group of four had sat in the little bar parlour over sixteen hours without once attempting to move, the old landlord grew loquacious : he told short anecdotes of his career, and at last Maydock asked him if "he couldn't tell them something in the cut-throat line."

"You must have been mixed up with some of these rum 'uns," he continued, "and as we're in for a swim, spin us a yarn."

"Well, look here : you've heard of Captain England."

"Who was he ?"

"A pirate."

"Well, what about him ?"

"Would you like to hear his story ?"

"Yes, if it's worth the trouble."

"Well, judge for yourself. Captain England was mate of a sloop that sailed from Jamaica, and was taken by Captain Winter, a pirate, just before the settlement of the pirates at Providence Island. After the pirates had surrendered to his Majesty's pardon, and Providence Island was peopled by the English Government, our captain sailed to Africa.

"There he took several vessels, particularly the Cadogan, from Bristol, commanded by one Skinner.

"When he struck to the pirate, he was ordered to come on board in his boat. The person upon whom he first cast his eye proved to be his old boatswain, who stared him in the face, and accosted him in the following manner:

"'Ah, Captain Skinner, is it you?—the only person I wished to see: I am much in your debt, and I shall pay you all in your own coin.'

"The man trembled in every joint, and dreaded the event, as he well might.

"It happened that Skinner and his old boatswain, with some of his men, had quarrelled, so that he thought fit to remove them on board a man-of-war, while he refused to pay them their wages. Not long after they found means to leave the man-of-war, and went on board a small ship in the West Indies.

"They were taken by a pirate, and brought to Providence; from thence they sailed as pirates along with Captain England.

"Thus accidentally meeting their old captain, they severely revenged the treatment which they had received.

"After the rough salutation which has been related, the boatswain called to his comrades, laid hold of Skinner, tied him fast to the windlass, and pelted him with glass bottles, until they cut him in a shocking manner; then whipped him about the deck until they were quite fatigued, remaining deaf to all his prayers and entreaties; and at last, in an insulting tone, observed, that as he had been a good master to his men he should have an easy death; and upon this, shot him through the head.

"Having taken such things as they stood most in need of out of the snow, she was given to Captain Davis, in order to try his fortune, with a few hands.

"Captain England, some time after, took a ship called the Pearl, for which he exchanged his own sloop, fitted her up for piratical service, and called her the Royal James.

"In that vessel he was very fortunate, and took several ships of different sizes and different nations. In the spring of 1719 the pirates returned to Africa, and, beginning at the river Gambia, they then sailed down the coast to Cape Corse, and captured several vessels.

Some of them they pillaged, and allowed to proceed some they fitted out for the pirate service, and others they burnt.

"Leaving our pirate upon this coast, the Revenge and the Flying King sailed for the West Indies, where they took several prizes, then cleared and sailed for Brazil.

There they captured some Portugese vessels; but a large Portugese man-of-war coming up to them proved an unwelcome guest. The Revenge escaped, but was soon lost upon that coast. The Flying King in despair run ashore. There were then seventy on board, twelve of whom were slain, and the remainder taken prisoners.

"The Portuguese hanged thirty-eight of them.

"Captain England, while cruising upon that coast, took the Peterborough of Bristol, and the Victory. The former they detained, the latter they plundered and dismissed. In the course of his voyage England met with two ships, but these taking shelter under Cape Corse Castle, he unsuccessfully attempted to set them on fire. He next sailed down to Whydah road, where Captain La Bouche had been before England, and left him no spoil. He now went into the harbour, cleaned his own ship, and fitted up the Peterborough, which he called the Victory.

"During several weeks the pirates remained in this quarter, indulging in every species of riot and debauchery, until the natives, exasperated with their conduct, came to an open rupture, when several of the negroes were slain, and one of their towns set on fire by the pirates.

"Leaving that port, the pirates, when at sea determined, by vote, to sail for the East Indies, and arrived at Madagascar.

"After watering and taking in some provisions, they sailed for the coast of Malabar.

"This place is situated in the Mogul empire, and is one of its most beautiful and fertile districts. It extends from the coast of Canora to Cape Comorin. The original natives are negroes, but a mingled race of Mahometans, who are generally merchants, have been introduced in modern times.

"Having sailed almost round the one-half of the globe, literally seeking whom they might devour, our pirates arrived in this country.

"Not long after their settlement at Madagascar they took a cruise, in which they captured two Indian vessels and a Dutchman. They exchanged the latter for one of their own, and directed their course again to Madagascar. Several of their hands were sent on shore with tents and ammunition, to kill such beasts and venison as the island afforded. They also formed the resolution to go in search of Avery's crew, which they knew had settled upon the other side of the island: their loss of time and labour were all the fruits of their search.

"They tarried here but a very short time, then steered their course to Juanna, and, coming out of that harbour, fell in with two English and an Ostend ship, all Indiamen, which, after a desperate action, they captured.

"They arrived the 25th of July, last, in company with the Greenwich, at Juanna, an island not far from Madagascar. Putting in there to refresh our men, we found fourteen pirates that came in their canoes from the Mayotta, where the pirate ship to which they belonged, viz., The Indian Queen, two-hundred and fifty tons, twenty-eight guns, and ninety men, commanded by Captain Oliver de la Bouche, bound from the Guinea coast to the East Indies, had been bulged and lost. They said they left the captain and forty of their men building a new vessel, to proceed on their wicked designs.

Captain Kirby and another concluding that it might be of great service to the East India Company to destroy such a nest of rogues, were ready to sail for the purpose on the 17th of August, about eight o'clock in the morning, when they discovered two pirates standing into the bay of Juanna, one of thirty-four and the other of thirty-six guns. We immediately went on board the Greenwich, where they seemed very diligent in preparations for an engagement, and they left Captain Kirby with mutual promises of standing by each other. They then unmoored, got under sail, and brought two boats a-head to row me close to the Greenwich; but being open to a valley and a breeze, made the best of his way from them; which an Ostender, in their company of twenty-two guns, seeing, did the same, though the captain had promised heartily to engage with them, and they believed would have been as good as his word, if Captain Kirby had kept his. About half an hour after twelve, Captain Mackra called several times to the Greenwich to bear down to their assistance, and fired a shot at them, but to no purpose. For though they did not doubt but he would join them, because when he got about a league from them, he brought his ship to, and looked on—yet both he and the Ostender basely deserted them, and left them engaged with barbarous and inhuman enemies, with their black and bloody flags hanging over them, without the least appearance of ever escaping, but to be cut to pieces. But it was determined otherwise; for, notwithstanding their superiority, they engaged them both about three hours; during which time the largest of them received some shot betwixt wind and water, which made her keep off a little to stop her leaks. The other endeavoured all she could to board them, by rowing with her oars, being within half a ship's length of us above an hour; but, by good fortune, they shot all her oars to pieces, which prevented them, and by consequence saved their lives.

" About four o'clock most of the officers and men posted on the quarter-deck being killed and wounded, the largest ship making up with diligence, being still within a cable's length, often giving us a broadside. There being now no hopes of Captain Kirby coming, they endeavoured to run ashore; and though they drew four feet of water more than the pirate, he stuck on a higher ground, and was disappointed a second time from boarding. Here they had a more violent engagement than before : all the officers and most of the men behaved with unexpected courage; and, as they had a considerable advantage by having a broadside at his bow, they did him great damage; so that, had Captain Kirkby come in then, we believed they would have taken both the vessels, for they had one of them sure; but the other pirate (who was still firing at them) seeing the Greenwich did not offer to assist them, supplied his consort with three boats full of fresh men. About five in the evening the Greenwich stood clear away to sea, leaving them struggling hard for life, in the very jaws of death; which the other pirate that was afloat seeing got a warp

out, and was hauling under the stern. By this time many of his men being killed and wounded, and no hopes left of escaping being all murdered by enraged, barbarous conquerors, he ordered all that could get into the long-boat, under the cover of the smoke of the guns; so that, with what some did in boats and others by swimming, most of them that were able got ashore by seven o'clock.

" When the pirates came aboard they cut three of his wounded men to pieces, and he, with some of my people, made what haste he could to the King's-town, twenty-five miles from us, where he arrived next day, almost dead with the fatigue and loss of blood, having been sorely wounded in the head by a musket-ball.

" At this town he heard that the pirates had offered ten thousand dollars to the country people to bring him in; which many of them would have accepted, only they knew the king and all his chief people were in his interest. Meantime, he caused a report to be spread that he was dead of his wounds, which much abated their fury. About ten days after, being pretty well recovered, and hoping the malice of our enemies was nigh over, he began to consider the dismal condition they were reduced to ; being in a place where they had no hopes of getting a passage home, all of them in a manner naked, not having had time to get off another shirt, or a pair of shoes, than what they had on.

" Having obtained leave to go on board the pirates, and gotten a promise of safety, several of the chief of them knew him, and some of them had sailed with him, which he found of great advantage ; because, notwithstanding their promise, some of them would have cut him, and all that would not enter with them, to pieces, had it not been for Captain England, and some others whom he knew. They talked of burning one of their ships, which we had so entirely disabled as to be no farther useful to them, and to fit the Cassandra in her room ; but in the end he managed the affair so well that they made him a present of the said shattered ship, which was Dutch built, and called the Fancy; her burden was about three hundred tons. He procured also a hundred and twenty-nine bales of the company's cloth, though they would not give me a rag of his own clothes.

" They sailed the 3rd of September; and he with jury-masts, and such old sails as they left him, made a shift to do the like on the 8th, together with forty-three of his ship's crew, including two passengers and twelve soldiers, having no more than five tons of water on board. After a passage of forty-eight days he arrived here on the 26th of October, almost naked and starved ; having been reduced to a pint of water a day, and almost in despair of ever seeing land, by reason of the calms they met with between the coast of Arabia and Malabar. They had in all thirteen men killed, and twenty-four wounded ; and they were told that they destroyed about ninety or a hundred of the pirates. When they left them there were about 300 whites, and 80 blacks, in both ships. He was persuaded, that had his consort, the Green-

wich, done her duty, he would have destroyed both of them, and got two hundred thousand pounds for owners and selves; whereas, the loss of the Cassandra might justly be imputed to his deserting them. He delivered all the bales that were given to him into the company's warehouse, for which the governor and council ordered him a reward.

"Captain Mackra was certainly in imminent danger, in trusting himself and his men on board the pirate ship; and unquestionably nothing but the desperate circumstances in which he was placed could have justified such a hazardous step. The honour and influence of Captain England, however, protected him and his men from the fury of the crew, who would willingly have wreaked their vengeance upon them.

"Captain England was so steady to Captain Mackra, that he informed him that it would be with no small difficulty and address that he would be able to preserve him and his men from the fury of the crew, who were greatly enraged at the resistance which had been made. He likewise acquainted him that his influence and authority among them was giving place to that of Captain Taylor, chiefly because the dispositions of the latter were more savage and brutal. They therefore consulted between them what was the best method to secure the favour of Taylor, and to keep him in good humour.

"Mackra made the punch to flow in great abundance, and employed every artifice to soothe the mind of that ferocious villain. A singular incident was also very favourable to the unfortunate captain.

"It happened that a pirate, with a prodigious pair of whiskers, a wooden leg, and stuck round with pistols, came blustering and swearing upon the quarter-deck, inquiring where was Captain Mackra.

"He naturally supposed that this barbarous-looking fellow would be his executioner; but, as he approached him, he took the captain by the hand, swearing that he was an honest fellow, and that he had formerly sailed with him, and would stand by him; and let him see the man that would touch him.

"This terminated the dispute, and Captain Taylor's disposition was so ameliorated with punch, that he consented that the old pirate ship, and so many bales of cloth, should be given to Mackra; and then sunk into the arms of intoxication.

"England now pressed Mackra to hasten away, lest the ruffian, upon his becoming sober, should not only retract his word, but give liberty to the crew to cut him and his men to pieces.

"But the gentle temper of Captain England, and his generosity towards the unfortunate Mackra, proved the origin of much calamity to himself.

"The crew, in general, deeming that kind of usage which Mackra had received inconsistent with piratical policy, they circulated a report that he was coming against them with the company's force.

"The result of these invidious reports was, to deprive England of his command, and to excite those cruel villains to put him on shore, with three others, upon the island of Mauritius.

"If England and his small company had not been destitute of every necessary they might have made a comfortable subsistence here, as the island abounds with deer, hogs, and other animals.

"It is even said that the shores are replete with coral and ambergris; but, had this been the fact, the Dutch would not have abandoned such a rich treasure.

"Dissatisfied with their solitary situation, Captain England and his three men exerted their industry and ingenuity, and formed a small boat, with which they sailed to Madagascar, where they subsisted upon the generosity of some more fortunate piratical companions.

"Captain Taylor detained some of the officers and men belonging to Captain Mackra, and, having repaired their vessel, sailed for India.

"The day before they made land they espied two ships to the eastward, and, supposing them to be English, Captain Taylor ordered one of the officers of Mackra's ship to communicate to him the private signals between the Company's ships, swearing that if he did not do so immediately he would cut him into pound pieces.

"But the poor man being unable to give the information demanded, he was under the necessity of e during their threats.

"Arrived at the vessels, they found that they were two Moorish ships laden with horses.

"The pirates brought the captains and merchants on board, and tortured them in a barbarous manner, to constrain them to tell where they had hid their treasure

"They were, however, disappointed, and the next morning they discovered land, and at the same time a fleet on shore plying to windward. In this situation they were at a considerable loss how to dispose of their prizes.

"To let them go, would lead to their discovery, and thus defeat the design of their voyage; and it was a distressing matter to sink the men and horses, though many of them were for adopting that measure.

"They, however, brought them to anchor, threw all her sails overboard, and cut one of her masts half through.

"While they lay at anchor, and were employed in taking in water, one of the above-mentioned fleet moved towards them with English colours, and was answered by the pirate with a red ensign, but they did not hail each other.

"At night they left the Muscat ships, and sailed after the fleet.

"About four the next morning the pirates were in the midst of the fleets, but, seeing their vast superiority, they were greatly at a loss what method to adopt.

"The Victory was become leaky, and their hands so few in number, that it only remained for them to deceive, if possible, the English squadron.

"They were unsuccessful in gaining any thing out of that fleet, and only had the wretched satisfaction of burning a single galley.

"They, however that day seized a galliot, laden with cotton, and made inquiry of the men concerning the fleet.

"They protested that they had not seen a ship since they left Gogo, and earnestly implored their mercy; but, instead of treating them with lenity, they racked their joints, in order to extort farther confession.

"The day following a fresh easterly wind blew hard, and rent the galliot's sails; upon this the pirates put her company into a boat, with nothing but a try-sail, no provisions, and only four gallons of water; and, though they were out of sight of land, left them to shift for themselves.

[It may be proper to inform our readers, one Angria an Indian Prince, of considerable territory and strength, had proved a troublesome enemy to Europeans, and particularly to the English. Callaba is his principal fort, situated not many leagues from Bombay, and he possesses an island in sight of the port, from whence he molests the Company's ships.

His art in bribing the ministers of the great Mogul, and the shallowness of the water, that prevents large ships of war from approaching, are the principal causes of his safety.]

"The Bombay fleet, consisting of four grabs, the London and the Candais, and two other ships with galliot, having an additional thousand men aboard for this enterprise, sailed to attack a fort belonging to Augria, upon the Malabar coast.

"Though their strength was great, yet they were totally unsuccessful in their enterprise.

"It was this fleet, returning home, that our pirates discovered upon the present occasion.

"Upon the sight of the pirates, the commodore of the fleet intimated to Mr. Brown, the general, that as they had no orders to fight, and had gone upon a different purpose, it would be improper for them to engage.

"Informed of the loss of this favourable opportunity to destroy the robbers, the Governor of Bombay was highly enraged, and, giving the command of the fleet to Captain Mackra, ordered him to pursue and engage them wherever they should be found.

"The pirates having sent away the galliot with her men, they arrived southward, and between Goa and Carwar they heard several guns, so that they came to anchor, and sent their boats to reconnoitre, which returned next morning with the intelligence of two grabs, lying at anchor in the road.

"They accordingly weighed, ran towards the bay, and in the morning were discovered by the grabs, who had just time to run under India-Diva-Castle for protection.

"This was the more vexatious to the pirates, as they were without water; some of them, therefore were for making a descent upon the island, but that measure not being generally approved, they sailed towards the south and took a small ship, which had only a Dutchman and two Portuguese on board.

"They sent one of these on shore to the captain, to inform him that if he would give them some water and fresh provisions, he might have his vessel returned.

"He replied, that if they would give him possession over the bar, he would comply with their request. But suspecting the integrity of his design, they sailed to Lacca Deva islands, uttering dreadful imprecations against the captain.

"Disappointed in finding water at these islands, they sailed to Malinda island, and sent their boats on shore, to discover if there was any water, or if there were any inhabitants.

"They returned with the information that there was abundance of water; that the houses were only inhabited by women and children, the men having fled at the appearance of the ships.

"They accordingly hastened to supply themselves with water, used the defenceless women in a brutal manner, destroyed many of their fruit trees, and set some of their houses on fire.

"While off this island they lost several of their anchors by the rockiness of the ground; and, one day blowing more violent than usual, they were forced to take to sea, leaving several people and most of the water casks; but when the gale was over they returned to take their men and water.

"Their provisions being nearly exhausted, they resolved to visit the Dutch at Cochin.

"After sailing three days, they arrived off Tellechery, and took a small vessel belonging to Governor Adams, and brought the master on board very much intoxicated, who informed them of the expedition of Captain Mackra.

"This intelligence raised their utmost indignation.

"'A villain,' said they, 'to whom we have given a ship and presents, to come against us; he ought to be hanged! and, since we cannot show our resentment to him, let us hang the dogs his people, who wish him well, and would do the same if they were clear.'

"'If it be in my power,' said the quartermaster, 'both masters and officers of ships shall be carried with us for the future, only to plague them. Now, England we may mark him for this.'

"They proceeded to Calicut, and attempting to cut out a ship were prevented by some guns placed on shore.

"One of Captain Mackra's officers was under deck at this time, and was commanded both by the captain and quarter-master to tend the braces on the booms, in hopes that a shot would take him before they got clear.

"He was about to have excused himself, but they threatened to shoot him; and, when he expostulated, and claimed their promise to put him on shore, he got an unmerciful beating from the quarter-master; Captain Taylor, to whom that duty belonged being lame in his hands.

"The day following they met a Dutch galliot, loaded with limestone, bound for Calicut, on which they put one Captain Fawks; and, some of the crew interceding for Mackra's officers, Taylor and his party replied—

"'If we let this dog go, who has overheard our designs and resolutions, we will overset all our well-advised resolutions, and particularly this supply we are seeking for at the hands of the Dutch.'

"When they arrived at Cochin, they sent a letter on shore by a fishing-boat, entered the road and anchored, each ship saluting the fort with eleven guns, and receiving the same number in return.

"This was the token of their welcome reception, and at night a large boat was sent, deeply laden with liquors and all kinds of provisions, and in it a servant of John Trumpet, one of their friends, to inform them that it would be necessary for them to run farther south, where they would be supplied both with provisions and naval stores.

"They had scarcely anchored at the appointed place, when several canoes, with white and black inhabitants, came on board, and continued, without interruption, to perform all the good offices in their power during their stay in that place.

"In particular, John Trumpet brought a large boat of arrack, and sixty bales of sugar, as a present from the governor and his daughter; the one receiving a table-clock, and the other a gold watch, the spoil of Captain Mackra's vessel.

"When their provisions were all on board, Trumpet was rewarded with about six or seven thousand pounds, was saluted with three cheers, and eleven guns; and several handfuls of silver were thrown into the boat, for the men to gather at pleasure.

"There being little wind that night they remained at anchor, and in the morning were surprised with the return of Trumpet, bringing another boat equally well stored with provisions, with chests of piece-goods and ready-made clothes, and along with him the fiscal of the place.

"At noon they espied a sail towards the south, and immediately gave chase, but she out-sailed them, and sheltered under the fort of Cochin.

"Informed that they would not be molested in taking her from under the castle, they sailed towards her; but, upon the fort firing two guns, they ran off for fear of more serious altercation, and, returning, anchored in their former station

"They were too welcome visitants to be permitted to depart, as long as John Trumpet could contrive to detain them.

"With this view he informed them that in a few days a rich vessel, commanded by the General of Bombay's brother, was to pass that way.

"That government is certainly in a wretched state which is under the necessity of trading with pirates, in order to enrich itself.

"Nor will such a government hesitate by what means an injury can be repaired, or a fortune gained.

"Neither can language describe the low and base principles of that government which can employ such miscreants as John Trumpet in its service.

"He was a tool in the hands of the government of Cochin; and, as the dog said in the fable, What is done by the master's orders, is the master's action.'

"While under the direction of Trumpet, some proposed to proceed directly to Madagascar, but others were disposed to wait until they should be provided with a store ship.

"The majority being of the latter opinion, they steered to the south, and, seeing a ship on shore, they were desirous to get near her; but the wind preventing they separated, the one sailing northward and the other southward, in hopes of securing her when she should come out, whatever direction she might take.

"They were now, however, almost entrapped in the snare laid for them.

"In the morning, to their astonishment and consternation, instead of being called upon to give chase, five large ships were near, who made a signal for the pirates to bear down.

"The pirates were in the greatest dread lest it should be Captain Mackra, of whose activity and courage they had formerly sufficient proof.

"The pirate ships, however, joined and fled with all speed from the fleet.

"In three hours' chase none of the fleet gained upon them, except one grab.

"The remainder of the day was calm, and, to their great consolation, the next day this fleet was entirely out of sight.

"This alarm being over, they resolved to spend the Christmas in feasting and mirth, in order to drown care and to banish thoughtfulness.

"Nor did one day suffice; but they continued their revelling for several days, and made so free with their fresh provisions that in their next cruise they were put upon short allowance; and it was entirely owing to the sugar and other provisions that were in the leaky ship that they were preserved from perishing.

"In this condition they reached the island of Mauritius, refitted the Victory, and left that place with the following inscription written upon one of the walls:—'Left this place on the 5th of April, to go to Madagascar for Limos.'

"This they did lest any visit should be paid to the place during their absence.

"They, however, did not sail directly for Madagascar, but to the island of Mascarius, where they fortunately fell in with a Portuguese of seventy guns, lying at anchor.

"The greater part of her guns were thrown overboard, her masts lost, and the whole vessel disabled by a storm; therefore she became an easy prey to the pirates.

"Conde de Ericeira, Viceroy of Goa, who went upon the fruitless expedition against Angria the Indian, and several passengers, were on board.

"Besides other valuable articles and specie they found in her diamonds to the amount of four millions of dollars.

"Supposing that the ship was an Englishman, the Viceroy came on board next morning, was made prisoner, and obliged to pay two thousand dollars as a ransom for himself and the other prisoners.

"After this he was set ashore, with the express engagement to leave a ship to convey him and his companions to another port.

"Meanwhile they received the intelligence that a vessel was to the leeward of the island, which they pursued and captured.

"But instead of performing their promise to the Viceroy, which they could easily have done, they sent the Ostender along with some of their men to Madagascar, to inform their friends of their success, with instructions to prepare masts for the prize; and they soon followed, carrying two thousand negroes in the Portuguese vessel.

"Madagascar is an island larger than Great Britain, situated upon the eastern coast of Africa, abounding with all sorts of provisions, such as oxen, goats, sheep, poultry, fish, citrons, oranges, tamarinds, dates, cocoa-nuts, bananas, wax, honey, rice, cotton, indigo, and all other fruits common in that quarter of the globe; ebony, of which lances are made, gums of several kinds, and many other valuable productions.

"The locusts on land, and the crocodiles in the river, form the principal inconvenience that the inhabitants experience.

"Here, in St. Augustine's Bay, the ships sometimes stop to take in water, when they take the inner passage to India, and do not intend to stop at Johanna.

"Though they are still few in number, compared to the natives, yet the Europeans, and particularly the pirates, have reared a mulatto race since the discovery of this island by the Portuguese in 1506.

" The natives are negroes, with short curled hair, active, and formerly malicious and revengeful ; but, on account of the presents they are accustomed to receive, they are become tractable and communicative.

" They live on terms of friendship with the Europeans who reside amongst them, and the latter can, on a minute's warning, muster two or three hundred.

" The natives find it their interest to cultivate their friendship, because they are divided into small governments, who carry on a continual war with each other ; so that the pirates render the party with whom they join always victorious.

" When the Portuguese ships arrived here, they received the intelligence that the Ostender had taken the advantage of an hour when the men were intoxicated, rose upon them, and carried the ship to Mozambique, from whence the Governor ordered her to Goa.

" The pirates now divided their plunder, receiving forty-two diamonds per man, or in smaller proportion according to their magnitude.

" A foolish, jocular fellow, who had received a large diamond of most immense value, was highly displeased, and so went and broke it in pieces, exclaiming that he had many more shares than either of them.

" Some, contented with their treasure, and unwilling to run the risk of losing what they possessed, and perhaps their lives also, resolved to remain with their friends at Madagascar, under the stipulation that the longest livers should enjoy all the booty.

" The number of adventurers now being lessened, they burnt the Victory, cleaned the Cassandra, and the remainder went on board her under the command of Taylor, whom we must leave for a little, to give an account of that squadron that arrived in India in 1721.

" When the commodore arrived at the Cape, he received a letter that had been written by the governor of Pondicherry to the governor of Madras, informing him that the pirates were strong in the Indian seas ; that they had eleven sail and fifteen hundred men ; but adding, that many of them retired about that time to Brazil and Guinea, while others fortified themselves at Madagascar, Mauritius, Johanna, and Mohilla.

" And that a crew under the command of Condin, in a ship called the Dragon, had captured a vessel with thirteen lacs of rupees on board, and, having divided their plunder, they had taken up their residence with their friends at Madagascar.

" Upon receiving this intelligence, Commodore Matthews sailed for these islands, as the most probable place of success.

" He endeavoured ineffectually to prevail on England, at St. Mary's, to communicate to him what information he could give respecting the pirates.

" But the pirate declined, thinking that this would be almost to surrender at discretion.

" He then took up the guns of the Jubilee sloop that were on board, and the men-of-war made several cruises in search of the pirates, but to no purpose.

" The squadron was then sent down to Bombay, was saluted by the port, and, after these exploits, returned home.

" The pirate, Captain Taylor, in the Cassandra, now fitted up the Portuguese man-of-war, and resolved upon another voyage to the Indies ; but, informed that four men-of-war had been sent after the pirates in that quarter, he changed his determination and sailed for Africa.

" Arrived there, they put in at a place near the river Spirito Sancto, on the coast of Monomotapa.

" As there was no correspondence by land, nor any trade carried on by sea to this place, they thought that it would afford a safe retreat.

" To their astonishment, however, when they approached the shore, it being in the dusk of the evening, they were accosted by several shot.

" They immediately anchored, and in the morning saw that the shot had come from a small fort of six guns, which they attacked and destroyed.

" This small fort was erected by the Dutch East India Company a few weeks before, and committed to the care of a hundred and fifty men, the one-half of whom had perished by sickness or other causes.

" Upon their petition, sixteen of them were admitted into the society of the pirates, and the rest would also have been received had they not been Dutchmen, to whom they had a rooted aversion.

" In this place they continued during four months, refitting their vessels, and amusing themselves with all manner of diversions, until the scarcity of their provisions awakened them to industry and exertion.

" They, however, left several parcels of goods to the starving Dutchmen, which Mynheer joyfully exchanged for provisions with the next vessel that touched at that fort.

" Leaving that place, they were divided in opinion what course to steer ; some went on board the Portuguese prize, and, sailing for Madagascar, abandoned the pirate life ; and others, going on board the Cassandra, sailed for the Spanish West Indies.

" The Mermaid man-of-war, returning from a convoy, got near the pirates, and would have attacked them, but, a consultation being held, it was deemed inexpedient, and thus the pirates escaped.

" A sloop was, however, dispatched to Jamaica with the intelligence, and the Lancaster was sent after them. but they were some days too late, the pirates having, with all their riches, surrendered to the governor of Portobello.

" Calming their consciences that others would have acted a similar part, without the least remorse they took up their residence here, to spend the remainder of their days in living upon the spoil of nations.

" Nor can the reflection be restrained, that if they had known what was transacting in England by South-sea Directors, they would at least have had one proof to adduce, ' that whatever robberies they had committed, they might be pretty sure that they were not the greatest villains then living in the world.'

"It is difficult to compute the injury done by this crew during five years.

"Whether to gratify their humour, to prevent intelligence, or for the want of men to navigate, or from the brave resistance made, or from wanton folly and barbarity, the moment the resolution was formed the vessels they captured were frequently sent to the bottom.

"After their surrender to the Spaniards several of them left that place, and it is reported that Captain Taylor accepted of a commission in the Spanish service, and commanded the man-of-war that attacked the English log-wood cutters in the Bay of Honduras.

CHAPTER LXVIII.

MARIE APPEARS IN PARIS FOR THE FIRST TIME— THE FRAIL PRIMA DONNA—MARIE'S GOOD FOR-TUNE.

AT the moment appointed Marie was at the stage-door of the Opera.

With the money advanced by the Signor she had arrayed herself in a neat and pretty costume, and presented a very different appearance to that which characterised her in the streets of Paris only a day previous.

"Who are you, mademoiselle?" demanded the porter of the Italian.

"I am a chorister, and I want to see the Signor Albertini."

"You will find him on the stage."

The man pointed to the direction in which the stage lay, and Marie passed on.

In a few moments she was on the stage.

She found her friend, Albertini, drilling a large number of choristers, whilst the principal characters in the opera were lingering about in little groups, conversing gaily.

At first the chorus-master did not recognise his *protege* in her altered costume, but as she smiled upon him he elevated his eyebrows with a pleased expression, and motioned her to approach.

He handed her a roll of music, which he drew from his pocket, and told her to fall in with the lady *soprani* of the company.

"Now," he said, "it will be as well to go over the opening chorus once more before the rehearsal really commences. Oblige me."

The leader of the orchestra gave the signal to his band, and next moment the whole choir broke out into full song.

The piece of music was a singular one, and there was a number of hitches in executing it; but Marie knew every note, and by her clever rendering of each passage soon brought the others into tune and time.

They looked at her with mingled amazement and jealousy.

But she persevered with her business and heeded them not.

In one part of the chorus there was a singular passage for the *soprano* voices, unaccompanied by the orchestra.

It was a very touching bit of melody, and appeared very difficult for the ladies to thoroughly appreciate.

At the opening notes they all suddenly stuck, and Marie alone continued the strain.

Here was her opportunity.

The manager, the chorus, the principals, and the orchestra, were all silent.

Seizing her opportunity, she exerted herself to her utmost, and, to the amazement of all, sang the whole passage with striking effect.

As she finished all those on the stage broke out into a loud roar of

" Bravas !"

Marie knew that her time was at last come.

She saw the manager approach Albertini, and could divine by the glances he threw at her from time to time that she was the object of their conversation.

Again the rehearsal progressed, and after some hours' work it ended, and they all dispersed.

As Marie was passing from the theatre, Albertini approached her.

"It is all right," he said; "the manager says you have a grand voice, and I am sure he will give you a chance."

* * * * *

Three days after this the opera was to be produced.

For the last time the company met for rehearsal, and everything went as smoothly as possible.

Night came at last, and it wanted but one hour to the moment of the rising of the curtain.

Marie, dressed as a nun, and lounging about the wings with a dozen other choristers, marked the arrival of the *prima donna* who was at that time delighting all Paris.

The lady, leaning on the arm of the manager, retired to her dressing-room.

Marie wondered how long it would be before a similar honour would be conferred upon her.

Just as the manager turned from the door of the lady's dressing-room, a young gentleman, elegantly dressed, and bearing in his hand a magnificent bouquet, approached, and, with a slight nod to the manager, passed into the room at the door of which that functionary had left the *prima donna*.

"It is the Count," whispered a little black-eyed girl to Marie.

" What Count?"

"The Count D'Almere. He is mad after the signora."

"Is he rich?"

"Very."

"And does she love him?"

"He is rich."

"Oh, I comprehend you," said Marie, with a smile.

Their conversation was now interrupted by the sound of loud voices in their immediate neighbourhood.

"You cannot pass!"

"I will pass!"

"I say you cannot!"

But I tell you I will. I saw her enter—I saw *him* enter, and I will follow."

Next moment Marie saw the door-porter dashed on one side, and a young man, rather meanly clad, rushed towards the spot where she stood.

"What means this intrusion?" demanded the manager, walking up to the new comer.

"Sir," said the young man, "I want my wife, and I want her villanous seducer. I saw them both enter this theatre, and I will find them."

"My good sir, there is an error. We know not your wife—we have not seen her seducer."

"Do not lie, old man, she is here. Could I be deceived?"

"Nonsense—nonsense; get away, you are creating a disturbance, and you will be heard in front of the curtain if you do not get hence quietly."

"Seek not to cavil with me," cried the intruder, "or it shall be the worse for you With these eyes I beheld her enter this place, and I will see her."

"Who is your wife?"

"Leonora Belvati."

"Then there is no Leonora Belvati here."

"You lie!"

"Monsieur!"

"I say again you lie. You are all in a conspiracy to tear her from me, but you shall not succeed. Bad as she is, I love her still, and would save her from her worst enemy—herself. Oh! you know not what I have suffered on her account."

"I have no doubt you are an ill-used man, whoever you are," said the manager, kindly, "but I really must protest against your creating this disturbance in my theatre. I assure you we do not know, and have not seen your wife. There is some mistake; so go out quietly."

The Count now left the *prima donna's* room.

"There," cried the young man, pointing to him, "there, am I mistaken now? Will you tell me now that she is not here?"

"That, sir—"

"Is the Count D'Almere. I know him too well."

The Count started back, and cried—

"Carl here!"

"Yes, here, villain!" cried the infuriated man; "here to settle accounts with thee at last."

"Do you know this man?" demanded the manager of the Count.

"Yes—that is—no. Take him away."

"Let them dare."

"Begone, fool, or you will bring trouble upon yourself."

"Or upon thee."

"Begone, I say."

"Where is my wife?"

"Begone. Will none of you remove him?"

"Where is she? Speak, or I will tear you into a thousand pieces."

The *prima donna*, attracted by the sound of voices, now left her room.

Seeing the intruder, she uttered a loud shriek, and fell back senseless.

In a moment the young man was by her side.

He picked her up, and, enfolding his arms about her, cried—

"Thank God! I have found you again, and he shall never more have you in his power."

"Release that lady," cried the Count.

"Never; wretch! She is mine, and if you but advance a step to lay a hand on her, I will blow your brains to the winds. I am armed and am desperate. Advance at your peril."

The Count fell back.

"Ah," continued the man, "you fear me now, but I will spare you, for I have found her again and can afford to allow you to live; but cross my path once more, and, by God, nothing shall save you, and now we will begone."

He lifted the insensible form of the woman in his arms with as much ease as if she had been a child, and made for the door.

The manager became alarmed.

"Sir, sir," he cried, running towards the young man, "you forget that lady is engaged to sing to-night. You must not remove her."

"Must not! Who will prevent me? She is my wife, and I choose to bear her away. Let me see who will prevent me."

"But listen to reason"—

"I will listen to nothing. Get from my path, and let me begone."

"No, no!"

"Out of the way!"

Knocking the manager to the ground, the young man ran with great speed from the stage, down the stairs, and into the hall.

The next moment he was gone.

Thinking less of the indignity he had suffered than of the position in which he stood with respect to the public and the opera, upon which the curtain was about to rise, the manager rose, and cried—

"Heaven bless us, what is to be done?"

"*Sacre!* But this is a *contretemps*. What does it mean?"

He glared at the Count for an answer.

"The fact is, my dear fellow," said the Count, "you have lost your *prima donna*. Our impulsive friend is, as he says, her husband, and nothing in the world will induce him to allow her to return. I know him of old."

"The devil take him and you too," cried the manager. "What am I to do?"

"The best you can," said the Count, coolly, as he walked away.

At this moment the chorus-master came to the scene of action.

"Oh, Albertini!" cried the manager, throwing himself into the old man's arms, "I am ruined —I am undone! What will become of me—of you—of us all? Our *prima donna* is gone—gone—gone!—and the opera cannot proceed."

" *Diable!*   What say you?"

"The truth.   They have borne her away, and there is not another lady in Paris who can play the part."

"The piece must be changed!"

"Yes, and the people will tear the house down. Two seasons running this opera has been announced and never performed, and if I go on to withdraw it to-night they will slay me."

"What can be done?"

"Where is Loscini?   Will not she attempt the part?"

"Loscini is hoarse ; besides, she knows not a note."

"Then I can find no one to play it."

At this moment the chorus-master caught the eye of Marie.

She pointed to herself.

"Ah!" he cried, "why did I not think of it? Of course ; yes, yes, she will play it divinely."

"Who?"

"This lady."

The old man advanced, and caught Marie by the arm.

"Your little soprano? Ridiculous."

"Not at all, monsieur; she will do it justice."

"Indeed I will, if you will only trust me with it."

"You play the part—you sing the music? Can I believe my ears? And why not? Yes, you sang the soprano part of the chorus magnificently, and may do it.   But consider, there is not ten minutes to spare.   Do you know the music?"

"Every note."

"And you will not disappoint me?"

"Try me."

"Go, then, and dress, and if you can but succeed your fortune is made."

"But the dress?"

"Ah, the dress.   Use that prepared for the wretched woman who is gone.   Diable! how fortunate the mad husband did not come a few minutes later, and bear her away in the dress."

Marie required no second invite.

In a moment she was in the dressing-room of the *prima donna.*

Without delay the robes of the nun were slipped off, and the glorious dress of the chief character assumed.

In five minutes she was again at the side of the manager.

Her comportment electrified the old gentleman.

"Ah," he said, "it cannot be possible that you now assume the part for the first time?"

"You shall see if I play it like a novice," answered Marie.

"And now I must make the announcement."

The manager threw off his hat, and stepped before the curtain.

In a few words he explained that sudden illness had deprived him of the services of the lady announced for the chief part; but that, at a moment's notice, the great character had been in the kindest manner assumed by Signora Laporte, for whom he claimed the indulgence of the audience.

The announcement was received with anything but satisfaction by the audience, for they had come expressly to hear the great *prima donna* in the new part; but still the dissent was not altogether so loud as might have been anticipated, and the manager came off with a smiling face.

"Now," he said, "let the overture commence."

The introductory movement was soon hurried through, and then the curtain rose.

The business of the piece proceeded tamely enough until the entrance of the chief tenor, who awakened some enthusiasm by his first *scena;* but all the interest was, as a matter of course, centred in the *debutante,* who, however, entered without the slighest demonstration of applause.

"We shall see whether that will continue," murmured Marie, as she proceeded with the business of the scene.

For some time she had not to speak, having to listen to the address of the tenor, who in a flood of melodious passion accuses her of treachery and falsehood.

The attitude of Marie was, during this part of the scene, quite a study.

She stood motionless as a statue, her arms grasping the voluminous folds of a large cloak, firmly clasped over her breast.

Her face calm and passionless, her eyes fixed and searching ; but as the last notes of the tenor's voice died away, she threw her white arms above her head, and gave vent to such a burst of passion as fairly took the house by storm.

Her acting was magnificent, but her voice excelled it.

The vast theatre seemed to reverberate with the tremendous volume of sound that filled it ; and, ere the scene terminated, the whole of the audience rose to their feet and gave vent to their delight in shouts of the most excited applause.

Marie acknowledged this but slightly, and left the stage with a calmness and dignity that seemed to create the greatest astonishment in the audience.

As soon as she came off at the wing the manager caught her in his arm, and almost shrieked with delight.

"It is grand! it is magnificent! it is marvellous !" he cried. "You have made my fortune ! You have immortalised me as well as yourself. Never was there such a voice !"

"Never, never," cried Albertini, rushing up to his *protege* ; "ah, they shall say in after years that it was old Albertini, the chorus-master, that introduced the great Laporte to the *Opera.* They shall say this, and it will be the best epitaph they can put on his tomb."

"I owe all to you," said Marie, "all—all to you, and I shall never forget your great kindness to me."

"Oh, mention it not.   I am overwhelmed with honour and happiness as it is."

"And let me not be behind-hand with my congratulations," cried the young Count, joining the group—"ah, monsieur *le directeur,* you in reality owe this to me ; for, had I not de-

prived you of one *prima donna*, you would not
have had occasion to seek another, and this
triumph would have been lost. Will you accept
these poor flowers," he continued, addressing
Marie. "They are an unworthy gift, but I
could get no better at so short a notice."

Marie took them, and thanked him with a
smile.

At this the face of the old chorus-master fell
again,

"Ah," he said, "it is ever so; these men,
these villians, they will not let a poor girl be
virtuous if she would. She took his favours
with a smile. Ah me! She may yet accept the
donor! I hope not, I hope not, but there is no
knowing. He is rich and she is poor."

Meanwhile Marie entered into animated conversation with the brilliant young noble.

CHAPTER LXIX.

PIPEY AND MRS. BOODLES DEPART FROM ENG-
LAND—THE CAPTAIN OF THE EMILIA.

WHILST business was almost at a standstill
with the three men, who were seated, telling
interminable tales in the bar-parlour of the
little inn by the river side, the vessel destined
to convey at least one of them from England
was making her way towards Deal.

The intelligence of her arrival in that vicinity
was soon conveyed to the man who lent his aid
to Maydock.

"It's all right," he said, on the third day of
their sojourn at the inn; "it's all right at last,
and all we have to do is to get down to Deal and
make off."

"And about my request," said Pipey; "have you forgotten that?"

"Well, you see," replied the seaman, "it don't altogether rest with me. I'm only second fiddle, and the captain is mighty particular who he takes on board, unless they join for food and all; but I'll do the best I can for you if you'll run down to Deal with me."

"It's best he should do so under any circumstances," said Maydock; "for I can go no further; it's dangerous, and you might want help."

"Just so."

"And if the captain will be advised by me—and I think my wish has some weight with him—he'll take our young friend out with him. He's likely to prove of service, if his looks don't belie him."

"Thanks," said Pipey. "You'll find you won't lose by putting in a good word for me."

Maydock left the room.

Strange! At the moment he stepped into the passage leading to the doorway, Grimer, the lawyer, entered hurriedly, and beckoned him into the open air.

"Lucky I've met you," said Grimer. "Come out, I've something important to say."

"What's up now?"

"Not much; but I want to know who these people are that will take the old woman from England?"

"Why do you ask?"

"I've my reasons, you may depend."

"Well, I believe them to be of the right sort."

"Do you know the captain?"

"I've had frequent dealings with him."

"But do you know him intimately?"

"No."

"Is he to be trusted?"

"Why do you ask!"

"Because I think he's playing a double game."

"I can't make out what you can possibly know about him, supposing that you are correct."

"I dare say not, and I'm not going to satisfy you. Where is the ship?"

"Skulking somewhere in the neighbourhood of Deal."

"I thought it was Dover."

"It was to be Dover, but there's been a change of tactics."

"Dover's too warm, I suppose?"

"Yes."

"Well, so far so well. The ship's at Deal, under false colours. Doing the lamb, eh? The old tale of the wolf in sheep's clothing. But, allowing the ship to be at Deal, where's the captain?"

"How should I know? Do you suppose that I can tell the whereabouts of the captain because the ship is at Deal? You might as well ask if a ship, of a thousand tons burthen, having one hundred men to work her, and carrying a cargo of grain, was bound for the Isle of Man, what would be the captain's name?"

"Ah! yes, I suppose that's funny, but I don't see it. Now, listen."

The old lawyer put his mouth close to the ear of the robber, and spoke for some moments.

"I can't understand the matter," said Maydock. "The captain may be, or may have been, in London. But how the devil—"

"Hush! Never mind, I have told you what I suspect. Now, what is to be done?"

"I can't tell."

"Is this fellow who has assisted you to be trusted?"

"I don't know, and I shouldn't like to try him. You see, he's thick in with his captain; and, although he may be glad to serve me, I doubt if he would do it at the expense of his superior."

"Well, then the woman ought not to leave the country."

"But to remain here is to fall directly into the hands of those who would give something to find her. Even here they have been selling this Pipey and the old woman; and by h—ll we had a narrow escape even as we entered the crib, quiet and out of the way as it is!"

"You don't say so?"

"I do."

Maydock then related the adventure with the thief-takers.

"Well," said the lawyer, "I suppose she must go, although it's an awful risk to run, and one I don't like having a hand in."

"Something must be done."

"Something *ought* to be done."

"I have it."

"What?"

"An idea."

"Give it mouth."

"Yes, that is it; it can't fail."

"What can't fail?"

"My idea."

"Well, is it a secret?"

"No."

"Then let me hear it."

"You see, there was a young fellow I picked up in London, a seafaring chap, who is down on his luck and wants work. He has been dead on to my mate in this job about getting him out with him this trip, but the fellow seems to hang fire over the job. If I could drift this chap over to my interests, and get him on board the Emilia, there will be an end of the difficulty, for he's just one of that sort who won't stand upon trifles, and will do what's required of him in a business-like manner."

"Well, he's your man; will you try him?"

"I will. As far as *our* business is concerned, I'll stake something he undertakes and performs his work properly; but it's the getting him on board that I'm afraid of."

"Manage it at any risk."

"I will."

"Do not fail to try; but should I by any chance be defeated?"

"Well, then we must take the risk, and she *must* go."

"All right."

They separated.

Maydock returned to the inn.

The sailor was asleep.

Pipey sat regarding him attentively.

Maydock winked at and beckoned Pipey from the room.

He placed his hand on his lips, and nodded, and pointed at the sleeping man to indicate that he was not to be disturbed.

"You really want to go out in this ship," said Maydock, when they were alone.

"I should *rayther* think I did," said Pipey.

"Well, I want you to go; but I've a commission for you to execute."

"What is it?"

"Listen! I've made arrangements for the captain of the Emilia to drop this old soul somewhere or other where there's no hope of her again reaching England, but, at the same time, I don't want her to die, or to be *altogether* lost sight of. To this effect I arranged with the captain of the Emilia, but I'm afraid, from what I have this moment heard, that he's been got at, and that he has a commission to pitch the old lady overboard."

"The devil!" cried Pipey.

"It's a strange affair, and quite beyond my comprehension; but it appears to be correct, and that's why I'm anxious that you should go."

"You want her protected?"

"At all risks."

"Then I'm your man. I tell you that, if I can but get out in that ship, I'll see the captain and all his crew blown to the devil before a hair of that old soul's head is harmed."

Pipey said this with a face that quite astonished Maydock.

"Hillo!" said the thief, "you seem to have taken a remarkable liking for the old lady."

"Not a bit of it; but I've taken an awful fancy to get out in the Emilia, and will do this for the man who will let me gratify my wish."

"I'll write to the captain. And now, how about terms?"

"Terms for what?"

"Your looking after the woman."

"I don't want anything for that. One good turn deserves another, and, if you do me one, it's hard if I can't do you a small service in return."

"A small service," muttered Maydock to himself; "what a fire-eater. He calls protecting a woman against a fiend of a captain, and a whole ship's crew, 'a small service,' and demands nothing for it. But there's more in this than I can see. He evidently wants to join this piratical set of bair-brained fools, and will do anything to succeed. But that's not my business;" and then aloud he said—

"Well, you're a good sort of a fellow, I see; but only reach England again, and tell me that the woman is alive, and bring me word where I can put my claw upon her, and I'll reward you after a fashion you can little dream of."

"I tell you I'll see to her, and, take my word for it, she will turn up again in England *the very moment she's wanted*"

There was a deep meaning in these last words that Maydock could not comprehend.

His astonishment would have been great had he divined who stood before him, and how deep an interest he felt in the fate of the woman he was asked to protect.

And so matters were arranged.

That very day the seaman, Pipey, and Mrs. Boodles set off for Deal.

The old lady hesitated not.

She knew Pipey was near her, and appeared to be quite contented.

But neither by word nor deed did she commit herself.

The alacrity and joyousness with which Mrs. Boodles moved certainly did puzzle Maydock, but he suspected nothing.

And so they at length reached Deal.

In a dingy inn, in a little, unfrequented lane in the town, they found the captain of the Emilia.

He was a tall, burly fellow, but his hands were wonderfully white, and his manners were those of a thorough aristocrat, although it was plain that he had no particular education to boast of.

He was an autocrat because it suited him to be so.

He had to deal with men who could beat him at blackguardism, and he had to resort to other weapons to maintain his supremacy.

If he blew a man's brains out, and such acts were not of unfrequent occurrence on board the Emilia, he raised his hat, apologised, pleaded the force of circumstances as an excuse, and then sent his victim to eternity.

This conduct completely puzzled, if it did not absolutely awe, his men, and they followed him, and his word was law.

"I knew I should find you here," said the second in command of the Emilia; "I've brought the lady who is to take the little trip with us."

The Captain rose and bowed to Mrs. Boodles, who, on her part, curtseyed and said—

"My dooty towards you, my dear sir."

Mrs. Boodles thought this polite.

"And who is our second friend?" said the Captain, glancing at Pipey.

"A young feller as wants to try a trip, leastwise to get out of England with us."

The Captain shook his head.

The mate then drew forth Maydock's note and handed it to the aristocratic ruffian.

"It won't do," he said, after perusing it. Maydock put it on at the highest amount of pressure a fellow can stand under, and uses the greatest amount of inducement he can hold out, but it won't do. I'm not to be bullied or coaxed into taking a stranger into my ship for a trip to suit his own convenience. If you'd like to join altogether," he continued, addressing Pipey, "I may listen to you."

"I'd rather not."

"Then I say again it won't do."

As he uttered these words he waived his hand loftily, and in doing so drew up his coat sleeve and exposed his wrist.

About it was a narrow band of scarlet ribbon.

This caught the eye of Pipey in a second.

"Won't it do?" he said, quietly diving his hand into his breast and drawing it forth with a narrow strip of scarlet over the fingers. "I thought it might, and I fancy you'll alter your tone,"

He flashed his hand before the captain.

The latter started.

"I will reconsider your determination," said Pipey.

"Well, I may."

"You must at once, for your friend to get out of England in the Emilia."

"Well, you look a lively hand, and I don't know but what for once I'd go out of my way—"

"To comply with my request. I thought so."

The mate looked astonished at all this; he knew nothing of the charm of the bit of ribbon.

"Well, quick decided," said Pipey after a pause; "and I'm to go."

"I think you may."

"That's right."

"You must all be on board to-night."

"At what hour?" asked the mate.

"Midnight."

"Where is she?"

"You'll find her fast enough. The boat will be on the beach. There will sure to be a moon, and the Emilia will be found getting about and in readiness."

*   *   *   *   *

"How the devil did you manage that?" asked the mate as they left the room.

"What?" asked Pipey, with extreme innocence.

"What!—the getting over the cap'n. I never saw him so licked in all my life. He must know you."

"He never set eyes upon me in all his life until that moment."

"I can't think it. And yet if he'd known you he'd have granted your request at first."

"Of course."

"Then what's at the bottom of it?"

"A charm my friend—it's in my eye! I may say it's all my eye; but there's no getting away from it, they must come to."

"Ah, you're a rum 'un."

"You may have cause to repeat the observation before we've done with each other."

"Well, I can't make you out."

"There's very few that can."

The seaman looked at Pipey with a puzzled expression, but hazarded no further remark.

It was plain that he was quite as much "knocked over" as he had avowed the Captain to have been.

*   *   *   *   *

It is now time that we speak more particularly of the mysterious Captain of the Emilia.

From what we have already let drop, it will be readily understood that here was the commander of a ship, that, although professedly having honest commerce for an aim, engaged somewhat largely in piracy and illegal trading.

The Emilia was the last of a half-score of vessels of a similar description that had been sailed in or commanded by Captain Dangerfield, or, to call him by the name by which he was better known, the "Jackal," probably from the constant grin that opened his large mouth, and exhibited his large and preternaturally white teeth.

But the Emilia was not the largest ship, nor was her present occupation the most daring in which Captain Dangerfield had sailed, as a brief glance at his career will testify.

His boyhood was one continued scene of daring adventures.

Unlike the majority of youths, from infancy he exhibited a coolness of demeanour and a contempt for danger almost marvellous.

Fear was entirely absent from his nature, and although possessed of no extraordinary gifts, he attracted great attention, and contrived to keep himself conspicuous from the time he was sent to school till the end of his life.

He selected the seafaring profession, and, even at the outset, by sheer force of will and a little bravado managed to begin almost at the top of the ladder.

Dangerfield sailed from the Thames, in the character of second mate in the Gambia, of sixteen guns and thirty men, belonging to the African Company.

There was a number of soldiers, under the command of John Massey, intended to garrison a fort which was destroyed.

The Gambia arrived safe, and landed Massey and his men; but the military power was overruled by the merchants and traders.

To them it belonged to victual the garrison; and, being scanty in their allowance, Massey was highly offended, and remonstrated in terms more suitable to his feelings than their interests.

He boldly declared that he had brought these brave men here under the assurance that they were to have plenty of provisions, and to be treated in the most handsome manner; therefore, if they were not so treated, he would be under the necessity of consulting for himself.

The governor was then sick, and, for his better accommodation, was taken on board the Gambia.

During this period the captain, being offended with Dangerfield, his second mate, ordered him to be punished.

The men interfered in behalf of Dangerfield, and the captain was disobeyed.

Dangerfield and Massey having become intimate during the voyage, they now aggravated their grievances to each other, and the result of their consultations were to seize the ship and sail for England.

When matters were ripe for execution, Dangerfield sent a letter to Massey, informing him " that he must repair on board, as it was now time to put their design in execution."

Massey then harangued the soldiers in the barracks, saying,

" You that have a mind to go to England, now is the time."

They in general agreed, and, when all things were ready, he sent off the boat with this message to the chief mate, " that he should get the guns ready, for the King of Barro would come on board to dinner."

Dangerfield knew the meaning; confined the chief mate, and prepared to sail.

In the afternoon, Massey came on board with the governor's son, having almost emptied the store-houses, and dismounted the guns of the fort.

The captain of the Gambia having gone on

shore to hold a council with the governor and others was not permitted to come on board.

He called to Dangerfield and his associates, and offered them what terms they chose, to restore the ship; but all in vain.

They put the governor's son on shore, and three others who did not choose to go along with them, and immediately sailed.

Scarcely were they out at sea, when Dangerfield addressed them in the following manner:

"That it was the greatest folly imaginable to think of returning to England, for what they had already done could not be justified upon any pretence whatever, but would be looked upon by the government as a capital offence, and none of them were in a condition to withstand the attacks of such powerful adversaries as they would meet at home. For his part, he told them he was determined not to run such a hazard; and, therefore, if his proposal was not agreed to, he desired to be set on shore in some place of safety; that they had a good ship under them, a parcel of brave fellows in her; that it was not their business to starve or be made slaves; and, therefore, if they were all of his mind, they would seek their fortunes upon the sea, as other adventurers had done before them."

The crew was unanimous, knocked down the cabins, prepared black colours, and named the ship the Delivery.

She was mounted with sixteen guns, and had fifty hands on board.

To enforce order, and to provide for the stability of this government, several articles were drawn up, signed, and sworn to.

They soon began their operations, by capturing a vessel belonging to Boston, emptied her of her stores, and allowed her to depart.

Proceeding to Hispaniola, the Delivery met with a French vessel, laden with wine and brandy.

In the character of a merchant, Captain Massey went on board, viewed the liquors, and offered a price for the greater part of them, which was not accepted of.

But, after a while, he whispered in the Frenchman's ears, "that they must have them all without money."

The captain understood his meaning, and, with no small reluctance, agreed to the bargain.

They took out of her about seventy pounds, besides thirty casks of brandy, five hogsheads of wine, several pieces of chintzes, and other valuable goods.

Dangerfield returned five pounds to the Frenchman for his civility.

But this commonwealth was soon to experience the effects of discord.

Massey had been trained a soldier, and was solicitous to move in his own sphere; therefore he proposed to land with fifty or sixty men, and plunder the French settlements.

Dangerfield represented the rashness, imprudence, and impracticability of such an adventure.

Massey remained resolute in his determination.

It became necessary to decide the matter by a reference to the community.

A great majority were of the opinion of Danger-field; but, though overruled, Massey was not convinced, so became fractious, and quarrelled with Captain Dangerfield.

The men also were divided; some were land pirates, and some were sea pirates, and, ere long, they were prepared to decide the matter with the sword.

But employment terminated dissension.

The man at the mast-head cried—

"A sail! a sail!"

In a few hours they came up with her, and found that she was bound for England.

They supplied themselves with necessaries, and took a few hands out of her.

Dangerfield proposed to sink her and all the passengers on board; but Massey interfered, and prevented this cruel action.

Accordingly, she was permitted to depart, and arrived safe in England.

The next day they captured a small sloop, and detained her.

Massey still remained uneasy, and declared his resolution to leave the Delivery.

Dangerfield proposed that he and all those who were of his sentiments should go on board the sloop which they had just taken, and seek their own fortunes.

This was instantly agreed to, and Massey, with ten more, went on board, and sailed directly for Jamaica.

With a bold countenance he went to the governor—informed him that he had assisted in running off with the vessel; but his object was to save the lives of his Majesty's subjects from perishing, and that his express design was to land them in England; but, in opposition to this determination, Dangerfield and the majority were for becoming pirates; and that he had embraced the first opportunity to leave them, and surrender himself, his men, and his vessel, to his excellency.

Massey was kindly received, and sent along with Captain Laws to cruise in quest of Dangerfield; but, not finding him, returned to Jamaica, received certificates of his surrender, and came home a passenger to England.

When he came to town he wrote a narrative of the whole matter to the African Company, who returned him for answer, "that he should be fairly hanged."

He was accordingly seized, and, upon his own letter, and the evidence of the late captain of the ship, who had been left at the fort, and the governor's son, and some others, he was condemned to end his course at Tyburn.

Dangerfield, cruising off Hispaniola, captured a small ship from Bristol, and a Spanish pirate.

He rifled and burnt both ships, sending the Spaniards away in their launch, and constraining the Englishmen to turn pirates.

In a few days they took another sloop, which they manned, and carried along with them, and then harboured at a small island to clean.

Here they spent their time more like demons than men, in all manner of debauchery, drunkenness, and rioting.

Having again set to sea, they met with Edward Low, a pirate, in a small vessel, with thirteen hands; and, upon the request of Dangerfield, he united his strength with theirs, Dangerfield retaining the command, and Low becoming lieutenant.

Proceeding on their voyage they met with a vessel of two hundred tons, called the Greyhound, commanded by Benjamin Edwards.

Piratical colours were hoisted, and she was commanded to strike.

The Captain declined, and an engagement ensued ; but, finding the pirates too strong for him, he surrendered.

Instead of treating the Captain and his men with generous lenity, they beat them in a merciless manner, drove them on board their own ship, and then set fire to it.

In their course they took several other ships, rifled and dismissed them ; but two they fitted up for their own service.

With this small fleet—viz., Admiral Dangerfield in the Happy Delivery, Captain Low in the Rhode Island sloop, and Captain Harris (who was second mate in the Greyhound) in a sloop formerly belonging to Jamaica—they sailed to Port Mayo, in the gulf of Matique, and made preparations to clean their vessels. With this view they made tents of their sails, stored their provisions in tents also, and then commenced their operations ; but scarcely were they at work when a body of natives came down upon them, drove them to their ships, seized their tents and stores, and set fire to the Delivery, which was stranded on shore.

Dangerfield and his men now went on board the largest sloop, called the Ranger, and left the other at sea.

They were soon reduced to great want, and commotion ensued ; but when they had got to the West Indies they took a prize which supplied their wants, and, having sank her, they sailed for America.

They in a short time captured a brigantine, and the company, being divided in their sentiments, Low, and those who were of his views, went on board the prize, and went off, while those who agreed with Dangerfield remained in the Ranger.

On his way to the mainland of America Dangerfield took several ships with very little resistance ; but, upon the coast of South Carolina, he met with a ship bound for England.

An engagement took place, and Dangerfield was so hard pressed that he was under the necessity of running aground and landing his men ; but when the Captain of the English vessels had taken the boat, in order to burn the pirate ship, a bullet from the pirates on shore put an end to his life, which so discouraged his men that they returned to their vessel.

After their departure Dangerfield got off his sloop, though in a very shattered condition, having suffered much in the engagement, and many of his men having been killed or wounded.

With no small difficulty he went into an inlet in North Carolina, where he remained during the winter.

In spring he again took to sea, steered to Newfoundland, took several vessels of small import-

ance, and, on his way to the West Indies, captured a brigantine, plundered her, took two men into their own ship, and sent her off.

Having cruised a considerable time it was necessary to clean, and, for that purpose, went into the Isle of Blanco.

While they were keenly employed in this work, the Eagle sloop, belonging to the South Sea Company, with thirty-five men, attacked Dangerfield, and constrained him to cry for quarter.

While they were surrendering Dangerfield and twelve of the crew escaped out of the cabin window, and fled to the woods.

Five of them were taken, but the rest remained upon the island.

Informed of this meritorious action, the Spanish Government condemned the ship to the crew of the Eagle, and sent a small sloop to the island, with twenty-five men, to search the woods for the other pirates.

Three others were found, but Captain Dangerfield, with three men and a boy, escaped.

Dangerfield returned to England. He had not long to wait for employment. He found the Emilia under the command of a man called Angerstoft—a German—and agreed to sail with him as first mate.

Ere a month had passed Angerstoft was dead, and the Jackall elected captain. He had commanded the Emilia, and carried on a splendid trade with her for over twelve months, when we introduced him to the reader.

His appearance we have yet to exhibit.

CHAPTER LXX.

PRIDE AND POMP—A CUNNING WOMAN'S DEVICE—SUCCESS OF A DEEP-LAID SCHEME—A FORTUNATE INTERRUPTION.

THE round of dissipation and unceasing pleasure into which the Duchess threw Olivia was fast hastening that young lady into an abyss of destruction.

Day by day her modesty and reserve disappeared, until at last not a vestige remained.

She was, in every sense of the word, a worldly girl ; dress, show, magnificence, pleasure, were the beacons by which she consented to be guided.

Making worldliness a religion, she became a stanch devotee—in fact a perfect martyr to her faith.

Soon the peach-blossom faded from her cheek, and art was called in to supply the shortcomings of nature.

Her mirror was now Olivia's constant thought, and the more praise she got for her beauty, the more fastidious care did she take to enhance it.

It may well be supposed that her cunning aunt observed this awful change with delight.

Having made up her mind for the betrayal of the girl, she set herself down determinedly to the task, and would have succeeded had her intended victim been a saint, but unhappily she found Olivia made of a different and more pliable material, and one that it was easy to weld into the shape required.

The young girl was day and night engaged in her delirious round of fashionable pleasures, and it was not to be wondered at that her morality took flight when exposed to and jostled against worldly vice so continuously.

Only one thing could possibly have kept her from a sudden and awful fall, and that was the image of that man she had and did still love —sincerely, deeply, truly love.

But even that affection was not proof against the *coup d'etat* prepared for her, and which we are about to describe.

The Prince had been in the society of this new enchantress every day for fourteen days, and in his own opinion was as far off from the accomplishment of his desire as on the moment of his first meeting Olivia.

His impulsive nature could endure this no longer, and he determined to bring matters to a crisis.

Fortune favoured him !

Starting off for the residence of the Duchess one morning, after a night passed in thinking of Olivia, he had determined that in one interview he would either at once take possession of the object of his new-born and awful passion, or seek a mistress elsewhere.

He found the Duchess, as usual, in her boudoir.

It was early, very early for a visitor, and her Grace started with unfeigned surprise as the Prince rushed rather than walked into her little paradise.

" To what am I indebted for this early visit ?" demanded the Duchess.

The Prince threw himself into a chair, and with much energy replied—

" To my broken peace of mind."

" How ?"

" Another night of unrest," he cried, " another night of misery! I can endure this no longer, and I am come to say so."

" You can endure *what* no longer ?"

" You know to what I refer. The torture of this unrequited love of mine."

" Unrequited !"

" Yes. For it must be so, I feel convinced, or I should have had Olivia in my arms before this."

" Psha !"

" It is well for you to sneer at me, because you know not my agony of mind, and can form no conception of the misery I feel as I look into that cold, passionless face, and find that I am no nearer the end you promised to this wooing than I was at the moment of my introduction.'

" Again I say, psha !"

" And again I say I cannot, I will not endure this any longer."

There was an earnestness in his tone that made the Duchess stare very seriously at her visitor.

" Do you mean this ?"

" I do."

" And you have determined to bring matters to a crisis ?"

" Unquestionably."

" Then you will commit a fatal error."

" I care not. I have determined on learning my fate, and I will this night sleep in the arms of your niece, or see her no more."

" What madness is this ?"

" It may be madness, but I have determined on the course, and no earthly power shall move me."

" You are wild, inconsiderate, mad !"

" Yes, you have told me so often, but it has no effect upon me."

" Then go your own way, but you will lose Olivia."

" I care not. With the gifts I have at my disposal, I can gain for a mistress whomsoever I please."

" Gifts !"

" Yes, the most coveted in the land. One of them I thought of offering you ; but, as you do not seem inclined to fall into my views, and make no effort to assist me, I shall present it to Lady Ellington, whose daughter—"

" Stay ! What is this gift ?"

" The office of Lady of the Bed Chamber, only left vacant last night. I thought I had heard you covet it very frequently, the more so because it would throw you so constantly in contact with the Queen, who has, unfortunately, rather shunned you of late, and I did my best to make peace between you, and get the office—"

" And you succeeded ?"

" So far that a word more from me will make it a certainty. But—"

" But ! No ' buts' for me. I have already lost *caste* through the coldness of the Queen, and this will restore me. I *must* be Lady of the Chamber."

" Unfortunately—"

" I know what you will say. You mean to barter the office for that chit of Lady Ellington's ; but it shall not be."

" And Olivia ?"

" Shall be yours."

" To-night ?"

" Yes, to-night."

" Are you sure ?"

" I am."

" There is doubt. I am not to be tricked ?"

" No."

" Swear it "

" I swear it."

" On your soul ?"

" On my honour."

" *On your soul.*"

" Yes ; on—my—soul !"

" That will do. Now I believe you."

And this other gift that you mentioned ?"

" It is for my mistress."

" And its nature ?"

" Maid of Honour."

"Ah! this, then, is the bait with which I am to catch the fish?"

"It is the only one I can offer."

"It will not do for Olivia. But no matter, I am not to be baulked."

"I knew you would not, and I only regret that I did not put on the pressure a fortnight ago."

"It would have been useless unless the office of Lady of the Bedchamber had been vacant."

"Ah! you women! you women! what an incorrigible set of place-hunters you are."

The Prince soon took his leave, and the Duchess sat down, with her hands clasped over her brow, to form a plot by which her oath was to be kept.

*   *   *   *   *

An hour later her Grace entered the sitting-room of Olivia.

That lady was attired, and prepared for a morning drive.

"Oh, aunt!" she cried, "I am about to visit Lady Ellington. Will you come?"

"No."

"Why not?"

"Because I should not be well received."

"I do not understand you."

"You will presently. Lady Ellington expected the post of Lady of the Bedchamber, and her pale-faced chit that of Maid of Honour; and by this time they will have learned that I have snatched the coveted prizes from them."

"You?"

"Yes love—that is, I *may do so* if I am so inclined. You and I have the chance of being the envied ones."

"I really cannot believe my senses."

"In all probability you cannot. It was as much as I could do to credit mine, but it is a fact, nevertheless, that the Prince has just left me, and that he has brought me the appointments. But ah, me! there is a condition attached to them that I fear will debar us from accepting them."

"What condition?"

"I dare not tell you, my pet."

"Dare not? Wherefor?"

"Because you would despise me for having listened to it."

"It must, then, be something very awful."

"Nay, it is but an act of every-day occurrence. It is, in fact, the acceptance of that which ninety-nine out of every hundred ladies of the land would give their ears to have the refusal of, but you are so young, so pure, so—I dare not say more."

"You must, aunt, you must."

"You will know all?"

"Yes."

"Thought of the revelation brings the scalding blush of shame into your cheek."

"Yes."

"Then I *must* speak. But Heaven knows I would not have done so had you not thus pressed me."

"Go on. A presentiment of evil creeps upon me, but I am prepared to listen."

"So far from evil threatening, fortune is preparing to shine with marvellous brilliancy upon us. But you look pale and ill; perhaps I had better say no more."

"Go on."

"I will do so. I see by your manner that you comprehend me, although you will have me speak. I will be brief in the revelation of this condition. It is that you become the mistress of the Prince!"

The girl staggered back, and would have fallen, had not her aunt caught her in her arms and placed her in a chair.

"I knew this would be the case," she said; I knew what the effect would be. Why, oh, why, would you make me speak?"

Olivia looked up into her aunt's eyes.

"And you," she said, slowly and determinedly, hissing each word through her set teeth, "and you would have me become this man's mistress —you would have me bargain away my soul for this brief and transitory honour!"

"Psha! that is the language of a silly, sentimental child, not of the woman of the world I thought you had become."

"*You* would have me sacrifice my *honour* to achieve this end?"

"If you call a sacrifice of honour throwing yourself into the arms of the future King of England, and reaping wealth, and titles, and position, then I would have you do this."

"Then know I *cannot*, will not do this evil."

"But listen to reason—"

"God forgive you for seeking to prostitute the child of your husband's dead brother. I have spoken!"

She uttered these last words in a tone calculated to stop further discussion of the subject, but the Duchess had not yet played her last card.

The cunning woman applied her handkerchief to her eyes, and burst into a pretended frenzy of grief.

"Yes," she cried, "God forgive me. I have sinned deeply in this, but I call Heaven to witness that it was only on the most awful pressure. It was only to save your position, only to hold you in your present place, only to pander to the pleasures you so love, only to advance your worldly welfare. Yes, I have sinned; but I think you *will* forgive me."

Olivia started, and came to the side of her aunt.

"I am sorry I have pained you," she cried, "I did not mean to do so; but what, what mean you by the words you have just uttered?"

The Duchess was too much overcome with grief to reply, but she placed her hand in her bosom and drew forth a note, which she gave Olivia.

The young girl hastily unfolded it, and read as follows:—

"To her Grace the Duchess of Grasmount.

"Your Grace,—

"We have most respectfully to request a settlement of the claims of Archer and Co. for £9 432 19s. 7d., amount due for jewellery supplied to yourself and Miss Besgrove. We have

further to intimate that, unless the amount mentioned be paid in full within three days from the date hereof, we shall proceed in the usual manner for its immediate recovery.

"We are,

"Your Grace's

"Most obedient servants,

"HALLINGTON and CONLEY,

"Solicitors.

"Dated — day of ——, 17—."

"I have read it," said Olivia, "every word, but what has this to do with the matter?"

"Everything. Unless that amount is paid forthwith I am certain be to dragged to a prison The disgrace—the disgrace!"

The Duchess covered her face again, and gave vent to several hysterical and heart-rending cries.

"But the amount," said Olivia; "the amount is such a trifle."

"It's more than I can raise by five thousand pounds."

"But a mortgage—"

"I cannot raise one."

"Wherefor?"

"The affairs of the Duke are in the most complicated state, and it will be at least twelve months before I can touch a shilling of his estates."

"You cannot mean this?"

"I am only too miserably in earnest."

"That is indeed dreadful."

"It is, it is. You will now see why I urged the suit of the Prince! He not only offered these honours to us; he agreed to settle the demands of these rapacious creditors."

"Indeed!"

"Yes, indeed!"

"And it is for me; for me that you are to be thus persecuted?"

"Name it not, my angel girl, I can bear it!"

"But it was to gratify my ambition, to pander to my pride that this fearful debt was incurred?"

"Do not torture me with those words. I would do this and twenty times as much for you at any time."

"It is terrible; it is terrible."

Olivia burst into tears.

"Do not weep," moaned the Duchess, between her own hysterical sobs, "do not weep. It is enough for one to suffer, and it is best that that one should be me. Cheer up, little love; I am growing old now, and the vanities of the world should leave me? Perhaps it is best that they should be torn form me thus suddenly."

"No, no. It cannot; it shall not be!"

"What would you do?"

"*You may tell the Prince that I consent!*"

"No, no!"

"Enough. I will have my own way this once. No words of yours can move me. Hasten and tell the Prince that I will receive him."

"I would rather—"

"Silence, dear aunt; I am prepared for my fate! You need not urge another word."

"Are you resolved?"

"I am."

"Then Heaven bless you, for you are saved."

*   *   *   *   *

"Saved!" cried Olivia, as she sank on the floor after her aunt had quitted her. "Saved! Great God! What mockery! Saved? Yes! *Her* credit; *my* position is redeemed, but, my precious soul! what of that?"

She cried long and bitterly.

She wrung her tiny hands, and beat her little feet on the floor, in the awful agony that had come upon her, and thus she passed the day.

The finery in which she had decked herself was thrown off and disregarded.

There were no calls made that day.

There was no reception of visitors.

Olivia kept her own room; and, fixing her mind upon the awful part she had to enact, strove to nerve herself for the task.

Night came at last, and with it the Duchess. She was full of life, brimming over with smiles now.

"I have communicated your determination to the Prince," she said, "and he sends back word that he is frenzied with delight, and that he will be here within the hour."

"Enough; I will retire to my chamber."

"'Tis well," said the Duchess, and then, bending over the young girl till her lips nearly touched her brow, she continued, in a low and rapid voice, "but when the Prince comes to your chamber in a few minutes, let him not be received with coldness and reserve. Be not unto him inanimate and passionless as a marble statue—"

"Oh, leave me, leave me, aunt," exclaimed the young lady, shuddering all over with the deepest sense of humiliation and shame. "There is something dreadful—aye, even horrible, in hearing such injunctions come from your lips. Let it suffice that I sacrifice myself—"

"Well, well, I will say no more," interrupted the Duchess; then hastily imprinting a kiss upon the cheek of her niece, she hurried away to await the arrival of the Prince.

Olivia then took up a small lamp, and hastened to her chamber.

She dismissed her maid on the instant, and sat down to think again, and to nerve herself for what was to follow.

At length she rose, and commenced slowly to lay aside her apparel.

She was armed, as it were, with the fortitude of a desperate resolution.

Having made up her mind to the worst, she abandoned herself to the current of what appeared to be her destiny—or rather to the control of the strong compulsion that ruled her with an imperious necessity.

In such a mood did she gather up and arrange the masses of her luxuriant hair for the night: and when in a state of semi-nudity she seated herself upon the couch to divest herself of her remaining apparel, she could not help clasping her hands with a sudden paroxysm of anguish at the thought of all the circumstances under which she was about to surrender herself into the arms of the princely voluptuary.

But, at the same moment, the door was gently opened, and his Royal Highness entered the chamber.

The moment he flung his gaze upon Olivia, he devoured, as it were, all her charms with a rapid, burning look. He beheld her, indeed, as finely formed as her wily aunt had often intimated that she was; and as the wing of the bird sweeps over the surface of the sea, thus passing from wave to wave with whirlwind speed, so did the glance of the royal sensualist travel quick from charm to charm—from contour to contour—from shoulders of firmness and whiteness to breasts still more plump and dazzling, rising like two swelling globes from the surface of an ample chest—well divided—rich in their sculptural proportions without being too luxuriant—and each crowned with a delicate rose-bud.

Thence did his looks sweep along the white and well-rounded arms so admirably modelled in their robustness—so glowing and warm even in their whiteness—and belonging to a figure which, though somewhat largely proportioned, was perfectly symmetrical, and all the flowing outlines of which were developed by the drapery that hung loosely about it.

Nor were the Prince's eyes averted or arrested in that first sweeping glance, ere they had likewise embraced the statuesque moulding of the lower limbs—so full and robust where fullness and robustness were proper—so slender where the well-turned ankles required such slenderness

—and with the shapely feet so long and narrow.

Notwithstanding her hands were joined and her looks were mournful, when the eye of the Prince thus rapidly scanned all the charms that were more than half exposed, there was, nevertheless, a kind of languid voluptuousness which hung at the moment about that young woman, and which at once seized like the intoxicating influence of highly perfumed flowers upon the senses of the Prince : so that his brain appeared to reel for a moment as he paused upon one of the descending steps.

The next instant he sprang forward—he caught her in his embrace—he pressed her in his arms.

But at that moment the door opened !

The Prince started back in amazement.

Olivia shrieked, gave one hasty glance at the figure before her, and fell senseless to the floor.

The intruder was Lewis Arndale.

CHAPTER LXXI.

ON BOARD THE EMILIA—PIPEY LEARNS WHAT JUST CAUSE MAYDOCK HAD TO SUSPECT DANGERFIELD—THE LETTER ON THE CABIN TABLE —THE PROPOSITION—HOW CAPT. DANGERFIELD WAS DEFEATED.

POOR Mrs. Boodles objected very strongly to enter the boat on Deal beach that was to bear off to the Emilia.

It required some pressing and a little force to induce the good old lady to seat herself in the frail skiff, but at last Pipey managed to get her in, and they were soon off, scudding merrily enough over the dark blue waters.

Although Pipey was in a new element he managed to conduct himself in a manner that disarmed suspicion, and with Tom Shattler, the mate, for a companion, he managed to get on very well.

Shattler had taken a great fancy for our hero from the night of their meeting ; but when he saw his mysterious influence over the Captain, whom he regarded as the sternest and least shakable of human beings, he became an enthusiastic admirer of the ex-thief-taker and officer of the secret service.

He regarded him as a superior being, and one whom it was a pleasure to know and be intimate with.

Pipey determined to make himself agreeable, and, despite the doubt and fears that agitated him, a great deal of his old devilry and good humour returned, and he kept the crew incessantly amused by sayings and antics.

The Captain he had not seen or spoken to since he met him in the little out-of-the-way tavern.

Dangerfield, as was not an uncommon practice with him, resigned the command to his lieutenant, and kept himself close in his cabin.

He was of a sullen and retiring nature, and cared not about mixing with the crew more than was necessary. Moreover, he had an objection to making himself cheap on board the ship.

He knew what strange, impulsive, superstitious, and credulous beings he had to deal with ; and by his reserved habits, coolness in danger, haughtiness at all times, and the arrangement of his cabin—which more resembled the chamber of an ancient necromancer than the apartment of a smuggler chief—he contrived to get a character for supernatural powers that he thought it advisable to keep.

But Pipey never troubled himself about Dangerfield ; he was too much absorbed in his own affairs.

Mrs. Boodles was decidedly out of her element on board the Emilia.

She had a cabin to herself, and every arrangement that the ship could afford for the convenience of a lady passenger was made ; but the resources of the Emilia were limited, and poor Mrs. Boodles was sadly at a loss how to conduct herself.

The cabin she described as " a cramped-up chaney cupboard with only one shelf, which they had made into a bed, and expected a Christian woman to sleep upon."

This shelf was the old lady's dread, for no sooner did she lay herself upon it at night than she would find herself sprawling on the deck, being tossed off by the rolling of the vessel.

Then there was the " pisenous " pea soup, the limited supply of water, the sour wine, and the salt beef to complain of, and Mrs. B. was decidedly unhappy ; and had not Pipey been near her, it is certain that she would have gone " out of the way " of her enemies for ever.

It was only the knowledge that the dear captain was near that supported her in her great trouble.

They had been out four days when Dangerfield summoned Pipey to his cabin.

" Tell him to bring in some wine," said the pirate to his black servant, " and that will save you the trouble of coming in again."

Pipey received the wine from the servant, and entered the cabin.

Dangerfield was seated near a table.

" Shut the door," he said, as Pipey entered ; " I want to have a talk with you."

Pipey did as desired, and then approached the table.

As he stood awaiting the further movements of the captain, his eagle eye wandered over the cabin, and at length rested on the table.

A letter, laying opened therein, caught his glance.

With a sidelong look he devoured its contents without attracting the notice of Dangerfield.

The letter was but a brief scrawl, and ran as follows :—

" Dear Dangerfield,—

" Since my interview with you I have seen the Duchess. She agrees with me, and imagines Grimer will keep the old woman safe, *if he can !* You *must* kill her. It is the wish of our sister, and we must obey. So if our friend the cunning lawyer thinks he has got us in a line, he makes a mistake. Had he suspected that Dangerfield was likely to fall in company with her grace, the possibility is that you would not have been honoured with your present charge.

"Adieu,

"Yours fraternally,

"The BLACK CAPTAIN."

"Oh, oh!" thought Pipey, "so Maydock really had a cause for asking me to come on board the Emilia. This has been a lucky chance."

The Captain, who had remained in a reverie for a few moments, now caught sight of his open letter, and looked up sharply into the eyes of Pipey; but that young gentleman was at the instant particularly engaged in examining a sword that hung against the side of the cabin.

Silently the Captain folded his letter and placed it in a desk.

"That letter must be mine," thought Pipey; "it will be useful one day, and I will have it before I turn my back upon the Emilia."

"Well," said the Captain, looking up, and motioning Pipey to a chair, "ours was a strange meeting, wasn't it? I little thought to see one of the brethren in Deal, I can tell you."

"Perhaps not."

"No, indeed! But I've had you down to say that, since I've been on board, I have had too much to do to spare you a moment until now."

"Don't apologise."

"I'm not about to do so."

"Perfectly right. There's no occasion."

The Captain looked at his strange hand with mingled wonder and suspicion.

The impudence of Pipey was a novelty to him, but he did not seem to relish it.

"I want to know what brought you on board the Emilia?" continued Dangerfield.

"Why, I've already said it was my wish to leave England."

"Nothing more?"

"Yes."

"What then?"

"The business of the Duchess of Grasmount."

Dangerfield started.

"You received orders to drown the woman in whose company I came to Deal?"

"Yes."

"And I've brought orders to the contrary."

"From whom?"

"The Black Captain."

"I can't see through this."

"But you will presently. By the laws of our society we are bound to assist one another."

"We are?"

"As long as we do nothing to injure the brotherhood in its integrity."

"Just so."

"Well, when the Duchess demanded the life of this old woman it was freely granted her, but the day after you received a letter from the Captain, ordering you to make away with the poor wretch, he found that the Duchess had been playing us false."

"How?"

"Using us only as a means for the furthering of her own ends, and caring so little for us as to drop hints that almost led to our betrayal."

"Is that so?"

"It is."

"The devil!"

"'Then,' said the Captain to me, 'follow Dangerfield; go to Italy. Get to Venice, if possible, with the old woman, and keep watch over her day and night until you hear from me. By right,' he continued, 'this Duchess should be entombed alive, but a worse death for her would be the scaffold. Therefore, see to this woman, and when I call on you to produce her see that you do so.' Then I planted myself on Maydock and your man, and so I am here."

"I understand."

"That's right."

"And, to tell you the truth, I'm not sorry for this. I hate killing women. I had a mother who loved me. She was the only being who ever loved me, and I can't forget it. I can't forget it, and I wouldn't willingly hurt a hair of a woman's head for her dear sake; but the laws of the Order of Scarlet Brethren is peremptory, and I had no choice in the matter, although God knows how my soul revolted against the deed. Drink, man; I'm glad you've come to save me from the crime I so much dreaded."

Thus Pipey saved Mrs. Boodles. He left the cabin, laughing in his sleeve at the success of his simple plot.

CHAPTER LXXII.

FALLEN AMONG DESPERADOES—A LONG AND TEDIOUS JOURNEY—A CHIEF OF BRIGANDS—TORTURE.

ALL the night, and until noon next day, did Lord and Lady Lovelace tramp over the blue mountains, seeking some path that would lead them back once more to the city. But in vain!

No human habitation met their eye.

No human being crossed their path; accordingly, they had to wander on, and hope for that relief which seemed, indeed, a long way off.

It may be supposed that they were but indifferent travelling companions.

Engrossed with their own thoughts they wandered silently on, both longing for the moment when they could part company for ever.

Fair Liz had not one little spark of love left for the man who had so deceived her; and he, seeing that his protestations and prayers were unheeded, began very seriously to think that he was wasting time, and resolved to blot her image from his mind, and instal another in its place.

His pride was wounded by her indifference; and as he ceased to think less and less of her, so the thought of Marie and her child oppressed him, and he began to long for the warm and passionate love he felt she bestowed upon him at the birth of their infant.

Liz, on her part, was thinking of the friend and protector of her girlhood, and wondered where he was now that the hour of her sorest need had come.

With thoughts like these engrossing their attention, the fugitives from the encampment of Zingari wandered through the intricate mountain passes, seeking some friendly guide to convey them to the city.

They had walked for more than twelve hours, when Liz, who had declined the assistance of Lovelace up to that point, sunk exhausted to the earth.

"I can go no further," she said; "go on your way and leave me to my fate."

"That I will not do. Rise, Lady Lovelace, I have yet strength enough to support you until we find some house and fall in with friendly aid."

"I cannot move. Do you go on, and if you find any one who is inclined to render assistance send them to me."

"Never! I swear I will never leave you thus!"

They were surrounded by a maze of low bushes, wild mountain plants, and the spot was as still and dreary as possible.

While Lovelace gazed about him in the hope of finding some sign to guide him to a pathway his eye caught something bright and glittering behind a little row of bushes.

In a moment he was conscious that a carbine was levelled at his head; he turned, as if for flight.

Behind another bush there was more glitter, and again did the muzzle of a carbine present itself to his gaze.

Next moment, as if by magic raised, a half score of black-bearded brigands of the very worst type surrounded him, and, with horrid grins on their cruel faces, raised their sugar-loaf hats with mock courtesy.

In the worst possible Italian they demanded him to stand still, politely informing him that if he attempted to move death would be his portion.

They then grinned at and bowed to him who stared at them in speechless amazement.

"What do you require?" demanded Lovelace, in Italian. "If you are brigands, and I cannot doubt that that is your calling, you will gain nothing by detaining us, for we have nothing for you."

"Oh, that point must be decided by the Wolf; we have not the right of arguing it with milor," said one, who appeared to be the leader.

"Stay," said Lovelace; "if money is your aim you may earn it by conducting us to Venice."

"To Venice?"

"Yes."

"Does milor know how far he is from Venice?"

"No."

"Over forty miles."

"Psha!—it must be close at hand; it lays somewhere in this direction."

"No, milor, in that."

The brigand pointed to the very route by which Lovelace had come to this spot.

"Unfortuate!" he cried. "But still, if you have a mind to earn a few English sovereigns, you may do so by conducting us to some point where we can obtain a vehicle to convey us to Venice."

"Ah, that will be impossible, for milor must first see the Wolf."

"What do you mean by seeing the Wolf?"

"The chief of our band."

"Do you mean to say that you will detain us?"

"I have no option."

"Confusion! I will not be detained."

"I am afraid milor cannot help himself."

The Italian said this with a grin of mischief that inclined Lovelace to level him to the earth, but the gleam of the deadly carbine checked this impulse.

"The signora looks tired," said the man. "That is sad, but she must be assisted."

"We are prisoners," said Lovelace to his wife. "These wretches will take us to their chief. There is no use in resisting, so rise and lean on my arm. Better *mine* than *theirs*."

Liz rose mechanically, and grasped the arm of her husband.

"How far?" asked Lovelace.

"About three miles."

"This lady can never walk that distance."

"Then we shall have pleasure in carrying her."

Liz shudderingly clung to the arm of her husband, and in a few moments, guided by the little band of brigands, they once more moved onward.

A few minutes' walking brought them to a roadway through the apparently interminable mountains.

As Lovelace saw it, he muttered a deep curse; for here, had he not been thus suddenly pounced upon, was the way out of the difficulty into which he had fallen.

Before the three miles were accomplished poor Liz had to depend entirely upon Lovelace for support. She was too exhausted to move hand or foot, and her husband threw his arm about her slender waist, and carried her the remainder of their journey.

A few minutes of struggling under his burthen brought the English noble to the retreat of the brigands.

Their encampment lay in a hollow between two hills; and here, sheltered from sight, were raised a score or two of white tents, gleaming in the bright sunshine.

The arrival of the party with the prisoners was hailed with loud shouts from a hundred throats, and as many pairs of eyes gleamed upon them as they passed to the tent of the chief.

There was more shouting, and cries of "The Wolf!"

They paused before a tent of more pretentions than the others, and there came therefrom a tall and grim-looking fellow, wearing the beard that characterised most of the others of his band; but in this respect only did he resemble them.

Their faces were unmistakably Italian; his was unmistakably English.

There was the bull-dog look of the lower type of British face about him, and his nationality could have been sworn to at any time and in any place.

This fellow, named by his band "The Wolf," was as uncompromising a villain as ever breathed, and the story of his life will be worth tracing.

Sam Dark was once known throughout Europe as a pirate of the most desperate character, but his fame chiefly rested on a daring attack made on a ship of the Great Mogul.

It was reported that he had married the Great Mogul's daughter, who was taken in the ship that fell into his hands, and that he was about to be the founder of a new monarchy; that he gave commissions in his own name to the captains of his ships and the commanders of his forces, and was acknowledged by them as their prince.

In consequence of these reports, it was at one time resolved to fit out a strong squadron to go and take him and his men; and at another time it was proposed to invite him home with all his riches, by the offer of his Majesty's pardon.

These reports, however, were soon discovered to be groundless, and he was actually starving without a shilling, while he was represented as in the possession of millions.

Not to exhaust the patience nor lessen the curiosity of the reader, the facts in this man's life shall be briefly related.

He was a native of Devonshire, and, at an early period, sent to sea; advanced to the station of mate in a merchantman, he performed several voyages.

To prevent the intrusion of French smugglers into the Spanish dominions, a few vessels were commanded to cruize upon that coast, but the French ships were too strong for them; therefore the Spaniards came to the resolution of hiring some foreigners to act against them

Accordingly, some merchants of Bristol fitted out two ships of thirty guns, well manned, and provided with every necessary; and commanded them to sail for Corunna, to receive their orders.

Captain Gibson commanded one of these ships, and Dark was his mate.

He was a fellow of more cunning than courage; and, insinuating himself into the confidence of some of the boldest men in the ship, he represented the immense riches which were to be acquired upon the Spanish coast, and proposed to run off with the ship.

The proposal was scarcely made when it was agreed upon, and put in execution at ten o'clock the following evening. Captain Gibson was one of those who mightily love their bottle, and spent much of his time on shore.

But he remained on board that night, which did not, however, frustrate their design, because he had taken his usual dose, and so went to bed.

The men who were not in the confederacy went also to bed, leaving none upon deck but the conspirators.

At the time agreed upon the long-boat of the other ship came, which Dark hailing in the usual manner, he was answered by the men in her.

"Is your drunken boatswain on board?" which was the watchword agreed between them.

Dark replying in the affirmative, the boat came on board, with sixteen stout fellows, who joined in the adventure. They next secured the hatches, then softly weighed anchor, and immediately put to sea without bustle or noise.

There were several vessels in the bay, and a Dutchman of forty guns, the captain of which was offered a considerable reward to go in pursuit of Dark, but he declined. When the Captain awoke, he rung his bell, and Dark and another conspirator going into the cabin found him yet half asleep. He inquired, saying, "What is the matter with the ship—does she drive? what weather is it?"

Supposing that it had been a storm, and that the ship was driven from her anchors.

"No, no," answered Dark, "we're at sea, with a fair wind and good weather.'

"At sea!" says the Captain, "how can that be?"

"Come," says Dark, "don't be in a fright, but put on your clothes, and I'll let you into a secret. You must know that I am captain of this ship now, and this is my cabin, therefore you must walk out; I am bound for Madagascar, with a design of making my own fortune, and that of all the brave fellows joined with me.'

The Captain having a little recovered his senses, began to understand the meaning.

However his fright was as great as before; which Dark perceiving, desired him to fear nothing, "for," says he, "if you have a mind to make one of us, we will receive you; and if you turn sober, and attend to business, perhaps, in time, I may make you one of my lieutenants; if not, here's a boat, and you shall be set on shore.'

He accepted of the last proposal; and the whole crew being called up to know who was willing to go on shore with the captain, there were only about five or six who chose to accompany him.

They proceeded on their voyage to Madagascar, and it does not appear that they captured any vessels upon their way.

When arrived at the north east part of that island, they found two sloops at anchor, who, upon seeing them, slipt their cables, run themselves ashore, while the men all landed, and concealed themselves in the woods.

These were two sloops, which the men had run off with from the West Indies, and, seeing Dark's ship, supposed that he had been sent out after them. Suspecting who they were, he sent some of his men on shore to inform them that they were friends, and to propose a union for their common safety.

The sloops' men were well armed, had posted themselves in a wood, and placed sentinels to observe whether the ship landed her men to pursue them.

The sentinels only observing two or three men coming towards them, unarmed, they did not oppose them.

Upon being informed that they were friends, the sentinels conveyed them to the main body, where they delivered their message.

They were, at first, afraid that it was a stratagem to entrap them, but when the messengers assured them that their captain had also run away with his ship, and that a few of their men, along with him, would meet them unarmed, to consult matters for their common advantage, confidence was established.

They were mutually well pleased, as it added to their strength.

Having consulted what was most proper to be attempted, they endeavoured to get off the sloops, and hastened to prepare all things, in order to sail for the Arabian coast.

Near the river Indus the man at the masthead spied a sail, upon which they gave chase. As they came nearer to her they discovered that she was a tall vessel, and might turn out to be an East Indiaman.

She, however, proved a better prize; for, when they fired at her, she hoisted the Mogul's colours, and seemed to stand upon her defence. Dark only cannonaded at a distance, when some of his men began to suspect that he was not the hero that they supposed.

The sloops, however, attacked, the one on the bow, and another upon the quarter of the ship, and so boarded her. She then struck her colours.

She was one of the Great Mogul's own ships, and there were in her several of the greatest persons in his Court, among whom, it was said, was one of his daughters, going upon a pilgrimage to Mecca; and they were carrying with them rich offerings to present at the shrine of Mahomet.

It is a well-known fact that the people of the east travel with great magnificence; so that these had along with them all their slaves and attendants, with a large quantity of vessels of gold and silver, and immense sums of money to defray their expenses by land; therefore the spoil which they received from that ship was almost incalculable.

They took the treasure on board their own ships, and plundered their prize of every thing valuable, and then allowed her to depart.

As soon as the Mogul received this intelligence, he threatened to send a mighty army to extirpate the English from all their settlements upon the Indian coast.

The East India Company were greatly alarmed, but they found means to calm his resentment by promising to search for the robbers, and deliver them into his hands.

The noise which this made all over Europe gave birth to the rumours that were circulated concerning Dark's greatness.

In the meantime the adventurers made the best of their way back to Madagascar, intending to make that place the deposit of all their treasure to build a small fort, and to keep always a few men there for its protection.

Dark, however, disconcerted this plan, and rendered it altogether unnecessary.

While steering their course, Dark sent a boat to each of the sloops, requesting that the chiefs would come on board his ship to hold a conference.

They obeyed, and, being assembled, he suggested to them the necessity of securing the property which they had acquired in some safe place on shore, and observed that the chief difficulty was to get it safe on shore; adding, that if any of the sloops should be attacked alone, they would not be able to make any great resistance, and thus she must be either sunk or taken with all the property on board.

That, for his part, his vessel was so strong, so well manned, and such a swift-sailing vessel, that he did not think that it was possible for any other ship to take or overcome her.

Accordingly, he proposed that all their treasure should be sealed up in three chests; that each of the captains should have keys, and that they should not be opened until all were present; that the chests should be then put on board his ship, and afterwards lodged in some safe place upon land.

This proposal seemed so reasonable, and so much for the common good, that it was accordingly agreed to, and all the treasure deposited in three chests, and carried to Dark's ship.

The weather being favourable, they remained all three in company during that and the next day; meanwhile Dark, tampering with his men, suggested that now they had on board what was sufficient to make them all happy.

"And what," added he, "should hinder us from going to some country where we are not known, and living on shore all the rest of our days in plenty?"

They soon understood his hint, and all readily consented to deceive the men of the sloops, and fly with all the booty; this they effected during the darkness of the following night.

The reader may easily conjecture what were the feelings and indignation of the other two crews in the morning, when they discovered Dark had made off with all their property.

Dark and his men hastened towards America, and, being strangers in that country, they agreed to divide their booty, to change their names, and separately to take up their residence, and live in affluence and honour.

The first land they approached was at the Island of Providence, then newly settled.

It, however, occurred to them that the largeness of their vessel, and the report that one had been run off with from the Groine might create suspicion; therefore they resolved to dispose of their vessel at Providence.

Upon this resolution Dark, pretending that his vessel had been equipped for privateering, and having been unsuccessful, he had orders from the owners to dispose of her to the best advantage, he soon found a merchant.

Having thus sold his own ship, he immediately purchased a small sloop.

In this he and his companions embarked, and landed at several places in America, where, none suspecting them, they dispersed and settled in the country.

Dark, however, had been careful to conceal the greater part of the jewels and other valuable articles; so that his riches were immense.

Arriving at Boston, he was almost resolved to settle; but as the greater part of his wealth consisted of diamonds, he was apprehensive that he could not dispose of them at that place, without being taken up as a pirate.

Upon reflection, therefore, he resolved to sail for Ireland, and in a short time arrived in the northern part of that kingdom, and his men dispersed into different places.

Some of them obtained pardon and settled in that country.

The wealth of Dark, however, now proved of small service, and occasioned him great uneasiness.

He could not offer his diamonds for sale in that country without being suspected.

Considering, therefore, what was best to be done, he thought there might be some person at Bristol he could venture to trust.

Upon this he resolved; and, going into Devonshire, sent to one of his friends to meet him at a town called Biddiford.

When he had unbosomed himself to him and other pretended friends, they agreed that the safest plan would be to put his effects into the hands of some wealthy merchants, and no inquiry would be made how they came by them.

One of these friends told him he was acquainted with some who were very fit for the purpose, and if he would allow them a handsome commission, they would do the business faithfully.

Dark liked the proposal, particularly as he could think of no other way of managing this matter, since he could not appear to act for himself.

Accordingly the merchants paid Dark a visit at Biddiford, where, after strong protestations of honour and integrity, he delivers them his effects, consisting of diamonds and some vessels of gold. After giving him a little money for his present subsistence, they departed.

He changed his name, and lived very quietly at Biddiford; therefore there was no notice taken of him.

In a short time his money was all spent, yet he heard no word from his merchants. He wrote to them repeatedly; at last they sent him a small supply, but it was not sufficient to pay his debts.

In short, the remittances they sent him were so trifling that he could with difficulty exist.

He therefore determined to go privately to Bristol, and have an interview with the merchants himself; where, instead of money, he met with a mortifying repulse; for, when he desired them to come to an account with him, they silenced him by threatening to disclose his character; the merchants thus proving themselves as good pirates on land as he was at sea.

After this reverse he recommenced the life of a pirate, and for some time prosecuted a most successful business along the Italian coast.

It then reached his ears that the government of the country was so incapable of protecting its people, and the thousands of travellers the classic renown and beauty of Italy attracted to its shores, that the business of brigand was one of great profit and no particular risk.

Dark put it to his crew if it would not be better to sell the ship, share the profits, and take to the mountains for the future.

He found the majority ready to fall into his views, and so establishing himself as chief, he stalked one day into the interior of the country, and soon numbered a band of one hundred scoundrels of all nations—the majority being Sicilians.

The renown of the Wolf spread far and wide, and there was no part of the country that was not at some time subject to the depredations of his band.

He was a hard, cruel man, hesitating at nothing in the pursuit of gain; sacrificing men and women indiscriminately, and inventing the most awful tortures that human mind could conceive, whereby to wring from his victims the gold that formed the idol he worshipped.

Dark looked at his prisoner for some moments.

"So," he said, after a long stare at them both, "so you are English?"

"Yes," said Lovelace.

"Ah, then I greet you as a countryman."

"I regret it."

"Wherefor?"

"Because I am sorry to see an Englishman in such a position."

"Humph! you will pay for that."

"And now let me ask you why I am brought here?"

"Ha! ha! why you are brought here? that is a good question. Why should you be brought here, but for the purpose of paying toll for passing through the mountains."

"Why should I do so?"

"Because I will it!"

"Then I will to pay you nothing."

"We shall see. Search him."

Lovelace was seized and roughly handled.

"Not a stiver," said one, after turning his lordship's pockets inside out.

"The worse for him."

"And now that I have been subjected to all these indignities, allow me to ask what is to follow?"

"That will depend upon yourself."

"What mean you?"

"You will understand me presently. Now, who are you?"

"An English traveller."

"I guessed as much. I want your name."

"Then you will not have it."

"We shall see."

"We shall."

"Who is the lady?"

"My wife."

"Indeed! She is very beautiful! It will not be a trifle that will ransom her. Are you staying long in Venice?"

"Yes."

"Have you friends there?"

"I have, as you will learn to your cost."

"Ah, that is what all my guests say, but I heed them not, for I know best. People say all manner of things under the torture of a forced sojourn with me. Now, are your friends rich?"

"Yes, and powerful."

"So much the better for you, so much the better for me."

"The worse you mean."

"The better I mean."

"Time will prove which of us is right."

"It will, and now that you have afforded me all the information I require, I am enabled to fix the amount of your ransom to a nicety. You are an English traveller, sojourning for some considerable time in Venice. Your friends are rich and powerful, and by your tone I am to comprehend that they will exert themselves in your behalf. Good! You are worth to me exactly six thousand English pounds, and the lady, although by far the greater treasure"—he raised his hat to Liz as he spoke—"I am only able to set the price of four thousand pounds upon."

"And I wish you may get the sum, or any part of it."

"That is a kind wish of yours, considering you will have to find it."

"I never will find it."

"I really think you will."

"Never! Never!"

"Humph! You have not heard me yet. I give you five days to find the sum I demand, and if at the end of that time the money is not forthcoming, I shall be under the painful necessity of hanging you, and shall have the extreme felicity of taking the lady under my own particular care, and making her queen of these mountains."

"Villain! Do you dare speak thus—"

"That's insult number two. I must teach you manners."

He beckoned to two of his men.

"Bind this man," he said ; "bind him as you know how, and just *warm his feet*."

The men grinned horribly.

"Remember," said Lovelace, "you shall suffer for this."

"Psha!"

"I pray you cease this violence," said Liz, advancing and addressing the chief; "do not lay hands upon him. We are rich, and will—"

"Silence, madam," cried Lovelace angrily ; "allow them to proceed, and be the consequences upon their own heads. I will have a fearful revenge for this."

"Yes," said Dark, coolly, "yes; that is the old, old tale ; but before my guests leave me their tone changes marvellously."

"Villain! ruffians!" cried Lovelace, as the cords of his tormentors cut into his wrists and ankles; "villains! you know not what you do, but you shall repent this."

The chief, without heeding him, beckoned to some women.

"Take the lady with you," he said, "and see that she is cared for ; but this husband of hers must undergo his punishment."

The women dragged Liz away with them.

"You have insulted me," said the Wolf, when Liz was gone ; "you have insulted me, and I never submit to insults. Moreover, I have a curiosity to know your name."

"You shall not know it ; and as to yourself, I spurn you, wretch that you are, and treat your threats with scorn."

"Ha! Take him to the fire ; he really must be thoroughly warmed."

The men caught Lovelace in their arms, and walked with him to one of the many camp fires, over which crocks were boiling.

"What are you about to do with me?" he asked.

"Oh," said one of his conductors, "you should not have offended the Wolf thus. He is a very tiger when roused, and, Heaven knows! you have roused him enough. Lie down."

"What for?"

"No matter ; lie down."

Lovelace hesitated.

One of the men, however, came behind him, and threw him forcibly to the ground.

"Oh, were my hands but free!" muttered Lovelace between his set teeth; "were my hands but free, you should suffer for this."

"It is not our fault," said the men; "you have chosen, and you must suffer. We dare not disobey the orders of the Wolf."

They knelt beside him, and stripped off his boots and stockings.

"What, I ask, what, in the name of God, are you going to do with me!"

"*Warm your feet!*"

They drew Lovelace to the camp fire, and set his feet close to the live embers.

At first he felt not the heat, but soon it grew unbearable, and he winced with pain.

Then the men sat down on his legs, and he could not move hand or foot.

"Oh, my God!" he yelled ; "how long is this to continue?"

"Until the Wolf gives the word to release you."

There was no sign of the Wolf, and the torture Lovelace was undergoing brought the sweat of agony to his brow.

In a few minutes he shrieked with pain, and his cries could be heard echoing through the mountain glades.

Then the Wolf was seen approaching.

He was smoking a cigar, and strolled leisurely to the spot.

"Well," he said, "how do you like feet warming?"

Oh, Heaven, save me, or I shall go mad !"

"Do you apologise for your insults ?"

"No."

"Then wait there a little longer."

"I shall die—I shall die!"

"Oh, no ; you can bear a great deal more than that."

"God spare me !"

"You should rather appeal to me."

"If you have one spark of manhood—if you have any human feeling—let me get away from this fire."

"You apologise?"

"Yes."

"I thought you would. And now, your name ?"

"Do not ask it."

"Your name ?"

"Lord Lovelace."

"Ah, I thought I had caught a rich prize. You will write to you friends for the ten thousand pounds ?"

"Yes."

"I knew you would. You see I am right, and you were wrong. I am always right—my guests are always wrong. Release him."

Lovelace had fainted.

CHAPTER LXXIII.

A CRASH — THE LAST DAYS OF THE SCARLET BRETHREN — ESCAPE OF THE BLACK CAPTAIN —THE DUCHESS AND THE YOUNG LAWYER.

THAT devilish institution the Scarlet Brethren was doomed to a sudden and ignominious end.

Despite the great care that had been taken to render its workings as complete as possible; despite the terrible laws of its organisation; despite the rigour with which its members were chosen, a black sheep had crawled in, and hesitated not, when the moment arrived, to crumble the whole edifice into dust.

The reader already knows sufficient of the tale to comprehend the fate of a delinquent, and the manner in which Pipey was treated is a sufficient guarantee for the punishment that would be meted out to a detected delinquent amongst the brotherhood.

But human passion overcame the fear of such punishment—jealousy was too strong to be controlled by judgment, and the fear of that awful death by entombment during life could not stay the tongue of Tom Rumbold.

He had quarrelled with the Black Captain, and had been threatened by that individual.

He let the sore thus made extend until it inflamed his whole system, and, meet when they would, words and blows passed between them.

At length, in a moment of passion, the Captain drew his sword, and lopped off the right ear of his antagonist.

The wounded man said nothing, but went his way with sullen looks.

The Captain thought that he was conquered, but he little knew what was passing in that man's mind, or he would never have parted with him.

Rumbold went straight to a magistrate, and, forgetful of his oaths, forgetful of all save the smart of his wound and the indignity put upon him, revealed the secret of the organisation of the Order of the Scarlet Brethren.

He, at his own request, was conveyed to Newgate and secured.

"I demand the king's pardon for turning king's evidence," he said; "but I will be a prisoner until the band is broken up, and the Captain swinging on Tyburn tree."

It so happened that one of the very officers to whom the information of the existence of the society was conveyed was a personal friend of Lewis Arndale, the lawyer, and, not for a moment suspecting him to be one of the brotherhood, he communicated the tale of Rumbold to him almost the moment he heard it.

Lewis Arndale knew that it was all over with him now.

It was certain that all connected with the society must be brought to justice, and the first thought was of immediate flight.

Then he thought of the Duchess, and, remembering that she was the aunt of Olivia, determined to inform her of the awful crisis in their fate.

With this view he was hastening to her house when he stumbled against the Black Captain, who was likewise bound to the same place.

As a matter of course he told him all, and the consternation of the Black Captain may be imagined.

"Hasten," cried the Captain; "there is only time to save the Duchess. We must think of flight."

They flew onward with lightning speed, and, without being announced, sought the Duchess.

On hearing what had come to pass she swooned, but the thought of her niece, to whose apartment she had but a few moments before conducted the Prince of Wales, flashed across her distracted brain, and she could not but think that this was a judgment upon her for the awful crime of which she had been guilty.

On her the magic word "Olivia!" burst from the lips of the wretched woman. Lewis was reminded that she was in the house.

"She must go with us," he cried; "I cannot leave her. I will seek her and ask her to fly with me."

He left the Duchess under the care of the Black Captain, and rushed off to seek the lady of his love.

Where and how he found her the reader already knows.

* * * * *

We now pause to take a retrospective glance at the career of this man Rumbold, who had thus suddenly brought about so much consternation.

It will repay the attention of the reader:—

Rumbold was the son of honest and industrious parents, who lived at Ipswich, in Suffolk.

In his youth he was apprenticed to a bricklayer; but evil inclinations having an ascendancy over his mind, he eloped from his employment before a third part of his time was passed.

In order to support himself after having absconded, and, having a great desire to see London, he repaired thither, and soon confederated himself with a gang of robbers.

In conjunction with these, he shared in many daring exploits; but, wishing to try his skill and fortune alone, he left them, and repaired to the road.

He travelled from London with the intention of waylaying the Archbishop of Canterbury.

Having got sight of the party between Rochester and Sittingbourn, in Kent, he got into a field; and, placing a tablecloth on the grass, on which he placed several handfuls of gold and silver, took a box of dice out of his pocket, and commenced a game at hazard by himself.

His grace observing him in this situation, sent a servant to inquire the meaning, who, upon coming near Rumbold, heard him swearing and rioting about his losses, but never paid the least attention to his questions.

The servant returned and informed the prelate, who alighted, and seeing none but Rombold, asked him whom he played with?

"Pray, sir," says Rumbold, "be silent—five hundred pounds lost in a jeffy!"

His Grace was about to speak again—

"Aye," continues Rumbold, always playing on, "there goes a hundred more!"

"Pr'ythee," said the archbishop, "do tell me whom you play with?"

Rumbold replied—

"With ——," naming some one who perhaps never had existence.

"And how will you send the money to him?"

"By his ambassadors," quoth Rumbold; "and, considering your grace as one of them extraordinary, I shall beg the favour of you to carry it to him."

He accordingly rose and rode up to the carriage, and, placing in the seat about six hundred pounds, rode off.

He proceeded on the road he knew the archbishop had to travel, and both, after having refreshed at Sittingbourn, again took the road, Rumbold preceding the archbishop by a little distance.

He waited at a convenient place, and again placed himself on the grass in the same manner as before, only having very little money on the cloth.

The archbishop again observed him, and now believing him really to be a mad gamester, walked up to him, and, just as his grace was going to accost him, Rumbold cries out, with great joy—

" Six hundred pounds !"

" What !" said the Archbishop, " losing again ?"

" No, by God," replied Rumbold, " won six hundred pounds. I'll play this hand out, and then leave off, while I'm well."

" And who have you won of ?" said his grace.

Of the same person that I left the six hundred pounds for with you before dinner."

"And how will you get your winnings ?"

" Of his ambassador, to be sure," says Rumbold.

" So, presenting his pistol and drawn sword, rode up to the carriage, and took from the seat his own money, and fourteen hundred pounds besides, with which he got clear off.

With part of this money Rumbold bought himself an eligible situation, but still he could not give up his propensity of appropriating to himself the purses of others.

For many miles round London he had the waiters and chamber-maids of the inns enlisted into his service ; and though, to appearance, in an honest way of gaining a livelihood, he continued his nefarious courses to a great extent.

He was not, indeed, always successful.

Having once been apprised of two rich travellers being at an inn, where one of his assistants were, he left London immediately, and waited on the road which he had been informed the travellers were to take.

Long, however, he might have waited, for the travellers were too cunning ; they pretended to be travelling to the place which they had last left.

Determined not to return without doing some business, he waited on the road.

The Earl of Oxford, attended by a single footman, soon appeared, and, being known to his lordship, he disguised himself by throwing his long hair over his face, and holding it with his teeth.

In this clumsy mask he rode up, demanded his lordship's purse, and threatened to shoot both the servant and him if they made the least resistance.

Expostulations were in vain, and he proceeded to rifle the Earl.

In his coat and waistcoat he found nothing but dice and cards, and he was very much enraged, until, feeling the other pockets, he discovered a nest of goldfinches, with which he was mightily pleased, and said he would take them home, and cage them, recommending his lordship to return to his regiment, and attend to his duty ; and, as an encouragement, gave him a shilling.

As Rumbold was riding along the road, he met a country girl with a milk-pail on her head, with whose beauty and symmetry of shape he was greatly taken.

They entered into conversation, Rumbold alighted, and, excusing himself for the freedom, sat beside her while she milked her cows.

They became very familiar, and desires were inflamed in him which they soon found an opportunity to gratify.

Pleased with each other's company, they made an assignation the same evening.

Our adventurer was to come to her father's house at a late hour, and pretending to have lost his road, solicit a night's lodging.

This plan was accordingly followed out, but they were disappointed in each other's society that evening, for some one of the family kept astir all night.

Determined, however, not to leave his fair convert, he pretended in the morning to be taken dangerously ill, and the good farmer rode off immediately for medical assistance.

All the power of surgery, however, could not discover his ailment.

The farmer kindly insisted upon his remaining where he was until he should recover, to which he, with great professions of gratitude, assented.

He had his paramour appointed to attend him, and they continued their criminal indulgences for several days.

At last, fearing too long an illness might alarm the farmer, he called on him one evening, and offered him money for the trouble and expense he had put them to, which the other refused, with many assurances of welcome, and telling him he had plenty to spare, and always wished to be hospitable.

Completely overpowered by such generosity, Rumbold wished to make some apparent return, and, borrowing a name, told him he was a bachelor of property in a certain county ; that he had hitherto remained secure against the attacks of beauty, but that he now was vanquished by the attractions of his daughter, and hoped, if their girl had no objections, that a proposal of marriage would not be unacceptable to the family.

The farmer, in his turn, overcome by such a mark of condescension, expressed himself highly gratified at the proposal ; and, upon communicating it to the family, all were agreeable, and none more so than the girl.

The idea of adding gentility to the fortune which the farmer intended for his daughter quite elated him, and made him extremely anxious to gain the favour of the suitor.

Rumbold followed out the design, and his endearments with the daughter were thus more frequent than he expected.

His principal design was to sift the girl as to the quantity of money her father had in the house, and where it lay ; but was chagrined when informed that there were only a few pounds; that a few days before they met her father had made a great purchase, which took all his ready money.

Seeing now that there was no chance of gleaning the father's harvest, though he had cropped the mother's labour, he resolved to leave the family, and, accordingly, one evening took his march *incognito*, leaving a present of twenty pieces of gold, enclosed in a copy of verses.

He proceeded on the road, and met with no person worthy his notice, until the following day, when a singular occurrence happened to him.

Passing by a small coppice between two hills, a gentleman, as he supposed, darted out upon him, and commanded him to stand and deliver.

Rumbold requested him to have patience, and he would surrender all his property; when, putting his hand into his pocket, he drew a pistol, and fired at his opponent, without the shot taking effect.

"If you are for sport," cried the other, "you shall have it," and instantly shot him slightly in the thigh; at the same moment, drawing his sword, cut Rumbold's reins at one blow, thus rendering him unable to manage his horse.

Rumbold fired his remaining pistol, and again missed his adversary, but shot his horse dead.

Thus dismounted, the gentleman made a thrust at him with his sword, which, missing Rumbold, penetrated his horse, and brought them once more upon an equal footing.

After hard fighting on both sides our adventurer threw his adversary, bound him hand and foot, and proceeded to his more immediate object of rifling.

Upon opening his coat, he was amazed to discover that he had been fighting with a woman.

Raising her up in his arms, he exclaimed, "Pardon me, most courageous amazon, for thus rudely dealing with you; it was nothing but ignorance that caused this error, for, could my dim-sighted soul have distinguished what you were, the great love and respect I bear for your sex would have deterred me from contending with you; but I esteem this ignorance of mine as the greatest happiness, since knowledge, in this case, might have deprived me of the opportunity of knowing there could be so much valour in a woman. For your sake I shall for ever retain a very high esteem for the worst of females."

The amazon replied that this was neither a place nor opportunity for eloquent speeches, but that, if he felt no reluctance, she would conduct him to a more appropriate place. To this he readily assented.

They entered a dark wood, and, following the winding of several obscure passages, arrived at a house upon which the sun had not shone since the deluge.

A number of servants appeared, and bustled about their lady, whose disguise was familiar to them, but were astonished to see her return on foot attended by a stranger.

They were then conducted to an elegant apartment, and, after having been refreshed by whatever the house afforded, they became very familiar, and Rumbold pressed his companion to relate her history, which, with great frankness, she related in the following words:—

THE STORY OF THE FEMALE ROBBER.

"I cannot, sir, deny your request, since we seem to have formed a friendship which I hope will turn out to our mutual advantage.

"I am the daughter of a sword-cutler; in my youth my mother would have taught me to handle a needle, but my martial spirit gainsayed all persuasions to that purpose.

"I never could bear to be among the utensils of the kitchen, but was constantly in my father's shop.

"I took wonderful delight in handling the warlike instruments he made. To take a sharp and well-mounted sword in my hand, and brandish it, was my chief recreation.

"Being about twelve years of age, I studied, by every means possible, how I might form an acquaintance with a fencing-master.

"Time brought my desires to an accomplishment, for such a person came into my father's shop to have a blade furbished, and it so happened that there was none to answer him but myself.

"Having given him the satisfaction he desired, though he did not expect it from me, among other questions I asked him if he was not a professor of the noble science of self-defence, which I was pretty sure of from his postures, looks, and expressions.

"He answered in the affirmative, and I informed him I was glad of the opportunity, and begged him to conceal my intentions, while I requested he would instruct me in the art of fencing.

"At first he seemed amazed at my proposal, but, perceiving I was resolved in good earnest, he granted my request, and appointed a time which he could conveniently allot to that purpose.

"In a short while I became so expert at back-sword and single rapier that I no longer required his assistance, and my parents never once discovered this transaction.

"I shall waive what exploits I did by the help of my disguise, and only tell you, that when I reached the age of fifteen, an innkeeper married me, and carried me into the country.

"For two years we lived peaceably and comfortably together; but, at length, the violent and imperious temper of my husband called my natural humour into action.

"Once a week we seldom missed a combat, which generally proved very sharp, especially on the head of the poor innkeeper; the gaping wounds of our discontent were not easily salved, and they in a manner became incurable.

"I was not much inclined to love him, because he was a man of a mean and dastardly spirit, and thought it inconsistent that a dunghill cock should crow over a game hen.

"Being likewise stinted in cash, my life grew altogether comfortless, and I looked on my condition as insupportable; and, as a means of mitigating my troubles, adopted the resolution of borrowing a purse occasionally.

"I judged this resolution safe enough, if I were not detected in the very act; for who could suspect me to be a robber, wearing abroad man's apparel, but, at home, that suitable to my sex? besides, no one could procure better information, or had more frequent opportunities than myself; for, keeping an inn, who could ascertain what booty their guests carried with them better than their landlady?

"As you can vouch, sir, I knew myself not to be destitute of courage; what, then, could hinder me from entering on such enterprises?

"Having thus resolved, I soon provided myself with the necessary habiliments for my scheme, carried it into immediate execution, and continued with great success, never having failed till now.

"Instead of riding to market, or travelling five or six miles about some piece of business (the usual pretences with which I blinded my husband) I would, when out of sight, take the road to the house where we now are, where I metamorphosed myself, and proceeded to the road in search of prey.

"Not long since my husband had one hundred pounds due to him about twenty miles from home, and appointed a certain day for receiving it.

"Glad I was to hear of this, and instantly resolved to be revenged on him for all the injuries and churlish outrages he had committed against me; I knew very well the way he went, and understood the time he intended to return.

"I way-laid him, and had not to wait above three hours, when my lord and master made his appearance, whistling with joy at his heavy purse.

"I soon made him change the tune to a more doleful ditty, in lamentation of his bad fortune.

"I permitted him to pass, but soon overtook him, and, keeping close by him for a mile or two, when at length I found the coast clear, I rode up and seized his bridle, presented a pistol to his breast, and, in a hoarse voice, demanded his purse, else he was a dead man.

"This imperious don, seeing death before his face, had nearly saved me the trouble by dying without compulsion; and so terrified did he appear that he looked liker an apparition than any thing human.

"'Sirrah,' said I, 'be expeditious.'

"But a dead palsy had so seized every part of him that his eyes were incapable of directing his hands to his pockets.

"I soon recalled his spirits, by two or three sharp blows with the flat of my sword, which speedily wakened him, and, with great trembling and submission, he resigned his money.

"After I had dismounted him, I cut his horse's reins and saddle-girths, beat him most soundly, and dismissed him, saying—

'Now, you rogue, I am even with you; have a care the next time you strike a woman, (your wife I mean), for none but such as dare

not fight a man will lift up his hand against the weaker vessel. Now you see what it is to provoke them; for, if once irritated, they are restless till they accomplish their revenge to satisfaction. I have a good mind to end your wicked courses with your life, inhuman varlet, but I am loth to be hanged for nothing—I mean for such a worthless man as you. Farewell, this money shall serve me to purchase wine to drink a toast to the confusion of all such rascally and mean-spirited things!'

"I then left him, and ——"

This extraordinary character was about to proceed with the narration of her exploits, when the servant announced the arrival of two gentlemen.

She left the room; and returning with her friends, apologised to our adventurer for the interruption, but hoped she would not find the company of her companions disagreeable, whom she soon discovered to be likewise females in disguise.

The conversation now became general, and, upon condition of Rumbold stopping all night with them, the amazon promised to finish her adventures next day.

This accorded with the wishes of Rumbold; and, when they retired to rest, he found the same room was destined for them all.

His curiosity was, however, overcome by his covetousness; for, rising early next morning, and finding all his companions asleep, he rifled their pockets of a considerable quantity of gold, and decamped with great expedition, thus disappointing the reader in the continuation of a narrative almost incredible from its singularity.

Our adventurer had frequently observed a goldsmith in Lombard-street counting large bags of gold, and he became very desirous to have a share of the glittering hoard.

He made several unsuccessful attempts, but having in his possession many rings, which he had procured in the way of his profession, he dressed himself in the habit of a countryman, attended with a servant, went to the goldsmith's shop, and proposed to sell one of those rings.

The goldsmith, perceiving it to be a diamond of considerable value, and from the appearance of Rumbold, supposing he was ignorant of its real worth, after examining it, he, with some hesitation, estimated its value at ten pounds.

To convince the countryman that this was its full value, he showed him a diamond ring, very superior in quality, that he would sell him for twenty pounds.

Rumbold took the goldsmith's ring to compare with his own, and, fully acquainted with its value, he informed the goldsmith that he had come to sell, but it was a matter of small importance to him whether he purchased or sold.

He accordingly pulled out a purse of gold, and laid down the twenty pounds for the ring.

The goldsmith stormed and raged, crying that he had cheated him, and insisted on having back his ring.

Rumbold, however, kept hold of his bargain

and replied that he had offered him the ring for twenty pounds; that he had a witness to his bargain, there was his money, and he hoped that he would give him a proper exchange for his gold.

The goldsmith's indignation increasing at the prospect of parting with his ring, carried the matter before a justice.

Being plaintiff, he began his tale by informing the judge that the countryman had taken a diamond ring from him, worth one hundred pounds, and would give him but twenty pounds for it.

"Have a care," replied Rumbold; "for if you charge me with *taking* a ring from you, which is, in other words, *stealing*, I shall vex you more than I have yet done."

He then told the judge the whole story, and produced his servant as a witness to the bargain.

The goldsmith now became infuriated, exclaiming that "he believed the country gentleman and his servant were both impostors and cheats."

Rumbold replied, "that he would do well to take care not to make his cause worse; that he was a gentleman of three hundred pounds per annum; and that, being desirous to sell a ring at its just value to the goldsmith, the latter endeavoured to cheat him by estimating it far below its value."

The judge accordingly decided in favour of our adventurer, only appointing him to pay the twenty pounds in gold, without any exchange.

The gold of Lombard-street still continuing to attract the attention of Rumbold, he, with longing eyes, one day traversed that street, attended by a boy whom he had trained in his service.

The boy ran into a shop where they were counting a bag of gold, seized a handful, then let all fall upon the counter, and ran off.

The servants pursued, seized the boy, and charged him with having still some of the money.

Rumbold approached to the assistance of the boy, insisted that the youth had not stolen a farthing of their money, and that the goldsmith should suffer for his audacity.

The goldsmith and Rumbold came to high words, and mutual volleys of imprecations were exchanged.

The latter then inquired what sum he charged the boy with having stolen?

The goldsmith replied that he did not know, but the bag originally contained a hundred pounds.

Upon this Rumbold insisted that he would wait until he saw the money counted.

He tarried about half an hour, and the money was found complete.

The goldsmith made an apology to Rumbold for the mistake; but the latter replied that, as a gentleman, he would not endure such an affront with impunity.

After some strong expressions on both sides

Rumbold took his leave, assuring his antagonist that he would hear from him.

The goldsmith was arrested the day following in an action of defamation.

The sergeant who arrested him, being bribed by our adventurer, advised him to compromise the matter; that the gentleman he had injured was a person of quality, and if he persisted in the action it would expose him to severe damages.

With some difficulty the matter was settled by the goldsmith giving Rumbold twenty pounds in damages.

A jeweller in Foster-lane next supplied the extravagances of Rumbold.

He had often disposed of articles for that jeweller, who had full confidence in Rumbold's fidelity.

One day, having observed in his shop a very rich jewel, he acquainted the jeweller that he could sell it for him.

Happy at such information, he delivered it to Rumbold, who carried it to another jeweller to have a false one, exactly similar, prepared.

He then embraced an opportunity to leave the counterfeit jewel with the jeweller's wife, in his absence.

Shortly afterwards he met the jeweller in the street, who said he never expected to have been so used by him, and threatened to bring the matter under the cognizance of a judge: but Rumbold retreated to a remote part of the city.

Rumbold was one day travelling in the vicinity of Hackney; his attention was directed towards a house, which he earnestly desired to possess.

He approached the house, knocked at the door, and inquired if the landlord was at home.

He soon appeared, when Rumbold politely informed him that, having been highly pleased with the appearance of his house, he was resolved to have one built after the same model, and requested the favour of being permitted to send a tradesman to take its exact dimensions.

This favour was readily granted; when our adventurer went to a carpenter, and informed him that he wished him to go along with him to Hackney to measure a house, in order that he might have one built of a similar construction.

They accordingly went, found the gentleman at home, who kindly entertained Rumbold, while the carpenter took the dimensions of every part of the house.

The carpenter being amply rewarded was dismissed, and, by the aid of the draught of the house taken by him, Rumbold drew up a lease, with a very great penalty in case of failure to implement the agreement.

Being provided of witnesses to the deed, he went and demanded possession.

The gentleman was surprised, and only smiled at the absurdity of the demand.

Rumbold commenced a law suit for possession of the house, and his witnesses swore to the validity of the deed.

The carpenter's evidence was also produced, many other circumstances were mentioned to corroborate the fact, and a verdict was obtained in favour of Rumbold's claim.

But the gentleman deemed it proper to pay the penalty rather than to lose his house.

Rumbold, disguised in the apparel of a person of quality, one day waited on a scrivener, and acquainted him he had immediate occasion for a hundred pounds, which he hoped he would be able to raise for him upon good security.

The scrivener inquired who were the securities, and Rumbold named two respectable citizens, whom he knew to be at that time in the country, which satisfying the money-lender, he desired our adventurer to call next day.

In the meantime he made inquiry after the stability of the securities, and found he had not been imposed upon as to their respectability.

Our adventurer again waited upon the scrivener, who having agreed to advance the sum, Rumbold sent for two of his accomplices, who personated those who were to be securities, and, after a little preliminary caution, signed the bond for him under their assumed names; and, upon Rumbold's receiving the money, they immediately took their leave.

The name which Rumbold assumed on this occasion was of further service to him, for it happened to be that of a gentleman of property in Surrey, whom he met with after this adventure at an inn.

Having learned what time the gentleman intended to remain in town, and the name and situation of his estate, he determined to render this chance-meeting of service to him.

He accordingly again waited on the same scrivener, and informed him he had occasion for another hundred, but did not wish to trouble any of his friends to become security for such a trifle, for that, as he possessed a good estate, it might be advanced upon his own bond; and that if the scrivener could spare a servant to ride the length of Surrey, he would then learn the extent of his estate, and be enabled to remove any scruple whatever.

A servant was accordingly sent, and directed to go and make inquiry after the property of the stranger whom Rumbold had met at the inn.

Returning in a few days, Rumbold found the scrivener very condescending, and free in his congratulations upon the possession of so pleasant and valuable a property, and said he would not scruple though the loan had been for a thousand.

Rumbold, finding him thus inclined, doubled the sum, and, after giving his own bond for two hundred pounds, left the scrivener to seek redress as he best could.

Thus Rumbold supported himself by exercising his ingenuity at the expense of others; and he had now amassed a considerable sum of money.

He was not so addicted to these bad habits but that he felt an inclination to retire from scenes so fraught with danger and infamy.

For this purpose he placed his money in the hands of a private banker, with a design of living frugally and comfortably upon the interest.

This banker unfortunately failed, and made off with all Rumbold's property, so that he was once more reduced to the necessity of having recourse to his old employment.

The first exploit recorded of Rumbold, after his re-appearance in public, is the following.

He stopped at a tavern, where he called for a flagon of beer, which was handed him in a silver cup, as was customary at that time.

Being in a private room and alone, he called for the landlord to partake of his noggin, and they continued together for some time, until the landlord had occasion to leave him.

Soon after he went to the bar, and paid for his beer, while the waiter at the same time went for the cup, missing which, he called Rumbold back, and asked him for it.

"Cup!" says Rumbold; "I left it in the room."

A careful search was made, but to no effect; the cup could not be found, and the landlord openly accused Rumbold with the theft.

He willingly permitted his person to be searched, which proved equally unsuccessful; but the landlord still persisted in maintaining that Rumbold must have it, or, at all events, that he was chargeable with the loss, and would have the matter investigated by a justice, before whom they immediately went.

The landlord stated the case, while Rumbold complained loudly of the injury done him by the suspicion; and from his never endeavouring to run off when he was called back, and submitting so readily to be searched, the justice dismissed him, and fined the landlord for his rashness.

During their visit to the justice, some of Rumbold's associates entered the same inn, where, according to arrangement, they found the cup fixed under the table with soft wax, and they made off with it without the least suspicion.

One of the adventures of Rumbold is now very common in the metropolis.

Having observed a countryman pretty flush of money, he and his accomplices followed him; but from Hodge's attention to his pocket they failed in several attempts to pick it.

Our practitioners, however, taking a convenient opportunity and place, one of them goes before and drops a letter, while another keeps close by the countryman, and, upon seeing it, cries out—

"See, what is here?"

But although the countryman stooped to take it up, our adventurer was too nimble for him, and having it in his hand, observed—

"Here is somewhat else besides a letter."

"I cry half," said the countryman.

"Well," said Rumbold, "you stooped, indeed, as well as I, but I have it. However, I will be fair with you; let us see what it is, and whether it is worth dividing."

Thereupon he broke open the letter, in which was enclosed a chain or necklace of gold.

"Good fortune," says Rumbold, "if this be real gold."

"How shall we know that?" replied the coun-

tryman; "let us see what the letter says;" which was as follows:—

"Brother John,—

"I have here sent you back this necklace of gold you have sent me, not for any dislike I have to it, but my wife is covetous, and would have a bigger. This comes not to above seven pounds, and she would have one of ten pounds. Therefore, pray get it changed for one of that price, and send it by the bearer to—

"Your loving brother,
"JACOB THORNTON."

"Nay, then, we have good luck," observed the cheat, "but I hope," says he to the countryman, "you will not expect a full share, for you know I found it; and besides, if one should divide it, I know not how to break it in pieces without injuring it: therefore I had rather have my share in money."

"Well," said the countryman, "I will give you your share in money, provided we divide equally."

"That you shall," said Rumbold, "and therefore I must have three pounds ten shillings, the price in all being, as you see, seven pounds."

"Aye," said the countryman, thinking to be cunning with our adventurer, it may be worth seven pounds in money, fashion and all, but we must not value that, but only the gold; therefore I think three pounds in money is better than half the chain, and so much I'll give, if you'll let me have it."

"Well, I'm contented," said Rumbold; "but then you shall give me a pint of wine over it."

To this the other also agreed, and to a tavern they went, where the bargain was ratified.

There Rumbold and the countryman quickly disposed of two bottles of wine.

In the meantime one of Rumbold's companions entered the inn, inquiring for a certain person who was not there.

Rumbold informed the stranger (as he pretended to be) that he would be there presently, as he had seen him in the street, and requested him to come in and wait for him.

Upon this the stranger sat down to await the arrival of his friend.

In a little time Rumbold proposed to remove into a larger apartment, where they commenced playing at cards, to amuse themselves until the gentleman expected should arrive.

Rumbold and his associate began their amusement, as the countryman was a stranger to the game.

After he had continued a spectator to the good fortune of our adventurer, who in general vanquished the stranger, the countryman was at last prevailed upon to run halves with the fortunate gamester.

For a while the same good fortune smiled upon them, and the stranger, in a rage at his great losses, refused to proceed.

But after a few bottles more were emptied and the long-expected gentleman never appearing, they renewed their amusement, and fortune deserting Rumbold and the countryman, who seconded him, in a short time the latter found himself without a shilling.

The landlord was then called to assist in drinking the money gained, and, being informed how they had cheated the countryman, he was resolved to exert his ingenuity at their expense.

Meanwhile, several associates of Rumbold, who had been respectively employed in similar adventures, entered the room, joined in their conversation, and participated of their wine.

The landlord was at last requested to bring supper, which was done with great alacrity.

The bottle continuing to move with considerable rapidity the company were, in general, intoxicated before they sat down to supper.

When it was brought in they commenced with great avidity, and soon despatched a shoulder of mutton and two capons; and, under the influence of wine, all fell asleep with the dishes before them.

The landlord embraced this favourable moment of silence to collect all the bones and remnants of the whole day's provision, and divided them upon the plates which were upon the table.

In a short time one of them, losing his balance, embraced the floor, and, by the noise of the fall, awoke the rest of the drowsy company.

They all renewed their attacks upon the victuals.

"How came these bones here?" cried one of them; "I do not remember that I ate any such victuals."

"Nor I," said another.

Upon which the landlord was called and interrogated.

"Why, surely, gentlemen, you have forgot yourselves," said he; "you have slept sound and fair indeed. I believe you will forget the collar of brawn you had, too, that cost me six shillings out of my pocket."

"How, brawn?" said one.

"Aye, brawn," answered the landlord; "you had it, and shall pay for it. You'll remember nothing presently. This is a fine drunken bout, indeed."

"So it is," replied one of the company; "sure we have been in a dream. But it signifies nothing, my landlord; you must and shall be paid. Give us another dozen bottles, and bring us the bill, that we may pay the reckoning we have run up."

This order was obeyed, and a bill presented, amounting to seven pounds, and every man was called upon to pay his share.

The countryman shrunk back, wishing to escape, but one of them pulled him forward, saying—

"Come, let us tell noses, and every man pay alike."

The countryman desired to be excused, and said his money was all exhausted; they, therefore, agreed that he should be exempted.

The company went to bed, and enjoyed a sound repose; but the simple countryman could not close his eyes for reflecting upon his sudden reverse of fortune.

In the morning the countryman, in order to procure money to carry him home, resolved to sell the chain in his possession.

He accordingly went to a goldsmith, but, to his additional mortification, he was informed that, instead of gold, it was only brass gilded over.

He informed the goldsmith of the whole matter, who went along with him to a justice, to obtain a warrant to apprehend Rumbold and his associates; but, before their arrival, the worthy knights of the pistol had prudently decamped with their spoil.

He after a while struck up an intimacy with the Black Captain, and, from his marvellous skill as a swindler, proving of use to that nefarious scamp, he was made prime favourite, and initiated into the mystery of the Scarlet Brotherhood, and enjoyed a long lease of popularity, until the quarrels between them commenced.

The end of their connection is before the reader.

* * * * *

The Captain exerted himself to the utmost to restore the Duchess, but it was many minutes before he succeeded.

He seated her at a table, so that she could support her head thereon, and then spoke to her with great rapidity.

"It is over with us!" he cried. "What have you that you can lay your hands upon? for, believe me, all that you have in this house is the sum total of what you will possess when to-morrow dawns."

"You do not mean that?"

"I do."

"We must fly then?"

"Yes, you are thrown upon me now. You

are mine at last, for I alone can aid you now."—

"Do not say so."

"I do."

"But the world—"

"The world must from this moment be nought to you. Your path has been chosen with deliberation; you knew what you risked in following it. The end is before you, and you must take the consequences of your indiscretion."

"Villain, I do not believe you. This is some vile *ruse* to betray me into your power."

"It is not. I swear it."

"I will not believe you."

"Here is one who will convince you of the truth of my assertions."

Lewis Arndale, ghastly pale, and sick at heart from what he had just witnessed in the chamber of his beloved one, entered the apartment.

"Convince her Grace of the awful position in which she stands, Arndale—to me she will not listen."

"Then let her meet her fate," cried the young man; "the fate she so richly merits. Vile hypocrite! cunning devil! infamous bawd! you have ruined the purest of earth's flowers—you have brought shame to the best of women. Would that I had the power of sending thee to the gallows you so richly merit."

"What mean you?"

"What do I mean? Great God! she asks me what I mean—she professes ignorance of the hell-devised work progressing under her roof, and by her own planning! Oh! was ever such deceit ere known?"

"Come," cried the Black Captain, "I don't understand this, and I do not wish to be enlightened; but there is no time for these heroics. Will you fly with me, Duchess of Grasmont, or will you remain and meet your fate?"

"I will go with you," said the Duchess, gasping for breath.

"Enough! secure what money and goods you can immediately lay hands on, and return to me instantly."

The Duchess swept past Lewis, and quitted the room.

The young lawyer followed.

In the passage he was met by Olivia.

Her hair was dishevelled, and clung to her snowy shoulders in disordered masses. Her eye was full of madness, and she wrung her little white hands in the deepest despair.

On beholding Lewis she rushed towards him, and caught him by the arm.

"Save me!" she cried; "save me from myself."

"Begone!" he yelled; "begone, vile one. Bad as I am I will not be contaminated by your touch."

"Oh, God, I am mad! Do not desert me now or I shall die—I shall die!"

"Begone!" cried Lewis, flinging the poor, trembling wretch to the earth; "begone, or I shall curse you!"

He tore himself from her puny grasp, and threw her into the apartment he had quitted, and she fell lifeless to the earth.

He turned, and was about to fly, when he encountered the Prince of Wales.

Regardless of consequences in that moment of fury, he seized the royal lover by the throat and threw him from him.

The prince fell heavily, and, his head encountering the sharp edge of a table in his descent, was instantly laid open.

Then Lewis Arndale rushed out of the house.

The Black Captain regarded the proceedings in the utmost bewilderment.

He could not comprehend what motive there could be for all this outburst on the part of Arndale; but he saw that the Prince had received an awful wound, and at once perceived that to be near him, under the circumstances, was rather dangerous work, and so he left the apartment, and closed the door, leaving the Prince and the insensible girl to shift for themselves, and recover or die as chance directed.

He allayed the suspicions of the servants—who, alarmed by the noise of the scuffle, were gathering in little bands in the hall and about the stairs—and there awaited the Duchess.

She came in about half an hour, and placed in his hands all her money and valuables.

"Quick," he cried; "there has been bloody work done by that mad fellow Arndale, and we had best not stay another moment. Now for the Old Mint."

"No, no," cried the Duchess: "first to my bankers. I may be in time to draw a large sum ere the report of this horrible business spreads too far."

"True; let us to the bankers, by all means, and then for the nearest *route* to France."

They quitted the house.

Many long years will have passed over their heads before we shall see them again.

CHAPTER LXXIV.

A DIGRESSION—TYBURN TREE—ITS HISTORY—A SKETCH OF ONE OF THE MOST NOTORIOUS CRIMINALS ASSOCIATED WITH THE LOCALITY.

FULL seventy members of the gang of Scarlet Brethren were captured and punished—many of them gracing Tyburn Tree with their bodies.

It was a brave time for the lovers of the horrible, for scarce a day passed without some of the most notorious members of the now world-famed Scarlet Brethren rendering up their lives to the laws of their country.

The history and mystery of the band was now as familiar as household words, and London was every hour congratulating itself on the narrow escape it had had, for every day the depredations of the band were becoming more alarming and promised to be without end, so well were the plots contrived and the work of plunder and blood consummated.

The escape of two such notorious criminals as the Black Captain and the Duchess of Grasmont was universally regretted, for their acts were of course published by those members of the gang who were brought to justice.

Nevertheless, there was enough and to spare of horrors at Tyburn, and the public should have been, in all conscience, satisfied.

So few know aught of Tyburn, although the word is familiar enough to Englishmen, that we deem a slight glance at its history will be acceptable here.

This celebrated place of execution, which figures so prominently in the records of crime, is said to have been first established in the reign of Henry IV., previous to which "The Elms" at Smithfield seems to have been the favourite locality for the punishment of malefactors.

The name is derived from a brook called Tyburn, which flowed down from Hampstead into the Thames, supplying in its way a large pond in the Green Park, and also the celebrated Rosamond's Pond in St. James's Park.

Oxford-street was, at an earlier period, known as Tyburn-road; and the now aristocratic locality of Park-lane bore formerly the name of Tyburn-lane; while an iron tablet attached to the railings of Hyde Park, opposite the entrance of the Edgeware-road, informs the passer-by that here stood Tyburn turnpike-gate, so well known in old times as a landmark by travellers to and from London.

The gallows at Tyburn was of a triangular form, resting on three supports, and hence is often spoken of as "Tyburn triple tree."

It appears to have been a permanent erection, and there also stood near it wooden galleries for the accommodation of parties who came to witness the infliction of the last penalty of the law, such exhibitions, it is needless to state, being generally regarded by our ancestors as interesting and instructive spectacles.

Considerable disputation has prevailed as to the real site of the gallows, but it now appears to be pretty satisfactorily ascertained that it stood at the east end of Connaught-place, where the latter joins the Edgeware-road, and nearly opposite the entrance to Upper Seymour-street.

A lane led from the Uxbridge-road to the place of execution, in the vicinity of which, whilst excavating the ground for buildings, numerous remains were discovered of the criminals who had been buried there after undergoing their sentence.

Among remarkable individuals who suffered death at Tyburn were the Holy Maid of Kent, in Henry VIII.'s reign; Mrs. Turner, notorious as a poisoner, and celebrated as the inventress of yellow starch; John Felton, the assassin of the Duke of Buckingham; the renowned burglar Jack Sheppard, and the thief-taker Jonathan Wild; Mrs. Brownrigg, rendered proverbial by her cruel usage of apprentices; and the elegant and courtly Dr. Dodd, whom pecuniary embarrassments—the result of a life of extravagance and immorality — hurried into crime.

The last malefactor executed here was John Austin, on 7th November, 1783, for robbery with violence.

At that period the place of execution for criminals convicted in the county of Middlesex was transferred from Tyburn to Newgate, where, on the 9th of December following the date just mentioned, the first capital sentence, under the new arrangements, was carried into effect.

We are informed that some opposition was made by persons residing around the Old Bailey to this abandonment of the old locality at Tyburn; but the answer returned by the authorities to their petition was, that "the plan had been well considered, and would be persevered in."

Our readers do not require to be informed that the place thus appointed is still the scene of public executions, now happily of much less frequent occurrence than formerly.

Those curious documents, called Tyburn Tickets, were certificates conferred under an act passed in the reign of William III., on the prosecutors who had succeeded in obtaining the capital conviction of a criminal.

The object of the enactment was to stimulate individuals in the bringing of offenders to justice; and in virtue of the privilege thus bestowed, the holder of such a document was exempted "from all manner of parish and ward offices within the parish wherein such felony was committed; which certificate shall be enrolled with the clerk of the peace of the county on payment of 1s. and no more."

These tickets were transferable, and sold like other descriptions of property.

The act by which they were established was repealed in 1818; but an instance is related of a claim for exemption from serving on a jury being made as late as 1856 by the holder of a Tyburn ticket.

The conveyance of the criminals from Newgate to Tyburn by Holborn Hill and the Oxford-road afforded, by the distance of space traversed, an ample opportunity to all lovers of such sights for obtaining a view of the ghastly procession.

A court on the south side of the High-street, St. Giles's, is said to derive its name of Bowl Yard, from the circumstance of criminals in ancient times, on their way to execution at Tyburn, being presented at the hospital of St. Giles's, with a large bowl of ale, as the last refreshment which they were to partake of on this side of the grave.

Different maxims came ultimately to prevail in reference to this matter; and we are told that Lord Ferrers, when on his way to execution, in 1760, for the murder of his land-steward, was denied his request for some wine and water, the sheriff stating that he was sorry to be obliged to refuse his lordship, but that, by recent regulations, they were enjoined not to let prisoners drink when going to execution, as great indecencies had been frequently committed in these cases through the criminals becoming intoxicated.

One of the most vigorous drawings by Hogarth represents the execution of the Idle Apprentice at Tyburn—a fitting termination to his disreputable career.

Referring to this print, and the remarkable change which has taken place in a locality formerly associated only with the most repulsive ideas, a recent writer observes—

"How the times have changed! On the spot where Tom Idle made his exit from this wicked world, where you see the hangman smoking his pipe as he reclines on the gibbet, and views the hills of Harrow or Hampstead beyond — a splendid marble arch, a vast and modern city— clean, airy, painted drab, populous with nursery-maids and children, the abodes of weal and comfort, the elegant, the properous, the polite Ty-burnia rises, the most respectable district in the habitable globe."

These remarks naturally call to mind one of the most celebrated of the many notorieties who have ended their days on the famed tree.

We pause to bring his name and career before the reader :—

Thomas Witherington was the son of a worthy gentleman of Carlisle, in the county of Cumberland, who possessed a considerable estate, and brought up his children suitable to his condition.

He received a liberal education, as his father intended he should live free from the toil and hazard of business.

The father dying, Thomas came into possession of the estate, which soon procured him a rich wife, who afterwards proved the chief cause of his ruin.

She was loose in her conduct, and violated her matrimonial obligations, which drove him from his house to seek happiness in the tavern, or in the company of abandoned women.

These, by degrees, perverted all the good qualities he possessed.

Nor was his estate less subject to ruin and decay, for the mortgages he had made on it, in order to support his luxury and profusion, soon reduced his circumstances to the lowest ebb.

Thus reduced to poverty, how could a man of his late affluent fortune, and unacquainted with business, procure a maintenance?

He was possessed of too independent a spirit to stoop either to relations or friends for a precarious subsistence; and to solicit the benevolence of his fellow-men was what his soul abhorred.

Starve he could not, and only one way of living presented itself to his choice—levying contributions on the road.

This he followed for six or seven years with tolerable success; and we shall now relate a few of his most remarkable adventures.

Upon his first outset he repaired to a friend, and, with a grave face, lamented his late irregularities, and declared his determination to live by some honest means; but, for this purpose, he required a little money to assist him in establishing himself, and hoped his friend would find it convenient to accommodate him.

His friend was overjoyed at the prospect of his amendment, and willingly lent him fifty pounds, with as many blessings and advices.

But Witherington frustrated the expectations of his friend, and with the money bought himself a horse, and other necessaries fit for his future enterprises.

One night he stopped at Keswick, in Cumberland, where he met with the Dean of Carlisle.

Being equally learned, they found each other's company very agreeable; and Witherington passed himself for a gentleman who had just returned from the East Indies with a handsome competency, and was returning to his friends at Carlisle, among whom he had a rich uncle who had lately died, and left him sole heir to his estate.

"True," says the dean, "I have often heard of a relation of Mr. Witherington's being in the East Indies, but his family, I can assure you, received repeated information of his death; and what prejudice this may have done to your affairs at Carlisle to-morrow will be the best witness."

The dean then told him his own history, and concluded with these words—

"And I am now informed that, to support his extravagance, Mr. Witherington frequents the road, and takes a purse wherever he can extort it."

Our adventurer seemed greatly hurt at this account of his cousin's conduct, and thanked the doctor for his information.

They were both fond of their bottle, and they spent the evening very agreeably, promising to travel together next day to Carlisle.

Having arrived at a wood on the road, Witherington rides close up to the dean, and whispered into his ear,

"Sir, though the place we are at is very private, yet, willing what I do should be more private, I take the liberty to acquaint you that you have something about you that will do me an infinite piece of service."

"What's that?" answered the doctor; "you shall have it with all my heart."

"I thank you for your civility," says Witherington.

"Well, then, to be plain, the money in your breeches pocket will be very serviceable to me at the present moment."

"Money!" rejoined the doctor: "sir, you cannot want money; your garb and person both tell me you are in no want."

"Aye, but I am; for the ship I came over in happened to be wrecked; so that I have lost all I brought from India, and I would not enter Carlisle for the whole world without money in my pocket."

"Friend, I may urge the same plea, and say, I would not go into that city without money for the world—but what then? If you are Mr. Witherington's nephew, as you pretend to be, you would not thus peremptorily demand money of me; for, at Carlisle, your friends will supply you; and if you have none now, I will bear your expenses to that place."

"Sir," said Witherington, "the question is not whether I have money or not, but concerning that which is in your pocket; for, as you say, my cousin is obliged to take purses on the road, so am I ; so that if I take yours, you may ride to Carlisle, and tell that Mr. Witherington met you, and demanded your charity."

After a good deal of expostulation, the dean was terrified at the sight of a pistol, and, delivering Witherington a purse containing fifty guineas, the doctor pursued his journey to Carlisle, and our adventurer set off in search of more prey.

Witherington, being at Newcastle, put up at an inn where some commissioners were to meet that day to make choice of a schoolmaster for a neighbouring parish.

The salary being very handsome, many spruce young clergymen and students appeared as competitors.

Being possessed of sufficient qualifications, Witherington thinks of standing a candidate, and for this purpose borrowed coarse, plain clothes from the landlord, to make his appearance correspond with the conduct he meant to pursue.

He repaired to the kitchen, and, sitting down by the fire, calls for a mug of ale, putting on a very dejected countenance.

One of the freeholders, who came to vote, observing him as he stood warming himself by the fire, was taken with his countenance, and entered into conversation with Witherington.

He very modestly let the freeholder know that he had come with the intention of standing a candidate, but when he saw so many gay young men as competitors, and, fearing that everything would be carried by interest, he resolved to return home.

"Nay," replies the honest freeholder, "as long as I have a vote justice shall be done ; and never fear, for, egad ! I say, merit shall have the place ; and if thou be found the best scholar thou shalt certainly have it, and to show you I am sincere I now, though you are a stranger to me, promise you my vote, and my interest likewise."

Witherington thanked him for his civility, and consented to wait for the trial.

A keen contest took place between two of the most successful candidates, when our adventurer was introduced as a man who had so much modesty as to make him fear appearing before so gaudy an assembly, but who wished to be examined.

He confronted the two opponents, and exposed their ignorance to the trustees, who were all astonished at the stranger.

He showed it was not a parcel of Greek and Latin sentences that constituted a good scholar, but a thorough knowledge of the nature of the book which they read, and an ability to discover the design of the author.

Suffice it to say that Witherington was installed into the office with all the usual formalities.

Conducting himself with much moderation and humility, the churchwardens of the parish took a great fancy to him, and made him overseer and tax-gatherer to the parish ; and the rector, likewise, committed to his care the collection of his rents and tithes.

This friendly disposition towards Witherington extended itself over the parish, and never was a man believed to be more honest or industrious.

Of the latter qualification, we must say, in this instance, he showed himself possessed ; but of the former he had never any notion.

His opinion had great weight with the heads of the parish, and he proposed the erection of a new school-house ; and for this purpose offered, himself, to sink a year's salary towards a subscription.

It was willingly agreed to, and contributions came in from all quarters, and a sum exceeding seven hundred pounds was speedily raised.

The mind of Witherington was now big with hope ; but, being discovered by two gentlemen, who had come from Carlisle, he made off with all the subscriptions and funds in his possession, leaving the parish to reflect upon the honesty of their schoolmaster.

He went to Buckinghamshire, and, being at an inn in the county town, fell into the company of some farmers, who, he discovered, were come to meet their landlord with their rents.

They were all tenants of the same proprietor, and poured out many complaints against him for his strictness and injustice in not allowing some deduction from their rents, or time after quarter-day, when they met with severe losses from bad weather or other causes.

He learned that this landlord was very rich, and so miserly that he denied himself even the necessaries of life.

Our adventurer, therefore, determined, if possible, to bleed him before he parted.

The landlord soon arrived, and the company were shown into a private room.

Witherington, upon pretence of being a friend of one of the farmers, and a lawyer, accompanied them.

He requested a sight of the last receipts, and examined them with great care ; and then, addressing the landlord—

"Sir," says he, "these honest men, my friends, have been your tenants for a long time, and have paid their rents very regularly ; but why they should be so fond of your farms at so high a rent I am unable to comprehend, when they may get other lands much cheaper ; and that you should be so unreasonable as not to allow a reduction in their rents in a season like this, when they must lose instead of gaining by their farms. It is your duty, sir, to encourage them, and not to grind them so unmercifully, else they will soon be obliged to leave your farms altogether."

The landlord endeavoured to argue the point, and the farmers, seeing the drift of Witherington, refrained from interfering.

"It is unnecessary," says Witherington, " to have more parley about it ; I insist, in behalf of my friends here, that you remit them a hundred and fifty pounds of the three hundred you expect them to pay you, for I am told you have more than enough to support yourself and family."

"Not a sous," replied the landlord.

"We'll try that presently. But pray, sir, take

your pen, ink, and paper in the meantime, and write out their receipts, and the money shall be forthcoming immediately."

"Not a letter till the money is in my hands."

"It must be so, then," answered Witherington; "you will force a good-natured man to use extremities with you;" and so saying, laid a brace of loaded pistols on the table.

In a moment the landlord was on his knees, crying—

"Oh! dear sir—sweet sir—kind sir—merciful sir—for God of Heaven's sake, sir!—don't take away the life of an innocent man, sir, who never intended harm to any one, sir."

"Why, what harm do I intend you, friend? Cannot I lay the pistols I travel with on the table but you must throw yourself into this unnecessary fear? Pray proceed to the receipts, and write them in full of all demands to this time, or else—"

"Oh, God, sir!—oh, dear sir!—you have an intention — pray, dear sir, have no intention against my life."

"To the receipts, then, or, by Jupiter Ammon! I'll—"

"Oh, yes, I will, sir."

With this the old landlord wrote full receipts, and delivered them to the respective farmers.

"Come," says Witherington, "this is honest and, to show you that you have to deal with honest people, here is the hundred and fifty pounds; and I promise you, in the name of these honest men, that, if things succeed well, you shall have the other half next quarter day."

The farmers paid the money, and departed astonished, and not a little afraid at the consequences of this proceeding.

Witherington ordered his horse, and inquired of the ostler the road the old gentleman had to travel, and took his departure.

He took the road by which the old gentleman had to travel, and soon observed him jogging away in sullen silence, with a servant behind him.

When he observed our hero he would have turned, but Witherington seized the bridle of his horse, and forced him to proceed.

He bantered him upon the folly of hoarding up wealth, without enjoying it himself, merely for some spendthrift son to squander after his death.

"No," says he, "money is a blessing sent us from Heaven, in order that, by its circulation, it may afford nourishment to the body politic; for, if such wretches as you, by laying up thousands in your coffers to no advantage, cause a stagnation, there are thousands in the world that must feel the consequences, and I am to acquaint you of them: so that a better deed cannot be done than to bestow what you have about you upon me; for, to be plain with you, I am not to be refused," and, so saying, presented his pistol.

The old gentleman, terrified for his life, resigned his purse, containing more than three hundred and fifty guineas; and Witherington, unbuckling the portmanteau from behind the servant, placed it on his own horse.

He left the old landlord with an admonition to be, in future, affable and generous to his tenants, for they were the persons that supported him; and if he ever again heard complaints from them, he would visit his house, and partake liberally of what he most fancied.

The county, after this adventure, were up in pursuit of Witherington, and he retired to Cheshire with great expedition.

The first house he put up at was an inn kept by a young widow, noted as well for her kindness to travellers as her wealth and beauty.

She paid our adventurer great attention, and invited him to be of a party, consisting of some friends she was to have that evening.

He was not blind to the charms of the widow, and gladly accepted the invitation.

The company he found to consist chiefly of gentlemen, whom he could discover were angling for the widow's riches.

Witherington received great favour in the eyes of the lady, and she asked him to favour the company with a song, as she was sure, from his sweet, clear voice, that he could perform well.

Witherington, wanting no farther importunity from a person he had fixed his affections upon complied with the request, and sung an amorous ditty, very applicable to his present situation, and, with the assistance of a side glance and a sigh, enabled the widow to draw the most favourable inferences.

He was completely successful, and the widow evidently was vanquished.

Witherington was now requested by the widow to relate some story concerning himself, "as certainly a person who could make himself so agreeable, and make others take such an interest in his welfare, could not fail to have met with something remarkable in his life-time."

Witherington was all compliance, and begged to give a short recital of his life; and the company were all anxious to proceed, expecting to be informed of something marvellous and mysterious.

He invented an artful story, the drift of which was to give the widow a high idea of himself, of the power that love had over him, and of the generosity of his own mind.

"His great misfortune," he said, "was disappointment in love, the object of his choice having been stolen from him by an old, rich uncle, against her inclination, and that he had just left home in order to divert his mind from the melancholy with which this had overcast him; and chance," said he, in concluding, "has thrown me into this hospitable house, where I cannot but own I have found as much beauty as I have been unfortunately deprived of."

This story excited considerable interest throughout the company, in particular in the breast of the widow, to whom Witherington now evinced unequivocal marks of attention, which seemed to excite considerable jealousy in some of the gentlemen present.

They all parted, however, on the most friendly terms, and our adventurer resolved to stay some time at Nantwich, in order to follow out this adventure.

Next morning Witherington renewed his assiduities, and both he and the amorous widow were equally gratified with each other's company.

At length, determined to carry his point by a *coup de grace*, he declared a most ardent passion for the widow, which, after much prefacing and many assurances, was returned tenfold.

She assured him, at the same time, that he had many rivals, but over these he had gained the pre-eminence in her estimation.

A few days after the first interview with the other suitors at the inn Witherington's ascendancy was so evident, that a rival, who imagined the game within his reach, was seriously alarmed, and had recourse to stratagem to free himself from such an opponent.

For this purpose he sent for Witherington, and, with every appearance of disinterested friendship, informed him that he had sent for him to caution him against further intimacy with the widow, to whom he confessed he once paid matrimonial court, but that he had thrown her completely off since he had discovered the measure of her guilt, and congratulated himself upon his escape.

Expressing his detestation of the character of a defamer, and solemnly avowing the purity of his motives, he informed Witherington that the widow was most fickle and insincere in her attachment, as any one might have discovered at the supper-party; and, in order to gratify this wavering inclination, she had poisoned her last husband.

He entreated him, then, as he valued his own happiness and security, to desist from prosecuting his attentions farther, and hoped Witherington would pardon the liberty he had taken, for that, hearing his acquaintance was to end in marriage, and considering the fortunate escape he had himself made, he was bound to prevent a stranger from being imposed upon.

Witherington at once saw the drift of his rival, and humoured him accordingly.

He seemed shocked at the baseness of the widow, and joined the other in self-congratulation.

He thanked the gentleman for his kindly warning, and told him to leave the affair to his management, and he would soon discover the depth of her guilt; and that, as they both seemed to have one object in view, namely, the possession of her money, they might then be able to make what use of the circumstances they found convenient and proper.

The gentleman seem satisfied, and they parted for the time.

Our adventurer returning to the inn acquainted the widow with the whole conversation between him and the gentleman.

She was greatly incensed, declared the world was very censorious, and vowed revenge at whatever price.

Witherington, judging a rupture was about to take place, thought it high time to make his advantage of the credulous woman; so that evening, taking her aside, he observed to her that the best way of revenging herself upon his rival would be, if she had any serious intention of marrying him, to show her inclinations by some mark of her favour that might distinguish him above his rival.

Glad of this opportunity, she conveys him into a closet, where, showing him all her money and plate, she told him that all these were at his service, provided he could deliver her from the importunities of the gentleman.

Witherington assured her that she might depend upon him, and, taking his leave for the night, retired to his chamber.

Here he wrote the following letter to the widow:—

"MY DEAR,—

"Ever mindful of what a woman says, especially one who has been pleased to set her affections on me, I have written this letter purely to acquaint you, that being obliged to go to London, and the journey being pretty long, I could not do better than make use of the money in the closet, which you was so good as to say was at my service. I was in exceeding haste when I began to write this, so that I can spare no more time than to request you to be sure of thinking on me till my return.

"I am,

"My dear madam,

"Your, most devoted lover,

"J. WITHERINGTON."

After writing this he went privately into the widow's closet, and secured all her ready money, which amounted to above three hundred pounds, then going into the stable, saddled his horse, mounted, and rode out at the back door, leaving the family fast asleep, and the widow and her gentleman lover to prosecute their amours as they thought fit.

Witherington, not yet content with the spoil obtained from the parish and from the widow, repaired to the London road, where he committed a robbery between Acton and Uxbridge, after which he was detected, and committed to Newgate, where he led a most profligate life until the day of his execution at Tyburn.

CHAPTER LXXV.

THE CATACOMBS OF PARIS—MARIE IN TROUBLE—
THE PURSUIT—THE PLACE OF REFUGE.

THE catacombs of Paris, like those of Rome, were originally quarries.

A considerable portion of the city is built of the stone dug up from beneath it.

The old quarries in the neighbourhood of Paris being considerably reduced architects find it necessary to seek for materials in Burgundy, in the department of the Oise, and in Alsace, suited to such constructions as the new additions to the palace of the Tuileries and the Grand Opera.

The extent of the excavations is said to be equal to a tenth of the whole superficies of Paris, and the quantity of material thus obtained 11,000,000 cubic metres.

The quarries were appropriated, in 1784, to the reception of the bones of the dead from the cemetery of the Innocents, and other burial-grounds.

According to the official report issued in 1857 the remains of 3,000,000 persons have been deposited here; but it is supposed that that estimate is decidedly under the mark.

The skulls and bones are built into the walls of the subterranean passages, with inscriptions stating the quarter whence they were removed.

About seventy different staircases lead down into the catacombs, but the chief entrance is in the Rue d'Enfer (this name is a corruption of Rue Inférieure).

This underground grave-yard extends under

the chief streets of the Faubourgs St. Germain' St. Jacques, and St. Marcel, and also under a number of important buildings, such as the Pantheon, Luxembourg, and Observatory.

Down into these fearful vaults one night, not many nights after having achieved her great triumph at the *opera*, rushed Marie, as if a thousand fiends were at her heels.

Her face was livid with terror, her form trembled in the throbs of a convulsive agony, and her eyes were being forced from their sockets from some inward pressure.

Never had she looked so ghastly.

To understand the cause of this terror we must quit the vault, and turn to a scene that had been enacted before we find Marie rushing at midnight into the catacombs.

It was the sixth night of her appearance at the *opera*, and, after singing as brilliantly as usual, she prepared to leave the theatre.

She rushed from her dressing-room, and, avoiding the look of old Albertine, who waited at the door of her dressing-room to see her to her home, speeded down the stairs, through the hall, and into the street.

At the door was a splendid equipage awaiting her, and into this she sprang with alacrity.

Next moment she was in the arms of the Count D'Almere.

"At last," he said; "at last you have consented to be mine, and make me happy. Ah! bless you, mine own."

"But Leonora Belvati?"

"Psha! what care I for her?"

The vehicle moved away rapidly, but not before a dark and dangerous face had peered in the carriage window and cast a fearful glance at its occupants.

"Home," cried the Count to his coachman.

The man who had glanced in at the carriage window hailed a vehicle.

"Follow that carriage," he cried, and in less than a minute the humble one-horse cabriolet was dashing after the splendid equipage of the Count.

On they went until they paused at the Rue Richelieu.

The Count sprang out, and assisted Marie to alight.

Next moment they were within the portals of a princely *hôtel*.

Then the cabriolet stopped, and the man who had followed the Count's carriage alighted.

"Whose *hôtel* is that?"

"It belongs to the Count D'Almere."

"Good."

The man was discharged, and he who had followed the Count and Marie walked in the direction of the *hôtel*, and took up a position opposite, and surveyed the Princess with the greatest possible attention.

Meanwhile the Count and Marie were seated in a charming apartment, discussing a light and elegant supper.

They sat together.

Their arms entwined about each other.

Their eyes fixed upon each other.

Marie was once more playing her old game of fascination, and playing it with marvellous suc-

cess, for the youth about whom she cast her spell appeared to be already desperately enslaved.

There was not, however, any affection on her part.

She had determined on growing rich.

Fame she had speedily acquired, and from her boy admirer she saw the means of gratifying her second great passion.

So the warning look and tearful eyes of the old man who had assisted her to fortune were disregarded, and she took to the evil course without hesitation.

"I shall love you for ever," said D'Almere, fixing his burning glance upon her.

"And Leonora?"

"Why do you always cry Leonora into my ears when I speak of love? Have I not said that for her I had but a momentary fancy: a boy passion! whilst for you I have only a deep and undying love."

"And you will love me ever, as you promise, and not turn from me at the sight of another pretty face or charming voice?"

"I swear to be your slave."

"Then I am yours."

"Wholly?"

"Wholly yours, D'Almere, wholly yours."

"Ah, then I am indeed happy."

He caught her to his heart, and imprinted many kisses on her brow and cheek, to which ordeal she submitted with the grace of a true voluptuary.

But at this moment a shadow fell upon them, and on glancing up they beheld in the room a dark and mysterious figure.

Marie uttered a cry and sprang to her feet.

The young Count placed his hand upon his brow, and indignantly demanded the cause of the intrusion.

"Ask her," said the man, pointing to Marie; "she will tell you."

"Begone, or I'll chastise you for your impudence," cried D'Almere: "begone, I say."

"I heed you not," cried the man.

"Oh, begone; I pray you, begone," said Marie; "what could have brought you here, Philippe," for it was Philippe. "Oh what mystic fate hangs over me?"

"You ask me why I am here," he said; "does not your heart answer that question. Where should I be when you are about to sin, but at your side, to snatch you from the peril. I am here, as I was at Marlborough House when you first stooped to temptation. I am here to rescue you. Where should I be at such a moment but at your side?"

"Wretched man, I know not, care not, who you are," cried D'Almere: "but I will not pardon this intrusion; I will not submit to this indignity; you leave not this roof alive."

"Psha! But that I believe this woman to have sought the embraces I saw you lavish upon her, you would have been ere now dead at my feet. I look not to thee, but to her."

"Oh Philippe, begone, begone."

"Not without you."

"I cannot, will not go with you."

"You have no choice."

"Indeed!" cried D'Almere; "you shall find

she shall have a choice; fellow, I will see that she stays in the place if she so chooses."

"She will not choose thus."

"Philippe, I must. Begone, I say."

"Not without you."

"This is persecution," cried D'Almere, in an extreme rage; "if you quit not this apartment on the instant, by Heaven I will send my sword through your black heart."

"Fool, I seek no quarrel with thee, and I warn thee do not enrage me, or you will repent it to the last moment of your existence."

"No harsh words, I pray," said Marie, and then addressing herself to Philippe, she continued—"Philippe, I have determined on remaining here, so begone at once; you have no right to command me, and you shall not do so. Begone, I say. I will not depart with you."

"By the God above us you shall!"

He advanced, and seized her wrist.

"Come!" he cried fiercely; "I drag you from infamy—from shame—from the depths of degradation! Come with me!"

"No—no! Unhand me!"

"Since you will tempt me," cried D'Almere, "take this!"

He drew his sword as he spoke, and made a rapid lunge at the man who held Marie's wrist; but he was too quick, and, springing on one side, the thrust was spent upon the air.

Meanwhile Philippe drew from beneath his cloak a short stiletto, and, with the rapidity of lightning, sent it home to the heart of the young Count, who dropped on the floor with a low moan.

"Heaven save us — what have you done?" cried Marie.

"I know not—I care not! He drove me to it, and must pay for his own rashness."

Finding herself released, Marie sprang to the door, and, ere Philippe could stir a step, she had flown down the great staircase, and had entered the street.

In a moment he followed her, and then ensued a race which only terminated at the catacombs.

What had induced Marie to rush into those awful vaults she knew not, but perhaps she had some vague idea of being able to baffle her pursuer in their tortuous windings, and in the awful darkness that reigned there.

She sped along amidst the ghastly piles of skulls and bones, but the sound of footsteps was ever behind her.

She rushed madly forward into the gloom, but the words of Philippe, calling in a hoarse and terrible voice, "Marie! Marie! you fly me in vain!" rang in her ears, and at last, overcome with terror and filled with an awful feeling of superstitious awe, she sank upon the ground, and next moment the ghastly face of Philippe was bent upon her.

The Italian drew a small lantern from his pocket, and illuminated a small space in the great vault in which they stood.

"You see," he said, "you cannot escape me."

"Why have you followed me?—why have you pursued me thus?"

"Is not my whole life devoted to you?"

"To my ruin?"

"No, to the ruin of those who have ruined you. You thought you had escaped me, but I was not to be put off the scent. It was a difficult matter to trace you, but I was in earnest, and nothing could baffle me."

"You will be my death yet."

"No. I will be life to you. Marie, your granddame is dead."

"Dead."

"Yes."

"I am glad."

"I knew you would be. To that woman I swore an oath to watch over and protect you, and to avenge your betrayers; whilst the Zingari lived I feared to allow the old passion I had for you to take possession of me, for I stood in awe of the old fiend's malice. She would have known that after the life you have led that I could not make you my wife, and she would have resented any other proposition, but when she died I was free, and I turned to possess you. I set off after you, followed you to Paris, traced out your child, secured it, and then sought you. I need not say how I found you. As jealous tonight as I was when you first sinned at Marlborough House, years ago, I burned with rage when I saw you seat yourself beside the Count in that splendid carriage. I said to myself 'I will follow, and snatch her from him. She is mine, and I will have her. No one has a greater right to her than I, so she shall be none of his.' He was a foolish young man, and has met with a death he little expected—perhaps little deserved, but I am not very particular about such a trifle now. He stood in my way, and I smote him down."

"Is he dead?"

"Dead! is it possible for him to survive after having this plunged to the hilt into his heart?"

"Villain!"

"Not at all."

"Assassin!"

"Psha! he would have played the assassin—I but acted in self-defence."

"Wretched excuse. You had no right to enter his house."

"No right?"

"No earthly right."

"Indeed."

He only acted as any other gentleman would have done, and your excuse is mean and paltry."

"Nay, I seek not to excuse myself, mistress. I killed him, and that is all about it."

"It was the act of a low bravo."

"You think so?"

"I do."

"Ah! it makes no great difference now. But enough of this, Marie. I am in no humour for bandying words; I am with thee, and I am happy."

"Happy?"

"Yes, happy. Should I not be happy on my wedding night?"

"Wedding night!"

"Yes. This is the night of our union. I promised myself that we would be inseparably united, though not by aid of priest, when we should first meet, wherever and whenever that might be. This is the time—it's an ominous one, for I have just shed a fellow creature's blood. This is the place; God knows it is quite as ominous as the time. Here, surrounded by the bodies of decayed men and women—here, in the presence of death, breathing the air of the grave, we will solemnise our unhallowed union."

"Never."

"You must. You are mine—mine, Marie, at last. I have waited years for you.

"I am not—I will not be."

"You must."

"I will not, I swear—"

"Swear not, for you will be foresworn."

"I will register an oath—"

"You must not. I have said you shall be mine, and I have the means of forcing you to the union."

"What means?"

"Your child is in my power, and I swear, by all my hopes of salvation, that you shall see that child no more if you decline to agree to my proposals."

"Fiend!"

"Do you decline?"

"Yes."

"Remember—I am in earnest, and the infant dies if you decline to become my mistress."

"You will not be so base."

"So help me Heaven, I will!"

Marie bowed her head in resignation.

"You consent?" he said.

"What can I do?" she cried; "oh, what can I do but consent?"

"True; you have no choice."

"Have you no heart?"

"Yes; I have a heart. Although you have done your best to crush it out of me, I have some heart left me still; and it beats for you—wholly for you; so be mine."

"It is awful."

"What?"

"My future."

"Why awful? You once loved me."

"Yes."

"Is that love all gone?"

"Yes."

"Has it turned to hate?"

"No."

"What then?"

"I fear you."

"You feared the Doctor; but you were his mistress."

"Yes; but do you remember the end of that ill-starred union!"

"I do."

"And you still wish to possess me?"

"Yes. I fear no such fate as you would have conferred upon him."

"Well, then, I am yours."

"You will have to swear to it."

"In what words?"

"Repeat after me. I take thee, Philippe, to be mine for life. I swear fidelity to thee, and in the sight of Heaven promise that this troth shall be as binding as if uttered in the church, and in the presence of a priest."

Marie repeated these words, and Philippe continued—

"And I also swear, by my hopes of salvation, to seek no other keeper, and to obey the man I now take to be mine in all things, even as if he were lawfully bound to me and I to him. He shall be as a father to my child, and in all the acts of life I promise to be guided by him, and obey his will."

Marie also repeated these words, and then Philippe proposed an oath to her, so fearful in its character that we forbear to record it.

Marie shuddered as she uttered it, and clung to the garments of him who now proposed it, as if terrified at its awful nature, and fearing some dire effects to follow the words.

Indeed some few skulls and bones did, at the instant, fall from their place, and rattle on the damp stones of the vault, causing Marie increased alarm.

Philippe stood erect, and his face gleamed in the light of his lantern.

It was livid, and filled with an expression of mingled fire and terror.

After he had extorted the oath of constancy from Marie, he, in turn, uttered one as fearful and as binding, and thus the horrible and revolting union was consummated.

"We are bound to one another," he said; we are one now, Marie—tied as sinful, Heaven-defying, abandoned wretches should be tied; and now we must prepare to pass the night."

"Surely not in this place."

"Yes."

"No, no."

"Yes."

"I could not close my eyes in such a den."

"Nor I; but here we must stay. Is it not fit place wherein to pass *our bridal night!*"

"God help me!"

"Amen."

"You will relent. You will come with me to my lodging."

"No; you forget I am dyed crimson with a nobleman's blood. Even now the *gendarmes* are prowling the streets after me, and Paris is in an uproar. I must not leave the catacombs to-night."

"Oh God!"

"It is fearful. Is it not?"

"It is indeed."

"We shall not rest happily on these dark stones and with all these grinning skulls about us, but still here we must lay, and in the morn devise some plan of escape."

"Escape."

"Escape. Can we remain in Paris? We should be apprehended the moment we appeared in the streets. I, as the murderer: you, as the accomplice."

"True."

"We must to England."

"To England!"

"Yes, it is the only safe place; besides, is there not work to be done there?"

"I do not understand."

"Have you forgotten your wrong?—forgotten the vengeance we are to work on your betrayer?"

"Prince George?"

"Yes."

"I have not forgotten."

"The time may yet be far off, but we must seize the opportunity. He is to be paid for his villany. I am sworn to be quits with him, and I will see that he comes not short of his reward. Ah! Prince, pampered, flattered voluptuary, rolling in the luxury of your palaces, those who rest to-night on the damp floors of these hideous catacombs will yet pull you down—will yet let you *know* what it is to be thoroughly wretched, deserted, despised, trampled upon. But enough of this."

"Philippe spread his cloak on the stones and invited Marie to throw herself thereon.

With fear, and trembling from head to foot, she obeyed, and next moment was clasped in the arms—it was like the embrace of a corpse—of her first lover.

CHAPTER LXXVI.

THE RELEASE OF FAIR LIZ—DEATH OF LORD LOVELACE—UNITED AT LAST.

IT was towards the close of a brilliant day; the fifth after the capture of Lord and Lady Lovelace by the band of the Wolf, that a young English traveller might have been seen wending his way, under the guidance of a peasant, to the encampment of the brigands.

He strode along fearlessly, and with an air of gaiety that was evidently a source of surprise to his guide, who ever and anon paused to glance at him.

At length they sighted the bright tents of the encampment, and the traveller quickened his footsteps.

His approach was marked by the band, who from their recumbent positions sprang to their feet, and advanced to meet.

The Wolf was there at the head of a gang of lawless rascals, and, leaning on a carbine, he calmly awaited the coming of the approaching stranger.

At length that person stood before him.

"Whence came you?"

"From Naples."

"What brings you here?"

"I bring the ransom of Lord and Lady Lovelace."

"Ha!"

"Yes; where are they?"

"His lordship is dead; her ladyship is in yonder tent."

"Lord Lovelace dead?"

"Yes; the five days expired *four hours ago*, and I cut his throat, as I promised him I would."

"But you are, nevertheless, welcome, for we can still relieve you of the ransom."

"Can you?"

"We can."

"But you won't."

"Oh, won't we?"

"No; I'm not to be taken in and done for in that style, Mr. Wolf, and so you'll find."

"Why what shall prevent me from stripping you of all you possess."

"My will."

"Your will."

"Yes; and it is a will that usually carries all before it."

"Who are you?"

"I am a man—an Englishman, and my name is Pipes—Captain De Pipes—at your service, to a limited extent! All Venice and all Naples rings with the story of the capture of his lordship and his bride, and, as I'm a friend of the family, I come to rescue them. I only set foot in Italy yesterday, or I should have been here before."

"You are too late. The lord is dead, and his lady is now mine. I said she should be queen of the mountains if the ransom did not come to hand within the given time, and I mean to keep my word."

"You do?"

"Yes; but I'll have no further talk with you. Seize him! Take from him his money and make him a prisoner."

"Stay."

"Do not pause a moment."

"Stay, I say! The man who stirs a hand breaks his oath!"

Pipey, for it was our hero, held up his right hand, and exhibited the badge of the Scarlet Brethren.

"You see," he continued, "*I know you all,* and came prepared to fight you with your own weapons. My beloved brethren, how are you? No nonsense about that; it's the genuine thing, and it's all the booty you are likely to get out of me. I, of course, knew how very willing you all would be to oblige a brother, so, instead of bringing you money, I brought you this scarlet token. Is it not sufficient?"

"Yes!" cried the band, but the Wolf was silent.

"I knew you would say so."

"They may say what they will—I say you shall be my prisoner, and I will not give up the lady I have here."

The band murmured.

"Do you forget your oath?" said Pipey.

"I don't; but it was never meant to bind a fellow down to such acts as you would have him do. You are a prisoner. Bind him! Now we will see whether you have any money about you or not."

The band did not hesitate another moment. Pipey was bound and secured, but there was no money about him.

"I shall have to release you," he said; "for I dare not kill you. But you shall stay with me in the mountains during my pleasure. And now take him to a tent, and let him reflect how little the Wolf cares for brethren and oaths."

"Well, you are a nice 'un, I declare; but I've not yet done with you. Just learn that Captain Dangerfield and the whole crew of the Emilia will be on my track if I do not return to the City before the morning. You know Dangerfield, and you know whether you can afford to stay and settle accounts with him. He is quite as well acquainted with this mountain fastness as yourself, and he will track you to death if I am not with him in the morning. You can reflect whether or not you are strong enough to risk battle with such an enemy."

"The devil!"

"So, I have touched you at last, have I?"

"You came into the wolf's den well prepared for an encounter."

"I always do. Nothing like plenty of precaution to my thinking."

"You are right, and I confess, for once in a way, that I am beaten. You are at liberty to go."

"And the lady?"

"She is mine; you may leave her to me."

"No."

"Well, she shall not go."

"She must."

"I won't part with her."

"Then I must go without her; and Dangerfield—"

"Oh, curse Dangerfield!"

"Well, I will give you till midnight to think the matter over. If by that time she is not handed to me, and a guide furnished us to get out of this infernal den, you may take the consequences."

*   *   *   *   *

The Captain of the brigands took the full time furnished him by Pipey to decide on the fate of his captive, but at midnight one of the band brought Pipey word that he could depart with the lady.

"I will conduct you to her," said the man; "follow me."

Pipey needed no second invite.

He sprang to his feet, and, pushing the brigand before him, strode out of his tent.

They approached another canvas awning, and here the guide signalled to Pipey to enter.

He drew aside the curtain that shielded the opening, and gazed upon the form of his beloved one.

She lay sleeping tranquilly on the ground, dreaming, perhaps, of him.

"Liz," he cried; "Liz; it is I—Pipey. Be not afraid. I am come to save you."

With a cry of surprise and joy Liz sprang to her feet, and threw herself into the arms of her old lover.

"I knew you would come," she cried; "I felt that you would be here to save me."

"Have I not sworn ever to be near you in your hour of need?"

"You have; and nobly have you kept your oath."

"And truthfully will I keep it to the last. Come."

"Whither?"

"To Naples."

"Why there?"

"Would you prefer Venice."

"No, no; Naples be it. I would see Venice no more."

"Come, then."

"And Lovelace?"

Pipey hung his head.

"You will save him—you will not desert him?"

"I came to save him, but I found that he was beyond human help."

"What mean you?"

"Liz, Liz—your husband is dead!"

"Oh God! My God!"

"It is sad, very sad; but this is no time to pause. We must away, or we may share his fate."

Silently they quitted the tent.

Silently they took hands, and followed the guide who was to conduct them to Naples.

Their further adventures will form the *Third Epoch* of the MYSTERY OF MARLBOROUGH HOUSE.

CHAPTER LXXVII.

WHICH ENDS THE SECOND EPOCH, AS THE FIRST COMMENCED, WITH A NIGHT REVEL IN MARLBOROUGH HOUSE.

THE Prince of Wales took a long time to recover the effects of that terrible blow received in his encounter with the young lawyer; but he *did* recover it, thanks to the thickness of his skull; and not only did he overlook the *contretemps*, but took its fair author to his bosom, and made her a maid of honour—curious contradiction of terms!

To Olivia he behaved, on the whole, very well, and after a while contrived to get her married to a young duke, whose brains were dealt out to him in a very stingy manner by his noble progenitors.

The duke was satisfied, the prince was charmed, and Olivia was by no means discontent, although far from happy.

Her wedded life was doomed to be but a short one, and we are about to describe how she lost her husband.

Three months after her marriage a certain young painter from Hamburg was discovered a great deal in her company.

It was notorious that the young artist was exceedingly well up in the good graces of the Duchess, for she made no secret of her preference for him over others.

But to this the Duke was blind. He suspected nothing, and would see nothing, so his wife was enabled to prosecute her intrigue as she thought desirable.

This young Hamburgh painter was, as our readers may suppose, none other than her old lover, Lewis Arndale, who had come back disguised and repentant to bask in her smiles and atone for the cruelty he had been guilty of on that awful night when the Scarlet Brethren were betrayed.

It was the night of a grand masked ball at Marlborough House, and the Duchess was there in the guise of a page of the court of Louis XI., and remarkably well she looked in her splendid attire.

It was a gay and magnificent scene, and one

not easily forgotten. The lights were dazzling, the music delicious, and the costumes enchanting.

But these the duchess marked not.

Her eyes wandered about the rooms in search of some object, and thus distracted her attention from the gay maskers.

At last a white plume, hanging from the bonnet of a cavalier of the time of Charles II., attracted her attention.

This plume waved in a little nook screened off from the saloon by a deep crimson curtain, and towards this spot speeded the magnificent page.

The cavalier caught her hand as she approached, and drew her into a little arbour, where they could not be well observed.

"I am glad you are come," Olivia said to Lewis, for he was the cavalier; "I am glad you are come, for I have so longed to talk with you, and have found no opportunity this last week. Poor fellow."

"I pray you do not laugh at me. Oh, you forget how I have loved you—how I love you still."

"And you forget that I dare no longer listen to such language."

"I do not forget, but I cannot resist the opportunity of repeating again and again how much I love you."

"And if the Duke heard this?"

"What then?"

"What then? why he would kill you."

"Psha, he is too great a fool."

"Fools are sometimes dangerous."

"Yes, but not frequently."

"I do not know that."

"But talk not of him. Can you not talk to me of yourself?"

"That would be wrong."

"Psha, do not tease me. Olivia, you are mine—you know you are mine for ever. The past is nothing to me—the present is but a dream. You are mine, and in the future we will be one."

"Oh, Lewis! the present is indeed but a dream, and your future is but a picture in that dream."

"Believe it not. I feel that you will yet be mine. I know that I am right."

"I doubt it."

"Do not doubt it, for there is no occasion."

"We shall see."

"We shall, indeed. But you love me, Olivia, you love me still."

"Yes, Lewis, I do, and ever shall, love you dearly."

"Better than all the world?"

"Better than all the world."

"Indeed!"

It was not the voice of Lewis that uttered that word.

Olivia looked up, and beheld two maskers standing over her.

One was her husband, and the other was the Prince of Wales.

It was her husband that had spoken.

"So," he said, "this is how I find the Duchess of Marklington employed?"

"Not a word to that lady," cried Lewis, "or I dash you to the earth."

"Take off that mask, sir," cried the enraged Duke; "let me see who is the betrayer of my happiness."

Lewis removed his mask.

"The painter, by all that's damnable!" cried the Duke.

"And quite ready to answer for his crime whenever he may be called upon."

"Can I fight such a fellow?" asked the Duke of the Prince as they walked away.

"You must," said the Prince.

"Must I? How deuced distressing."

"Fly!" cried the Duchess to Lewis—"fly, and save yourself; I fear some horrible end to this drama."

"No matter," said Lewis, "I must go through with my part, and Heaven have mercy upon him!"

"You will not kill him?"

"I shall do my best to do so."

"Lewis!"

"Olivia, this is a matter which men fight about to the last gasp. Do you keep tranquil. Take no notice, and go home as quickly as possible."

"But if you should fall?"

"I shall not fall."

"You know not what may happen."

"True, there are chances against me, but I think I can defend myself against such a foe as the Duke. Do as I bid you, and go speedily; do not wait another moment."

"I will obey you."

"You are just in time; see, a couple of gentlemen approach. This affair will be settled speedily."

He kissed her on the cheek, and she, trembling from head to foot with fears but half defined, hastened from the house.

The new comers unmasked, and proved to be two officers of the Guards.

"We are the friends of the Duke of Marklington, whom you have outraged. Need we name our errand?"

"I presume not, unless you are come to tell me that his grace resigns to me the Duchess, and wishes me joy."

"This is insolence."

"You had best be careful what language you use to me, gentlemen," said Lewis, "or I may tweak your noses."

The Guards looked astonished.

"Now," continued Lewis, "your errand."

"It is to announce to you that his grace awaits you in the park."

"Is it a moonlight night?"

"Yes."

"So much the worse for his grace. He does not fence well, I think."

"You will soon prove that, if you desire to learn."

"So I shall. I follow you."

"Have you no friend?"

"I want none. I shall kill his grace without the slightest humble assistance."

The Guards looked remarkably glum at this avowal of Lewis', but they said nothing in reply.

In a short time Lewis and the Duke were facing each other in a retired nook in the park.

Lewis came coolly up to his man, and, drawing his sword, declared himself quite ready.

The other was stripping off his domino, and preparing for a long and and arduous engagement.

Lewis waited for him with the greatest *nonchalance*, whistling a dance tune the while, and balancing his sword on the tip of his fore finger.

At length his Grace was ready.

"You have taken great pains with the toilet in which you chose to quit the world," said Lewis, glancing contemptuously at the Duke; "but I am glad to see that you have at last arranged matters to your satisfaction."

They crossed weapons, and in a short time were parrying and thrusting at each other with great vigour.

After a few passes, Lewis hurled the sword of his antagonist clean out of his grasp, and, ere he could recover from his surprise, a sword had grated its way through his heart.

He fell back dead.

"There," said Lewis, "I knew how it would be. What a silly man he was to hasten his end in so ridiculous a manner."

*   *   *   *   *

Her Grace was a widow.

Did she remain long in her weeds?

The *Court Chronicle*, nine months after the duel, announced that she had married for the second time.

Her bridegroom was the slayer of her late husband.

Such is life!

END   OF   THE   SECOND   EPOCH.

QUEEN CAROLINE (From the Portrait by James Lonsdale.)

THE THIRD EPOCH
OF THE
CHRONICLES OF MARLBOROUGH HOUSE.

THE SHADOW OF THE HAND OF FATE.
The Romance of the Life of Queen Caroline.

No. 37.

CHAPTER I.

1810—THE SEVEN DIALS—A DEN OF INFAMY—
HOW ROYALTY AMUSED ITSELF—A YOUNG MAN'S
INTRODUCTION TO LIFE.

MANY years have passed since the last epoch of our tale was penned, and we now enter upon the nineteenth century and shall have to introduce our readers to new scenes and people.

The Prince of Wales is no longer a single man, for Caroline of Brunswick, the herone of this epoch of our tale, has come over to share his name and fortune.

Terrible fate!

On the fifth of April, 1795, Caroline of Brunswick disembarked from the Jupiter and went on board one of the royal yachts, and a few minutes before twelve o'clock landed at Greenwich.

The Princess was received on her landing by Sir Hugh Palliser, the governor, and other officers, who conducted her to the governor's house, where she took tea and coffee.

Lady Jersey did not arrive at the governor's till an hour after the Princess had landed; and soon after they both retired into an adjoining room, and the dress of the Princess was changed, from a muslin gown and blue satin petticoat, with a black beaver hat and blue and black feathers, for a white satin gown and very elegant turban cap of satin trimmed with crape and ornamented with white feathers, which were brought from town by Lady Jersey.

It is impossible to conceive the bustle occasioned at Greenwich by the Princess's arrival.

The congregation at the Hospital chapel left it before the service was half over, and even the pulpit was forsaken for a sight of her highness.

The acclamations of the people were unbounded.

A little after two o'clock her Royal Highness left the governor's house and got into one of the king's coaches drawn by six horses.

In this coach were also Mrs. Harcourt and Lady Jersey.

Another of his Majesty's coaches and six preceded it, in which were seated Mrs. Harvey Aston, Lord Malmesbury, Lord Clermont, and Colonel Greville.

In a third coach, with four horses, were two women servants whom the Princess brought from Germany, and were her only attendants from thence.

The Princess's carriage was escorted on each side by a party of the Prince of Wales's own regiment of light Dragoons, commanded by Lord Edward Somerset, son to the Duke of Beaufort.

Besides this escort the road was lined at small distances by troops of the Heavy Dragoons, who were stationed from Greenwich all the way to the Horse Guards.

There were, besides, hundreds of horsemen, who followed her to town.

Westminster Bridge, and all the avenues leading to the park and the palace were crowded with spectators and carriages; but the greatest order was preserved.

The people cheered the Princess with loud expressions of love and loyalty, and she, in return, very graciously bowed and smiled at them as she passed along.

Both the carriage windows were down.

At three o'clock her Serene Highness alighted at St. James's, and was introduced into the apartments prepared for her reception, which look into Cleveland Row.

After a short time the Princess appeared at the windows, which were thrown up.

The people huzzaed her, and she curtseyed; and this continued some minutes until the Prince arrived from Carlton House.

At a little before five o'clock the Prince and Princess sat down to dinner.

The people continuing to huzza before the palace, his Royal Highness, after dinner, appeared at the window, and thanked them for this mark of their loyalty and attention to the Princess, but he hoped they would excuse her appearance then, as it might give her cold.

This completely satisfied the crowd, who gave the Prince three cheers.

The Princess of Wales travelled in a mantle of green satin, trimmed with gold, with loops and tassels, *a la* Brandenburgh, and wore a beaver hat.

In the evening, when the populace had become rather noisy in their expressions of loyalty and attachment before the Princess's apartments, she addressed them from her window, and these are the words she uttered;—

"Believe me, I feel very happy and delighted to see the good English people, the best nation upon earth."

The Prince then addressed the masses, and all London was gay.

Perhaps all London was thinking that with his marriage his Royal Highness was about to cast off his anything but royal pursuits, but such was not to be the case.

From the moment the Prince beheld his destined consort he detested her.

After receiving her he rushed off and cried to his mother, but, having fortified himself with brandy, went through the mockery of addressing the people on his newly-acquired happiness.

Three days afterwards his Royal Highness reeled into chapel in a state of filthy intoxication, and took Caroline to wife.

In 1810, the year in which we re-open these chronicles, we find the royal pair plunged into the very depths of wretchedness, and we shall have to record their lives from that date till the last scene of all.

Thus much by way of introduction to our new epoch.

* * * * *

It was a wretched night in December, and the Seven Dials were as desolate and dismal as could be.

The usual crowds of low ruffians hung about the corners.

Dog fanciers and low pugilists abounded, and from the public-houses came sounds that made night hideous.

At a corner of one of the many streets leading out of this wretched neighbourhood was a small shop occupied by a chemist and druggist.

It was the only shop, with the exception of the places where liquor was sold, now open, for it was after eleven o'clock.

Near the door of this place hovered a poor woman.

She was clad in a thin and dirty shawl.

She wore no bonnet, and her feet were without coverings.

This wretched being, whose pale face and wasted form looked hideous in the lights reflected from the coloured bottles of the shop window, paced up and down before the door.

She peered into the shop, and placed one foot on the door-step, as if to enter, and then drew back and walked away.

Again and again she repeated this manœuvre, and withdrew to a short distance.

At length she appeared to summon up as much courage as she possessed, and beating her bosom wildly, cried—

"Yes, yes, it must be done—it must be done. Better now than later—better now than later!"

She again approached the door, and this time her hand rested upon the latch, and she entered.

The opening of the door rang a small bell attached thereto, and in answer to the summons a little wheezen-faced, bald-headed man came from an inner room, and demanded what his customer required.

"I want laudanum," she said, "two penn'orth, that's what I want."

"What d'ye want it for?"

"My husband's complaint, and the doctor ordered it for him, that's all I know."

"And who's your husband?"

"Tomy Squall, of Maid's-lane."

"Oh, and the doctor ordered him laudanum?"

"Yes."

"Can't he sleep?"

"No; he tosses, and turns, and raves in his sleep; the doctor said he was to have twenty drops or more to the dose, according to circumstances."

"Just so."

"Pray be quick, I can but badly wait."

"Have you a bottle?"

"No."

"Never mind, I'll give you one; it's not much out of me, but a penny out of your pocket to pay for one *would* be something, I suspect."

"Twopence is all I have in the world."

"Poor soul!"

The old man busied himself in putting up the drug, and the woman's eyes followed him about the shop.

"Here you are," he said, at length, bringing her a small phial containing a dark-coloured fluid; "there's your laudanum; mind how you use it."

"I will, sir."

The woman tendered the two pence.

"Take it away, take it away. God forbid I should take the last money from such a poor wretch as you; go home to your husband and give him his laudanum."

"The saints protect you. The Blessed Virgin watch over you," cried the woman. "If the world were made of such as you there would be but little misery in it."

"Tut! tut! get away with you. You are a foreigner, are you not?"

"Yes, sir, a foreigner."

"I thought so, although your accent is nearly gone."

"It should be. We have not seen Italy for nearly twenty years."

"You are an Italian, then?"

"Yes, sir, an Italian; and I've seen better times, even in this country."

"It would appear so, by your manner. What is your husband?"

"He rented an organ when he was well and had plenty of money, but now he has nothing, and lies all day groaning and raving on his bed."

"He drinks, I suppose?"

"Yes; he has given way to drink."

"Ah! the old, old tale. Dear me, it's very sad, very sad. Good night, and better fortune attend you, my good soul."

"Good night, and God bless you."

She went into the street. "Yes," she said to herself, as she hurried along the wretched street, "Bless you, for you have given the most wretched of God's creatures the means of ridding herself of a dark, hopeless, and detestable life. Bless this little phial; its contents will end a life of wretchedness and suffering."

She hurried along, and made all the haste she could towards a dark and desolate alley that branched off from the Dials.

As she was turning into this place, a band of half-a-dozen revellers rushed out and stumbled against her.

It was easy to divine, from their manners and voices, that they belonged to the superior class, and that they had no manner of business in such a place.

"Hillo!" said the foremost of the men—a magnificently-built fellow, who had passed his fortieth year, but who had an extremely juvenile carriage—"Hillo, my good soul, we have almost crushed you."

Singular as it may appear, the woman started at the sound of his voice, and clutched his arm violently.

"Yes," she cried, wildly, "it is you. I know you. I cannot forget you, though so many years have passed since we last met."

"My good soul," said the man, "you mistake me for some other person; it is impossible that we could have met before."

"You think so because you do not recognise me. How should you in this guise?"

"Psha! you are demented."

"Say you so? Come with me to yon light, and see if I am mad."

She tightened her hold, and dragged him to a lamp that swung near at hand, whilst his companions stared in amazement.

Under the lamp the woman tossed back whole streams of jet black hair from her face, and, raising her eyes to those of the man she held in her grip, said—

"Now what say you ? Now tell me if you do not recognise me ?"

"No, not a feature."

"And yet you once swore that that face would dwell in your memory for ever."

"Nonsense, nonsense—some mistake. I really do not know you."

"But I tell you I know you, and I repeat you know me well. Do you remember Marlborough House and Rooker ?"

"Ha !"

"Have you no recollection of the little Italian girl he brought there one night, many, many long years ago ?"

"What ! Marie Lavrouffe ?"

"The same. I am she; and you—you, I see, are the same—George, Prince of Wales."

"Hush ! not that name in this place."

"I am glad we have met," continued the woman; "very glad, for I am near the brink of the grave—dying of starvation. You will help me."

"Heaven save us, yes. Here, take my purse, and let me get away."

"Thanks."

"Good-night, and much good may the money do you."

"Good-night."

The man tore himself from the woman's grasp, and walked rapidly away to where his companions awaited him.

"So," cried the woman, looking after him, "you are still the same cold, brutalised pleasure-seeker as of old. Ah, the sight of you stirs up old recollections — awakens old thoughts of wrongs which I thought were forgotten, opens old wounds anew. I swore a great oath of vengeance against thee once, for thou wert the author of my ruin. The memory of that oath is now strong upon me. Shall I fulfil it ? Yes, George of Wales, yes, hateful, accursed Prince, I will keep that oath. The money you give me puts new life into me. I will use it in strengthening this worn and weakened frame. I will use it in plotting and scheming how to make you as wretched as I have been for years. To the kennel with the poison; I have here money to buy life, and life is dear to me now, for I live for vengeance."

As she spoke the woman dashed the phial of laudanum to the earth, and, gathering her thin shawl closer over her shoulders, ran as fast as she was able up the dark passage.

* * * * *

Meanwhile the Prince rejoined his companions.

"By my faith," cried one, "a strange adventure ! What did it amount to ?"

"It amounted to a recognition."

"Oh, yes; she recalled herself to my memory."

"And who is she ?"

"One of whom you fellows might have heard your fathers speak, that was no other than the once famous Italian singer, and my no less favourite mistress, Marie Lavrouffe !"

"Nonsense."

"It is a fact."

"We can scarce credit it."

"I presume so ; but it is, nevertheless, a fact ! Ah ! when I knew her first she was a very different individual."

"So I should say."

"Yes; a sparkling little, black-eyed gipsey, with a laugh like a bell, and a voice as soft and musical as the note of a nightingale."

"How could she have become reduced to this sad plight ?"

"Worn out, I suppose, and too improvident to make hay when the sun was condescending enough to shine."

"Poor thing !"

"Poor thing, indeed. When she quitted me she must have been worth half a million, and now—"

"And now she's a poor devil of a street beggar in the Seven Dials. It's an uncommon, but by no means extraordinary case."

The Prince and his four friends took arms, and walked on gaily to one of the streets leading out of the Dials, and in which was situated a house well known as the resort of the famous pugilists of the day.

"Come," said the Prince, "let us go and have a look at the Game Chicken, who is to fight to-morrow at Moulsey. He is just returned from his training, and is to be seen to-night. What say you, Jackson ?"

He addressed a tall, well-built man with whom he walked, and who was no other than the famous Gentleman Jackson, the well-known prize-fighter and manager of the prize-ring in those days.

"Ah," said that worthy, "we will take a glimpse at the Chicken if your Highness pleases, but the house is by no means a nice one for you to enter."

"I care not."

"Well, no one will molest you whilst I'm with you, but you will meet a rough set."

"What matters it ? We are out on the lark, and our young friend, Lord Larkleigh, here, fresh from Oxford, must be initiated into the mysteries of the metropolis sooner or later, and he may as well begin with the house of Nobby Bill, the prize-fighter."

"Just so, your Highness."

They walked on, and in a few minutes stood at the door of a low public-house, which was immediately opened to admit them, on the summons of Jackson.

They entered.

A low drinking room, filled with a crowd of the greatest vagabonds the world could produce on an emergency, was revealed to the aristocratic excitement-seekers.

The landlord, a broken-nosed, beetle-browed, old pugilist, recognised Jackson, and, tipping him the wink, invited him to ascend a flight of dingy stairs, which led to the upper apartments of the house.

Jackson bade his friend to follow him, and, mounting the stairs, they reached a front room garnished with many ill-drawn portraits of famous boxers and athletes.

In this room was seated a dozen well-dressed,

though showy and slangy-looking individuals. At the head of the table, with cropped hair, hard, swarthy face, and the look of a human tiger, sat the Game Chicken, who was, the next day, to do battle at Moulsey.

Recognising the importance of the new comers the assembled guests rose to their feet, but at a motion from Jackson resumed their places, and took no further heed of the new arrivals.

The little party under Jackson's escort approached the Game Chicken, and Jackson spoke to him.

"Well Chicken," he said, "and how is it with you to-night?"

"Pretty well," gruffly replied the Chicken.

Jackson stooped down and whispered something in his ear, whereupon the Chicken rose and doffed his cap to the party of aristocrats.

"My dooty to yer, gentlemen, and I hopes as you'll be down to see the mill to-morrer."

"We shall see, Chicken, we shall see," said the Prince.

"You'll see a good fight for your money, gemmen."

"Indeed."

"Yes, the Slogging Butcher's all a good 'un, and can stand and be hit, and them as knows me knows as I don't run away."

"You don't," said Jackson approvingly, "you don't, Chicken."

"And I won't to-morrer if I knows it. Yes gemmen, it'll be all a good fight."

"I'll back the Chicken for a pony," said a youthful member of the company, whose hook-nose and flash jewellery bespoke the Israelite. "I'll back the Chicken for a pony, or anything more or less as the fancy of the gemmen may indicate."

Nobody appeared willing to accept the challenge of the youthful Israelite, and he immediately relapsed into silence.

Meanwhile the Game Chicken stripped off his clothes and exposed his brawny chest, muscle-covered ribs, and terrific arms to the admiring gaze of the visitors.

"There's no flesh there," he said admiringly.

"Not an ounce," said Jackson, "you're as well looked after as could be. I never saw a fellow in better condition."

"And I mean winning."

"Of course you do," broke in the Israelite, in a voice that said as plainly as possible—"show me the lunatic who would dispute the fact."

"I can smash him in forty minutes," said the Chicken, bending his ponderous arm.

"Yes," cried enraptured Moses; "in thirty-four minutes and a half, Chicken. I'll take three to one it don't last thirty-three minutes and a half."

Again there was no speculation, and the son of Israel had to keep his money, if he had any, in his pocket.

Lord Larkleigh was evidently much surprised at what was passing before him, and opened his noble eyes very wide indeed, but he said not a word.

After the condition of the fighting man had been further tested, and his muscular develop-ment still more admired, our party prepared to withdraw, first throwing on the table a few guineas for the benefit of the Game Chicken.

They descended the stairs again, and in the bar were mobbed by the crowd of roughs assembled there.

"Come gemmen," cried one burly ruffian, bustling the Prince, "it ain't often real tip top svells come here, but when they do they pays for it. Tip us a suv'rin, just to drink yer 'elth vith."

"Ah," cried another, "that's yer sort, my boys; just a suv'rin, we ask no more; ve'll take no less, as Cheap Jack says, so stump up."

"Hurrah for the svells who's goin' to stand lush to the tune of a suv'rin?" cried another, and in a few minutes the party of gentlemen were surrounded.

"Now," whispered Jackson, "look after your pockets, and leave me to settle this matter."

The party obeyed their leader.

Jackson then threw out his great arms, and in a moment cleared a tolerable space about him.

He next buttoned his coat across his chest, and then fell upon the assailants of his friends.

Every time his tremendous arm was launched out some one fell to the floor; in about the space of a minute the twenty brutal roughs who had attacked the party were laying crushed, maimed, and bleeding on the floor of the bar-room.

The gentleman pugilist then elbowed his way to the door, and, opening, pushed his companions into the street.

"By Jove," cried the Prince of Wales, "but that was warm work."

"It was," said Jackson; "but it strikes me they had all the worst of it."

"They did, indeed."

"They didn't know with whom they were dealing," said Jackson, "or they wouldn't have interrupted me."

"So I should say," said Larkleigh. "By Jove, they went down like so many bullocks."

"It's the only argument they comprehend," said the pugilist.

"I shall know better than to go there alone," said the young lord.

"So I should presume," said Jackson, "after the specimen you have had of the peculiarities of the St. Giles's roughs."

"And now where shall we go?" asked the Prince. "We must go some where to finish."

"Let's go to Nan Hicks," cried the others. "It is better to go to Nan's than elsewhere. The fun is always more furious there than at any other house."

"All right," said Jackson; "Nan's be it then. The place is in its glory at midnight."

They now struck out into the neighbourhood of the Haymarket, and in one of the several turnings out of that great artery of the metropolis brought themselves to a halt before a little ordinary-looking house, in which no lights or sign of life could be seen.

They knocked three times, and, in reply to their summons, the door was pulled open a little, and a head thrust out.

The party were immediately recognised, and entered.

Led by Jackson, they mounted a flight of steps, and thrust open a green baize door in the wall.

A flood of light and a burst of wild laughter saluted them.

They entered a magnificent corridor, from which opened three or four glorious saloons, and Larkleigh now says that the building in which he stood formed no part of that which he had entered, which was, to all intents and purposes, merely an entrance to this great set of saloons, which extended over at least three houses.

They were so constructed, however, that light and sound could not penetrate into the street. Fat Nan's, as the den was called, was unknown but to the initiated few.

In the saloon which they had entered they found at least two hundred gaily-dressed men and women.

The men were, for the most part, young fellows from the Horse Guards, and naval officers, mixed here and there with a black coat, which evidently covered a gentleman recognised in the world as " Reverend," and who was generally supposed, in his own corner of the world, to be a model of morality and a marvel of sanctimoniousness.

The women were all courtesans—poor painted, gaily-caparisoned wretches, against whom society had shut its portals—who strolled the streets at night for a livelihood.

In one of the saloons was dancing, in another drinking, whilst a third was devoted to the exhibition of *poses plastique* (a Parisian importation), and a fourth was a mere lounge—a retiring room, set apart for conversation ; perhaps, on occasions, adapted to worse purposes.

The dancing was conducted on the wildest principle, and with no possible regard for decency.

Men and women whirled round and round in that new excitement the " waltz," which just then was the rage, and of which Byron sang—

" To you husbands of ten years, whose brows
Ache with the annual tribute of a spouse,
To you of nine years less, who only bear
The budding sprouts of those that you *shall* wear,
With added ornaments around the roll'd,
Of native brass, or law-awarded gold ;
To you, ye matrons ever on the watch
To mar a son's or make a daughter's match ;
To you, ye children of whom chance accords
Always the ladies, and *sometimes* their lords ;
To you, ye single gentlemen, who seek
Torments for life, or pleasures for a week,
As love or Hymen your endeavours guide,
To gain your own or another's bride,
To one and all the lovely stranger came,
And every ball room echoes with her name.

*   *   *   *   *

Hands may freely range in public sight
Where ne'er before—but, pray ' put out the light.'
Methinks the glare of yonder chandelier
Shines much too far, or I am much too near.
And true, though strange, Waltz whispers this remark—
' My slippery steps are safest in the dark.'
But here the Muse with due decorum halts,
And lends her longest petticoats to waltz.''

It was evident that the Muse had not lent her

longest petticoats to those waltzers at Nan's, for those they wore barely sufficed to cover the knees of the lady dancers, who clung with barefaced immodesty to their male partners, and whirled round until, what with heat, wine, and music, they fairly boiled over with fierce excitement and desires, and failed not to give expression to them in the most disgusting manner.

Leaving this wild orgie we enter the saloon of the *poses,* and there we find at one end of the place a stage erected, which, as we take our place, is covered with long crimson velvet curtains.

Soft music steals through the saloon. The heavy curtains draw on one side, and exposed to view is a picture of the ocean dazzling in the silver moonlight.

Gradually there rises through the water a splendid young girl in a state of semi-nudity.

Her golden hair streams down her back and falls in a veil over her shoulders and bosom.

A gauze is about her waist ; otherwise she is without covering.

Gradually she rises until the whole of her figure is exposed.

Her attitude is the most graceful that can be conceived.

Her face is remarkably beautiful, and the grace of her white and rounded limbs beyond exception.

She represents Venus rising from the sea.

The Dolphin on which she stands revolves so as to show the whole of her form, and sufficient time is given to allow the mob to feast their eyes upon the sight, and then the curtain descends again.

" By Jove !" cried the Prince, " a glorious little girl. Who the devil is she ?"

" Consult Nan," said Gentleman Jackson ; " no one but she will be able to tell you."

" And where is Nan ?"

" She is sure to be behind the curtain."

" Can we go there ?"

" Oh, yes, on payment of a guinea each.''

" That's but a trifle. Come along."

The whole party approached a little door at the end of the room that led to the stage whereon the *poses* were exhibited.

Jackson tapped at the door, and in a moment a woman opened it.

They passed in, threw down five guineas, and demanded an audience of the famous Nan.

A magnificent female, clad in a robe of claret velvet, made very low about the shoulders and bosom, approached.

A glance was sufficient to enable her to recognise the Prince.

" Oh ! my sweet," she said, catching the Prince in her great white arms, and smothering him in a voluptuous embrace, " to what am I indebted for this pleasure ?"

" We have come, Nan, to inquire who is Venus."

" Oh, my little Venus has attracted your attention, has she ? Well, I supposed she would not be long here without finding a host of friends."

" But who is she ?"

" That's more than I know. She is here with

an old grandfather. Would you like to see him ?"

"Directly. Is she a new importation ?"

"Yes. This is her first appearance."

"Indeed. Then she has no friends ?"

"Not that I'm aware of."

"Good—we will be introduced. But," continued the Prince, turning to his companions, "this is my affair, young fellows ; so don't seek to cut me out. I'm the most desperately smitten, and I claim to have the first chance."

The others acquiesced.

Only Larkleigh remained silent.

"And this," he said to himself, "this is seeing life. God knows how little I expected to become acquainted with such scenes."

CHAPTER II.

THE INTRODUCTION TO VENUS—A TERRIBLE GRANDSIRE—A YOUNG GIRL'S TRIALS—SOLD TO A PRINCE—A CRY FOR HELP—A MOTHER'S ENTREATY—THE RESCUE.

"CALL Lavrouffe," cried Nan, to an attendant.

"Lavrouffe !" exclaimed the Prince.

"Yes," continued Madam Nan ; "Lavrouffe, the grandfather of our little Venus."

"That name," said the Prince.

"Ah,' said Madam, "I see you are acquainted with the name of Lavrouffe. The old fellow is the father of the great Marie of that name, the once famous Italian singer.

"You do not say so ?"

"It is a fact."

"Great Heaven ! and this child——"

"Well. I presume this child is the great *Marie's daughter*, though I really can't say, for the old fellow will not speak on the subject. I only guess this, mind ; for aught I know the girl may be the daughter of some other child of the old man."

"This is strange," said the Prince, turning to his friends, "a very strange adventure, is it not ?"

"It is."

"What do you refer to ?" asked Madam Nan.

"Why, we have seen Marie Lavrouffe to-night, and now we meet her daughter."

"You do not say so ! Marie in England ! Then old Lavrouffe must not be informed of it, or he will fly with his child, and that would be ruin to me. Strange as it may appear, the old fellow has a great objection to meeting Marie."

"Indeed !"

"Yes ; but here he is. Not a word of Marie, as you love me."

At this moment old Lavrouffe, now over seventy years of age, and tottering on the brink of the grave, came to the spot.

"Here are some gentlemen," said Nan, bawling into his ear, "some gentlemen come to see you, and to be introduced to Azaline."

"Indeed," said the old fellow, nodding to the party, "indeed ! Azaline is a fine girl—a very fine girl, gentlemen."

He put on his spectacles, and peered into the faces of the new comers.

At length his eye rested on the Prince.

"Ah," he said, "ah, your Highness ; we have'nt met for fifteen years and upwards, but I know you."

"The devil ?"

"Yes ; I've a good memory," said the old fellow, not noticing the exclamation ; "a very good memory."

"So it appears."

"And so your Highness wishes to hear little Azaline ?'

He took the arm of the Prince, and walked away with him.

After a pause he said—

"Your Highness once knew another child of mine, but she was a bad-disposed girl, and served your Highness cruelly."

"She did."

"I remember, I remember. But Azaline is a different girl ; she is gentle and good, not a bit like Marie, not a bit."

"Is Marie her mother ?"

"No, no, no. Who said she was ?"

"No one ; but I merely thought—"

"Then you thought wrong. This is no child of mine—this is a stranger in blood. I found her in Paris—starving in Paris, and adopted her."

"Very good."

"And so your Highness wishes to be introduced to her ?"

"Yes."

"And should she leave the old man who has been so good to her—leave him, I say, and deprive him of support, will your Highness remember the poor old man, and recompense him for the loss ?"

"Yes, yes," said his Highness, with a shrug expressive of disgust ; "yes, yes ; to be sure."

"Well, then ; I will introduce your Highness. This way."

He led his Royal Highness to a little room on the right of the stage, and, pushing open the door, dragged his Highness in.

What took place in that room we will not reveal.

Suffice it to say that in that interview a human being was bartered—a human soul—a Christian girl was bought and sold for gold !

The wretched creature scarce understood what was being done, for she was young and without guile.

She only knew that she dare not disobey the old villain who stood over her, and so she became a passive spectator. The kisses and embraces she submitted to as passively as if she had been but a mere clay figure.

At length the Prince issued forth, with the girl hanging on his arm.

"Get out of the way, you fellows," he said to his friends, "get out of the way. I don't want anything more to do with you to-night, so don't come near me."

They knew his meaning, and withdrew.

The Prince then left the saloons.

"Where am I going ?" asked the young girl, when they reached the street.

"To a palace, my darling," said his Royal Highness.

"But I would rather go home."

"You will have no home from this moment but with me."

"Say you so?"

"Yes."

"And grandfather?"

"He has given you to me."

"And who are you?"

"A Prince."

"I desire you will let me go. I do not wish to remain in your company."

"Oh, nonsense. Come along."

"I will not go with you."

"You must."

"I will cry for help."

"Psha! your grandfather will not permit any nonsense of that sort."

"Heaven help me!"

"Better trust to me for help."

"I will not. I know you not, and I will not go with you. Help!"

"Good God! are you mad?"

"No; but I was mad in the *salon*—mad or dreaming. I begin to understand now, and I will not submit to this degradation."

"Psha!"

"Help."

"Silence."

"Help."

"I must call your grandfather."

At this moment a woman came upon the scene.

A pale, haggard, raven-haired woman, who peered into the face of the Prince and then into that of the girl.

"Great God!" she cried as her eye fell upon the girl, "my child."

"Mother!"

"Marie!" ejaculated the Prince.

It was his old flame, Marie Lavrouffe.

The girl whom he was carrying off was her child — the child of her amour with Lord Lovelace.

Marie regarded the Prince fixedly for one instant, and then sprang upon him and attempted to tear the young girl from his embrace.

But the Prince did not choose to be baffled after this fashion, and clung with extreme tenacity to his prize.

"Release her," cried Marie; "release her, Prince, or it shall be the worse for you. You have brought me to the abject being you now behold, but, for God's sake, have mercy on my poor child."

"Psha. You rave, I say."

"I do not rave."

"This is no child of yours."

"She is—she is."

"I say not. Ah! here is her grandfather."

The old villain now left the house and approached the two.

He seemed much startled to see Marie, but in an instant his self-possession was regained.

"How now? Is this girl the child of you, woman?"

"No," unhesitatingly answered Lavrouffe.

"Yes, yes, I say," screamed Marie. "This is some awful plot to tear my child from me. Oh! father, it was you who stole my child from me in Paris; it was you who would bring her to that awful abyss into which your cupidity and the heartlessness of this man have plunged me. I see it all now."

"Does she speak the truth?"

"I have said so," answered the old man doggedly.

"You here," said the Prince; "you here. Now be gone, woman, or I will give you in charge of an officer for creating a disturbance and causing me annoyance."

"She is my mother," cried the young girl; "she *is* my mother, and I will go with her."

A carriage now rolled up to the door, and at a sign from the Prince the driver stopped.

"To Carlton House," he said, thrusting the girl into the vehicle.

The driver seemed to know his hirer, touched his hat, and prepared to start.

As the foot of the poor trembling girl was on the step, as she was being forced into the carriage despite the efforts made by her mother to detain her, a young, slim man ran to the spot.

"What is this?" he cried.

"Oh, sir," cried Marie, "sir, they are tearing my child from me!"

The young man glanced at the Prince.

"His Highness of Wales is occupied as I never expected to find him," said the youth in ironical tones that stung the Prince deeply.

"And who are you who dare comment upon my behaviour and occupation?"

"I am a nobleman; that is sufficient."

"There is something in your voice I seem to remember," said Marie, "something that reminds me of the past. You seem kind and manly. For God's sake, let me entreat you to free from them my child."

"Silence, my good soul, and let the young lady speak."

He then addressed himself to Marie's child—

"Are you the daughter of yon woman?"

"Oh, yes, yes."

"And are you being forced into that carriage against your will?"

"Yes, against my will."

"This conduct is unmanly," said the youth to the Prince, "and I will not sanction it. Get you gone, sir, and hand this poor girl to her mother."

"Dare you—"

"Your Highness will make no impression upon me by big words or big looks. *I dare* raise my voice, and, if needs be, my hands, in the defence of the innocent."

"Oh, most virtuous noble, whom I do not know, this shall be severely chastised."

"I care not for any chastisement you can inflict. Thank Heaven, there is a means of publishing both sides of the question, and allowing the public to judge between the right and the wrong."

"I shall not have to resort to any such measure as that."

"I presume so; but *I shall.*"

"Take your rescued damsel, and begone; I wish not to detain her."

"You dare not."

"Dare not?"

"I repeat the assertion—Dare not!"

And the Prince dared not; for, turning on his heel, he slunk back to the house, followed by the crest-fallen Lavrouffe.

"Your name," said Marie, hugging her child to her breast; "your name, good sir, that I may speak of it night and day for ever.'

"What can my name matter to you, good woman?"

"Much—pray give it me."

"You are welcome to it—I am Lord Lovelace."

The woman staggered as if stricken by a bolt of iron.

Recovering herself, she approached the youth and gazed into his eyes.

"Lovelace," she cried; "his nose, his eyes, his mouth. My lord, my lord, you have this night saved from infamy *your sister*."

"*My sister!*"

"The child of your own father.'

"Great God!"

The young man would have spoken more, but, catching her child by the arm, Marie ran with her from the spot.

CHAPTER III.

PITT'S ALLEY, MAID'S LANE—CONCERNING VEN-
DORS OF VEGETABLES—RAGS AND BONES—
THE ATTIC LODGERS—BODY SNATCHING.

MAID'S-LANE culminated in Pitt's alley.

The latter thoroughfare, as we hinted two chapters back, was an artery that drained off the scum from the Dials.

The lane was bad enough, but the alley was something to remember.

It was rectangular in form, and was composed of houses for the most part aged, tottering, and rotten and filthy.

The inhabitants of the alley were a singular set of beings, evil in disposition, dirty in habits, and loose in morals.

Most of them were in some way of business.

Rag merchants were in abundance, but coster-mongers predominated.

The smell arising from their respective wares was anything but pleasant; at times, in the height of the summer, it was positively obnoxious.

The perfume of rags, bones, and stale vegetables enclosed in a place of narrow limits, otherwise filthy and fetid, was constantly telling upon the health of the Pitt's alleyites, and King Fever fixed his throne in their midst, and reigned supreme amongst them.

The place, too, was disgustingly overcrowded.

In every room, scarcely large enough to swing the proverbial cat in, was established a family of from four to eight persons, eating, sleeping—rotting there, but with no notice taken of them.

Boards of Health did not extend their influence over these quarters.

Suffice it that they kept the streets of palatial residences of the West-end thoroughly swept and watered ; enough that they removed nuisances from under aristocratic noses.

What were the poor wretches in these dens to them ?

What if pestilential fever swept them down in scores ?

What if the cesspools poisoned them at the rate of twenty per *diem*?

What if the whole neighbourhood was but a field of corruption—a home of vice—a den of infamy —the hot-bed of plague ?

What all this to them? Nothing.

The inhabitants of the place were only poor, illiterate, drunken swine, about whom the world cared nothing.

So they might live or die, as chance directed, and the world was to go on as usual, for all this dirt, crime, and misery was to be hushed up by the officers of *health*, and the money forced from the public to alleviate these horrors was to be pocketed by fat officials, and no one the wiser.

The most extraordinary part of this affair was, and still is, the number of children born and reaching years of maturity—a cramped, crabbed, brutal, illiterate, crime-stained maturity, but maturity for all that.

Is it possible that children, like pigs, thrive best when wallowing in filth ?

It would appear so, if the Seven Dials specimens may be taken as illustrative of the fact.

Never clean, never kept, seldom clothed, seldom fed, these beings appear, grow up, and disappear (on the gallows), apparently strong, certainly hearty, most positively shrewd, and cunning to an extraordinary degree.

There is something in this that should be sifted to the bottom.

Let these children escape fever, and nothing else appears to affect them.

Consumption they do not know, starvation is a joke to them, and minor disorders and troubles never vex them.

But unhappily the majority do not escape fever.

It is ever present in their hamlets, mowing them down in droves and swarms, crushing them in multitudes.

To all appearances Pitt's-alley is, at the moment of our visit, very much fever-troubled.

Gaunt men and emaciated women hang and crawl about the place with great glaring, supernaturally brilliant eyes, hollow white cheeks, with just one bright red spot beneath the black vein of the eye, with tottering legs, burning palms, parched throats, cracked lips, and reeling pains.

They all appear to be more or less infected in this manner.

The children, barring the healthy ones, lie about the gutter that runs down the middle of the alley wallowing in mud, apparently glad to place their heated brows in the dull, stagnant pools that settle in the broken stones, and thus still the throbbing and torture within.

It was evening, the alley was quiet, and the hum of the day was over.

The costermongers had returned home, more or less drunk.

The rag merchants had purchased and carted off as much of that day's filth as could be conveniently purchased and carted off, and the time of rest was drawing near.

Suddenly a shriek rent the air ; it was the cold, piercing shriek of a woman.

All those that were able rushed out of their houses and listened.

At length the shriek was repeated.

It came from a little court on the left of the alley.

The court was attached to a rag shop, and in it was a tenement consisting of one large kitchen or wash-house, over which were two old and fast decaying rooms or lofts, approached by a stair broken and ricketty.

No one would have imagined it was a human habitation, but the shriek told that the den had its inhabitants.

" What's that ?" said one.

"Can't think," said another.

" There must be something up," ejaculated a third.

" Murder," suggested a fourth, with awful indifference.

" No. Who's to do it ?"

"I don't know. Who lives there?"

"Tony Marks, the old tailor, and his sister Jane in the front room, and Tommy Squall and his wife in the back. It can't be Tony or his sister, 'cos they can't move; and it can't be Tommy and his wife, 'cos he ain't home.''

"Well, what is it?"

"Hadn't we better see?"

"Well, that would be best, p'raps."

Having come to this conclusion, several of the people, men and women, rushed in the court, and prepared to mount the stairs.

Their progress was at once checked by a great black cat, seated in the stairs, glaring down on them with his fiery and awful eyes, and preparing to spring.

They at last dislodged this impediment, and mounted the few stairs.

The den rented by the Squalls was empty.

So they ran into that occupied by Marks and his sister.

It was an awful place.

The floor was black with filth; an old broken chair stood in one corner, a ricketty table was in the centre of the room, and in one corner was a bundle of shavings, on which were thrown a few rags.

At first it appeared that the apartment had no occupant, but, on rushing to the heap of rags, it was discovered that on it lay two bodies bearing something of the semblance of humanity, but very little.

The first form was that of a little emaciated man, almost destitute of covering.

The eyes were open, but fixed on the ceiling with a glazed stare of death.

The lower jaw had fallen, and had stretched the beastly skin-bag that had once been a cheek to its full extent. A beard of many months' growth hung on a breast through the skin of which every bone could be plainly counted, and the shape determined upon.

The hands resembled the claws of a beast, and the legs scarcely the size of an infant's.

Across that ghastly spectacle lay a woman.

She was breathing; otherwise she would have been the counterpart of the stark corpse.

They raised her.

Seated in the old chair, her senses returned in some measure.

She gazed about her wildly, and then made a clicking noise with her tongue, expressive of requiring drink.

"Get her some vater," said a man; "get her some vater, and be quick."

"Put a dash of gin it," said another; "it'll bring her to."

"Yes," said a third, "better put some Old Tom in it; she vants it bad enough."

Old Tom was the remedy in that neighbourhood for all evils.

Two women ran over for the stimulant; a third was despatched for a doctor, and two men and a woman were left with the corpse and the insensible woman.

"Tony's cut it at last," said one man to the other.

"Yes, he's gone · poor devil."

"He couldn't last for ever at this game," struck in the woman; "how could he?"

"Just so, how could he? poor devil, since the fever took him, and the old thing can't have had anythink to eat or drink."

"Devil a bit or sup. Who was to give it 'em?"

"Just so; where wos they to get it?"

"And this," said a woman, "this is the place where they perfesses to have relieving officers."

"Relieving officers! Bah! what a sham! why they ain't seen von in the alley for more nor a month."

"No, nor 'spectors either."

"'Spectors! vot's the use o' them. They only bullies and blackguards, and threatens to have us poor devils up afore the beak if we don't be cleaner, and do unpossible things, just like so many swells would."

"Aye, that's it."

Just then the women returned, and the restorative was administered to Tony's sister.

In a few minutes she recovered sufficiently to speak.

"So," she said, slowly and lowly, "so you heard me call?''

"Yes, we heard yer."

"Ah! ah! yes, to be sure; and Tony?"

"Tony's dead."

"Aye, dead. I thought he'd die."

"O' course."

"Of course. It was five days ago he touched anythink"

"Five days!"

"Yes; he's been going ever since."

"i should think so."

"At first he did not seem to care much as long as there was water."

"Yes."

"But when the pitcher was empty, and I tumbled down in trying to get over the stairs to fill it, he got awful."

"And nobody came a-nigh ye to get ye a drop of water?"

"Not a soul."

"I tumbled down at the head of the stairs. The pitcher smashed, and it was hours before I could crawl back again to Tony."

"Yes."

"And then I laid down by his side and couldn't move again."

"Not move?"

"No, I haven't moved for three days."

"And haven't you called?"

"Yes."

"And haven't them Squalls been in to see how you're gettin' on?"

"They ain't been home for more'n three days."

"So you've been here alone?"

"All alone!"

"Good God!"

"And Tony kept on murmuring, 'Water! water!—I want water—get me water!' and I'd try and try, but neither hand nor foot could I move, and so—"

"And so?"

"It went on till just now. Then he started

up, he glared at me with his great wild eyes, clutched me by the throat, and screamed, ' Water!' I tried to move—God knows how I tried—but it was no manner o' use. I couldn't move hand nor foot, and so he cried in vain."

" Go on."

" Then he went mad, and, with more strength than you'd a' thought he had in 'him, dragged me to him, crying, ' I'm parched—I'm dying—and if I can't have water *I'll drink your blood!*"

" Good God!"

" He drew me close to him, and I couldn't move away from him. He opened his jaws, and, as I thought to have felt his teeth meet in my throat, he let me go, and fell back. That's when I screamed. After a bit I looked at him again, and I saw what had happened then. I cried out again, and that's all."

Accustomed, as these people were, to see and hear of such scenes, the narrative of this woman, told so abruptly and ungrammatically, fairly appalled them.

It was a tale of terror that even in their imagination they could not have conjured up, and for many minutes they were speechless.

At length the doctor came.

He was a tall, snake-like man, who seemed to coil himself up and dart about rather than use the ordinary mode of locomotion.

He was all glitter and rattle.

His eyes glittered, his teeth glittered, his very hands seemed to glitter; and, as he moved about, from down in the depths of his throat came a snake-like rattle that seemed peculiar to him.

"Pagh!" ejaculated Dr. Python, as he entered the room; "pagh!" and he spat. "What an atmosphere; u-r-r-h!"

He went to the heap of rags, looked at it, drew from his pocket a bottle, held it to his nose, spat again, uttered his peculiar " U-r-r-h," and then turned the corpse about with his foot.

" Dead!" he said.

"Yes, doctor, quite dead."

"U-r-r-h! then why was I sent for, u-r-r-h ?"

" Not for him, but for this poor soul."

"U-r-r-h! What's the matter with her?"

He put this question as if he imagined the people about him could give him an answer.

Then he advanced, told the people to stand on one side, and looked at the woman.

" Hold up her hand," he said, to a man.

The man did so.

He placed two fingers on the bony wrist, and held them there.

" Open her mouth," he said, again.

This was done.

"U-r-r-h! Fever! She's had your d——d poison; u-r-r-h! Too low to recover. Must die! U-r-r-h."

" Must die!"

" Yes; bound to die. U-r-r-h!"

" But you'll give her something?"

"Give her something! D—— me, u-r-rh! What should I give her? D'ye think the parish of St. Giles hasn't enough to pay for without having the expense of drugs put upon it

for cattle like this, and without any chance of doing 'em good. U-r-r-h ?"

" But—"

"But d——n me, no but I've said my say, and that's all; she will die, die and be d——d to her, like a dog, and who cares? The parish don't care. The public thinks itself victimised because it has to pay rates and taxes to feed and physic the cattle; the overseers don't care, because the cattle give them such a d——d lot of trouble: and I don't care, because I'm underpaid, and can't afford to give any attention to such d——d, Ur-rh! cattle, so there you know all about it, d—— me? Ur-rh, and you may all go the devil, and be eternally d——d, the whole lot of ye, for bringing me to such a den to make me sick for a month. U-r-rh!"

With this beautiful and Christian-like speech and benediction, Doctor Python went as rapidly as possible down the stairs.

As he reached the bottom step, he lighted upon the great black cat.

The animal cried, and, turning its lithe neck, caught the doctor by the heel, and made him cry out with the pain of the bite.

"Ur-r-r-h!" rattled the doctor, in extreme agony, "d——d wretches can keep d——d things like that to make their teeth meet in respectable people's heels. U-r-r-h! Yes, d—— me, I will give *you* a small drug—*you* want it."

He took from his pocket a piece of bread, drew from his pocket a minute phial, poured a few drops of its contents on the bread, and flung it to the cat.

The ravenous animal swallowed it immediately.

There was a pause.

The poor brute sprang into the air, and fell down dead.

From its body arose a thick vapour, and a smell that at once told that the action of the drug was to burn up its entrails.

"U-r-r-h! That's right.

Muttering this between his teeth, Doctor Python turned on his heels, and stalked into the court.

*   *   *   *   *

It was dark now.

The doctor was walking rapidly out of the alley when an old man, bent, crippled, and tottering, ran after him, and touched him on the shoulder.

"Ah," said the doctor, recognising the old fellow, " what do you want?"

"That's what I was going to ask you."

" What d'ye mean ?"

" You know."

" How should I ?"

" You know *me* ?"

" I know no good of you."

" But *you know me* ?"

" Yes."

" Well, you may guess why I stopped you."

" I can't—I'm not good at riddles."

" Perverse as a donkey."

" What's that ?"

" Oh, you needn't fluster, Python, if you know

me." I, at least, have a little knowledge of you."

"What's that—a threat?'

"No. I can't afford to threaten."

"What the devil do you then stop me for?"

"You've been into the court yonder?"

"Well?"

"Well; I know what is going on there."

"What is going on there?"

"Death."

"What's that to me?"

"A great deal."

"How so?"

"How stupid you seem to have grown of a sudden. It's all in all to you. It's your living. Since you force me to speak, don't every student in London know who to come to when they want a body, or any part of it, for anatomisation?"

"Well?"

"And don't Doctor Python, who supplies the student, and who professes to lecture them on anatomy, know who to come to when he's hard up for subjects."

"Again, well?"

"Well; the said doctor's hard up for subjects now, and the demand's large."

"How do you know that?"

"Because Doctor Python wouldn't give a poor wretch of a woman a simple draught that would have saved her life, because he knew that he should want her corpse to-morrow night."

"Oh, oh!"

"You see I know your game pretty well."

"You are quite a genius."

"But you're quite a fool if you think you can cheat me. Ha! ha! I'm too old a soldier for you."

"Well, since you are so clever, and seem to know so much, what about those two bodies?"

"They are yours on the old terms."

"All right. I shall want 'em by midnight to-morrow."

"They're yours."

"Well, that's all right. Good evening."

"I've not finished yet."

"The devil you haven't."

"No."

"What next?"

"A little matter that concerns me privately."

"Speak quickly, then, for my time is precious."

"I've no doubt."

"No sneers, old fellow, or it will be the worse for you."

"Bah!"

"You dare me."

"Oh, yes, if you like; I'd as soon dare you as another, for I've no cause to fear you."

"Did you stop me to tell me so?"

"Scarcely that; although there's no harm in your knowing it."

"Well, what have you to say to me? Quick, I say!"

"What! is there another *life to save?*"

"What mean you?"

"I didn't know if you had another case as urgent as that of the tailor's sister on hand, and I know your kindness of heart wouldn't admit of your staying if such was the case."

"Devil!"

"Nonsense. That language is not polite."

"A truce to this! What have you to say to me?"

"Nothing particular."

"Then I will go."

"Don't! you had best not."

"Why?"

"Because I want you."

"Do you mean to madden me? Will you tell me why you have detained me?"

"All in good time."

"Hell!"

"Hush, hush! that's bad language for a professional man to use."

"Come, come, speak?"

"Well, then, I will."

"Do, and be brief."

"As brief as possible."

"That is well."

"Just now I observed you kill a cat!"

"Well."

"Well; I thought it a very interesting experiment in chemicals."

"You did?"

"I certainly did."

"And was it for *that* you have detained me this infernal while—u - r - rh!"

"Not quite, but it was to say I am also fond of experementalising with chemicals."

"What mean you?"

"I mean that I like to watch the effect of poisons on animal bodies."

"And what's that to me!"

"Nothing. I told you I wanted to speak to you on a purely personal affair."

"Confusion! I think you want to madden me."

"Nonsense; I would'nt do no such thing for the world."

"Then why do you bother me with such trifling conversation as this?"

"To you it *may* be a trifle, to be sure, but to me its of the very utmost importance."

"Speak on then."

"Well, doctor, I certainly admired the skill with which you disposed of that unhappy black Tom cat, and I said to myself that's a marvellous poison."

"It is."

"Just so. My reflection is verified as having determined in my own mind that that was an invaluable poison, my next thought was *how much I should like to possess it?*"

"To what purpose would you use it?"

"For the disposal of a feline annoyance! My house, my neighbourhood is swarmed with cats. I should like to rid myself of them."

"Storrocks," said the doctor.

"You had best mind. You're playing some desperate game, I can see."

"What odds to you?"

"Just so."

"Well, doctor, having made up my mind that the poison was invaluable in the case of the feline race, I determined to ask you how it would affect the human frame."

"In precisely the same manner."

" Ah, instantaneous death !"

" Instantaneous !"

" Well, I must trouble you, then, for that phial."

" My phial ?"

" Yours."

" You can't have it."

" O, pardon me ; I *must*."

" I will tell you the name of the poison, and—"

" And that won't do. You know no chemist would sell it me."

The doctor answered not.

" Come," said the old man, " the phial. '

" I can't spare it."

" You shall."

" Shall !"

" Yes, shall."

" You can't force me."

" I will."

" You dare not."

" Daren't I ? You know not what I dare do. For twopence I'd let the authorities know who is the receiver of all the bodies—"

" Hush, fool."

" You know how to stop my tongue."

" But—"

" I don't want any 'but's.' I want the phial.'

" You will have it ?"

" I must. Deeply as I regret taking it from you, who know how to put it to such good use I must have it. My need is pressing."

" But had you not seen me use it ?"

" I should have had to resort to such ugly weapons as the knife, the bludgeon, or the pistol and I don't feel inclined to run any such risks.'

" And you will have the poison !"

" Of course. Hand it to me."

The doctor hesitated but a moment. Then he drew forth his small case, and from it extracted the small phial we have before spoken of.

He looked at it lovingly for a moment.

He seemed to hesitate about parting with it and would have perhaps returned it to its place had not the old man snatched it from him, and placed it in his pocket.

" There," he said, " that's all right, doctor that's all right ; and now you may go. The bodies of the maids will be in your house at midnight to-morrow. Good night."

The doctor did not reply, but walked rapidly away.

" Ha !" said the old man, looking after him, " it's good to have such a fellow under one's thumb—very good ; it gives one such a pull over the world generally. Ah ! my little phial. you will be an invaluable friend, and I shall know how to use you to advantage. Killing cats, forsooth ! Goodness guide us, to think that such splendid drugs should be wasted upon paltry Tom cats, whose brains one is at liberty to dash out against any wall in London. And, for the matter of that, there was a time when the same mode of getting rid of a man might be put in force in this place with almost as little risk. But times have changed, and the metropolis is better watched, better watched !—and if

it were not better watched, it would be all the same in my case. I'm old now, very old, and can't do the things I once did. The lion's all gone out of me, and I'm obliged to descend to the tricks of the jackal."

He glanced at the phial again, and finally placed it in his bosom.

" There," he said ; " there it will be safe ; and now for home, and the work that's to be done."

He walked away.

He was a peculiar old man was that who stopped and had the foregoing interview with Dr. Python.

He was bent almost double, but there was something like elasticity left in his step, and his eye was as bright, and his mind evidently as active, as that of a youth of twenty.

His style of conversation was not at all in accordance with his general appearance.

The former was sharp, epigrammatic, and characterised by something approaching refinement ; whilst, on the other hand, the dress was old, musty, worn, and mean in the extreme.

But the chief peculiarity was in the face.

It was a face that, once seen, was never to be forgotten.

It was a ghastly white face, and every line was as hard, rigid, and motionless as if it had been graven in granite, or as if the nerves and muscles had been of steel.

Whatever expression the eye wore, there was the same meaningless expression in the face.

There never was a change.

It had always the same terrible, hard, unvarying character.

We have said the dress was old and worn, but we have not said that it's cut was of a *by gone era*—that it was *black*, and that hanging to the skirt, down the front, and about the cuffs was the remains of a trimming of *black* bugles ; but now that we have given these facts, the reader will begin to discern that he has met an old acquaintance.

*   *   *   *   *

As this old man darted away a figure, closely muffled, came out from the shadow of a doorway close by where the conversation between the doctor and the body-snatcher had had their conversation.

This figure glided after the old man with extreme velocity, dogged his footsteps, followed in his wake, and seemed to track him with the unvarying certainty of a well-trained bloodhound.

It was the figure of a short but rather stout man, whose face was characterised by wonderful vivacity and shrewdness.

" Ah, my friend, my very old and *dear* friend, the BLACK CAPTAIN, who once so considerately buried me alive, I am on your scent again, am I ? Again at the old game of thief-taking. Well, it's pleasant sport, after all, and I relish it all the more for not having practised it of late years. We shall see if any of the old ability that once made all London stare with wonder yet remains."

It was our old acquaintance, Pipey.

CHAPTER IV.

THE PRINCE AND A VICTIM—LADY BAUKSFORD
AND THE BILLETS—HIS HIGHNESS TRAPPED
AND BEATEN AT HIS OWN GAME.

LORD and Lady Bauksford lived in one of those magnificent squares that form the grand *quartier* known as Belgravia.

They were an exceedingly happy-going couple, and had only lately put in an appearance in the metropolis.

They had both spent the greatest part of their lives abroad, where they had been educated under the surveillance of the most accomplished masters.

There was a feud between the fathers of the young people such as raged between the Capulets and the Montagues in Shakespeare's play; but the young Lord and Lady Alice met, and straightway assumed the characters of "Romeo" and "Juliet."

As a matter of course, they married against the will of their parents, and equally, as a matter of course, were abandoned to their fate by their noble sires.

But fate was kind to them, and after a brief twelve months of misery both the heads of their houses dropped off, and they returned to England, home, and love.

The season in which they came under our notice was only the second in which they had been known to the world of London.

Lady Charlotte Bauksford, the young lord's sister and elder by some few years, had, however, been "out" some five seasons and had not "gone off."

She was now eight-and-twenty years old, but only just becoming perfect in her beauty.

Her reputation was world-famed, but, singular enough, no one had attempted to win and wear her.

How was this?

The mystery must have some explanation if it could be but fathomed.

There was *a mystery*; that was admitted on all hands, but few were able to fathom it, very few; and Lord Bauksford returned to England to find his sister single and hear men speak of her with something like a sneer on their lips.

This for some time escaped him, but at last —at last he could not fail to notice it, and the dawning of the truth smote him to the heart.

He strove to hide the fact from his wife, but, with a woman's penetration, she had already divined the truth, and with a woman's tact she had wormed herself into the confidence of the sister-in-law herself, and had come at the truth, which lay hid down the bottom of the deep well of her heart.

That truth she strove to keep from her husband, for she well knew the awful effect it would have upon him.

So that while *he* was endeavouring to hide from his wife the consciousness of an implied frailty on the part of his sister, *she* was plotting to conceal the awful secret of the past from him. That secret may be told in a few words.

Lady Charlotte had fallen—had become the mother of a child of whom the Prince of Wales was the father.

*   *   *   *   *

Time passed, and the face of Lady Charlotte paled and grew wan, for she much feared the knowledge of the awful facts of her case coming to the knowledge of her brother.

That brother, whose high sense of honour, whose frenzied temper, and terrible pride she so dreaded.

Lady Alice undertook the task of disarming the Prince, and restoring Charlotte to peace and happiness.

Her plans were very simple, but singularly dangerous and bold.

It was to throw herself in the way of the Prince, pander to his awful passions, and thus lead him on to relinquish the letters, written to him by Lady Charlotte, he held.

So far she had succeeded.

The Prince was a frequent visitor at his lordship's house, and Lady Alice played her cards so well that she had extorted from his royal Highness the promise to effect an exchange of letters, and also to extort from the Prince an oath of secresy concerning the unfortunate woman he had betrayed.

*   *   *   *   *

It was the night on which the plan of the Lady Alice was to be tested.

It was between four and five o'clock in the afternoon, and we shall find Alice in her elegantly furnished bed-room.

The chamber was appointed with the most exquisite taste; the atmosphere was warm and perfumed.

Numerous bottles of the rarest scents and choicest perfumes might be seen upon the toilet-table—near which there stood a full-length mirror, or Psyche, in which the fair mistress of the place might survey her entire form at pleasure.

Alice was now not alone there; another young lady was present; and in order to avoid any unnecessary mystery, we may as well at once observe that this young lady was the Lady Charlotte.

Lady Charlotte was now disapparelling herself in her sister-in-law's chamber at the house at Belgravia; and Alice was taking from a box certain articles of raiment which she was spreading out upon the bed.

But these articles of raiment all belonged to a masculine costume!

What could either of these ladies have to do with the apparel of a gentleman?

We shall soon see.

Lady Charlotte presently finished the process of laying aside the costume which properly became her sex; and then, with Alice's assistance, she began to clothe herself in the masculine vesture which had been produced from the box.

There was some little mirth and raillery on the part of the two young ladies as the process went on : but there was a certain sternness and resoluteness of purpose in the looks of both, as if it were no masquerading pleasantry which was in contemplation, but as if the assumption of that male costume by the Lady Charlotte were connected with some purpose of real sterling importance.

Lady Charlotte, being tall for a woman, appeared, when dressed in male costume, to be a young gentleman somewhat under the medium stature.

That costume fitted her most admirably ; and by degrees, as she put on garment after garment, by the succour of her sister-in-law Alice, she evidently strove to adopt a more dashing, fearless, and off-hand demeanour than that which was naturally her own.

" And now let us gather up this beautiful hair of yours, Charlotte ; and then you shall put on this hat, and it will complete your attire. There ! —now you are indeed perfect. Ah ! and how interesting !" ejaculated Alice, with looks of admiration.

" And yet I feel to a certain extent awkward and embarrassed, notwithstanding all my endeavours to adopt as manly a demeanour as possible."

" Oh, but you must succeed in throwing off that embarrassment. Recollect you have undertaken to play a particular part, and you must perform it. Nothing but a bold, courageous, and indeed desperate demeanour will strike terror into the heart of the cowardly fellow !"

" Ah ! now that your words so vividly remind me of all my wrongs, I feel that I am capable of any proof of courage and daring that may be required of me. Here, give me a pistol, my dear Alice !"

Lady Alice lost not a moment in complying with the desire of her sister-in-law, to whom she handed a small rifle pistol of most exquisite workmanship,—she herself retaining its companion.

" Take care," she said ; " the pistols are always kept loaded."

" Ah ! why so ?" exclaimed the young lady in male attire, as a pallor flitted across her countenance ; and for a moment she seemed as if she had rather have nothing to do with the weapon.

" Oh, because Charles keeps them loaded for security's sake. There have lately been some very daring burglaries in this neighbourhood. But surely, Charlotte—"

" No, no, I am not afraid," ejaculated the young lady. " It was only a passing reluctance to hold the weapon—but I am already accustomed to it, and I can even play with it—"

" At all events, my dear Charlotte, keep the muzzle turned in the other direction, for you have just been pointing it most disagreeably towards myself."

" Good heavens ! if it had gone off !" cried Charlotte, now again becoming very pale.

" Then I should have been stretched dead at your feet," was Alice's reply, still given in a tone of calm, quiet courage. " But do not be agitated and nervous—assert all the powers of your mind—be resolved—be determined—say to

yourself that you *will* be bold and at the same time collected—and you know not how easy it will become to accomplish that which you are bent on doing."

" Ah, if I were only like you, Alice. But yet I feel that I am gathering courage, fortitude, and self-possession from your example. Now see ! do I not at present hold the pistol in a becoming manner ? In a few minutes I shall be quite expert ; and you will fancy that I have been taking lessons in a shooting gallery. Yes, truly—I feel every minute more and more at home in this costume. I really think it has its advantages over that which belongs to our own sex."

" Ah ! at that moment," ejaculated Alice, with a peal of merry laughter, " you were, indeed, admirable. You had precisely the graceful, negligent, lounging air of a young fashionable."

" And what do you think of this ?" asked Charlotte, laying down her pistol, folding her arms across her bosom, and leaning them upon the back of a chair, while she looked up with arch seriousness into Alice's countenance. " Is this indicative of self-possession ?"

" The attitude is inimitable," exclaimed Lady Alice, still laughing merrily with delight. " Really, my dear, if it were not that the contours of the bust are somewhat too richly developed, you might pass yourself off as a very pretty young gentleman—a trifle effeminate, of course, and with a face so remarkably smooth that it would appear as if the growth of a beard were impossible. Ah ! I should like to see the attitude you would take if imitating some exquisite when smoking a cigar."

" If we had a cigar here," responded Charlotte, " I would very soon gratify you on the point. I feel that I am becoming quite manly ; and as for courage, rest assured, my dear, all your kind advice and aid shall not have been thrown away. But the purpose which we have in view," she added, her countenance becoming serious and almost severe, " shall be accomplished."

" I am delighted to hear you speak in a tone so confident. Indeed, my dear, when the moment for action comes, you must say to yourself—"

" I will say to myself that I am about to deal with a villain !" she exclaimed energetically, at the same time stamping on the carpet with her foot, which was imprisoned in an exquisite patent leather boot ; " and rest assured, Alice, that I can deal most remorselessly with him. But tell me, why are you yourself so bitter—"

" Bitter, my dear Charlotte ? That is not the word, because I personally know so little of the Prince."

" Yet, if you be not bitter against him," said Charlotte, " you at least have a very strong feeling—"

" Am I not taking your part ?" exclaimed Alice ; " and to take your part naturally inspires me with all the enthusiastic feelings of a partisan. Besides, this Prince is indeed a most accomplished villain——"

" Yes—a villain such as there exist but few

in this world!" interjected Charlotte with passionate vehemence. " To suffer me to believe myself seriously married to him."

" And at the very time when you were suffering so deeply on his account, he was elsewhere performing the part of a vile seducer! He was then beguiling others, even perhaps more cruelly than he beguiled you."

" Yes, the Prince is a villain in every sense!" exclaimed Charlotte; " and the conduct which he is now pursuing stamps him almost with the blackness of a fiend! The wretch! to endeavour to replenish his empty purse by means so vile. Ah! I wish that I were indeed a man, for then with this arm of mine would I bestow upon him such chastisement as only a masculine hand can inflict."

" Bravo!" exclaimed Alice; " say everything to sustain your courage—think of everything to inspire you with additional fortitude. Lash yourself up into a rage."

" By heavens," she replied, "it requires but little to do that. You know that naturally I am meek and mild—perhaps I have been called amiable—but ah! I can assure you that there have been moments when it has appeared as if a veritable fiend were existing within me; and *this* is one of those moments."

"Well, my dear Charlotte, you will soon have an opportunity of punishing that villain. It is now close upon five o'clock, and at about that hour he is to be here. We do not dine until six; and thus, by the time dinner is served up, we shall have accomplished all the task that we have set ourselves, and we shall have had leisure to compose our feelings, and suffer our excitement to cool down."

"And what if Charles were to return unexpectedly?" exclaimed Charlotte; "what would he think?"

"Do not be afraid, Charlotte; Charles has accepted an engagement to dine at his club, and I know that he will not fail to keep it. It was for that reason I selected this particular evening for the business which we have in hand."

"Ah, my dear Alice, how deep a debt of gratitude do I owe you! You have behaved towards me with so much goodness and generosity! Oh, yes, dearest Alice, never, never can I forget how you ministered unto me, how you sustained me when I felt as if I were actually dropping and sinking out of existence."

There was a pause, and then she spoke again.

"Look, my dear Alice. Does my hand now tremble as I take up this pistol? Do I look like a novice in the handling of it?—and do you feel as if there were any awkwardness on my part which might place you in bodily fear, as just now you were? Pshaw! I have already the spirit of a man; and if the villain, when he comes, does not accede to the demand which I shall make upon him, I swear to you, Alice, that without pity and without remorse—"

"Hush, my dear friend, we do not want murder's work to be done beneath this roof! Display as bold a front and as strong a heroism as you are now showing, and it will be sufficient. He will be overawed—he will crouch at your feet—and the game will be all in your own hands."

"And so I mean it to be," ejaculated Charlotte, whose manner for the last few minutes had been displaying a vivacious hardihood and a wild recklessness which were something more than the mere harum-scarum exuberations of a young girl, but which rather resembled the devil-may-care boldness of a young man. Yes, yes, Alice," she continued; "if success depends upon me, it shall be realised. But ought he not to be here by this time?"

"It is only just five, and he will be here about that hour. Are you afraid, Charlotte, that if his presence be delayed a reaction will take place in your feelings—your courage will evaporate——"

"Alice, this jesting on your part is too bad," cried Charlotte, ; then, turning towards the Psyche, she surveyed herself with considerable satisfaction, while tutoring the countenance, which was naturally so soft and interesting in its beauty, to put on the severest and sternest expression. "No, no, my courage will not ooze out. Ah, this is fortunate. Here is Charles's cigar-case lying on this side table. And is there not something very manly, my dear Alice, in smoking a cigar?"

Alice could not help laughing at the *naivete* and ingenuousness which were thus blending with the study and desire on the part of her friend to maintain as fierce and dauntless a demeanour as possible; and she said, "By all means take a cigar, Charlotte, if you do not think the tobacco smoke will make you sick."

"It will be useless for me to study to become as manly as possible for the nonce," said Char-

lotte, "if you, by your raillery and banter, keep constantly reminding me of the weaknesses of my real sex. But look, Alice."

Thus speaking, Charlotte took a cigar from the case, lighted it, and placed it between her beautiful red lips.

A wreath of fleecy vapour curled upward from those lips; and Alice, who had a vein of mischief in her mirthfulness, exclaimed, laughing,

"I really thought to see you suck in the smoke instead of puffing it outwards, and if such had been the case—"

"I should now be sick and ill," added Charlotte; "and the villain might have yet had the laugh against me. You do not know, Alice, with what a spirit I am imbued at the present moment?"

At this moment Alice's confidential maid entered the bed-chamber, saying, in a low voice, and with a significant look—

"He is here."

Alice made a sign to the abigail, which she evidently at once understood; for she withdrew with the air of one who was ready to perform a duty of which she had been previously made aware.

But at the same moment Charlotte, taking a pistol in her hand, passed behind the curtains of the bed; while Alice deposited the other pistol on a piece of furniture near the door.

Alice then issued from the chamber, but leaving that door more than three parts open behind her.

The adjoining room was Alice's *boudoir*, if we may borrow the French term for that which was really an exquisitely-furnished little parlour communicating with the bed-chamber.

Tapers were burning upon the mantel: a lamp stood upon the table in the centre of the room; and Alice flung a glance into the mirror to assure herself that her looks were sufficiently composed for the part which she had to perform, and that her toilet was of an elegance sufficient to give a species of coquettish support to the winning and seductive mien which she was now all in a moment adopting.

Scarcely were her eyes withdrawn from that mirror, with the full conviction in her mind that she never in her life looked better, when the door was noiselessly opened, and the Prince was ushered into the room by the Abigail, who immediately disappeared.

He bowed with a kind of familiar courtesy, and then he rivetted his eyes upon the lady who awaited him there.

Smiles were upon her countenance, blended with a certain look which seemed to be that of a softly sensuous confusion; and as the eyes of the Prince slowly wandered over the richly-developed contours which the costume so completely delineated, it was soon with devouring regards that he gazed upon the fine person of Alice.

"Be seated," she said, placing herself upon a sofa with a sort of half-air as if she left him to choose a seat for himself, but yet with a sort of half-invitation for him to sit down by her side.

And this he did, still bending upon her glances that were full of passion, and which seemed to be in voluptuous response to the semi-overtures that were made by herself.

"And now," she said, in a soft tone, and yet with a sufficient degree of seriousness to inspire the belief that business matters were to be entered on first, whatsoever the next topic of discourse might be, "let us begin by settling the subject which induced you to favour me with a visit the day before yesterday, and then again yesterday."

"Ah," he replied, with a look of languishing meaning, "I would almost rather that I might be permitted at once to explain the hopes with which I have been inspired——"

"Let that topic follow," she said with a winning smile, as for a moment she laid her white hand upon his arm in that pretty way which a woman has of enforcing her will by a gesture and a touch. "Come, your Highness, let us, in the first instance, speak seriously and in a matter-of-fact strain. Look upon me therefore at the beginning only as——what shall I call myself?—the friend to whom Charlotte has referred you for the purpose of arbitrating between you both in a matter of some little difficulty and delicacy. Ah! and I ought to add that I am fully prepared to settle this matter; for as I on my own side have a pocket book full of notes here, you on your side will have the kindness to tell me whether you have brought all the correspondence to which allusions have been made at previous interviews?"

As she thus spoke, Alice placed a pocketbook on the table, and the Prince at the same time produced a small packet of letters; but, having shown them, he returned them into his pocket, saying—

"I can assure you that every letter which I ever received from Charlotte is here."

Alice bit her lip for a moment at the almost insulting want of confidence which was displayed by the Prince, who even at the very instant when he was presumptuously aspiring to the favours of the lady, nevertheless exhibited his own utter selfishness by the fact that he would not part from the letters, nor even risk the chance of their being snatched up until the bargain for their redemption should be fully concluded.

"I pledge my most solemn, sacred word of honour," said the Prince, "that I am acting fairly, and that every letter received from Charlotte is included in this packet. If there be any means by which I can give an additional proof of my good faith—"

"Yes; there is a means," interrupted Alice. "There are writing materials. Take your place at that table, and pen me a letter to this effect, —that whatsoever calumny or scandal may have whispered in reference to yourself and Charlotte is utterly false. Ah! you can write the letter as if it were in reply to one received from me, and in which I, as Charlotte's sister-in-law, deemed it my duty on hearing of those whispered scandals to address you on the point, and demand an explanation. Believe me, your Highness," added Alice, in her most winning tones, and with her most voluptuous looks, "that the more completely you thus vindicate and clear up Charlotte's character, in case anything should hereafter be said in reference thereto, the higher will be the opinion I myself shall entertain of you; and—and—" here Alice threw into her voice the tremulousness of a soft confusion—"the more readily shall I be inclined to listen to you—"

"Say not another word!" ejaculated the Prince, rejoiced at the prospect of obtaining not merely a considerable sum of money, but likewise the favours of the lady by whose side he sat. "You shall see what I will write, and I feel convinced you will be satisfied!"

He accordingly placed himself at the table, and he began to pen a letter in the strain which Alice had already dictated.

He had really withheld none of Charlotte's letters—not because any sense of honourable feeling remained to him, even in the midst of the performance of a rascally deed — but simply because so refined a piece of villainy had never occurred to him as that of keeping back one or two of the letters to be similarly used for a future purpose of extortion.

Thus as he was already prepared to surrender the whole correspondence, and thereby settle the matter at once and for ever, he had no hesitation in writing precisely such a letter as Alice had suggested.

On the contrary, he had an additional motive for so doing, on account of the hint which she had thrown out that such conduct would prove the surest passport to her favour.

The letter was accordingly penned: Alice read it, she was completely satisfied, and she suffered it to remain on the table, whence the Prince himself did not dare remove it.

"And now," she said, all at once assuming a most winning look, "tell me what you ventured to hope—repeat to me the language which you yesterday addressed to my ears——."

"Oh!" exclaimed the Prince, "was it possible for me to remain unmoved in your presence——"

"Ah your Highness,' said Alice, with that species of hesitation which seemed to imply that he had only to prosecute his addresses boldly and fervently in order to win her; "but how can I place confidence in you, even if in the weakness of my own heart I were to forget my duty towards my husband?"

"Did I ever betray Charlotte's secret?" asked the Prince passionately. "No, no; and if now that everything has long been at an end between her and me, I have availed myself of the power which circumstances gave me over her—"

"To that subject," Alice interrupted him, "we will not again allude. It is your business, and not mine; and, I repeat, it has not altered you in my estimation. On the contrary, the generous readiness with which you penned that letter ought after all to inspire me with the fullest confidence."

"Oh, let it be so, beautiful Alice," ejaculated the Prince, seizing her hand and pressing it to his lips.

"But, oh, reflect, your Highness," she said, slowly, and as if hesitatingly withdrawing that hand; "you would render me false and faithless to my husband; and if he were to discover—"

"Ah, dearest Alice," interrupted the Prince, "have you not already gone very, very far with me?—did not your looks yesterday bid me hope, and even your words, when you bade me come to you under circumstances of such privacy this evening? Are you not already compromised with your maid in respect to the manner in which I have been introduced hither?—and must you not have every reason to rely upon her fidelity when you resolve to trust her thus far? Who, then, can betray the secret? Oh, render me happy, Alice. I know—I feel that I cannot be altogether indifferent to you."

Alice appeared to be hesitating and yielding. The Prince again took her hand—again pressed it to his lips, and then she whispered in his ear—

"You will be the cause of my undoing; but, oh, it is impossible to resist you!"

From the spot where this colloquy took place the eyes of the Prince could plunge into the bed-chamber, the door of which stood three parts open, and lights were burning there.

Alice made a gesture as if bidding him to proceed thither, and she would follow.

Full of rapture, forgetting also the letter which lay upon the table, the Prince hastened into the chamber, Alice being close behind him.

The moment they had both crossed the threshold, she snatched up the pistol which she had left ready to be thus grasped—she closed the door, and placed her back against it.

At the same moment there was a rustling of the bed draperies; and forth emerged an individual who at the first glance struck the Prince to be some stripling of sixteen or seventeen.

But the light of the tapers flashed on the pistol which this individual likewise carried; and at another glance hastily flung upon the youthful countenance, the Prince recognised Lady Bauksford!

"Ah!" he ejaculated, as the sudden idea of treachery now smote him—or at least what *he* deemed to be treachery; then perceiving that Alice was also armed, he exclaimed, "Good heavens! you would not murder me?"

"Villain!" cried Charlotte, presenting the pistol at his head; "down upon your knees to implore your wretched life!"

"And to surrender up the packet of letters which he has about him!" exclaimed Alice. "Oh, despicable, contemptible creature that you are—did your silly vanity induce you to believe that you were so strong in your fascinations, and I so weak in my principles, as to insure you an easy conquest after the acquaintance of but a few days?"

"It is all very fine, ladies," said the Prince, endeavouring to put a good face upon the matter; "but I am not to be thus duped; and if you drive me to those extremes which may create a disturbance, you will only have yourselves to thank for such a disagreeable result."

"Fool that you must be!" exclaimed Charlotte; "as great an idiot as you are a villain! to suppose that we should not have provided against all contingencies. This chamber was selected for the purpose. It is remote from that part part of the house where the domestics now are: no sound can penetrate beyond its walls—and the report of fire-arms would not be heard out of doors. Ah, it is no longer a weak woman with whom you have to deal. Look upon me as a man—for, by Heaven, I possess the spirit of one—and this garb does not in that sense belie me."

It might have at first seemed to the reader a mere silly and puerile idea for Charlotte to dress herself up in masculine apparel for the proceeding in which she was now engaged; but the calculation which had suggested that course was founded on a knowledge of the character of the Prince.

Like all villains of the mean and despicable stamp, he was more or less a coward; and the presence of that injured girl, apparelled as a man, impressed him with the conviction that it was likewise a man's stern and desperate energy which was inspiring her.

Her features, which were wont to be so soft and pensively interesting in their expression, indicated a stern resoluteness: her face was pale, but her lips quivered not, and her eyes were rivetted vindictively upon the young man.

She held the pistol levelled at his head; and as he glanced aside, he beheld Alice at the door in an equally menacing attitude.

"Good heavens, they will murder me!" he thought within himself: and then in an audible tone he faltered forth—

"What—what do you intend to do?"

But at that instant the door was violently burst open—Alice was thrown forward by the fury of the impulse—and Lord Bauksford, pale with rage, rushed into the chamber.

* * * * *

That the reader may comprehend the cause of this sudden and unexpected appearance of Alice's husband, a few words of explanation must be given.

It was perfectly true that he had made an engagement to dine with a couple of friends at his club; but on arriving there he found a note to inform him that some other engagement prevented them from keeping the appointment.

He knew that his sister Charlotte was to dine with Alice, and finding no one at the club whose society he particularly coveted, he resolved to return home and take his place at the dinner-table at his own house.

On arriving there he inquired of the lady's maid where her mistress was; and he was instantaneously struck by the confusion and bewilderment of the young woman's manner.

"Has my sister come?" he demanded.

"Yes, sir—that is to say—I think so," faltered out the maid; "but I am not quite sure——"

"Well then, I will see for myself," ejaculated

Bauksford abruptly. "I suppose your mistress is up in her own room?"

"Yes, sir—but—but—she is engaged. Pray don't——I mean you had better not disturb her——"

Lord Bauksford regarded the young woman with increased astonishment and suspicion: he hesitated for a moment whether to ask any more questions; but quickly making up his mind, he strode past her and ascended the staircase.

The Abigail withdrew in terror, wondering how it would all end; for she herself did not rightly understand the purpose for which his sister had been dressing herself up in men's clothes, or why the Prince had been so stealthily admitted up into Alice's boudoir.

Of course, however, the maid imagined that some intrigue or love affair was going on, and this was the reason why she was so terrified and confused when questioned by her master.

Meanwhile, as we have said, Bauksford ascended the staircase. and on tiptoe he drew near to the door of his wife's boudoir.

There were strong suspicions in his mind—which was natural enough, considering the perturbed look and manner of the lady's maid; and he thought the statement which had been made to him in the morning that his sister Charlotte was going to dine with Alice might after all have been an invention or pretext to throw him the more effectually off his guard.

Bauksford listened at the door of the boudoir, and the sound of a man's voice met his ears.

Ah! then his suspicion was only too correct—and Alice was a wanton.

But who could her paramour be?

Bauksford continued to listen. He did not at once burst into the room to confront the guilty pair, as he believed them to be; he wished to learn particulars—to ascertain, if possible, how long the amour had progressed—in a word, he was curious to ascertain the circumstances of his own presumed dishonour.

But, ah! the name of his sister was now mentioned.

Surely she was not implicated in any intrigues that were now progressing.

He listened with suspended breath. It was assuredly his wife Alice's voice which he heard in conversation?

Yes! *her* well-known voice that was now speaking seriously of some business-matter which had to be discussed, and then changing into the languid, tremulous accents of love.

Bauksford's ear was now retained motionless at the key-hole; and he soon began to comprehend what the business-matter was which had to be discussed.

The person who was there, in the boudoir, was the Prince.

Was it possible that the Prince had accomplished the dishonour of Charlotte?

Yes, yes! it was but too evident!

A bargaining for the return of her letters was progressing in the boudoir; and Alice was conducting the negotiation.

But how was this?

Was the Prince Alice's paramour?

No—not as yet; for now something was said which showed Lord Bauksford that his wife had only known the Prince for two or three months.

But ah! now that the negotiation was concluded in respect to Charlotte's letters, the Prince was pleading his own cause with Alice.

What would be the result?

Would she not now indignantly command him to quit her presence? Had she not been hitherto temporising and dissembling in order to gain the point on Charlotte's behalf?

Every moment Bauksford expected to hear his wife start up and order the audacious man to quit her presence; but no—her voice was becoming lower—it sounded tremulous in its tone, and Bauksford could no longer catch the sense of the words that were breathed.

He strove to peep through the key-hole, but the sofa where Alice and the Prince were seated was in such a position that he could not command a view of it.

At length he heard footsteps in the boudoir, and the door of the bed-chamber closed.

Ah! then his wife had yielded!—yielded like the veriest wanton to a man whom she had known but a few days.

Bauksford's blood was boiling; and he resolved to wreak a deadly vengeance upon him whom he now looked upon not merely as the seducer of his sister, but likewise of his wife.

He glided along the passage—he traversed the landing—he reached his own dressing-room—and there he provided himself with a brace of loaded pistols.

Hastily retracing his way, he again reached the door of the boudoir; he tried it—it was unlocked—and he entered.

Three strides brought him to the opposite door—his fingers grasped the handle—he pushed the door forward with desperate violence, for he felt that there was some obstacle on the inner side, and he burst into the chamber.

A very different spectacle from what he had anticipated burst upon the eyes of Lord Bauksford.

Instead of discovering his wife embraced in the arms of a paramour, he found that he had hurled her forward from the door; and at the first glance he beheld, as he thought, two persons of the other sex with her.

CHAPTER V.

A DARK NIGHT'S WORK—AN OLD FRIEND ON THE WATCH—CONVEYANCE OF A BODY FROM ITS RESTING-PLACE—THE TRACE OBLITERATED.

THE man whom the Doctor called Lorrocks, but whom we know as the notorious robber, and leader of the Scarlet Brotherhood, the Black Captain hastened away from the Dials, and struck into that interminable labyrinth of dirty streets and lanes leading into Leicester-square on the one hand, and Regent-street on the other.

He walked rapidly until he arrived at a small court, not far from the first-mentioned place.

It was better in its aspect than Pitt's-alley, but it was not a whit more moral in its peculiarities, although its inhabitants were some degrees removed from those who lived under the auspices of Pitt's.

Cragg's-court was the home of the worst class of prostitutes and dissolute foreign mechanics.

It was also the home of Lorrocks, for by this name it is best to call him now.

Plunging into a house, he ran hastily up the stairs and so disappeared.

But he had not shaken off the man who followed him.

That individual clung to his footsteps, and saw him safe into his house before he left him.

"There you are," he said, regarding the door by which Lorrocks had entered, " there you are, my aged sinner ; and now that I know where to put my hand upon you I may retire."

Making a note of the number of the house, he turned on his heel and walked away.

Meanwhile Lorrocks had opened a door on the second floor, and entered a dirty and meanly-furnished room.

Over the fire, nursing her knees, and swaying her aged body to and fro, was a woman of about the same age as the Lorrocks, perhaps a few years younger, but certainly not many.

Her face was shrivelled and distorted, and her hair was scant and silvered ; but in spite of this and her mean attire, there was an air of dignity about her that it was impossible to mistake.

She was quite the woman of whom one would say, in passing her,

" She has seen better times."

On the entrance of Lorrocks she looked up, shuddered, and bent still further over the embers.

" So," he said, fixing his eyes upon her—" so, still moping—still repining."

" What else can I do ?"

" Be merry and enjoy yourself for the remainder of the days that are allotted to you."

" Merry—Heaven and earth !—I have much cause for mirth."

" As much as others."

" As much as others !—and with my past to look back upon ?"

" Your past ! always your past. Haven't you had time enough to forget the past ?"

" No, and it never will be forgotten."

" Bah ! you're a fool."

" I was when I listened to you, and fled the country with you."

" You could do nothing else ; you were a criminal, branded and infamous, and had I not snatched you from the hands set on you by the law, you would have swung on the gibbet with the other members of the Society of Scarlet Brethren — rich, noble, and powerful as you were."

" Psha ! the Prince of Wales would have saved me."

" He would not, and you know it. But I will not say what he might have done had not that unhappy *contretemps* taken place between Lewis and your niece. That, I should say, was sufficient to make him withdraw his countenance, even from her Grace the Duchess of Grasmont."

" Don't — don't mention that name again. Spare me that—for God's sake spare me that !"

" Why should you not hear it ?"

" Why not ? Heaven ! can you ask me that ?"

" Well, I suppose it's bad for you great ones of the land to come down to this. Even I, without a noble name to blush for, sometimes feel my position, and would gladly change it ; but I'm all but callous, and a very small amount of work or excitement drives the past out of my head, and teaches me to live only for the future."

" And the future," said the woman, " the future—what is there in that to live for ?"

" Much. I shall be rich yet—rich, very rich, and then I shall know something of happiness— know something of happiness."

The words were repeated again and again by the woman, but in a tone that plainly indicated the words conveyed no hope to her bosom.

This, then, was the once notorious Black Captain, and the no less notorious Duchess of Grasmont.

This was the pass that crime had brought them to.

The property her crimes had forced her to abandon now lay fallow in the grasp of the law, and there was no claimant for it.

What the real heiress was doing all this time we have got to see.

Lorrocks knew that she was alive, knew that she was in London, had determined to possess himself of all the wealth of the dukedom of Grasmont, but of his plans the duchess knew nothing.

He did not intend that she should just then.

It was one hour after his entrance into the house that a knock came at his door, and roused Lorrocks from the reverie into which he had fallen after the conversation with the wretched woman he had helped to ruin and degrade.

" Ah," he said springing to his feet, " Ah, that's him, now you get up stairs and stay there till I call you down."

" That's a nice way to speak to——"

" A Duchess ! I know what you're going to say. But it's no use to keep eternally dinning that into my ears. Now get out ; my business is important."

" Who is it with ?"

" You shall see."

He opened the door as he spoke, and admitted a very old and broken-down old man who appeared to be tottering to his grave.

The old fellow carried a musty blue bag, and had all the appearance of having been a lawyer.

There is a something in this profession that stamps those who follow it with a mark as indelible as that placed upon those who follow the profession of arms, or " go down to the sea in ships."

The old fellow entered with an affectation of brusqueness, and raised his hat to the lady.

"My duty, madam. I suppose you've forgotten me; but I know *you* full well—full well. You're the Duchess. Oh, don't fear me—don't fear me; I wouldn't betray your presence for the world; not I—not I. I'm seventy-five – seventy-five; and you were a client of mine once. Yes, yes; old friends have claims, and I wouldn't sacrifice yours. No, no!"

"Ah, I know you now. Years have passed since we met, but I remember your face, changed though it is."

"You remember me?"

"Yes; you are Grimer, the lawyer."

"I was, I was; but times are changed. I can't do now what I did then. I *was* a sharp practitioner, *I* was. No one ever got over me. No one ever got a bit the better of me. No, no; I was too sharp for them all—too sharp! Ah, ah, ah! But there's something of the fire left in me still; something—something. It's not all gone, and I'll prove it yet. I will—I will."

Muttering these words, he advanced into the apartment, and the old lady made for the door.

It was held open for her by Lorrocks.

"You here!" she whispered to him, as she passed; "then *I know* what your business is."

"Well?"

"Well, I shall ask you the result of this interview, and I shall insist on knowing."

She went out.

"You'll insist upon knowing, will you? Oh, indeed, madam; that's it, is it? Now, if you're troublesome I shall begin to imagine you a *cat!*"

He put his hand inside his vest, and it rested on a small phial.

A gleam of triumph passed over his face, and he turned to confront his visitor.

"Well, Grimer—well old man, what news, what news?"

"Ah, you're obliged to come to me for news after all, you are—you are—you can't help it. It was Grimer who started this game. It was Grimer who found the daughter of the Duke of Grasmont. It was Grimer who foraged up the proofs; it was Grimer who received and kept your secret. It was Grimer who secured the girl—"

"It was Grimer who lost her; and it was Grimer, and no one but Grimer, who kept his paper in a place so accessible that a non-professional man found them, and would have secured them had I not stepped in and taken them."

"But who found out the return of the heiress to England? Who knew where to put his hand upon her?"

"And who," mentally asked Lorrocks, "who was drivelling old imbecile enough to come and tell me all about it, and thus put the game into my hands?"

But these queries he kept to himself.

"And, now, what news?" asked Lorrocks.

"News? No news that I know of. I've been on the watch, and she's here all right, and easily got at. That's all."

"Well."

"Well, her husband, Lord Lovelace, died abroad, and now she's the wife of that boy—"

"What boy?"

"Pipey. Oh, a fine sharp boy he always was. He, he!—my boy, my boy."

"Yes, a sharp boy indeed, but I've no affection for him. He once sold me. Ah! the way in which he got out of that dungeon, after being sealed up for life, beats me—beats me!"

"Take my advice," said the old lawyer, "take my advice and don't cross his path. He's dangerous, and the only way to get through this business now is to keep out of his sight. Open warfare must'nt be thought of."

"True, true; I've thought of that. I won't cross him, and I'm sure he won't recognise me."

False security. Did he but know that the enemy he so dreaded had marked all his acts and had been following him for hours that very night.

"But we must drop the great game for a while," said the old lawyer, "smaller fish want frying and must be attended to."

"What's to be done now?"

"There's work at St. Sepulchre's to-night."

"Oh!"

"Yes, I've a job for you."

"A doctor's job?"

"No: a better paying one."

"Well?"

"You know that Lady Hawkshaw died suddenly last week?"

"I read of it."

"Well, it was thought that all was right—heart disease, and all that sort of thing, but now the relatives of her ladyship have come suddenly from Spain, and demand an inquest."

"Well."

"To-morrow the body will be disinterred."

"Again—well."

"It is not well. On the contrary, it's bad—very bad, and mustn't take place."

"Who says so?"

"Sir John Hawkshaw."

"Then there was foul play there."

"I suspect so."

"Has Sir John been to you?"

"No; but his paramour, and, as I suppose, the murderer of his wife, has done me the honour of calling at my office."

"And the result?"

"Was a reward of one hundred pounds for snatching the body to-night, and effectually destroying it."

"Whew! St. Sepulchre's, hey?"

"Yes."

"A dangerous game to play there."

"Yes."

"And a hundred pounds is the reward?"

"No more, nor less."

"Well, then, you had best go elsewhere and find some one to do the work. I'm not going to jeopardise my neck for one hundred pounds."

"The devil!" wheezed the old miser. "Do you mean to say you refuse?"

"Most distinctly."

"But you can't. I've undertaken the job."

"More fool you."

"But—"

"Nonsense! A baronet, a murder, and the danger of doing such a job in the centre of London. It's preposterous."

"How nonsense? I don't want *much* of the money. I'll give up my just share, and give you seventy-five."

"It won't do."

"But what am I to do? It's too late to go further to look for one, and the job's on my hands."

"Let it stop there."

"Nonsense, nonsense; be reasonable. Now, let us talk it over: I'll give up *all* my share— you shall have the whole hundred! Think of that—the whole hundred. I've pledged my word, you know, and to keep it I must make a sacrifice; I must, indeed."

"Poor fellow."

"Now, don't sneer so; say you'll do it—say you'll do it."

"I will."

"Ah, I knew you would."

"For the sum of five hundred pounds!"

The old lawyer looked as if he would fall from his seat with amazement.

"Five hundred pounds," he repeated.

"Just that sum."

"But I—I only had one hundred for the job, how can I."

"Now don't think to humbug me? your old and downy, but I'm a degree above you. You never could best me, so don't try it now, for I know you too well to suppose you would undertake such a job at the sum of one hundred pounds, absurd, absurd."

"But I assure you."

"Don't take the trouble."

"But Lorrocks, dear, good, Lorrocks."

"I'm nothing of the sort. I'm old, griping, grasping Lorrocks, and you know it, so no more oily words to me."

"You've settled on the matter?"

"Quite."

"Well, as I've pledged my word, I *must* carry out this business at a sacrifice. I'll give one hundred and fifty."

"No you won't."

"Now—now."

"Now now, *don't* try it on, it's nothing more nor less than a waste of time, and you will have the satisfaction of knowing, after a while, that your labour has been lost."

"Well, then, I must say the two hundred."

"It won't do."

"Why, three then."

"Say five at once, or *I'll make it seven, and I won't budge without it.*"

"Oh, you're awful, you're incorrigible," said the lawyer, pretending to look beyond measure astonished.

"Well, what say you?"

Think of the sacrifice I'm making and be merciful."

"I know the nature of your sacrifices, old fellow."

"And you won't hedge under five?"

"Another word and it's seven."

"Well five be it."

"I thought I should get it."

"Ah, you know how to do me. It's awful— to think on the manner in which I am victim-ised."

"It is."

"You're sneering at me, but I declare myself to be a perfect martyr."

"I know you are."

"Well, then, be more merciful."

"Not this time."

"Hard as flints; but I'll be even with you for it, I will, I will."

"Now no more mumbling, but just explain what's to be done, and let us understand one another."

"That's best."

"Is it a vault, or a common grave."

"A common grave."

"Ah! The baronet had an eye to business when he selected a common grave."

"Perhaps so."

"I shall want a mate."

"You will."

"There's old Death's Head; he'll go with me to-night."

"Yes: and there's a third party to be there."

"Yourself?"

"No; the lady I mentioned just now. She won't give up the game till the body is destroyed."

"What a devil."

"You would say so if you only knew her."

"Perhaps I shall to-night."

"No doubt of it. Well, I must go now, but mind, St. Sepulchre's at midnight."

"At midnight."

The two hoary villains grasped hands, and the lawyer went his way."

"A devil of a job this," muttered the body-snatcher, as his friend disappeared.

*   *   *   *   *

It was quite midnight before Lorrocks stood at the gate of St. Sepulchre's.

With him was an old man, who appeared to be a living skeleton.

After waiting for a few moments, this pair of worthies were joined by a young woman of great personal beauty, and by her side tottered the old lawyer.

"This is the man," said Grimer, introducing Lorrocks. "This is the man who will do the business."

The woman scrutinised his face with great anxiety.

"You are to be trusted?"

"Trusted?" said Lorrooks. I've kept far more important secrets than this in my time."

The woman said no more, but motioned im-patiently for him to enter the churchyard.

Old Death's Head, as Lorrocks called his com-panion, produced a key which he applied to the lock, and in a moment they stood within the yard.

"You keep watch from this place," said Grimer, "the signal will be a whistle."

They were gone out of sight, and the lawyer was left to his vigil.

*   *   *   *   *

"That's the grave," said the woman to her companion, pointing out a recent mound.

"All right."

"Be speedy. '

"I shall for my own sake, you may depend."

Lorrocks produced an implement, which he lowered into the mould by a screw-like process.

At length he applied a strong leverage and the earth was raised.

Up it came.

Still up.

And at length the head of a coffin presented itself.

More implements were produced.

Marvels of ingenuity, which appeared to perform the work by magic.

One of these tools was placed against the head of the coffin.

"Now for it," said Lorrocks, with a grin.

He exerted some little strength, a circular saw was set in motion and the head of the coffin came away in his hand.

"Faugh!" he said. "This job is worth as many thousands as hundreds have been paid for it. I can smell the *Prussic acid* now."

The woman shuddered.

"Prussic acid s a devil of a tell-tale," continued Lorrocks. "I wonder people will use it."

"Silence."

"Why ?'

"We may be overheard."

"Not much fear. Grimer is at the gate, and that's the only means of approach."

"But do not speak. I cannot bear to hear you."

"Poor soul! and yet, if report speaks true,

you are not given to be so very shakey in the nerves."

"Silence."

"Oh, yes, with all my heart. Here, old Death, pull her out; she's too far gone for me. I've a strong stomach, but I shouldn't relish my supper after touching *her*."

"Old Death" placed his hand in the head of the coffin, and dragged forth a body in a most advanced state of decomposition.

"Now then," said the grim old man, "what next?"

"Just this. Bear her to the north side of the church. Fever's reigning awful just now, and there's about twenty paupers' graves open for to-morrow's work. We'll use one of 'em, and when the traces are wiped off no one will be the wiser."

Applying his implements again, the coffin from which the corpse was abstracted was forced back into the grave, and all traces of its being disturbed was skilfully wiped out by Lorrocks.

They then all three repaired to the south side of the church, Death carrying the awful corpse, and then it was found that Lorrocks was right.

Many shallow graves were open.

"Any one will do," he said. "Toss her in."

Death did as desired.

"Is this safe?" said the woman.

"Quite safe," said Lorrocks.

"Quick, then; I tremble with fear."

"All's well."

"I trust so."

But at this moment Grimer gave the signal of danger.

CHAPTER VI.

CAROLINE OF BRUNSWICK—STATE OF AFFAIRS IN THE ROYAL FAMILY OF ENGLAND—PERSECUTIONS, AND THE FORESHADOWING OF RETRIBUTION.

LORD BANKSFORD was speechless on beholding the real state of affairs in his wife's chamber.

As a matter of course he could not avenge himself as he would wish on the royal betrayer of his sister.

That he thirsted to wipe out the stain upon his name with blood may readily be supposed; but the libertine was a prince, and that sacred rank forced the young noble to hold his hand.

His wretched sister he at first spurned from him, but at length relenting, he consented to forgive her crime, take her to his heart, and forget the past as far as she was concerned in it.

For her betrayer, however, there was no forgetfulness.

His lordship joined the ranks of those fierce radicals who were then becoming formidable, not alone in the country, but in the House of Commons.

Daily and hourly a tremendous party was springing into existence, bent on changing the aspect of affairs; resolved on righting the neglected and injured Princess, and reforming the Court of the poor old imbecile George III., under the sway of his prodigal son.

Truly at that time England was in as fearful a state as could possibly be conceived.

Hear what Thackeray says on this theme:—

"Nature and circumstances had done their utmost to prepare the Prince for being spoiled; the dreadful dullness of papa's court, its stupid amusements, its dreary occupations, the maddening humdrum, the stifling sobriety of its routine, would have made a scapegrace of a much less lively prince.

"All the big princes bolted from that castle of *ennui*, where old King George sat, posting up his books and droning over his Handel; and old Queen Charlotte over her snuff and her tambour-frame.

"Most of the sturdy, gallant sons settled down after sowing their wild oats, and became sober subjects of their father and brother—not ill-liked by the nation, which pardons youthful irregularities readily enough for the sake of pluck, and unaffectedness, and good-humour.

"His biographers say that when he commenced housekeeping in that splendid new palace of his, the Prince of Wales had some windy projects of encouraging literature, science, and the arts—of having assemblies of literary characters, and societies for the encouragement of geography, astronomy, and botany.

"Astronomy, geography, and botany!

"Fiddlesticks!

"French ballet-dancers, French cooks, horse-jockeys, buffoons, procurers, tailors, boxers, fencing-masters, china, jewel and gimcrack merchants—these were his real companions.

"At first he made a pretence of having Burke, and Pitt, and Sheridan for his friends.

"But how could such men be serious before such an empty scapegrace as this lad?

"Fox might talk dice with him, and Sheridan wine; but what else had these men of genius in common with their tawdry young host of Carlton House?

"That fribble, the leader of such men as Fox and Burke!

"That man's opinions about the Constitution, the India Bill, justice to the Catholics—about any question graver than the button for a waistcoat, or the sauce for a partridge—worth anything!

"The friendship between the Prince and the Whig chiefs was impossible.

"They were hypocrites in pretending to respect him, and if he broke the hollow compact between them, who shall blame him?

"His natural companions were dandies and parasites.

"He could talk to a tailor or a cook: but, as the equal of great statesmen, to set up a creature, lazy, weak, indolent, besotted, of monstrous vanity, and levity incurable—it is absurd.

"They thought to use him, and did for awhile; but they must have known how timid he was—how entirely heartless and treacherous, and have expected his desertion.

"His next set of friends were mere table companions, of whom he grew tired, too; then we hear of him with a very few select toadies—mere boys from school or the Guards, whose sprightliness tickled the fancy of the worn-out voluptuary.

"What matters what friends he had?

"He dropped all his friends: he never could have real friends.

"An heir to the throne has flatterers, adventurers who hang about him, ambitious men who use him; but friendship is denied him.

"And women, I suppose, are as false and selfish in their dealings with such a character as men.

"Shall we take the Leporello part—flourish a catalogue of the conquests of this royal Don Juan, and tell the names of the favourites to whom, one after the other, George Prince flung his pocket-handkerchief?

"What purpose would it answer to say how Perdita was pursued, won, deserted, and by whom succeeded?

"What good in knowing that he did actually marry Mrs. Fitz-Herbert according to the rites of the Roman Catholic Church; that her marriage settlements have been seen in London; that the names of the witnesses to her marriage are known.

"This sort of vice that we are now come to presents no new or fleeting trait of manners.

"Debauchees — dissolute, heartless, fickle, cowardly— have been ever since the world began.

"This one had more temptations than most, and so much may be said in extenuation for him.

"It was an unlucky thing for this doomed one, and tending to lead him yet farther on the road to the deuce, that, besides being lovely, so that women were fascinated by him; and heir apparent, so that all the world flattered him; he should have a beautiful voice, which led him directly in the way of drink; and thus all the pleasant devils were coaxing on poor Florizel: desire, and idleness, and vanity, and drunkenness, all clashing their merry cymbals and bidding him come on.

"We first hear of his warbling sentimental ditties under the walls of Kew Palace by the moonlight banks of Thames, with Lord Viscount Leporello keeping watch lest the music should be disturbed.

"Singing after dinner and supper was the universal fashion of the day.

"You may fancy all England sounding with choruses, some ribald, some harmless, but all occasioning the consumption of a prodigious deal of fermented liquor.

"The jolly muse her wings to try no frolic flights need take,
But round the bowl would dip and fly, like swallows round a lake,"

sang Morris, in one of his gallant Anacreontics, to which the Prince many a time joined in chorus, and of which the burden is—

'And that I think's a reason fair to drink and fill again."

"This delightful boon companion of the Prince's found 'a reason fair' to forego filling and drinking, saw the error of his ways, gave up the bowl and chorus, and died retired and religious.

"The Prince's table, no doubt, was a very tempting one.

"The wits came and did their utmost to amuse him.

"It is wonderful how the spirits rise, the wit brightens, the wine has an aroma, when a great man is at the head of the table.

"Scott, the loyal cavalier, the king's true liegeman, the very best *raconteur* of his time, poured out with an endless generosity his store of old-world learning, kindness, and humour.

"Grattan contributed to it his wondrous eloquence, fancy, feeling.

"Tom Moore perched upon it for awhile, and piped his most exquisite little love-tunes on it, flying away in a twitter of indignation afterwards, and attacking the Prince with bill and claw.

"In such society no wonder the sitting was long, and the butler tired of drawing corks.

"Remember what the usages of the time were, and that William Pitt, coming to the House of Commons after having drunk a bottle of port wine at his own house, would go into Bellamy's with Dundas, and help to finish a couple more.

"You peruse volumes after volumes about our Prince, and find some stock half-dozen stories —indeed, not many more—common to all the histories.

"He was good-natured; an indolent, voluptuous prince, not unkindly.

"One story, the most favourable to him of all, perhaps, is that, as Prince Regent, he was eager to hear all that could be said in behalf of prisoners condemned to death, and anxious, if possible, to remit the capital sentence.

"He was kind to his servants.

"There is a story common to all the biographies, of Molly the housemaid, who, when his household was to be broken up, owing to some reforms which he tried absurdly to practise, was discovered crying as she dusted the chairs because she was to leave a master who had a kind word for all his servants.

"Another tale is that of a groom of the Prince's being discovered in corn and oat peculations, and dismissed by the personage at the head of the stables; the Prince had word of John's disgrace, remonstrated with him very kindly, generously reinstated him, and bade him promise to sin no more—a promise which John kept.

"Another story is very fondly told of the Prince as a young man, hearing of an officer's family in distress, and how he straightway borrowed six or eight hundred pounds, put his long fair hair under his hat, and, so disguised, carried the money to the starving family.

"He sent money, too, to Sheridan on his death-bed, and would have sent more had not death ended the career of that man of genius.

"Besides these, there are a few pretty speeches, kind and graceful, to persons with whom he was brought in contact.

"But he turned upon twenty friends.

"He was fond and familiar with them one

day, and he passed them on the next without recognition.

"He used them, liked them, loved them, perhaps, in his way, and then separated from them.

"On Monday he kissed and fondled poor Perdita, and on Tuesday he met her and did not know her.

"On Wednesday he was very affectionate with that wretched Brummell, and on Thursday forgot him; cheated him even out of a snuff-box which he owed the poor dandy; saw him years afterwards in his downfall and poverty, when the bankrupt Beau sent him another snuff-box with some of the snuff he used to love, as a piteous token of remembrance and submission, and the king took the snuff, and ordered his horses, and drove on, and had not the grace to notice his old companion, favourite, rival, enemy, superior.

"In Wraxall there is some gossip about him.

"When the charming, beautiful, generous Duchess of Devonshire died—the lovely lady whom he used to call his dearest duchess once, and pretend to admire as all English society admired her—he said—

"'Then we have lost the best bred woman in England.'

"'Then we have lost the kindest heart in England,' said noble Charles Fox.

"On another occasion, when three noblemen were to receive the Garter, says Wraxall—

"A great personage observed that never did three men receive the order in so characteristic a manner. The Duke of A. advanced to the sovereign with a phlegmatic, cold, awkward air like a clown; Lord B. came forward fawning and smiling like a courtier; Lord C. presented himself, easy, unembarrassed, like a gentleman!'

"These are the stories one has to recall about the Prince and King—kindness to a housemaid, generosity to a groom, criticism on a bow.

"There are no better stories about him; they are mean and trivial, and they characterise him.

"The great war of empires and giants goes on.

"Day by day victories are won and lost by the brave. Torn, smoky flags and battered eagles are wrenched from the heroic enemy and laid at his feet; and he sits there on his throne and smiles, and gives the guerdon of valour to the conqueror.

"He! Elliston the actor, when the 'Coronation' was performed, in which he took the principal part, used to fancy himself the king, burst into tears, and hiccup a blessing on the people. I believe it is certain about George IV., that he had heard so much of the war, knighted so many people, and worn such a prodigious quantity of marshal's uniforms, cocked hats, cock's feathers, scarlet and bullion in general, that he actually fancied he had been present in some campaigns, and, under the name of General Brock, led a tremendous charge of the German legion at Waterloo.

"He is dead but thirty years, and one asks how a great society could have tolerated him?

"Would we bear him now?

"In this quarter of a century what a silent revolution has been working! how it has separated us from old times and manners! How it has changed men themselves!

"I can see old gentlemen now among us, of perfect good breeding, of quiet lives, with venerable grey heads, fondling their grandchildren; and look at them, and wonder at what they were once.

"That gentleman of the grand old school, when he was in the 10th Hussars, and dined at the Prince's table, would fall under it night after night.

"Night after night that gentleman sat at Brooke's or Raggett's over the dice.

"If, in the petulance of play or drink, that gentleman spoke a sharp word to his neighbour, he and the other would infallibly go out and try to shoot each other the next morning.

That gentleman would drive his friend Richmond, the black boxer, down to Moulsey, and hold his coat, and shout and swear, and hurrah with delight, whilst the black man was beating Dutch Sam the Jew.

"That gentleman would take a manly pleasure in pulling his own coat off, and thrashing a bargeman in a street row.

"That gentleman has been in a watchhouse.

"That gentleman, so exquisitely polite to ladies in a drawing-room, so loftily courteous, if he talked now as he used among men in his youth, would swear so as to make your hair stand on end.

"I met lately a very old German gentleman, who had served in our army at the beginning of the century.

"Since then he has lived on his own estate, but rarely meeting with an Englishman, whose language—the language of fifty years ago that is—he possesses perfectly.

"When this highly bred old man began to speak English to me, almost every other word he uttered was an oath: as they used it (they swore dreadfully in Flanders) with the Duke of York before Valenciennes, or at Carlton House over the supper and cards.

'Many of my readers, no doubt, have journeyed to the pretty old town of Brunswick, in company with that most worthy, prudent, and polite gentleman, the Earl of Malmesbury, and fetched away Princess Caroline for her longing husband, the Prince of Wales.

"Old Queen Charlotte would have had her eldest son marry a niece of her own, that famous Louisa of Strelitz, afterwards Queen of Prussia, and who shares with Marie Antoinette in the last age the sad pre-eminence of beauty and misfortune.

"But George III. had a niece at Brunswick; she was a richer princess than her Serene Highness of Strelitz. In fine, the Princess Caroline was selected to marry the heir to the English throne.

"We follow my Lord Malmesbury in quest of her; we are introduced to her illustrious father and royal mother; we witness the balls and fêtes of the old Court; we are presented to the princess herself, with her fair hair, her blue eyes, and her impertinent shoulders—a lively, bouncing, romping princess, who takes the advice of her courtly English mentor most generously and kindly.

"We can be present at her very toilette, if we like, regarding which, and for very good reasons, the British courtier implores her to be particular.

"What a strange Court!

"What a queer privacy of morals and manners do we look into!

"Shall we regard it as preachers and moralists, and cry, ' Woe, against the open vice, and selfishness, and corruption; or look at it as we do at the king in the pantomime, with his pantomime wife, and pantomime courtiers, whose big heads he knocks together, whom he pokes with his pantomime sceptre, whom he orders to prison under the guard of his pantomine beefeaters, as he sits down to dine on his pantomime pudding?

"It is grave, it is sad, it is theme most curious for moral and political speculation; it is monstrous, grotesque, laughable, with its prodigious littlenesses, etiquettes, ceremonials, sham moralities; it is as serious as a sermon, and as absurd and outrageous as Punch's puppet-show.

"Malmesbury tells us of the private life of the duke, Princess Caroline's father, who was to die, like his warlike son, in arms against the French; presents us to his courtiers, his favourite; his duchess, George III.'s sister, a grim old princess, who took the British envoy aside, and told him wicked old stories of wicked old dead people and times; who came to England afterwards when her nephew was Regent, and lived in a shabby furnished lodging, old, and dingy, and deserted, and grotesque, but somehow royal.

"And we go with him to the duke to demand the Princess's hand in form, and we hear the Brunswick guns fire their adieus of salute, as H.R.H. the Princess of Wales departs in the frost and snow; and we visit the domains of the Prince Bishop of Osnaburg—the Duke of York of our early time; and we dodge about from the French revolutionists, whose ragged legions are pouring over Holland and Germany, and gaily trampling down the old world to the tune of ça ira; and we take shipping at Slade, and we land at Greenwich, where the Princess's ladies and the Prince's ladies are in waiting to receive her royal highness

"What a history follows? Arrived in London, the bridegroom hastened eagerly to receive his bride.

"When she was first presented to him, Lord Malmesbury says she very properly attempted to kneel.

"He raised her gracefully enough, embraced her, and turning round to me, said,—

"' Harris, I am not well; pray get me a glass of brandy?'

"I said, 'Sir, had you not better have a glass of water?'

"Upon which, much out of humour, he said, with an oath, ' No: I will go to the Queen."

What could be expected from a wedding which had such a beginning—from such a bridegroom and such a bride?

"I am not going to carry you through the scandal of that story, or follow the poor Princess through all her vagaries; her balls and her dances, her travels to Jerusalem and Naples, her jigs, and her junketings, and her tears.

"As I read her trial in history, I vote she is not guilty.

"I don't say it is an impartial verdict; but as one reads her story, the heart bleeds for the kindly, generous, outraged creature.

"If wrong there be, let it lie at his door who wickedly thrust her from it. Spite of her follies, the great, hearty people of England loved, and protected, and pitied her.

"' God bless you! we will bring your husband back to you,' said a mechanic one day, as she told Lady Charlotte Bury with tears streaming down her cheeks.

"They could not bring that husband back; they could not cleanse that selfish heart. Was her's the only one he had wounded?

"Steeped in selfishness, impotent for faithful attachment and manly enduring love,—had it not survived remorse, was it not accustomed to desertion?

"Malmesbury gives us the beginning of the marriage story;—how the Prince reeled into chapel to be married; how he hiccupped out his vows of fidelity—you know how he kept them; how he pursued the woman whom he had married; to what a state he brought her; with what blows he struck her; with what malignity he pursued her; what his treatment of his daughter was; and what his own life.

"He the first gentleman of Europe! There is no stronger satire on the proud English society of that day, than that they admired George.

So much for Thackeray's picture of the Court life of the period.

It can, however, be heightened in its colouring without any exaggeration in the details.

At Windsor there was the poor old blind man, the third George of England, reduced to a state of idiotcy.

In the grim old castle he might have been seen groping his way about the apartments allotted him, and chattering unintelligible gibberish to his keepers.

This, too, whilst his son, the heir to the throne, and the virtual ruler of the nation, was framing the most awful debauches at the Pavilion of Brighton; seducing all the poor wretches chance threw in his path, and plotting to rid himself of the wife who had grown detestable in his sight.

The nation was growing furious, and that fury was in every conceivable way augmented by the characters who have played conspicuous parts in this tale.

The Prince had wronged them shamefully; he had cut their honour to the quick; he had stamped out the virtue of the women, and betrayed the friendship of the men.

The time was now coming for retribution.

It was to be awful in its intensity.

How awful will soon be apparent to the reader,

for a few more chapters will bring these chronicles to the end.

We draw near the last scene.

We approach the climax, but the horrors we have detailed, the intense suffering we have depicted in these pictures of *trial and temptation*, have not yet reached the culminating point.

The youthful Lord Lovelace, Lord Banksford, and hundreds of other nobles, were agitating in the upper circles.

Young Lovelace had learnt the history of his unhappy father from his mother, and became the deadly enemy of the Prince. Banksford was implacable, and when the Princess went to Italy in 1814 he followed her, and swore fidelity to her.

He had many imitators.

CHAPTER VII.

THE SIGNAL—GRIMER AND AN ACQUAINTANCE FACE TO FACE—THE ESCAPE OF LORROCKS—THE PURSUIT AND CAPTURE.

THE consternation in the churchyard on hearing the danger signal given by Grimer was nothing short of tremendous.

"Hark!" said Lorrocks; "that's Grimer."

"Is there danger?" asked the woman.

"Danger! D'ye think Grimer's fool enough to disturb us without occasion?"

"What is to be done?"

"Look here," said Lorrocks, hastily addressing his ancient companion, "get the traces of the work wiped away quickly. You are known to assist the sexton here, and nobody will take any notice of you. We must run for it," said he, addressing the woman; "there's another gate, and for that we must make as fast as our feet will carry us."

He seized the hand of the woman as he spoke, and hurried off with her.

We will return to Grimer.

*   *   *   *   *

The old lawyer had kept watch until the instant of giving the signal without seeing or hearing anything to alarm him.

Suddenly, as if it had started out of the earth, came a figure before him.

"Hillo!" said Grimer, his teeth chattering with fear, "what's this? Who are you—and what d'ye want here?"

"I'm not unknown to you, and my business is very simple. I want you and your friends."

"Eh?—what?"

"Don't you recognise me?"

"No."

"I'll bring myself back to your memory by one word—PIPEY!"

The old man started.

"Saints protect us!" he cried, in an agony of fear, "it's the boy himself!"

"So you *do* remember me!"

"Yes, yes! But I'm busy now. Get away—get away! You know where to find me: come and see me to-morrow."

"To-morrow won't do for me, because your friend the Black Captain, *alias* Lorrocks, may not be with you. I want *him* as much as yourself."

"Lorrocks! I know no such person."

"Oh! Don't you?"

"No."

"Well, that's a pity; because you ought not to keep the society of people you do not know."

"What mean you?"

"I mean that this Lorrocks is in the churchyard. I know his business here—I know your business here. But *that* has little to do with me. I'm on a different matter."

"What is it?"

"I want *the will bequeathing the Grasmount property to my wife!*"

"Your wife?"

"Yes, my wife; once Fair Liz, the ballad singer; then Lady Lovelace; *now* Mrs. De Pipes."

"Goodness gracious!"

"You appear astonished, but that's nothing to me. What about that will?"

"I know nothing of it."

"It's a lie!"

"It's the truth!"

"If you have it not—and I am willing to believe that it is not in your possession—tell me who has it?"

"I—I—"

"No hesitation. The Black Captain *had it*—has he got it *now?*"

"As far as I know—"

"He has?"

"Yes."

"And he is in that churchyard. Well, the opportunity is an admirable one. Farewell, Mr. Grimer; you may rely upon it I'll soon relieve your friend of my personal property."

Pipey—for the individual coming thus suddenly on the scene was no other than our hero—here bounded through the gate of the churchyard, and hastened up the gravel path.

He had not proceeded far when Grimer gave the signal of danger.

"Confound it!" said Pipey. "I should have gagged the old bird; but no matter."

He now quickened his pace, but as he came near the spot where he thought to find his birds, he beheld them flying.

The old Death's Head was there, but Lorrocks and the woman were disappearing through the second gate.

Pipey paused not an instant.

He dashed forward at an immense rate, and was soon upon the heels of the pair.

Finding himself so hotly pursued, Lorrocks quitted his companion, and darting into a lane on his left, immediately disappeared.

His pursuer was not, however, to be baffled.

He pressed on, but unfortunately he had lost the scent.

Pipey paused to reflect.

"He will not go to his home," he said to himself; "he is too wise for that. Where shall I seek him?"

A moment's thought, and he started off again.

He took the nearest route to the spot where he had witnessed the interview between Lorrocks and Dr. Python.

It was daylight when he reached the dismal den in the Dials.

He darted up the dark passage we have before described, and, as fortune would have it, caught sight of his man hastening with as much speed as he could use into the little tenement in which Dr. Python exhibited his humanity towards the dying woman.

With a leap, such as would be made by a leopard in pouncing upon his prey, Pipey darted upon Lorrocks.

He seized him by the throat, and forced him off his legs.

"Villain!" he cried; "I have waited years to repay you for the trick you once served me, and to force from you the will of the old Duke of Grasmount. You are in my power now, and by Heaven, I'll have revenge!"

CHAPTER VIII

THE RETURN OF THE PRINCESS FROM ITALY— THE TRIAL—THE SENTENCE.

WE now arrive at that momentous point in the life of Caroline when she had to undergo that awful trial which was to end in her degradation and shame.

Caroline had returned from Italy!

The news spread, and London was in a frenzy of excitement.

Of the life she had been leading during her exile there was many an unfavourable, and even foul whisper; she had been followed in her wanderings, and all the reports that were multiplying against her were collected, and sent to London, as fresh matters of accusation, should circumstances compel such a step.

Ambassadors, instructed from home, refused to recognise her as Princess of Wales, and the Courts at which they resided were closed against her entrance.

But when her name was struck out of the Liturgy, and the recognition of her rank as Queen withheld at the accession of her husband, she felt as if her silence would justify her condemnation—that she must come to England to demand an open trial, and vindicate her innocence and her claims.

She may have felt, too, that from the irritated state of public feeling, and the unpopularity of George IV., the bulk of the nation, right or wrong, would be ready to advocate her cause.

Mr. Brougham (now Lord Brougham) her principal legal adviser, received her commands to meet her in France.

He left London on the 1st of June, bearing the following proposition to the Queen, which had been placed in his hands by Lord Liverpool, the premier :—

" The King is willing to recommend Parliament to enable his Majesty to settle an annuity of £50,000 a year upon the Queen, to be enjoyed by her during her natural life, and in lieu of any claim in the nature of jointure or otherwise, provided she will engage not to come into any part of the British dominions, and provided she engages to take some other name or title than that of queen, and not to exercise any of the rights or privileges of Queen, either with respect to the appointment of law officers, or to any proceedings in courts of justice. The annuity to cease upon the violation of these engagements, viz., upon her coming into any part of the British dominions; or her assuming the title of Queen; or her exercising any of the rights or privileges of Queen, other than above excepted, after the annuity shall have been settled upon her."

The Princess, who ever proclaimed that she was supported by the consciousness of her own innocence, rejected these propositions with disdain, and declared that she would presently be in England to confront her enemies, and to appeal to a generous people.

She was at Calais, on her way to London, on the 5th of June, 1820, and the intelligence was conveyed to Whitehall by telegraph.

A cabinet council was assembled hereupon, and it sat through nearly the whole night.

On the next morning—the morning of the 6th—the King went in state to give the royal assent to such bills as had passed Parliament; and, this being done, he left Lord Liverpool to deliver the following message to the Lords :—

" The King thinks it necessary, in consequence of the arrival of the Queen, to communicate to the House of Lords certain papers respecting the conduct of her Majesty since her departure from this kingdom, which he recommends to the immediate and serious attention of this House."

The papers referred to were laid on the table in a green bag, which was sealed.

This was the famous green bag which made such a figure in the chronicles of the day.

A similar message was delivered to the Commons by Lord Castlereagh.

Both ministers announced the intention to move an address to the King, and to refer the papers to a secret committee on the following day.

The Lords were silent; but in the Commons there was some vehement debate.

On the 7th Lord Liverpool proposed that the papers should be submitted to a secret committee of fifteen peers, to be appointed by ballot.

Lord Liverpool, however, announced that the course to be pursued against the Queen could not be an impeachment for treasonable conspiracy, seeing that Bergami, the alleged partner in her guilt, being an alien, was not amenable as a traitor to the crown of England, and that to constitute conspiracy there must be at least two criminals.

The secret committee was appointed by ballot on the following day.

While this was passing in the Lords there was another vehement debate in the Commons.

Mr. Brougham presented a message from the Queen, which set forth that she had come to claim her rights and maintain her innocence; that she protested against a secret tribunal appointed by her accusers; and, finally, that she appealed to the justice of the House of Commons.

Lord Castlereagh declared that ministers were neither persecutors nor prosecutors in this matter; and that the illustrious personage would not and could not be judged without an open inquiry and examination of witnesses.

Mr. Canning, who entertained a kind and generous feeling towards the Princess, solemnly vowed that he would never place himself in the situation of her accuser.

The same eminent orator and statesman declared that he would take no further share in these deliberations; and, finding the cabinet resolved to proceed, he very soon resigned his office.

Mr. Wilberforce moved the adjournment of the question to the next day but one, in the hope that during the interval some amicable arrangement would prevent a disgusting investigation, which might go far to taint the public morals, and which could not but degrade the two contending parties—the King as well as the Queen.

This motion was agreed to, and for several days there was silence in the House upon the subject.

Caroline of Brunswick had landed at Dover from the ordinary packet on the 6th, accompanied by Alderman Wood and Lady Ann Hamilton.

Her entry into London was a kind of triumph, for she was received with joyful acclamations by the common people, and an immense mob followed her carriage, shouting, "The Queen for ever!" and heaping vituperations and curses upon the heads of her husband's ministers.

On the 14th the somewhat radically composed Common Council of the City of London presented an address, congratulating her Majesty on her arrival in this country.

The example was speedily followed, and for many months the metropolis was kept in a ferment by addresses and processions, got up by all manner of people, of trades, and of bodies, corporate and not corporate, in honour of the Queen's happy return.

In truth, from the first moment of her arrival, all the discontented and disaffected – all the radicals and all the reformers, of whatsoever kind—all who wished for change, and all who wished for commotion and strife—rallied round this hapless, reckless woman.

The cries for annual parliaments, universal suffrage, and vote by ballot, were all drowned in the louder shouts of "Long live the Queen!" "God save the Queen, and destroy her enemies!"

For any one to have intimated in the streets of London a suspicion of her innocence and spotless purity would have been to make a very perilous experiment on the popular temper.

It was very soon observed that the hosts of her admirers and champions were not made up of the respectabilities, and that the most ardent of her followers and processionists marched from the lower parts of the town, from St. Giles's and the Whitechapel suburb.

With a very few exceptions, the ladies of rank, station, and character were exceedingly shy of her, whatever may have been the Whig politics of their husbands, or the speeches delivered by them in Parliament: and the warmest of her supporters and panegyrists in the two Houses showed no anxiety that their wives and daughters should visit her Majesty in her own house.

By a certain party, or rather by two certain parties—the Whigs and the Radicals—she was seized upon as an instrument proper to work out their own designs.

They calculated that through her means the unpopularity of the King might be brought to a climax, and the long-seated ministry utterly overthrown.

They were, therefore, determined, from the first, to set their faces against any amicable arrangement or compromise; to support her flagging spirits by incessant addresses, processions, and highly-seasoned compliments; and to prevent, by every means in their power, her withdrawing from the conflict.

They had brought her to the stake and they were resolutely determined upon keeping her at it.

Yet apart from these political views, and wholly unconnected with them, there was a strong and generous feeling in a very considerable part of the community in favour of the unhappy Princess.

The heart of the people revolted at anything like oppression exercised upon a woman; her illustrious birth, the misfortunes of her family (her father and her brother had both fallen in battle during the late revolutionary war); her own misfortunes and sorrows, which had commenced from the hour of her union with George, Prince of Wales; her natural kindness, benevolence, and generosity of disposition; the long state of abandonment in which she had been left by her husband; her husband's youthful profligacy, the irregularities of his mature age, and certain connections which he was notoriously maintaining at the very moment he was causing his wife to be charged with adultery; all these, and many other facts and circumstances, pleaded powerfully in behalf of Caroline of Brunswick.

The utter failure of the attempt to arbitrate was announced to the House of Commons on the 19th of June.

Upon this the Government pressed proceedings.

On the 26th of June, whilst the secret committee was still sitting, Lord Dacre presented a petition from the Queen, in which she protested against any secret inquiry, demanded time to bring her witnesses from abroad, and requested to be heard by her counsel.

Messrs. Brougham, Denman, and Williams, being allowed to present themselves at the bar of the House, dwelt eloquently upon the hardships of the Queen's case, and on the necessity of delay.

On the 4th of July the secret committee gave in its report.

On the next day Lord Dacre presented a petition from the Queen to be heard against the report by her counsel.

This was refused.

And Lord Liverpool, in pursuance of the report, brought in a bill of pains and penalties, intituled "An act to deprive her Majesty Queen Caroline Amelia Elizabeth of the title, prerogatives, rights, privileges, and exemptions of queen-consort of this realm, and to dissolve the marriage between his majesty and the said Caroline Amelia Elizabeth"

The bill was read a first time, and a copy of it was ordered to be sent to the Queen.

We cannot detail the proceedings, or quote the eloquent pleadings of Brougham and Denman.

On the 19th of August, Lords Grey and King made successive attempts to quash the investigation by motions ; but the respective divisions were 181 to 65 and 179 to 64.

After these divisions had taken place, the Attorney-general stated his case in support of the bill.

His statement occupied two days, the 19th and 21st of August.

As it was ending, on the 21st, drums, trumpets, horns, and the shoutings of a tremendous multitude, announced the approach of her Majesty.

She entered the House of Lords.

Then in her presence the examination of witnesses was commenced ; and then, in a few minutes there was an incident and a scene.

Upon hearing the clerk of the house call the name of Teodoro Majocchi, the third witness, the Queen started from her seat with a faint cry, and rushed out of the house. This man had been her servant, and a close eye witness of most of her proceedings for a long time.

It was assumed by some that her emotion and her cry proceeded from conscious guilt, taken by surprise at the production of such a witness; it was reasoned by others that she might have been excited only by disgust and indignation at the ingratitude and treachery of an old servant.

The scandalous investigation went on, and day by day the disgusting reports of proceedings and examination of witnesses filled the newspapers, until it came to this—men who regarded the purity of their wives and daughters interdicted the journals in their houses.

On the 7th of September the case against the Queen was closed; and an adjournment took place to allow time to her counsel for preparing her defence.

On the 3rd of October, Mr. Brougham delivered the defence at great length and with astonishing eloquence and effect

He was ably followed by Mr. Williams.

The examination of the Queen's witnesses continued till the 24th of October.

When it was closed, Mr. Denman went over the whole case with vast ability and with equal boldness.

The witnesses against the Queen had in some instances prevaricated; and although a good deal of their testimony was perfectly convincing (and particularly to such persons as had lived in Italy, and were conversant with Italian manners), the case, in the apprehension of what was perhaps the majority of the nation, was left in that state which Scotch lawyers call "not proven."

Yet none but political fanatics or utter enthusiasts in generosity and charity could doubt but that this daughter of a most ancient and illustrious house had, during her foreign sojourn and rambles, behaved with the greatest levity and indecorum.

Those who judged of her with most severity were travellers who had followed her footsteps, or who had lived in Italy at the time that she had resided in that country; those who judged most favourably of her were such as had never quitted their own shores, who knew nothing of foreign life, and who knew nothing of her foreign story except what they took upon trust from the newspapers of the day.

Dr. Lushington supported Mr. Denman.

The King's Attorney and Solicitor-general occupied the 27th, 28th, 29th, and 30th, in replying.

The bill of pains and penalties was read a second time on the 6th of November, by a majority of 123 to 95.

The House having gone into committee, a discussion was raised on the divorce clause of the bill.

Some bishops, and other supporters of the bill, resisted this clause from religious scruples, or from the dread that the Queen would recriminate upon her husband.

In fact, such recrimination had been threatened by Mr. Brougham at the very outset of the proceedings.

But a Parliamentary manœuvre was resorted to; the opposition peers voted for the divorce clause, and it was carried by a majority of 120 to 62.

This majority proved highly injurious on the third reading.

Many peers who would have voted for the bill without the divorce clause, voted against it when the divorce clause was made a part of the bill; and thus, on the 10th of November, the third reading was carried by only nine votes, the numbers dividing being 108 against 99.

Lord Liverpool declared that, looking at this small majority, and at the state of the public feeling, he and his colleagues abandoned the bill.

The House adjourned to the 26th of November.

On that day, just as Mr. Denman was commencing to read a message from the Queen, the Usher of the Black Rod presented himself at the bar; and at this unexpected apparition, the Speaker left the chair, and, followed by ministers and the members of the ministerial party, proceeded to the House of Lords, there to be informed that the session of Parliament was prorogued by his Majesty.

And thus ended, in defeat and disgrace to the King, an indecent, obscene contest, which had filled right-minded men with unutterable disgust, and which had made every Englishman residing or travelling on the Continent, hold down his head and blush for his sovereign and his country.

The Parliament of 1821, which commenced its session on the 23rd of January, was characterised by the exhibition of a new spirit.

From the late commotions it had perceived what was absolutely needed for the progress of the age and the wants of the nation, and that neither peace nor order could be assured until the demands of the nation were complied with.

But before any step in this direction could be taken, it was felt that the present ministers must be got rid of; and for the purpose of defeating them, the Whigs coalesced with the Radicals, and adopted the Queen's name as their watchword and signal of attack.

Here, however, their calculations were at fault, for the Queen's popularity was now on the wane.

Calm reflection had succeeded the wild enthusiasm that had welcomed her to England, and her trial had convinced many of her warmest adherents that, however free she had been from actual guilt her conduct had been chargeable with much imprudence and indecorum.

Accordingly, when Lord Archibald Hamilton moved for a vote of censure on ministers, for the omission of her Majesty's name in the Liturgy, the motion was defeated by a large majority.

A next motion of Lord Tavistock, for a direct censure on the whole of their proceedings in the case of her Majesty, which was brought forward for the purpose of procuring the ejection of the ministers, was in like manner defeated.

Thus also it fared with the third and last

effort, by which it was proposed to replace her name in the Liturgy. It was decisively negatived.

While important Parliamentary proceedings were going forward, the tables of both Houses continued to be inundated with petitions in behalf of the Queen

The opening speech had recommended a suitable provision to be made for her, instead of that which she had enjoyed as Princess of Wales; but she had expressed her firm determination to accept of no settlement while her name was omitted in the Liturgy.

Not deterred by this declaration, £50,000 had been voted to her for life; and after some demur the pressure of poverty prevailed: she consented to accept the boon, and by doing so lost much of that popularity which her previous rejection had procured for her.

But the coronation, which her arrival had delayed, must now be so emnised at every risk, for George IV. valued the pomp of royalty more than even its power, and he could not feel himself "every inch a king" until his head had been surmounted by the crown.

The 19th of July was therefore fixed for the pageant; and here the Queen had determined to take her final stand. On the 25th of June, she lodged her claim to be crowned, like her royal predecessors, and her claim was ably supported by her law advisers Messrs. Brougham and Denman; but after a long antiquarian and historical exploration, it was found that the coronation of a King did not necessarily imply that of his consort, and that, since the reign of Henry VIII. only six out of thirteen queen-consorts had been crowned; so that, on the strength of these precedents, her claim as a right was rejected.

Caroline then wrote to Lord Sidmouth, stating her determination to be present at the ceremony, and desiring that a suitable place should be provided for her accommodation; and when this was refused, she made a similar application to the Duke of Norfolk, as earl-marshal of England, but with the same result.

Rejected in these appeals, she now tried one that looked like downright insanity; she requested the Archbishop of Canterbury to crown her alone on the following week, while the Abbey of Westminster was in preparation for the final ceremony, which could be done without further national expense.

But to her letter containing such a singular request, the astonished primate returned the following brief reply:—

"The Archbishop of Canterbury has the honour to acknowledge with all humility the receipt of her Majesty's communication. Her Majesty is undoubtedly aware that the Archbishop cannot stir a single step in the subject matter of it without the commands of the King."

The coronation took place, with unwonted splendour and magnificence, on the 19th of July.

The Queen resolved to be present, or to make a scene by seeking admittance in the eyes of the people.

It is said that the more prudent of her friends endeavoured to dissuade her; but it is to be apprehended that most of those who surrounded her, and who were making use of her merely for party or factious purposes, without any regard to the shock her feelings might sustain, very strongly urged her to go down to the Abbey.

She went, and stopping before the Abbey door, was there refused admittance by the doorkeepers and military officers on guard.

She then wandered round the Abbey walls, in a vain search of some other entrance, and having thus exhibited her humiliation, she retired through the dense multitude, applauded by some, but hissed and hooted, and called foul names by others.

The yells and excitement were fearful, and the scene perhaps the most novel that ever took place in this country.

There was the grand old Abbey bathed in a flood of sunlight.

From within pealed the notes of the organ, and the eye rested upon a mass of glitter and magnificence of which we seek in despair for a parallel.

The vast concourse of sight-seers were roused, as it always is, by royal pageants, to a great pitch of excitement, and the cheering and cries of astonishment and delight were terrific.

It appeared that the partisans of the King and Queen were pretty nearly balanced in numbers, for when a shout for his Majesty rent the air, it was always followed by a counter cheer, quite as loud and enthusiastic, for the Queen.

But who shall describe the appearance of Caroline on that scene?

Who can do justice to the intense feeling aroused by the sight of her well-known figure, hustled by the mob, grovelling in the dirt, whilst her husband was having placed upon his brow the crown of England?

Truly this was the moment for the bringing to a crisis the conflicting opinions that were agitating England.

Let us be more minute in our details.

A carriage, well appointed, and attended by numbers of gentlemen on horseback, dashed up to the Abbey.

Not long before George IV. had entered with a magnificent train.

The carriage we allude to was that of the Queen of England.

As it drew up many of the horsemen dismounted, and with a great show assisted Caroline from her vehicle.

As this was being done, Lady Banksford, closely followed by young Lord Lovelace, rushed to the side of the Queen.

"I implore your Majesty to retire," cried Banksford; "these people," he continued, turning and casting a look of withering contempt upon those who appeared anxious for Caroline to advance to the Abbey, "these people bring you here to further their own vile ends. Pray retire, or evil may come of it."

The Queen hesitated.

"Listen to my Lord Banksford," urged Lord

Lovelace; "your Majesty will find that he advises well."

"Psha!" said one of the officious attendants on the Queen, "these are childish fears. Pray do not listen to them, your Majesty."

"I will not," said the Queen, and next moment she was in the crowd.

Then arose the uproar to which we have alluded.

The tumult was unprecedented.

Lovelace and Banksford followed in the wake of the Queen, and prevented the mob from pressing too closely upon her.

As she forced herself towards the Abbey, a woman of haggard appearance stood before her, and, waving her hands aloft, burst forth into a fierce invective against the King.

This woman was Marie Lavrouffe.

She recited her wrongs, told the tale of her betrayal, hinted at the attempt to ruin her only child, and called on the young Lord Lovelace to corroborate her words.

"For God's sake, retire," said Lovelace to her; "do not appeal to me; get you home."

"I will not go home," she cried. "I will remain here and recite my wrongs, so that the people may hear and avenge them."

"We will avenge them," was yelled by the mob.

"Down with the King," cried Marie.

"Aye, down with him, and long live the Queen!"

"Let us break open the doors, and make them crown the Queen."

"Aye, smash in the doors—down with the doors. Let us have the Queen crowned."

The authorities were becoming alarmed.

There were symptoms of a terrible riot in the crowd.

The guards were put on the move, and at one time the aspect of affairs became most serious.

Meanwhile the Queen pressed on to the doors of the Abbey.

Admittance was demanded for her.

She personally appealed to the guards, but no one would give way for her to enter, and she walked about the sacred edifice until she sank exhausted into the arms of Lovelace and Banksford.

Finding that their efforts to create the confusion they had anticipated would result in failure, those who brought the Queen to the Abbey cruelly left her, and had it not been for the two lords we have named, there is no knowing what might have been the result of the ill-advised step.

"Bear her to her carriage," said a well-disposed officer of the Guards; "carry her away, or I fear something sad may happen."

"We will do so," said Lovelace, and with his companion he forced his way through the yelling crowd, and bore off the Queen.

But the excitement of that day had done its work.

The Queen of England had received the blow which was to bear her down to the grave..

Meanwhile his most sacred Majesty George IV. feasted and dissipated, after his usual style.

There was no thought of that wretched Queen in those moments.

CHAPTER IX.

CONCERNING THE FAMILY OF MR. DE PIPES, AND FURNISHING SOME PARTICULARS OF ONE MR. ALFRED WARE, TOGETHER WITH HIS ELOPEMENT WITH AZALINE LAVROUFFE.

FROM hints scattered over the foregoing pages, the reader will comprehend that on the death of Lord Lovelace the fair Liz at last became the wife of her devoted admirer, Pipey. The ceremony was performed in Italy, and after a few years of foreign travel, the happy couple returned to England to pass in happiness the remainder of their days.

Two months after the barbarous death of Lord Lovelace, Liz brought a child of his into the world.

To this child Pipey was more than a parent.

He loved it as fondly as if it had been his own, and Liz rejoiced that her infant had found so good and true a friend. It is only necessary to add that the boy was worthy his parent; the young lord was, indeed, a noble youth, and proud and happy was Pipey to be his friend, instructor, and guardian.

Pipey and his wife had ample means, and it was at the urgent pleadings of Liz that our hero forbore to seek that vast inheritance, the Grasmount property, to which Liz now knew she had a claim.

But after a while Pipey could no longer refrain from seeking it.

The task pleased him; and Liz, on being dazzled by Pipey into the belief that the possession of the estates and titles would be appreciated by her darling boy, consented that he should attempt their recovery.

Our readers have seen him on the track.

A singular incident in the lives of this united and happy family was the appearance in the circle of Azaline Lavrouffe.

Young Lovelace would not hear of parting with his half sister, and forced Marie to consent to making him her guardian.

It required immense persuasion, but at last the consent was given, and the sweet girl found herself under the roof of the woman who had rescued her from a watery grave on a moonlight night years and years ago in Venice. How they all grew to love the little Azaline can readily be understood.

Let us briefly say that very soon she became as one who had never lived out of that happy circle.

But Azaline did not appear to be happy.

It was not her mother she pined after. Her friends assured themselves of that; and they also knew that the love and care they lavished upon her left her nothing to wish for.

But the truth was Azaline loved!

She had met a man, some years her senior, who had been introduced to her as the Hon.

Alfred Ware, and on this man she had fixed her heart.

Had she known who in reality was the supposed Ware, whose face gleamed beneath the mask *she saw*, she would have been heart whole; but, as it was she loved this Ware, and we have to note to what end this ill-fated attachment led!

Ware carefully abstained from introducing himself to the family of Pipey.

He contrived to meet Azaline in society, and particularly at the house of a Mrs. Brown, to whom he had got a lady friend to introduce her.

Poor girl, she was rushing into a trap of the most desperate kind, and, unfortunately for her, the lynx eye of Pipey was taken off from her, as he was now fully engaged in tracking those who had so long defrauded his wife of her inheritance.

So matters went on until this supposed Ware proposed to Azaline. The young girl naturally referred him to her friends.

But Ware palmed off on her an elaborate excuse, which freed him from the ordeal of meeting Pipey and his wife.

He hinted at his present poverty, urged that her friends would object to it, and also said that he dared not publish his marriage, as his expectations would be considerably damaged by such a course.

Under these circumstances Azaline consented to receive his addresses in secret; and although the household of Pipey was tolerably familiar with the name of Ware, and all understood that Azaline had some affection for the man who owned that name, the eyes of none were open to the truth

One day Ware called at the mansion occupied by Pipey.

All the family, with the exception of Azaline, were out. Cunning Mr. Ware!

His visit appeared to the young girl to be an accidental one, but by bribing the servants and keeping watch he had convinced himself that he could have an uninterrupted interview with Azaline before he ventured near the house.

That interview was sought for the purpose of concocting a scheme of elopement.

He had that day induced his friend Mrs. Brown to send an invite to Lord Lovelace and Azaline for that evening.

He *knew* Lovelace could not come, and he meant to persuade Azaline into accepting the invite, and also certain terms which he proposed.

Ware pressed his suit with ardour, and begged the young girl to trust him and fly with him.

At first she strenuously refused. Again he pressed his suit, and she wavered.

He poured out a perfect flood of impassioned words, and—she was won.

"Oh, Azaline!" he said, "will you not place implicit reliance upon me?—have you not every faith in my love, my honour, my sincerity?"

"Yes, dear Alfred, yes—every faith," answered the young lady. "Oh, I am sure that you love me, and you know that I love you in return! Tell me that you love me, Alfred."

"Devotedly!" and Alfred, winding his arms round Azaline's waist, strained her to his breast, covering her lips and cheeks with kisses so impassioned—so fervid, that, filled with confusion, she at length gently disengaged herself from him.

"And you will consent to become mine—mine without delay? Oh, as years shall I esteem the minutes which are yet to elapse ere you can become indissolubly mine! But why should our happiness be delayed? If your half-brother should bid you reflect and deliberate, rest assured that he will never view with pleasure the alliance that your own heart prompts you to form. If, therefore, our union must, for every reason, take place stealthily and privately, may it not as well be solemnised to-morrow as a week, or a month, or a year hence? Oh, Azaline, consent to make me happy with the least possible delay, and all the most devoted love which man can show for woman shall be testified by me towards you."

In this manner did Alfred continue to plead, and Azaline yielded to his supplication.

She consented to elope with him, if he could so arrange all the details of the proceeding that Lord Lovelace should not suspect her design until it was too late for him to take any measure to prevent it.

With flushing cheeks, with eyes swimming in mingled tenderness and confusion, and with palpitating bosom, did Azaline thus in tremulous whispers, signify to Alfred Ware that she yielded to his supplications.

He assured her that every arrangement should be conducted with the utmost circumspection, that he would lose no time in procuring a special license, that they would journey to some secluded village where the marriage could be solemnised, and that immediately on their return to London, he would lead her into his protector's presence, and they would throw themselves upon their knees before Lord Lovelace.

Azaline listened to all these assurances, which more than ever convinced her of the honourable character and devoted love of her admirer; still there was one difficulty to get over.

How could she leave the villa unperceived by his lordship?

They deliberated for some little time, and at length a plan was arranged.

Alfred then again embraced Azaline fervently, and he took his departure to carry out the arrangements which had been settled between them.

At a distance of about a mile from the mansion resided a lady named Brown, to whom she had been introduced, and to whom she had rather taken a fancy, considering her to be an agreeable and entertaining person.

It happened that, on the very day of which we are writing, Mrs. Brown had sent a note, inviting Miss Lavrouffe to take tea with her in the evening.

She now resolved to accept that invitation, and the instant Alfred had taken his departure she sent a note to this effect to Mrs. Brown.

"I shall pass an hour or two with Mrs. Brown," said Azaline to Lord Lovelace, on meeting him.

"If I had thought that you desired to go, I would have gone with you."

"Oh, I have no particular wish," exclaimed Azaline, "only I fear that it would seem strange, as Mrs. Brown has on two or three occasions invited me, and I have always refused hitherto."

"Go, then, my dear sister," said the unsuspicious Lovelace.

It was shortly after eight o'clock in the evening that Azaline entered a hackney vehicle which had been engaged to take her to Mrs. Brown's.

She felt a tightening at the heart as she took leave of her more than brother, and she could scarcely prevent herself from embracing him with a degree of fervour which might have raised a suspicion that the leave-taking was felt to be one which would prove of longer duration than a mere two or three hours.

But Azaline thought to herself that she had gone too far to retreat, and having, therefore, to play a particular part, she succeeded in veiling whatsoever emotions she felt on the occasion.

She went, and the unsuspecting Lovelace remained alone that evening.

It was a very small party which Mrs. Brown gave on this occasion; just, as she expressed it, a few of her neighbours dropping in to see her quite in a friendly way, without formality or ceremony.

She appeared a well-meaning woman enough, and her weaknesses did not appear to amount to vices.

There were about a dozen guests at Mrs. Brown's house. Four old people sat down to whist; the more juvenile portion of the company recreated themselves with music.

Azaline seemed more than usually gay; her spirits were partially forced, and partially borne up with the bright hopes in which she was cradling herself.

Whenever for a moment a sensation of remorse on account of her duplicity to Lovelace, or of regretful emotion at having separated herself from that much-loved brother, crept into her heart, she took refuge in merry-sounding laughter, or flew to the piano to play a cheerful air; or she started some gay and joyous topic of discourse.

Every one present thought that Miss Lavrouffe had never before proved herself so amiable, and had never seemed in better spirits.

There was an ormulu time-piece upon the mantel in Mrs. Brown's drawing-room: and as the hands drew near towards the indication of the hour of eleven, Azaline's heart fluttered more and more; she had all the greater difficulty in concealing her real agitation beneath a semblance of outward natural gaiety.

The time-piece struck the hour, and then Azaline, watching an opportunity when the whist players were deep in their game, and the rest of the company were gathered about a young lady at the piano, glided unperceived from the room.

The domestics were employed in laying the supper table, of this Azaline assured herself. She caught up her veil and scarf in the breakfast parlour, where she had left those articles, and, unperceived by a soul, she passed out into the garden at the back of the house.

This she threaded, and in a few moments reached a gate opening into a lane, where a post-chaise was waiting, and where Alfred was in readiness to receive her.

At that instant a severe pang shot through the heart of Azaline.

It was almost a sense of consternation which seized upon her brain, and if the hand of any guardian genius had been stretched forth to hold her back she would have yielded to the friendly intervention.

And if, too, there had been a saving voice to whisper a single syllable of warning in her ear, she would not have remained deaf to it.

It required at that moment but the weight of a straw thrown into the balance to induce that young girl—hitherto rash, self-willed, and wilfully self-blinding also—to retract all that she had been resolved to accomplish.

But no guardian hand was there—no saving voice mingled with the breeze, which was whispering along the lane, and ruffling the autumn-tinted foliage of the trees.

One last look did Azaline fling behind towards the house which she had thus so stealthily quitted—a look in which there was a momentary expression of anguished entreaty, as if imploring that some one would even yet come forth thence to save her.

But the next moment she was inside the chaise, clasped in the arms of her lover; and then in the rapturous feelings which took possession of her soul, all remorse was forgotten.

Rapid and varied, however, were the transitions of feeling which Azaline was doomed to experience; and this, indeed, is ever the case with those who are taking a step that hovers in doubt betwixt the approval or disapproval of their own consciences.

A moment before, while she stood upon the steps leading down from the garden gate, she would have consented to be saved if anyone had been there to save her.

Another moment, and she experienced feelings of soft ecstatic rapture when clasped in the arms of her lover.

Then, yet another moment, and a strong revulsion of feeling took place within her.

Her soul received a sudden shock as the thought flashed to her mind that she was alone in that chaise with Alfred Ware.

"Where is the maid whom you promised to have in attendance for me?" she softly and tremulously inquired, with scarcely courage to put a question which might seem to imply distrust of her lover, and yet on the other hand impelled by delicacy of feeling to put it.

"You know not, dearest Azaline, how distressed I am at this disappointment. But believe me, it is not my fault. An elderly lady-friend of mine faithfully promised to supply the requirement; but at the last moment the girl whom I expected made not her appearance. I was bewildered how to act——But heavens, Azaline, you are weeping."

And so it was.

Again had the sense of her imprudent conduct returned to Azaline's mind.

The tears were trickling down her cheeks—they were glistening in the light which was shed by moon and stars into the vehicle.

"Oh, Alfred!" she murmured, "what must you think of me that I consent thus to travel with you—alone?"

"If you had refused, Azaline," he answered, "I should have fancied that you had no trust nor confidence in me; and I should have considered, therefore, that for some reason I was held unworthy to become your husband."

"I feel that there ought to be every confidence between us," exclaimed Azaline, wiping away her tears—for an instant smiling softly and tenderly upon her lover, and then casting down her looks beneath the luminous earnestness of his own.

He passed his arm round her waist, drew her towards him, and covered her cheeks with kisses, until those cheeks glowed with burning blushes, and she felt that there was a fervour of passion in his embraces which made her tremble and shrink away from them.

For be it remembered that Azaline was strictly chaste in her virgin thoughts; no gross ideas had ever entered her imagination; and, though naturally of a warm temperament, yet the unimpaired purity of her soul would have been proof against the wiles of deliberate seduction, while it would also have shielded her from any attempt to surprise her virtue in a moment of seeming weakness.

Giddy and thoughtless she was—self-willed and rash, as the reader has seen—too much prone to regard superficial or ephemeral circumstances as the elements of happiness—too confiding in her disposition—too indolent to reason deliberately when it was for her good; and yet, on the other hand, too ready to conjure up a thousand arguments in support of any project whereon she had set her mind.

Thus, though her character was without strong moral stamina, she was purely virtuous: her innate sense of modesty was not marred by the element of levity that was in her disposition; and so she trembled and vague fears sprang up in her mind, as she felt that there was something more fervid, more passionate, in the kisses which her lover imprinted upon her cheeks, than was completely consistent with the chastity and purity of love.

Ware saw that he had shocked and frightened his beauteous companion; and he hastened to efface the impression which his passionate fervour had thus made upon her mind.

He spoke to her in the softest and tenderest manner—in the most delicate terms did he assure her of his affection; he expatiated on the happiness they would enjoy when united beyond the power of any human law to separate them; and thus in a few moments Azaline was completely reassured—she was likewise completely happy.

It was sweet for her to listen to this tender language: she had sufficient vanity to be flattered by the compliments, which, delicately and without fulsomeness, Ware interwove with his protestations of imperishable affection, and with his expatiations upon their prospects of happiness.

Again were all remorse and regret forgotten: Lovelace was only remembered as one who in a few days would be happy to welcome her as the bride of Alfred Ware; and when he again kissed her cheek, she felt neither shocked nor frightened—she trembled not, neither did she immediately withdraw from his embrace—because now there was no passionate fervour in those kisses; they seemed to be but the chaste testimonials of a pure, manly and honourable love.

The post-chaise proceeded at a rapid rate; the first stage was soon accomplished, the horses were changed, and away sped the equipage again.

It was a little past one o'clock in the morning when the second stage was accomplished, and a small town was reached.

The night was frosty, and at this hour the chill set in with bitterness.

Ware gently suggested that it would be well if his beloved were to take a few hours' rest at the place which they had thus reached, adding that they could pursue their way at eight o'clock towards the village where he proposed that the ceremony should be solemnised, and where he promised that they should arrive before mid-day.

Azaline, now all confidence, expressed her willingness to leave every arrangement to her lover; and, moreover, she felt the bitterness of the chill, for she was but lightly clad, and, though his cloak was wrapped round her, she had no warm furs to protect her.

A halt was accordingly resolved upon at the inn where the post-chaise now drew up.

All the inmates had retired to rest, but a chambermaid was speedily summoned from her room and she signified her readiness to attend to the requirements of the travellers.

Ware intimated that they needed two rooms, and he asked whether it were possible to have any warm negus supplied at that hour, observing that both himself and his companion were well-nigh perished with the cold.

The chambermaid conducted them into a parlour, where there happened to be a remnant of fire in the grate, and she promised that all their wants should be quickly attended to.

In a few minutes she returned, bearing a tray containing wine in a decanter, hot water, sugar, and all that was requisite for making the negus that had been ordered.

Ware displayed the most delicate attentions towards Azaline—conducting himself, alike in speech and in looks, in a manner calculated to maintain all the confidence with which he had succeeded in inspiring her—and that confidence was complete.

"You must have suffered much from the cold night air, my sweetest," he said; "for I myself felt its bitterness. It must be many hours since you partook of any refreshment, and this negus will warm you."

While thus speaking, Ware was standing at

the table mixing the beverage; while Azaline sat cowering over the remnant of fire in the grate.

She did, indeed, feel bitterly cold; and she could scarcely keep her teeth from chattering.

Ware approached her with the steaming glass in his hand, and he delicately pressed her to partake of its contents.

She did so—but drinking merely a portion of the negus; for she was naturally most abstemious in respect to any except the weakest beverages.

The chambermaid soon returned to intimate that the rooms were now prepared for the reception of the travellers; Ware respectfully wished Azaline good night—simply pressing her hand, and not offering to embrace her in the presence of the domestic.

The young lady followed the chambermaid to the room prepared for her reception.

The domestic had considerately lighted the fire, which was now blazing and sparkling in a manner to diffuse an air of cheerfulness about the room.

The maid retired, and Azaline used all possible speed in disapparelling herself, for she felt drowsy, which she attributed to the numbing influence of the cold.

She sought the couch, and not many moments had her head rested upon the pillow when she sank into a profound slumber.

* * * * *

The consternation in the household of the Lovelace family on hearing of the disappearance of Azaline Lavrouffe can easily be imagined.

Lord Lovelace gave way to a frenzy of grief from which he only recovered on hearing the sweet voice of his mother entreating him to be calm and calling upon him to act.

Unhappily Pipey was away from home—tracking the Black Captain to his lair.

They knew that she must have flown with the fascinating young Ware, of whom she spoke so much and so warmly, but beyond this they had no clue.

Poor Lovelace knew not what course to adopt.

He felt so uneasy, wretched, and afflicted, that it seemed as if he must do something, but he was bewildered by his own thoughts.

If he could only find the slightest clue to the track which Azaline had taken, he would speed after them—he would not allow his sister to proceed to the altar without at least being accompanied by himself.

But that clue was utterly wanting; for though he discovered that a postchaise had departed from Mrs. Brown's gate in a northerly direction, how could conjecture hit upon the precise road which it had taken; or how could inquiries be instituted upon such a point?

Lovelace therefore came to the conclusion that there was nothing to be done in the matter, and that he must endeavour to remain quiet until he received some tidings of his sister.

He thought to himself that Azaline would not be so cruel as to leave him very long in suspense, and that she would be certain to write immedi-

ately after the ceremony should have made her an honourably wedded wife.

CHAPTER X.

ONE MORE ATTEMPT TO CARRY OFF FAIR LIZ—
A DESPERATE PLAN DEFEATED BY LOUISE.

OUR readers will have no difficulty in remembering the name of Portman.

It has appeared in these pages often enough beside that of the Prince of Wales.

Portman, the companion of his early revels, now an old but, unhappily, sinful man, was in the enjoyment of great favours and distinction.

He had been raised to the peerage, and held several remunerative posts at Court.

Moving in the best of circles, it was not surprising that he should meet the wife of our friend Pipey.

No sooner had the old reprobate set eyes upon her, than he determined to make himself agreeable to her—with what view the reader may guess.

As a matter of course, his advances were repulsed with scorn; but Liz, dreading to arouse the anger of her husband, failed to acquaint him with the persecution she had undergone; and so submitted to a torture which might have been ended on the instant had Pipey but known of its existence.

It chanced that Portman revealed his passion for the wife of Pipey to the King; and that worthy, wishing to punish Liz for her former coldness and indifference to himself, urged him on in the matter.

The result was, that on the very night following the disappearance of Azaline, Portman had concocted a plan for carrying off the woman who had so inflamed his passions.

But it so chanced that the flight of Azaline had attracted to the mansion of Pipey a lady, whom we introduce as Mrs. Captain Marchmont, but in whom the reader will recognise an old friend when we call her Louise.

The history of this beautiful girl, from the moment we left her until we now find her again, we have yet to relate.

Suffice it now to say that she is the wife of an honourable and gallant man, and the near friend of the wife of Pipey.

They had no wish to receive Louise on this painful occasion; but she would not be put off, and forced herself into the presence of Liz.

She, to their astonishment, said she should remain there for the night; and, accordingly, preparations were made for her accommodation.

It was about eleven o'clock at night when the ladies separated, to retire to their chambers.

An apartment adjoining the one which Liz occupied, had been prepared for Louise; but upon being conducted thither she made no immediate preparation to seek her couch.

On the contrary, the instant she found herself alone, her proceedings were of a strange and singular character.

Having evidently made up her mind to pass a day or two at the mansion, she had ordered a box containing changes of apparel and the requisites of the toilette to be sent by a carrier; and this box had arrived in the course of the evening.

She now opened it, and from amongst the dresses which it contained, she drew forth *a pair of pistols!*

These she deliberately began to load, and when the task was accomplished she looked at her watch.

It was then half-past eleven o'clock.

"At midnight it is to happen," she muttered to herself; and a singular expression of mingled rage, distress, and firm resolution passed over her countenance.

She now extinguished the tapers; and with-out disapparelling herself, or making the slightest preparation for rest, she sat down in the dark, and soon fell into a profound reverie.

But we must leave her for the present, and direct the attention of the reader to certain incidents that were passing elsewhere.

A few minutes before midnight a postchaise drew up at a little distance from the mansion, and two persons alighted.

One of them bade the postilion make a little circuit in the neighbourhood, for fear lest the circumstance of such an equipage stopping there should attract the attention of any belated persons returning to their homes.

The postilion was further directed to be at the iron gate of the mansion in about a quarter of an hour's time.

The chaise accordingly rolled away; and the

two individuals who had alighted from it proceeded to the gate which has just been alluded to.

This was locked, as those persons indeed expected to find it; but having satisfied themselves that no observer was nigh they at once scaled it.

Without maintaining any further mystery on the point, we may as well at once inform our readers that these two persons were Portman and his valet.

The latter was a man of about five-and-thirty years of age—thoroughly unprincipled—fond of money—and ready to do anything to obtain it.

His name was Marks, and he had been for about a twelvemonth in the service of his present master.

"Now," said Portman, so soon as they were within the garden, "you thoroughly understand all that we have to do?"

"Everything," was the man's response. "It is not a very difficult matter to carry off a lady, provided you can prevent her from screaming in such a way as to alarm the household."

"There will be no fear of that," rejoined Portman; "thanks to the discovery of chloroform. But remember, if we happen to meet any one of the servants——"

"I will grapple her at once, and trust to me that not a word shall issue from her lips provided that you will be prompt in applying the handkerchief with that stuff you speak of to the nostrils, so as to quiet her altogether."

"All our proceedings," rejoined Portman, "shall be conducted with promptitude and energy. You have your mask with you?" he added, taking one from his own pocket, and adjusting it upon his countenance.

The example was immediately followed by Marks; so that master and man, with those black vizards, had the air of burglars.

The precaution of concealing their faces had been suggested by Portman in case they should have to deal with any of the domestics—his object being to involve in as much mystery as possible the authorship of the bold outrage which he contemplated.

The diabolical plan which he had formed may be briefly explained.

His purpose was to carry off Liz to a secluded house which he had hired some ten or a dozen miles distant, and where he resolved that her honour should be sacrificed to his passion.

He calculated that when once she found that his triumph and her own disgrace were accomplished, she would of necessity accept the position of his mistress, and that no disagreeable consequences would result from the villanous outrage by which it was intended to make her his victim.

Portman had been for the last few days hatching this plot in concert with his valet; and when in the course of the day which had just passed the intelligence reached him of Azael's elopement, fortune appeared to be favouring his nefarious scheme by the removal of one whose presence in the villa had previously appeared to constitute no mean difficulty, inasmuch as

Portman knew, or at least believed, that, when Pipey was away, the ladies occupied the same chamber.

Having adjusted the masks upon their faces Portman and his valet approached the villa.

In one front room only was a light to be discerned, and this was glimmering through the curtains which were closed within the casement of that chamber.

Portman had no doubt that this was the room in which his intended victim slept, and he instantaneously comprehended its position in reference to the staircase, which he hoped very shortly to ascend.

Passing round to the rear of the premises, he and his valet at once commenced their operations; for Portman was well acquainted with all the arrangements and details of the establishment, alike from a knowledge of the interior as from observation made in respect to the exterior in those times when he was accustomed to call at the house, and had walked in the garden with the young ladies.

There was a glass door which had a shutter fixed up within.

A glazier's diamond, with which the valet was provided, speedily and noiselessly cut out one of the squares of glass; and a small centre-bit, plied dexterously, soon made a hole sufficiently large for the introduction of a hand.

The screw which retained the shutter was now quickly removed by taking off the nut fastening it on the inner side.

Then the shutter was cautiously lowered; and the extraction of another pane of glass enabled Portman to introduce his hand and unlock the door.

If the key had not been found in the lock, or if there should have happened to be bolts which could not be reached from the outside, the alternative would have been to cut away a sufficiency of the glass framework to admit a human form; and for all these eventualities the valet was provided with the requisite implements.

But the key *did* happen to be in the lock, and no bolts proved to be fastened.

The entry into the house was thus effected.

Portman and the valet found themselves in a passage communicating direct with the hall.

A complete silence reigned throughout the villa; and treading with the utmost caution, they advanced towards the staircase.

This they ascended, and they gained the landing communicating with the principal chambers.

But now a chance had to be encountered against which at the outset it was scarcely possible to provide, and which, therefore, had to be left to the chapter of accidents.

It was whether the door of Liz's room should be found locked or unlocked.

On this chance Portman knew full well depended the success or failure of his nefarious project.

Noiselessly, on tiptoe, did Portman advance to the door of that chamber where the glimmering light had been seen through the curtained windows from the outside.

He grasped the handle—he turned it with the utmost caution—his heart leapt with a

criminal exultation as the door yielded to h
touch.

Slowly he opened it sufficiently to listen : all
was silent within.

A little further he opened it, so as to be enabled to look into the room ; and at the same
time his hand clutched a kerchief which was
strongly impregnated with chloroform.

Liz was wrapped in a profound slumber.

The light which was burning on the toilet-
table played upon one side of her countenance,
thus revealing with a Rembrandt effect the regularly formed and beautiful profile.

The luxuriant masses of the golden auburn
hair lay floatingly over the pillow : one fair arm
was beneath her head—the other reposed,
softly curved, upon the counterpane.

It was the slumber of angelic innocence in
which she was steeped : a halo of purity and
chastity appeared to surround her ; and yet
the better feelings of the profligate patrician
were not touched by the spectacle—on the
contrary, his evil passions were all the more
powerfully excited.

He was advancing on tiptoe towards the couch,
when all of a sudden Marks kicked his foot
against some piece of furniture as he was following his master, and Liz started up in affright.
Terror and consternation, however, sealed her
lips long enough to enable Portman to reach
the side of the couch ; and the kerchief which
he clutched in his hand was thrust into the
lady's face at the very instant when a cry for
assistance was about to peal forth.

She sank back upon the pillow in a state of
unconsciousness ; and it was all the work of a
moment from the time that her eyes opened
until they thus closed again.

But just as Portman was on the very point of
winding his arms around her form to lift her
from the couch an ejaculation burst from his
valet Marks ; and, on looking round, he beheld
another person upon the scene.

This was Louise, with a pistol in each hand.

Her countenance was pale, but it expressed
the firmest decision, mingled with indignation
—almost with rage.

Portman, who had little expected to find the
victim of his master beneath that roof, was
transfixed to the spot ; and through the eyelet
holes of his mask his looks were rivetted in confusion, bewilderment, and dismay upon Louise.

A glance had shown her that Liz was lying in
a state of unconsciousness, and she lost no time
in profiting thereby.

Noiselessly closing the door, she made an imperious gesture for Marks to pass further into
the room, so as not to be betwixt herself and
that door, and he at once obeyed her ; for the
man seemed utterly overwhelmed with terror at
the appearance of Louise.

She then levelled the weapons that held
the lives of master and man hanging as it were
on threads ; and Marks crept like a grovelling
coward towards the spot which she so peremptorily indicated.

Then Louise, motioning towards the door,
gave utterance to the single imperious word—
"Begone !"

Utterly crest-fallen, discomfited, yet full of an
impotent rage to which he dared not give vent,
Portman stole forth from the chamber, followed
by his valet.

But ere Marks passed the threshold, he turned
his head for a moment, and through the holes
of his mask he flung upon Louise a rapid look.

She answered it with a glance of triumphant
intelligence ; and then the men disappeared
from her view.

Louise now advanced towards the couch ; and
finding that Liz was still wrapped in the pro-
foundest unconsciousness, she stole back to her
own chamber.

"Had he attempted the least violence," she
murmured to herself, "I would have consummated my vengeance ruthlessly and remorselessly !"

She then returned into the other chamber, but
she did not immediately adopt any measures for
the restoration of the young lady.

It did not suit her purpose that an alarm
should be raised until Portman and his valet
were safe out of the premises, and consequently
beyond pursuit.

The house was all quiet.

The entire scene had passed unheard and unsuspected by the domestics ; and thus Liz could
never know that Louise had suffered some
little while to elapse ere she adopted the requisite means to bring her back to conscio
ness.

When Louise fancied that a sufficient interval
had gone by to place Portman and Marks beyond
the reach of any danger, she began to bestow her
attentions on Liz.

Our heroine slowly opened her eyes, for the
stupefying effects of the chloroform did not pass
immediately away ; and now Louise thought it
prudent to summon the domestics, and to
assume an excited expression of countenance.

The villa was, therefore, speedily a scene of
consternation and dismay.

But Louise soon began to perform a part of
heroic boldness, by descending to ascertain (as
she said) whether the burglars were still upon
the premises.

The servants would not suffer her to proceed
alone ; and the means by which the entry had
been effected were very quickly ascertained.

We need hardly observe that Liz was powerfully excited when, being brought back to complete consciousness, she remembered how she
had seen two individuals with black masks in
her chamber.

<hr />

CHAPTER XI.

LOUISE TOLD LOUISE—HER STORY TRACED—THE
YOUNG NOBLEMAN IN FERVENT LOVE.

WHEN last we referred to the unfortunate
Louise, who has so frequently figured in these
pages, it was to behold her refusing temptation,
and accepting poverty rather than again embrace
the splendid dissipations of Colton House.

She sank into poverty, and became the drudge of an old woman, who kept a second-rate beer-house near the docks at Blackwall.

It was a hard life, but it was a honest one, and she strove hard to bear her lot with patience.

Twelve months of labour was, however, rewarded with a future of which she could scarcely have dreamt.

One day, a fine, dashing young sailor entered the house of her mistress, and accosted her.

He was a light-hearted, free-spoken fellow, and at once made himself quite at home !

On seeing Louise, his eye followed her about the room for some time, and he notified to her that there was something in her voice that he seemed to remember !

She, on her part, was no less stricken on beholding the seaman, and they entered into a conversation which resulted in mutual recognition.

The seaman was no other than Harry Lanyard : the man to whom Louise owed her incarceration in a felon's cell.

"By the bright blue waters," cried Lanyard, tossing his hat to the ceiling, and catching Louise in his arms, "I'm right glad to see you, lass. Ah! many's the long night I've lain awake, and thought of your darling eyes, and cursed myself that I was ever the cause of bringing a tear into them."

"Hush !" said Louise, "pray, do not remind me of a past so dark and terrible !"

"That I won't, lass, and I ought to be kicked for mentioning it, but I didn't think—I didn't think."

"No matter ; I'm glad to see you again, and trust we may be friends in the future."

"*Friends !*" said Lanyard, scratching his head, and looking gloomy ; "*friends !* why, aye, lass, if you will it that way ; but it wasn't to be friends with you in the future, supposing we met again, that I thought of during the long watches of the night, far away on the ocean ! I did dream of some nearer tie ; but, if you say it's to be friends, why—why—friends be it ; but, hang it ! the word sticks in my throat and chokes me."

"Ah !" said Liz, "would that I could claim that nearer relationship at which you hint. But you must not forget my past life. No, Harry, I am not the woman that you should have for a wife."

"Not the woman ! curse—but no, I'm not going to swear. Not the woman ! why you're the only one ! Talk you of your past life ? I remember it. You told me the whole sad story, and I've thought it over and over, and I've said she has been unfortunate, but not otherwise culpable. She went astray when she knew no better ; but it's not her fault, and she will do better when she's got the chance, and that chance she shall have, as sure as my name's Lanyard ! Yes, Louise ; that's just what I've said to myself, and I mean what I say. I've lived for many long months in the hope of seeing you, and making reparation for the wrong I unintentionally did you. I loved you before I parted with you. I love you still, so don't say no, girl ; consent to be my wife, and make me happy."

What more could Louise urge ?

She could only repeat again and again her one objection, but this was talked down, and she *did* consent, and in a short time they were married.

*   *   *   *   *

Five years passed away.

Lanyard made frequent voyages, and at length obtained the command of a vessel.

This was only the first step upward.

A series of lucky voyages produced immense sums of money for his proprietor, and he became a prime favourite.

Mr. Marchmont, the merchant in whose service Lanyard sailed, was a widower, and childless.

Suffering made him prematurely old, and at length he invited Lanyard and his wife to take up their abode with him.

They did so, and added some little comfort to the last days of a dying man.

At length the old man died ; on his will being opened, it was found that the whole of his enormous wealth had fallen to Lanyard—the only condition being that he assumed the name of Marchmont.

*   *   *   *   *

To the happy pair whose history we are now tracing was born a son, who, in a few years, became the light of their home.

Frank Marchmont was gifted with an artistic taste, which, in the course of time, ripened into perfection, and the boy, although so young, became one of the best painters of his time.

There is, however, no bright home uncrossed by a shadow, and that of the Marchmonts proved no exception to the rule.

The skeleton in their golden cupboard was found in the strange conduct of the idolised Frank, who had formed an attachment for some obscure girl, and this caused his parents great anxiety.

He made a secret of this passion, and his behaviour excited the greatest alarm, but no unkind word was spoken to him, and although he was closely watched, no restraint was put upon him. But this secret attachment was the bane of his parents' existence.

———

CHAPTER XII.

CONCERNING LEWIS ARNDALE AND HIS WIFE—THEIR DOWNFALL—THE EXILE—THE HOME IN THE MINORIES.

THE death of the Duke of Marklington did not at first excite any particular commotion, but on the speedy marriage of the Duchess with his slayer, the friends of the young noble suddenly awoke to a sense of wrong, and urged the authorities to take the matter in hand.

On the death of the Duke, the Prince of Wales wished to renew his intimacy with the widow.

But the rivalry of Arndale was too powerful, and his suit was scorned.

One day he met Olivia in the Park.

They were both on horseback.

The fair widow never before looked so charming, and the Prince was enraptured.

He watched her for some time, and at length drew close to her side, and seized her riding habit.

"You must hear me," he said; "I love you, Olivia, as dearly as ever, and you must be mine once more."

"Your Highness had best leave me," said Olivia, indignantly.

"I will not, by Heaven !"

"Pray, pray leave me ; your presence is painful to me."

"I will not listen to you. Pray turn, and leave the park with me."

"If your Highness does not desist, I will cry for aid."

"Olivia, I will not listen to such words."

He seized her habit as he spoke, and attempted to turn the head of her horse towards the park gates.

At this moment Arndale rushed into the Row, and by a single blow knocked the Prince from his horse.

This was sufficient.

He was seized, his disguise torn from him, and he stood before the world as the hunted felon—a leader in the band of Scarlet Brethren—a man whose life was forfeited to the laws of his country.

The extreme sentence of the law was not, however, carried into effect, and Arndale was transported for life.

The Prince proved his relentless foe, and his persecutions did not end with his transportation.

The very maid who waited on Olivia, and who was the *confidante* of her every action, was bribed into the service of the Prince, and whilst performing her offices, acted the part of a spy.

Others followed.

Trumpery charges were raked up against her, and at length she was imprisoned as an accomplice in the death of her husband, notwithstanding the well-known fact that he fell in fair fight. The effect was that her vast property was confiscated to the Crown ; and when she left the prison-house, it was with an infant daughter in her arms—born to poverty, and the inheritor of the scorn of a would-be sanctified world.

They worked hard, these two poor women, for many years, while the father wandered in a far-off land.

They worked that they might, one day, join him, and live in comparative happiness.

But it was a hard battle to fight ; and they found that they had all they could do to keep the wolf from the door—much more, to save money !

Meanwhile, Arndale wandered abroad. He had freed himself from the life of a galley slave in the dockyards, but he had never been able, even in foreign climes, to free himself from the brand upon him, and so passed away many years.

At length, Amelia, the daughter of the unfortunate Arndale, was thrown by chance in the path of a young man, for whom she at once conceived a liking.

He was rich, but she was steeped deep in poverty ; but still she saw that the affection he professed for her was pure and holy, and she listened to his addresses ! Listened to him trustingly, and that trust was never once abused.

But, as may be supposed, the poor mother, who had suffered so much, could not be brought to believe in his professions, and attempted to discourage his addresses ; but Frank Marchmont, for it was he who was the lover of Amelia, was not to be thrust off thus ; and, although not permitted to enter the doors of her he loved, still persisted in seeing her, and renewing those protestations that had won her heart.

CHAPTER XIII.

MOTHER AND DAUGHTER—THE PRINCE FRUSTRATED.

OUR readers will not be surprised to hear that the Prince had not lost sight of Olivia.

He could hate as well as love, and his vengeance was as great as his passions were strong.

He employed two men, named Bill Haggiss and Tim Larkall, vagabonds of the worst description, to watch over Olivia and her daughter.

He was Regent now, and the most powerful man in the universe.

He pursued these wretched women for two motives—the first to avenge the coldness of the mother ; the second to gratify his passions by gaining possession of the daughter.

To this end he engaged the ruffians we have named, and we regret to say that this was not the only instance in which they had acted for him, and under his orders.

Once the wretched Olivia was drawing water from an old well at the back of the house in which she resided.

It was one of those old-fashioned machines now no longer seen but in remote country places.

The water was drawn in a bucket, attached to a rope worked by a windlass.

As she bent over to seize the bucket she had raised to the brink, Haggiss, who had watched her, stepped forward and tipped her in.

He paused not a moment to contemplate his work, but fled at the top of his speed.

Well for him that he did, for at the instant Frank Marchmont came upon the scene.

He heard the piercing shriek of the mother of the woman he loved, and in an instant comprehended what had occurred.

Seizing the rope in his hand, he descended into the well, and soon re-appeared, bearing the half-drowned Olivia in his arms.

This act insured for the young painter Olivia's eternal gratitude ; but it could not induce her to admit of any intimacy with her child.

She shuddered at the disparity between their stations in life, and thought the wisest plan they could pursue was to forget each other.

But Marchmont was not to be daunted, and he persevered with his suit *sans intermission.*

Well for him, well for Amelia, well for all concerned, that he did so.

*   *   *   *

We must now introduce our readers into a house in St. James's-street, known as the most fashionable "Hell" of the metropolis. We do so in order to pursue the thread of this narrative.

"Liar."

"Ha!"

"I am cheated, robbed;" and the speaker, a handsome young man, threw his hand of cards on the table.

It was a private room of the gambling house in London.

A group of all characters were gathered round the table.

There were to be seen the professed aristocratic sharp—the easily gulled pigeon—the accomplished profligate and *roué*—the man who gambled for mere excitement, and he who indulged from infatuation and desire of gain.

The eyes of all were turned upon the excited young speaker, who, flushed and angry, had risen from his seat, and upon the individual to whom his observations were addressed.

This latter, a tall man, had also risen, but, unlike his adversary, he was cool and collected, and replied to the other's anger only by an ironical smile.

But when the word false was used, and he was accused of cheating, a dark flush tinged his cheeks, and he placed his hand on the shoulder of the other.

"Young man," he said, "I am not accustomed to be the subject of such charges. I must call upon you to retract your words before these gentlemen, who have seen me openly insulted."

"Never," returned the other impetuously; "I repeat I have been robbed; whether by you or by others of the players I am not able to state. I am no tyro, and know that not by fair means should I have been beaten every time."

"Insomuch as the charge affects me as one of your adversaries, I must request instant retraction and apology."

"Retract," said several; "apologise to his Highness."

"I will do neither. I am not to be juggled out of both money and honour."

"In that case," said he whom he had first charged, "I must have instant satisfaction. This is not a common fleecing-house. The nobility of England are present; they will hear my justification, but my wounded honour must be satisfied."

"Then I am ready," said the hot-headed young man. "I have fallen amongst thieves, and must prepare to defend my life."

"I have five minutes to spare," exclaimed the other, his eyes gleaming fiercely upon him; "choose your weapons, and let us be expeditious."

"Oh, let us have pistols. I will see them loaded; at any rate I will not be cheated of life."

"Fool!" said his unmoved adversary; "you would provoke me to anger."

Several of those present now strove to interfere, that they might prevent bloodshed: but the fiery young stranger would brook no interference, and soon the deadly weapons were loaded and handed to them by their hastily-chosen seconds.

The tall man took his place with steady precision, but his hot opponent, still labouring under the excitement of the wine he had imbibed, and the losses he had experienced, was more hasty in his movements, though unflinchingly resolute.

A deadly silence reigned. The two men whom the occurrence of a moment had thus placed in deadly antagonism, stood waiting the signal to fire; the cold steel barrels containing the murderous lead steadily poised for effective use.

The rest, who had risen from their play to witness this hastily got up duel, stood in expectancy of the result.

The seconds gave the words.

The reports were simultaneous, and the more youthful of the combatants staggered, reeled, and fell to the ground.

The other remained untouched.

"Wounded, but not dangerously," exclaimed one of the players, as he knelt beside the prostrate man.

"Let him be taken to his carriage," said the tall man, as he doffed his cloak and hat.

"Cheat," cried the wounded man; "there is armour beneath your dress, or that ball would have reached your cowardly heart. But we shall meet again; then guard your heart—I will reach it by other means."

The tall man bestowed a haughty glance upon him, but, disdaining a reply, left the room and the house.

"I must have hit him," again exclaimed the young man. "I could cut the stem of a flower at ten times the range; and it is not likely I should miss the part I covered."

"Who is he?" he inquired, as they were raising him from the floor.

"Don't you know *him?* He is the *gallant* Prince whom English dames love and fear."

"I shall know him and remember him, for, if I am not mistaken, I have a long account to settle."

Let us go before the Prince, and follow whither he is bound.

It is a lonely part of the Minories—a place that scarcely seems the fitting haunt of one of such high estate. A lonely spot, and a lonely house—tall, massive, and grim; the street is dark, and the place seems uninhabited.

There is much mirth afloat within, but not of an innocent, pleasing kind; the glances of the masculine portion of the guests are lit by an unholy fire as they gaze into the ravishing faces of the fairer beings by their side, who, in their turn, show, by the lascivious sparkle of their eyes, that they are not insensible to the ardour of the looks they encounter.

There would seem to be some of the noblest of England congregated, and some of the fairest of its dames.

The discourse is animated, the wine flows freely, and love and recklessness seem to bear the sway.

This is in one room of that large house; in another there is a different scene.

An apartment, somewhat luxuriously furnished, has for its occupant a fair young girl, whose deep blue eyes seem to beam with an all-absorbing love. Her complexion is as fair as the hue of the lily, but traced with the rose's bloom; her lips like softest-hued coral, and her hair like the golden skein of the Nereid's tresses.

But in those tremulous orbs there is a glistening tear, and the play of that lip bespeaks a spirit sad.

Why sits she, silent and sorrowful, in that lonely room, when at so little distance there is so joyous a gathering of mirth and gaiety?

A loud summons at the outer door—a heavy tread—resounded along the vestibule; the stairs were slowly ascended, and the key turned in the lock of her chamber door.

She was, then, locked in. Let us see for what purpose.

The door was opened abruptly, and the same tall man whom we have seen at the gaming-house strode into the chamber.

"Let us have no interruption," he said, as he shut the door and secured it on the inside.

At the sound of the key being turned the young girl had risen hurriedly and looked inquiringly towards the door, but as her glance rested on the Prince a shudder passed through her frame, and she wrung her hands in anguish.

An exultant smile rested on the face of the Prince as his eager glance scanned the shrinking maiden.

He was a somewhat austere-looking man; stern and dignified in countenance, with a cold piercing eye and a broad clear forehead.

There was, however, a voluptuous cast about the whole face that stamped him as a consummate roué and libertine.

His was a dangerous expression—implacability alternating with sensual profligacy, cruelty with amorous passions—the gleam of his eye, at one time cold and still, was the next instant fired by the light of unholy desire.

The young girl was the first to speak.

"It is for this, then, I have been inveigled here; it is a villany of *your* concoction, that you might foully triumph where you have failed to conquer."

"Amelia, I have offered you my love, and under such conditions that the highest born of England might have been proud to listen to my proposals; from you I have received scorn where I should have received gratitude—insult where I should have obtained your yielding love."

"Your offers have been insults," retorted the maiden, her blue eyes sparkling with a passionate glitter; "by what right dared you presume upon your rank to make me the object of your debasing proposals?"

"The right which love confers on all—the high or low, the meek, the proud. I beheld you, and your charms inspired me with that passion which still burns like a volcano within my breast—soon to be quenched, fair maiden. I hold you in my power; there are none here who will heed your cries; I have laid my plans securely. Decoyed by artifice, you will perforce become mine, even as I wished you to become of your own free will. You have caused this mode of procedure, and it will now rest with you what treatment you receive *after* my love has received its reward."

Amelia became more pale as she listened to his address.

His was no idle boast.

She was in his power, and the thought of what she might be subjected to by his lawlessness was agonising in the extreme.

Proud in his triumph the Prince advanced; but the fair girl, rendered brave by the peril in which her honour was placed, seized an ornamented poker from the handsome fire-place.

"Do not lay hands on me," she exclaimed, "I hold my honour dear, and will defend it with my life!"

She brandished the bright instrument in such a manner as to make the royal libertine shrink back apace; but recovering from the surprise in which her unexpected act had thrown him, he uttered a contemptuous laugh, and stepped towards her with the glittering poker yet in her hand, she eluded his grasp, and stepping round by the table, made for the door.

The Prince followed, and, as her hand was upon the bolt, grasped her by the shoulder.

"Cease this foolery," he exclaimed; "this house is filled with creatures of mine; rush where you will, you must eventually be taken. Why, then, by useless opposition, arouse my hate?"

Amelia slowly faced him.

"If I am thus in your power, I at least know how to defend myself. Dare not to commit this outrage; by Heaven, all London shall be ringing with it to-morrow."

The Prince smiled in derision.

"The ear of London would only open when a royal tongue spoke. Your words would be unheeded even if you were free to depart to-morrow —an extremely improbable contingency. Come, fair one, be reconciled to your fate. To-morrow you will be more contented, believe me, with the position in which I shall place you."

His hand, as he spoke, tightened upon her; she drew abruptly away and the jacket of lace torn from her shoulder revealed her white bosom to his lewd gaze.

A forward movement on his part was followed by the upraising of the shining poker.

It descended sharply on his head, causing him to stagger back.

Without waiting to see the effect of the blow, the beautiful maiden hastily opened the door and darted forth.

But whither now should she fly?

She knew not in what direction to proceed, for at every turn she might meet those who would be too willing to aid the profligate in his designs.

A muttered ejaculation from within the chamber told that the Prince was recovering from the effect of the blow, and, hearing him scrambling over the furniture, she darted up the staircase.

The door opened, and the Prince, uttering deep curses, followed. Up every flight of stairs the young girl passed with the speed of a doe, and when she arrived at the top, darted into the first room that presented itself to view.

She had heard her persecutor ascending after her; she flew to the window.

To look down upon the street made her giddy, the height was so great; escape was cut off that way, and retreat was impossible. She was safely penned and at his mercy.

As she was giving way to her despair, she caught sight of a small trap-door in the ceiling; a chair quickly placed on a table, enabled her to reach it, and she pressed through just as the Prince, angry and scowling, entered the room.

The trap-door took her to the top of the roof.

It was flat, and she rushed to the side; it was terrible to contemplate the darkness on which she gazed—still more terrible to contemplate the fate that awaited her if she hesitated. At some distance below her, she noticed what appeared to be the roof of another house. The leap would be a frightful one, and she paused. As the hand of the Prince touched her she, with a cry, flung herself off.

The roof to which the young maiden leapt, when escaping from her persecutor, was a flat one.

It was coated with lead, and had near the centre a very old glass trap or skylight.

In the gloom the heroic girl could not perceive this arrangement ere she took the terrific jump; and when, after whirling for a moment through the air, she passed, with a frightful crash, through some intervening obstacle, it seemed to her that the house was falling with her.

Almost instantaneously was her rapid descent arrested, but not, as she had anticipated, by her being crushed in the ruins of the building, or shattered to pieces on the pavement.

She alighted on a yielding substance; and, though the shock almost shook the remaining breath from her body, she retained sufficient consciousness to know that she had not sustained any severe injury.

At the same instant a startled shriek broke on her ears; lights flashed for a second before her eyes—then there was the deep tones of a man, and she was involved in darkness.

While she was pondering in her mind what had befallen her, she felt herself rudely grasped by the throat, and dragged from where she had fallen.

Stupefied by the whirl of events, she could offer no resistance, and she gave herself up for lost.

Anticipating, every instant, the plunge of the fatal knife, she lay perfectly passive—scarcely, indeed, breathing; and was considerably relieved when the man, who had before spoken, exclaimed:—

"Show the glim, it is a woman."

Presently, a light was struck, and the young girl was able to look around her.

The first object her eyes rested on was the inquiring face of a man not very far advanced in years.

He was bending over her, and held a long dagger in his hand.

There was not, however, that threatening expression on his countenance that would have boded her harm; he seemed, indeed, more startled than angered, and his features, somewhat refined, though marked by a dissolute

licentiousness, chased from her mind the dread that had at first been awakened there, though it created another feeling, tending to fear, in a different direction.

The woman now came forward. Her features, pretty in themselves, were improved by the rouge on her cheeks; but there was something in the glance of her eye that was far from prepossessing; of a light blue, large, but with small pupils, there was in them a cold, cunning glitter, to which a trace even of cruelty was added.

No other beings were in the room, and the real aspect of affairs now flashed to the mind of the young maiden.

She had fallen through the skylight, fragments of which were plentifully bestrewn about her, and her further fall had been broken by the bed in the room, from which she had been unceremoniously dragged by the man who upheld her, and who now again spoke.

"Where have you come from? How came you up there? Answer, before I stick you like a pig."

"I jumped from the house-top."

"From the house-top. What's your name?"

"Amelia."

"What were you up to on the roof?"

Now, it occurred to Amelia that if they were, as she conjectured, in any way connected with her titled prosecutor, it would not at all tend to obtain for her that liberty she so much desired, if she informed them why she had taken that desperate leap. She, therefore, hesitated, which the man observing, he repeated his question, this time in a more peremptory tone.

The woman, too, joined in.

"She's a spy; she's been prying about the house, I daresay. Better take her to the guv'nor."

"How came you in the house?" asked the man.

Amelia, who was now recovering from the stupefying effect of her fall, struggled to rise, and her captor permitted her to gain her feet; she was deadly pale, and her appearance tended considerably to soften the roughness of his manner towards her.

"Oh, sir," she exclaimed, "it is in your power to aid the innocent and unfortunate; brought here by violence, imprisoned in a chamber of this house, only that I might be a victim to the evil passions of a bitter and powerful enemy. I have, to escape from so terrible a fate, taken a leap that has been attended by a miraculous result; do not further oppress me; suffer me to depart, I implore you."

The man seemed doubtful how to act, and Amelia was about to renew her entreaties when Sail exclaimed, laying her hand upon the shoulders of the man—

"Do not let her go; she may be a spy upon us, and will betray us if she is permitted to leave. We must be cautious—better, far, that she should be altogether *silenced* than let her go to work our ruin."

There was something exceedingly horrifying in the words of that young being, who could so coldly recommend the murder of one of

her own sex, and Amelia shuddered as she listened.

"Hark!" again exclaimed the woman, "some one is approaching; we are betrayed."

She spoke this time in tones of terror, and, turning her cruel glance upon Amelia, drew a long thin knife from her dress, and, while her arm was raised threateningly, listened intently to the sound outside.

Amelia also strained her sense of hearing to the utmost, to discover whether the approach of her most dreaded foe were thus signalled.

A light footstep, but which echoed distinctly from without, was heard.

Whoever it was came very near the door, and, passing by, went slowly up the stairs.

It was curious to watch Sall while the footsteps were near. Her eyes were fixed with a glare, like that of the basilisk, alternately on the door and Amelia; and, with the keen blade in her hand, she seemed ready to spring upon the young girl immediately on the entrance of those whom she appeared so much to dread.

When the sounds had totally died away, she drew a long breath, and, replacing the dagger in her dress, opened the door, and gazed out.

It was very dark in the passage, and Amelia, actuated by a sudden impulse, sprang from the side of the man, and, darting past the surprised woman at the door, fled with a low shriek down the stairs.

"After her," exclaimed Sall, in dismay; "she will alarm the house. We are lost if she escapes."

The man bounded through the room, and was soon lost to view.

The part of the house in which Amelia found herself appeared but seldom visited; there was no light in any of the staircases, nor could she hear any sound, except her pursuer's footsteps, as he leapt hastily after her; arrived at the bottom of the stairs the passages ran to the right and left as well as before her, and uncertain which way to take to gain safety, she paused a moment to deliberate.

But each direction seemed alike dubious, and she had just rushed along the one before her, when the man, who had leapt over the banisters, sprang upon her and clutched the end of her flying dress.

Her flight was too impetuous for her to stop on the instant, and she dragged her pursuer after her; but her strength was not equal to the exertion, and, half-way down the passage, she sank helplessly on her knees.

Her assailant grasped her by the shoulder, and drew his knife.

"Necessity, and regard for the honour of that lady, compels these measures," he said, as he placed the deadly weapon to her throat.

But even as the terrified Amelia, shrinking from the cold touch of the fatal steel, momentarily anticipated her horrible death, a hand was placed on the arm of the man, and the knife was wrenched from his grasp.

"Return to your vile partner in guilt," said a voice, whose cold, stern accents filled him with awe, "and leave unmolested this innocent and much-outraged being."

A tall woman, dressed in a long, dark robe, stood by his side.

Her touch was like ice, and the man, awed to cowardice, turned and fled, pausing not to look behind him, till he again stood before the guilty woman whom he had left cowering in the chamber.

Grateful for her deliverance the young girl sank sobbing at the feet of her mysterious protectress, who, taking her kindly by the hand, raised her from the floor.

"Come," she said, "I will conduct you from this cursed abode of crime and mystery."

Joyously the young girl followed; and her conductress, leading her through a lofty room, conveyed her by a secret door to a corridor leading from the house; a smaller door she opened, and the cold air of the night blew in upon them.

"You are now free," exclaimed her guide; "beware that you fall not again in the power of that evil being, from whom you have this night, as a reward for your heroic defence of your virtue, been most miraculously saved.'

"Lady, I know not who you are," murmured the young girl, "who have so kindly delivered me from this house of ill. Nor know I how sufficiently to thank you for the good service you have rendered me. Receive the grateful blessings of a defenceless girl, who, in her prayers, will remember one who has befriended her in her utmost need."

"Thanks are not due to me, fair maiden; thank rather him who befriended you when you took that terrible leap. Go, now; lose no time in returning to your home; the hour is late, and these are unsafe times for innocence and virtue to be abroad."

Amelia, yet mystified by the events of that night, hurried to her home, there to ponder upon what had befallen her, and to revolve in her mind those things which, though she knew it not, were hereafter to involve her future destiny in a complication of trouble.

Her escape from the voluptuous Prince only made him the more than ever determined on effecting her ruin; but that night he had made another enemy. The man with whom he had fought was Frank Marchmont, the son of the woman he had years ago betrayed and deserted.

CHAPTER XIV.

THE RETURN OF THE WANDERER—AN ATTEMPTED ABDUCTION FRUSTRATED.

It is midnight—cold, wretched and gloomy; the rain pelters through the streets, and the wind soughing by, seems to speak of misery and destruction.

The streets of London are deserted; and the good people, cosy between their sheets, pity the unhappy mariners compelled to brave the fury of tempestuous seas.

Coarse-minded ruffians, intent only on their nefarious plans, associate in unknown kens and secluded corners, there to scheme fresh deeds of villany.

In a dismal quarter of the city, a part where shrinking poverty and hardened vice jostle each other; where the huddled hovels of the wretched congregate, far from the lofty palaces of the wealthy, we will now direct our steps, and follow the course of events.

Amidst the beating rain and sweeping wind, heedless of the elements' fury, a man, clad in a long and tattered cloak, proceeded with tottering steps through the sloshy streets.

He was weary and weak, and often when the rude blast bore fiercely against him, he leant upon his staff to steady himself from the raging tempest.

In appearance, he was somewhat singular: his face unwashed and careworn, his hair unkempt and straggling; his long beard, fluttering in the wind, added to the effect produced by his drenched and tattered garments, and bespoke extreme poverty and wretchedness; yet there was a something in his aspect that seemed to speak of a past dignity: it was like the remnant of a by-gone grandeur clinging to him in the shattered wreck of his fortunes.

Occasionally he paused: and, leaning against some friendly doorway, took momentary shelter from some sweeping gust, which dashed the cold rain in his prematurely aged face; and then, with lips quivering, and eye bedimmed with tears, looked mournfully around and about, now gazing dreamily at the humble habitations and the darkened sky.

And at length his thoughts found vent in

words, and, while a tear trickled down his cheek, he cried—

"Will it never have an end—will my wanderings never cease, my sufferings never terminate? Long, long, I have plod my weary way; spurned where I should be caressed, degraded where I should be exalted; will it never, never, have an end; must I for ever, with the brand of shame and misery on my brow, wander over the earth an outcast and an alien?"

The winds, as they tore by the old houses, moaned drearily, and swept the words from his quivering lips; a peal of thunder boomed, and his grieving tones died away unheard.

"Oh, God," he continued, "why am I thus accursed—shall not my years of agony and toil, ages of sorrow—of shame—during which my tears have been blood, and my food misery—shall not these atone for the deeds of the past; must they ever remain searing on my brain, burning in my heart? Oh, God, hear me, and deliver me from my appalling doom."

In torrents fell the rain; gloomily the cannons of heaven rumbled in the distance, and a sheeted gleam of lightning encircling the city with its one, played about the gables of the dim building, and showed the aged wayfarer in his wretchedness and pain.

More unavailing prayers he murmured, his hot tears the while trickling on the wet pavement, and when he found that all were unanswered, he drew his rags of poverty around him, and leaning for support on the staff his hands but slightly held, passed on his weary way.

He was not so very old—that sorrow-stricken man—though his form was bent and his hairs were grey; the iron hand of grief and shame had borne upon his stooping frame, and his limbs shook and yielded in age, toil and famine.

For he had wandered far, unto they food, and receiving no rest; with the crushing weight of misfortune on his form, and the fiery brand of crime upon his brow.

Crime! For he reaps in his old years the fearful fruits of early crimes.

He has sinned, but only as an atom in the scale have been his crimes, compared to the wrongs that have been perpetrated against him. And this has silvered his tangled hair, and whitened his majestic beard.

Feeble and staggering he tottered on: the rain pelted in his eyes, and the wind snatched at his gasping breath; still the man bore up bravely, and wandered on.

Wandered whither—and whereof so?

Anywhere, that he might hide his head, and rest his aching limbs.

Down a lowly, dimly-lighted street he wends his way; his limbs are becoming weaker, and he leans against the houses as he pass, for the trusty staff can scarcely now support his frame.

The rude wind buffeted him to and fro, and he sways like a drunken man; but, ere he reaches the end of that dismal street, a dizziness overtakes him, his limbs gave way, and he lies fainting on a lowly doorstep.

His head falls upon his breast, his matted locks, soiled with toil and travel, cover his head:

his staff, a ghostly pallor overspreads his features, and he feels that he is dying.

The wind sweeps by in triumph; the rain beats down in fury; and the old man sits where, in his weakness, he has fallen.

Shall he thus perish, unaided and alone?

Is there no succour at hand—no good Samaritan to administer reviving cordial, to arouse his ebbing faculties? No attending angel to moisten those parched lips, and win that heart from the sway of death?

The lamplight sheds its ghastly glare upon him, playing with strange effect on his half-shown countenance.

Half of his form is shown in the gaslight; the remainder is lost in the gloom of the doorway.

A groan escapes his lips—a thrill creeps through his shivering frame—the head sinks lower—he falls inanimate.

Is he to die?

No!

The door is opened slowly, and a young maiden stands upon that threshold. She has heard that smothered groan, and has come to see what human being can be so superlatively wretched even in that haunt of misery.

Her inquiring glance changed to one of pity as she looks upon the stranger; and she stoops over him, to see if he yet breathes.

She is herself but meanly clad; though her dress is neat, and her appearance prepossessing.

She is evidently one of that humble class who, if they have but one loaf, will share it with those who have none.

Softly she spoke to the drooping wayfarer; tenderly she took his arm, and endeavoured to raise him from his lowly posture.

There was magic in the touch—a talisman in her tones.

The traveller was partially aroused from his death-like stupor.

He raised his head dreamily, and seemed to be listening again for those sweet, cheering accents.

"Alas! good sir," said the young girl, "you are ill and weary; let me assist you to rise, that you may enter our humble dwelling."

Still dreamily, and with a vacant stare, the old man regards her; then, with his trembling hands he grasped her wrist, and muttered, almost inaudibly—

"Speak again—let me hear your voice; speak, if I am not dreaming."

"You are too weak to rise," rejoined the maiden; "stay here, and I will call my mother."

"No, no," murmured the old man hastily, and in a voice broken with emotion, "do not leave me—do not leave me. Speak again, and let me look into your face. Those tones, so like the tones of bygone days, have called me back to life; let me hear them again. Come, I am strong now, I will accompany you in."

With his palsied hands he grasped her delicate arm, and, slowly rising to his feet, looked wonderingly into her face; and, with lips trembling and eyelids quivering, leaned his head upon her shoulder, and entered the house.

A touching sight it was to see, by the light of the garish lamp, that fair young girl, with the stricken, drooping man resting on her for support—his eyes swimming in a sort of delirious joy, and his broken accents pleading for her to speak, but not to desert him.

He was shaking and tottering in his weakness, and his progress was slow.

He clung to the young maiden, and murmured in thankfulness and joy when they were safely inside.

She led him into a humbly-furnished room, where a low fire was burning in the grate. A small lamp, placed on the table, threw a flickering light round the room, playing upon the careworn features of a benignant-looking, elderly female, who, habited in the garb of woe, sat by the scanty fire.

She rose as the young girl, with her trembling charge, entered.

The old man's face was resting on the shoulder of the kind-souled maiden, so that she could not even get a glimpse of his features; but when he stood in the middle of the room and, still tremulously holding his fair preserver, endeavoured to support himself, and gazed round the apartment, a sudden shriek broke from her lips, and, with open arms, she darted forward.

What can blind the eye of love?

Will it not trace out its object even when the lapse of years have furrowed the youthful cheek and seamed the placid brow?

The eyes of that aged pair, encountering at the same time, caused a thrill like an electric shock to pass through their frames; and as that cry escaped from the woman's lips, the weary stranger, endowed with fresh life and vigour, sprang forward to meet her.

"My wife—my child!" he exclaimed, and, with a sob of joy, fell senseless into her arms.

And mutely wondering stood that gentle girl.

This man was Lewis Arndale; the women were his wife and child.

*　　*　　*　　*　　*

While the weary wanderer was tottering on his way, previous to his being guided by an unseen Providence to the house of those so dear to him, a scene, of a very different character to that which shed its cheering sunbeams on his troubles, was occurring at a house not two hundred yards from that which had given him shelter and welcome.

It was an old-fashioned inn, situate in one of the lowest streets of the capital.

Surrounded by wretched tenements, within which dwelt the miserable victims of penury and vice, it was the focus of every crime and villany; the favoured resort of those whose deeds were the deeds of desperate criminality.

The house was closed, and, to all appearance, the inmates had betaken themselves to rest.

The interior, however, told a different tale.

Here, in a large, dreary room, dimly lighted by several flaming lamps, were assembled a disorderly group, comprising half a dozen ill-looking men, and one or two jaded and tawdrily-bedizened women.

Some were standing near the expiring fire of logs; others, sitting on low stools, were busily engaged in the concoction of fresh plans of villany, or in coarse and jocular reminiscences of past well-executed schemes, refreshing themselves the while by imbibing largely of the strong liquors before them.

Among these latter may be classed two men of evil aspect, who, closely seated at a table, appeared to be indulging in lively anecdotes of their bygone sports.

Self-satisfaction was depicted on the ruffianly faces of each; and so eager were they in their discourse that they did not heed the proximity of a third individual, who, closely jammed in a corner behind them, his arms folded, and his back against a wall, was in such a position that he could easily overhear every word that passed between the two confederates in crime.

He was a burly-formed man, with broad, thick-set shoulders, a deep chest, and short, thin legs, attached to which were two huge feet, encased in boots that made them seem literally Titanic in proportion.

His features were squatty and close. A low forehead, rendered more repulsive by the thick, coarse eyebrows above his restless, cunning eyes, a flat, heavy chin, whereon not a vestige of hair appeared, and a mouth, the expression of which was indicative of brutal ferocity, imaged his personal beauties.

He wore a short rough jacket, a fly cap, from beneath which straggled a few tufts of hair; his legs were clothed to the knee in short cords, and a pair of leather gaiters reached to his lower extremities.

A formidable cudgel, tightly grasped, rested between his knees, and needed not the peculiar twist of his blue cotton necktie to convince the beholder that he was one of that class of British ruffians, familiarly known under the term of "bull-dogs."

He was unmistakably English — the worthy representative of a type more famed in the Newgate Calendar than in virtuous annals; and as he sat, squeezing himself into the smallest possible compass, he seemed to take a great interest in the conversation going on between those who surrounded him.

This man was no other than Hammer, once the friend of Yellow Maydock.

The elder of the two ruffians was speaking, a villanous look in his sunken eyes as he discoursed.

"Ah! those were jolly times: not a week but some bit of business was in hand; the cracking a crib, the overhauling of some traveller's luggage, the battering in of some skull, for which we were well paid, or the kidnapping and strangling of some squeaking kid—those were good times, indeed. Things are getting dull now; travellers leave their load at home, now; and there don't seem to be no one whose head's wanted to be cracked. Even our old employer, the King, has shut up shop, and there's hardly a chance of turning in a penny."

"Truly, Bill," returned the other, "the times are hard; they'll be better soon, I hope, or we must drive the nail deeper into the King."

"Not much chance there, he's getting as chary of cash as he is of business, and don't seem to want too much of our considerate company."

"He is a tough skinflint, but we've seen the colour of a few of his shiners."

"And done a few awkward jobs for him."

The two worthies laughed, and the third rough seemed by the restless gleam of his eyes to be intently listening to every word.

"And now, comrade, about that little matter that you said you had got in hand."

"Oh, that's an old task, and one that we've been on for a long time, though it's only now that we're at all near the job. You recollect the old party as used to live some years ago at the big crib close alongside of the artillery house?"

"What him as had the woman that the King was always a-trying after!"

"The very identical. Of course you know all that happened—how the King tried all he knew to get hold of her, and how the old man found him there and pitched him into the street? Ah, there was always something pretty deep between them two, or he'd never have gone to work the way he did; they were old pals, I reckon, in many a deed as won't bear the naming; but that kick cost him dear—he was had up for murdering that gal as was found with her breasts cut off in his chambers, and it cost him nearly all his fortune to get clear of that mess; and then we had to do that little job that helped him off his stray articles of plate—that didn't make him much the richer, and when the King managed to carry off his wife it near upon drove him mad. It's a mystery to me how she ever got out of his clutches, though I daresay he made the most of the short time he did have her. But old Arndale never believed her anything but untouched. He didn't half know the King, or he wouldn't have thought so, nor yet have openly accused him of the act and challenged him to fight it out. The King wasn't over fond of making himself a target for other people to shoot at, and when he appointed the meeting in the park he might have guessed what was up; but not he—he walked straight into the trap, and only found out what he was invited there for when they clapped hands upon him. That was another mystery—how she got notice of what was going on in time to make off with her child afore we had time to put our mauleys on her; perhaps his ghost comed to her. Anyways, she was off in a jiffy, and we didn't gain much for finding the nest empty."

"Except threats and oaths," put in his companion.

"Plenty of them; they always was very plentiful; and many's the time, when I've been all alone with him, that I've had a good hard job to keep my sticker out of his back. But he pays well, and that makes up for it. Howsoever, as I was saying, that's been our job ever since, to find out what became of her and her precious little girl that he's been so anxious about; and a long time we've been about it, looking in every crib but the right one; for hang me if I should ever have thought of looking after her in the quarter where I found her."

"Found her?"

"Found at last, girl and all. And hasn't she grown a stunner!"

"Where—where did you find her?"

"Why, you see, it was the other night, or rather morning—for it was precious late—after I had been to see our old pals at the helm, that I was coming on to this crib, when I sees in front of me a girl, walking at such a rate that when I comed up to her I took a hard squint, to see if she had any slipping machines, instead of boots, on. After I'd looked at her feet of course I took a twig of her face, and, blow me, if I wasn't nearly staggered; for if she wasn't as like the very party we'd been so long hunting for, only that she seemed to have grown younger by a good deal. I was rather puzzled, and, as I didn't know but what she might have been a ghost, I took the liberty to convince myself by putting my arms round her waist and giving her a kiss. Such a screaming and tussling as she commenced nearly scared me out of my wits, and I was just thinking about pulling out my hand-chopper to stick into her, when I got a tap under the ear that made me see seven lamps where there was only one. Her fellow, I suppose it was (I shall know him again), had been watching about, to be near her window while she was sleeping—the angel. He walked her off while I was finding the softest stone to lie on till I comed round; but I twigged where he took her—a house with a lamp at the corner. He gives a peculiar knock, and, blow me, who should come out but the very woman herself. I seed it then at a go; it was the daughter that I'd first come across."

"This is a lucky go," exclaimed his accomplice in guilt.

"I reckon on it; not that I think he'll want the mother now, hot as he was after her. She's got rather old and looks all the worse for her trials and misfortunes, as the chaplain kiddy at the jail would say. But there's the girl; she's young, blooming, and lovely, and, as far as I can judge from the hug I gave her, she'd turn out just the plump sort of article that the governor's so mad after."

"We're born under a lucky star. What do you mean doing? Bring the King where he can see her at her house?"

"No," returned the ruffian: "I have taken a bit of a fancy to her myself, and I'd like to leave that cove of hers a sweetener for the lump he put on the back of my skull. I'll get her clean off, take her to our crib, and then, if I shouldn't be tempted first myself, bring the governor there. I think the job would be a handsome one."

"When shall we set about it?"

"In a few nights. I've got a little more to find out before we can do it, and there's a little more to tell you, which I'll explain as we go along."

The two worthies rose and left, and the listener, eyeing them from beneath his bushy brows, was about to follow, when a sudden com-

motion that rose in the room checked his pere-
grinatory movement.

The commotion in question consisted of a
most violent and noisy outbreak, directed, as he
plainly saw, against himself.

*   *   *   *   *

Who that, after weary wanderings in distant
realms, has returned to his native land and
home, has not felt within his heart a bounding
joy, a melting emotion, so soul enthralling, that
he or she has felt contented to die at the feet of
some idolised object, or lie before some cherished
spot and calmly die?

Who but they, who, in toil and travail, have
journeyed in alien lands, where the soothing,
dear tones of kindred were never heard, and
where the soul was as the sun-scorched desert,
consumed by that yearning for the sympathy
and love of kindred friends, has not looked with
tear-dimmed eye and heaving breast on the distant orb setting, to rise on the land of their
birth?

Happy, happy, they who, when their feet rest
once again on their beloved shores, know where
to turn to the hearts that joyfully beat for their
coming; desolate and bleak, indeed, those who
come only to find the home of old deserted and
silent—the hearts of love, throbless and cold!

Long was it before the wanderer—whom we
left newly restored to those from whom wide
years had marked the separation—was sufficiently recovered again to speak, and when once
more his faculties returned, and his eye rested
upon the face of that being whom he had
deemed lost for ever, fresh tears trickled down
his furrowed cheeks, and in piteous tones he
besought them not to leave him.

It was evident that the memory of his deep
sufferings were strong upon him, and that he
dreaded lest the fearful cup of joy should be
dashed from his lips ere he had time to quaff its
delicious fulness.

The young girl, who had stood timidly apart,
rushed to his arms when she heard that it was
indeed her long-lost parent who had thus returned, and when the now-assured old man sat
with his hands clasped upon those of his
cherished wife, and his daughter, scarcely seen
since her birth, resting with her arms about his
neck, and her face pressed against his grey
hairs, he felt that the sum of his happiness was
complete.

But joyful as was that hour, his prostrate condition prevented its continuance; and, when
such refreshments as were best calculated to
restore his enfeebled system were administered,
he was conducted to his bed, his faithful wife
remaining up to watch by the returned one's
bedside.

For a few days he hovered between life and
death, for, so weakened had he become, that it
seemed he had but reached them that he might
die; and as, from fear of discovery, he would
not suffer any physician to be fetched, his recovery depended solely upon the skill and attention of those who were with him.

And this availed; for, after a short time, he
slept more composedly, not starting in his sleep,
as he had been wont to do at first, but with a

tranquil look of felicity on his features, and a
smile of joy about his lips.

After this his strength returned by degrees,
and he was at length enabled to leave his bed,
and to sit by the window, to again seek such
fresh air as the close jumble of buildings in that
poverty-stricken corner permitted him to
breathe.

Much had the restored husband and wife to
discourse upon, their confidences were not half
told; and in their lengthened conversations they
learned how much each had suffered for the
other.

Darker grew the look of Arndale when his
wife revealed the persecutions and indignities
she had received at the hands of their implacable
foe; and, as he listened, the hot blood again
rushing through his veins told that the vigour
of yore was not entirely shattered.

"We must leave this place," he said; "it is
dangerous to remain. I tremble lest the eye of
officious curiosity, or cunning malice, should
light upon us—discovery would be death, for
the machinations of the Satan-like enemy have
so cast their web around me that it is not enough
that dishonour has overtaken me, but I must
suffer more. In my bitter hours of suffering
and agony, when drooping by the way, I have
lain as I thought to die, many have been the
terrible oaths I have breathed that if I were
spared he should render a terrible reckoning;
but much as I seek that vengeance, which must
and shall come, I know too well his power to
brave it here. In security I may continue my
plans, long nourished, but for the present our
safety only must be regarded."

"Let us," replied his wife, "in our thankfulness that we were again permitted to meet in
this world, suffer the past to be buried for ever.
Let us hence in some other land, where the
power of the oppressor shall be vain; we may
attain those sweets of felicity that may recompense us for our years of bitter grief."

The colour rose to the man's cheek, and the
light of old burnt in his deep blue eyes.

"Think you," he exclaimed, "that I would
tamely pass over those long years of torture,
when the hand of misfortune has been like a
burning ploughshare in my heart? Shall I forget those deep injuries that have galled my soul
till my blood has changed to liquid bitterness.
Am I to relinquish the sole desire which has put
vigour to my frame, and strengthened my sinews
when they have been warped by the wear of toil and
misery? No! I have lived for this revenge, and
in a terrible retribution will I wash out the
memory of those blighting sorrows, caused and
accomplished by that fiend alone."

His passion increased, and as he proceeded,
his aspect was majestic in the extreme. His
wife heard in silence: she dared not say more
lest she should provoke him to anger, but her
heart misgave her when she saw him so bent on
avengement, for she knew the power of their
unrelenting foe, and was too well aware that
he would not rest if he discovered them till he
had dragged them down to the abyss of destruction.

So she pursued the matter no further, and the

old man absorbed in the remembrance of his wrongs, and in anticipation of their avengement, relapsed into a moody silence.

But afterwards, when their daughter came softly into the room, his heart was touched, and he regretted any measures that might tend to involve her in misery and tribulation.

"Come hither," he said. "tell me how you like the haunts of London?"

"Alas, father, I like not the place; even for my young years, it teems with bitter reminiscences; there seems to be ever resting over me an unseen peril, which sooner or later must overtake me; I dread the very air, and never tread these streets at dark that I do not feel that I am doomed never to reach home again."

"This is a maiden's timidity; you will subdue it as you grow older; but why are you out so late—and is it often so?"

"It will never occur again, now that you have come, dear father; I had heard from my mother that in the gloomy prison in the Fleet you were incarcerated; and I had dreamed once that at midnight, by its walls, I should meet you returning to us; and though the sight of its heavy-looking walls has appalled me with terror. I have wandered continually on the recurrence of the night of my dream, about the precincts of the frowning old castle, trembling at every sound, and shuddering whenever my eyes have rested on the grim walls. Midnight after midnight have I waited in fear and horror, but you came not: a thousand such nights would I have freely passed to have been blest by your return. May the heavens be praised that you have come at length."

The old man caught the pale-faced, devoted daughter in his arms.

"Bless you, my child," he exclaimed, "yours was indeed a most romantic devotion; but were you always alone in that dreary spot?"

Amelia blushed as she replied: "At times I have been accompanied by a youth who has, more than once, protected me from insult; but more frequently I have been alone."

"And this youth, who is he?"

"His name is Frank. He is a painter, poor in purse, but rich in honour."

"I have not seen him since my return," said her father.

"He does not visit us; my dear mother has led me to believe that it would be wrong to encourage his attentions. I have refrained from doing so, and have, indeed, treated him coldly even when his services have stood me in great need."

"I have done so," said the wife, "that there might be formed no attachment which might have afterwards proved perplexing."

"You have done right, wife."

"Still I believe him to be honourable and true; and I doubt not, though we have not seen him, that he has more than one night kept guard and watch beneath Amelia's window."

At this the old man started violently, and the colour left his cheeks.

"He will betray me! he will betray me! Oh! why did you not tell me of this before?"

Alarmed by the thought his fears had suggested,

the old man's terrors returned in all their force, nor could all the efforts of mother and daughter pacify him.

"I am betrayed," he moaned; "all my dangers are lost in this; my past miseries rise before me, and I know that I shall be again torn from your side, perhaps never to see you more."

"Be assured," said his wife, while Amelia shed tears at her father's distress; "the youth is too noble, too upright to breath a word to anyone, even if he ever heard or saw you; besides his love for Amelia would keep him silent."

"The reverse," cried the agitated man; "he may make use of this discovery as a means of compelling you to give him our child, if you say you have led him to believe he cannot have her; it is the way of the world, and you will see it will be so now."

"I don't think it; but to make all sure, I will summon him to our presence."

"No, no; in Heaven's name do not so rash a thing. He may not have seen me; but, if he has not, that would be a sure way of placing me in his power."

"Indeed you may trust him——"

"I will trust no one; I have trusted too often, and been betrayed. No, we will hasten from this spot—from this land; only when on a distant shore shall I breathe freely."

The old man's terror was pitiful in the extreme, and it was long before his alarm could be sufficiently toned down for him to listen to the suggestions made to ensure his safety; but finally it was decided that as soon as his strength would permit, they should depart from the city, and embark on board some vessel bound for the Continent.

When this was settled, the old man became much quieter and retired early to rest, where he slept that fitful slumber of the weary and fearful; in his dreams he looked for the shores of France, whither he resolved speedily to journey but that night occurred events that not only scattered his newly-made plans to the winds, but threatened again to involve him in the meshes of danger and suffering.

*　　*　　*　　*

The house in which the returned exile and his wife and daughter dwelt was, as we have before mentioned, situated in a low quarter of the purlieus of the city, and was itself ancient, gloomy, and tumble-down.

A small, antique window, constructed when glass was less known and dearer priced than at present, overlooked the street; this was the window of Amelia's humble room.

From the limited size of the dwelling, it did not boast of many rooms, and the chamber in which the old man slept with his wife was contiguous.

The mother and daughter had sat up rather late that evening, for the words of Arndale had created some commotion in the breast of Amelia, and a lengthened conversation was held, as to the best means of bringing about an introduction between him and the youth whose devotion to their cause they knew would, if anything, be increased by the knowledge of the wanderer's presence.

They needed, besides, the clear head and vigorous energy of the young lover, to combat those difficulties which it was too evident would be inadequately met by themselves; and having determined upon again breaking the matter to Arndale in the morning, they retired, Olivia to rest by the side of the husband of her youth, and her daughter to sleep in her lonely chamber.

A very timid, and yet very brave, girl was Amelia.

Her's was a soul shrinking in terror at a sound; yet desperately nerved to heroism when the hour of peril arrived.

She was sensitive in the highest degree, but, docile and obedient, she followed implicitly the guidance of those who had the right to counsel her.

That the handsome young Frank had made a deep impression on her heart cannot be denied; she loved him with the sacred feeling of maiden tenderness, which makes of the loved object an idol upon the highest shrine.

It was with grief, then, that she heard her father so positively set his veto against his being admitted into their confidence, and, with the unfathomable gloom still overhanging her, she retired to rest with a mind troubled at the view into the dim and teeming future.

She lay deeply meditating, till she sank into a slumber.

Restless dreams attended her, and she occasionally awoke with fitful starts—soon, however, sinking to sleep again.

From the last of these she awoke with a start; it seemed that she had slept an age; and, hardly yet in the clear possession of her faculties, she gazed around.

The moon was dimly flickering through the interstices of the blind at her casement, and lighting with a feeble radiance the apartment.

Such furniture as the room possessed was thrown into obscurity by the deep gloom, and the light, playing upon the surfaces, threw them into all kinds of shapes and outlines, suggesting a thousand fears to the timid maiden's fancy.

After lying for some time—kept awake by an oppressive dread—she was just about to drop off to sleep again when a slight noise awoke her fully with a start.

It was on the outside of her door, and sounded like the creaking of a man's boots.

What could it be? Surely not her father walking about the house.

It could not be her lover, for he would never have dared thus to approach.

Her dreading mind pictured all sorts of horrid fancies, in the midst of which she suddenly thought of the ruffian who had waylaid her when returning from her romantic and devoted expedition in search of her father, and from whom her lover's timely arrival had rescued her.

Another moment and her worst fears received their confirmation.

The door was slowly opening.

Spell bound and unable to utter a cry, she lay, her heart palpitating and her brain teeming with the wildest apprehensions, while the door continuing to open, revealed the form of a man, clad in a rough attire, and his face concealed by a crape mask.

He held in his hand a lantern, but its light was unnecessary, for the faint moonbeams revealed him to the shivering maiden as plainly as it disclosed her to his lawless gaze.

It was one of the ruffians of the tavern.

His confederate in villany having communicated to him the whereabouts of their intended victim, it had occurred to him that he might make use of the opportunity for doing a good stroke of business before his accomplice had time to join him.

Accordingly he had quietly stole to the house; the door, old and rickety was soon forced, and, closing it softly after him, he crept stealthily upstairs to the chamber of the unfortunate maiden.

The impulse to cry out that had at first occurred to Amelia was overcome by prostrating fear, and she still lay in that half comatose state, while the hardened ruffian crept on tiptoe to her bedside.

Any outcry that she might now have made was immediately prevented, for the scoundrel, though scared at first by beholding her with her eyes wide open gazing upon him, quickly recovered from his surprise, and with the rapidity of an adept at the art, placed a muffler over her mouth.

"Get up," he said coarsely, "dress yourself, for you're going a journey along of me, and I don't want you to catch cold by being naked."

Amelia did not move, and the brutal fellow, seizing her by the arm, dragged her from the recumbent posture in which she was lying, his iron grip leaving the marks of his fingers on her delicate arm.

"Come," he continued, as he drew his large, broad-bladed knife, "put on your rig, and come without any trouble: if you make any noise, I'll stuff this cold sticker into your chest. So if you don't want any of that business, dress, and be quick."

That icy dread which had so long possessed her, grew stronger upon her; she felt that the terrible and long anticipated crisis had come, and, under the influence of that unknown spell proceeded to obey the ruffian's brutal dictates.

It was not without a shudder at being compelled thus to appear unrobed before him that she left her bed, fortunately her night-robe was long, and she was thus screened from his rude gaze.

Over this she hastily threw her dress, and the ruffian, casting a large mantle over her, caught her in his arms, and passed with her out of the room.

So quickly was she whirled from her chamber, and down the stairs that she had not time for reflection, and when safely away from the spot where her father slept, and no longer awed by the sight of that terrifying knife, she struggled with her assailant, and, in the hurried moment, taking him by surprise, freed her arm so as to reach the gag on her mouth.

This she removed, and forgetful of everything save the outrage offered her, gave vent to a loud shriek of agony, that echoed wildly through the house.

The brutal fellow dropped her instantly to the floor, and again drawing his knife, stood over her menacingly; but she heeded not his threats; her excited mind was beyond control; and springing to her feet, she dashed away from him, at the same time repeating that terrible shriek.

It was answered by one from above; and the voice of the old man was heard in hurried accents of alarm.

Another voice was heard—a voice well-known to the young girl—and which assured her that she would be saved.

She was not mistaken in her conjecture as to who owned that voice, for just as she fell fainting at her assailant's feet, and the ruffian upraising his knife, was about to plunge it into her breast, a figure was seen flying by the balustrade, and her lover swiftly descending the stairs, leapt upon the desperate scoundrel.

With a terrible oath the ruffian turned upon the youth, and the two struggled with determined fury.

The former still held the deadly weapon, but the grip of his youthful assailant rendered him powerless to use it; in vain he tried every method in his power to overcome him; the young painter was strong and powerful, and he wrested the knife from his grasp at the very moment that Arndale, who had tremblingly descended the stairs, struck the fellow a terrible blow with his staff on the back of the head.

The ruffian fell senseless to the ground, and Arndale with an exultant cry, bent over him.

The victim of his brutal indignity lay fainting on the floor, and the young painter and Arndale stood gazing at each other.

Only for a moment did the mistrustful glance of the old man rest upon the deliverer of his daughter.

A beam of joyful confidence replaced it, and outstretching his arms, he clasped the young painter to his breast.

And here it may be as well to explain how the lover came thus opportunely to the aid of Amelia. As Olivia had surmised, he had kept watch over her night after night, and on that eventful evening he had been at a distant studio, from which he returned only when the predatory villain had, unseen, obtained an entrance.

Unaware of the outrage to which she was being subjected, he stood thoughtfully before the house, and was only aroused by that terrible scream which, ringing through the house, awoke the old man and his wife.

Rushing to the door, the young painter wildly strove to obtain admittance, but, unprovided with the implements used by the burglar, he was unable to enter.

Meanwhile Lewis and his wife, who, hearing their daughter's scream of distress, had hurried into her chamber—came to the window to call for help. Had not Olivia recognised the young artist, it is probable that Lewis would, in his frenzied alarm, have hurled some weighty piece of furniture upon him, deeming him to be an accomplice.

Satisfied that he was a friend, they implored him to enter, and Frank failing to gain ingress by the door, in his desperate energy, actually climbed up the front of the house and entered by the window, a means he had often contemplated, when on his lonely watch he had thought upon the readiest means of rescuing her in case an outbreak of fire should render her in need of swift aid.

There were tears in the father's eyes as he thanked the young painter.

"You have indeed rendered me a service, and now that I am assured of your fidelity and heart, I will take you to my confidence. I am the parent of that dear child whom you have guarded while I have been wandering an outcast upon the face of the earth. I am proud to call you my friend, though, alas! the friendship of the unfortunate is less a blessing than a curse to him who is the recipient of it.

"Sir, you indeed honour me," exclaimed the painter, "it has been my only solace to be near your beloved child, whom these villains seek to ensnare. Call not your friendship a curse; it is a boon—a honour I do no merit. Yes, will I strive to render myself worthy of your esteem. My services are yours. Name any task you wish executed, and if possible of accomplishment I will perform it."

"I thank you. But let us look forward to brighter views. In the meantime you can aid me: by-and-bye I will explain, but first let us remove from the house of this ruffian, whose foul presence yet pollutes it."

Glancing towards the maiden who, unconscious, lay in the arms of her mother, Frank assisted Lewis to raise the prostrate ruffian, who now, slowly recovering from the effects of the knock down blow, staggered half conscious to his feet.

They conducted him to the door, and thrust him forth, the father exclaiming as he went:—

"Scoundrel, you have this time got off free; remember that in future I keep loaded pistols in my house; set your foot again inside my door and I will lodge a bullet in your skull."

At the first sound of that voice, the ruffian started as if electrified; as Lewis concluded, he turned slowly round and faced him; but when his glance rested on that face, a spasm passed through his frame, and reeling, as if from a sudden shock, he fell back against the wall of the house. For a moment he seemed spell bound, and while Frank amazed at this strange change, glanced from one to the other, he shook off the lethargy that had held him in its spell, and staggered away speechless.

He turned the corner, and was out of sight; and the young painter was just about to close the door and seek some explanation, when another figure stalked by. He was a tall stately man, attired in a long rich cloak; his bearing was erect, his steps dignified and measured, and his features, marked by an iron resolution, were handsome and distinguished. As he passed the door, the lamp shone full on his face; Lewis, whose attention had been attracted to him from the first, tottered back as his glance rested upon those features; and, placing his hand over the region of his heart uttered a faint cry.

That sound reached the ears of the tall stranger who immediately turned his gaze into the doorway.

The glimpse that he caught of that pale, noble face seemed to petrify him, he halted in his course, and while a wild light beamed from his eyes, his features showed the perplexity and doubts of his mind.

But in the second glance all that play of the features vanished, and only a cold look of triumph and hate was visible on those haughty features. With that smile playing about his lips, he was about to step forward to the doorway, when the young painter, in obedience to a horrified whisper from Lewis, abruptly closed the door in his face.

The tall individual pushed against the door and tapped with his knuckles, but after waiting some moments he abandoned his intentions and stalked haughtily away.

Arndale leant against the passage wall; all the strength he had acquired was departed.

His face was white, and his limbs shook, and he experienced every indication of the most dreadful terror. In vain Frank tried to soothe him, or dispel his alarm.

"Shivered, wrecked," he moaned, "my new-found happiness shattered to the winds; after all my weary toils, to have but this short respite; oh, Heaven, it is bitter—bitter indeed!"

"Is he then so deadly a foe," inquired Frank, as he supported him.

"The deadliest enemy man ever knew; all my accumulated miseries are traced to him—he has heaped burning coals upon my heart, and singed my brain with liquid fire; his hate is remorseless, and his power only too great. He has seen me, and I am lost; for never will he let me rest till he has hurled me to a terrible doom."

"We will endeavour to baffle him; he is not all-potent; there is One above whose power can shiver his strength, even in his hours of pride. Let us ascend to your chamber, that we may devise means for meeting this difficulty. I, too, am acquainted with him. If I err not, there is overhanging *him*, a vendetta of the most relentless kind; more sharp and more imminent than the sword of Damocles. I will attach my cause, and that of my mother, to yours; combined we shall have strength to oppose and vanquish him. Let me now conduct you to your chamber."

"Your words should cheer me," said Arndale sadly, "but I know too well the hateful malignity of that glance, whose beam is more deadly than the malaria of the death-odoured Upas tree."

CHAPTER XV.

HAMMER GETS INTO TROUBLE.

DURING the interview between the two ruffians to which Hammer listened, there had been a poorly-clad, wretched looking woman, with her face bedizened with powder and paint, conversing with two men, whose appearance denoted them of the class termed crimps, or bullies.

Their discourse had been excited and frequently attended by gestures of a most violent kind.

The woman, apparently in a state of extreme terror, was speaking pleadingly and earnestly, when the taller of the two men, suddenly uttering a loud oath, turned round, and, pointing to Hammer, quitely ensconced in his corner exclaimed:

"He is here, and you have betrayed us."

Ere the woman could speak in reply, he struck her a blow in the face, felling her to the ground as if she had been struck with a thunderbolt, and, drawing his long knife, sprang towards Hammer.

Attention being thus turned towards him, the others glanced in that direction, and, for the first time being cognisant of his presence, rose to their feet.

Hammer, too, rose, and, as threatening cries raged on every side of him, and knives gleamed in all directions, grasped firmly his formidable stick, and coolly surveyed the excited groups surrounding him.

The unfortunate girl still lay where she had fallen, and was trodden over, unregarded, by the angry men of crime.

"He's a spy," cried the ruffian who had so cowardly struck the woman; "she's given him the password. Scrag him, before he goes out to tell tales of this crib."

"What's up, my fine kiddies?" said the object of their vengeful manifestation; "is this the way you're going to treat a stranger? Don't come too close with them pickle-carvers, in case any cove among yer get's his head cracked."

He described a circle with his bludgeon as he spoke, and the fellows who seemed most eager to attack him stood for a moment at bay.

Then one—a tall, wiry-faced, grey-headed scoundrel, with a knavish look that would have been his sure conviction had he been on his trial—advanced from the rest. Hammer raised his cudgel, with an unmistakable pugnacious intent, and the man halting where he stood, exclaimed:

"What little business brought you here, my bird? There's a rule against strangers, and you'll have to pay the penalty."

"Vot brought me here? Vell, that is a good 'un. Strike me dumb, old cocoa-nut, if I don't like you. Vy, as if you didn't reg'lar invite me, along vith that voman, to come in and drink vith you."

"What does he say?" asked several.

"He's been listening to all we have been talking about," said one.

"He must have good ears, then," said the old villain.

At this moment the girl rose, staggering, from the floor, her face bleeding, and her eye already blackened from the force of the ruffian's blow.

She looked wildly round, till her glance rested on Hammer, surrounded by those angry men, with their sharp-pointed knives, and then with a faint shriek, she sprang towards where he stood.

But the fellow who had before treated her with such violence, rudely seized her, and, with a terrible oath, hurled her backwards.

She reeled, and, falling heavily, her head struck against the floor, and she lay senseless.

Hammer's fingers tightened on his bludgeon.

"Vell," he exclaimed, "of all the cowardly varmints I ever come across, you bang 'em out and out. Look sharp arter your blocks, for if I don't make some of 'em ache before you're ten minutes older, my name's not Hammer."

Suiting the action to the word, he let the end of his bludgeon fall with such crashing effect on the skull of the old man near him, that he dropped all of a heap to the floor; and the next sweep of the weapon encountering the sconce of the ruffian who had so brutally ill-used the woman, sent him staggering to her side.

The din that now arose was terrific.

Armed with short knives, the men, swearing and threatening, closed in a body round Hammer whose stout weapon, falling where it listed, favoured the heads adjacent with a visitation only equalled by a cudgel encounter at Donny-brook fair.

While his assailants, excited and furious, were pressing round him, but still keeping as far as possible from the swoop of the thick stick, carefully loaded with lead, he, cool and unmoved, dealt his blows with a business-like aim, and soon cleared for him a way to the door.

Here his foes gathered to obstruct his egress; and Hammer, seeing that in the narrow passage his difficulties would increase, retreated hastily to the fire, and snatching thence a blazing log, rushed with it, blazing and smoking, into the midst of those who opposed his progress.

The clearance was instantaneous; those whose thick skulls had been fearlessly presented to his battering cudgel were daunted by the fiery log which he thrust burning into their eyes; a futile stand was made, and as the red hot wood dashed about their faces they yielded, gave way, and finally breaking, scattered in all directions, eager only to escape the fiery visitation.

At the door a short, thick-set ruffian was placed; Hammer not pausing in his charge, went full at him, but the fellow quite willing to forego the pleasure of the salute, skillfully ducked to the ground, and the flaming firebrand, thrust with such impetuous force, struck violently against the door, hurling its myriad of sparks around.

"A very good thrust," soliloquised the man crouching to the floor; "a very clean thrust, but I am quite satisfied with its effect on the door, and am truly glad my head was not there to meet it."

Meanwhile Hammer, bludgeon in hand, rushed out into the street, and, overturning a stout old watchman coming round the corner, continued his headlong way, pausing not in his flight till he had placed a considerable distance between himself and those who he knew, if they had the chance, would have no hesitation in hacking him to pieces with their knives.

Satisfied that he was safe, he leaned his back against the door of a house, and resting on his trustworthy cudgel, took breath.

"Well," he muttered, "it was lucky I went in there arter all; I've heerd jest enough to tell me my fortin's made. Von't I keep a sharp lookout on them lads, that's all? Strike me, by jingo; and now, marm, or your ladyship, or whosomdever you may be, I'll lose no time in letting you know what you'll be so eager to hear. I've had a rest and a blow, now I'm off."

The mutability of earthly affairs is proverbial, and the old proverb respecting who proposes and who disposes is well known; both were exemplified in the case of the worthy Hammer, who had scarcely uttered the last word of his soliloquy than, just when he was grasping his cudgel and pressing for a start, the door behind him gave way, and, much to his astonishment, he found himself falling backward, when his intent was to have gone forward.

As the interesting Hammer was very heavy, and the door opened very quickly, he had no power to save himself, and did not come to a stop till he sat suddenly on the hard floor, coming down with a bump that shook his newly-recovered breath out of his body, and made his teeth rattle together like a box of dice.

Muttering a curse low and deep he was just thinking of rising when he was kindly helped to his feet by an unseen hand behind him, at the same time his cap was knocked cleverly over his eyes, and a voice exclaimed, as his cudgel was quietly taken out of his hand—

"Allow me, my dear man, to relieve you of this heavy encumbrance. Dear me, how hot you are—quite out of breath, I declare. Now, now; pray don't struggle, you will become so disagreeably warm if you do. There, there; I've just put that (don't be restive) that slender band round your body in order that you may not hurt yourself by tossing your arms about in the dark, as you will presently be when I have put this soft cambric before your eyes."

The word "flabbergasted" has been often used, and, indeed, is admitted in many dictionaries to express that state of stupifying dismay in which a man finds himself when, by some untoward event, he suddenly becomes upset in his calculations and overthrown in his interests.

The word only can express the state of mind in which the worthy Hammer found himself when he was thus quietly disposed of, and his obfuscated faculties had not become altogether clear when, after being gently conducted by his mysterious friend along the passage and upstairs into a room, the bandage was removed from his eyes and he found himself confronted by several men, whose inquiring and threatening glances were turned upon him.

———

CHAPTER XVI.

RUIN AND DESOLATION ONCE MORE—A PRISON—
A DAUGHTER'S TEARS—A FRIEND IN NEED.

THE one glimpse of the muffled figure at his door caught by Lewis Arndale was sufficient to fill him without violent fear.

He knew that the man before him was the King of England, and he *felt* that he was recognised.

What was to be done now?

To stay there was certain destruction.

Fly he could not.

No hope.

No gleam of sunshine through the heavy clouds.

He turned back, bolted the doors of the house, and gently told his wife the nature of the position in which they now stood.

Filled with anguish she suggested instant flight.

To this Lewis agreed, and making their daughter aware of their intentions, they prepared to leave the great city.

At daylight all was prepared for flight.

A flight as dangerous as remaining, for they had neither money nor means for pursuing a journey.

Nevertheless fly they would, and so, as the clocks were striking the hour of three, they issued from the house.

They stole down the little street and were about to hasten away at a great rate when from a contiguous alley rushed two men.

In a moment father, mother, and daughter were prisoners.

Their captors were the two men of the inn, who, by their conversation, betrayed that they were in the interest of the King.

A vehicle at the same moment appeared, and Lewis and his wife were thrust in.

The ruffians were about to deal similarly with the daughter when a tall and powerful woman rushed upon them, and catching Amelia by the arm, tore away from the spot.

The men did not attempt to interfere in this.

They appeared to recognise the woman who had completed this bold manœuvre, and to appreciate her strength and agility, for, jumping into the cabriolet after the old pair, they cried aloud to the driver, "NEWGATE," and, securing the door, were soon rolling away.

The word Newgate rang in the ears of the poor girl like a funeral knell.

The awful syllables seemed to strike coldness to her heart and terror to her soul.

NEWGATE!

She knew sufficient of the history of her unhappy parents to be aware of the awful import of the word in connection with them.

"Aye," said the woman who had effected the rescue, "Newgate! That means either transportation for life, or death, which is the preferable alternative."

"Say not so."

"Why deceive you?"

The tones of the woman's voice now appeared to be quite familiar to the young girl, and as at that moment they passed under one of the swinging lamps that threw its rays over the dirty road, she looked up into the face of her deliverer, and at once recognised the woman who had so opportunely snatched her from the Prince in the mysterious house into which she had fallen after making that awful leap from the roof, of which we treated a short time back.

Surprise and terror seized the poor girl; but the kind words of the woman reassured her.

"Listen to me," said this mysterious being. "You are now friendless and alone in the world. I know much of, though not all, your history. London is no longer a place wherein you can live in safety. Your parents are dead to you; the world is but a blank if you cannot begin it over again. I will give you the opportunity. Accompany me to Clifton, and I will find a home and friends for you."

"Why should you, a stranger, take this interest in me?"

"No matter; will you accompany me?"

"My poor mother—"

"It is useless to remember her. Her enemy has her now in his power. Believe me, nothing can be done for her."

"But to quit the scene in which they suffer—"

"Is your best plan. Will you come?"

"Yes."

Broken-hearted and desolate, the poor girl at once placed her hand in that of the woman who had offered her so much assistance.

They sped onward, and at length reached Holborn.

They entered the old Blue Post's booking office, and there, in the grim and antique coffee-room, awaited the moment for the starting of the Bath coach.

*   *   *   *   *

In two hours they were *en route* for the fashionable city of the west.

*   *   *   *   *

In a couple of days poor Amelia found herself domesticated at Clifton, under the roof of a Mrs. Alkington, whom her mysterious friend introduced as her sister.

"In this place," said the woman, "I am Mrs. Freeman: never call me by any other name."

Amelia remembered the injunction.

Mrs. Alkington, the sister of her deliverer, proved to be a little snappish woman, who, after a short battle for supremacy, beat down all the air of mystery and dispelled all the cold superiority surrounding her majestic sister, and appeared to overawe her.

Amelia was sadly puzzled to understand the organisation of this household. Mr. Alkington was a tall thin man, who laughed and sneered at everybody and thing, whilst his wife was simply offensively snappish. They appeared to be independent in position, while adding to their income by letting furnished apartments.

Mrs. Freeman did nothing but promenade and spend money, and, although there was not the least ostentation in her manner, she was continually perpetrating acts which would lead one to suppose that she was possessed of an ample fortune, which she was spending right royally.

Amelia did not admire her position in this household. She dreaded being a dependent, and the thought of her isolated position, added to the poignancy of her grief at parting in so sudden and awful a manner; but her parents and her young artist lover made her so sad and desolate that her health gave way.

After a while she recovered, and then suggested to Mrs. Freeman that it was time she looked about her for some employment.

Mrs. Freeman at first smiled at the idea, but as Amelia was fixed on this point, she had to give way, and exerted herself to find work for her *protège*.

Being skilful at embroidery, plenty of work was to be had for the asking, and Amelia soon earned enough to pay for her board and lodging, and this made her feel more independent and a little happier.

* * * * *

One day when walking on the cliffs with Mrs. Freeman, Amelia and her friend were accosted by a well-dressed man, whom the lady recognised and addressed as Sir Matthew May.

She introduced, Amelia and the baronet became most attentive.

Time after time they met this gentleman, and one day, through Mrs. Freeman, he proposed marriage to Amelia.

The poor girl was struck dumb at so unexpected a proposal, and, without hesitation, declined it.

Mrs. Freeman merely shrugged her shoulder, and sneered.

They saw nothing of Sir Matthew for some time after this, but it was evident that he had not given her up.

Mrs. Freeman had evidently entered into a plan to make the baronet's proposal acceptable, and set about her work in a very systematic and business-like manner.

She knew that she had only to crush out Amelia's spirit of independence to bring her into a fit frame of mind for listening to the propositions of the baronet.

Her plan was a simple but effective one.

She deprived Amelia of her work, and made no effort to assist her.

She let her run into arrears with Mrs. Alkington, and that lady forthwith flew out upon her, and snapped at her with extreme malignity.

Mr. Alkington followed suit, and laughed and sneered at her with unremitting perseverance.

In a short time her position was far from being an enviable one.

She felt it, and prayed for the moment when she could release herself from it.

"Nothing can be easier," Mrs. Freeman would say, when Amelia appealed to her for advice. "Marry Sir Matthew, and you will be well cared for."

Amelia was always silent after this for some days.

When matters became desperate and Amelia thought seriously of throwing herself off the cliffs into the silent water beneath, Mrs. Free

man altered her tactics; bestowed upon her as much love and kindness as she was capable of.

She paid Amelia's rent and lavished money on her without intermission, but she never lost sight of her great object, in trying to induce her *protege* to listen to the suit of this mysterious Sir Matthew May.

———

CHAPTER XVII.

PLEASANTLY as Amelia's time seemed now, for the most part, to pass there were hours when bitter reflection and remembrance would still intrude.

She was still without employment, and every day added to the debt of obligation which she had contracted towards Mrs. Freeman, who continued to force on her acceptance more even than what Amelia considered it proper that she should expend, even had she possessed a much better prospect of being able to repay it, which it was understood between them both, she was to do whenever it should be in her power.

It was true that Mrs. Freeman's apparent thoughtlessness and habits of self-indulgence often led Amelia into expenses which she would never have incurred had she been left alone and could have exercised her own judgment and discretion.

But, how could she object to paying for an extravagant repast at a fruiterer's or a pastrycook's, when the money had but a few hours, perhaps, before been given to her by her companion? Or how decline to invite the latter to share her dinners, her tea, or provide supper for her, when, but for her, she Amelia would actually have been without those meals; and when, too, Mrs. Freeman declared, as she often did, that from her sister's sordid disposition and irritable temper she never sat down without reluctance, and always rose without enjoyment, from her (Mrs. Alkington's) table.

Totally unwittingly, and without, indeed, being able to assign the slightest reason for it, Amelia found that Mrs. Alkington's manners towards her had undergone a total change.

She had, in accordance with a hint from Mrs. Freeman, regularly paid her rent from the funds which the latter furnished; but, though the landlady could not be said to be actually uncivil to her when they met, every Monday morning —on this occasion and at no other time was there any intercourse between them—Amelia felt uneasy, and mortified, and humiliated, at the pert tone in which the former would inquire whether she had got her work back yet; and her significant mode of remarking, that it was well some people could live as well without work as with it; for her part, she was obliged to work hard for what she got, and could hardly make a living after all.

These, and numerous insinuations of similar import, at length rendered Amelia's situation so unpleasant, that she could no longer keep silence on the subject to her friend and adviser, to whom, from motives of delicacy, she had hitherto refrained from mentioning this grievance.

But Mrs. Freeman's surprising her in tears after one of her hebdomadal visits to Mrs. Alkington's little parlour, when the latter had been more than usually caustic and severe upon her weak-spirited lodger, at length led to a thorough explanation between them.

"I have long been wanting, my dear girl, to tell you that I am myself wretchedly uncomfortable here," observed Mrs Freeman. "My sister, to tell you the truth, is of such a miserable disposition, that she is jealous and envious of our friendship, and would do anything in her power, I know, to break it. We have constant disputes about you; and her not having heard for these seven weeks, from her lodger, whose rent is now in arrear, has made her quite unbearable: in short, but for you, I should have, long ago, quitted the house in which I meet nothing but sneers and impertinence, for my brother-in-law's jeers and laughs are almost as bad as her sourness. But I cannot leave you, dear Amelia, till I see you settled in some way. And, indeed, I will confess I am not quite disinterested in this; for I know I am sure that an event which you won't let me speak of, will yet take place; and then, I know dearest Amelia's heart too well to doubt that she will forget her faithful though humble friend."

Amelia's tears redoubled.

"I cannot deceive or mislead you, my dear Mrs. Freeman," she replied. "I cannot certainly, pretend to be unconscious that Sir Matthew regards me with a—a—"

"That he loves you ardently—loves you, adores you, Amelia," interrupted Mrs. Freeman, hastily. "It is impossible you can mistake that, I am sure. You know I have said, all along, that you would be Lady May. I have told you that he is a man so much superior to common prejudices, that he would think nothing of what other men would regard as barriers between you."

Amelia smiled mournfully.

"I was not thinking of what, as you say, might justly be considered as barriers between us," she observed, "but of what I know to be an insuperable one."

"And what is that, Amelia?" demanded Mrs. Freeman, hastily.

"My own wayward heart," said Amelia, blushing deeply; "or rather, my having no heart to give," she added, in a faltering tone.

"Nonsense, my dear girl! I will not believe that story," replied Mrs. Freeman. "You in love—so deeply in love as to refuse a baronet with three thousand a year! But, now, do tell me, for I am dying with curiosity to hear: who is the peerless swain who has made such a lasting and incurable wound that rank and wealth, and the adoration of a handsome, elegant man, cannot cure it? Where does he hide himself? and by what magic charm does he keep alive his influence with you? For I have been here three months, and during that time I am sure you cannot have seen or heard from him. But I suppose the fact is you have exchanged vows, and they are to remain unshaken by time,

absence, or death. Come, now, confess the truth, Amelia, ; have you broken a sixpence between you, and do you wear it, with the bit of blue ribbon he bought you at the fair, next your heart? Nay, never bend that frowning brow on me! I do not mean to say that you were ever guilty of such childish ceremonies in reality, but I would lay my life that the chain that binds you to this nameless swain is equally frivolous; for he cannot be deserving of you who can for so long—"

"You are mistaken," interrupted Amelia, eagerly, "he is worthy. But I will tell you all our sad history; and then you shall judge whether it is likely that I can think of—"

"Sir Matthew and three thousand a year," interrupted Mrs. Freeman, laughing; "but, go on, my dear; I am all attention."

Amelia began with diffidence. She described the early attachment existing between the young artist and herself, her father's misfortune, and the tragic events which had totally overthrown all her hopes of happiness—everything, in fact, in her brief but eventful history was told without reserve; and Mrs. Freeman's "crocodile" tears flowed plentifully over the tragic tale.

"But, after all this, Amelia, dear Amelia," she observed; "though I acknowledge it was hard to be separated, when your hearts were so united, I still remain true to the interest of Sir Matthew, and, you must allow me to add, your own interest. I am not one who laughs at the tender ties of a first affection, and thinks it is to be broken without pain or remorse; but I am convinced, Amelia, that your romantic disposition, and the tenderness of your heart, has led you to magnify the merits and attractions of this young man in proportion to his misfortunes. But, even supposing he is all you say and think he is, my dear; how slight is the chance that you will ever meet him again? Besides, Amelia; if you did but know as well as I do the little probability that a man will retain his constancy towards a female, however amiable and estimable, when he is absent for years, months, or even weeks—for I have known weeks, even, eradicate a passion so violent that—"

"I would pledge my existence upon his faith," interrupted Amelia, warmly.

"Well, we will not dispute it," rejoined Mrs. Freeman, hastily. "Put on your bonnet and dry your eyes, for I want you to go out with me, that we may have some sober counsel together upon another subject."

This subject proved to be the annoyances of which both complained from Mrs. Alkington's conduct, and which originated this conversation.

Mrs. Freeman, indeed, had a proposal to make, to which, as usual, she soon, by her persuasive mode of putting the case, even though it appeared at first repulsive, eventually brought Amelia to agree. This was, that they should, without giving Mrs. Alkington any intimation or explanation of their motives, leave the house, and retire to a little cottage about a mile from Clifton, which belonged, Mrs. Freeman said, to a near relation of her's, and which had been offered her, free of rent.

It was contrary to Amelia's disposition to act with duplicity, or, more properly speaking, to act clandestinely, that it cost Mrs. Freeman a long hour's oratory—eloquent as she was on subjects in which she was interested—to reconcile her to the measure; but when Amelia had once given her consent to it, became even more anxious than her friend that it should be speedily put in execution.

So irksome, indeed, it was to her to meet Mrs. Alkington under the consciousness that she (Amelia) was going to act in a manner that the latter would feel she had a right to complain of, that she would infinitely have preferred, if it had been possible, never to have returned to the house again; and her feelings resembled more those of a condemned culprit than anything else when her landlady herself opened the door to them on their return.

To make the matter still worse, Mrs. Alkington was in the humour to be gracious.

Amelia's downcast and agitated look, and the hurried manner in which she attempted to pass her, excited the good woman's interest and curiosity; and she detained her, by putting her hand, with an air of familiar kindness, on her (Amelia's) arm, as the latter was hastily following Mrs. Freeman up stairs.

"What a hurry you are always in now, Amelia," she observed; "surely you have enough of my sister's company, all day and night, sometimes to bestow a few minutes on an old friend."

Amelia murmured a confused and indistinct apology.

"It's no compliment to tell you so," continued Mrs. Alkington, "but I can't help noticing that you don't look well to day. Your long walks don't seem, indeed, much to agree with you; for I've noticed two or three times, that you've come home looking much worse, and more out of *sperrits*, than you was when you went out. But, come into the parlour; it's my birthday, and you must have a glass of my own gooseberry wine; I've just tapped a bottle, and very good it is, I assure you. Now, I won't be refused, you know, so don't put on that no-thank-ye face, or else I shall be affronted, I assure you."

Amelia could no longer decline the unusually friendly invitation; she ventured, indeed, to hint that it would be better to include Mrs. Freeman, who lingered half way up the stairs, listening, and waiting for her to join her; but Mrs. Alkington hastily and snappishly put a negative on the proposal.

"My sister's got no such good will towards me, that I should ask her to drink my health," she observed. "Besides, it's very odd that I can't have a minute's talk with you, but Susan must be lugged into it. She may wish you well, and I dare say does, but she can't wish you better than I do, and that you ought to know, Miss Amelia, though you seem to have forgot it lately."

It cost Amelia a most painful effort to contradict this assertion, and assure Mrs. Alkington that she had never doubted her friendly feelings, but she saw it was expected she should do so, and she had not courage to disappoint her com-

panion, or to avow that she had indeed, for some time past, learned to regard her rather as an enemy than a friend.

The gooseberry wine was, as the maker of it declared, so good, that it tempted her to add a second and third glass to the one which she had taken before; and, in proportion as Mrs. Alkington became more elevated, her professions of friendliness and kind intentions towards Amelia became warmer.

"You think, I dare say," she observed, "that because I'm too busy, and got too much to think of to run up and down to you, or spend all my time with you, as my sister does, that I don't care anything about you; but you're quite mistaken, I assure you.

I pass many an hour, when I ought to be asleep in my bed, in thinking and contriving what can be done for you; and I assure you, too, that when I'm fretting and stewing about that lodger's unaccountable silence and neglect, it's more on your own account than my own; because, I'm pretty sure I shall get my money, some time or another.

"And, indeed, as you know, I've no reason to think otherwise, for that there is that in the large trunk he's left behind him that would pay me double and double; he told me to be careful of it, for that there were articles of great value in it; and, I'm sure, I never found any reason to doubt his word. So, you see, my dear, if I'm a bit cross and fidgetty about him sometimes, it can't be on my own account half so much as your's."

Amelia was unable to contradict this, though the assertion gave her more pain than pleasure; for it seemed to convict her of ingratitude, and render the act she meditated, in quitting Mrs. Alkington's house, one of the vilest treachery.

Mrs. Freeman's shrewd and penetrating look instantly detected the cause of Amelia's uneasiness, when the latter, at last, got away from her too obliging landlady, who was just now as prodigal of her kindness and favours, as she had latterly been the reverse.

"You surely are not silly enough to be imposed upon to think my sister's professions really sincere, my dear Amelia," she demanded, when the latter, in reply to her questions, acknowledged the feelings which Mrs. Alkington's unexpected kindness had produced in her bosom.

"What motive can she have for attempting to impose upon me?" returned Amelia.

Mrs. Freeman laughed.

"Do you not know, my dear, that an extra glass or two always makes my sister very sentimental? If you had not have happened to come in her way, just now, she would have found some one else to lavish her extraordinary kindness upon. I have actually seen her embrace her poor servant, in her overflowing kindness, one evening; and you know, as well as I do, how much sincerity there could be in that. Indeed, as the poor girl said, she dreaded to see her *missus* so loving, for she was sure to be ten times more cross and dissatisfied the next morning. I should be sorry to see you mortified, Amelia," continued Mrs. Freeman; "but if you are still inclined to believe in my sister's professions, I would certainly advise you to make trial of them, to-morrow morning, by requesting of her some trivial favour: you will soon be convinced that all her liberality and kindness vanishes, as the spirit of her gooseberry wine evaporates."

Amelia, however, was spared the proposed trial, for Mrs. Freeman took especial care that during the day, she should have no opportunity of encountering her sister, who, as it appeared, had herself no disposition to oppose her, Mrs. Freeman's, intended removal, which, by accident, she discovered, without, however, suspecting, as it appeared, that Amelia had any concern in it, or intended to share it.

The real fact was that Mrs. Freeman had contrived to impress her sister with a belief, that she had at length procured a situation, in a family; and Mrs. Alkington at once felt rejoiced that Susan, as she called her, was once more getting into the way of making money, and that she would thus be relieved of the presence of one whom, for many reasons, she disliked being her inmate.

Unsuspected and unobserved Amelia's trunk was carried out, together with her friend's, to the coach which the latter had sent for.

"You may as well see me to my new home, Amelia," said she, contriving that Mrs. Alkington should hear her; "the ride will do you good, and it will not be far for you to walk back."

Amelia made no reply; her heart recoiled from the deceit she was practising, but in obedience to Mrs. Freeman's instructions, her bonnet and shawl were hastily thrown on, and in a few minutes she was in the coach, and out of sight of the house which had been the scene of so many misfortunes and sufferings to her.

To Amelia's surprise, instead of proceeding at once to the cottage which was to be their future residence, the coach drew up to the door of a house at a very short distance from the place they had quitted.

"Will you forgive me, dearest Amelia, if I acknowledge I have practised a deception on you?" said Mrs. Freeman, as soon as they were alone in the little parlour to which they had been shown. "Nay, do not look so alarmed," she continued, "for it is not yet too late to recede, if you refuse your consent to my plans. I have, it is true, ventured to deceive you, so far, because I feared that, had I told the whole truth, that I am going to London instead of remaining in this neighbourhood, your timid nature would have induced you to have shrunk from the risk of accompanying me."

"To London!" repeated Amelia with consternation; "my dear Mrs. Freeman, what should you—what can I possibly do in London?"

"Everything, my dear, that you cannot do here," replied Mrs. Freeman; "you will there be able to turn your industry and talents to good advantage, and those, with my experience and knowledge of the world, and a few respectable connections which I can boast of, will soon set us above the frowns of the world; but, as I said before, Amelia, it is not too late for you to recede, if you dislike the plan. It will be easy for you to return to my sister, and lay all the blame

on me; I do not care what she says or thinks of me."

To London—it was a formidable undertaking—she dare not run the risk; and she turned to Mrs. Freeman to express her dissent, but the look she met was so earnest, so imploring, that her resolution failed her, and she remained in silent perplexity, unable to come to a resolution how she should decide.

"Dearest Amelia, can I have any motives but for your interest?" said Mrs. Freeman, in her most insinuating tone of voice; "but I will not attempt to influence you. I am sorry, heartily sorry, I have so far tried to bias you, for your look reproaches me."

"Oh, no, no, you mistake—indeed you do; how can I reproach you—how can I feel otherwise than grateful to you!" exclaimed Amelia.

"There can be no place, now, that you can consider your home, more than another, you have no one you can reckon upon as friends. But I am wasting time, dearest Amelia, and doing, too, what I did not wish to do, trying to persuade you."

Amelia again tried seriously and calmly to run over in her own mind, the various motives, both for and against the step Mrs. Freeman proposed; but her thoughts were all a chaos, the project had come so suddenly upon her, she was so totally unprepared for a serious consideration of what she would, but a few minutes before, have considered totally impracticable, that she still wavered and hesitated, without being able to adduce a single argument, either for or against, except that which forced itself upon her, by the recollection, that her purse did not contain a third part of the sum, which she reckoned, would be necessary for her travelling expenses.

"How can I possibly think of going with you," she observed, "without the means of paying even ——"

"If that is the only objection, dearest Amelia," replied Mrs. Freeman; "set your heart at rest, for I will confess to you, that relying, perhaps, too sanguinely on your attachment to me, I have actually paid your coach hire; and see, they are already putting the luggage into the coach, you must decide, therefore, my dear girl, immediately, for in ten minutes more, we must be either separated, perhaps, for ever, or our interests have become one, and inseparable."

Amelia could no longer hesitate.

"I will go with you," she exclaimed, grasping Mrs. Freeman's hand.

"There spoke my own dear Amelia! Oh, how happy you have made me. Oh, yes, I knew you would not desert me, that you would see my little stratagem in its true light, as only arising from my attachment to you; but stay, Amelia, there is a person whom I can send a message by, to my sister, for I shouldn't like to leave her in suspense, as to what has become of us both."

Mrs. Freeman flew out of the room, as she spoke, and the moment after, Amelia beheld her in conversation with *a man, whose eyes were directed with a look of earnest curiosity towards the window, at which she was seated.*

In another minute, he disappeared, and Mrs. Freeman, returning to the room, with a flutter of exultation and triumph, exclaimed,

"Now, Amelia, the coach is ready, dear."

CHAPTER XVIII.

A PASSIONATE admirer of the beauties of nature, and powerfully impressed with the striking contrast of the cultivated scenery which now surrounded her to the wild and rude charms of her native hills, Amelia soon forgot all unpleasant reflections in their contemplation. Mrs. Freeman was all kindness and attention to the inexperienced traveller.

There was only one passenger beside themselves, an elderly man, who, muffled up in great coat, Welsh wig, and flannel stockings, seemed totally absorbed in his own contemplations, and at length gave audible notice that he took no interest in their discussions, by covering his face with his handkerchief, and snoring in the corner into which he had settled himself, on his first entrance into the coach, as if determined to make himself extremely comfortable, without any regard to, or even appearing to heed that he had any fellow passengers.

Amelia was, therefore, totally unrestrained in her observations and comments, except that she delivered them in a tone so soft that it could not interrupt the slumbers of their companion, and Mrs. Freeman did her best towards keeping up her interest in the passing scene, by pointing out the remarkable places, naming the different gentlemen's seats they passed, and relating anecdotes connected with their owners.

"You have travelled this road often, then," observed Amelia.

"Yes, so often, my dear, that I know every mile of it as well as I do the streets and squares in the west end of London. Ah, Amelia, there will be the sights and wonders for you to see—such shops, such magnificent shops, and dresses, and company, and promenades. Oh! Bath is nothing to it!"

Amelia's thoughts were in a moment subtracted from the present scene; she was recalling to her memory her first impressions of London, the despair she had felt at living perpetually in in such a crowd of people.

The recollection brought with it a train of melancholy thoughts, and banished the expression of surprise which she was about to give utterance to, at the enthusiastic tone in which Mrs. Freeman spoke of the metropolis, though she had always professed the most extreme weariness and dislike of crowded cities, and their accompaniments, empty show, and parade, and luxury, and noise, and extravagance.

"You must not look so grave, dearest, or I shall begin to think that you already repent accompanying me," observed Mrs. Freeman with her usual tenderness; "but sure I am, Amelia, that I have done the very best for your interest, and that, before long, you and I both shall have reason to congratulate ourselves on having ventured on this step; but a truce to all moralising, we stop here to dinner, and my appetite is too keen to admit of my talking."

Their sleepy companion now began to give signs of returning animation, his handkerchief was consigned to his pocket, his wig drawn still lower over his eyes, his immense travelling shawl brought higher over his chin, and due attention bestowed upon the other parts of his accoutrements.

"I wonder whether this dummy dines with us, or whether he will be as unsociable at his meals as he has hitherto appeared," whispered Mrs. Freeman, as she leaned her head—together with Amelia, who was seated opposite to her, out of the coach window.

Amelia, ten minutes before, would have thought it a matter of very little consequence which he did; but, within those ten minutes, her thoughts of him had undergone a considerable revolution; for, once she had accidentally encountered his eyes, and had felt them so overpowering, so totally unlike what she should have expected from his age and infirmities, and seeming apathy, that she was absolutely startled; but she had been, if possible, still more starled by, the moment after, detecting Mrs. Freeman frowning at him, as if to suppress any similar manifestation of his — what should she call it? not admiration, for that word would not express what his eyes conveyed.

"I don't half like that old man, my dear," said her companion, when they were alone in the room to which they were shown, and in which the cloth, &c., was already prepared for dinner. "I saw he quite confused you with his stare; but I don't think he'll do it again, for I gave him a look which he seemed to understand."

Had Amelia known more of the world than she did, or had she been prone to suspicion, or could by any possibility have attached suspicion to her warm-hearted and affectionate friend, she would certainly have thought, if she had not said, that the old man and Mrs. Freeman understood each other much more readily than strangers usually do, between whom not a word had passed; for, their fellow traveller's grunting, wheezing observation of "Beg pardon, ladies; hope I don't disturb you," when he first entered the coach, had neither received, or seemed to expect to receive, a reply from either of them.

But the innocent, unsuspecting girl found, in Mrs. Freeman's explanation, a perfect solution of the riddle that for the last few minutes had tormented her; and she felt still more gratitude to the kind friend who had been thus roused from her usual timidity in her defence.

"'Take the good the gods provide you,' as the poet says," replied Mrs. Freeman, laughing. "Don't you remember the line? I don't know who wrote it, but I recollect it's in the Speaker that we all learnt in at school, and I believe it's almost all I do remember about it; but it's quite a maxim with me, I assure you, never to stand hesitating about consequences, but to enjoy life wherever I've the opportunity. And, indeed, Amelia, after all, what *is* the use of standing shilly-shallying, and making faces at trifles? We've got but a few years to live, and why shouldn't we enjoy them as much as ever we can?"

Amelia could not deny the wisdom of this observation; yet there was something so flippant in its delivery—something that seemed so unlike the gentle, reflective, sentimental, and decorous Mrs. Freeman, and that appeared to insinuate so much more than the precise words conveyed, that she involuntarily shrunk from continuing the subject, and, with a feeling of indefinable distrust and dissatisfaction, took her place at the table in silence.

"I beg your pardon, ladies," said the innkeeper, who himself waited upon them, as he placed one of the dishes on the table, "but the deaf gentleman that came by the same coach with you, and, it seems, can hardly understand a word that's said to him, made a mistake, and did not order any dinner for himself, thinking that the coach company all dined together. It's too late now to provide him any; but if you would have the goodness to allow him to dine with you—"

"Upon my word, sir, it is an intrusion I don't approve of. I am not fond of associating with strangers,' said Mrs. Freeman with a great deal of assumed dignity. "But, however, if the person is really likely to go without a dinner, Amelia, my dear, I think we must admit him." Amelia, of course, could not dissent; and in a few moments the host introduced the stranger, observing at the same time—

"He needn't be any incumbrance to you, ladies, for he's as deaf as a post; and I've been obliged to bawl till I'm hoarse to make him understand how matters stood."

During the whole time of dinner the stranger's attention seemed entirely absorbed in the good things which were placed before him, and to which he did ample justice, Mrs. Freeman assiduously helping him, and, at the same time, indulging many arch and free remarks on the excellence of his appetite, and the gusto with which he relished his dinner.

Amelia, indeed, felt, sometimes no slight embarrassment at the liberties in which her friend indulged herself, when they were left alone with the old man; and she could not help sometimes raising her eyes, with a look of fearful investigation, to his countenance, to be certain that he really was incapable of hearing and comprehending the remarks which she thought would have better fallen from any one's lips than those of a delicate female.

The traveller, however, still ate on, without seeming to be conscious that he was the subject of those arch smiles and grimaces which Mrs. Freeman so liberally bestowed upon him; and at the conclusion of their repast, and after hastily swallowing a glass of wine from the bottle which the waiter, evidently by his previous direction, had set before him, bowed and departed, without having uttered a single word from his first entrance.

"The gentleman begs you will take a glass of wine, ladies," said the innkeeper, re-entering the room. "The bill is all settled, and the coachman will be ready in ten minutes."

Mrs. Freeman expressed some surprise and some reluctance at being thus indebted to a stranger; but the man remarked, with a significant smile, which brought a deep crimson into Amelia's cheek, that he was sure the obligation lay on the other side, and then withdrew, leaving them with the decanter and glasses before them.

"Come, Amelia, we may as well profit by the old fellow's liberality as leave it to the waiter," said Mrs. Freeman, filling the glasses. "I hope," she continued, "that your scruples about extra expense are now removed; and, to tell you the truth, I had a kind of presentiment, when I ordered the dinner, that such would be the case; for I've always been particularly lucky in travelling, and hardly ever paid a shilling for anything I've had on the road."

Amelia felt still more dissatisfied.

Could this be Mrs. Freeman, whom she had looked up to as a model of propriety of behaviour, and as possessing a delicacy and refinement of ideas far, infinitely far beyond what might reasonably be expected for one of her confined education and subordinate situation in life?

"Now, don't look so serious, Amelia," rejoined her companion. "You think, I see, that I am wrong in accepting these favours from a stranger; but, my dear, when you have seen as much of the world as I have, you will see the matter in a very different light. And, after all, what matters it what he thinks of our eating a dinner or drinking a bottle of wine, at his expense? In a few hours we shall part: we go west; he, in all probability, due east; for he looks like an old carcase-butcher in Whitechapel, or a substantial sugar-baker in Thames-street, or Ratcliff Highway—places that your delicate little feet will never visit again. Besides, I will lay twopence that, with all his gallantry, he has got some fat, old, burly woman at home that calls him husband; and, perhaps, a whole brood of gawky sons and daughters, or even grandchildren. I'm sure he looks old enough to have as many as old Methuselah; so there's no great danger, even if he was to meet us in our promenades, of his claiming acquaintance with two smart young women like you and I."

It was impossible for Amelia, whatever were her real sensations, to refrain from smiling at the arch and *naïve* tone which so well became her gay companion; yet, even while she, in compliance with her repeated and pressing solicitation, at length accepted the glass of wine the former had poured out, she felt that it was not consistent with her own sense of right, and that whatever might be her real character—that which she had formerly appeared in, or her present, gay, light, and accommodating one—she must possess considerable artifice to be able thus to appear so totally distinct at one time from another.

It was a source of increased dissatisfaction, too, to Amelia, that, before they quitted the dining-parlour, her friend had actually finished all the wine that had been left in the decanter.

Amelia herself had absolutely refused to taste a single drop more than one glass.

"Well, I don't get Madeira every day," said Mrs. Freeman; "and as I know it can't hurt me, I shan't leave a drop for those that come after. Do, Amelia, be persuaded, only one little glass more."

Amelia, however, was positive in her refusal; and she rejoiced as much at her own resolution, as she felt ashamed of her companion's self-indulgence, when she beheld the significant glance with which the stranger surveyed the flushed cheeks of the latter, and then turned his inquisition upon herself.

Never, perhaps, in her life, had Amelia assumed so proud, so cold, and so haughty a look as at that moment. She felt, indeed, in reality humiliated; but she felt it also necessary to let this mysterious and penetrating old man know that she knew how to respect herself, and that she was not to be compromised by the imprudence of her companion.

A very short time elapsed before Mrs. Freeman's hearty dinner and indulgence afterwards had the effect of quieting her somewhat unruly vivacity, she fell into a profound sleep, and the stranger, again drawing himself up into his corner, followed her example.

Amelia, however, felt no inclination for repose. For the first time in her life she experienced the misery of self-reproach.

She had felt conscious, from the moment that she had yielded to Mrs. Freeman's proposal to leave her home clandestinely, that it was wrong; yet she had continued to surrender up her own judgment to this woman,—nay, she was still doing so,—though now more than half convinced that she (Mrs. Freeman) was far from being a proper person with whom to associate herself, far less to rely implicitly upon as a director and guide. It was now, however, too late for her to recede; and Amelia, as she acknowledged to herself that it was so, became still more miserable and depressed, as the distance between her and her late home rapidly increased.

During the remainder of their journey little occurred to withdraw Amelia's attention from the harrassing and disquieting thoughts which had taken possession of her mind. All, indeed, which she now beheld tended to confirm her worst fears, for at the next place they stopped at, Mrs. Freeman recognised in the waiter an old acquaintance, and the twenty minutes that they remained there seemed lengthened to hours, by her (Amelia's) impatience to get away from a scene so revolting to her ideas of delicacy and female decorum, as was now presented to her.

It was not merely that Mrs. Freeman threw aside all reserve, and behaved towards her quondam acquaintance with a levity and freedom so totally at variance with her former manners, that Amelia would have found it difficult to recognise in her the same person that offended the latter; but it was evident from the waiter's recurrence to former transactions, his low, impudent winks and inuendoes, and disgusting personal familiarities whenever he entered the room, that his former knowledge of Mrs. Freeman had been such as led him to regard her with no feelings approaching to respect.

Towards herself, even, his looks and manners were most offensive; and Amelia looked anxiously towards the door of the room, before which she had seen their deaf coach companion pass and repass several times after they entered the room, with a feeling that even his presence would be a protection.

"You're a devilish pretty girl," said the impertinent waiter, as she turned away from his intrusive looks. "What situation are you going to seek in London, my dear? for I suppose it's your first appearance there in any character, as the play bills say; I can tell that by the pretty rose pink that flushes your cheek at being stared at. But you'll soon get rid of that in London, won't she Susan?"

Recalled, apparently, to more sobriety of feeling by this observation, Mrs. Freeman resumed her usual sedateness of look and manner, as she replied—

"That young lady is not going to seek a situation, I can assure you, Richard; and, if I thought London likely to banish the modesty that is so becoming at her age, I should be very sorry to have been the means of taking her there."

"Modesty!" repeated the man with a sneering laugh; "modesty, and Sue Freeman's companion! I like that."

Mrs. Freeman frowned.

"It seems very plain, at any rate, that you have long dismissed all pretensions to modesty, or even decency of behaviour, or you would not have made such an impudent and unjust remark," she observed.

"Psha! nonsense, what's the use of trying to play the hypocrite with me?" returned the man; "the young lady, I dare say—"

"The coach is ready, ladies," said a female servant, hastily putting her head into the room; "and you, Mr. Dick, I wonder at your impudence to stand prating there when you ought to be—"

Amelia did not await to hear the rest of this remonstrance, nor did she even, as she had hitherto done, regulate her movements by her companion's, for, without even looking to see whether the latter followed her, she instantly obeyed the welcome summons, and was seated in the coach before either of her former companions.

The saucy waiter, in spite of his fellow servant's reproof, accompanied Mrs. Freeman to the coach door.

"How I wish I was going along with you, Sue," he observed. "Do you remember when you and I went down from London to Brighton together? You could blush then almost as pretty as your companion there."

Amelia turned from his impertinence, and beheld the eyes of their deaf companion peering over the handkerchief in which the lower part of his face was muffled, as if watching the effect of the man's insolent remarks upon her.

"I have surely seen those eyes before," thought Amelia, almost starting as she encountered the keen glance, which, however, was immediately withdrawn as with apparent apathy and inattention ; the stranger occupied himself in buttoning himself up to the chin, drawing his large gouty stockings, which were rolled above his knees, still higher, and altogether seeming intent only on making comfortable arrangements for the remainder of the journey.

"The fellow is grown quite a puppy," said Mrs. Freeman, as she drew in her head from the adieus of the waiter, who continued to talk to her until the coach drove on. "He was a footman, my dear, in the family that I first lived with," she continued, addressing Amelia in a tone of apology ; "and as he was then quite a raw country boy, and I a simple inexperienced girl, and were, besides, both from the same part of the country, we naturally clung to one another, and were almost like brother and sister, as I may say. Richard, indeed, I believe would fain have looked upon me in a more tender light, but I never gave him any encouragement, and all he said now, is nothing but mere impudence and rhodomontade."

Amelia made no reply to this attempt at apology or explanation, for she felt convinced that whatever might have been the origin of her companion's acquaintance with this man, he had certainly during it lost all respect for her, if he had ever felt any, and she therefore felt no inclination to discuss his present conduct.

During the remainder of their journey, nothing occurred of sufficient consequence to withdraw her thoughts from the unpleasant subject that occupied them, and it was with a heavy heart, and with no disposition to share the satisfaction that was visible in her companion's countenance and manners, that she at length found herself in London.

At the White Horse Cellar they alighted, a hackney coach was called, the deaf gentleman with more solicitude and gallantry than he had before shown, superintended the placing their luggage in the coach, handed them both into it, and waited until Mrs. Freeman, having directed the coachman to drive to No. —, Crawford-street, Marylebone, bade him adieu.

CHAPTER XIX.

"Now, then, dear Amelia, let me welcome you to London, and I trust to wealth and happiness," said Mrs. Freeman, in her most fascinating tone, as she threw herself on a sofa, in a smartly furnished apartment, on the first floor of the house at which she alighted, and where, it appeared—from the greeting of the female who received them at the door, and immediately ushered them up stairs—they were expected guests.

Amelia sighed deeply, but made no reply.

"You do not appear satisfied, my dear girl," resumed her companion, after looking at her for some time, as if scrutinizing the thoughts which were passing in the poor girl's mind. "Does not this place answer your expectation ?" And she glanced round the room with an air of conscious satisfaction, which was totally at variance with her question.

"A much more humble home would satisfy my expectations," returned Amelia, in a desponding tone ; "and I will confess the truth, I have been thinking that a less expensive one would be far more suitable to our finances."

"Excuse me, Amelia," returned Mrs. Freeman. "I cannot but consider that you ought to allow me to be the best judge of this matter ; we have come here, you know, dear Amelia," she continued, resuming her sprightliness, "to seek our fortunes, and if you knew as much of the world as I do, you would know that there's nothing to be done without appearance and show. Do you suppose, if we were to take a garret, such a beautiful apartment for instance, as the one you have left behind you ; do you think, I say, that it would be likely we should have many lady customers climb up to us, or whether any body would think very highly of the fashions we should exhibit at our windows ? I forgot, though, that it would not be very easy to make that exhibition, though we might, to be sure, suspend a dashing cap, or bonnet, or turban, at the end of a long pole, from the parapet, as the dyers do their goods. Well, you are determined not to laugh, I see, and so to be as serious as yourself, Amelia, I must, once for all, assure you, that if you think I will consent to live in the hugger-mugger way we did at Mrs. Alkington's, you are quite mistaken. Nothing venture, nothing have, is a good old proverb, and so I'm determined to act upon it."

Amelia was completely silenced by these remarks ; she felt, indeed, that what Mrs. Freeman asserted, had hitherto been confirmed by her own observations, for certainly, it had been most painfully forced upon her, that show and confidence, almost uniformly triumphed over modest unassuming merit. Still, however, she could not feel satisfied how Mrs. Freeman's plans were to be accomplished.

She had heard, repeatedly, from the latter, within the course of a few weeks, that her resources were nearly exhausted ; she (Mrs. Freeman) had even hinted, that unless something turned up to her advantage, she should be obliged soon to dispose of some of her superfluous articles of finery, such as ear-rings, rings, necklaces, &c., of which, indeed, she possessed, what—considering the station she had always held in life—appeared to Amelia, a surprising variety.

Yet, now, though their journey to London must have cost her a considerable sum, and there certainly could be no immediate prospect of a supply, she seemed perfectly at her ease, and, indeed, not to give the slightest consideration to what she was accustomed to style the ways and means.

The first day of their residence in London, was, of course, devoted to rest from the fatigues of their journey ; but, on the second morning, Amelia, anxious to lose no time in commencing that course of industry, which she felt could alone enable her to triumph over the difficulties of her situation, ventured at breakfast, to hint to her companion, that it would be expedient to commence work without further delay.

Mrs. Freeman smiled.

"You are a strange girl, Amelia," she observed; "I don't believe there's another in the world who would, immediately after their arrival in London, be content to sit down to work without having seen anything of the lions, as they call the sights; however, you may set your mind at rest, for there are a thousand little things to be done before we can go decidedly to work. In the first place we must have cards printed and distributed, and a brass plate with our names engraved, for the front door, that's quite indispensable; they will sound well enough, though there's nothing like French names, for bringing fashionable customers; and then, there's our stock to buy, we must have some stock, you know, to work up; but, Lord, it's time enough to bother our brains about that, we'll go first and have a look about us, and see what revolutions have taken place, since last I saw London; and I must go among my friends too, and see how many of them are disposed to give me a helping hand in my new undertaking. I shall be able, then, to calculate my strength better, when I know what I have to depend upon; and we must have a turn, too, among the milliner's shops, and see what they are doing, or else, perhaps, our Bristol fashions will prove a month or two behind the London ones."

Amelia could not, of course object, to this; it was in fact but another means of forwarding her project, to that which she had herself proposed, and she certainly was by no means indifferent to the promised pleasure, of seeing some of the splendours of the metropolis, of which she had heard so much.

It was, however, with considerable chagrin, she learned from her companion that it was too early yet, by some hours, to think of going out.

"I don't know, indeed, what I was thinking of," observed Mrs. Freeman, yawning, "to let you entice me out of bed at this unseasonable hour. Why, my dear girl, the very housemaids are not yet stirring, nor the shop boys taken down their shutters in any of the fashionable streets. We should not meet a soul worth meeting, before one or two o'clock; but, however, to indulge your impatience, which is very natural, we'll for once be unfashionable enough to go out an hour or two earlier, so you may hold yourself in readiness by eleven o'clock. Let me see," and she looked at her watch, "it's only half-past eight now, I don't know how you'll contrive to kill time till then, especially as I want to step to see an old friend of mine, that lives a few doors up the street, but I won't stay long."

Amelia requested she would not hurry herself on her account, and wrapping herself up in a shawl, and drawing Amelia's straw bonnet over her night-cap, she shuffled away, not even troubling herself to exchange her slippers for shoes.

Amelia felt surprised at this, but she had seen too much within the last two or three days, in Mrs. Freeman's conduct, that was new and surprising to her, to allow her to dwell long upon so comparatively trifling an inconsistency, as her setting off in such a hurry to visit her friends, after saying a few moments before, that not a creature, above the rank of housemaid, would be out out of their beds at that early hour.

For the first hour of her absence Amelia remained alone seated at the window, sometimes so absorbed in thought of the past, or anticipation of the difficulties of the future, as to forget the novelty of her present situation; while occasionally her attention, on the contrary, would be so forcibly arrested by the busy scene which the street now presented, that, in spite of melancholy regret and uneasy foreboding, she could not help being surprised and interested by the passing scene.

From this occupation she was at length roused by the entrance of the landlady of the house, whom she had only casually seen at their first arrival, she having been called from home, as Amelia understood from the servant girl who waited, to attend some relative who was supposed to be at the point of death, and from attending upon whom it appeared she was only that morning returned.

Towards this woman Amelia had felt no very great prepossession, at the moment she had first beheld her; for, in addition to a very coarse and masculine set of features, and a corpulent, unwieldy person, Mrs. Maggs, as she was called, was also excessively dirty and slatternly, while her manners wore a mixture of cringing servility and insolent familiarity, which appeared to Amelia much more repellant than absolute rudeness.

"So, my dear, you're all alone by yourself, as the Irishman says," she observed, as she entered the room.

Amelia bowed, in silent acquiescence.

"Well, and how do you like Lunnun?" continued Mrs. Maggs, throwing herself into a chair, immediately opposite to Amelia, who shrank back almost in alarm, as she beheld the flushed face and unsteady eye of her visitant, and smelt the hot steam of spirituous liquor which issued from her parched lips.

"I can scarcely answer your question, madam," she returned, "having as yet seen little more of London than is to be seen from this window."

"And no bad sight of it either, miss, I can assure you," observed Mrs. Maggs. "This is a wery ginteel street, and nothing to be seen in it that can give offence, even if people are much more ginteel than they seem to be."

"I did not mean to insinuate anything," commenced Amelia, mildly.

"Insinivate! No, ma'am, I should think not," interrupted Mrs. Maggs, with violence. "I'd defy you, or any other paltry, little country miss, to insinivate anything against the character of my house; for there arn't a house in Lunnun more orderly behaved, or more quiet, than mine. I never takes nobody in but what's proper and well-behaved; and, though I say it, I've had ladies live in this very 'partment, that rides in their carriages now, with their livery sarvants behind them."

"I dare say, madam, it is very possible," observed Amelia, who found she was expected to say something in reply to this elegant effusion, and yet dreaded to add, by any untoward remark, to the irritation which the woman seemed to feel.

"Possable!" the virago repeated. "Who axed you whether it was possable, or unpossable, either? Lord bless me! I'm come to a pretty pass, indeed, when such bits o' pale-faced, country hawbucks as you sets yourselves up to talk about possables, in my house. And you're a beauty, too, in some people's opinion. Well, there's no 'counting for people's taste; but, as I said to Mrs. Freeman, when I first seed you—"

The sudden entrance of the last-mentioned person, prevented the conclusion of this sentence.

"Why, what the devil have you been doing, Sue, to go out that figure?" exclaimed the woman, transferring, at once, all her attention from Amelia to her friend. "What a guy you do look!" she continued; "I say, if a certain party could see you this figure, he wouldn't say there wasn't a prettier little vixen in——"

"Nonsense, Mrs. Maggs; it's years ago since that was said of me," interrupted Mrs. Freeman, giving her a significant look to be cautious, which did not escape Amelia's observation, confused and alarmed as she had been at Mrs. Maggs' vituperation.

"I am a very different person now to what I was then," she continued, "and have more serious things to think of than my looks. I've been out now upon business, I assure you. But come down stairs; I've something in the parlour that I want to show you."

Again Amelia detected the significant wink with which Mrs. Freeman enforced her observation, and which was a sufficient corroborative, had there been any wanting, of the perfect understanding which existed between her and her landlady.

Mrs. Maggs muttered something which Amelia did not understand, but which seemed to have a relation to the late colloquy between them, from the sarcastic expression of her maudlin eye, which was still fixed on her (Amelia's) expressive features.

"Don't be a fool," murmured Mrs. Freeman, as, with pretended playfulness, but evidently real anxiety to get her out of the room, she gently pushed Mrs. Maggs before her into the passage.

"Merciful goodness! to what have I exposed myself by my ill-placed confidence!" ejaculated Amelia, resuming her seat, from which she had arisen in alarm, at the moment Mrs. Maggs had, in the exuberance of her wrath, drawn her own chair violently forward, and, placing her hands on her knees, pushed her face almost close into the mild, retreating one of her gentle opponent. "What shall I do?—where shall I go?—what will become of me?" continued the poor girl, wringing her hands, as the discordant tones of the landlady, in apparent anger with Mrs. Freeman, whose voice was exalted also beyond its usual pitch, reached her from the parlour beneath.

Long after the hour appointed for their ex-

cursion, Amelia continued alone, and ruminating upon what had passed. The very thought of remaining in a house, subject to the unprovoked insults of such a woman as Mrs. Maggs, was of itself sufficiently horrible; but still more so when to this was added the fact, that Mrs. Freeman seemed perfectly *au fait* in such affairs, and evidently felt no other annoyance than that which arose from her (Amelia's) observation of the scene she had witnessed—

"Yes,?" exclaimed the latter, in continuance, "it is but too plain that I have been grossly, cruelly deceived, and that I have fallen into the hands of an artful, unprincipled woman; for, what else can Mrs. Freeman be, to be the associate of such a creature as this woman? And yet," she thought, "Mrs. Freeman can have no interested motives in inducing me to become her companion. It was always in her power—at least I have always had reason to believe so—to secure herself a good maintenance by her own exertions. Let me not, therefore, be ungrateful to her because she is not what my sanguine fancy believed her. It is, perhaps, my ignorance of the class of people with whom, as a servant, she has probably been unwillingly associated, and to whom custom has reconciled her, that makes them appear thus repellant and disgusting to me. And yet, Heaven forbid I should ever become accustomed to such manners, such looks, such habits, as distinguish this woman! Alas! how different—how different from those——"

She burst into tears as the recollection of her home rushed upon her mind: and was followed by the distressing conviction that seemed to arise from her present situation and prospects, that she was separated from them for ever.

"Come, my dear; I suppose you are quite tired of waiting for me, and thought I had forgotten all about our walk," exclaimed Mrs. Freeman, bursting into the room, with all her usual cheerfulness and vivacity of manner.

Had Amelia told the truth she would have acknowledged that the intended walk and all connected with it had been by her totally forgotten for the last half-hour, and that she had in imagination been retracing scenes and walks which she had but too much reason to fear it was her doom never more to behold.

"I'm afraid that foolish old woman downstairs frightened you this morning, my dear," observed Mrs. Freeman, as she hastened to dress herself for the intended excursion. "But you need not be afraid, she means no harm, and is as good a creature as ever lived, only she is sometimes apt to take a little drop too much; and, indeed, there's every excuse for her just now, for she has been sitting up all night with a person that died this morning, and after all her trouble she finds that she won't get so much as a suit of mourning, for the widow has come this morning from the country, and taken possession of everything."

Amelia could not at all understand how this was an excuse for a woman disgracing herself, or how it was Mrs. Jennings could have formed any extraordinary expectations of benefitting by a person who had, it appeared, connections to whom, of right, all belonged; but she did not venture to make any other observation than to express a hope that she should "never again be exposed to such undeserved insult, or witness manners so revolting and disgusting in a female."

Mrs. Freeman coloured.

"She is a foolish, ignorant, old woman, Amelia, certainly," she observed; "but she could have had no intention of deliberately insulting you; you will know her better by and bye. I used to be like you, frightened at her, once, when she got into her tantrums, but I don't care a farthing for her now, and that's the reason why she never attacks me."

The subject was dropped, for Amelia, though she thought, did not give utterance to those thoughts, that no time would, she was sure, accustom her to meet with composure, or submit without reluctance to such manners as she had that morning beheld.

With infinite difficulty, and not until after long disputing on the subject, Amelia was allowed by her dissatisfied companion to follow the dictates of her own judgment in equipping herself for their projected excursion.

Mrs. Freeman, indeed, was evidently seriously vexed that she could not prevail on her companion to follow her example in arraying herself in the most striking manner she could possibly devise; but in spite of all her assumption of knowing best what was suitable to London, and of the necessity there was of appearing fashionable and attractive themselves if they expected to be thought capable of directing the taste of others, Amelia was not to be convinced that it was either suitable or becoming to load herself with finery, or to be conspicuous by wearing all the colours of the rainbow in flowers, ribbons, &c.

"Well, I declare, after all, Amelia, I do believe you know best what sets you off to advantage," observed the former, when having at length, as it appeared, conquered the ill humour which her companion's opposition to her mandates had created, she turned round to look at her as they crossed Oxford-street to Bond-street. "Certainly that simple cottage bonnet is very becoming to your face, though I do still wish you would have had the pink ribbon and roses, instead of that plain white satin—it is so very childish; and that quaker coloured silk, too, though it looks well upon you, is quite old fashioned."

Amelia smiled, but she made no reply, for at that moment her eye rested upon a face and person which, even at the distance of some hundred yards or more, she was convinced was familiar to her.

Before, however, she could utter an observation to her companion, or decidedly and satisfactorily ascertain the fact, the gentleman turned into a shop on the opposite side of the street to that on which they were walking, and Amelia's eager glance into the shop as she passed at that distance, was baffled by several ladies coming out, and pausing at the door to converse.

"Did you see anybody you knew then, Amelia?" demanded Mrs. Freeman, whose quick eye

had instantly discovered the change in her countenance.

"I thought—I am almost sure it was—and yet it is very strange that he should avoid me, for whether it was him or not, I am certain the eyes of the person were fixed on me. I saw him—I am almost sure I saw him start, as he looked first at you and then at me."

"Well, but who was it, child?" demanded Mrs. Freeman, impatiently.

"Mr. Alkington's lodger," replied Amelia, her eyes turned towards the shop, in the hope that the person she spoke of would recognise her.

Mrs. Freeman's countenance betrayed evident confusion.

"Good gracious! do come along; I'm sure I don't want to meet him, of all the people in the world!" she exclaimed.

"And why not?" demanded Amelia, in surprise. "I would give the world, almost, to speak to him," she continued, looking back over her shoulder, as her companion hurried her onwards.

At that moment she saw Mr. Lovell come out of the shop, and she saw, too, distinctly, that his eyes followed her and her companion, while his usually stern countenance assumed a still sterner look, and told her plainly that his avoiding her did not arise from chance or accident, but that he deliberately shunned speaking to her.

"What can I have done to excite his displeasure?" she observed to Mrs. Freeman, as they proceeded on their walk.

"What does it matter, whether he is displeased or no, the old savage?" returned the latter. "I can't think, for my part, Amelia, how you can make him of such importance as to bestow a thought upon him; I always told you he was either mad or much worse, and I hope you'll believe me now. Pray don't keep looking back at him—what will people think of us?"

Thus reprimanded, Amelia at once relinquished all hope of renewing her friendship with one whom, in spite of all Mrs. Freeman could say, and in spite even of her own experience, which certainly proved him inconsistent and capricious, she could not help regarding with feelings of respect.

During the remainder of their walk, Amelia was silent and abstracted, it was in vain her companion pointed out to her the splendour of the shops and carriages, or named to her different gay and fashionable people as they passed, whom she either recognised, or pretended so to do.

"I declare, Amelia, it's quite a bore to walk with you," exclaimed Mrs. Freeman, peevishly. "Three times have I asked you a question without getting a word of answer, and you look so wild and miserable, that people are actually staring in your face with curiosity, wondering what such a woe-begone—— Lord, Amelia, brighten up, do, there's a dear girl, do you see who that is on horseback, there, talking to a lady in that carriage? Come, I've found out an old acquaintance as well as you, and one, too, that I'll be bound for it won't shun us, or look black at us, as your Mr. Lovell did just now."

Sir Matthew, for it was him whom Mrs. Freeman thus pointed out, did not indeed look displeased at this *rencontre*, nor did he apparently shun them, for he affected to be so deeply engaged in conversation as not to see them, though a slight hesitation in the midst of the speech he was making, and an additional brightening of his florid complexion, would have betrayed to one even less observant than Amelia, that he was not ignorant that they were near him.

But it was notonly the conviction that he saw and recognised them that rushed into Amelia's mind, at the moment she beheld him; a thousand minute circumstances which she had at the time noted, and then tried to believe accidental—tried to believe herself blameable in misinterpreting—for which she had even blushed at her injustice, now forcibly rushed into her mind, confirmed a suspicion, that there was a mutual understanding between Mrs Freeman and Sir Matthew, and that their meeting now in London was not purely accidental.

Without a moment's hesitation she turned her piercing eye upon the face of her companion.

"You expected this," she observed; "but what motive induced you to be so silent on the subject?"

Mrs. Freeman looked for a moment abashed, but she speedily recovered her self-possession.

"Expected!" she repeated; "that is rather a curious observation. Certainly I knew; and so might you, too, if you had taken the trouble to listen to Sir Matthew's observations the two or three last times we saw him, that he was soon going to London; but as to any expectation of meeting him here to-day, I beg leave to deny it. What was it you meant to insinuate, Amelia, by that observation?" she continued, after some moments' silence, during which Amelia, though daunted by her manner, was still revolving in her mind all that could confirm or lessen her suspicions.

"I meant to insinuate what I said," returned the latter, calmly; "that you knew Sir Matthew was coming to London, and were prepared to meet him; and I still do not retract what I said."

Again Mrs. Freeman looked confused; but the moment after she burst into a loud laugh.

"I see it is no use to attempt to deceive you, Amelia, and so I may as well acknowledge the fact. My views in coming up to London have been very different to those of commencing milliner; but not a word of this, if you love me, before Sir Matthew, who, I see, has turned his horse's head this way, and will overtake us in a few minutes. I must play my cards cautiously, Amelia; but yet I hope, before many weeks are passed, you will have to wish me joy as Lady May!"

Totally thrown off her guard by this seeming confidence, Amelia's whole fabric of surmises and suspicions—founded on Sir Matthew's former professions towards herself, and the late conviction that had broken on her mind, that Mrs. Freeman was far from being the correct, disinterested, and kind-hearted woman she appeared to be—all fell at once to the ground.

Every circumstance that had appeared unaccountable to her, Mrs. Freeman's new-born assumption, her recklessness of expense, her self-indulgence, and, above all, the glaring change in her style of dress, from extreme neatness and propriety to the most flaunting and showiest attire that she could make up—all was now accounted for; and Amelia, in the simplicity of her heart, sighed at her own injustice in having attributed worse motives to her companion than she really deserved.

Not that she, for one moment, believed that there existed any solid foundation for Mrs. Freeman's assertions; on the contrary, she was convinced that Sir Matthew had never entertained a thought of the kind towards her companion. But Amelia believed that vanity had misled her into believing what she wished to be true, and that she really deceived herself with the hope of bringing about the event of which she spoke so confidently.

As she had said, before they had reached Piccadilly Sir Matthew overtook them; and, flinging the reins of his horse to his servant, alighted, and instantly accosted them.

"I could scarcely believe my eyes, when first I saw you," he observed. "How long have you been in town? and where are you staying? It is your first visit to London, is it not? We must show her all the sights. I shall be delighted to accompany you anywhere. Where are you going this morning? because I am quite disengaged, and will feel proud to become your Ciceroni."

All this was uttered with so much volubility that there was neither room nor necessity for an answer to any of his questions except the last.

"We are not going anywhere particularly," said Mrs. Freeman, with one of her prettiest, most demure looks and tones.

"Oh, then we will go to Somerset House. It is the first day of the exhibition. Miss Amelia is a great admirer of pictures, I know: and all the world will be there."

Amelia had no time to say she knew nothing about pictures, and had no wish to mingle with all the world—she had no time, indeed, to reflect upon the manifest impropriety of two females, in their situation in life, being ushered about to public places by a young, gay man of fortune and title—for the the hackney coach, to which he had given a signal, in an instant was at the side of the pavement; the step was down, Mrs. Freeman seated, and, without another word of explanation, Sir Matthew turned to offer her (Amelia) his hand to get in.

A conviction that all this was wrong and imprudent, however, sent the deep colour into Amelia's cheeks, and occasioned her, for one moment, to hesitate; but there was no alternative. She could not, strange as she was to the streets and ways of London, say she would rather walk home alone, and accordingly she obeyed Mrs. Freeman's impatient—

"Come, Amelia; what are you waiting for?" and was the next moment seated by her side.

Sir Matthew was so full of his self-congratulation on his own good fortune in meeting with them, and his anticipations of the pleasure he should take in initiating Amelia into the enjoyments and gaieties of a London life, that it was some time before either of his companions could find an opportunity of uttering more than a single negative or affirmative to all his numerous questions and observations. Amelia, however, had time to remark that, though his attentions were divided between them, and though he certainly spoke more of her herself, and more to her possibly than Mrs. Freeman, there were certain looks and smiles passing which seemed to confirm the idea of a more intimate acquaintance between Sir Matthew and her companion than Amelia had hitherto observed.

"Well, and what sort of a journey had you up to London?" he at length inquired. "I wish I had known you were coming, as I certainly should not have trusted you to have come up alone."

"Amelia will not give you credit for that assertion, Sir Matthew," said Mrs. Freeman, smiling; "she has taken it into her head that you and I are quite *d'accord* on this occasion, and that our meeting to day—— You cannot, indeed, believe half the flattering things she has said to me, on your account."

She looked down as she concluded the sentence, as if overcome with timidity at what she had said; and Sir Matthew, who appeared evidently embarrassed, and unable to take the hint she had given him, was, for a moment, completely posed what to say.

"It is no use attempting to deceive you, Sir Matthew," resumed the lady, after a few moments' silence. "I have been compelled to acknowledge to my friend the attachment between yourself and me, and the circumstances that compel us, at the present time, to be secret; and now, having, I trust, removed all restraint between us, I will tell you that we had a very humdrum sort of a journey, not a single companion but a deaf old fellow who paid, it seems, for two places (it was the four inside coach), that he might have room, I suppose, to stretch his long legs, and snore, as he did, most musically, two thirds and seven-eighths of the way."

"Indeed," said Sir Matthew, laughing, Mrs. Freeman's lively sally having apparently given him time to recollect and perfectly recover his composure; "I ought to be very thankful, I suspect, to the deaf old fellow; for a stage coach affords such facilities of making acquaintance. I have, myself, known two elopements, and several most interesting love affairs, all attributable to stage coach adventures."

"You would not, I hope, infer that Amelia was in any danger," said Mrs. Freeman significantly: "as to me, it would be doing yourself great injustice indeed—" and she looked at him with peculiar meaning in her eyes—"if you could suppose a stage-coach acquaintance, or any other acquaintance, could for a moment withdraw my—"

"You are really too good, too kind, too condescending," said Sir Matthew, interrupting her.

Amelia looked hastily in his eyes.

If the tone of his voice was equivocal—and it certainly was so, or Amelia would not have ventured to look at that moment—certainly the

expression of his countenance was not so, for so far was it from corresponding with the words he uttered that Amelia thought Mrs. Freeman must indeed be blind if she did not see that he was absolutely laughing at her.

There was nothing, however, in the latter's manner that could induce the belief that she saw this; on the contrary, her expressions became every moment more and more unrestrained.

She even hinted at the event, which she acknowledged she had confided to Amelia, as being likely soon to take place, and, as if deprecating his anger at her incautiousness, added, hastily,

"It was necessary, my dear Sir Matthew, that I should be candid with Amelia, because she very naturally would have objected to our associating with you, or admitting you as a visitor under any other circumstance; but now all our scruples are removed, and I may venture, without fear, to ask you to my humble apartments."

Sir Matthew bowed in silence; to any impartial observer, it would have been at once evident that he was playing an irksome part in this affair; but Amelia was now completely thrown off her guard.

It was true she still suspected, still, indeed, firmly believed that Mrs. Freeman deceived herself and was deceived by him, if Sir Matthew in reality made her believe that he intended to marry her; but that there was any more deep deceit hidden under all these pretences, never once occurred to her mind.

All the world, as Sir Matthew had said, were at the exhibition; that is to say, there was an immense crowd of all sorts and descriptions, and Amelia, half frightened and half amused, for a while forgot all uneasy sensations in the novelty of the scene around her.

CHAPTER XX.

FULLY established now upon the most unrestrained terms of intimacy, Sir Matthew was scarcely ever absent from Crawford-street, and even Amelia's unbelief began to give way when she witnessed the constant assiduity and anxiety for their comfort and accommodation which he manifested.

At home and abroad, too, he was during the first week of their residence in London, their constant companion; and Amelia, thoroughly deceived by the manners and confidence which appeared to exist between Mrs Freeman and him, was at length lulled into the belief that the latter had really superseded her in his affection, and that, in despite of all that seemed to oppose such a disproportionate union, the pert, flippant, half-educated self-sufficient lady's maid—for such, and no more, Mrs. Freeman certainly was, although the possession of considerable shrewdness, and the capability of successfully imitating the manners of her mistresses, had enabled her, for a short time, to appear superior to her station—would be merged in the lady of fortune, and title, and fashion.

There were moments, indeed, when it could not fail to occur to Amelia that it depended on herself alone to overturn in a moment the fabric which Mrs. Freeman seemed to think stood upon so secure a foundation—moments in which Sir Matthew betrayed not only coldness and in-difference towards Mrs. Freeman, but that he, without apparent design or intention, contrived to insinuate that nothing but the hopelessness of his love for her had induced him to transfer his attentions to another.

Mrs. Freeman was, or affected to be, blind and deaf to all this.

She seemed to consider all his attention to Amelia as arising out of his regard for her ; and when the latter once, in the openness of her heart, and stimulated by some recent observa-tion which, in her opinion, amounted to complete treachery on the part of Sir Matthew, ventured to insinuate a doubt of his sincerity towards her friend, the latter completely disarmed her by saying, with archness, and, at the same time, patting the fair cheek, which was glowing with confu-ion at what its possessor had said—

" And so the pretty child thinks that it could even now rival me, if it would ? Well, I ac-knowledge it is very likely that you are right, Amelia ; and, to tell you the truth, I have more than half suspected it for some time. Indeed, I feel that it would be excessive vanity on my part to suppose that my feeble attractions could have entirely effaced your image from his heart; for—I may say it now, without offence, Amelia— I know that Sir Matthew did adore you, and that, had you listened to his suit, he would never have bestowed a thought on me. Nay, I will go farther than that, Amelia ; I will acknow-ledge to you that I believe in my heart, that he deceives himself, now, in thinking that he can be happy with me. But what is to be done, Amelia. On the one side stands poverty, obscu-rity all that is horrible and to be dreaded ; on the other, wealth and distinction."

Amelia was at once silenced and dismayed at this candid confession.

How cruelly and unjustly had she accused her friend of levity and vanity, and want of proper principle.

How delicately had the latter now stated her situation, without once letting a word drop from her lips which could be construed into that which Amelia nevertheless felt to be the fact— that, but, for her own unfortunate circum-stances, and her (Mrs. Freeman's) having so identified herself with her, the latter would in all probability, never have been placed in a situa-tion in which her feelings and interest were so evidently at variance with each other.

Towards Sir Matthew, too, Amelia felt differ-ently than she had for some time past, whom she had looked upon as a heartless, unprincipled, deceiver.

It was not in human nature—not in woman's nature, at least—not to feel some kindness to-wards one who, she believed to be, in secret, so devotedly attached to herself, as Mrs. Freeman had represented Sir Matthew to be ; and, though she certainly gave him no reason to think that she regarded him in any other light than she had always done, as a friend, she almost uncon-sciously assumed a more familiar, confiding tone, and shrunk less from him than she had hitherto done.

Three weeks passed away in this security, and Amelia, though melancholy forebodings would sometimes rush unbidden into her mind, and the most heartfelt regrets for the past steal unconsciously over her gayest moments, be-came more familarised to, and entered with more zest into, the gay life into which she was introduced by her companions, than she could have ever believed it possible she could.

The hurry of diversion and amusement, in-deed, in which they lived left her scarcely time for sober reflection, and prevented her dwelling, as probably she otherwise would have done, on several inconsistencies in both Mrs. Freeman's conduct and that of Sir Matthew, which would otherwise have excited suspicion, and become the subject of her serious investigation.

That Mrs. Freeman should feel the most per-fect confidence in her (Amelia's) intentions and principles, was certainly, she felt, nothing but her due ; but it certainly argued worse than indifference towards Sir Matthew, if she believed him, as she had said, devotedly attached in his heart, to leave him hour after hour, with the object of his affection, which she constantly did under the most frivolous pretences.

Often, too, on some trifling plea, Amelia was made Sir Matthew's sole companion, either in his walks or drives, for his curricle was now con-stantly at the service of the ladies ; and Amelia, though with secret uneasiness, and a conviction in her inward heart that she could not conquer, though she stifled it, was persuaded to take her seat in it, as the companion of the future Lady ——

Soon, however, it became evident to her that Sir Matthew was much better pleased when Amelia alone accompanied him ; and though she at first hesitated to do so, by degrees her scruples were silenced.

The sense of propriety, and the necessity of suiting her appearance to her finances and situa-tion in life, which had at first, in spite of all Mrs. Freeman's ridicule and persuasions, kept Amelia within the strictest bounds as to her dress, was now, too, almost imperceptibly done away with.

" It would be disgracing Sir Matthew to appear with him otherwise than as dressed suitably to his rank," was Mrs. Freeman's mode of reasoning ; and though Amelia and she dif-fered greatly as to the style of dress that was becoming to rank and fashion, the former could not refuse to wear the handsome presents for which she was equally with her friend indebted to Sir Matthew's munificence ; and consequently she now appeared dressed in a style quite, as Mrs. Freeman declared, suitable to the dashing vehicle which daily conveyed her through all the fashion-able rides, to the admiration, as Sir Matthew very often observed, of one sex, and the envy of the other.

" How I wish you were a horsewoman, Susan,"

observed the baronet, as he lolled over his breakfast one morning, discussing their plans for the day. "My friend, Colonel Beet, has got the prettiest creature to dispose of that ever eyes beheld. It has always carried a lady, and he would not sell it for any other purpose. He offered it to me quite a bargain; but as you can't ride—"

"Don't be too sure of that," returned Mrs. Freeman; "at least I am not too old to learn, and if it will please you I will begin taking lessons to-morrow; and in the meantime Amelia will ride the animal if you will buy it for me."

"That will be just the thing," returned Sir Matthew, starting up. "I will go directly, and see Beet about it. I shall catch him in bed now, and so make sure of the bargain, for I know two women of my acquaintance who want it, and if it was only to disappoint them—"

"Really the women are much obliged to you," said Mrs. Freeman, as he quitted the room. "But come, Amelia, you must go and put on your riding habit.

It was one of Amelia's weak points to be dotingly fond of being on horseback.

She was ready in a short time.

An expression of pleasurable surprise was visible in the countenance of the baronet as he surveyed her particularly neat and symmetrical figure, which certainly appeared to more advantage in that habit than any other.

"This is a pleasure I scarcely anticipated," he observed. "I was not aware that you were so well prepared for an excursion; and I have, therefore, sent Joe to my tailor's, to desire him to come and measure you and Susan for habits. However, she can see him, and give her orders, and you can——"

Amelia would have protested against unnecessary expense, but Mrs. Freeman's observation was decisive.

"Your habit will do very well for a makeshift, child," she observed; "but after all, it's old fashioned, and so not another word."

"Come to the window, Amelia, and see what a pretty creature it is," said Sir Matthew, passing his arm around her slender waist, and leading her, as he spoke, to the window, beneath which a servant in livery was walking the animal in question, while another led Sir Matthew's horse and his own, up and down.

It was indeed a beautiful creature, and Amelia did not withhold her praise from it; while Mrs. Freeman, peeping over her shoulder, lavished upon it her usual phrases of sweet, lovely, elegant, &c., &c.

But Amelia hesitated about the propriety of going out with the baronet, and sat herself moodily at some little distance from the window.

* * * * *

"Sir Matthew will be dreadfully disappointed if you do not go with him," said Mrs. Freeman, in a low voice. "I should be very sorry, on more accounts than one, that you should offend him just now. Do, there's a dear girl, try to compose yourself, and tell him that you will go."

Before Amelia could, however, command herself to appear composed, Sir Matthew, who had been leaning out of the window talking to his groom, advanced to her.

"I presume Miss Arndale is too much engaged to bestow a thought on such an insignificant personage as myself," he observed in a tone of excessive pique; and then, after a short pause, he added, re-assuming his usual mild insinuating manner—"Must I send away the horses, Amelia? I do not wish to force you, dear girl; but, indeed, I do think that air and exercise, and change of scene, will do you much more good, just now, than sitting at home brooding over vain regrets and useless recollections."

Unfit as she was to engage in any pleasure, Amelia knew not how to refuse the pressing entreaties with which Mrs. Freeman seconded this observation, and in a few minutes her tears dried up, and an assumed smile concealing the anguish of her heart, she was seated on the beautiful animal, which seemed proud of its burthen.

The day was fine, the park crowded with fashionables, and Amelia, as they cantered along the ring, felt her cheeks glow at the observation their appearance excited, while Sir Matthew, though he affected to be only solicitous for her pleasure and comfort, evidently felt not a little elated and gratified at the praises and expressions of admiration, which from time to time reached his ear, on his fair companion's appearance and horsemanship, as well as the animal she rode.

Repeatedly he was joined by gentlemen who, by their looks, and in some instances by words, expressed their desire of knowing something more of the fair and modest girl, who shrank with confusion from their earnest gaze; but Sir Matthew was determinately deaf and blind to their hints and their curiosity, and though several found opportunities of addressing a few words of compliment to her, under the pretext of examining Sir Matthew's new purchase, the baronet contrived effectually to elude all their attempts at a further introduction to his charge.

It could not but occur, however, to Amelia that all this apparent kindness and courtesy to her was entirely confined to the male part of Sir Matthew's acquaintance, and that the ladies seemed, on the contrary, disposed to view her with sentiments of a very opposite nature.

More than once, indeed, she drew back with a feeling of surprise and almost consternation at the looks of pointed scorn with which her casual glance was returned by some young and handsome females, whom she immediately recollected as the same with whom Sir Matthew was conversing on the morning when she had first recognised him in Bond-street; while scarcely less appalling, or less inexplicable, was the look of pity and sorrow which beamed from the dark eyes of a matron who now accompanied them, and to whom it was plain, by her earnest bending from the window of the carriage, as for the second time Amelia and her companion passed them in the circle, the former had been especially pointed out.

Amelia felt as if fascinated by those dark expressive eyes; again and again she sought them out, but they were now bent on Sir Matthew with an expression very different to what they had worn before, for they now betrayed resentment and severe reproof.

"Who is that lady?" was just hovering on Amelia's lips; but its utterance was prevented by her observing that Sir Matthew had totally averted his head, and affected to be busily engaged in examining a new carriage with most extravagantly gorgeous liveries, which was passing.

But the moment the lady who was seated in it beheld the baronet she pulled the string.

"So you wanted to sneak past, did you?" she observed, addressing the latter; "but it wouldn't do. I want to wish you joy of your bargain there," pointing to the animal Amelia rode. "Fred told me you had bought it of him; but now, if you don't wish to commit deliberate murder, take that poor girl off its back directly, for there isn't such another vicious devil in England; she spilt me twice the last time I rode her."

"You!" said Sir Matthew in a tone of derision. "You surely don't mean that as any proof of the animal's viciousness, because she wouldn't keep such a rider as you on her back?"

"Why, you saucy varlet! do you mean to say I can't ride? Do you know I was out with the hounds every day last season, at Melton?" said the lady.

"Indeed! you do surprise me now," observed Sir Matthew; "not that you went out, but that you ever came back again. Good morning."

"Stop a moment, I have some news to tell you," vociferated the lady.

Sir Matthew reined in his horse, and Amelia, though she had proceeded a few paces, was yet within the reach of their conversation.

"First of all, tell me who is that pretty girl who sits so well on that mare—she makes me almost regret I have parted with her," demanded the lady, looking at Amelia.

"It's very odd," she continued; "I could never make her obey the hand as she does."

"Amelia is an excellent horsewoman," said the baronet, with conscious pride in his looks.

"Amelia," repeated the lady; "but who is she—who are her friends? They can have but little grace, I think, to trust her with such an ungracious wretch as you."

"Nonsense! What were the news you were going to tell me? Do make haste, for I can't stay here all day," returned Sir Matthew very unceremoniously.

"Well, then, your uncle is in town—come on purpose to make his will, and some other pretty little arrangements which—"

"In town," repeated Sir Matthew, "and I not know it! Tell me, Clara, have you seen him? Does he know I am here? What did he say—tell me all, there's a dear girl?"

"Oh, yes, I am a dear girl now; you can be civil enough now to answer your own purposes; but it would serve you right, were I to leave you to burst in ignorance; however, I am too good-natured, as you well know, and so I'll tell you at once the whole story. It's just three weeks ago, I think, that a note was delivered to my right honourable papa, as we sat at breakfast: I saw

his colour change, he seemed surprised and agitated, and without the slightest apology to me, for running away, just as I had condescended to sweeten his chocolate with my own fair hands, off he marched with the servant. Well, I waited and waited till the chocolate was cold, and then I poured it into the slop basin, and prepared to make a fresh cup. 'Who knows, after all,' I thought to myself, as I held the sugar suspended in the tongs, 'whether he'll come back in time to drink this before it's spoiled; he can't surely condemn me, as he has often done, for inordinate curiosity, if I just try to learn what probability there is of his coming.' 'Where is your master?' I inquired of the servant, who answered the bell."

"'In the library, madam.'

"'In the library; surely he has forgotten that he has not breakfasted.'

"'I beg your pardon, madam, I ought to have let you know before; he is breakfasting with the gentleman in the library.'

"You may be sure I didn't ring a pretty peal in Thomas's ears for his carelessness in keeping me waiting so long without my breakfast.'

"'And pray, who is this person with whom your master is breakfasting in the library?' I inquired, with seeming carelessness. 'My gracious papa particularly objects, you know, to my making inquiries of his servants as to his private proceedings, afraid, I suppose, that I should discover some of the state secrets which he confides to his *valet-de-chambre*, or be shocked at the intelligence that his last new *chere amie* has ——'

"For shame, Clara! how you talk!" interrupted Sir Matthew. "Do pray let the old gentleman's amour's rest in obscurity, and proceed at once to my uncle; was it him who was closetted with your father?"

"I won't tell you a word more, if you don't let me go on in my own way," said Clara, assuming a pretty pouting look and tone. "You don't suppose that my father is so bad a politician, as to suffer me to make a thorough discovery at once of his secret? No, no; all I could learn of Thomas was, that the stranger was a tall, surly-looking, old gentleman, who refused to give any name when he sent up the note.

"'I told him,' said Thomas, 'that I was ordered not to take in any notes or letters, without knowing who they came from, because master and my young lady had been so often taken in to open begging letters.'

"'Mine is not a begging letter, you puppy!' said the old gentleman, grasping his great bamboo, as if he would knock me down, if I hesitated any longer. 'And if it was,' he roared after me, 'it's your master's duty, and your young lady's, too, to read every letter sent them, and then treat the writers according to their deserts, and not reject them all in a lump.'

"If I'd had a grain of sense, as you well know I have not," continued Clara, "I should instantly have set this impudent stranger down for my uncle the earl; for though I had never seen him since I was ten years old, I had a perfect recollection of the lecture he preached me then, about my frippery and trumpery, as he called the beautiful lace frock, white satin slip, and splendid suite of pearls, in which my poor mother had decked me to go to her Majesty Queen Charlotte's juvenile fête at Frogmore; and how he brought tears into my eyes, as much with the grasp of his powerful hand, as he held me fast between his knees, as with the eloquent picture he drew of the naked and hungry children who might be clothed and fed out of my superfluities, and I enjoy no less pleasure, admiration, and distinction.

"Fine stuff, you know, cousin Matthew; but I knew no better then than to take all for granted that he said, and cried for an hour because mamma would not let me pull off all my finery, and sell it to clothe and feed naked beggars and their brats.

"I went to the ball, but the old stern earl's face and voice, and the description he had given of some starving family that he had just come from that morning, in some dirty hole or nook where nobody but himself that had any regard for themselves—as my father observed—would have ventured, haunted me all the evening, and spoilt the harmony of the music, and the taste of the dainties with which we were regaled.

"My uncle went abroad the very next week, and I never saw him from that time to this; but though I forgot his lesson, or learnt to know better than to practise it—'

"That is false, Clara," interrupted Sir Matthew; "you have faults enough, but insensibility to your fellow-creatures is not one of them."

"It is well you qualified that compliment," returned Clara, "or I should have been proud, indeed, of the only one my dear and well-beloved cousin ever thought proper to pay me; but *apropos de brebis, retournons, a nos moutons.*

"I had forgot, for the moment, all about the tall surly old gentleman, and therefore did not find out it was him whom Thomas so graphically described; and it was all in vain that, in my own pretty little innocent undesigning roundabout way, I tried to get out of my politic and crafty papa who it was, and what was the important business which had kept him five hours shut up in the library.

"So far, however, I got upon the right scent, as they say at Melton, that I learned my hopeful cousin Matthew was in some way concerned in the affair; for my father abruptly observed, the moment we were alone after dinner—

"'So, Clara, that precious rascal Matthew is in London I find; though he has not condescended to let me know it, and, indeed, acts altogether as if there were no such person in existence. But, it's no wonder; I am a very insignificant person, no doubt. The Right Honourable Harvey Fitz-Harvey, one of his gracious Majesty's commissioners—'

"'Dear papa,' said I, in my silly way, 'I dare say Matthew does not know of your new dignity; let me write to him how highly the king has honoured you, and I'll be bound he will hasten to show you all manner of respect; for, with all his faults, Matthew, you know, is the very

reverse of disloyal, and honours, I am sure, even the very shadow—'

"You think yourself, I dare say, a very facetious young lady, Miss Clara,' said my dignified papa; 'but really I see nothing in this affair to joke about. Sir Matthew, I hear, has already deserted Lady Albina Mandeville; so that the three thousand pound damages he paid for that pretty affair, and the risking his own life in his encounter with her brother, and wounding the poor young man so that he will be an invalid for life, has been all to gratify—"

"'Don't you know, papa,' said I, very wisely and sententiously, ——Nay, Matthew, you shall listen to me; I have not yet told you half——"

"I have heard quite enough of your rhodomontade, Clara, I ought to have known that you only detained me to gratify your malice."

Clara burst into a loud "Ha! ha! ha!' as he put spurs to his horse, and rode off.

"Shall I tell your uncle I have seen you?" she called out, putting her head out of the carriage window.

"You may tell him you have seen the devil, if you like," muttered Sir Mathew, between his closed teeth, as he rode close up to Amelia's side, and endeavoured apparently to read in her countenance how much of this conversation had reached her ear, and what impression it had made on her; but the investigation was anything but satisfactory to him, for her embarrassed look and total silence betrayed, as plain as words could have done, the nature of her reflections.

"I hope you do not give any credit to what you may have heard my rattling cousin Clara say," he observed; "because, I assure you that there is not a word of truth in all she uttered. You may yourself, indeed, judge how little what she says is to be depended upon, by what she asserted as to the cause of her parting with the horse you ride on; for the fact is, she can scarcely sit a horse without being tied on. You, who ride so beautiful, would die of laughter to see Clara's awkward figure. She was vexed, as you might observe, to see the animal the property of one who shows it off to such advantage; and my rallying her induced her to invent one of those malicious tales for which she is famous."

Amelia, however, was not to be so easily deceived, even by the cool indifferent tone, and the insidious smile, with which her companion uttered these assertions.

She had happened to have a full view of his countenance, as his cousin had uttered her remarks respecting Lady Albina Mandeville; and she had seen confusion and shame, which even his bold and resolute effrontery could not wholly conquer, striving for the mastery.

Besides, was it probable a female—a young, and, by her station in life, a respectable female, could have invented such a revolting tale?

It was bad enough, indelicate enough, or rather more than enough, to have recurred to it, and uttered her remarks with so much levity as this young lady had done, but it was utterly incredible that any female could invent such a tale; and during the remainder of their ride Amelia's thoughts were divided between the unhappy lady whom Sir Mathew had deserted, as his cousin had phrased it, and the still more unhappy one whom according to Amelia's belief was destined to be the next victim.

And yet there were moments even now when she could not help indulging suspicions that Mrs. Freeman was acting a part—that she did not in reality believe that Sir Matthew intended to marry her, though, for some reason, she judged it expedient to pretend to believe it.

Amelia, indeed, was completely puzzled, and often very unhappy, at what was passing before her, without being able to comprehend it; but she was now, at least, at no loss to comprehend Sir Matthew, when, after again paying her some well merited compliments on her horsemanship, observed—

"It will be time enough to buy Susan a horse when she has learned to manage it; and, therefore, I must request you will consider this as your own, Miss Arndale."

Amelia without a moment's hesitation, refused the present.

"You forget, Sir Matthew," she observed, "that you actually gave it to Mrs. Freeman—I beg your pardon, Susan I should have called her; for, I believe, you do not like to hear her called by that name."

Sir Matthew burst into an ironical laugh.

"Indeed, Amelia, it is very indifferent to me what she is called," he observed; "though I have certainly preferred calling her Susan, because it was the name she was called by when she lived in my mother's service, and therefore I am more accustomed to it."

Amelia looked grave and thoughtful; there was an expression of more than indifference, of contempt in his manner, which she could not mistake, and which she felt at once gave a complete contradiction to all that her companion had asserted respecting Sir Matthew's real devotion to her, although there was nothing in his manner which could prove it.

A long silence ensued; Sir Matthew looked earnestly in her face, for some moments, and then observed—

"You and I have long been playing at cross purposes, Amelia, yet I think you have all along suspected that I have been forced, by other people's manœuvres and artful devices, into assuming a character which has sat all along very ill on me, and which, at this moment, I have determined to drop for ever. Tell me now, candidly, Amelia, have you ever believed that it was possible I could have any serious intentions towards such a woman as your companion Susan, or Mrs. Freeman, as you call her?"

"It would not become me to doubt it, sir," returned Amelia. "But, be that as it may, I have no ambition to become your confidant."

"Psha! my dear girl, let us deal plainly," he observed; "you must have seen, for women are never blind on such subjects, that I am devotedly passionately, fervently attached to you; that I in reality adore you, and that I have foolishly been led into a labyrinth by that artful woman, who persuaded me that you would at once take alarm if I professed my love and flattered my vanity; that you would find me irresistible upon a nearer acquaintance—and forgive the stratagem, for the sake of the passion that prompted it. From day to day, and week to week, however, she has persuaded me to delay, though I have been as miserable as any poor dog could be, at the deceitful game I've been obliged to carry on. It's no easy thing, Amelia, to pretend to make love to a woman you hate and despise, and that, too, before the very face of the only woman you can like or love," he continued in a hurried tone; "for I swear to you, my dear girl, that you are the only woman I ever saw in my life that I really did——"

"You may spare all your protestations, sir," said Amelia, interrupting him, and endeavouring to conceal, under the assumption of coldness and indifference, the terror and alarm she really felt at the discovery of the deep-laid and treacherous plot which had been laid against her. "It is a matter of perfect indifference to me, I assure you, in what light you regard me, but I beg to be distinctly understood that this conversation puts an end to all communication between you and me. I will deal frankly with you, Sir Matthew, more frankly, indeed, than your deceptive conduct towards me deserves, and tell you at once that, even were you sincere, and did really mean all you profess, there is an insurmountable barrier between us. Mrs. Freeman could have told you, and ought to have told you, that my heart, my affections, my faith, were given to another, long before I beheld you, and that from those engagements no temptation on earth could make me swerve."

Sir Matthew looked astonished and confounded at the firmness and even boldness with which she spoke.

He had evidently prepared himself for a very different scene.

He had expected that she would have overwhelmed him with reproaches, have accused him of base and dishonourable intentions, and reprobated the treachery and deception of Mrs. Freeman.

To all this he was prepared to reply by a thousand passionate protestations of honour and sincerity on his part, whatever Mrs. Freeman's views or opinions might be.

But all this was now totally uncalled for.

Amelia displayed neither surprise, alarm, nor distrust.

She simply told him that she was already engaged; and, therefore, that it would be quite an useless waste of time for him to say any more on the subject of love to her.

Completely disconcerted by the course she had taken, his vanity mortified, and his consequence piqued by her cold indifference and composure, Sir Matthew for some time scarcely uttered a word as he rode homewards by her side, beyond an indistinct and unconnected murmur at his hard fate, and a complaint of Mrs. Freeman's insincerity in having led him to believe that she (Amelia) was wholly disengaged, and that it was mere timidity, and a fear of acting contrary to the rules of prudence, that induced her to keep up her reserve and distance towards him.

To all this Amelia turned a deaf ear.

Her mind, in fact, and her thoughts, were in a complete state of tumult.

She saw—she believed she saw—to its fullest extent the dilemma in which she was involved, and she was now revolving, with the deepest anxiety, the means by which she should free herself from all connection with the base, unprincipled woman in whom it had been her misfortune to place such implicit trust.

She was in a strange place, without a friend, and without money, for, though living in what she considered luxury and extravagance, she had never, since her arrival in London, been in possession of five shillings.

The clothes which she had brought up with her, she was well aware, were worth but little, even if she knew how to dispose of them; and of the articles presented to her since her arrival, and which she was aware were all purchased at the cost of Sir Matthew, she was resolutely determined not to retain a vestige.

"Oh, no, no; it would be acting as mean and dishonourable as themselves," she murmured, while the deepest crimson suffused her pale cheeks at the thought. "No! I will prove to them how little they knew me, if they thought I was to be purchased with their gewgaws, or deceived by them into—"

She turned involuntarily her eyes upon Sir Matthew as she spoke, and beheld his fixed upon her with a look of intense scrutiny.

"You despise me, I see, Amelia," he observed; "yet, if you could but see my heart at this moment—if you could but know how ardently, how devotedly—"

"I cannot listen to this language, sir," Amelia interrupted, with decision; "but there is one means by which you can confer a great obligation on me, and prove, indeed, that you are sincere in your regret for the unworthy deception in which you have joined."

"Name it, Amelia; anything, everything that man can do—all that I possess—"

"No, no — no further obligations," said Amelia, with energy; "I am already oppressed, cruelly oppressed with those I have so unconsciously incurred, for I now see—at least, if I may believe what you have asserted—that it is me, instead of Mrs. Freeman, who—"

"Name it not, Amelia; would to heavens that the sacrifice of my whole fortune could convince you of my sincerity. of my devotion; but I see you bear even the offer of my services with impatience, and yet, just now, you said it was in my power to oblige you."

"It is—and at very little expense," returned Amelia, "for all I ask of you is to conceal for the present—for a few days, at most, but probably only for a few hours—the explanation that has taken place between us. Suffer Mrs. Freeman to believe that I am still deceived, until I think proper to acknowledge I am no longer so."

"I will give you my word and honour that I will be guided solely by your wishes, however painful it may be to dissimulate longer with that woman," returned Sir Matthew; "but tell me, Amelia—for as a friend you must allow me to inquire, though you will not suffer me to interest myself as a lover—what end do you propose by this, and what are your final intentions? I feel, indeed," he continued, observing her hesitate, "that it is my duty to see that no evil arises to you, from your connection with Mrs. Freeman, for be assured, dearest girl, that, unless she had had some object in view to accomplish, that woman would never have endured for an hour the society of one whose every word and action were a reproof to her. There have been times, indeed, Amelia, when, even with all her artifice, she could not deceive you, unsuspicious as you are and have been. I know that, within a few short hours of your quitting Bath, she so far threw off the painful restraints of decency of manners that you were alarmed and shocked, and, I believe, tempted sorely to repent having trusted your destiny so far in her hands as—"

"You are right, indeed, perfectly right," said Amelia, with earnestness; "but how was it possible that *you* should know all this?"

"Oh! the deaf old man could see, if he could not hear." he replied with a significant smile.

Amelia was again completely astonished.

"How have I been deceived," she exclaimed; "but did Mrs. Freeman know that that person——"

"Know it, yes, certainly my dear girl, though she was not aware that my motive for assuming the disguise was in reality distrust of her. I knew that she would not hesitate for a moment to betray my interest, if she thought it would advance her own, and therefore, in addition to the delight I experienced at being an unsuspected observer of all your actions, and gazing unrestrainedly——"

"You—you—Sir Matthew, it could not possibly be you, who——"

"It was me, indeed, Amelia. Do you suppose I would delegate to any individual on the face of the earth the supreme pleasure of guarding you from all danger of insult, as well as of enjoying your society for so many hours? You slept, too, Amelia, and during that sleep, I had the supreme felicity of taking Mrs. Freeman's place by your side. It was with difficulty, indeed, Amelia, that I then preserved my disguise; but let it plead with you as a proof of my real esteem and regard for you, that I contented myself with silently supporting you, and thought it luxury enough for so undeserving a mortal as myself, to feel your sweet cheek laid on my shoulder, and inhale——"

A sudden pause, much to Amelia's satisfaction, relieved her from hearing the conclusion of this speech, which she had been prevented, effectually interrupting by the surprise, the confusion, and the resentment, she felt at the discovery she had made.

Surprised, vexed, and angry as she felt, however, all those emotions were for a moment suspended, as at the sudden pause he made in his extravagant rapture, she involuntarily turned her eyes upon his face, and beheld the change that had taken place in his countenance, from which every vestige of colour had fled, as he bent his earnest look on a travelling chariot, which at a very slow pace was advancing towards them.

"It cannot be, and yet it certainly is," he murmured, apparently totally unconscious of Amelia's observation, or that her quick eye instinctively followed the direction of his.

A lady was seated or rather was reclining in that carriage, for she seemed totally unequal to the task of supporting herself, and was propped up with pillows, while the front and side glasses were all let down, to give her air, by her attendant, who was seated by her side, and regarded her pallid face with evident alarm and interest.

Amelia, had never in her life seen anything to compare with the beauty of that face, though it was the beauty rather of a statue, than a living being, the complexion vying in colour and transparency with the purest marble, while the jet black tresses that were crossed on the high forehead seemed, by the contrast, to render the paleness of that beautiful face but the more striking.

The eyes were closed, and Amelia almost thought, as she gazed, that they were closed for ever, and that the fair statue was indeed as insensible to the cares and griefs of this world as she appeared, but that, at an exclamation from her attendant, who had casually turned her eyes on Sir Matthew, as they drew near, suddenly aroused her, she lifted the heavy lids that seemed a moment before to have been weighed down in death-like slumber, and a loud shriek, as Sir Matthew desperately urged his horse on past the carriage, told that she had recognised the unfeeling destroyer of her peace, who, trying to veil his consternation and dismay from Amelia, dashed on at a pace that soon brought them to the door of the house in Crawford-street, at the window of which Amelia beheld, with secret disgust and abhorrence, the treacherous Mrs. Freeman awaiting with smiles their return.

CHAPTER XXI.

It needed no words to explain to Amelia that, in the strikingly beautiful, but evidently wretched and dying female, whom she had thus transiently seen, she had beheld the unhappy woman whose disgrace and desertion she had overheard spoken of with so much apparent apathy and levity by Sir Matthew's relative; and though, as we have before said, not a word was uttered by Sir Matthew which could betray anything like an acknowledgment of the fact, Amelia beheld with a feeling of satisfaction the effect that this interview had had upon him.

Never, indeed, had she seen Sir Matthew so totally subdued, so unable to disguise his agitation, or to veil his feelings under the mask of levity and nonchalance, which, though he at first tried to do, was soon dropped, and he sat silent and abstracted on the sofa on which he had thrown himself on his first entrance into the room.

"What is the matter with you, Sir Matthew?" said Mrs. Freeman, after having twice spoken to him without having received an answer.

"You look as strange and as startled as if you had seen a ghost. If it wasn't broad daylight I should swear you had been frightened—and, I declare, there's quite a cold perspiration on your forehead. What—"

"Nonsense!" interrupted Sir Matthew, throwing off her hand, which she had placed on his forehead, with violence. "I wish you would not annoy me by your ridiculous remarks and conjectures."

"Well, upon my word. sir, you are really very polite; but you need not have bruised my hand so against the sofa," said she lady, with great anger.

"I didn't want to bruise your hand," he returned; "but I wish you would mind your own affairs, and not trouble yourself about mine."

"Really! Indeed, this is a curious change!" she began, in a high tone.

"Don't make a fool of yourself," he uttered, in an expressive whisper, which, though apparently intended only for her own ear, was sufficiently audible to be distinctly heard by Amelia. "I am not in the humour," he continued, "for trifling. Who do you think I saw in Piccadilly just now."

"I don't know, indeed. But, whoever it was, you needn't be spiteful to me; I couldn't help it."

"You couldn't help my seeing her, certainly; but, perhaps, if it had not been for you and your artful schemes—"

"Bah! Now I know who you mean," interrupted Mrs. Freeman. "It is not the first time you have said that, but you know better; you know very well that it was all your own planning, and that I only did as you bid me."

"She is dying, however, between us; that can't be denied," observed Sir Matthew.

"Dying! Who? Lady Albina? I thought you said just now you saw her in Piccadilly?" exclaimed Mrs. Freeman.

"So I did," returned the baronet; "but so altered—so horribly altered! I did not mind her letters, for I knew you women are very fond of talking of death and the grave, and all the rest of it, if they are disappointed; and—but it's plain she did not exaggerate. I would give ten thousand pounds, at this moment," he added, starting up, and beginning to pace the room with a hurried step, "yes, that I would, if I could only see her look as she once looked. And that scream, too, I shall never get it out of my ears!"

"What nonsense you are talking," said Mrs. Freeman, in a tone of remonstrance, and darting at the same time a look at Amelia, as if to discover whether the latter was attending to what was passing.

Amelia, however, appeared lost in a deep reverie; and though her countenance betrayed that the subject of her reflections was anything pleasant, it was impossible to be certain that it was in any way connected with what Sir Matthew had inadvertently betrayed,

"I never saw a man so nervous as you are,"

continued Mrs Freeman, after a short pause, significantly winking at the baronet. "Why should you fret yourself about what you can't help? And after all, perhaps, there is no danger of Lady Albina's dying; for I recollect when I lived with her, three years ago, Mr. Mandeville and all their relations took it into their heads she was going to die, because she looked so pale and thin, and lost her appetite; and yet she got as well and as hearty again as ever."

"She will never get well and hearty again now," said Sir Matthew, in a desponding tone.

"Well, and if she don't, I suppose you need not break your heart about it?" returned Mrs. Freeman. "I own it's a melancholy thing to see a fine young woman cut off in the spring of life. But perhaps there's less to regret about Lady Albina than most. She lived very unhappy, I know, with old Mandeville; and they ought to blame themselves who made such a match. At any rate," she added, with peculiar significance, "it would be very foolish of you, who have nothing to do with it, to fret yourself—"

"It won't do," said Sir Matthew, in a low tone; "she," nodding his head at Amelia, "knows all about it. We met that malicious devil, my cousin Clara, in the park, and she took care to let out all about Albina."

"What an unfortunate wretch I am!" he continued, again resuming his walk. "And there's my uncle, the earl, come to town, too, and has heard some fine stories about me, it seems. I wish I was dead!" he added, with vehemence, catching up his hat, and flying out of the room.

For some moments Mrs. Freeman remained totally silent, as if resolving in her own mind what part she should take; but, at length, she broke into a forced laugh.

"Well, I always thought the man a fool," she observed, "but he proves himself a worse one than I suspected. Now, would you believe it, Amelia, this Lady Albina, that he is making all this fuss about, and, I dare say, thinks is dying of love for him, and penitence, and so forth, was notorious long before she ever saw him, and had had two or three *liasons*, as the French say, though she had only been married four or five years. For my part," she continued, "I'm sure I thought it the worst day's work I ever did when I engaged myself to her; for it was a miracle almost that saved my name from being brought forward in the trial, by which her old husband got a few thousands out of poor Sir Matthew's pocket, and got a divorce from his wife into the bargain; and if I had been brought forward in such a disgraceful affair, it would have been quite the ruin of me, you know, my dear."

Amelia could scarcely conceal her contempt and disgust at this vile hypocrisy and assumption; but she felt that it would be bad policy to let Mrs. Freeman discover her feelings until she (Amelia) had formed some plan to withdraw herself entirely from the hateful connection, and she, therefore, merely replied with as much indifference as she could possibly assume.

"You lived, then, with this lady, at the time she eloped with Sir Matthew?"

"Lord, yes, my dear. I wonder I never told you the story before," replied Mrs. Freeman; "and yet I don't know why I should, for I always hated to think of it. He was completely duped, for he thought it would settle his reputation as a man of gallantry, and be a fine feather in his cap among his gay companions; but, instead of that, he found he was only laughed at, for it was well known Lady Albina would have run away half a dozen times before if she could have persuaded any rich fool into running away with her. As to her dying, it would be all very pretty, if she could persuade him into marrying her now she's at liberty again; I fancy he'd find that her dying fit would soon go off again when once she had him fast."

"You would alter your opinion, I think, if you were to see her," said Amelia, who inwardly shuddered at the levity and cruelty of these observations.

Mrs. Freeman's pretended smiles vanished at the earnestness with which Amelia spoke.

"Why, you don't really think—but, Lord, what nonsense! If she was really dying, you know, she could not be out and about," she observed.

"She was in a travelling carriage, which from its appearance, had come a long way," returned Amelia; and, I confess, the thought struck me directly that she was come up to London to die, with her friends. Poor creature!" and Amelia sighed from the bottom of her heart.

For a time Mrs. Freeman's effrontery seemed to forsake her, and it seemed as if she was in some measure conscience-stricken at hearing that her victim was really in the state Sir Matthew had represented. But this feeling was but transitory; and a few extra glasses of wine after dinner, a luxury which she now regularly partook of, at Sir Matthew's expense, restored her to her usual spirits.

It was in vain, however, that Amelia attempted to veil from her keen and shrewd observer, that she was unusually low-spirited and thoughtful.

"One would think, my dear Amelia, positively that you were in love with Sir Matthew, and took the discovery of his wickedness to heart," she observed. "But, Lord, my dear, even if it was so, if you knew as much of the world as I do,——"

"Heaven forbid!" ejaculated Amelia, involuntary; "at least, that I should ever know so much of the world, as to be able to look upon such subjects as these as a mere matters of course, as it seems you do."

"You are quite right," said Mrs. Freeman, laughing; "in fact," she added, after a few moments' pause, "I will own to you Amelia, that——"

"Excuse me, let us drop the subject," interrupted Amelia; I cannot speak of it, without seeing so forcibly before my eyes that beautiful woman dying, evidently dying a victim——"

"Bah! For goodness' sake, Amelia, don't horrify one with your description," interrupted

Mrs. Freeman. "But where the deuce is Sir Matthew?" she continued, seeming suddenly to recollect herself; "it's past nine, by my watch, and he was to have been here by seven, to take us to Drury Lane, to see the new comedy."

"I do not wonder that he has forgotten his engagement," said Amelia; "I should think his feelings would not suit much with comedy to-night"

"Feelings!" returned Mrs. Freeman, with a bitter sneer; "there's few people in the world beside yourself, I suspect, Amelia, that would give Sir Matthew credit for very tender feelings."

"Indeed!" returned Amelia, with quickness," "I have heard you hold very different doctrine.

"Ah, that was when I wanted to recommend him to your favour, Amelia," she replied, laughing: "but though I tried to deceive you for your own good, mind I was never deceived. I knew all along that there is not a more heartless, selfish libertine in the world than he is."

"Is it possible?" said Amelia—who saw that she was now completely off her guard—"that, with this opinion, you could wish to make a husband of him?"

'To be sure it is possible, Amelia, very possible," she replied. "It is not him I want; I want his fortune, his title; and, above all, I want to have the power of mortifying those that have tyrannised over me. I want to have the opportunity of treading on the necks of some of his proud family; and that I shall have, if I become his wife."

There was so much earnestness—such an evident impress of truth in what she had last uttered—that Amelia was startled and confounded.

How could she reconcile this with what Sir Matthew had acknowledged to her, that there was no reality in his pretended addresses, and that she (Mrs. Freeman) had herself planned the deception, to aid his views towards herself.

For some minutes she sat silently revolving these considerations in her mind, while Mrs. Freeman, with her eyes fixed on hers, appeared to be endeavouring to read her thoughts.

Suddenly, however, the recollection of the latter reverted to Sir Matthew's protracted absence.

"I hope he is not going to make a greater fool of himself than ever," she muttered. "If, after all, he should be drawn in by Lady Albina's pretended——"

"Do not say pretended," said Amelia, warmly. "I assure you you are mistaken; the poor lady is really dying."

"Well, then, if she is really dying," returned Mrs. Freeman, in a tone of extreme levity, "I can have no reason to fear her rivalling me."

"What can all this mean?" thought Amelia, as, wishing to drop the painful subject, she arose to seek a book which Sir Matthew had that morning lent her.

"Sit still, can't you, Amelia. I don't like to be left alone, you know; and especially just now, when I am so vexed and low-spirited. I could cut my throat."

Amelia reseated herself.

Mrs. Freeman, evidently unable to dismiss the train of thoughts from her mind which Sir Matthew's absence, coupled with his having met Lady Albina in the morning, had excited, commenced questioning her minutely as to all that passed.

"Pshaw! stuff! All art! She always was so sentimental, and so theatrical," she exclaimed, as Amelia, wishing, if possible, to awaken something like remorse in her mind, painted, in the most forcible language she could command, Lady Albina's appearance and distracted manner.

All that the lady, whom Sir Matthew had designated his cousin Clara, was repeated, too, as far as she could recollect; and the interest with which she evidently entered into the detail, and the regret she expressed that Sir Matthew was on such bad terms with his uncle, confirmed Amelia in the belief that, whatever might be Sir Matthew's views or intentions, she (Mrs. Freeman) certainly indulged the belief that she should become his wife.

The evening passed away, and no Sir Matthew.

Mrs. Freeman evidently began to grow very uneasy.

Amelia, on the contrary, hailed his absence as a good omen, believing that it was occasioned by repentance on his part for the misery he had brought on the unhappy Lady Albina.

The usual hour arrived for his visit in the morning.

Never since their residence there had he neglected calling before noon.

But now one, two, three o'clock struck without his making his appearance.

The woman of the house, who herself waited on them, entered to lay the cloth for their dinner.

Amelia now began to brighten up amazingly, for she felt happier.

But her joy was to be of brief duration, as the following chapter will show.

CHAPTER XXII.

AMELIA FINDS HER MOTHER — A STRANGE MEETING.

ONE day Amelia walked into the City. Her object was to make some purchases at a well-known French house.

She had progressed as far as Ludgate-hill, when a crowd in front of one of the shops attracted her attention.

She paused and looked at the scene.

"It's only an old woman fallen down in a fit," said one.

"Let her alone," said another, "she's only shamming; call a policeman."

These remarks excited the interest of the kind-hearted girl, and she made her way through the mob to the place where the woman lay on the ground.

A shriek drew the attention of the bystanders upon herself.

She staggered forward and fell.

"Mother! mother!" she uttered, as she dropped senseless by the side of the poor soul lying groaning and writhing on the pavement.

Yes, it was the once beautiful Olivia! the once proud Duchess—now the wife of a pardoned criminal, and living on the charity of the public, doled out to her in half-pence in the crowded thoroughfares through which she once rode in her own chariot.

* * * * *

Suddenly a young and elegantly dressed man elbowed his way through the crowd.

He hailed a passing cabriolet, and, lifting the two senseless forms from the ground, thrust them into the vehicle, and, mounting the box beside the driver, bade him drive to a square situated in the most fashionable part of the West-end.

The young man was the artist she loved—the son of Lady Lovelace.

* * * * *

In a short time the vehicle drew up at the door of a house indicated by the young artist, and the occupants were carried from it and placed in the care of a lady who presented herself at the door.

The young artist whispered a few hurried words and withdrew.

The astonishment of Amelia on finding herself, on the recovery of her senses, lying in a strange bed by the side of her mother, may readily be understood.

She made all sorts of inquiries as to how she came there, and what had happened; but was told to be silent—that she was among friends who cared for her, and that under no circumstances was she to excite herself in the least.

"A kind gentleman," said Mr. Stevens—for such was the name by which the lady of the house introduced herself to Amelia—"a kind gentleman has brought you here, and he will look after you, if you only remain quiet."

"But at least you will tell me his name?"

"Oh, yes; his name is Mr. Lovell."

"Mr. Lovell?"

"Yes; bless his dear old heart!"

"He is old, then?"

"Not particularly so; but you will see him ere long."

Amelia did see him.

Mr. Lovell and her artist lover were one and the same person; but this Amelia knew not, for the young gentleman had taken particular pains "to make himself up" as an old and fussy medical-looking man, with a bad memory and a bad temper.

The young artist was evidently determined to do good by stealth.

Amelia was certainly not much prepossessed by his appearance or his behaviour.

For he took particular care to render himself most obnoxious in his behaviour when in her presence.

Nevertheless he attended unremittingly to her wants, and those of her mother, and in a few days both were much better.

It must not be supposed that the thoughts of Amelia did not run on those she had left, during the time of her illness.

Sir Matthew and Mrs. Freeman were constantly in her thoughts, but only to be thought of as altogether objectionable people.

In spite of every care and attention Olivia remained for many days in a state lingering between life and death; and when, at length, all immediate apprehensions of the latter event were removed, and she began to show symptoms of returning strength and perfect consciousness, Amelia was shocked by discovering, from the observations of the indefatigable and skilful attendant, Mr. Lovell that, the distortion of her features, and the impediment which prevented her distinct utterance, were likely to continue lasting mementoes of the severe attack the unfortunate patient had suffered.

During these melancholy days Amelia's attention had been unremitting; and Mr. Lovell, though still maintaining the same harsh abruptness of manner, whenever he had occasion to speak to her, yet proved by his observations to Mrs. Stevens, that he was not unobservant of that filial affection which rendered her so insensible to fatigue, so utterly neglectful of her own comfort, or even her health.

"Can you not get some one to relieve that poor girl, up stairs, from constantly watching at her mother's bedside?" he inquired; "get some trusty woman, if you can, and say it's by my orders."

Amelia was at first inclined to demur, when, in consequence of these instructions, Mrs. Stevens introduced an elderly woman, whom she represented as an expert and careful nurse; but Mrs. Stevens' remark, that it would appear very ungrateful to Mr. Lovell to refuse his offered assistance, silenced her opposition; and Mrs. Carr, as she was called, entered upon her office, to which, indeed, she seemed, by the quietness, yet intelligence, of her look and manner well adapted.

"You will go to bed, to-night," said Mr. Lovell, as he turned away from the bedside of his patient.

Amelia made no reply; she was unwilling, it might be said she was afraid, to offer any opposition to her singular visitant, whose piercing eye dwelt on her changeful countenance with a look of deep interest, though he tried to veil it by knitting his brows, and compressing his lips together, thus adding harshness to a set of features which were naturally stern and repellent, though not exactly unhandsome.

"I say I desire you to go to bed to-night," he repeated, "I cannot afford to pay money to people for doing nothing; and if I had not seen the necessity that you should be relieved from your labours, I should not have sent you an assistant."

"You are very kind, sir, and I am deeply grateful," faultered Amelia.

"Prove it! prove it then by obeying me! I like actions, not words."

Amelia bowed her head in silent acquiescence, and he hurried from her, to give some directions to the new comer.

"Mind, he observed, as he quitted the room, turning to Amelia, and holding up his finger, as if to enforce his words; "till eight o'clock to-morrow morning you give up the care of your mother."

"What a strange gentleman," said nurse; "but it is not the first time I have seen him, though he does not know me again; indeed, I don't think he ever looked me in the face, either then or now, though he attended morning and evening for nearly a month, the person I was with."

"Yet Mrs. Stevens says he is not a physician," observed Amelia.

"He is the best of physicians," returned the nurse, smiling; "for he cures all his patients without a fee, at least, I know he not only attended them without any, but he paid all the young man's expenses besides."

"Heaven will repay him!" said Amelia, fervently; "and yet, though I feel so grateful to him when he is absent, I cannot but confess that his manners make me fear, rather than love him, when he is present."

"At all events you must not make him angry by disobeying him," replied the nurse; "for, I will answer for it, the first thing he will ask to-morrow is, how you passed the night, and I'll defy anybody to deceive him; besides, you may safely trust your mother to my care, for I will not leave her for a moment."

Thus reassured, Amelia retired to her bed, where sleep soon buried all her cares in deep oblivion.

It was not till after the hour that Mr. Lovell had named for her rising that Amelia awoke, and then, hurrying on her clothes, she hastened to the bedside of the invalid, who she found, to her great satisfaction, had passed a very quiet night.

"It's well for you you were a-bed, miss," observed the nurse, smiling; and well for me that I was not napping on my post, for the gentleman stole up here at daybreak this morning, and, after taking a look at your mother, he asked me where you were? I said, 'A-bed in the next room;' and away he went, looking quite satisfied. I'm sure if he was your own father he could not feel more for you."

"I only wish he would speak a little milder," thought Amelia; "and I am sure I should love him almost as well as if he were ever so nearly related; but now, in spite of all his kindness, I tremble whenever I hear his voice, or see his keen eye fixed on me."

From Mrs. Carr, the nurse, Amelia learnt, during the time they sat over their breakfast, the particulars of that act of benevolence which she had before alluded to, as having been the means of her first introduction to Mr. Lovell. A young man from some distant part of the country, she said, had been suddenly seized with a brain fever. He was a total stranger in London, and the people of the house, where he had lodged a few days, were in such consternation at the thoughts of his dying, and their having to bury him, that they were about to send him to the workhouse.

Mr. Lovell, who had entered the shop, a small turner's, to buy some trifling article, overheard the conversation on the subject, between the man of the house and one of his neighbours, who was advising him not to delay a moment in getting rid of one who might prove such a heavy burthen to him.

Mr. Lovell, it appeared, requested to see the poor young man, who, it was said, could not live. He thought differently, however, and he undertook to cure him, or, at all events, to defray every expense attendant on his remaining in his lodging, and being properly looked to.

"And well did he keep his promise," continued Mrs. Carr; "for, night and morning, and sometimes three times a day, he was at the poor young man's bedside; and handsomely, too, he paid me, and everybody; and when the young man got well, and could give some account of himself, he, that is Mr. Lovell, put aside all that roughness that arn't natural to him, though he keeps it up so. Howsoever, poor Belgrave, as he called himself, though that wasn't his right name, seeing his linen was all marked B. M.—"

Amelia held her finger up in token of silence.

"We will talk of this another time," she hastily whispered, seeing her mother's attention was excited by the woman's exclamation of surprise.

With mingled pain and pleasure Amelia listened to a detail which revived in her heart recollections that the pressure of care and misfortune had for some time stifled, though not extinguished.

"And to this man, who will scarcely suffer me to speak to him, and who never looks at me without seeming to despise and contemn me—to him do I owe the preservation of my mother?" were Amelia's reflections as Mr. Lovell entered the room.

His stern eye, as usual, took a hasty glance at her countenance, and was, as usual, as hastily withdrawn; and Amelia's warm emotions, which a moment before would have urged her to throw herself at his feet, and try to give utterance to her fervent gratitude, were again all chilled by the expression of that look.

From this time his visits became less frequent. Olivia recovered as far as it was likely she would ever recover, and Amelia, who felt grieved and humiliated at being the constant object of his bounty, to a man who treated her with so much apparent contumely, summoned courage to say to him that there was no longer any occasion for the nurse to remain in attendance.

"And when she is gone, sir," continued Amelia, faltering, and not daring to raise her eyes to his, "I shall be able, I trust, to supply, by my own exertions, all our wants. I am conscious that we have been a very serious burthen—"

"There, please to say nothing about that, young woman," he interrupted; "but have the goodness to tell me how you propose to support yourself and your mother?"

"All my means are exhausted," said Amelia.

"Indeed! that is a rather curious expression; but you are a curious young woman altogether, I really am at a loss to comprehend you."

Amelia could scarcely suppress a smile, but it was followed by a deep sigh, as she timidly replied—

"I am sorry, sir; for I am sure I would not wish to have any concealment from you."

Mr. Lovell replied, at first, only by one of those searching looks which had so often made Amelia shrink beneath them, though unconscious why she should do so.

On the present occasion, however, instead of casting them to the ground, she raised them to his face, with that peculiar look of confidence and innocence which gave such attraction to her countenance.

"I must certainly have strangely mistaken," murmured the artist to himself; "and, yet, my own eyes—pray, young woman," he added, "answer me one question with sincerity—What brought you to London, where, it seems, you have neither friends nor money?"

Tears rushed into Amelia's eyes, and again they were dropped to the ground, as she replied—

"I must refer you to my mother, to answer that question, sir."

"Well, then, I will ask you another, which you can answer," said Mr. Lovell, after another pause—"Who was that man with whom you rode one morning in the park? Where did you get acquainted with him? and—but, there, answer first what I have asked you."

"I know but little of him, sir."

"Nor wish to do so?" added Mr. Lovell, in a tone of inquiry.

"Nor wish to do so," repeated Amelia, firmly.

"Hum!" said Mr. Lovell. "Yet, if I mistake not, you accepted his present; one, too, totally unfit, I should think, for a girl that intends to get a honest living."

This was uttered in a tone so austere and contemptuous that poor Amelia's spirits sunk completely, and for a few moments she remained unable to answer.

"Whoever gave you that information, sir," she at length observed, "also should have done me the justice to tell you the circumstances which led to that gift, the only one I have received; and they ought also to have told you that nothing ever gave me more real pain and mortification than being compelled to retain it."

"Compelled! What compelled you?" demanded Mr. Lovell.

"Oh!" cried Amelia, "well did I foresee that that horse was doomed to be the cause of bitter mortification to me."

"I should be sorry, very sorry, to inflict mortification where it was undeserved," observed Mr. Lovell, in a softened tone; "but I *will* ask my authority, since it appears so painful to you to give an explanation which appears to me very simple and easy; but be it as it may, young woman, I would advise you, if you really are all you pretend and appear to be, to avoid all communication with one whose situation in life, independent of his principles, which I know to be bad, decidedly bad, mark me, render

him a most unfit person for you to have anything to say to."

"I am quite aware of it, sir—"

Before Amelia could finish the sentence, Mr. Lovell was gone.

In a few hours after Mrs. Stevens entered the room.

"What do you think, Miss Amelia? I really do believe our old gentleman is in love with you; for when I carried up his dinner, instead of walking into the other room, or standing at the window with his back to me, as he usually does, he came up to the table, and said—

"'I want to ask you a few questions, good woman; sit down there,' pointing to a chair.

"Well, you may be sure, I couldn't think of taking such a liberty, though I've *set* in greater folks' presence before now; but then, there's something so proud and so distant, somehow, about Mr. Lovell that, if it was the king's majesty himself—God bless him!—I don't think I could feel more daunted and 'bashed. Howsomever, he cut me short at once."

"'Sit down, do; if I did not wish you to do so I shouldn't ask you,' he shouted, at the top of his voice, and you know what a voice it is when he raises it. Well, down I popped into the chair, for I felt as if I could have sunk through, it was so strange to me to find myself sitting right opposite, and the old gentleman's fierce eyes fixed full upon my face.

"'Don't be frightened, good woman,' says he, 'I only want to ask you a few questions about those people upstairs. Do you know who and what they are? I don't ask for mere curiosity."

"'No,' thinks I, 'there arn't much curiosity about you, I'm answerable.' So, with that, I went as straightforward as I could about it to tell all I knew, and, would you believe it, he let me talk on a full half hour, without ever interrupting me, or saying, as he usually does, 'There, there, that's enough, don't talk, I hate talk!'"

"It was, indeed, strange," observed Amelia, whose expressive face had changed from white to red, and red to white, half a dozen times during Mrs. Stevens' remarks.

"There must be some peculiar reason which could induce Mr. Lovell thus to lay aside his usual reserve, and curb that impatience which scarcely allowed him to listen, even when it was absolutely necessary, much less to such circumlocution as Mrs. Stevens' discourse displayed."

Such were the thoughts which occasioned those changes.

"You needn't be afraid Miss Amelia, that I said a word to hurt your feelings," she observed; "and, indeed, if I could have avoided mentioning anything altogether, I would; but he's such a man, if you drop but half a word, he catches hold of it, and then he questions, and cross-questions you, so that there's no help for it, you must tell the whole truth. But laws, what a fright I was in.

"He'd sat all this time with his dinner that I'd cooked so nicely, and brought up so smoking hot, getting as cold as ice before him, and never touched; but when I mentioned *his* name—Sir Matthew, I mean—he gave his plate a push that sent the dish with the chicken and the sauce-boat to the other end of the table, spilt all the gravy, and oh! such a mess; but he never took a bit of notice, but walked up and down the room, muttering to himself, and I won't be sure, but I think I heard him swear.

"'Won't you be pleased to take some dinner, sir?' said I, when I'd wiped it all up, and put it tidy again ; ' No !' says he, as sharp as if I'd asked him to take poison.

"I know his way, so I wouldn't say another word, but began to clear the table ; but just as I'd put all the things in the tray, he turned sharply round—

"' Don't go yet, Mrs. Stephens,' says he, 'this poor girl up stairs then, is quite destitute of friends, and nothing to depend upon but her industry.'

"I told him you had told me so, and, that he might depend upon it, all was correct that I had told him ; and then he became quite mild again, and seemed to take such a pleasure in listening to what I said in your praise, that really I don't know where it will end ; to be sure he is rather elderly for you, Miss Amelia, but there, better be an old man's darling than a young man's slave, as the saying is. Well, after all I should like to see you rich and happy, and ——"

"For mercy's sake, do not talk so, Mrs. Stevens!' whispered Amelia, who saw that her mother, though she was unable to take any part in the conversation, was yet attentively listening ; and saw also that her eyes betrayed more pleasure and satisfaction than had beamed in them since the commencement of her illness ; "such preposterous hopes and expectations," continued Amelia, raising her voice, "have been the bane of my happiness ; but you, I am sure, have too much sense to mean any thing more than a joke, at my expense."

The unexpected entrance of the very person of whom they were speaking, prevented Mrs. Stevens' reply ; Mr. Lovell stopped for a moment, as if disconcerted at the presence of the latter ; but his habitual commanding manner was in a moment resumed, and he desired her to go down stairs, as he had something to say to Amelia.

It was the first time that Amelia had ever been addressed by any softer title than "young woman," or "girl," and she felt the blood rush into her face, as Mrs. Stevens, in passing her, smiled expressively at his unusual familiarity.

"Sit down, sit down here, Amelia," said the supposed old man, drawing a chair close to the one he had taken himself.

Amelia obeyed, trembling, however, in expectation of the scene that was to ensue.

"I'm very sorry," continued Mr. Lovell, "that I hurt your feelings so much, this morning, about that horse ; but I will tell you, candidly, that I happened to be in the park, a short time after, and overheard the jokes and observations which were made upon Sir Matthew's generosity, in making such a present to a girl whom one of the shopmen declared was nothing by a milliner's workwoman, he having repeatedly seen her in Bath, bring home her work when he went with parcels, and being rather struck with her as a pretty girl, had

asked some questions, and thus learnt her name and residence.

"The man laid the parcel down close to me, and I thus saw that it was directed to the very house I lived in. I need not now explain why I felt particularly interested in Sir Matthew's actions.

"I determined, however, to watch his proceedings—but all this is no consequence to you, Amelia now ; all I wish is to tell you that I am convinced I wronged you, and now I'm going to make a proposal to you. What is the matter with the girl?—why do you start and shrink away?—surely you do not suppose that I am going to propose anything improper?"

"Oh, no, sir ;" and Amelia glanced towards her mother, who, propped in her easy chair, sat silently regarding them, and evidently listening with high-fraught expectation.

"Well, then, I will tell you, at once, what I propose. The price which he gave for that horse was one hundred guineas. You may well look surprised, for it is not worth above half the money. But that is not the point ;' and he drew out his purse. "I will give you the cost price for it, if you will allow me, in your name, to return it."

Amelia was about eagerly to reply that she should be most happy but that she could not think of taking the money, when she recollected the necessity of consulting her mother on the subject.

Mr. Lovell's quick eye saw instantly the direction of her's.

"You are right," she said ; "it is your mother I ought to have said this to. Are you satisfied, woman, with my offer?"

Mrs. Arndale nodded assent, and he threw the purse into her lap.

"Oh, no, mother, dear mother—do not, pray do not think——"

Mr. Lovell interrupted Amelia, whose distress was strongly pained both in her face and in the accents of her voice, at this proof of her mother's mercenary disposition.

"Be quiet, foolish girl," he observed, in a tone of kindness ; "this is all fair—it is a matter of bargain between your mother and me ; and she is perfectly right, having once made up her mind to keep it, not to part with it to gratify my whims, without its full worth."

Amelia turned away, to conceal the tears of bitter mortification which streamed down her cheeks.

Mr. Lovell took her hand.

"Amelia," he said, "do not grieve ; I understand your feelings, and appreciate them ; look upon me, henceforth as your friend."

*   *   *   *   *

Not long after the foregoing conversation Amelia sought her true friend in his apartment below.

"Is it you, my child?" he said. "Excuse me, I was totally lost in recollections of the past—recollections which you have forced upon me."

"I should be sorry," said Amelia, timidly, "if I should be the cause of giving pain where I am so deeply indebted."

"No, no; you are not indebted to me," he hastily replied. "What is the value of paltry coin? Between you and me, Amelia, I have greatly wronged you—I have done you great injustice; but you are amply revenged by the pangs which you have, this night, excited in my bosom—pangs that I have long stifled. I loved a maid once, Amelia, young and innocent, but she deceived me. There, go along child, this is all folly. I will take care that the horse shall be returned, and returned so that you shall not again be troubled by that libertine. There, now go, my child; I cannot talk to you."

Amelia reluctantly left him: she was shocked at the agony which his looks betrayed he had suffered, and she would willingly have tried to divert him from dwelling on those melancholy thoughts, which, as he said, he had so long stifled, and which had now, perhaps, on that account, broken out with redoubled force; but his manner was, even now, too decisive for her to dispute for a moment his commands, and she slowly returned to her mother.

"Mr. Lovell's respects to you, Miss Amelia, and will be glad if you will come down and make his breakfast for him at eight to-morrow morning," said Mrs. Stevens, opening the door of Amelia's bedroom, just as she was retiring for the night.

"The poor gentleman seems quite ill to-night," she added; "and no wonder, for he has not taken a morsel of food to-day. He seems to have something on his mind, but I dare say you'll hear all about it to-morrow. Lord, Miss Amelia, what a lucky thing, after all, your mother's being taken ill so very suddenly may prove to you! It's plain the gentleman has quite taken to you, and he hasn't, I do believe, a relation in the world. If you play your cards well who knows what may happen?"

"I have no cards to play, Mrs. Stevens," replied Amelia, who felt hurt and offended at the expression she had used. "Depend upon it, Mr. Lovell is one with whom—"

"Lord bless me, Miss Amelia, you do take one up so sharp. All I meant was, that if you contrived to keep the good opinion he's got of you, there's no knowing but that you might come in for a good fortune, after all; and, I'm sure, there's nobody in the world would be more glad to see it than me; for, as I said to Sir Matthew, last night—by the bye, Miss Amelia, you can't think how anxious and concerned Sir Matthew has been since he heard of your mother's dangerous illness. He wanted to send a physician, but I was afraid it would affront Mr. Lovell, and so I put him off that we had got one that you could put great confidence in. Well, then he wanted to give me money to pay for necessary expenses; but I told him there was no occasion for it at present, and I knew you would be angry if I took it without consulting you."

"You were very right, perfectly right," said Amelia. "Dear Mrs. Stevens, you cannot think how much obliged I feel to you; and now excuse my giving you advice, but I am sure the less encouragement you give to Sir Matthew to come here the better, for Mr. Lovell has a very ill opinion of him."

"Well, I declare I thought so," observed Mrs. Stevens; "for, when I was telling him all about the horse—which, by the bye, I can't think how he knew anything about; but he did, and so I was obliged to tell him the rights of it."

"It was most fortunate that you did so," observed Amelia, "for he knew all, except my reluctance to keep it."

"Well, I declare, I thought as much," returned Mrs. Stevens, "and so I took care that he should know that; for, indeed, Miss Amelia, though I really don't believe Sir Matthew means anything but what's honourable and respectful, yet, still, after what has happened, you can't—as I said to him yesterday, when urging me to persuade you to see him—you can't, I say, be too cautious; and, as I told him—

"'Miss Amelia says, she will think all the better of you for not intruding upon her while she is in trouble, and so you must wait patiently till the old lady is well enough to be left.' But you can't think what a deal of trouble I've had to persuade him; and how he has watched and waited, backwards and forwards, here, two or three times a day, with first one excuse and then another. I really do think, if ever a man was sincerely in love, he is. He's as dull and demure as a mouse."

To all this Amelia made no reply.

"Mr. Lovell will put an end to it all to-morrow," she thought to herself, "and therefore it is useless for me to enter upon the subject at all."

Precisely at the appointed hour, Amelia, having first given her mother her breakfast, entered Mr. Lovell's apartment.

He was already risen, and busily engaged writing; but he laid it aside the moment he saw her, and returned her salutation with kind courtesy.

"It is long since I had this pleasure, Amelia," he observed, as he took his seat at the breakfast-table, "and it will, perhaps, be long before I shall again, for I am going to quit you. Yes, I have been soberly considering the subject all night; and I have come to the resolution of setting out for Paris at daybreak to-morrow."

"To Paris!" repeated Amelia, in surprise.

"Yes, Amelia. I am going to see one who shall restore your father to you. Do not thank me, Amelia; I have a deeper interest in this affair than you can guess. I have for some days meditated this step, but it was not until yesterday that I learned the whole truth—learned that the unhappy man was, in reality, more an object of pity than condemnation."

Amelia's eloquent eyes thanked him through her tears.

"If you had but known my poor father," she faltered,

"Well, well," he added, "I do not wish to give you pain; and perhaps I have no right to blame her, for a defect of understanding seems inherited—for what but a want of common sense can have influenced that mother of yours? Do not look vexed, child; I would not wish to think worse of your mother than that she is a fool. I cannot think better of her ; for none but one devoid of understanding, or one devoid of all principle—in short, the most depraved of human beings—could act as she has done. I do not blame you, my poor girl, for wishing to think well of your mother: but, whatever you may think and believe of her intentions, do not let your kind feelings blind you to the utter folly, the madness of her life. But I need not say all this to you ; for you have already proved, by your conduct, that you have both sense to discriminate, and firmness to act up to your own sense of what is right and proper. And now to business. In the first place you will, perhaps, want money while I am gone. Now, do not begin to object and protest, as I see you are preparing to do. I do not want to overwhelm you with obligations, and I respect the spirit which makes you shrink from them. Your mother may be attacked with a relapse of her disorder, and you will want, perhaps, more than you can at present command, and if so, there is an order to pay you, at sight, ten pounds, so that you can use it, or let it alone, as you find necessary ; only premising this, that I shall consider it a proof of your want of confidence in me, if you do not freely resort to it, in case of necessity."

Mr. Lovell now proceeded to give her some direction as to the management of her mother, all of which Amelia listened attentively to, and promised faithfully to abide by.

"Now, then," he observed, "I have nothing to add. Oh, yes, there is one thing; here is a direction to a poor family, whose hovel I accidentally entered in one of my walks. I have allowed them five shillings a week ever since ; and, as I do not think them careful and prudent enough to trust them with the money in advance, you must be my treasurer, and continue to pay them the allowance every Monday. Here are three guineas, and before those are gone—"

"Oh, long before that, I hope and pray," exclaimed Amelia—"long before that I shall see you again."

"I hope so, child," he returned, turning away to conceal a starting tear ; "but life is uncertain, and I never part with one I love, without reflecting how many chances there are that I shall never behold them again. God bless you, Amelia. I shall not see you again before I go ;" and, without waiting for her reply, he walked into his bedroom, and closed the door after him.

Before the sun had risen, Amelia heard the chaise roll from the door, which conveyed her new friend on his important journey ; and earnest and fervent were her prayers that his mission might be successful.

Never since the hour when she had become assured that her father had been blameable every way had she felt so happy ; and she continued to hope and conjure, up visions of happiness, until they were all buried in sleep.

A long and loud groan awoke her from a dream, which had, in part, embodied all her waking thoughts ; and, without a moment's pause, she flew to her mothers' bedside, to behold her in the last agonies of death.

Oh, how frantically did Amelia now call on him who was far removed beyond the reach of her prayers, to save her mother.

Mr. Lovell's skill, his prompt attendance, had before rescued her mother from apparent death ; and if he were but here now!

Alas! vain were all Amelia's regrets, and equally vain the assistance that was as quickly as possible afforded to the sufferer; she was now beyond the reach of mortal help.

A second attack of her disorder had proved fatal, and, in less than half an hour from the time she had been roused by her groans, Amelia beheld her mother a lifeless corpse.

*   *   *   *

It was not as one who "sorrows without hope" that Amelia mourned the death of her mother ; there were many reasons why she should indeed acknowledge that it was a merciful dispensation which had removed her from a scene which could henceforward be only one of endless trouble and discontent.

Disappointed in every hope—condemned to linger on a only half existence—life could afford few charms ; while to those who were compelled to behold her sufferings, and consequent regrets, she must have been, indeed, a constant source of melancholy and disquiet.

But though Amelia acknowledged that it was better that she was taken from "the evil to come," still she could not but feel with bitter agony the forcible rending of that sacred tie which bound her to her only remaining parent ; could not but mourn, with almost hopeless regret, that she was now totally alone in the world, without one heart to feel, beyond the common sympathy of strangers, for her loss.

The dreadful distortion of her once handsome features, which had rendered Olivia, for the last few weeks of her life, a painful spectacle to look upon—an awful memento of the weakness of vanity—had all vanished ; and Amelia, as she contemplated the calm, tranquil countenance, which seemed almost to smile, as if pitying the fate of those who are still condemned to struggle in the troublesome world which she had quitted for ever, gradually felt that extreme despair, that utter hopelessness, which had at first rendered her insensible of everything but the magnitude of her loss, subside ; and though, for her own sake, she mourned that she was left desolate and alone, for her mother's she ceased to regret that the scene of trouble and suffering was over.

Tears, however—bitter tears—forced their way, and for a time, disturbed that calmness which had succeeded the first intense burst of sorrow, when Mrs. Stevens, who had been busily engaged, with two or three others, in performing those offices towards the deceased which custom renders necessary, put into her hands her mother's pockets, which she (Mrs. Stevens) had taken from under the pillow on which she died.

"You had better see what there is in them, Miss Amelia, before I put them with the other things to be washed."

Scarcely reflecting what she was doing, but mechanically obeying this direction, Amelia drew forth the contents.

"Lord bless me! whatever could your poor mother keep that money for, and you so short as you have been!" exclaimed the landlady, looking with surprise at the gold which rolled on the table. "Surely," she continued, "she must have felt that she had not long to live, and so have hoarded this up, to pay for a decent funeral."

Amelia did not think it necessary to explain how her mother had become possessed of this sum, but it recalled to her mind, forcibly, how her eyes had sparkled with pleasure—almost childish pleasure—as she, with feeble hand, counted it over, and deposited it where it was now found.

"Alas! it was not then of death that she thought," reflected Amelia, "though she concealed from me to what purpose that sum was to be appropriated; and he, who, with such indulgence for human frailty and weakness placed that money in her hand, even he little anticipated the purpose to which it would be appropriated."

The sight of this, the necessary means to procure what Mrs. Stevens had so emphatically styled a decent funeral—secured that good lady's most zealous and indefatigable services, and saved poor Amelia from repulsive details, which break in, with seemingly heartless coldness, upon the sanctity of sorrow.

Mrs. Stevens took it all upon herself.

She had a cousin, or uncle, or something, who was an undertaker, and he would do everything in the best and genteelest style, at the lowest possible prices; and Stevens and herself would follow with her (Amelia), that proper respect might be shown to the poor dear departed.

Amelia felt grateful for everything, but she requested that she might be left as much alone as possible, till the time appointed for the ceremony.

"I shall feel more fortitude and resolution by myself," she observed; but Mrs. Stevens could not believe that—she was sure it was enough to drive her quite melancholy, for a young creature like her to be shut up, hour after hour, in that manner, with a corpse; and, in spite of every remonstrance, Amelia was condemned to have her sorrows intruded upon by the visits of half a dozen strangers to her, but friends of Mrs. Stevens, who were actuated by curiosity, or led by real commiseration, to attempt to console the poor orphan, who was thus left destitute, under such peculiar melancholy circumstances.

Among those, whose well-meant but fruitless endeavours to administer comfort by the usual commonplace condolences on such a subject, was a sister of Mrs. Stevens, whom Amelia had once or twice seen in the house, during the first part of her residence there.

Mrs. Freeman, as she was called, was a ladies' maid by profession, and having, in the course of her various services, picked up considerable knowledge of the world, and rather pleasing and superior manners, was by no means an unpleasant companion, on ordinary occasion.

She possessed, too, that strong letter of recommendation, a handsome face, and good, though rather vulgar, person; she was capable of discriminating, and always kept the straight path in great matters, though, in small ones, she could sometimes conveniently wink, and step a few paces out of it.

Thus, *par example*, her lodgers might have safely trusted her with their money, their clothes, or any other valuables; but it was by no means the same case with their tea-chests, their butter, bread, wine, everything, in short, that could pay toll, without being likely to be detected.

In like manner, Amelia was perfectly safe in her hands, as far as regarded the little she possessed; but she had no scruples in adding a few shillings to the bill for mourning, though the poor girl, in the gratitude and generosity of her heart, had desired her to purchase, for herself, what she considered necessary, as far as the money would go.

"But, my dear, if this fifteen guineas are all you have,——"

Amelia recollected Mr. Lovell's generous deposit.

"It cannot be used for a better purpose," thought the poor girl, "and I am sure he would wish it should be so appropriated;" and, without scruple or reserve, Amelia put into her hands the draft for ten pounds which he had given her.

"Ah, we shall be all right, now, my dear," said Mrs. Stevens, her eyes sparkling with pleasure; "my husband can advance you the money, and then, after the funeral, you can go, and get it from the bank, for it's made payable only to you. Ah, poor dear Lovell, I dare say he foresaw how soon you would want it."

But, to return to Mrs. Freeman, of all those who

CHAPTER XXIII.

SIR MATTHEW AGAIN.

ONE morning, shortly after the sad event last chronicled, Amelia was startled by the presence of Mrs. Freeman.

That lady had dogged her to her hiding-place at last, and, what was more singular, appeared to hold such singular sway over Mrs. Stevens as to force that person to coincide with all she urged.

She announced that it was her pleasure to remain with "her dear young friend" for a few days; and on the instant Mrs. Stevens placed her best apartment at the disposal of the new comer.

Amelia felt as a fly in the web of the spider.

She had lost all power of action.

She felt the long arms of the mysterious woman about her neck, and she knew that it was useless to struggle.

Passively she submitted to everything that was urged by the woman she felt to be her worst enemy, and who was leading her to perdition.

She seemed to consider herself the obliged party in sharing Amelia's lodgings, and assisting in making her "customary suit of solemn black," observing that, having recently left a situation, she should else have been under the necessity of seeking a lodging, and putting up with accommodations and society not very pleasant to her, who had been all her life used to the superior manners of ladies, though in the humble station of their attendant,

By degrees Amelia, who had at first recoiled from the proposal that Mrs. Freeman should sleep and remain with her till the funeral, and, but that she felt too grateful to Mrs. Stevens, would have decidedly rejected it, became reconciled to her presence.

Mrs. Freeman's advice was always given with gentleness and deference, her compassion and sympathy were expressed rather by looks and tears than set words and phrases, and she encouraged rather the measures with which Amelia soothed her sorrows, instead of violently opposing, and declaring that she would kill herself with grief, and do no good to the poor dear departed, as was the common phrase of those who sometimes surprised Amelia weeping over the pale features which were soon to be taken from her for ever.

"I, too, have lost every one that I loved, Miss Arndale," sighed Mrs. Freeman; "and I know how useless it is to try by words to stifle natural feelings. Time is the only soother of grief; and, besides, as the poet says—

'The grief that does not speak
Whispers the o'erfraught heart, and bids it break.'"

It was into Mrs. Freeman's arms that Amelia, after her return from the mournful ceremony which consigned her mother to the cold grave, threw herself, to vent that burst of irrepressible grief which broke from her heart at returning to her now desolate rooms.

It was Mrs. Freeman's care which had removed every vestige, during her absence, which could administer to her grief, by reminding her of her loss; and it was Mrs. Freeman's silent sympathy and soft voice that first spoke hope and comfort to her heart, when the first agony of sorrow had subsided.

"You will not leave me, Mrs. Freeman?" said Amelia, when those who had attended to "show respect" to the deceased had withdrawn, and Mrs. Stevens was beginning to busy herself in, to use her own expression, setting all to rights.

'Leave you," returned Mrs. Freeman, tears glistening in her eyes. "Oh, no, Miss Amelia, certainly not, now; and, if it was in my power to say so, never. But at least, for this week, I shall, with your leave, defer my departure."

Amelia's looks, rather than words, proved how welcome was this supposed kindness.

The week passed away, and Mrs. Freeman still deferred her departure.

She had not been very careful, she acknowledged, or she might have had it in her power, perhaps, to have indulged the first wish of her heart, by remaining with Amelia for the rest of her life.

But still she was not unprovided for on emergency; and, if Amelia would allow her to pay a joint share of their expenses, she would still defer her intention of taking a new situation.

Amelia had now become so habituated to the society of this insinuating woman, that she would willingly have made any sacrifice to have retained her; but she felt doubly grateful for the kindness which thus conferred an obligation without seeming to consider it as such.

Time, as Mrs. Freeman had truly said, is the only soother of sorrow.

That which Amelia now felt for the loss of her mother was not diminished, but it was softened into melancholy remembrance and regret; and even those were sometimes lessened by the contemplation of the difficulties which seemed to threaten her.

At length Mrs. Freeman, who had been Amelia's constant messenger to the person for whom she worked, because she could not bear, as she said, to see Amelia demean herself by trudging backwards and forwards to wait upon people who ought to be waiting upon her—returned with the disheartening intelligence that Mrs. Somerford had no more occasion for Miss Arndale, nor would be likely to want her for two or three months.

"Cheer up, my dear girl, I have told you the worst, because I hate myself to be deceived by people deluding one with false hopes," said Mrs. Freeman, "and there is no occasion to despair. Come, put on your bonnet, and we will go to your pensioners, or rather Mr. Lovell's pensioners; you have never been yet to see them, and it will do you good—not only the walk, but to see how contented and comfortable people can be that have no ideas or wishes beyond those of the most complete ignorance. Who knows, besides," she added, assuming a livelier tone, "but some good luck may turn up for us, which cannot be expected while we sit looking at one another in these dull rooms. We may find a letter, perhaps, from your friend Mr. Lovell when we return. Come, I have a presentiment that something will happen to compensate for this piece of ill fortune."

Amelia complied, though she was far from feeling that buoyancy of spirit which seemed to animate her friend; and, for the first time since her mother's funeral, she left the house which had been to her the scene of so many miseries.

"Lawks! is it possible you are going out? Well, to be sure; I'm so glad Mrs. Freeman has persuaded you, at last. To be sure, how well you do look in black; and that is the most becomingest bonnet that ever was made. Well, if somebody as I know was to see you—. Well, well; I won't say who I mean; but you need not frown so."

Such were Mrs. Stevens' parting exclamations as Amelia quitted the threshold.

"What does that silly person mean!" demanded Mrs. Freeman, after they had proceeded a few paces. "I know she is a famous hand at match-making; has she been attempting to try her skill with you?"

"No, not exactly," returned Amelia, with some confusion.

"Well, I will not be intrusive, dear, if the subject is painful to you; but I hope she did not act so as to hurt your feelings."

"I should be very ungrateful if I was to attribute any blame to Mrs. Stevens," observed Amelia; "but I will tell you the whole affair, lest you should think it more serious than it was."

As briefly as possible Amelia recounted the circumstances attending her introduction to Mr. Lovell.

In the very midst of her detail Sir Matthew suddenly made his appearance from a pastry-cook's shop, which they were passing, and, without a moment's hesitation, approached them.

After a hasty but respectful salutation to Amelia, he addressed Mrs. Freeman.

"Is it possible," he observed, "that Lady Molyneux is in London again? I thought they were gone to the Continent."

"They have, Sir Matthew," she replied, "and that is the reason I am here. I was unwilling to leave England for so long a time as they propose to be absent, and so I was compelled to leave my lady."

"Indeed! I am sorry to hear it; they will not, I am sure, soon meet with one to supply your loss," he observed. "But, tell me, what was the cause of their sudden resolution to quit England?"

Mrs. Freeman entered into a long detail, in which Amelia could take no interest, and which she scarcely heard.

She could not reasonably object to walk on with Sir Matthew at her side, whose whole thoughts seemed engrossed by the subject on which they were talking, and yet she felt uneasy and uncomfortable that he should just at this precise moment make his appearance.

Still they continued to walk on, and Sir Matthew, having exhausted, it appeared, the subject on which he seemed so interested, now turned to Amelia.

"I scarcely know, Miss Arndale, whether, after the cruel misconstruction which your friends were pleased to put on some former transactions, I dare address you," he observed; "but I cannot resist the impulse of my feelings to assure you that, whatever your opinion of me may be, I have heard with the deepest concern and sympathy of the misfortune you have sustained."

It was impossible for Amelia to reply otherwise than with civility to this address, which seemed to occasion the greatest surprise to Mrs. Freeman.

They continued their walk for some minutes in silence.

Again, however, Sir Matthew found some subject to renew his conversation with Mrs. Freeman, and they continued it until they reached the row of hovels in which the latter pointed out the one which contained the objects of Mr. Lovell's bounty.

"We are on a visit of charity, Sir Matthew," she observed. "Such, I know, are not totally unknown to you; but, perhaps, it will not be pleasant to you to enter such a place."

"Where Miss Arndale goes, I am sure I shall never shrink from," said Sir Matthew, for the first time renewing that tone of gallantry, and the look of ardent devotion, which had, from their first meeting, distinguished him.

"Do not hinder his going in with us, dear," whispered Mrs. Freeman; "he is such a generous, humane man, that it wouldn't be justice to the poor people, to keep him from seeing them."

Amelia's scruples were disarmed; and without farther hesitation, she accompanied her companion into the house, followed by the baronet.

There was a family of seven children, all rosy, clamorous, clean, and happy, though so ragged, that they were literally half naked; and the efforts of their mother, as she dragged, first one little urchin, and then another, up from the low stools on which they were seated, having their dinner of potatoes, with a little bit of fat bacon, to serve, as she said, for a "say so"—meaning, that the name of meat would content them—her efforts to drag their sleeveless frocks over the brawny shoulders of the girls, and pull up the bit of shirt collars which served the place of the whole garment to the boys, showed that, though she did not possess the means, she understood the comforts of decency and appearance, even in her humble station.

"You must be hard put to it, my good woman, I should think, to get victuals for so many mouths?"

"Oh, no, bless you, sir; we're pretty well off for that; we're seldom quite without, though they are sometimes a little short; but, then, it's the father and I that feels it, more than they. But if I had but my health and strength, as I used to have, we should do very well; though thank God, I've no right to complain; for since I've had the rheumatiz, and have not been able to help myself, I've had a power of friends that I never had before."

"This is really quite a lesson, Miss Arndale," said Sir Matthew, apparently deeply affected at the cheerful resignation and humility of the poor creature who could thus draw good from evil. "You must allow me to be on your list of friends, my good woman," he added, putting a guinea into her hand; and then, as if to avoid her thanks, he walked hastily away, observing, that he should have the pleasure, he hoped, of meeting Miss Arndale again, either upon that or a similar occasion.

"This can never be the libertine he has been represented," thought Amelia, as she walked slowly by the side of Mrs. Freeman to their lodgings; "surely Mr. Lovell must have been mistaken."

Within a very short time again the baronet's name was introduced; and then Mrs. Freeman contrived to throw in some strong praises of his liberality, the kindness of his disposition, and his extreme sensibility.

Again and again the subject was renewed, although every time apparently undesignedly on the part of Mrs. Freeman; but it was so natural, in speaking of acts of kindness and humanity, to praise one who had performed more within her certain knowledge than any other person she could mention.

Such was Mrs. Freeman's reply when Amelia, somewhat struck with the warmth of her eulogies, now ventured to observe, smilingly, that it seemed the baronet had secured her (Mrs. Freeman's) good report.

"He is a great favourite, too, of Lady Molyneux," she continued; and, if it were only for that reason, I should respect him."

Lady Molyneux was Mrs. Freeman's model for everything that was pure, elegant, and refined; and Amelia had herself learned, from hearing her ladyship's opinions, and precepts, and example quoted as an ornament to her rank and sex, to consider her as, indeed, a most amiable and estimable woman.

And if Sir Matthew was really a professed and notorious libertine, as Mr. Lovell represented him, could it be possible that Lady Molyneux would not only afford him her countenance, but that he should have been the constant associate of her sons and daughters!

Oh, no, it was quite impossible; Mr. Lovell must either have misrepresented him, or have been misled respecting him by some calumnious reports.

"It does not strike me that you particularly admire the baronet, my dear," observed Mrs. Freeman, laughing. "And, yet, it is rather surprising, because I certainly think there is a great similarity between you and him, in many respects; and, indeed, I will confess the truth, my love, that while you and him were speaking to each other, it struck me that, if you were in the same sphere of life, you would be just cut out for each other. I am mistaken, too," she added, with a sly look, "if the same thought, or something very like it, did not come into Sir Matthew's head; and who knows, after all, Amelia, whether I may not yet have the pleasure of wishing you joy, as Lady ———? Love has done many more strange things than to bestow title and fortune on one who seems born to adorn it. But I am, perhaps, talking very foolishly," she added, in a graver tone, "though I know my dear Amelia will forgive an error which is solely occasioned by my regard for her."

It would have been very unnatural if Amelia had indeed felt any very serious displeasure at observations so flattering, and yet so delicate; and while she truly, and with sincerity, disclaimed all ambitious views, she also ingenuously acknowledged that she had especial motives for distrusting Sir Matthew, and, therefore, totally declining his attentions.

By degrees Mrs. Freeman drew from her the whole history of Mr. Lovell's remarks, and her consequent rejection of the munificent present.

Mrs. Freeman listened as attentively as if she had never heard a word of the story before.

"I cannot pretend to say what this Mr. Lovell's motives might be for such false aspersions, my dear, or whether he had himself been deceived by some enemy of Sir Matthew's," she observed; "but this I am bold to affirm, that

there never was a more false, scandalous, and malicious charge ever uttered; and, besides, what should this man know of Sir Matthew, who never went into any company, and knew nothing about what was passing in the world, except what he saw from walking about the streets of a morning, before any body else was out of their beds, or gaping through the Venetian blinds at the opposite neighbours half the day, as Mrs. Stevens tells me he did? And, indeed, to tell you the truth, Amelia, I have had more than a hint—and I firmly believe it true, too—that this Mr. Lovell himself was a man of no very excellent character, though Mrs. Stevens worships him, because he paid her well. But giving away money is a very poor proof of goodness, if people don't show it in other ways, and really I never heard—"

"Oh, indeed, you are mistaken," interrupted Amelia with warmth; "Mr. Lovell is, though harsh and austere in his manners, one of the most humane, kind-hearted men in the world. He may have been in error with respect to Sir Matthew, but I am sure he would not designedly injure a worm."

Mrs. Freeman smiled significantly.

"You know but little of the world, my dear," she replied; "and it is almost a pity that you should be taught how deceitful appearances are; though as to Mr. Lovell, I really don't know what he may have assumed towards you for his own purposes. No doubt, but—"

"I cannot bear to hear you speak so," again interrupted Amelia; "indeed, indeed, you wrong him. Mr. Lovell is—"

"My dear Amelia, I know better than you what he is, but I have my reasons for not telling you at present all I *do* know. But now let me ask you a question or two, and you will see how much you overrate Mr. Lovell's merits. He attended your poor mother, you say, with the greatest assiduity; prescribed, paid for her medicine, and administered it. Granted he did so, he might mean well, but the real fact is, that it is his hobby to act the physician; though as Dr. Jahourdin said to me one day, that he never knew a case where Mr. Lovell had been beforehand with him that the patient recovered. How, indeed, could he know anything about diseases, as the doctor said, that had no regular education? Indeed, to tell you the truth, Amelia, though it is painful to me to say it, I think Mrs. Stevens was very wrong—very wrong indeed, not to call in a proper medical man. As to you, my dear, you cannot be supposed to have experience enough to know anything about it, and, of course, thought everything was right and correct; but, had I been here, then, I assure you, I should not have been satisfied with leaving your poor mother to the care of Mr. Lovell, whose blunders, Dr. Jahourdin told me, were quite notorious."

"Good heavens!" ejaculated Amelia, whose distress at these observations was only equalled by her surprise, "I thought Mr. Lovell was totally unknown in London, and you speak of him—"

"He is, to use the vulgar proverb, my dear, better known than trusted—at least, as far as his medical skill goes. The truth is, Amelia, he is a very strange, out-of-the-way, eccentric man, and his being worth a considerable deal of money gives him the power to indulge all his whims, though they often cost other people very dear. But we won't say any more about him, you will see him in his true colours some day, if you ever see him indeed ; for perhaps before this time he's red hot in some other chase, and has forgotten you, and all belonging to you."

There was something in the manner in which this last observation was made that struck Amelia forcibly that Mrs. Freeman had indeed some hidden and powerful reasons for her evidently contemptuous opinion of Mr. Lovell.

And yet Amelia could not be brought to believe that there was in reality any foundation for that contempt.

She recalled to herself every act, every circumstance in which Mr. Lovell had been engaged, and all alike confirmed her belief that though he was, as her companion had observed, a strange eccentric character, he was nevertheless humane, considerate, and benevolent.

One circumstance only tended to confirm Mrs. Freeman's opinion of him, that he had been influenced by caprice, and was now, to use her expression, red hot in some other pursuit—and that was his total silence towards her, Amelia, ever since she had written to him, according to the directions he had given her, to announce her mother's death, and the non-performance of the promise he had made.

"What but benevolence, the purest benevolence, could have influenced Mr. Lovell in the case," said Amelia, exultingly to her friend Mrs. Freeman.

She smiled significantly.

"Time shows all things," she replied ; " besides, this has cost him little, as I said before, but a little money that he does not well know how to dispose of, and he is well paid for it, by appearing a great man ; and what, perhaps, is of still more consequence in his eyes, securing your good opinion and gratitude."

"For which I do not verily believe he cares one farthing," said Amelia ; " at least, this I am sure, that he has ever repressed every expression of it ; but we shall never agree, I see, on this point, and, as you have more than once said, I must leave it to time to bring you round to my opinion."

"You are vexed, my dear girl," returned Mrs. Freeman ; "and yet, why should I not be equally displeased that you should continue to doubt and suspect a person whom I have much more reason to esteem and respect than you have Mr. Lovell ? I saw to-day, when I told you that I had met Sir Matthew, and that he had inquired with kindness and solicitude after you, that you looked rather displeased than gratified ; and yet I am very sure that Sir Matthew holds you in much greater respect and estimation than Mr. Lovell has done."

The repetition of these and a thousand similar insinuations, the apparent delicacy and reserve of Sir Matthew's manners, when again and again he (accidentally, of course) crossed their path, when Mrs. Freeman and she were walking, at length had their effect.

Amelia became thoroughly convinced of what she had from the first been inclined to believe, that the baronet had indeed been misrepresented and calumniated, and the cold reserve and distance of her manners towards him, gradually yielded to increasing familiarity and confidence.

Sir Matthew was now the friend who was to be consulted on all occasions, his opinion was received as decisive, both by her and her friend ; the sense of impropriety which had at first made Amelia shrink from his society, and wish that he less frequently fell in their way, was gradually forgotten, in the pleasure of conversing with one so well informed, so intelligent, and so vivacious, and there was at length scarcely a day pass d in which some portion of it was not spent in his company.

It was true that Amelia sometimes felt some compunctuous visitings of that prudence which she now seemed in a fair way of totally neglecting when, after a long ramble, or an interesting conversation, in which she had totally lost sight of the distance between them, they had come suddenly upon some of Sir Matthew's acquaintance ; and she had beheld the free and bold glances with which the males had regarded her, and the averted and disdainful glances of the females.

But, on these occasions, Mrs. Freeman was always her kind counsellor and consoler.

"Why should you heed the looks or the opinions of a set of thoughtless insipid triflers," she would reply, "when you are conscious, not only of doing what is strictly right, but that you are as far superior to the generality of them as the sun is to the little stars that twinkle round him ? Besides, my dear, if you knew as much of these people as I do, you would think their disdain, nine times out of ten, a compliment. For instance, there was that painted, withered, old piece of mortality, Lady Araminta Thomson, that passed us this morning, and gave me, as well as you, such a stare, as if she would put us quite out of countenance. Lord, my dear, if I was to tell you what things I have heard of her ! Why, nothing but Sir Thomas Thomson, her husband's death—which, by the bye, was a very sudden and mysterious one—saved her from being divorced at the age of forty-five ; and, ever since that she has been dressing, and painting, and flirting at every young man that came in her way ; and, it is actually whispered, is at last reduced to make love to her footman ; so that, you see, my dear, how foolish you were to let her looks at you and Sir Matthew give you a moment's uneasiness. The real fact is that she has been trying, in vain, to entrap Sir Matthew into a noose, and it is nothing but sheer envy and disappointment that made her try to mortify us. For my part, I was pleased at the opportunity of plaguing her. I shouldn't at all wonder to hear that she has gone home, and either hung herself, or married some John Trot in despair."

Amelia had now become too much accustomed to Mrs. Freeman's tone of raillery and sarcasm, whenever she spoke of people she disliked, to give implicit belief to all she had chosen to say of this lady; but, though she did not actually believe it in its fullest extent, it removed the sting of that expressive contemptuous look which Lady Araminta had bestowed on her and her companion, and she forgot again the resolution which she had at the moment formed, that she would not again be seen as Sir Matthew's companion in the walks.

CHAPTER XXIV.

THE BLACK CAPTAIN AND PIPEY—THE RACE TO PARIS.

WE left the once fearful Black Captain in the grasp of his worst foe.

Our readers will remember that the neighbourhood in which the capture was made was the old alley in the turning out of Drury-lane.

Just as the villain fell paralysed under the fearful grip of the ex-detective, several men came rushing from the neighbouring houses.

The Captain saw them.

"Help—help!" he cried, "a rescue."

They had no profound admiration for the law; those half-starved, diseased marauders, and an officer of the law was to them legitimate game.

Moreover, the Black Captain was known to them, and was a pal.

Quick as lightning they surrounded the prostrate man, and two of them bore him off, whilst Pipey was hustled and pushed until he found himself in Drury-lane.

*   *   *   *

Two hours from that time the Black Captain was seated with Grimer, in the dingy office of the latter.

"What's the matter now?" asked the lawyer.

"Matter!" said the Captain, "just this—I've had a narrow escape from that devil, your friend Pipey."

"Ah! he always was a clever boy, was Pipey," was the remark of the lawyer.

"D——n his cleverness; he nearly ran me to earth."

"What's his game?"

"His game! why the will, to be sure."

"He musn't have it."

"I'll see him ——"

"Never mind where you'll see him. I expect you'll see more of him than you wish for. But now what's to be done?"

"I must fly."

"Of course you must."

"Where?"

"Paris."

"Why there?"

"Because, according to your own account, you know Paris so well that the devil himself would not find you there."

"True. Paris it must be."

"And at once."

"At once."

"Have you anything more to say?"

"Only this. Take care of my wife."

"What, the Duchess?"

"The Duchess."

"All right."

Another moment, and the Black Captain was gone.

*   *   *   *   *

An hour later Pipey was in the office of the old lawyer.

By threats of the most emphatic kind he extorted from the old lawyer the course pursued by his ally.

"Paris," muttered Pipey, as he heard the destination of the old highwayman, and leader of the Scarlet Brethren. "Paris; it's an awful place to hunt a fox in; but there's one blessing, I'm troubled with the best scent in the world."

That night he was posting to Dover.

But the Black Captain had got a capital start, and the chase promised to be a long one.

CHAPTER XXV.

THE LAST ESCAPADE OF THE KING OF ENGLAND.

IT was announced that the King's health was shattered, and that he had been recommended to try the waters of Bath.

He assumed the cognomen of Lord Frederick Melverley, and the noble companion of his journey was known as Mr. Grant.

They went into the West, unattended except by two body-servants.

They crossed the Channel, and went into Wales.

After a short stay at the residence of the Duke of ———, they one day mounted the roof of the mail coach, and prepared to return to the city of fashion.

On the same vehicle was an old lady and two beautiful girls.

Evidently mother and daughters.

With these unsophisticated Welsh women his Highness entered into conversation, whilst his friend kept perfect silence.

"Here's the milestone, mamma," said one of the young ladies; "I declare we are a mile from —— already. How pleasant it is to get on so fast."

"Did you never travel by the mail before?" inquired the King, in a familiar tone.

"Never, sir; indeed I have never travelled at all," she added, with *naïveté*.

"Is it possible! and have such charms been confined to this secluded spot of earth?" returned the gentleman.

"My daughter has never been from home before, sir, except when she went to boarding-school, and then she went in her father's own chaise, so that she knows nothing about travelling," said Mrs. Woodford—for that was the lady's name— who seemed by no means disposed to let the conversation drop.

The stranger appeared equally inclined to be upon good terms with his companions, and after another compliment to the young lady who had first spoken, and whose name was Maria, he observed—

"That young lady, who seems to regret her departure so much, of course has not the happiness to call you mother, madam."

"She is my daughter, sir; but I am sorry to say she has very little of the feelings of one, or she would not give way to this nonsensical grief at leaving a place which, I am sure, has nothing to recommend it to people of any refinement," returned Mrs. Woodford, dwelling with peculiar emphasis on the last word.

"But perhaps it is not the place itself the young lady so much regrets," observed the stranger significantly. "There are sometimes persons who—"

"Oh, dear, no, sir—nothing of that kind I assure you," interrupted Mrs. Woodford, pertly. "There is no person there, indeed," she added, with an air of consequence, "whom my daughters could consider worth bestowing a thought upon."

"Indeed; it is something singular for a lady so young to regret so deeply leaving the country to enter into gayer scenes; for I presume you are going to the metropolis, madam."

"No, sir; we stop at Bath. I have been recommended to try the waters there,"—and Mrs. Woodford's consequential tone became still more important as she gave utterance to this falsehood.

Grace, the other daughter, had in the meantime succeeded in stifling the tears which had provoked this discussion, though it was impossible for her to banish the feelings which had given rise to them, or to take any part in the conversation which ensued, and in the course of which the stranger contrived to learn all he possibly could respecting them, their connections, situation in life, and intended mode of living—all of which were, however, considerably embellished and modified by Mrs. Woodford's usual habit of speaking of herself, and all that concerned herself.

With the same apparent thoughtless candour that prompted his questions, the stranger contrived to let them know that his visit to Bath—he also was to stop in Bath—was one of mere pleasure, that he was independent of all control, and sufficiently at ease in his circumstances to indulge his inclinations.

Quite undesignedly too, as it appeared, he named several persons of rank, as his intimate friends, and Mrs. Woodford in return, talked of her cousin Sir Walter, and her father, who was very near marrying Lord Loppington's daughter, which would have been sure to have gained him a seat in Parliament, but that the lady preferred her own cousin, and ran away with him.

"Do you know the Melverleys, of Cardiston Hall?" inquired the stranger, after listening patiently to her pompous and tiresome description of some festivities, which she, after all, could of course only know by hearsay, since they had taken place at the marriage of her father and mother; but they served to show, as she was used to observe, that she was not sprang from the dirt, and that was the point aimed at with

her new acquaintance, whose account of himself, as far as it went, was highly satisfactory to her.

"Do I know the Melverleys," she repeated; "yes, my father's estates and their's joined, and many a romp I've had with Frederic and Henrietta Melverley, poor things; their father was a shocking rake, he used to spend all his time and money in London, and leave Lady Melverley and her children at the hall, with scarcely the necessaries of life; but he's dead now, and Frederic has got the title and a large fortune, which was left him by his mother's uncle, and they say he is as saving as his father was the contrary—but that he's got a son that is likely to tread in his grandfather's steps, and spend what his father saves."

"But they do not live at the hall," said the stranger; "how, then, can people in this remote part of the world pretend to know so much?"

"I don't know; evil fame flies fast, they say; but it is reported, I believe, that the family are coming down to live at the hall again, they have been abroad for many years."

"Yes, it was there I knew them," said the stranger.

"Oh, indeed! but Henrietta is dead, is she not?" demanded Mrs. Woodford.

"Lady Alston you mean, of course. Yes, she died in giving birth to a daughter."

"She was reckoned very handsome," observed Mrs. Woodford; "I wonder is her daughter like her."

"I do not remember my ——, that is Lady Alston," replied the stranger; "but Julia is the most beautiful creature ——; at least people say she is, and certainly I once thought myself that she could not be surpassed."

The stoppage of the coach for supper put an end, for the present, to the conversation which had become so interesting.

The stranger, with great patience and attention, assisted Mrs. Woodford to alight, and supported her into the house, and Grace, who had at first felt considerably annoyed by his levity, and the flippant freedom of his remarks, was now greatly reconciled to him for the humanity with which he attended to her mother's infirmities.

She shrunk, however, with great confusion from the scrutinising survey which he took of both sisters, as soon as they came into the full light of the supper room, and pulling her large bonnet closer over her face, to conceal her swollen eyes, she quietly seated herself in the most unobtrusive corner she could find.

Not so Maria. Under the pretext of heat and headache, her bonnet was pulled off the moment she entered the room, and her long and beautiful hair instantly fell over her shoulders in the most graceful confusion.

"Heavens! I declare I had quite forgotten I have no comb to fasten my hair," and she made an attempt to gather it up together.

"It would be a sin to hide such beautiful tresses by torturing them into form," said the stranger, viewing her with evident admiration. "Let me entreat that you will not concern yourself about that which becomes you most admirably."

"Oh, but I must; I can't sit in this manner;" and Maria, with a deal of well-acted confusion, gathered up her curls and replaced her bonnet.

The stranger's eyes seemed fascinated; and Mrs. Woodford, with ill-concealed pleasure, beheld the tribute which he paid to her daughter's charms.

From this moment, indeed, until the termination of their journey at the White Hart, in the Market-place, Bath, the stranger's every effort was directed to conciliate Maria and her mother.

Business of importance, he said, compelled him abruptly to leave them at the moment of their arrival; but he should live only in hopes of meeting them again in the course of a few hours.

Mrs. Woodford was in high spirits, and loud in his praise, the moment he was gone, "so truly polite, well-bred, and genteel," she observed.

"And so handsome too, mamma," chimed in Maria.

"There is no goodwill lost between you, my dear, for it is plain he thinks you very handsome," returned her mother. "I wonder who he is? Something strikes me he will prove to belong to a great family. Did you observe how familiarly he talked of lords and ladies? Yet we must be careful, Maria, for I have heard there are many impostors at Bath."

"Impostors!" returned Maria. "Surely no person with common understanding could be doubtful that this is a perfect gentleman."

"Well, well, we shall see him again, and have further opportunities of judging," replied the mother, who fancied that in thus qualifying her praise of him, she was displaying necessary and prudent caution, and immediately after launched out again."

"How fortunate it is for us that we came a day sooner than we intended, or we should have missed making this acquaintance, my dear, and we should have felt quite lonely for a time, even in this beautiful place, without some friend."

Maria cordially assented; she was in raptures with the place, and never tired of standing at the window of the room to which they had been introduced, to admire the dresses of the passersby, and wonder what could bring so many people out into the streets.

The number of carriages, too, excited her astonishment; and as she gazed at them with interest, fresh hopes that her mother's constant predictions that she was born to ride in her carriage, arose in her bosom, and she sighed only that she could not immediately realise the delightful prospect.

The day passed away in wondering, admiring, and consulting.

"What a fright the girl has made of herself," observed Mrs. Woodford, when she at length found leisure to look at Grace. "I am sure if Sir Walter was to see you now, with your eyes swollen out of your head, and your cheeks as pale as death, and the tip of your nose as red as if it was a frosty morning, it would be enough to frighten him away again."

Many hours passed away, and their fellow traveller, on whose coming both Mrs. Woodford and Maria seemed to rely, as on that of a friend, did not make his appearance; and too much fatigued to bear up any longer the whole party retired to rest, determined to lose no further time, but on the morrow proceed to establish themselves in apartments, and commence their career of pleasure.

The breakfast was over, and no appearance of their expected visitors; and reluctantly the mother and daughter left the inn to seek for lodgings, leaving Grace with strict orders to detain him, if it were possible, should he come in their absence.

Grace earnestly hoped he would not, but her hopes were not fulfilled, for they had scarcely left the inn, when he was shown into the room by the waiter.

The most friendly inquiries as to their health, accommodation, and so on, showed that the interest he had expressed for their welfare had suffered no diminution.

The air of levity which he had worn during the first hours of their acquaintance had totally disappeared.

His manners were gentle, soothing, and respectful towards Grace, whom timidity and inexperience rendered awkward and confused at first, but whom he soon contrived to render quite at ease with both herself and him, though she could not agree with him in thinking that Bath was such a delightful place, that she would soon forget all her regret at leaving the country.

Grace was still less inclined to believe this; when in an hour or two after, at her mother's command, she followed the porter with their luggage to a lodging in ——street, two small rooms and an attic; looking out, the dining-room on a dead wall opposite, at the distance of about twelve feet, the back bedroom into a small yard, around which were tailors' workshops, and the attic upon an interminable range of red tiles and chimney-pots.

And this was to be their future residence; and for this they had left the range of a large, substantial house, with nothing to intercept the pure breath of heaven from entering all the windows, but clusters of eglantine and jasmine, or the delicious fruit of the vine.

Poor Grace looked disconsolately around her as the mistress of the house preceded her into the apartments, as she called them, apologising at every step for their not being so nice as she could wish them, but the ladies that had them last had only left last night, and she had not had time to put every thing to rights.

"All the cleaning and putting to rights in the world," thought Grace, as she gazed at the greased and stained sofa cover and curtains, the dusty, discoloured carpet, and the fancy chairs, on which a patch here and there alone remained to tell that they had once been decorated with wreaths of flowers; "not all that hands could do could ever make this place and furniture look wholesome and comfortable."

The bedroom was even more repulsive.

The counterpane looked as if it was years since it had been acquainted with the washing-tub, the hangings were of dingy, drab moreen, loaded with dust, the dressing-glass was cracked, and everything looked slovenly, close, and unwholesome.

"There is another room at the top of the house, miss, with two beds; one, I suppose, for you—for the lady said her youngest daughter would sleep there—and the other for the maid that I am to get for you. You will like, perhaps, to have some of the things carried up there, out of the way?"

Grace acquiesced.

The top of the house seemed to promise, at least, more air and better light than the first floor.

She followed the dirty-looking servant girl, who was called from her occupations in the kitchen to carry the lady's things up stairs.

The first view of the attic, however, convinced her that her expectations had overrated its attractions.

It might once, indeed, have been light and airy, but economy had closed up two of the windows, and the third was scarcely large enough to show the dismal obscurity of the room.

Two mean-looking beds, with a scanty piece of white, or what had once been white, calico, as an apology for drapery, a rickety deal table, and two equally rickety chairs, completed the paraphernalia of the room which Grace was to consider hers.

"Did my mother see this room before she took the lodgings?" she inquired of the girl, who stood staring at her after depositing the trunks and band-boxes which she had assisted her to bring up.

"No, miss; the old lady was too lame to come up stairs; and, besides, the beds wasn't made, for master's 'prentices slept here, and deuced mad they'll be when they come to know they're turned out of their beds, and must pig in the workshop."

"Is there no other room I can have?" said Grace, whose horror at the appearance of this miserable place was increased by finding she was to be the successor of the tailor's apprentices in their wretched bed.

"Lawk! no, miss," said the girl; "all the rest of the house is let, except the back parlour, where master and missus sleep, and the back kitchen, where we cooks for the lodgers, and where I sleeps."

"Good heavens!"

Grace had never formed an idea that it was possible for human beings to exist thus cooped up, and to eat and drink, and cook and sleep all in one kitchen.

Poor Grace!

What would she have given at this moment, to have been an inhabitant of the meanest cottage in Llan——!

There they all had light and fresh air, and room to be cleanly.

"The old lady said there was no occasion to be very particler about your room, miss," said the girl, seeing that Grace still stood with dissatisfaction strongly painted on her countenance; "but if there's anything you want, such as a washing-stand, or a bit of carpet, to make you

comfortable, why, I'll try if I can't get it for you of missus, or out of one of the t'other lodger's rooms. There's one as isn't werry good pay, for missus ain't seen the colour of his money these three weeks, so she won't be werry particler what she takes out of his room. And, now I think of it, there's a fender there will make this fireplace look quite comfortable, with a bit of a chimbley-board that missus 'll get Sam to knock up, when he's done work in the shop; for he's the only one out of our six boys—great hulking fellows, as missus calls 'em—that knows how to handle a hammer, or drive in a nail."

"Not for me, I beg," said Grace, recalled from her melancholy thoughts by the maid's preparing to leave her, to commit the proposed spoliation on the lodger's room who was so unfortunate as not to have paid his lodgings.

"I do not wish to have anybody put to inconvenience for me; this place will do very well as it is—at least, I will try to be contented with it."

"Laws, bless you, miss! there was a very nice lady and her little girl—a real lady they said she was in her own country—a Spanish woman she was, and had had houses, and lands, and servants at her beck and call, and yet she was glad to put up with this room nigh upon two years, and there was less furniture, too, in it than there is now; for missus, finding she was very unsartain pay, took out the best of the things after she'd been here six or seven months. Indeed, she wouldn't have let her stay at all, only that she taught our Miss Matilda, missus' daughter, French, and dancing, and music, and needlework, and so saved the expense of schooling. But, poor thing, my heart often ached for her, after she took bad in the winter, and sometimes could hardly crawl out of bed to light her bit of fire and get the child victuals; and often and often I used to run up on the sly, when I'd a minute to spare, and do any little odd job for her; but, laws, I've got sich a hard place—six single men, besides the first floor lodgers, and missus is sich a dragon (in a low whisper), that, between you and I, I couldn't do half what I would have done for the poor thing. She used to promise me sometimes, that if she lived to go back to her own conntry she would take me with her, and I should never work again. But there was no such luck for Becky, for she went to the country where people never come back, poor cretur."

"Died?" said Grace, raising her tearful eyes to the good-natured, begrimed face of the loquacious Becky.

"Yes, miss, in that werry bed there," pointing to the meanest looking one of the two.

"And the poor child?" demanded Grace.

"Oh, God Almighty was pleased to take that first," returned the girl, "and so saved it from going to the workhouse—for it must have gone if she'd have died first, and I should have fretted my life out to see it, for I was a parish orphan myself once, till they put me 'prentice to missus, and I knows what it is not to have a friend in the world to look arter you."

Grace slid the shilling with which she had intended to reward Becky's civility and eviden_t

wish to oblige back again into her purse, and substituted half-a-crown.

"I'd rather, miss, if you please, that you'd keep it," said Becky, retreating; if you likes to give me a cap, or an apern, or anything of that sort, I shall thank you kindly; but missus takes all my *wails*—she says she lays 'em out in clothes for me, but I've a hard matter to get a pair of shoes out of her once in half a year, let alone other things, which I never have, only what the lodgers is kind enough to give me. Oh, Gemini! if there isn't missus raving like a mad woman. I suppose she thought I'd gone down before, and has just missed me. How I shall catch it," and Becky, without waiting for farther observation from Grace, clattered down stairs, leaving the latter standing alone in the middle of her desolate-looking room.

It was not of herself, however, that Grace thought, as she seated herself on one of the chairs, her eyes still dwelling on the shabby bedstead, the paltry patchwork counterpane, and the dingy-looking blankets to which Becky had pointed. It was of the delicately-reared, perhaps, nobly-born female, who, amid strangers even to her language, and still more strangers to her feelings, had there watched over the deathbed of her child, the last remaining link between her and perhaps the husband of her love, the all that was left her to hope for and to cherish; and then, when that last blossom was blighted, laying herself down and patiently waiting God's own time, when she would be permitted to follow it. And she was young, too, and beautiful, and accomplished. How must she have shrunk with disgust from the people whose paltry spirits could induce them to insult her, even by depriving her of the wretched comforts such a place afforded. How in the long dreary winters she passed here, deprived of every comfort, must she have looked back with sickness of heart, and longing for her own warm genial climate, its bright cloudless days and splendid moonlight nights, while all around her now was cold, and gloom, and darkness.

"And shall I then murmur at being obliged to make this my resting-place," thought Grace. "No, let me learn patience and humility from her example, who had much less right than me to expect such a lot."

In a few hours Mrs. Woodford and her daughters were established in their new lodgings, and Maria, though she felt somewhat disappointed at their obscurity and comparative meanness to what she had expected, was compelled to acknowledge that it would not have been prudent for her mother to have gone to a higher price than she had done for apartments. A guinea a week, indeed, appeared an extravagant sum for such accommodations; but their morning's promenade had convinced them they were lucky in getting them even at that price, the place being so full of company that it was scarcely possible to get rooms at any price.

——

CHAPTER XXVI.

DOUBTS AND FEARS.

For the first two or three days of their residence in Bath, Mrs. Woodford and Maria were delighted with all they beheld; the weather was beautiful, the streets were thronged with fashionables, and not unobserved or undervalued by either mother or daughter was the notice and admiration which the latter excited. Even Mrs. Woodford's infirmities were less felt, and less painful than ever, for she beheld many among the rich, the great, and apparently even the gay, who might have been glad to exchange situations even with her; but the novelty faded, the admiration went no farther than looks, or at most, an audible whisper, which always terminated with, "Who are they?"

And both mother and daughter began to feel it tiresome to be thus perpetually in a crowd, without recognising a single face that they could claim the most distant acquaintance with, or who even seemed to take the slightest interest in them, except honouring them with a stare, and not unfrequently with a smile of derision, at the singular discrepancy which Mrs. Woodford's habiliments and person exhibited.

Maria's natural good taste and personal beauty, rendered her appearance, though considerably far behind the reigning fashions, sufficiently becoming not to create ridicule; but it was not so with her mother, who was never satisfied unless she was loaded with finery, and whose *petite* and deformed person was thus rendered ten times more conspicuous, as she slowly paraded the promenades, or tottered to a seat amidst the smiles of most, and the pitying looks of others.

"We want somebody to introduce us properly, my dear," she observed, when, after a week's dull round, they found themselves still in the same situation—still isolated amidst a crowd, who were now become too familiarised with their appearance to bestow even a look of curiosity on the odd-looking little woman and the beautiful girl who had at first excited so much.

It was true that Maria seldom met a glance from the gentlemen which did not express admiration; but it went no further than glances, for her demeanour was too modest to encourage levity, and even had that not been sufficient to repel assurance, she had always her mother at her side.

And where all this time, was their stage-coach acquaintance?

He had called, as was before mentioned, on the day following their arrival at the hotel, had chatted away nearly two hours with Grace, who had found him, as she told her sister, a very pleasant, kind-hearted man, and had heard with very sincere satisfaction that he meant, with Mrs. Woodford's permission, to be a frequent visitor during his stay in Bath.

He had announced himself, too, as Captain Frederick, a distant relative of Lord Melverley, and had, with apparent sincerity and candour, assured Grace that he should be most happy to render them any services which, as strangers, they might require.

But more than all this, he had spoken in such terms of her sister that Grace, in the innocence of her heart, believed him actuated by the best and purest principles.

Maria's beauty, he observed, in such a place as Bath, could not fail to attract a number of admirers; but he hoped and trusted Mrs. Woodford would be extremely cautious in forming acquaintances, since, perhaps, in no place in the whole world were there collected so many reckless, heartless profligates,—men, indeed, of rank and fashion, but totally destitute of feeling and principle, and who would laugh at and triumph in the destruction and degradation of beauty and innocence.

"He talked to me," said the artless Grace, in repeating their conversation to her mother and sister, "just as a kind brother or long-tried friend would; and I am sure I felt as much at my ease with him as if I had known him for years instead of only the day before yesterday."

In spite, however, of all these promises and professions, Captain Frederick, for one whole, long, tedious week, never visited them in their new lodgings.

Several times indeed, Maria, in her promenades with her mother, had caught a distant view of him, but it was always in company with two ladies and a gentleman, and he had always appeared to be in such earnest conversation, that he could not see his stage-coach acquaintance.

Once, indeed, they had met face to face in one of the libraries to which they had subscribed, having learned from their landlady, that it was fashionable to do so, and Mrs. Woodford still retaining her old predilection for novel reading; and then, Captain Frederick, finding it impossible to shun them, had vouchsafed to bestow a distant bow, and a mere familiar smile on them; but this had rather mortified than pleased either Maria or her mother, the ladies whom he accompanied were remarkably plainly dressed, and extremely unassuming in their manners; the gentleman was absolutely a shabby-looking, old-fashioned fright, to use Maria's own terms in describing the party, and why he should think it necessary to look strange, and take airs in such company, they (Maria and her mother) could not possibly imagine.

"I am sure?" observed Maria, "he need not have been ashamed to own us, for all the ladies had on, was not worth as much as my Leghorn bonnet. By the bye, mamma, did you see how the young lady turned away from the young man behind the counter, when he wanted her to look at the beautiful ear-rings that we are to raffle for, to-morrow. I suppose she wanted to pretend to be above such things—but I rather suspect, the truth is, they are above her."

"I am sure her gingham gown never cost above a shilling a yard," replied Mrs. Woodford; "and as to that great straw bonnet that hides her face, so that I declare I hardly know now,

whether she was a black or a white, it would be dear at seven shillings."

"And yet, mamma," said Grace, who had, on this occasion, for the first time been of their party; "from the manner of the shopman, as well as that of several persons who I saw bowed to her, I cannot help thinking that she is a lady of some consequence; and as to her face, I caught a full view of it, when she turned suddenly round to give some money to that poor woman, who stood at the door with a poor sick child in her arms, and I thought I never saw such a sweet beautiful countenance in my life."

"Oh! you are a judge of beauty, I dare say," retorted Mrs. Woodford, contemptuously; "and by the bye, Miss Grace, it was very impertinent of you to step back and give that beggar woman something, but I suppose you thought it pretty to imitate your lady of consequence."

Grace did not reply, as she might with truth have done, that so far from imitating, she had been the first to notice the poor woman, and unostentatiously, and as she imagined unobserved, had stolen back to slip a sixpence into her hand, with a gentle half-murmured wish that she had in her power ——

"God in heaven prosper you, young lady, and grant you may never know the want of it," had been the exclamation of the woman on receiving it, and the tone in which this benediction was uttered, whether true or false, had roused, it appeared, the feelings of the young lady, who had been the subject of Mrs. Woodford's disquisition, and she had, after glancing on Grace's blushing face a look of kindness and sympathy, turned back and added something to her gift, which had sent the poor woman away, evidently astonished and overwhelmed with pleasurable surprise.

More than once, in the course of the two or three following days, some ill-natured remark on the part of Mrs. Woodford, or expression of mortification on that of Maria, recalled to Grace what she would otherwise, probably, have forgotten, the meeting with Captain Frederick and his friends; and she was compelled to own that she had been hasty in forming so strong a predilection in his favour, for that, certainly, his conduct did not at all correspond with his very warm asseverations of friendship and respect for Mrs. Woodford and her family.

"It is not that I value him a bit," said Mrs. Woodford one evening, after having, as usual, made his extraordinary neglect of them the subject of a thousand animadversions; "for after all, what is he? some poor relation, no doubt, of the Melverley family, and as to his captaincy, we all know captain is a fine travelling title, and it's ten to one if he's more than an ensign or lieutenant, at most; but even if he's captain, he would be no catch, for they can none of them manage to live on their pay, and can have very little to spare for a wife."

"And yet mamma, Captain Barnet's lady, that was down at Llan—— all last summer, made a great dash," observed Maria; "and wore very expensive dresses, you know."

"Yes, but she had a private fortune, child, or

she could not have done it. No, no, depend upon it, no woman could live on her husband's pay as an officer; and so, if Captain Frederick, as he calls himself, has nothing more, he's quite in the right of it, not to think of marrying."

"And yet," thought Grace, "I would wager my life he does think of marrying, and has chosen his wife, too, and that sweet, beautiful, young lady that hung so familiarly on his arm is destined to bear that title, or I am much mistaken."

Aware that such an observation would only draw from her mother some ill-natured remark, Grace, however firmly convinced in her mind of the fact, suppressed her thoughts, and she felt doubly glad she had done so, when, some days after, Captain Frederick, having first sent up his name, followed the maid-servant into the room, before Mrs. Woodford had time to say whether she chose to be visible to him or not.

A whole torrent of surprises, reproaches, insinuations, and affected resentment, on the part of Maria and Mrs. Woodford, was listened to with patience and pretended sorrow on the part of the gentleman; but Grace, who was perfectly silent, though she had replied to his greeting with as much freedom and kindness as ever, read in his countenance that he was far better pleased with this reception than he would have been with a more quiet and indifferent one.

"I plead guilty," he at length observed with a smile, "to the charge of having designedly avoided you, but my motives were anything but disrespectful to you; the fact is, my dear madam," addressing Mrs. Woodford, "the two ladies you have seen with me are my aunt and cousin, the gentleman I have the honour to call my uncle, and three more tiresome, determined bores never existed. My aunt is a bigotted methodist, and she has made as great a fool of her pretty little daughter as herself. Their whole and sole aim here is to make converts, and had I yielded to my own inclinations, and made you acquainted with each other, the consequence would have been that you would have been bored to death, as I have been, with their fanatic nonsense; but thank goodness I am at last rid of them: they have gone off to Devonshire to-day, and the moment I was free I have hastened to you."

Maria did not seek to dive very deep into the truth of this account of Captain Frederick's motives, his present avowed devotion soon effaced all past mortifications.

"He was henceforth wholly devoted to their service," he said, and, as a proof of it, he had brought tickets of admission for the theatre for that very night, and requested to be allowed to escort them there.

Mrs. Woodford was in raptures.

At last her Maria was in a fair way to be introduced to the world, and as she accepted his offer she acknowledged that he had quite made the *amende honorable*, for what she had prematurely considered his unpardonable neglect.

To Maria it was an epoch which seemed to be of the utmost importance to her future life.

Alas! how little did she dream that, in reality, it would decide what the tenure of that life was to be? And some hours were spent in dressing for this momentous appearance, which, in both Maria and Mrs. Woodford's estimation, was not of less consequence than that of a first-rate beauty in the court circle. During all this arduous task, in which Grace, not without many secret sighs at the meanness and frivolity which even filial duty could not blind her to in her mother, had been actively and usefully employed. Not one word had been said as to her (Grace's) own appearance; and when, at length, she timidly inquired whether she should *now* go and change her frock, Mrs. Woodford's look of astonishment, whether real or affected, at once bespoke what her words speedily confirmed, viz., that she had never for a moment thought of Grace, and that it was now too late to commence the task of dressing.

"It wants but five minutes of the time Captain Frederick appointed," she observed; "and, of course, we cannot keep him waiting. But what in the world can you have been thinking of, Grace, to leave till this time — but, no matter; you can go another night; this will not, of course, be the only time we shall visit the theatre. And, besides, I don't at all like trusting Jane (the servant their landlady had recommended them) to sit up alone for us; she looks stupid and sleepy, and if she was to fall asleep she might set fire to herself and the place, so it will be better you should stay at home, and then you can finish altering Maria's pelisse, in case she should want to wear it to-morrow."

Grace, perhaps, had never felt more keenly than at that moment the immeasurable distance which existed in her mother's heart between herself and her sister.

She looked at the latter, for the thousandth time surveying herself in the mirror, smiling in anticipation of approaching pleasure, and triumphing in the consciousness of being enabled at last to display, to the utmost advantage, that beauty which she had been taught to consider so inestimable.

But Maria was too much absorbed to bestow even a thought on her (Grace's) disappointment; and when, at length, she did turn from the glass, and caught a glimpse of Grace's mournful features, conceiving only that it arose from the disappointment the latter felt at not being of the party, she exclaimed—

"My dear Grace, how sorry I am; and this is the first time, too, that ever I saw you anxious about pleasure."

"I am not anxious now, Maria," returned Grace, in a grave tone; "a few minutes ago, indeed, I acknowledge I anticipated an evening's agreeable entertainment, but now—"

She cast down her eyes, and her voice faltered.

"Now, miss!" repeated Mrs. Woodford, sharply; "and pray what has happened now to make you think otherwise?"

"Nothing has happened, mamma," replied Grace with emotion; "but my feelings are changed, and I would not now go if it were in my power."

"I understand all this perfectly well, Grace,"

observed Mrs. Woodford, after surveying her for some moments in silence; "it all arises from a mean jealousy of your sister; this is not the first time I have seen it. But let me advise you not to give way to it, for it can only serve to make you miserable.'

Without waiting for a reply she turned to Maria, and again commenced her survey of her, turning her round and round, to see that every plait of her dress was properly disposed, and nothing omitted which could heighten her beauty, and totally regardless of the feelings which swelled Grace's bosom almost to suffocation at this undeserved and cruel reproof.

Grace jealous of Maria's beauty!—she who had patiently employed three long hours in assisting her to set off that beauty to the greatest advantage—who had arranged and re-arranged her ringlets and her flowers, clasped her necklaces and bracelets, and brought forth her own little stock of ornaments for Maria to try whether there was any of them she would like better than her own, and had, without a murmur, submitted when the capricious beauty, after being once completely dressed, and, as even Mrs. Woodford allowed, never to greater advantage, had suddenly torn off the coronet of flowers, pulled the combs out of her hair, and, shaking loose all the ringlets and bandeaux which, in compliance with her taste, Grace had formed, declared it was frightful altogether, and she would have it all done over again.

Even the partial mother had loudly exclaimed against her caprice, and declared it was a shameful waste of time and trouble.

Yet Grace had not only borne all with a smile, but had instantly commenced again combing, brushing, and forming round her pliant fingers the long glossy ringlets which had been thus deranged, without a single word of reproof, but, on the contrary, agreeing with her sister that, although she looked well, still it was not exactly the most becoming style to her features.

"She would look well anyhow," said the doating mother, gazing with a look of approval on her daughter's beautiful face.

"Yes," replied Grace; "and, in my opinion, never so well as totally unadorned. Look, mamma, now at her; if it was but the fashion to wear the hair loose, hanging over the shoulder in such curls as these, would not she look better than ever?"

And she was accused of mean jealousy!

Grace turned one look upon her sister, but Maria was again absorbed in the alteration of her sash, which she had now decided looked most graceful fastened at the side.

"Do, Grace, just tie it for me; nobody can tie a bow so well as you."

Grace laid down the work which she had taken up to hide the emotion which her mother's observation had created, and, without uttering a single word, obeyed her sister's request.

At that moment Captain Frederick was announced as awaiting them in the drawing-room.

"You need not come down, Grace," observed Mrs. Woodford, hastily; "I will make a proper apology to him for your not going, though I don't suppose that will be any great disappointment to him, unless, indeed, he is inclined to be a second Sir Walter, and fancy you into a beauty."

There was only wanting this to complete Grace's discomforture; but again she bent over her work, and resolutely avoided a single expression of those rebellious feelings which she felt it totally impossible to suppress.

"God bless you! Grace," said Maria, tripping good-humouredly back into the room, and affectionately kissing her cheek. "I wish you were going with us; but, never mind, do not be low-spirited, it is only for one evening your pleasure is delayed. Good gracious! is it possible that you take it so seriously to heart, Grace?" she continued, as she beheld the tears, which Grace could no longer prevent flowing down her cheeks; "I am sure I would rather stay at home altogether, than that you should fret so about it."

"And is it possible, Maria, that you, too, so grossly mistake me as to suppose that I envy you the pleasure you are going to enjoy? or that it would at all reconcile me to the loss of it, that you should be deprived of it, too? No, no; you ought to know me better, though my mother is determined to believe me so base and little-minded;" and again she wept, as she recurred to her mother's cruel observation.

"She does not believe you any such thing, Grace. How can you be so foolish as to fret at anything mamma says? You know it is only a bad habit she has got into of saying sarcastic things at everybody's expense."

"Except yours, Maria," said Grace emphatically. "But, do not again mistake my meaning; I do not envy you that you are beloved by your mother, but I do lament that I have no portion of that love. But, do not let me detain you, dear Maria; this is no new theme of sorrow to me, and, unfortunately, there will be opportunities enough for me to speak of it, if, indeed, it would not be wiser and better to bury it in oblivion."

"I shall talk to mamma about her injustice," said Maria thoughtfully, as if it had but just occurred to herself that Grace had a right to complain of the preference shown; and, repeating her affectionate good-bye, she hastened to join her mother and her companion, and, in a few moments, Grace heard the coach which had been sent for drive from the door.

Never, perhaps, in her life, had Grace passed so dull and utterly comfortless an evening as this; the noise of rain beating heavily against the windows was only interrupted by the click of pattens on the pavement, and occasionally the heavy lumbering of a coach or cart, of which few passed down the narrow, unfrequented street they inhabited. It was cold and chilly, too; but she could not have a fire, for her mother would have, perhaps, considered it a useless luxury. The task of completing Maria's pelisse, which Mrs. Woodford had so unfeelingly extorted, prevented her for a moment beguiling her melancholy thoughts with a book, though a novel of Miss Edgeworth's, which Captain Frederick had recommended, was temptingly placed on the table before her; but Grace soon forgot the novel, though she had glanced through the two or three first pages, and found in them a strong incentive to go on; and mechanically she continued, for hours, to ply her needle, for her thoughts were busy with past scenes, and the present were forgotten.

"What soothing recollections throng,
    Presenting many a mournful token,
That heart's remembrance to prolong,
    Which then was blest, but now is broken!"

The coach stopping at the door, gay voices speaking, and light footsteps ascending the stairs, aroused her from her dream, and before she could gather up her work, or light the second candle, which, in obedience to her mother's instructions, stood ready to be kindled on the table, Maria, her face radiant with pleasure, and accompanied, not by Captain Frederick, but his friend, equally handsome, fashionable, and captivating, entered the room.

"Here is my sister, Mr. Grant," said the former, as the stranger drew back and respectfully made room for Grace to pass with her bundle of work into the next room.

"Do not run away, Grace," she continued; "mamma is coming up, and Captain Frederick, but she is rather slow. Do pray be seated," and she pointed to a chair to the gentleman she called Mr. Grant, who was still standing gazing at Grace, whose usually pale cheek was now lighted up with a deep glow at being thus surprised in a confusion and litter, as her mother would have called it, and which would not have failed, she knew, to have called forth the severest reprehension from the latter.

"I cannot consent to sit down, if I am to be the means of disturbing your sister," said the stranger, still keeping his eyes fixed on Grace, who, having hastily thrown her work into the adjoining room, ran back to gather up her thread, silk, &c., from the table.

"Oh, no; Grace will sit down with us directly," returned Maria; "Only mamma is a little particular, and she is afraid of being scolded for littering the drawing-room."

Mr. Grant threw a look round the room as he repeated—

"Scolded! Heaven forbid that any one should think of scolding such a gentle, timid being."

But Grace, though she saw the look, and felt her cheeks burn still more painfully at the derision it conveyed of the elegant apartment which was thus pompously designated, did not hear the accompanying words; for she had—somewhat alarmed at her mother's remaining so long in the cold passage below—ran down to meet her.

Mrs. Woodford, however, was ascending the stairs, leaning on Jane, the new servant, and pausing at every step to give her some directions, from which Grace learned that the two gentlemen intended staying to sup with them.

"Grace, do you go down to the kitchen, and see that everything is sent up properly," she observed, the moment she beheld her anxious daughter.

"There's nothing ma'am, but the bone of the leg of mutton left," said Jane earnestly, "down stairs, and the pie you have locked up in your cupboard."

"You need not mind about supper, Grace," said Mrs. Woodford, without noticing her servant's pert observation; "only see that a clean table-cloth, and knives and forks, and everything proper is put in the tray; the rest will be brought presently.

A loud knock at the door now announced the arrival of Captain Frederick, and while Jane, at her mistress' desire ran down to let him in, the latter whispered to Grace.

"Our fortunes are made, Grace; Captain Frederick is desperately in love with your sister, and his cousin, Mr. Grant, who we met with again to-night—"

Captain Frederick ran hastily up the stairs, and prevented the conclusion of her communication, which, far from producing, as she seemed to expect, a corresponding pleasure to that which danced in her own eyes, had only the effect of rendering Grace more confused, uneasy, and embarrassed.

"Surely, surely these men will penetrate my mother's intentions, and we shall all become the subjects of their ridicule," she thought to herself, as she proceeded to the kitchen, to superintend the sleepy and more than half-reluctant Jane, who by no means relished the additional work of waiting upon the supper-table, after having, as she grumbled more than once, "been slaving like a horse at the wash-tub all day."

"Missus told me she kept very little company," she observed, "when she hired me; but this don't look much like it, bringing home gentlemen to supper at this time o' night, to keep poor servants out of their beds; and how it looks, Miss Grace, to see Missus and Miss Maria stuck up, all over flowers, and lace, and ribbon, and you with nothing but that plain muslin frock. I never see such a difference made between children in my life, and I wonder how you can bear it. I wonder what the gentlemen can think."

"I care nothing what any one thinks, Jane," replied Grace. "I am perfectly contented—"

"Oh, no, miss, don't say that, for as I was saying to the young man that lodges in the front attic—"

"I hope you do not make me the subject of your conversation, Jane, with the young man in the front attic," interrupted Grace, hastily; "but come, carry the tray up, and lay the cloth, and I will remain here, and attend to the door, if the person comes with the supper, whatever it is."

Grace, however, was not a little surprised and confounded, when, a few minutes after, in obedience to her promise, she answered the summons at the street door, and beheld no less than three persons loaded with every delicacy that could be procured at so short a notice, and learned that there was yet another to come, with wine.

All suspense, however, was soon at an end.

"Mercy! Captain Frederick," exclaimed Mrs. Woodford, approaching the supper-table, having during its preparation, affected to be totally indifferent to it, and wholly occupied in conversation with her visitors. "Mercy, what an extravagant man you are; who would ever have thought of your ordering such a supper. I thought, to be sure, you were only going to send in a lobster, or something of that sort, to make up with my cold leg of mutton, or I should have put a stop to it, I assure you. Why, here's a supper fit for a prince."

"A prince might think himself honoured to partake of it in such society," returned Captain Frederick, looking at Maria significantly.

"Well, I am sure, you are polite," returned Mrs. Woodford, whose spirits seemed exhilirated beyond all prudence; "but I really don't know how I shall ever make you amends for putting you to so much trouble. Maria, dear, you take this seat, and Captain Frederick will sit next you; Mr. Grant, will you honour me by taking this chair at my left hand."

Mr. Grant's eyes had, until this moment, been fixed on Grace's deeply glowing and expressive countenance; he had marked the deep flush of vexation and the start of surprise, which she could not control, at hearing her worst fears thus confirmed, and he seemed totally absorbed in endeavouring to penetrate the meaning of this emotion.

The mention of his name, by Mrs. Woodford, recalled his recollection to what was passing, and he was about to seat himself in the chair she pointed to, when he saw that Grace was still standing, looking irresolutely at her mother, as if doubtful whether she was expected to sit down, or whether she was at liberty to withdraw.

"Miss Woodford, I beg your pardon," he observed, eagerly; "you are not seated, pray ——"

"Oh, Grace will sit any where, Mr. Grant," said Mrs. Woodford, hastily; "pray do not give yourself any trouble about her; sit down where you are, child, and then you can make yourself useful, without incommoding any one."

"Do you understand Italian, madam?" inquired Mr. Grant, turning the conversation.

"Very little," she replied, with an affected toss of her head; "but my music master was an Italian, and after hearing him, I could never bear English songs."

Grace's eyes were fixed more firmly than ever on the table-cloth; she felt, though she could not see, that their guests were laughing at her mother, and she felt, too, most acutely that her mother deserved to be laughed at.

Hour after hour passed away, and the gentlemen's hilarity became still more unbridled, though even Mrs. Woodford had been at last so far awakened to the imprudence she had been guilty of as gradually to sink from the most unbounded familiarity and ease to comparative reserve and silence.

The sun had long risen before the visitors could, as they said, resolve to tear themselves away, and Grace, miserable, dejected, anticipating evil to which she could give neither shape nor make, retired to her gloomy chamber, without remaining to hear the remarks which Maria

eagerly commenced on their evening's amusement and companions.

* * * * *

"What is the matter?" exclaimed Captain Frederick, walking into the apartment of the Woodford's, and looking from one to the other.

The same look of gloom and constraint was on the countenances of all.

"What can have possibly happened to occasion this change, my good friends?"

"Nothing very particular," returned Mrs. Woodford, assuming a tone of indifference; "only the girls are fretting, because I have made up my mind to leave Bath at the end of the week."

"Leave Bath!" re-echoed Captain Frederick, in astonishment. "Surely you cannot be serious, dear madam?"

"Perfectly serious, sir, I assure you," she replied. "Why should I not? I came here only on account of my health, and as I do not find it at all bettered, the sooner I try some other place the more likely it is to be of advantage."

"And whither then do you propose to go?" inquired the Captain, after a few moment's thoughtful silence, during which his eyes had glanced from one to another, as if desirous of finding there an explanation of the mystery of this sudden resolve.

"I have not yet resolved where I shall go," said Mrs. Woodford; "perhaps," she added, with a consequential air, "I shall travel for some time before I again settle; I don't know that I mayn't take it in my head to go abroad, it would perhaps be the best thing I could do for the girls, to give them a polish."

Grace felt her cheek colour, and she caught a hasty glance at their visitor, who, while he tried to assume a look of sorrow and dismay, evidently struggled to conceal a smile at her (Mrs. Woodford's) mock-importance.

"This is unexpected, indeed," he at length observed, "and it is the more singular as I came to announce, that I have this morning received a letter, which obliges me to go to London, and thus put off for two or three weeks, an event, which I had joyfully anticipated would take place much sooner," and he looked at Maria with tender significance.

Mrs. Woodford's countenance underwent an instantaneous change, its previous gloom and dissatisfaction disappeared, and she darted at Grace a look of triumph, which did not escape her wily visitor.

"Well, that is curious," she exclaimed, "that we should both be going to leave at the same time; but you, I suppose, will soon return, Captain Frederick?"

"Not if you quit the place, certainly, my dear madam," he replied; "Bath will have lost every attraction to me, when it loses you."

"You are very polite, sir," said Mrs. Woodford, who evidently anxiously expected a farther and more direct elucidation of the Captain's views and intentions.

"Polite, my dear Mrs. Woodford," he repeated, in a tone of regret; "what can induce you to use such a cold formal word to me, after suffering me to hope that you regarded me with such different feelings? I had hoped, indeed," he continued, after a few moments' pause, during which Mrs. Woodford seemed studying how best to draw from him that explicit avowal she so longed to hear. "I had hoped that all unnecessary ceremony and reserve were banished from our intercourse, but I see something has happened to prejudice me in your opinion. I have some secret enemy—some one who takes advantage of my being compelled, by family circumstances, to postpone for a short time the avowal of my dearest wishes and intentions, to misrepresent and calumniate me. Yes, yes, I see it all," he continued, with warmth; "and I am so wretchedly tied down and hampered at the present moment by family arrangements, that I cannot at once, as I would do, dispel all misconstructions and suspicions, by at once explaining candidly my wishes; but you, Maria," he continued, affectionately taking her hand, "you, I trust, not doubt me; you can confide in my honour."

"Yes," returned Maria, her beautiful face lighted up with a smile of perfect confidence and exultation; "I do, and will confide in you, Frederick; I have never doubted you, myself, though I have been made miserable and wretched by the suspicions of those who are always thinking themselves wiser and more prudent than me."

The look which she significantly directed to Grace at the conclusion of this speech, could leave no doubt on the mind of her lover, as to whom it was that he was indebted for the catechising he had undergone, and Grace timidly shrunk from the sarcastic expression with which he fixed his eyes upon her, as he observed, he hoped the time was not far distant when he should have to congratulate himself on being allied to one so eminently distinguished for prudence.

It was impossible to mistake the sneering tone in which the last word was pronounced, and Grace, roused by the implication it conveyed, summoned all her courage, and looking him stedfastly in the face, observed—

"I have heard nothing this morning, Captain Frederick, that could change my opinion as to the prudence you sneer at."

"Grace, hold your tongue, instantly, interrupted Mrs. Woodford, with extreme anger. "How dare you take such impertinent airs? Upon my word, Captain Frederick," she continued, "I am quite ashamed of this bold girl; but the fact is that I never had anything to do with her bringing up; she was her father's pet, and she is just like him, rude and abrupt, and so opinionated, always fancying himself in the right, and I in the wrong, although, poor man, he knew so little—"

Grace could bear it no longer, she cared nothing for her mother's harsh and undeserved reproof of herself, but she could not stay to hear the memory of the best of parents profaned by her mother's unjust and unfeeling remarks, and, without uttering another word, she flew from the room.

When Grace was summoned to dinner Maria was in a high state of excitement.

"Which dress do you think I look best in, Grace, the peach-coloured crape, or my green gros-de-naples?"

"I like you in the green best," said Grace, in a tone which betrayed that she had paid little attention to the subject in dispute.

"And yet I look so very pale to-day," continued Maria, rising and looking at herself in the glass; "and green makes me always look paler. I think I had better wear the crape."

"Where are you going then?" demanded Grace, for the first time comprehending that some engagement, to which she was not a party, had been made during her absence.

"I am going to a concert with Captain Frederick," replied Maria, in a tone of joyous exultation.

"Yes, and your sister is to be introduced there to some ladies, near relations of his," added Mrs. Woodford in the same tone; "and so now, I hope, all your wise suspicions and observations will be at rest, Madam Prudence."

"I shall be most happy to have them set at rest," returned Grace, sighing. "But you are going too, mamma, are you not?" she added timidly, but with evident earnestness.

"No, I am not going, indeed, Grace," replied Mrs. Woodford in a composed tone; "it is a private concert," she added, after a moment's pause, "and Captain Frederick cannot procure a ticket for more than one lady and himself."

Grace was answered; it was impossible for her to suggest a doubt that all was not exactly as Mrs. Woodford was determined to believe it; yet she listened with an incredulity she could not conquer to all the remarks, and suggestions, and anticipations to which her mother and sister gave utterance respecting the valuable female acquaintance that this evening was to introduce them to.

The green, the peach-coloured, every dress and every ornament she possessed, were successively tried on before Maria could make up her mind as to what she should wear to appear to most advantage, and do honour to Captain Frederick's choice, for, as his affianced bride, she felt convinced she would be introduced on that important evening, and her toilet was scarcely concluded before her attentive conductor arrived.

Contrary to his usual custom on such important occasions, not a word of compliment escaped his lips, as he hurriedly glanced over her dress.

"We shall be late, my dear," he observed, hastily throwing her shawl over her shoulders, and then uttering a hurried "good bye," he led her, without another word, to the coach which was waiting for them.

"They are a beautiful couple," said Mrs. Woodford, with exultation, retiring from the windows from which she had watched them get into the coach; "and, handsome and elegant as he is, Frederick will have no reason to be ashamed of his partner to-night, even though the first people in Bath will be there, he says."

Grace made no reply.

A vague sensation of fear and uneasiness had

taken possession of her mind. She longed for the evening to be over, for Maria to come back, and to hear whether her reception had answered her expectations.

But the very anxiety she felt served but to make the time seem longer and more tiresome.

Mrs. Woodford was little inclined to talk: her mind was, indeed, fully occupied by the imagined certainty, now, of her hopes being all realised. Captain Frederick had, indeed, insinuated that there were obstacles which prevented his fully avowing himself; but, at the same time, he had greeted her ears with the welcome information, that his private fortune was quite sufficient to enable him to provide handsomely for his intended bride, even should his family object, and that he was determined that no consideration on earth should part him from his beloved, adored Maria.

"He is going to London to-morrow on purpose to try to get his father's consent," she observed, when, at length, Grace ventured to ask whether Captain Frederick had relinquished his intention of leaving Bath. "From what I can learn, there's a lady of title and great fortune in the way, that his friends have long wished him to marry, so he's obliged to act cautiously ; but one thing is certain, that before the end of another month your sister will be his wife, whether his family like it or not."

"It will be very unpleasant, though, for Maria to be upon such terms with her husband's family," said Grace, who tried to persuade herself that she had really been wrong in suspecting Captain Frederick of dishonourable intentions, and that all was really as he had made her mother believe.

"Oh, they will soon come to, no doubt, when they find it can't be helped," returned the sanguine mother.

One o'clock, two, three, passed ; and then, Grace, no longer able to endure the uneasiness she felt, ventured to awake her mother.

"Maria is not come home yet, mamma," she observed.

"Well, and is that your only reason for waking me out of the soundest sleep and the pleasantest dream I have had many a night?" returned her mother peevishly.

"It is past three," said Grace, by way of excuse.

"Three! bless me, how the time flies! But, they will not be long, now, I dare say ; and Mrs. Woodford, after two or three yawns, again composed herself to sleep.

Grace was now again left to her own painful reflections ; another hour dragged slowly and tediously away, and then a coach was heard rattling swiftly over the stones.

"Thank God!" exclaimed Grace, who had been watching through the window, though it was still too dark for her accurately to distinguish objects.

Mrs. Woodford awoke with the exclamation,

"Are they come?" she inquired, beginning to adjust her cap, which had half fallen off.

"Yes," said Grace, in a half doubtful tone: for it now struck her that the coach was coming in a different direction from that which they had gone.

Mrs. Woodford was now quite roused, and she looked surprised at the agitation which Grace's countenance and attitude betrayed as she stood in the middle of the room, listening to the sound of the carriage, which she was too soon convinced had passed the house, and stopped some doors off.

"What is the matter with the girl? what have you taken in your head, Grace?" demanded the former; "there can be no fear of any accident, for they had not above three times the length of this street to come home," she continued ; "but, I shall give Frederick a scolding for keeping her out so late, though, as it's the last night for a week or so, it's hardly to be wondered at."

Grace did not reply; she dared not give utterance to the fear that had taken possession of her mind; and again she returned to her post at the window.

"This is very strange," observed Mrs. Woodford, after another interval of silence. "Grace, do you recollect where it was he said the concert was to be?"

"Oh, no, I never heard any place named," returned Grace; "if I did but know," she hastily added, "I would find my way there at all risks, and put an end to this suspense."

"What suspense? what is it you are afraid of?" demanded Mrs. Woodford, with an eagerness that spoke too plainly that she herself was far from being so completely at her ease as she had hitherto appeared.

"I know not what I fear," replied Grace; "and yet, oh, how I do wish she had never gone," she added, passionately clasping her hands.

"Heavens! why do you frighten me so, Grace?" ejaculated Mrs. Woodford, seeming at once to comprehend the fears that were floating in Grace's mind; "he cannot, surely he cannot —oh, no, he would not have been so wicked as to deceive me."

"I hope he has not; oh, how fervently do I pray that he has not," said Grace, tremulously; "hark, there is five striking, and it is getting quite light. Oh, if I did but know which way to go."

"What would be the use?" returned Mrs Woodford, petulantly, and evidently still struggling with her fears; "if she is coming back," she continued, after a moment's pause; your going after her could do no good, and if she is not —but I cannot, will not, think it; she cannot be such a wretch as to have deserted her mother."

Unwilling, however, as she was to believe the fatal truth, it soon became too palpable to be doubted, and Grace had soon to struggle with her own overwhelming grief, that she might endeavour to support her wretched mother, who was now in an agony of terror and self-reproach at her wilful blindness to the artful machinations of the man, whom she loaded with every epithet that rage and despair could suggest.

One hope, and only one, remained, and to that she still continued for some time to cling with pertinacity.

He had hinted that, in the case of his father's

refusal, he would instantly, but secretly, make Maria his wife, and the moment prudence would allow, openly avow his marriage.

It might be, that he had suddenly determined to put it out of the power of fate to disappoint him, by marrying her first; and still in despite of common sense, she indulged the fond idea, that he would speedily return and present her darling child to her as his bride.

The day, however, wore away nearly to the close, without the slightest intelligence of the fugitive; and totally unable to bear the tortures of fear and self-condemnation any longer, Mrs. Woodford, after a paroxysm of despair and rage, which Grace in vain tried to calm, was seized with strong convulsions, and continued for many hours in imminent danger of her life.

It was impossible to conceal from the house, the event which had occasioned her mother's illness; and Grace, while she felt grateful for their well-meant efforts to serve her, was, nevertheless, mortified and pained to excess at the freedom of their remarks and censures, both on her mother's folly and imprudence, and the irretrievable ruin and disgrace her sister had brought upon herself.

"I have never believed any good would come of it," observed the landlady, as she assisted Grace to undress the wretched mother, who exhausted by the violent sufferings she had undergone, had at last become totally unconscious of what was passing around her; "I said to my husband," continued the former, "the very first time I saw Captain Frederick, as he called himself, in the house, that he came on no good errand, no, nor his sly quiet friend either; but you had a little more prudence, miss, than your sister it seems, for Jane tells me you wouldn't have anything to say to him, and—"

"Oh, how I wish I could see Mr. Grant," interrupted Grace; "he might, perhaps, if he were to behold the misery his unprincipled companion has brought upon us, give some clue as to where he has conveyed her."

Mrs. Stevens shook her head.

"I'm afraid, miss, they are all birds of a feather, and will stick by one another hard and fast; however, if it will be any easement to your mind, my husband shall try and find him out, and see if he can learn any thing of him about this Captain Frederick, if that's his name, though to tell you the truth, I've my doubts of it."

Grace anxiously inquired her reason for this assertion.

"Why, then, I'll tell you, miss. No longer ago than yesterday there was a customer of my husband's, a gay young gentleman, and one that we've taken a deal of money of; and so he was waiting in the parlour for my husband to come in, and who should come flying up to the door, in his usual harum scarum kind of way, but this Captain Frederick. And so Sir George looked over the blind, and says he, ' What does Lord— Lord '—I can't, for the life of me, now think of the name; but, however, it was Lord something —'does he patronise Stevens?' 'No, Sir George,' says I, ' it's not Stevens that gentleman comes to see, but he's a visitor to my first floor lodgers. But he's not a lord; his name's Frederick, Captain Frederick. And so then he laughed, and he said, 'Indeed, may I ask who your first floor lodgers are?' and when I told him an old lady and her two daughters, he laughed again. And then he asked whether the girls, meaning you and your sister, were handsome, and a whole load more questions, till at last I was half affronted, for I thought he was reflecting upon the credit of my house; and so I told him that, in my opinion, the ladies were more respectable than their visitor, whether he was a captain or a lord; and I was quite sure so, if he was imposing upon them in a false character. And, so then he wanted to draw in his horns, and say that it was very likely he was mistaken; he could not boast of having any acquaintance with the gentleman, and daresay his name, after all, was Frederick.

"'Perhaps its Lord Frederick?' says I, looking at him full in the face. 'Very likely it may be,' says he, growing very grand all at once, and snapping me up very short. So I was just going to beg his pardon, if I'd affronted him, when Stevens came in, and I left them together."

"This is another proof of deliberate deception," thought the agonised Grace, who could no longer indulge a hope that her unfortunate sister had not fallen a prey to the designs of a villain. Again, however, she recurred to the faint prospect which an interview with Grant might realise; and, at her earnest request, Mr. Stevens, who was a good-natured, civil man, and seemed deeply interested for her, departed in search of Grant, to whose residence he had got a clue by knowing the livery stables at which his horses were put up.

The composing medicine, which had been administered to Mrs. Woodford by the medical gentleman whom Mrs. Stevens had recommended Grace to send for, had the happy effect of throwing her into a comparatively calm and tranquil sleep; and Grace, relieved from the immediate terror of her dissolution, had now more time and opportunity to reflect on the situation in which her unhappy mother was placed by this overthrow of all her hopes.

"I am a ruined, miserable wretch, if she is not his wife, Grace! I have not ten pounds in the world, and what is to become of us if she has indeed deserted me!"

Such had been her despairing exclamation when first the fatal truth had flashed upon her mind; and Grace, as she now sat by her bedside, and contemplated her pale-worn cheeks and feeble frame, shuddered at the thought that poverty and want would, in all probability, embitter the remaining days of her frail existence, and add pangs to those of mortified ambition and disappointed maternal affection.

From these, and a long train of similar reflections, she was roused by Mrs. Stevens' appearance at the chamber door.

She beckoned her out; and Grace, having whispered a charge to Jane not to leave the bedside till her return, followed her conductress anxiously down stairs.

"My husband is come back, Miss," said the important landlady; "he's met with no luck, but he'll tell you all himself."

From Mr. Stevens Grace heard, after listening with ill-disguised impatience to the good man's exhortations to her, not to fret, and to recollect that she was now her mother's only stay and support, and therefore it would not do for her to let herself be cast down, that he had succeeded in finding Mr. Grant's residence, and had learned that he had quitted it for London three days since.

"I was determined, however," continued Mr. Stevens, "that I wouldn't come back with half an errand; so I asked the servant-maid that answered the door whether his friend, Captain Frederick, was gone, too.

"'Captain Frederick!' said she; 'I don't know no such a person. There was nobody of that name come here to see him, I'm sure.'

"'I mean the gentleman that used to ride a roan horse, and his servant a grey; you must know him, I'm sure.'

"'Oh, that was Lord Frederick Melverley,' she replied; 'but he's not a captain.'

"'May be not,' said I, 'but I didn't rightly know. But is he gone, my dear?'

"'Why, I can hardly tell,' said she, 'whether he's gone for good or not; but his valet was here this morning, and he said his master was off, and he didn't know whether he was coming back or not, but he was to stay at the hotel till farther orders.'

"This was just what I wanted," continued Mr. Stevens; "so I got out of her which hotel it was, and the valet's name, and away I went, without stopping a moment.

"The young man is a very decent, well-behaved sort of a person, considering whose servant he is; and so, when I had told him that I had a little business with his master, and should be glad to know when I could see him, or how I could write to him, he told me at once that he knew no more where his master was gone than I did, but that he rather suspected he should hear shortly, as Lord Frederick had only taken one change of linen with him.

"'It was a sudden journey, then, I suppose,' said I; 'is his lordship used to such frolics?'

"He shook his head.

"'It's not for one in my station to make observations on what gentlemen do,' he said; 'but I can't but say I'm sorry to see my lord so harum scarum,'

"'Then, I'll tell you what it is,' said I; 'as you're not one that would encourage your master in his bad ways, I'll just tell you the business I come about, and perhaps it may lay in your way to do us some service; and I'm sure it will be doing him good, as well as your lady, and the poor young creature that he's taken away from her friends, if a stop could be put at once to his journey.'

"So, then, Miss Grace, I up and told him all about his coming here, pretending to be honourable, and how the old lady, your mother, had been foolish enough to swallow all he led her with, and what the upshot of it had been; and

then he told me that he had long suspected that his master was after no good, for that he had sent his lady and her mother off to Brighton, and made some excuse for staying behind. I could make out," continued Stevens, "that the family had put this young man as a bit of a spy upon his master; but, though he did'nt approve of his doings, he said he thought it was no use to be tittle tattling everything he heard and saw. But he wished now he'd wrote and told the old lady that there was something amiss; but, however, he said he'd promise me that the minute he did hear from his master, he'd let me know all he could."

Maria was then indeed utterly, irretrievably ruined; for it was not in the power of her heartless seducer to repair the wrong he had committed, even if it were possible that he had the inclination.

Unconsciously almost to herself, Grace had, up to this moment, felt a lingering hope that Frederick, as she had used to call him, might even yet be induced to do her sister justice.

But this faint ray of hope had now vanished; and, in the deepest agony, Grace wrung her hands, as she repeated the fatal word which had at once pointed out to her the certainty of her poor Maria's infamy and degradation.

* * * * *

A month, a miserable month of grief and regret, and suspense, passed away, without a single word of positive intelligence having reached the unhappy relatives of the lost Maria.

Slowly, and by almost imperceptible degrees, Mrs. Woodford's health mended, and she became able to quit the chamber, in which, from the moment she entered it, Grace had been, day and night, her constant, never-tiring companion.

It was in vain that Mrs. Stevens remonstrated with her on her thus sacrificing herself to one who felt neither affection or gratitude to her in return, but received her most devoted attendance as only a matter of course, and repaid her most affectionate assiduity with petulant murmurings and the most incessant lamentations for the loss of one who seemed totally to have forgotten that there was such a person as her mother in existence.

At Grace's earnest request, Mrs. Stevens had carefully kept secret their discovery of the real situation in life of the *soi-disant* Captain Frederick; and the former regularly, with the bitterest anguish, was compelled to listen to the fond mother's anticipations of even yet beholding her "child" the bride of the supposed Frederick.

Other cares and anxieties, however, soon superseded all that Mrs. Woodford felt upon her favourite's account.

The small sum of money which she was in possession of at the commencement of her illness was nearly exhausted in the necessary expenses of a sick chamber; and Grace heard with terror her mother's despairing anticipations.

"Yes, the ungrateful wretch has brought me to want as well as shame," she would exclaim; "the money that should have been saved to support myself in the decline of life, has all been wasted upon her, and I shall be left to die of want."

"No, no, do not say so, dear mother; I am young, and strong, and active, and willing to work, and though ——" Grace burst into tears at her mother's angry and contemptuous look.

"And do you think then that I would consent to live upon your earnings?" she replied; "and if I would, pray, what is that you flatter yourself you could get a living at, haymaking, or weeding, or something of that sort I suppose; but you would find working in the fields a very different sort of thing, I can tell you, to what playing at it was in your father's lifetime. No, no, Grace; it is all very fine to talk of working for your living ——"

"I did not mean, of course, that I could earn a living at such labour as that," observed Grace, mildly; "but even that," and she turned away to hide the tears that were swelling in her eyes; "would be preferable to seeing you want."

"Well, well, you are a good girl, Grace," returned the mother, somewhat softened; "but we must try to find some better way of getting a living."

"Do not let us ever trust to chances again," interrupted Grace, who could not conceal her impatience at her mother's continuing to indulge her visionary schemes of aggrandisement. "There is a most excellent living to be got here," she continued, with liveliness, "by possessing taste and ingenuity; and you know both you and Maria have always allowed that I possess some; I am sure I could make far prettier, and more tasty caps, and bonnets, and pelisses, than any we have seen in that milliner's window, that we pass round the corner; and yet she can afford to keep a footman, and employs, Jane told me, who once lived with her, sometimes twenty or thirty young people to work for her."

"And pray, how would you make your wonderful taste and ingenuity known?" inquired Mrs. Woodford, in a contemptuous tone; "you have not got a shop, or connections, or friends."

"No; but a shop might be had, or at least, a handsome front parlour, and Jane says, Mrs. Somerford, the milliner, only had a parlour, and then I could make up some showy things——"

"And pray, where's the money to come from for this fine scheme, and I have not a guinea left, and owe more than that to the doctor?"

Grace did not dare reply what was in her thoughts, that they possessed many, many superfluous articles, which if sold, would produce the necessary money.

Her own share was indeed comparatively small; but she knew nearly fifty pounds had been expended upon Maria's finery, since their arrival at Bath, and surely now, there could be no use in keeping what was utterly useless, and must every time she looked at it, remind her (Mrs. Woodford) of the folly and vanity of her expectations.

"And they must be parted with," sighed Grace, who saw that the scheme she had so sanguinely planned in her own mind, would all

fall to the ground, from the want of her mother's concurrence. "Yes, poverty will compel her to part with even these treasured relics, and then it will be only to prolong the miserable day of utter want, without affording the means of trying to extricate ourselves."

As she had predicted, Mrs. Woodford acted, the dresses, the trinkets, all the mementos of her ungrateful daughter, were preserved as something too sacred to be touched, till every other means of raising money were totally exhausted; the silver spoons, tea pot, candlesticks, &c., &c., which she had, to Grace's infinite regret and shame, brought away from Llan——, were the first sacrifices. Mrs. Stevens, who was given to understand by Mrs. Woodford, that her embarrassment was only temporary, having agreed to take them as security for rent due, and in addition, advanced her a few pounds; but week after week passed on, the remittances she had pretended to expect did not arrive, and Mrs. Stevens began very plainly to hint that the rent was fast mounting up, and that Mrs. Woodford had already had more than it was prudent to advance on such old-fashioned plate, which wouldn't fetch a farthing more than its weight as old silver.

Jane, too, was evidently fidgetty, as she expressed it, about her quarter's wages; she wanted shoes, and a new dark gown for afternoons, and she dinned her wants so often in Grace's ears that the latter was compelled to purchase her silence by presents from her own little wardrobe, which, without paying the debt, were worth more than it came to.

Incessant had been Grace's prayers to her mother to discharge at once this useless incumbrance to their sinking state.

"What will Stevens think? What will everybody think?" was her reply; "they will know directly we are ruined."

Convinced that it was useless to hope that her mother ever would be brought to a reasonable view of her situation, or be persuaded to take reasonable measures to obviate the wretched state towards which she was fast sinking, Grace at length determined upon taking at least one decisive step, by acquainting Jane of the little probability there was of her being paid her wages if she remained, and prevailing on her not only to discharge herself, but to assist her (Grace) in procuring the means of secretly paying her what was due.

"Laws of mercy on me, Miss Grace, you make my hair stand on end to think that you should be brought to work for to pay me my wages, and my missus keeping up her consequence and—but there, I won't say another word about her, only that you are over and over too good to belong to such a—"

"And will you, then, Jane," interrupted Grace, mildly, "will you speak to Mrs. Somerford about your going back to her, as she said she wanted you, and that will be a good excuse to my mother for leaving her; and then, if Mrs. Somerford will give me work, she can pay you for it, and that will set all right between us."

"I declare I can't help crying to think of it,"

and Jane burst into a loud sob; "but howsomever, I'll go to my old missus this wery arternoon, and if so be as she's perwided with a maid, I'll be bound it won't be many days afore she can recommend me to some of her customers; and I know, too, that if I tell her about you, miss, she'll find you work, for she's a real good-hearted woman, only so passionate, which was the cause of my leaving, for I'm wery passionate myself, and won't be put upon by nobody, and that Charlotte which lived housemaid with her—"

"Yes, she behaved very ill to you, Jane," interrupted Grace, who had heard the story of Jane's wrongs from Charlotte at least ten times; "but now I'll go to my mother, for fear she should want me."

"She is a nice dear young lady," ejaculated Jane looking after her; "only she's so fidgetty, she can never listen to one."

Grace, however, listened with patience and undisguised pleasure to all Jane's long rigmarole story when she returned in the evening from Mrs. Somerford's, having asked leave of Mrs. Woodford to step out for a quarter of an hour, a permission she extended to nearly three hours, to her mistress' great annoyance.

"I am really surprised, Mrs. Jane, at the liberties you take," observed the latter, when Jane at length entered to know if missus wanted anything for her supper; "but I assure you, if you think to take advantage of me, because I have not paid your paltry wages, you are mistaken."

"I don't want to take any advantages, I'm sure, ma'am," replied Jane, pertly; "and as to my wages, I shall never ask you for them; but I've got another place, and shall be obliged to you to spare me as soon as ever it's convenient, because I hope you won't stand in a poor servant's light of getting a good place, and good wages."

"This is very sudden," observed Mrs. Woodford, in whose mind there was an evident struggle between her wounded pride and her hope of getting rid of Jane, not only without her wages, but without being humiliated by acknowledging that she could no longer afford to keep her.

"Oh, no; it's nothin' sudden, ma'am; only my old missus has often wished me back again since I left her, and so, as she's without a servant, I thought I couldn't do otherwise than offer myself, and, if you please, I'd be glad to go as soon as convenient."

"Oh, you may go as soon as you like, but it is not convenient, at present, for me to settle with you," replied Mrs. Woodford.

"Oh, never mind that, ma'am; I arn't partickler about the money, for my old missus will advance me enough to buy shoes and that, and a dark gownd to wear of arternoons."

Grace stole out of the room, leaving Jane to settle with her mother when she was to go.

In a short time she was followed by the latter.

"I've settled it all, miss; I'm to go to-morrow night. And Mrs. Somerford says she's got plenty of work for you, if you're capable, as I told her you was; but how you're to do it without missus finding it out passes me."

"Leave that to me, Jane," returned Grace, who felt, at this moment, as if a heavy burthen had been removed from her heart by this annunciation.

"But you'll be obliged to call on Mrs. Somerford, miss, for she must talk to you; and, indeed, she's mighty curious to see a young lady as has got such honest principles as to go to to work to pay a poor servant their wages. She says there arn't many such to be met with, now-a-days."

Grace did not much approve of appearing as an object of curiosity to the milliner.

But Jane assured her that Mrs. Somerford could not give out her work without proper directions; and it was concluded that Grace should attend her future employer's commands the morning after Jane had entered upon her service.

For the first time since she had entered Bath, Grace retired to her bed with the happy anticipation of possessing the means of, at least, warding off the extreme destitution which she had so often contemplated as the inevitable result of her mother's thoughtless and improvident conduct.

"Of course, if I continue to give satisfaction," she reflected, "Mrs. Somerford will not refuse me employment after my debt to Jane is paid; my mother will, by degrees, become reconciled to my working, we must remove into less expensive lodgings, and we shall be—oh, no, no! Never, never shall I be able to say happy again while Maria—"

A burst of grief interrupted her sanguine enumeration of the comforts that would spring from her humble but zealous exertions, and it was some time before she could again return to the tranquil contemplation of her plans for the future.

On the morning appointed Grace readily found an excuse for going out for half an hour, for they had now no servant to fetch in what was necessary.

The disposal secretly, through the means of Jane, of her coral earrings, necklace, and other ornaments, which the latter had found a purchaser for in one of Mrs. Somerford's *young ladies*, at a tolerably fair price, compared to what they had cost, had provided Grace with the means of going to market.

Mrs. Woodford expressed no surprise when, with a large shawl thrown over her shoulders, and a coarse straw bonnet, which she had carefully preserved, as having been the gift of her poor father, who had brought it himself from Bristol, to keep his pretty Grace from burning herself, and freckling her face in the sun—not that he thought freckles or a tanned skin any disadvantage to her, but that they afforded Mrs. Woodford an everlasting subject for finding fault, and scolding both him and his favourite—she presented herself at her bedside, and inquired what she should purchase for dinner.

"Whatever you like, Grace," was the reply, in a tone half petulant, half dejected. "It's no use

to ask me," she continued, her usual peevishness
surmounting even the little natural feeling
which had been for a moment excited by beholding the child, whom she had taken so much
pains to spoil and alienate from her, thus cheerfully setting her the example of sacrificing pride
and vanity at the shrine of independence. "You
have chosen to act, without consulting me, in
getting the means to play the market-woman,"
she added, turning coldly away, "and it's only
mocking at me to pretend to ask me for orders."

"My dear, dear mother! how can you so
cruelly misinterpret my motives?" exclaimed
Grace.

"There, again, you've returned to your old
custom of *mothering* me upon every occasion,
though you know how I hate the word. Your
sister never called me mother in her life, though
your low-minded father was always ridiculing
her for obeying me, and calling me—"

Grace had glided out of the room without
waiting for the conclusion of this censure upon
her father, whose memory was too justly dear to
her to allow of her listening with composure to
aught that could reflect upon him.

Before Mrs. Woodford had finished upon the
comparative gentility of her daughters, the gentle
and really dutiful girl was standing, with glowing cheeks and a throbbing heart, waiting, with
her basket in her hand, at the counter of Mrs.
Somerford; while the latter was assiduously endeavouring to satisfy the capricious taste of an
elderly over-dressed lady, who was examining,
and trying on, and rejecting, with expressions of
affected contempt, all the showy silk bonnets the
milliner offered to her.

"They are all *ojus*, I declare, Somerford,"
said the fat old lady, in a discontented tone.
"But really, since I've been to France, I hate
everything English. There isn't a bit of taste in
one of your women; all they make is somehow
so frumpish and dowdy. I wish to goodness
you'd get a French woman to manage your business; it would be pounds in your pocket.

"I'm sure, madam, I'm very sorry we can't
give you satisfaction," said Mrs. Somerford, in a
humble tone; "but I expect a young woman
that's highly recommended for taste to join my
establishment in a day or two, and perhaps she'll
be able to please you better.

"Well, then, I won't have any of these frightful things; I'll wait till I see what she can do;
but she must be decidedly Frenchified or she
won't do, I can tell you   Wait, I think I'll make
that French white, with the blonde lace round
the edge, serve me for a day or two; for it's
quite impossible to go to the rooms in this
thing;" and she threw aside a handsome pale
blue one, which she appeared from its freshness,
to have scarcely worn.

"That is the best, though one of the most
troublesome customers I have got, Miss
Woodford," said the milliner, who had seen
Jane's greeting to the latter as she entered into
the shop, and readily guessed that she beheld, in
the pretty, unpretending girl before her, the new
workwoman of whose taste her maid had spoken
so highly. "If you can manage to please Mrs.

Spriggs," she continued, "I can promise you
constant employment; for it's as much as one
person can do to work for her, she's so whimsical,
and so fond of change; but come in, and we will
have a little talk together. Jane talked of nothing else but you, ever since she came back;
and, I assure you, she's made all my young
ladies quite envious of you."

Grace felt that it was not any great subject for
exultation, to be the object of envy on account of
her capabilities to manufacture handsome bonnets or tasty caps; but she silently followed
Mrs. Somerford into a room, where about a dozen
young women were working: and she humbly
and patiently submitted to the chatty milliner's
directions, as to the disposal of the silk, and lace,
and ribbons, and flowers, and all the numerous
etceteras which were entrusted to her.

"It's not at all in my way, you see, Miss Woodford, to give such work out of the house; and I
did not intend to employ you, except in dress-
making, where, of course, I should know what
you were about. But I wish, if possible, to
please Mrs. Spriggs, who is an uncommon good
customer; and so, perhaps, as you're a new
hand, and will follow your own taste, you may
have a chance of hitting her fancy; but you
must be very quick, and let me have two or
three caps, and a couple of bonnets, as soon as
possible, for it's ten to one but she'll be here to-
morrow, teasing me again."

Grace promised attention, and the exertion of
all the ability she possessed; but she almost
trembled at the task she was undertaking, when
she saw the neat and delicate articles which the
young women around her were fabricating, and
heard that none of them could give satisfaction
to the difficult Mrs. Spriggs.

"I'll put them all up in a bandbox for you,
my dear, for you cannot crush them into that
basket," said Mrs. Somerford, who was evidently
disposed to be very kind to her timid little
workwoman; "you won't mind carrying them
home, I suppose."

Grace gulped down the small remains of pride
which made her feel somewhat humiliated at the
thought of appearing in the street with the em-
blem of her new vocation.

Her mother had so often descanted on the impropriety and meanness of being seen even with
a small parcel, that Grace had imbibed the idea,
though contrary to her usual good sense; and
she now felt ready to sink, as she beheld the
immense large bandbox which Mrs. Somerford
fetched out, and began to pack the materials in.

A long whisper from Jane, who had been
watching Grace's countenance, however, put a
stop to Mrs. Somerford's proceedings.

"You are right; that will be best" she
observed. "Never mind, Miss Woodford, Jenny
will bring the things for you, as it is such a
large box; because, as she says, if your mother
was to happen to see you it would betray you at
once; though, indeed, I can't think what sort of
a mother she can be to make this necessary."

Grace looked her grateful thanks to Jenny,
for having thus contrived to spare her the anticipated mortification, and departed, having pro-

mised to use her utmost ability and expedition to please the difficult Mrs. Spriggs.

In a few hours Grace, having easily obtained her mother's permission to retire early to her room, was assiduously at work at her new employment, to which she devoted nearly the whole of the night.

The next and the next night were passed in the same manner, and on the morning following, before her mother had risen, or it was likely she should meet many people in the street Grace proceeded, with the fruits of her assiduity, to the milliner's.

"Beautiful! charming! tasty, indeed!" were the epithets with which every single article was received by Mrs. Somerford, as Grace drew them out, one by one, and timidly held them up for approval. "Look here, ladies," continued the milliner, "here's patterns for you. I wonder when any of you will show me anything like these? But there's one thing to be said, to be sure; none of you have ever been in Paris, as Miss Woodford has."

Grace was about to disavow her having enjoyed this opportunity of improving her taste; but a significant look, and a sly pull at her frock, explained to her that Mrs. Somerford had her motives for this assertion, and that it was no mistake on her part.

She was not a little mortified, however, at the manner in which the productions of her fancy were received by the young women to whom Mrs. Somerford's observations were addressed. Contemptuous tosses of the head, half-suppressed titters, and significant looks at one another, accompanied the display which their mistress made of the taste of her new workwoman; and Grace felt heartily rejoiced when the latter observed—

"Well, now, Miss Woodford, if you will come into the parlour, we will have a little talk about terms, and so forth, while I get my breakfast."

The "terms, and so forth," as the milliner had phrased it, proved sadly beneath even Grace's moderate expectations; but, then, she had drawn her inferences from the extravagant prices which she had seen given for similar articles, and her knowledge of the comparatively trifling value of the materials.

Such as they were, however, Grace was compelled to submit, for Mrs. Somerford assured her they were higher than she gave to any of her other women.

"But, as I mean to tell Mrs. Spriggs they're made by a French milliner," she observed, "I think I shall succeed in pleasing her, and so I can afford to pay you something more on that account."

"It will be a long time," thought Grace, as she walked slowly home; "a long time, indeed, before I have even paid Jane her four pounds at this rate; and how shall I, in the meantime, contrive to keep my mother from finding me out; and how, too, is she to be supported in the meantime, and even when I am free to work entirely for her, and she, as she must do, consents that I shall devote all my time to it, shall I

ever be able to make sufficient to satisfy her wants, much less her wishes."

These reflections were most dispiriting, and added to the effects of her extreme fatigue, broken rest, and the recollections, which in the long hours of silence and solitude had perpetually forced themselves upon her, made her look the image of melancholy and dejection, as she slowly walked into their usual sitting-room, where, to her utter surprise, she found her mother already seated at the table, which she had, with the assistance of Joe, who now took the most active part in the household business, set ready before she ventured out.

"Upon my word, you seem to act quite independent, Miss Grace, going out and coming in just when you please," observed Mrs. Woodford, but, at this moment raising her eyes to the face of her daughter, she absolutely started.

"Good gracious, child!" she exclaimed; "where have you been? and what have you been about, for you look so deadly pale—"

"I am not very well," interrupted Grace, beginning to take off her bonnet, and turning away to conceal her tears; indeed, I felt so unwell that—"

"Well, well, if that was your reason for going out, that is enough; but now, do make me a bit of toast."

Grace proceeded with alacrity to do as she desired; but whether from the heat of the fire, or the agitation suffered, she had scarcely begun her task before her head grew giddy, her sight failed, and making an effort to rise, she fell senseless on the hearth rug.

* * * *

"What is the meaning of this, Grace? what is Mrs. what's-her-name talking about?" demanded Mrs. Woodford, turning with an air of offended dignity from Mrs. Stevens, who had commenced a strong outburst of feeling.

"Oh, it's of no use to ask her, poor thing, for she'll tell you nothing about it," interrupted the officious landlady; "but if she won't, there's plenty that will; ask my husband there, or ask either of them two gentlemen that live in my front two-pair, and that's just gone up stairs, when they see the poor girl wasn't dead—just ask any of them, I say, and they'll tell you what they think of your keeping up your consequence, and living in these apartments at a guinea a week, and wanting as much attendance as a duchess, and your poor daughter sitting up all night, night after night, when she ought to be at rest, working her fingers to the bone, to keep you up in your grandeur; but it won't do, pride must have a fall, as the old saying is, and it may as well come sooner as later; and so, Mrs. Woodford, I beg you'll look out for a place that will suit you, for I shall want these rooms for an old lodger of mine, that's coming next week to Bath."

Mrs. Woodford looked thunderstruck.

"This is really quite incomprehensible to me," she observed, still striving to keep up her consequence. "Do you mean, then, my good woman, to say that you turn me out of my lodgings?"

"It's better for me to turn you out of your lodgings, than to be turned myself out of my house," replied Mrs. Stevens; "and that I must be, if I don't pay my rent, and I fancy, if I depend on you, it will be a long time first. Good woman, indeed; I think you might condescend, ma'am, to give me my proper name, and not good woman me, as if you was talking to you inferiors."

"Come, come; this isn't a time to be scolding and pecking at one another," interrupted Mr. Stevens, good humouredly. "She didn't call you out of your name, I hope, when she called you a good woman; and, as to turning out, why I should be sorry to behave so sharply, or put anybody to a *non plush*, and so—"

"And so just go down stairs and mind your shop-board, and your 'prentices," interrupted Mrs. Stevens, angrily; "I shan't do or say anything but what my conscience tells me is just and right, and you know what you said yourself this morning, when you saw this poor girl stealing out of the house before her mother was up, to carry home the work that she's been poring her eyes out at for these three nights."

'What work? what does the woman mean, Grace?" demanded Mrs. Woodford, in a violent passion.

Grace, in vain, tried to give utterance to a word, so completely was she overcome, with the fear that her mother would attribute to her well-meant exertions all the mortifications which she had received, and was likely still to receive, from Mrs Stevens.

The explanation, which she was unable to give was soon, however, and without any qualifications, given by the landlady; and Mrs. Woodford had the mortification, not only of hearing Grace's honest and upright principle commended in opposition to her own conduct, but also of being told over and over again that no one respected, or pitied, or would even endure her, were it not for the sake of the poor girl whom she had always treated with so much coldness and contumely.

She was told, too, again and again, for Mrs. Stevens was determined, as she said, not to mince matters, that the sooner she gave up her present apartments, and paid the month's rent that was due, the more agreeable it would be to her landlady; and to complete the measure of her mortification, the latter wound up the whole by observing, that as, of course, the cheapest lodgings now would be the best, and she respected Grace so much, that she didn't wish to turn them out, she thought the best thing they could do would be to make up their minds to have the two attics, which she would make comfortable for them, and only charge seven shillings a week, and the boy could sleep with their 'prentices; or, if they liked to have one room on the second-floor, at the same price, she could accommodate them that way; but one thing was certain, they must, without delay, give up their present apartments.

With infinite difficulty, Grace succeeded in persuading her mother to check the torrent of indignation, which was ready to break forth at the indignity which she conceived was offered her in these propositions; but Mrs. Stevens, satisfied with having had the opportunity at last of saying, without reserve, all that had been for the last week or two rankling in her mind, was by no means in a hurry to press for a decided answer, and, therefore, readily yielded to Grace's suggestion that she should give her, Mrs. Woodford, a few hours to consider what she should determine on.

It was some time after they had been left alone together before Mrs. Woodford thoroughly comprehended all that Grace had to tell her in explanation of Mrs. Stevens' assertion; but even her stubborn heart relented, when she learned that her daughter had actually submitted to the mortification of engaging herself as a workwoman, and devoted to the completion of her task the time that ought to have been given to rest.

Grace's pleasure at finding that her mother did not feel angry with her, was, however, greatly damped by the latter's indignant resolution to remove instantly from the house in which she had been so insulted.

"We will go this very morning and look out for other lodgings, Grace," she observed; "and so try and eat some breakfast, for you look still so pale and——; why do you sigh and look in that manner, Grace? Surely you would not wish me to humble myself so as to take their wretched attics?"

"My dear mother, do not be angry with me, for saying that I do not see that you can do better. There are only two shillings left of the last trifle which I raised, and how can we afford to remove, even if we should get rooms as cheap—and then there is the fortnight due, which, of course, if we remove——"

"I see how it is," interrupted Mrs. Woodford, in a tone of mingled petulance and despondency. "I see it is all settled, and so I may as well give myself up at once. Well it matters not, I suppose, where I spend the short remnant of my days; and so you may do just as you like; I shall not interfere again."

"Do not say so, my dear mother," said Grace, with affectionate earnestness; "would to heaven it were in my power to secure you every comfort that your heart could wish! but—"

"I know it, I know it, child; you cannot do more. But it's hard, very hard, Grace, after such prospects as I've had, to submit——. Oh! if your sister—if Maria could see—"

"There is another reason why I think it best to remain here, mother," said Grace timidly. "Should any information arrive, and we should be removed to another—"

"You are right," interrupted Mrs. Woodford, with an eagerness that showed how much more deeply she was interested when Maria was concerned, than when even her own comfort and almost existence were at stake.

"You are quite right," she repeated; "and besides, it will show her at once what misery she has brought upon me, and prove how cruel it was of her to desert me in such a manner."

Grace was silent.

She was thinking at that moment how probable it was that Maria, with more real truth and justice, was upbraiding her mother as the cause of all that had befallen her.

"She cannot, I know she cannot be happy," thought Grace, whose mind was still totally absorbed in the subject which her mother had thus brought so strongly to her mind; "no, even though she may now be enjoying all the luxuries and pleasures that wealth can purchase; still, I am well convinced her heart would not let her be happy, and if the time should come, as unfortunately it too surely will come, that the villain who has robbed her of her fair fame, should become tired of and desert her. Oh! what then will her reflections be!"

Thus did the Prince of Wales plunge another family into the depths of misery.

Need we dwell on the history of Maria?

No; for it is that of many characters who have already appeared in this narrative.

CHAPTER XXVII.

WHAT TOOK PLACE IN PARIS—THE MYSTERY ABOUT TO BE REVEALED—ARRIVAL OF THE ARTIST—RETURN TO LONDON.

PIPEY dogged the Black Captain with the perseverance of a bloodhound.

The captain had ensconced himself in the lowest of the low dens of Paris, and imagined himself perfectly safe.

But he was not yet thoroughly acquainted with the character of the man by whom he was followed.

ht and day was Pipey on the scent, and at length they met.

It was in an old, deserted attic, in one of the worst houses of the French metropolis.

Here the Black Captain had paid well for the quarter extended him, and the owner of the house had promised him the safety he so longed for.

It was many days before Pipey could gain access to the house.

The owner was true to the trust reposed in him, and nothing would induce him to betray his lodger.

What threats and money could not do, Pipey at last brought about by strategy.

Assuming a disguise which lent him the air of a professed thief of the Parisian type, he mixed with some members of that fraternity, and, by this means, at length wound himself into the retreat of the captain.

Once within, he took care to make all the inhabitants beastly drunk.

He discovered that their weakness was old cogniac, and with this he plied them freely.

So freely, that in an hour they all rolled under the tables.

This was his opportunity.

Seeing it, he locked his sottish tools into one apartment.

And then commenced the exploration of the house.

From cellar to attic he went, when, despairing of success, fortune stood his friend, and placed victory in his hand.

In a corner of an out-of-the-way landing place he had nearly overlooked, was a little door that apparently opened on a cupboard or closet.

This he tried to open.

It was fastened.

Applying his eye to the keyhole, he discovered that the key was turned on the inside.

He called upon the occupant of this retreat to open the door.

Assuming the voice of the master of the den, he called aloud for admittance.

At first there was no notice taken of this summons.

On its being repeated, however, a voice from within demanded who was there.

"*C'est moi, Jules*," answered Pipey, continuing his imitation of the lodging-house keeper.

"It is well," answered the man within, and next moment the door flew open.

Pipey was in the apartment on the instant.

As he expected, the tenant of the little den he had entered, was no other than the Black Captain.

With a cry of rage and despair the trapped man sprang back.

"Ah!" said Pipey, regarding him coolly, "hunted down at last! It has been a long chase, but it ends well."

"Yes; but not for you," cried the captain, drawing a pistol, and aiming at Pipey, "so take the reward you merit!"

He discharged the weapon full in the face of his antagonist.

But Pipey was used to this sort of thing, and, by a lightning-like movement, ducked, and escaped the shot.

"Now, don't try that on again," he said, with his usual gravity, "it won't do."

"Baffled!" yelled the Captain, "baffled!—lost!"

"No, found; and precious glad I am of it. Now, then; the will."

"The will!"

"Ah, the will. That's plain enough, isn't it?"

"What will?"

"Ah, you're very innocent. You haven't the slightest notion of what I mean, no doubt; but it won't do. Come, I say; the will!"

"Damnation!" yelled the old wretch, "take it."

With that he threw a heavy packet of papers on the table.

"Ah!" said Pipey, gathering them up, "very good, very good indeed. I've taken them as desired, now, my friend, you'll excuse me if I pay you the same compliment, for I mean to have you."

"When you catch me?" cried the captain dashing open the little lattice of the attic, and springing out on the parapet, "follow me if you dare."

"I've dared do more than that before now," cried Pipey, as he darted after his victim.

In another moment they both stood on the awful parapet.

It was a bright moonlight night.

The stars shone in myriads.

They were at an awful distance from the street.

Below passed the thousand pedestrians looking like pigmies at the extreme distance.

A false step, a tremble, and one or both may be precipitated below.

The parapet ran along the top of half a hundred houses.

At some little distance a light gleamed from an attic window.

To this point the Black Captain evidently inclined.

He crawled with cat-like agility.

Pipey was no less active.

On they went, until the superior strength of Pipey began to lessen the gap between them.

On they went, running their race on this fearful course.

On—on!

Pipey still gained on his intended victim.

At length his hand almost touched him.

With a cry of fear the captain made a leap, and again put a gap between himself and his pursuer.

On—on again.

Again the gap decreases.

This time Pipey's outstretched hand falls on the shoulder of the captain.

There was another cry.

Another spring!

The captain alighted.

His foot slipped.

A momentary stagger, and then he is precipitated over the awful parapet.

A heartrending cry followed.

Pipey listened.

A dull, blood-freezing crash below.

The body of the Captain lies mangled on the pavement.

"So," said Pipey, "that's the end of the poor devil. Well, I'm sorry—he would have been such an ornament to the gallows."

Deeming it not worth while to be seen, he got off the parapet, and crawled back to the attic over the roofs.

He entered without being seen.

Noiselessly crawling down the stairs, he opened the door and quitted the house.

In a moment he was mingling with the excited throng, who viewed the crushed body lying on the pavement.

There was universal wonder how it could have happened.

Pipey might have told the tale, but he deemed it more prudent to keep silence.

*   *   *   *   *

On arriving at his hotel, he found an unexpected visitor awaiting him.

It was his son-in-law, the great artist—philanthropist—the young Lord Lovelace.

"And what brings you to Paris?" he asked, on seeing this gentle youth.

"The want of your help."

"In what direction?"

"In the furtherance of a scheme to set at liberty the father of her I love."

"You mean Lewis Arndale?"

"Yes."

"The husband of Olivia Hargrave?"

"Real," said the young lord.

He placed a paper in the hand of Pipey.

It was the announcement of the death of the once beautiful Olivia.

"Heaven be merciful to her," said Pipey; "she sinned, but she was sorely tried. She erred, but she was chastened by suffering."

"She was, indeed."

"And Lewis?"

"Lingers in a goal."

"I think not."

"They imprisoned him for a while, but at length the King had him quietly sent out of the country. He had seen his daughter, and, bad as he is, he could not make love to her while he held her father in a felon's cell. He liberated him, and he is in Paris."

"You do not say so!"

"I do; and what's more, I know where to find him."

"Let us hasten—"

"All in good time. Meanwhile let me congratulate you. I have at last solved THE MYSTERY OF MARLBOROUGH HOUSE."

He placed the rescued will in the hands of the young lord, who read his mother's real name for the first time.

Fair Liz, the street ballad singer, was no other than Charlotte Duchess of Grasmount. The infant, born at Marlborough House, was the legitimate offspring of the late Duke.

There it was, acknowledged in his own hand.

Years and years the truth had been buried; generations had come and gone; but at length the secret was revealed, and virtue held its own.

*   *   *   *   *

By right, this story should have ended with the above words, but readers like to hear *just a little more than all;* and so, we presume we must say, that Pipey and his son-in-law returned to London with Lewis Arndale, and that, in the end, all the good people of this tale were perfectly happy, and all the bad were punished according to their deserts.

L'ENVOI.

BY MRS. BOODLES.

"WHICH I says it, and stands by it! Never was there a sweeter family in all the world. As to that dear Captain de Pipes, the way he takes to them blessed infants of the Duchesses, and the children of his Grace, is more than wonderful. And then there's the darling Mrs. Louise, and her husband, and her infants—which they're the finest as ever was and all safe through the vaccination. and the hooping cough, and the measles! And then there's the daughter of that poor soul, Madame Marie, who died broken hearted two years agone. Ah! it were a blessing that the Captain followed that Prince, disguised as he was, and tracked them and brought her safe back, and made him burst a blood vessel. Which reminds me of that poor old creetur, the Duchess, who did serve me out by walking me off on that awful night they murdered the old Duke—which, I will say it such sperits and such pheasant never was. And to myself I'm hearty. I was ill before they hung old Grimer, the lawyer, and his accomplice Yeller Maydock; but the news of them wretches meeting their end brought me round, and made me jolly, which I wasn't on hearing the death of the poor queen, who never recovered being served so bad at Westminster, and the day the king was crowned. Well, he's served out; thanks be to Heaven! Anybody looking at his sunken eyes, his fat figure, and bloated face, will know what's in store for him. which appoplexy it is or my name ain't SAIREY BOODLES, widow, and housekeeper to the Honourable Captain de Pips, and his noble lady the duchess, which I says it is, and stands by it—*If anybody has spasms let 'em try three drops of brandy on a lump of sugar—them's my last words.*"

THE END.